UNITED N[ ]

TO: Legal Staff, Zurich/New York
FROM: A. Conworth

Please supply departmental comments on a notice that will be issued by the Global Revitalization and Environmental Enforcement Service for Edict 31 in the United States. Comments are due back by April 22.

GLOBAL REVITALIZATION ENVIRONMENTAL ENFORCEMENT SERVICE

FINAL NOTICE !

VIOLATION

YOU ARE HEREBY INFORMED
EDICT 31 THE GREENHOUSE LAWS

As drafted by the U.N. and accepted by Congress and the President of the United States of America.
YOU, AND YOUR FAMILY are **IN VIOLATION** of the following:

- ☐ • Automobile Usage without Permit
- ☐ • Travel without Permit
- ☐ • Excessive Home Power Consumption
  - o Overuse of Heat/or Water Privilege
  - o Overuse of Communication Privilege
  - o Overuse of Entertainment Privilege
  - o Overuse of Refrigeration
- ☐ • Failure to Report Monthly Wattage
- ☐ • Violation of Vacation Allowance

Failure to Reply to this notice within 72 hours can result in
REDUCTION OF WATTAGE ALLOWANCE,
FINES TO $10,000,
5 YEAR IMPRISONMENT IN THE GENERATORS,
or ALL THREE

DO YOUR PART
WE CAN BEAT
GLOBAL WARMING!

Canopy Publishing
Post Office Box 1026
Eastsound, Washington 98245
www.canopypublishing.com

Cover Art by Martin Gerad

Library of Congress Control Number 2004104285
ISBN 0-9753655-0-9

Printed in the United States of America

The
GALILEO
Syndrome

Daniel H. Gottlieb

CANOPY PUBLISHING
Washington   2004

Preface

In 1971, while pursuing a degree in biomedical engineering, a professor of mine suggested that perhaps my interests might lie someplace other than physics, engineering, and biology. He prompted me to read Loren Eisley, Aldo Leopold, John Muir, and others. At the time, I was interested but not impressed by the job prospects available to an environmental philosopher and so followed a track similar to most people: My interests were one part of my life, my revenue generation, another part--there were of course many others.

Over time I took part in the phenomenon called Silicon Valley. Working for Hewlett Packard, Lockheed, and other companies I became involved with the intricacies of advanced software as a system for integrating the heretofore disparate activities in engineering and manufacturing and their impacts, fiscal and otherwise, on the overall performance of an enterprise.

It was during this time that the notion of an environment, an ecosystem began to change for me. As we worked to translate the actions, and functionality, of subsystems into a patterned language--an acceptable software environment--for all members of the enterprise it became obvious that the problem seemed totally unbounded, i.e.; irreconcilable.

Until, through the process of modeling, it became clear that the esoteric software (intelligent software, non-linear software, AI) only needed a certain set of attributes to be truly helpful in integration. That set of attributes was the software needed to understand it was software and network needed to understand it was a network--and of course, that understanding could change over time. For you bit-heads out there: object systems.

While I had very little to do with the actual coding and architecture, I was lucky enough to work with the very best software people Silicon Valley had to offer. And while I was no where near as technical as them--I learned a great deal. Probably because, during that time I had carte blanche into the top R&D labs in the country helping to address incredibly complex problems, all needing advanced software. There were manufacturing applications, engineering applications, power generation, safety, and space applications--to name a few. I worked with a some of the national labs and spent quite a bit of time working with the utility industry and its R&D arm: The Electric Power Research Institute

While managing a project for EPRI, with a technical lead, I began to stumble across the problem of climate change--back then, 1985--it was a curiosity worthy of science fiction, and gobs of dollars for the modeling of climate and weather systems. The science seemed plausible and the effect too compelling for me to ignore.

It took no time to see our notion of ecosystem, of environment, was too bounded. Environmentalists could not understand economists. Corporate boards could not understand their own insulation--and no one seemed to see, and give weight to, our human environmental impacts were more than an interrelated set of physical events quantifiable by "good science."

The Galileo Syndrome was started in 1990; I had, and I still have, respect for "good science." But as I grew, partially though this event called Climate Change, I saw that true change develops only from the inside, that Jung's collective unconsciousness is merely a scratch on truth. Our environment will change, it always does, but if environmentalists are blind to a major part of the system they live in; a corporate culture, its economy, and its power structure, they will forever antagonize decision makers. As well, for the decision-makers of our culture to foolishly discount awareness that will certainly shape their markets is more than fear, ego, and greed. It is, for our species, a collective misunderstanding of our environment and the magnificent impact we humans, and others, have on this planet--and that sometimes we truly do need to make dramatic mid-course corrections.

Daniel H. Gottlieb

For Ama and La.

Thank you.
Without you both, my life is meaningless.
Thank you for being here, now.

Prepare To See The Future

The Fiftieth Anniversary of Earthday

Chapter One

"My father beats my mommy.
My mommy clobbers me.
My grandpa is a trekkie.
My grandma pushes tea.
My sister wears a phaser.
My brother...."

"Hold it. Now children, this piece of music is sixty-years old. Haven't you heard it enough in the last two months to get it right--yet?" The music teacher raps his baton on the music stand and pushes back his vagrant brown hair. Beneath a gray goatee, he pulls on a loose green bow tie. Regis Van Waters raises his baton like a saber ready to strike. The baton slashes toward the students with two broad, crossing strokes. To most it looks like the beginning of another temper tantrum. "What's so difficult here, children?"

Carlos Jordan stamps his foot on the bass drum peddle.

Boomp.

The high school teacher's glare shifts to the seventeen-year-old behind the trap set. Carlos Jordan's bony face remains passive, except for the hint of disdain that lights his blue eyes. "It slipped, Mr. Van Waters, sorry."

Head shaking, "Back at you, Champ. Now look, we're two weeks away from having an audience out there. I, for one do not wish to be embarrassed by a ragged orchestra, lame actors, or insolent drummers who belong in a cage. Am I clear, Mr. Jordan?"

Carlos' gaze remains open but defiant.

A burp erupts from the young male actors bunched on stage. Outflanked but determined to remain in control, Van Waters turns to the actors. "Now look, Jets. This is a baton, for those of you who have forgotten. It's your responsibility to occasionally look, and maybe--just maybe--pay attention to it."

On stage, a blond boy shakes his head slowly side to side--as if he has never seen a baton before. He glances at Carlos, winks, and then returns to slack-jawed gawking at the frustrated conductor.

"And you people in the orchestra. Is it too much to ask you to play the right notes?" His voice a plaintive song, he continues with: "Without the correct notes, the rest of us cannot play our music correctly."

A blond girl, a flute player in second chair, looks as if she is going to cry; she nods her head emphatically. The music teacher's hard stare drops her like kill. A music stand falls over in the trumpet section. There is unanimous dislike for the pompous Mr. Van Waters.

His eyes narrow. "Last, and certainly least," he shifts his gaze back to the percussion section, "you two dummies on the drums please be a little quieter, hmmm? When the Jets and the Sharks fight, you'll have plenty of time to make all the noise you want, but for now, try to keep the noise down." The other percussionist, Sheffield Pard, bows formally behind his timpani and looks down at his vest watch.

The three-thirty buzzer sounds. "Well, I guess that does it for today. I wouldn't want to keep you socially conscious people from your appointed activities. Tomorrow we'll do a complete run-through of the last act."

The students stand.

"I'm not finished. Sit. Now look." A sly leer rises across his face then drops like a curtain. "I know some of you kids don't think much of our New United Nations. I know some of you don't approve of our President's decision to accept the Greenhouse Laws initiated by the New United Nations. On the other hand, my precious artists, the planet is telling us something with these hurricanes, tornadoes and fifteen-inch rainstorms. The President's decision to join with U-dot-N-dot will stop global warming...."

"It will also limit our mobility," says a male voice from the stage crowd.

"We must follow our leaders." Van Waters is a Neo-hippie; and to him any act of defiance is a waste of time. His sarcastic smile immediately melts as he scans the bored students. He considers them dullards.

He leans forward over his black music stand: "I think our President's decision is a good decision. So should you. Remember this is a Republic." He straightens up. "Of course, voicing your opinions for, or against the decision, is part of what this country is about; however violence is not." He taps his baton on the stand. "Listen up. You each have the right to speak. But there is no place for violence in a free society. This isn't Columbia, and this isn't Berkeley. This is a rich-kid high school in the suburbs of New York City. Try to remember that. And while you're at it, try to remember there's really nothing you can do about the Greenhouse Laws anyway." He scans the students before him. "United Networks took over the old United Nations, and we had a referendum. Most voted against it. The New U.N., the U-dot-N-dot happened anyway. This is the same deal: Tis a fait accompli. In other words--a done deal. So learn your music well, kiddies."

"Yes, Mr. Van Waters," peeps the young girl who received the rock-like stare.

"Good." He smiles at her. "You're dismissed." Chairs scrape on the floor. The students run out the steel side-doors and hastily put their instruments away. The expected confrontation will be located in the middle of the fortress-like high school--and safe seating will be limited.

Sheffield Pard pushes his shoulder-length black hair away from his face. "Carlos," Sheffield's grey eyes look open and friendly. "Are you going to be with us?"

Carlos considers every conversation with Sheffield Pard a diplomatic training session. "I thought the class officers decided to be neutral." He points to the black armband.

"Oh, thanks." Sheffield's face sports an easy grin as the black armband slides down the pressed white shirtsleeve and disappears in the pocket of his slacks. "See I am neutral. So are you with us, Mister Diplomat?"

"Not me. I learned from Harry and May not to take sides in a fight."

"The riot will not be as bad as that." Sheffield stares down at Carlos' athletic shoes--as if he could see the missing pinky toe. Deftly tying his hair into an executive ponytail--one where the hair falls straight in a single tightly greased bunch beneath a topknot--Pard smiles a brilliant white grin.

Carlos shifts uncomfortably.

"Think about it. I will see you later." Sheffield turns; his black hair swings pole-like between his shoulder blades. Carlos curses the reaction he has to Sheffield's gaze. A good diplomat needs more cool than that he tells himself.

Lars, the blond boy from the stage with the gastric disturbance, ambles past Pard. Pard acknowledges him with a wave of his hand and continues walking.

"I see Pard is still practicing for the executive suite by keeping his head up his butt. Just what do you two have in common besides who pounds louder on the drums?"

"The only thing he and I have in common is the planet. He wants to rule the world. I want to keep it friendly. Your stomach settle down yet?"

"Yup, seems to only get upset when Herr Van Waters is speaking. Pard ask you to join his side of the argument?" Lars plays the cowbell projecting from the trap set with the backside of his hand.

"Pushed it all rehearsal." Carlos rubs his thin nose with the pair of claves clenched in a wiry hand.

"I am surprised Sheffield did not try to punch you out for not agreeing about humanity's God-given right to piss all over the planet."

"Pard and I made peace after I caught him stealing a math test. I tell him nicely to take a hike and he makes cracks about my parents. Diplomacy in action."

"Let's bat some balls. I do not want to be around here any longer than I need to be," Lars says.

They cross the carpeted floor and exit the auditorium. Carlos stops, lips pursed. A second later, face composed he opens one of the lockers built into the grey-green walls of the hall.

"So where do you want to go?" Lars asks warily. Carlos had mentioned something this morning about helping out this afternoon at the Greenhouse Laws protest rally. "Does the batting range still sound good to you? Or do you want to play some Ping Pong?"

"Actually, I was thinking about the courtyard."

Lars slams the locker door and faces Carlos. "I guess I must have been dreaming when I heard you say only an idiot would intentionally attend a riot."

"Maybe it will not be a riot. You are far too excitable."

"Carlos, my noble but foolish friend, I have never seen this place more alive. This will not be a forum today. It will be a feeding frenzy. Anyone who has been pissed off is going to use this excuse to beat the crap out of someone."

"I think not. A riot is like love. It is not a necessary evil. You have to want it to happen."

"You need help," Lars points at Carlos. Carlos nods as if he agrees and opens the locker door. After putting the music book away, they walk in silence.

In the hallway they pass a large blond girl from the trumpet section stretching her back in a forward fold. Her powder blue cashmere sweater sits on the tan tile floor. A black armband lies on the sweater. She stops stretching and rolls a black armband up her arm then wraps her right hand in a small leather belt. She tests the fit by punching a locker door. A moment later she begins to stretch her legs.

"Carlos," Lars says as they pass the girl, "you hate fighting. Why go to this?"

"Lars, the world is going crazy." Carlos stops and checks a door into the music storage room. It is still open. "I can't just go play Ping Pong while that happens."

"Our parents did. And two hours ago you were going to do just that, my friend." Lars follows Carlos inside watching Carlos check the windows. Lars rests his arm on a circular chrome frame that holds a Chinese gong. "Why not let them kill each other? These are barbarians who love to make messes. Why do you need to clean it up?" He taps the gong with his knuckles. A deep melodious tone fills through the room. "I love that sound."

"Lars, you know what happened with my toe?"

"Everyone does. So what?"

"I didn't turn the hose on my parents that night because a scissor lopped off my toe. I did it because I was worried about the rest of me."

Lars shrugs. "And they are still rabid."

Carlos narrows his eyes. "Not funny."

"Sorry."

"The point is if I had not waited, I would still have all my appendages. This rally today seems no different to me."

"But we do not need to be here. How about this? We can sit here a minute and think about something less important? I have a smoke on me," Lars says slyly. It is his final ploy.

"After. I may be stupid enough to go to this free-for-all today and try to stop it--I am not stupid enough to go trashed."

"Stop it? What for? Carlos, this is the social event of the year here at Vertwall High."

"Whoa'. Wait a minute. A few weeks ago you were arrested trying to get food shipped to Eritrea. A month before that you defended that Asian kid against those three clowns from Jersey. What is the difference here?"

Lars produces a lighter from his pocket. "You have a thousand bored rich kids out there. They want this riot. Just like your parents, they want to fight. They do dumb things because they enjoy it. I do not enjoy dumb things. I am not going to participate."

"Lars, I am scared to death about getting my face pounded in today.

And, to tell you the truth, I would really like to leave and go play Ping Pong."

"Now that is sensible." Lars lights the joint, takes a puff, and then hands it to Carlos.

"But I am not going to leave."

Lars sighs smoke. "Carlos, eight million people died in China six months ago because they couldn't read the U-dot-N-dot mandated language of English. One hundred and fifty thousand were washed away in Peru three weeks ago because they couldn't read the signs either. That kind of thing is worth stopping. Hell, I will risk my life to save people who want to be saved. These people do not want to be saved. This designer riot is not worth our time."

"It is all the same, Lars."

Lars throws his hands up in disgust. "So you are going?"

Carlos is silent as he exits the room.

Lars takes a long hit. "Damn." He snuffs the red tip between his fingers and pockets the remainder. After a pause he taps the gong and leaves the music room. Lars admires Carlos.

A few seconds later Lars reaches the bank of windows that looks out on the courtyard seeking Carlos. Two distinct groups fill the courtyard. One group is made up of shorthaired students wearing white shirts and black armbands. The other group is composed of bald-headed boys wearing ankle length kilts and girls in tight Indian print dresses. He sees Carlos walking distractedly, watching the crowd, then bumping into a pretty cheerleader by the name of Debbie Gold.

"Hey yo, Carlos. When I said I wanted your help, I didn't mean knocking over my woman." Sheffield Pard stands beside Debbie Gold as she peers around the courtyard.

She speaks: "Look at those bald-headed Freaks and their goofy-looking girlfriends. Those clothes went out years ago. I swear." She watches the unstylish group across the courtyard. She faces Sheffield, her eyes glowing. "The Freaks have started calling those who support the Greenhouse Laws, Greenies. We are not going to stand for that." A hint of lust colors Debbie's voice.

"Quite a recipe for fun," Lars looks for the school security guard, nowhere to be seen. Lars thinks she is probably under the bleachers in the gym, strung out again. He thinks about asking Debbie to join him under the bleachers to look for the guard. He smiles at Sheffield.

"I think the Greenhouse Laws are good, and I don't care if they do try and fight. They are not going to keep me from expressing myself. No way are those Freaks going to tell me I cannot support the New U.N. and the Greenhouse Laws. I am an American. And what's the problem anyway? We own the U.N." Debbie stares malevolently at those who protest the Greenhouse Laws--laws which limit the amount of energy one can use. "Give me your armband, Sheff," she says.

Sheffield smirks handing her his armband: "So which side are you on, Carlos? The neurotic side that says our ecological disaster was ignored so we would lose our freedoms, or the Greenies' side representing boldness, freedom, progress, and commerce?"

"You want to see the Freaks beat up because they are upset about losing their freedom?" Lars asks Debbie.

Pard answers for her. "Not at all my excitable friend. My dad works for the U.N.'s Growth Revitalization and Environmental Enforcement Agency. I plan to also work for them. And I do not want anything to get in my way. Therefore I am with the Greenies. Don't you agree, Deb?" He smiles at Lars.

"Your President agreed that a foreign military presence on your soil might be acceptable," Lars says baiting Sheffield.

"Ah, they are all our soldiers, Lars, you know that. You're just torqued Sweden doesn't own the New U.N.. Someone has to enforce the laws that say 'stop using so much energy.' So you're with us, Carlos?" Pard says.

"Nope. I already told you, no fighting for me--on either side."

A measured astonishment crosses Debbie's face. "Well, that is a surprise. I might think you would be used to it." She tosses words like spikes when she is angry.

Innuendos about Carlos' parents' well-known arguments were a soft spot, but they would not help in recruiting Carlos. Sheffield shoots Debbie an angry glance. Secretly he is glad to have an excuse for failing to recruit Carlos. He detests this boy he considers too old-fashioned "Carlos, the class officers will be on the north wall trying to keep order. You are welcome to sit with us."

"Thanks Sheffield--but no thanks." Carlos says. He and Lars step onto the concrete path that meanders through the center of the courtyard.

Lars examines the opposing factions in the courtyard. "It looks an even fight. Shall we pick a side, or do you want punch out a small cripple in each group and leave?"

Carlos looks around, smiling at his friend's dark humor. The excitement of battle in the air scares him momentarily. "Let's leave the cripples alone."

"Ya' can't have commerce on a dead planet, stupid," yells a bald-headed boy across the courtyard.

Another voice responds. "Who says we have to listen to the New U-dot-N-dot fascist Greenies? We know people are dying from global warming. We can solve this problem."

A can sails out in response from the New U.N. supporters' crowd and lands near the "Freak" crowd. Middle fingers shoot into the air like salutes.

"So where do you want to sit, freedom or survival?" Lars keeps an eye out for more flying pop cans.

"Rather a shitty choice to make. It is a shame this debate didn't take place twenty years ago. How about we sit in the middle?"

"The middle of what?" Lars asks uneasily, knowing Carlos meant the free-form concrete walkway between the crowds. A yellow pencil flies end over end across the courtyard and bounces off the back of a short African girl. She turns with a sneer.

Carlos and Lars are in no-man's-land. Carlos, careful to pick a spot exactly in the center, prepares to sit on the edge of concrete and grass. Lars grabs his shoulder before he sits.

The pencil sails back across no man's land hitting one large window of the cafeteria. "Why the center?" Lars finds himself less fearful than amazed at Carlos' apparent ignorance to his own danger.

Carlos continues scanning the two groups. "Well, I will let you know when I find out. You can go hang out with the class officers."

"My ass. I am not going back to Sweden and say I sat on the sidelines while you Americans had one of your famous eco-riots. I will neighbor with you. I just wanted to know why we are going to get our heads busted by everyone instead of only half of the school body."

"No reason." Carlos and Lars sit in unison. This moment will remain with Carlos long past his friend's death. "I am so scared," Carlos mumbles. More people notice where they sit than Carlos would ever have guessed.

Lars looks around. He has decided protecting Carlos is now a priority. When asked about it in the years ahead Lars will quip. "He was just too stupid for me not to protect him." Lars looks about for a weapon. "What do you really think, Carlos? I know it is a major invasion of privacy to ask you to answer a direct question, but do you think the restrictions on energy consumption are fair?" He is talking just to calm himself. Lars scans the schoolyard for the pencil.

"The greenhouse effect is wiping humanity off the planet," Carlos replies. "We have no choice. We need to reverse the greenhouse effect by restricting energy consumption--or it will eliminate us. The US oligarchy owns the New United Nations: They own the stock markets; they own the media. They own the armed forces. Therefore we have to restrict the energy used because they tell us to--otherwise they'll kill us."

"They're killing us anyway." Lars sees a fat girl in a brightly colored sari holding a small canister of mace in her chubby hand. Nearby stand two boys with dirty sweat socks filled with coins. Any hope of today being just a shouting match dissolves in his mind. "Sure does look like once again the population has no choice."

"The people who administer the laws will abuse them, but Van Waters was right. It is already a done deal. Besides, no cars, no shopping trips, no Orlando vacations, no plastics. It does not seem so bad to me," Carlos says apparently oblivious to the mounting fervor. "The ghost of Kyoto comes out of the bush."

Lars forces a laugh. "For some people, this is a living hell."

Carlos turns to his friend. "Your problem is you are just not selfish enough."

Carlos starts locating the troublemakers on each side.

"Looking for guys who want to kick your butt, I bet. You couldn't have made it any easier," Lars says.

"I have it figured. They'll have to stand in line. It might not be so bad. Or you can take care of them."

"Count on it," Lars says quietly. As he scans the crowd he finds himself wishing he had smoked the entire joint.

"Eco-Nazi pig," a voice screams.

In the courtyard now, thirty hard-core supporters of the Greenhouse Laws pull into a huddle against the east wall. Lobbing the term 'Freaks' as if it were a mortar round across the yard a bubble of sinister laughter erupts. Those against the laws huddle as well. Their return round of "Damn greenie fascists," has even more hatred. On the north wall, the class officers huddle among themselves.

Carlos waits; sweat pouring down his forehead, as the sun seems to point directly at him. Lars watches.

A girl's voice electronically crackles from the west side of the courtyard. Although Carlos does not remember her name, he knows the voice. She organized the anti-Greenhouse Laws movement in the school. Her strawberry blond hair and dark, intelligent eyes lure him with a quick glance. Her brightly colored clothes silhouette her young body. She is the sexiest woman Carlos has ever seen.

"With the Greenhouse Laws no one will have any freedom. You get an allotment of energy. Then you do as they say--or get put to work in those damn generators they're building everywhere. People are not hamsters to be locked in cages and run for hours a day..."

From the south wall, the side doors swing open and the beer-gutted security guard walks out followed by the principal, the vice-principal and three gym teachers. The rest of the staff is nowhere to be seen, except for a couple of the young English teachers who stand near the Greenhouse Laws supporters chatting with a student in a wheelchair.

The pretty blond girl--Carlos remembers her name: Roxanne Gladstone--waits until the administration takes up positions near the class officers. She speaks again in a clear, but tense voice. "This is the first Freedom Day at Vertwall High School, but freedom has been slipping away from us for years. Our President has made an agreement with Asian, European, and Mid-Eastern power junkies to condemn our generation to a nineteenth-century lifestyle of limited movement, rationed power, and U-dot-N-dot laws for our entire life. They say these laws are supposed to save the ecosystem of this planet by limiting our energy consumption. Where were these laws thirty years ago? The truth of the matter is the Greenhouse Laws are only meant to enslave us so the privileged can live as they please." The crowd around her cheers. "The global laws called the Greenhouse Laws have never been approved by the people. And it is up to clear-thinking Americans to force our Congressmen and Senators to preserve our freedoms and--"

Another electronic crackle thunders from the booing crowd across the courtyard. A tall fat boy with a beard and buzz-cut hair speaks. "Friends, that Freak thinks this is just a game of politics. But she is wrong. This is survival. Without the Greenhouse Laws we will perish and the cockroaches will inherit this planet. The Greenhouse Laws say you have to give up your car and eliminate energy usage after dusk." He stops and his eyes open in mock surprise. "So what? Look here." His arms reach out. "Friends, I do not like it either. But if our parents, all of our parents, had not been so gutless, we would not have to solve global warming by ourselves.

"And dig it, giving up cars is not so much. Adhering to recycling laws is not so much. Not traveling more than ten miles from your home is not too much. Even the jobs lost to save the hundreds of endangered species including man, are not too much. Disease, death, and extinction though, they are too much."

The boy looks around melodramatically. "My friends, if you want to know the real truth: I do not want the laws either. But I am not going to shirk my responsibility like my parents."

His crowd cheers while the other crowd hisses.

The boy continues speaking. "The alternative to the laws is extinction. We must rally together and support the Greenhouse Laws." Cheers and whoops roar from his supporters.

"Why didn't they do it earlier, Dupe?"

"Eco-Nazi."

Carlos looks back at Roxanne Gladstone. Her crossed arms accentuate her breasts beneath the bright yellow cloth of her blouse. She brings the bullhorn to her full and slightly crooked lips. He admires them as she speaks. Carlos has found a way to forget his fear.

"We students here at Vertwall High School must show solidarity to solve our problem. I agree. But the people who wrote these laws want to control us by using ecological disaster to control the population. No energy equals no freedom." She continues speaking but her voice is drowned out by the opposition.

"Baloney. Fellow students," another voice booms out, "no one can deny the disasters of the last few years. The hurricanes, the tornadoes, the hundreds of millions of dead in India, Greece and Mexico, the loss of New Orleans--these events are fact. Yet our friends over there say: 'Who are we going to trust?' Oh come on. Get a clue, pooh, trust? Oh make my day. Are we going to be like those reactionaries over there and only trust the people who tell us our leaders are money grubbing business-people and power-crazed politicians? What is the secret there? Our society is corrupt. Duh, no kidding. Things are not going to change. It is just the way things are now. Look, here is the fact: The only difference in our lives, beside some inconvenience, is that after the Greenhouse Laws, privileges will be formalized. So damn what? We can all use a little clarity in our lives. We need to cope, not hide."

"Do not give away your freedom because it is convenient," Roxanne yells back.

The boy smiles at her. "As realists, we must recognize the reality of our planet getting fed up and fixing to burp us out. We must support the Greenhouse Laws. In spite of the likelihood that it might diminish our freedoms. This will take guts. Do we have what it takes? Or will we join the dinosaurs and the eco-ostriches over there and just complain?"

A boy with a can of beer and an arm full of black armbands stands up. "One thing is for damn sure. We are not going to let them get away with not supporting the laws at this school." The voices of support grow louder from the New U.N. crowd. "Hell, yes." The boy launches his beer can across the courtyard. It lands at Roxanne's foot, hitting her in the ankle. She stares at it a moment, her pale complexion reddening.

Lars' head moves back and forth as if he were watching a tennis match. Roxanne kicks the can with her sandaled foot. Another can flies back across the yard flipping end over end before it rests near the other speaker.

A third empty beer can flies across the courtyard just missing Carlos. Lars reaches over and stands it up. "That was meant for us." Lars says.

Carlos studies Roxanne and the tall brawny boy who appears beside her. He looks like a college student. The stranger's sneer momentarily fixes on Carlos.

Lars looks at the stranger, then at Carlos. "That's smart, piss off a stranger. You will make a great diplomat. What are you smiling at now?" Lars asks. "That guy wants to rip your throat out."

"That guy would have only one reason to fear me so much: Her."

Roxanne speaks: "Don't you people realize that this is not just a discussion about giving up your cars and having less time to watch TV? Think about it. Who is going to decide who has the privileges? Who is going to decide who gets use of private transport? And who is going to decide what industry is critical? Not us, and not you. It will be the people who invoke the Greenhouse Laws. They will control us."

A thin boy with a buzz cut hairdo steps to within five feet of Carlos. Lars tenses. "The cowards who are against these laws are against them because they are chickens." He grins at Carlos.

The battle-pot boils.

"Who's chicken--you dumb Mick," yells a tall basketball player making a fist. The crowds each step closer to the center.

"Do you want to sit and be trampled? Or shall we stand and be trampled?" Lars' head darts left and right as the crowds begin to inch forward. Carlos stands up and Lars bounces to his feet. But then, when Carlos puts one knee to the ground and spreads his arms, Lars freezes. --What the hell-- he says to himself.

Carlos bellows.

"The Jets are gonna' have their way tonight!...Rah Rah Rhee, kick 'em in the knee! Rah Rah Rass, kick him in the other knee!" Carlos explodes up in the air arms and legs wide. He lands on his feet and drops to one knee. "Go, Sharks. Go Jets!"

The crowd, advancing to the center of the courtyard slows, mystified at the apparent riot-cheerleading section made up of Carlos Jordan and a befuddled Swedish exchange student apparently caught in a madhouse.

"...The Puerto Ricans grumble, fair fight. But if they want to rumble, we'll rumble 'em right." Both arms spread to the azure sky and Carlos takes a very short breath: "We're gonna' cut 'em down to size--tonight." Carlos winks at Roxanne, then the college student. "We said okay, no rufus, no trick. But just in case they jump us, we're ready to kick..." Carlos stands and begins to parade back and forth in the center of the courtyard kicking his feet in the air and leaning forward after each kick. The crowd is thrilled but appalled by his lack of decorum; he seems to be cheering both sides into a fight. But they no longer edge closer together.

"Tonight." He yells, pointing his index finger into the air.

The would-be rioters stare at Carlos, angry at his interference, certain that he is crazy.

Carlos, as if he could read their minds, hunches his shoulders and begins to walk like an ape. "When you're a Jet, you're a Jet all the way, from your first cigarette, to your last dying day. When you're a Jet, you've got brothers around. You're a family man. You're never alone. You're never disconnected. Your home is to loan; the company's expected." Carlos, swinging his arms, lumbers back and forth. "You're well protected."

"I told you that son of a bitch was crazy," someone says. "Some diplomat you'll be--"

"On Mars." Laughter follows from both sides, and they remain apart.

"To-night, to-night, won't be like any night...." Carlos pirouettes, interlaced hands beneath his chin, and then begins to dance between the two opposing sides. The two opposing sides share smiles.

Roxanne walks over to Lars. "He is just looking to start a fight, isn't he?"

Lars looks at her. "Tsk, tsk, you judge him harshly. Perhaps thine own eyes speak in blind horror of the mirror's word." Carlos completes an aerial turn and falls. Lars knows if there is a fight now, Carlos will be beaten to a pulp. He holds his breath.

"Well then, what does he want?" Roxanne asks in a yell. Carlos gets up and begins to clap his hands. "Fight, fight, we want a fight."

"I think he is too scared to know what he wants. He is just doing 'something'." Lars turns from her, hunches his shoulders, and lumbers over to join Carlos in a chorus of the Jet song.

Roxanne scans the crowds and notices the angry mood of both camps is replaced by surprise and amusement. There will be no fighting today.

A moment later the woman who plays Maria in the school's Spring musical production steps out of the Greenhouse Laws-support crowd and joins them. Krupke, Biff, and Bernardo follow from the anti-law group. They all continue to dance and sing. Slowly, the mobs on either side of the courtyard break into small knots of people and student officers begin to circulate. Then, amazingly, people start to leave. Roxanne watches, then swings her backpack over her shawled shoulder and joins in on the final chorus of "Officer Cupcake."

Minutes later, Carlos, who is exhausted, looks around. Lars and Roxanne dance a waltz. "The crowd is almost gone," he says in quiet amazement. The concert is over. Carlos sits down on the concrete.

Students pass Carlos making unkind comments about how he tried to start a riot. Lars' robotic repetition of "Up yours," follows them to the doors as he dances. Finally, Carlos, covered in sweat, lies down.

Roxanne flops on the grass beside Carlos a moment later. Her Madras print shawl falls to the grass with her pack. Her tanned shoulders are soft and round.

"I am Roxanne Gladstone." She holds out her hand and presses his.

"Where is your escort?" Carlos says, scanning the small knots of people still left in the courtyard.

Roxanne smiles slyly. "I don't know. How about some pizza...Lars? You can come also, Carlos."

Chapter Two

Above him, shattered tree branches poke through the remains of a white-framed greenhouse. Broken glass litters the concrete floor like thrown spears. "It's not my fault the damn storm knocked everything down." Harry Jordan kicks a broken blue bucket. He leans on the wooden rake; his hands capping each other. Harry waits for his wife's response. None comes. "So what are you bitching at me for, May?" Looking around the punctured greenhouse, his eyes narrow--still no response. Harry hates it when she ignores him. "Damn storms." He kicks a glass shard. It tinkles across the floor. "This is the fourth time in three years the glass needs replacing. Carlos, hurry up with that trash bucket. Hey, May."

Across the shattered remains of the family greenhouse, behind a potting table, May, the wife, straightens up a tin of fuchsias. She is a thin, angry woman in a cheap red flowered dress she hates. She stares at a mound of dead red and purple fuchsias that has glass in it--no good even for compost. May stands, pulling a small metal shard from the bench. It had been driven into the wood during last nights' storms. She wipes the metal with an old gray sweatshirt sleeve. The words: "Milan 2003" are smeared with dirt.

"May."

May is too angry to talk. At times like this she sees her husband as foolish. Even the distant elms she planted when Carlos was born seem ridiculous to her. They are torn back to twigs.

--They bend in such strange ways after a large storm--

She glances over her shoulder at the house. One wall ripped away, the second floor bathtub in the kitchen below, the new couch full of water and flat as a pancake. May rolls the shard of metal over in her hands.

--Too cheaply built, Harry is always looking for a deal. And now we do more time in Rent-A-Shelter. God, I hate those concrete boxes--

She glances at her watch.

--Carlos will be leaving soon to see his latest girl--

May wonders what this girl looks like and it hurts. She knows why they have never met any of his girls: he is ashamed of his parents' renowned anger. "I found another part of the neighbor's metal roof. The insurance gal will want to see it. Where is the pile?" She pushes back graying brown hair with her forearm. "And why does the red cross always give us flowered dresses?"

"I'm gonna' goddamn sue those bastards," Harry says, stepping down on a foot high pile of broken glass to hear it break. "I told Harrelson."

"Those are the Quarlys not the Harrelsons--"

"Who cares? I told them not to use one of those metal roofs--especially a cheap one." He wipes his muscular hands on his brown coveralls and sniffs his armpits. Fit and trim, he pulls on the front of his blue tank top wondering if it is getting too tight.

"If you had listened to me and put in the plastic panes, we wouldn't need to sue anyone," May tosses the piece of metal through the greenhouse frame like a Frisbee. It lands on the remains of the neighbor's hedge. She looks away quickly. "Where the hell is Carlos? I bet he's hiding again."

"Or he went to play Ping Pong again. Carlos," calls his father. In some ways it is a tribute to the human spirit that these two can continue their pettiness in the midst of the destruction around them. It is also a proof of madness, as they have no idea what is bothering their son this morning. Neither of them has given a second thought to the young woman who pounded and cried at the door of their storm shelter last night.

Carlos, still as a fawn, sits behind a wall of tall brown trash cans. His hands at his side; he stares at the ribs of a dead cat. His vision of the world petrifies him.

Silently, he again curses those who have placed humanity in hell and further tightened the reigns of his imprisonment. Carlos worries about Roxanne. Last night, just before evacuation to the storm cellar, he tried to reach her through the Internet. A message came up saying "...use of Internet for student chat-sessions has been banned because they are a non-essential activity and energy usage is now on a need to use basis." At the bottom of the screen it also said "We need team players like you, Carlos Jordan. Call us when you graduate college. Thank you. The Global Revitalization and Environmental Enforcement Network"--the Greenies. Carlos had laughed at the message calling him a team player. For him, a team player has no conscience and never talks about the world falling further into chaos. In a few years Carlos will work for the Greenies. He will never talk about the chaos. It will be a difficult time.

"Carlos, get out here. There's work to be done." Carlos slowly stands and pours glass into large brown recycling cans. Hands shaking as pieces spill all over the concrete pad, he steadies himself on the brown cans and tries again.

"He spilled it again," decries his mother. Carlos leans over to pick up the glass. "Damnit, Harry. I told you--you were too rough on him last night."

"Me?" The battle continues.

"First it was the storm. Then there was your raving about that woman. Then teasing Carlos, then fighting with me, then the greenhouse damage, then complaining about the neighbors' roof..." Their battle shifts to who did what to Carlos. The battles never end here.

Tears fall from the boy. Moments later he tells himself it is fear from the roar of the winds last night, the thumping of the door as object after object bounced off it; anyone would cry. But it does not help. A truth deep inside Carlos hurts like a red-hot hook. The boy sits and buries his face in his hands. He tries to face it all.

--My parents are crazy--

Last night during the horrific storm as they were ranting at the winds and cursing at everything under heaven his parents heard a woman kicking at the door of the storm cellar. The woman was begging for help: "My daughter is trapped in the basement. The water. She'll drown. Help me. Please." Harry and May ceased yelling. They looked about the small concrete bunker for signs of intruding water. Carlos rose to open the door--only to be kicked in the small of the back by his dad. The furious blow sent him sprawling onto his moldy folded cot.

"Sit the hell down. You want to get us killed?" His dad had said. Carlos still could not catch his breath. He sat panting like a dog all night. The grieving woman had heard the voices and called louder to them. "My baby--help me. Please." Her pounding and howling drowned out the storm for Carlos. When he tried to stand again, his father made a fist. It was all he needed to do.

After a loud thump and silence from the voice, his parent's accusatory screams rose to a crescendo. It changed to cursing, then silence, then laughter--at his stupidity in wanting to open the door in the middle of a deadly storm. The merciless teasing went on for hours. When the storm subsided his parents slept. At some point in the calm, Carlos felt his heart go blank.

When his father opened the door, Carlos wept over the battered body. That was four hours ago. In those hours Carlos relived what happened. Clearly I had no choice; he now tells himself. His soul moans louder pleading with him to see further--to what has happened.

Carlos steels himself and stands again; he circles back around the bins. Wiping his hands, he steps through a huge hole in the side of the greenhouse. No one has found the door yet. He glances up at the black clock clunking as it rocks back and forth above the torn doorway. He gains comfort from the clock's ability to still function after last night's storm.

Carlos' vision about his parents is now quite clear.

--Well the hell with them--

"I am going now," he calls to his parents.

"Did you clean the glass you spilled?" Replies his mother.

"Yes." He grabs his backpack.

"Did you spread the manure on the beds?" Asks his father.

"Yes." He is lying and does not care. Carlos walks to the house. A blank heart has little conscience.

"Why don't you stay and help us clean?" Says his mother. "Or is Ping Pong more important?"

"I missed that already, mom."

"So you're off to see what's-her-name," says his mother.

"The kid's got a date. Let him be," says his dad.

"She is probably helping her family clean up," May Jordan says, picking up a battered dark red beet. She drops it back onto the ground when she sees it is too torn up to be eaten. Ten years from now beets just like this one will be sold in markets. "Trust me, what's-her-name won't be sailing after the storm we had last night."

"You don't know Roxanne--"

"No. I do not," retorts May.

He ignores her comment. "--Or the rest of those sailing nuts. Its a point of pride to race regardless of the storms." He grabs a small plastic water bottle and turns to leave.

Harry Jordan waits at the greenhouse opening as Carlos approaches. A well-muscled man with wispy brown chest hair that pokes out the blue tank top he has his arms akimbo. Carlos slows. Harry Jordan suddenly sports a bright fatherly smile. "Son, you be back here by four so you can spread the manure like we told you." He steps back to let Carlos pass, but leans over to whisper in his ear. "Don't worry. It'll be enough time. If she doesn't suck you by four, you're wasting your time."

Carlos grits his teeth. Normally he would have answered with a comment about his father's crudeness. Today he says: "See ya'." Carlos bolts down the trail behind the house.

"Damn. May, will you look at this mess? He didn't clean up the glass he spilled or spread the manure. Carlos, get back here." Carlos hurries away, over fallen trees and past debris that covers the roadside trail.

About five hundred feet down hill he reaches a road. Across the littered street, a paramedic sits on a log that has fallen across a driveway. Head buried in dirty hands, the paramedic sobs; at his feet sit, a crumpled, wet, Raggedy Ann doll.

Before the man can look up, Carlos sprints away; he knows the drowned child belongs to this man. Carlos trips over a tire on the side of the road. He gets up without looking back and runs more. At the first sight of the Hudson River he stops.

Calm white sails fill the basin.

Carlos looks back. The man is gone; the doll remains. Weeks later Carlos will walk down that drive and talk to a woman. She will describe herself as a former grandmother. They will talk about the weather and he will leave. Before the end of the month, the grandmother will also commit suicide. Her grave, her son's grave and the child's grave, will have fresh flowers until Carlos leaves for college. Carlos will steal the flowers from his parent's flower shop.

He trots slowly downhill wondering about Roxanne.

The news will report fourteen thousand people dead in the New York metropolitan area. A somber, well-dressed news person will further say: "Most died in collapsing structures or were hit by falling objects. Fire has taken others. Only handfuls have drowned in basements."

Along the entire east coast of North America sixty thousand more will have died in the monster storms that are common. In the next few days another ten thousand will die from untreated wounds and exposure. Fifteen students from Carlos' school have also died; a weakened limb falling on a bus that was taking them home from a democracy lecture.

Had this actually been a so-called "thousand year storm," many could have been saved. But now the time between killer storms is weeks. In North America--the battered infrastructure of America can no longer take the beating. It is on the same route as Europe and Africa--Chaos. Emergency systems, though far more efficient than ten years ago, have much less in the way of resources. They are about to fail. It is the reason why military troops now wander the land.

In the South, constant hurricanes have cut into food production. In the Midwest, floods and brutal winter storms cripple heavy manufacturing. In the West, a cycle of drought and rain forest rainstorms brutalize the high technology industry. Everywhere screaming winds grow increasingly malevolent. Disease escalates. As a result, those who can, hoard resources. Nature is pounding America--as it has the rest of the world--into submission. The vaulted wealth of the country is disappearing.

A few gloat: To them this is the force that will rid their world of corruption. For many others the horrors that grip Southern Europe and Northern Africa are more to the point: Roving bands of marauders, warlords, unending starvation, death from exposure, disease and pain, these are the results of chaos. Fear of the same scenario in the US makes the Greenhouse Laws palatable for the population. America is finally scared. A few in power delude themselves with the notion that the laws are just another way to surf the crests in the spittoon. Others, with better access to information, know the truth: Humanity is in a mortal battle with the planet, hands tied by its own greed.

Only denial is an unlimited resource: The death tolls will rise for twelve more years and then the numbers will begin to drop. The government, the media, and the industrial councils will proclaim: "Humanity takes the upper hand in the Global Climate Battle." It is the decrease in population density that causes the drop in the death toll: In twelve years the population of the planet will halve. There will be no discussion of that fact just as there is no discussion now of how deadly the threat is to humanity. This is not the time of heroes. Everyone in this generation knows heroes die first.

Carlos jogs down the hillside visualizing the Flower's mansion. He sees a red-painted porch filled with long white tables bearing fruit, vegetables, and breads: the twin mahogany doors wide open and that smell of lilac pouring into the Hudson's breeze. He guesses the Ping Pong games will be finished inside but a few joke games will be going on in the parlor. Vivacious women and polite men lounging about the porch's rounded corners will wink and say hello to him. He smiles for the first time today as he climbs over a large fallen pine tree blocking the road.

Carlos decides to ask Emile, the owner of the mansion, if he can live there for a while. Emile is Carlos' friend and mentor. It is he who has suggested to Carlos a career in the diplomatic corps might well suit him. Emile Flowers had been the coach of the US Olympic Ping Pong Team--as well as an agent for NOAA. It is through him that the Greenies know of Carlos Jordan.

A thin man with gold hair and brown eyes, Emile talks often with Carlos, teaching him the facts of his life. To that end, Emile makes sure Carlos understands the fierce matches played in the ballroom center on

"a silly little white ball traveling back and forth over the small green net."
Emile discusses how every mistake is taken advantage of and how every
mistake is always telegraphed. Carlos takes it in, but he also notices the
onlookers cheer the tough volley. He likes that more than most.

Of course whenever Carlos plays he loses--but that is okay. These are
world-class athletes. He really wishes to just sit and be part of the bright
conversation and witty humor that springs from young, good-looking men
and beautiful women. When they make urbane jokes about the inconvenience
of global climatic change their laughter betrays knowledge of the absurdity of
their circumstance. Carlos understands this implicitly. He adores easy humor
as a way of coping with the incomprehensible tragedies of life. And especially
this morning, Carlos wishes to be part of that.

--If only I could accept the facts of life the way they accept them. They
keep emotions at a distance; they take care to think before speaking. They
keep an even keel--

It is this control, more than anything, which attracts Carlos to these
people. Carlos treasures polite distance and detests anger. He finds control
intoxicating, this ability to converse without a fearsome edge or malicious
intent. Some day he hopes to deflect his parents' anger with a joke or a
clandestine jab. It is a skill he practices diligently.

Once when they asked about his parents, Carlos waved a hand saying
"...they closed their minds long ago to being rational. They're not like us."
Many smiled, and no one ever asked him anymore about them. For months
afterwards he had nightmares about the players meeting his parents. The
dream always ended with a fusillade of rabid yelling and guttural slurs spilling
from his parents and his friends running from him. The dreams faded when
Emile told Carlos he would always be there for him. Carlos plans to test that
today.

When Carlos reaches River Road--the street that runs parallel to the
Hudson's east shore--he slows, mouth aghast. Fallen trees lie on almost every
home. The wind, rain and mud have shattered the rest. Household goods
clutter the roadway and lawns. Clothes decorate the tree limbs. The smell
of the sea is everywhere. The ten-foot sea wall, which had been put in last
year to stop the Hudson's storm-surges, is reduced to a low pile of rocks.
Looking closer at the homes he sees mud inundating everything. The verdant
lawns are caked with it; the dripping carpets in the houses are streaked with
it. Everywhere lays driftwood, mud, rounded rocks, broken furniture, and
clothes. As far as he can see, there no one.

Nine hundred people died along River Road last night--most of them
swept out into the river. The once-prized real estate will be available to all
now. It is too low to be of use to anyone.

--Emile--

Running down the street, he trips over the bloated carcass of a dead dog. Carlos stumbles to his feet not even noticing what has tripped him. Around an overturned car, passed a brass bed stand, down the street and across a deep gully in the road, running, running, he suddenly stops. A pile of battered boards replaces the porch: Pieces of Ping Pong tables float in the Hudson. Mud and water drip from the grand house. Shattered windows hang above the shadow of the porch. Mahogany doors lean against the front of the house. A lone figure moves inside the building.

"Emile?" Carlos climbs the front of the building. A dirty man pushes a broom back and forth apparently trying to get the muck from the house. It is a futile activity. "Emile?"

The mud-covered man looks up at Carlos. A deep sadness has worn clean rivulets in the man's face. He tries to smile. "No more Ping Pong, Carlos."

"Can I help?"

Emile lets the broom drop straightening his dirty white collar and approaching the boy. "No. But this all belongs to you now. I am leaving. The whole screwed-up world is yours in fact. It is a shabbier place than when I was a boy, but that cannot be helped. We were so foolish..."

"Where are you going? Take me." Carlos looks into the man's weary face. The brown eyes seem dead.

Emile pats Carlos on the shoulder with a sigh. Then looking outside he points to the sailboats jibing in the Hudson's shining water. "Nothing stops the rich. They still believe we are protected by our wealth. I cannot curse you like that." He leans against a broken Ping Pong table and gazes at the racing sloops. "Your girl is out there, right?" He watches the boats heel over in the winds and cut through choppy waves.

"Yes." Carlos does not see the boats. Instead he focuses on Emile. Somewhere in the distance, a wall collapses.

"My mutilated green lawn is yours also. You can give it all to her, if you like." It is a poor joke. Carlos turns away looking for the private dock that gently bobbed in the Hudson River; a pile of debris remains. Carlos remembers the guests that used to come across the river from Westchester, or down from Nyack. They were so bright and elegant. Carlos wonders where they are--now that Emile needs them. He looks back into Emile's empty eyes.

"The rich will desert the Hudson now just like they deserted the southeast. When it becomes too dangerous, we move on to new lands. We're locusts. But soon we will see there are no places to go. Soon we will wonder why we fed the places we love to the hoards--and we will be sanctified."

"Emile, you need to rest."

"Carlos? Are your parents all right?"

"I wish they were dead," Carlos says.

"I'm sure you do." Emile Flowers shakes his head in pity. "Carlos, there is something I have wanted to say to you for a long time: The hell with them."

"I have come to the same conclusion." Carlos replies with a wink.

Spinnakers flap open. They call Carlos.

"But stay with them until you go to college in the fall. Then see them when you can, however keep your distance. There will be little grace in the world now. But you'll fair well. I promise." Emile picks up the broom. "Take a look around. See if there is anything you can use. I have some work to do."

Carlos stands. "Go ahead." He walks into the living room. The muddy line on the wall almost reaches the ceiling. No furniture remains. The kitchen is a pool of food because the refrigerator has fallen over and it acts like a dam to the retreating mud. This is too much for Carlos.

"Emile, a message came up on my browser about joining the Greenies. Did you have anything to do with that? Emile?" Carlos reenters the parlor looking for his mentor but cannot find him. He searches for tracks in the mud, but he can only find the broom. "Emile." Carlos suddenly finds himself short of breath. "Emile, I have to get Roxanne. The race is almost over. Where are you?" A tear forms. Loudly he screams: "Emile." He looks about, lost in a whisper: "I thought you would always be here for me, Emile."

Silence, except for the winds.

"Fine." Full of sadness, Carlos climbs from the porch. Midway down the mud-caked lawn he stops and screams back: "Thank you, Emile." Carlos waits, but there is no response. He turns away telling himself he will get Roxanne and they will come back to look for Emile--but they will not. Carlos knows Emile was only waiting to say good-bye to him. He also knows the message on his browser was the result of Emile's connections. In the innocence of youth he assumes Emile will show up one day dressed in his white sweater and white pants.

Carlos arrives at the concrete dock; most of the sailboats have folded their sails and masts, or sailors cover them with bright blue canvas gloves. A set of five boats, already wrapped in their blue gloves, sits waiting to be placed into a watertight submersible dock. Out in the Hudson a small red tug steams back with a bright yellow five-boat unit. Once the boats are inside, and the unit sealed, the tug will tow the submersible dock out into the Hudson and lower it to the bottom of the river where the boats will ride out the next storm. The laughter of comrades drifts over the water from the community clubhouse. It seems to him the same laughter used to come from Ping Pong players.

--Fools--

Carlos scolds himself for thinking these people fools.

--I'm not like my parents--

He then catches sight of Roxanne walking next to a handsome middle aged man whom Carlos has seen many times on television. The sight of the news anchorman named Holden Caufield, with his silver hair and vacuous smile over a cleft chin, annoys Carlos. His melodic peanut butter voice had often comforted people by saying: "The storms are part of a weather cycle. There is nothing to worry about." Anger surges though Carlos' body.

The anchorman leans over Roxanne and kisses her head. The transparent sexual intent in his nodding head and benevolent smile are a spark to Carlos' rage. Carlos steps onto the middle of the concrete dock to stand legs wide and arms akimbo.

Caufield stares straight at Carlos. The anchorman's hand comes up to stroke the side of Roxanne's cheek. She has not seen Carlos yet; she fiddles with her field glasses putting them in a case. Carlos nods unconsciously and his fists clench. Roxanne looks up. Her distracted face freezes. A dark-haired woman pushes past him and storms down the dock. The couple ahead of her moves farther apart. The well-coiffured woman slaps Roxanne on the cheek.

"Tramp," the woman screams. "You sleazy little harlot. Did you think I wouldn't find out? How dare you. And you, Holden, you gold-plated creep."

"Now dear, we're just sailing. There is nothing going on."

"How dare you lie to me. Do you think I'm one of them?" She hits the anchorman squarely on the center of his chest.

Roxanne's face flushes in embarrassment. She finally sees Carlos. Real pain sets in. The woman turns back to Roxanne cursing her and grabbing Roxanne's long blond hair. "And you, you little tart--"

Roxanne seizes the woman's hand; pivoting swiftly, she hauls the woman over her back, off the dock and into the cool waters of the Hudson. Laughter pours forth from the crowd that has formed behind Carlos. Holden, however, is as a man encased in ice.

Eyes spitting fire, Roxanne faces him. "You lied. You said she left you. You jerk."

He shrugs his shoulders. She kicks him in the shin.

Roxanne hurries up the dock, embarrassment filling her face. Looking at Carlos closer, she notices a practiced serenity. Roxanne puts on a cheery smile. "So, what do you think of my skeletons?" She is certain it is clear to everyone, including this thin, strange boy that the famous Holden Caufield, News Weatherman to Millions, has been sleeping with her.

"Your skeletons are rather lively," Carlos quips. He leans forward to kiss the slapped cheek. He stops when dark eyes and a ridged brow greet his gaze. His expression remains calm and open. "What is wrong?"

"I'm just waiting for the explosion," She scans the mud that covers Carlos and worries his parents may have done something to him last night. "Did you sleep out in the storm?"

Carlos sees Lily Caufield emerge from the water. Her makeup has run and her black-banded eyes glow with hate. Her hair hangs like frayed brown strings. Her tan leather coat drips. She and her husband--barking indictments at each other--stride straight toward them. "Oh-oh."

Carlos focuses on Lily's face. Carlos again sports an even, blank expression. Roxanne notes all of it and wonders what is wrong with Carlos. She hears Lily hiss to her husband, "...I'm not going to touch her, Holden. I promise." The woman fears Roxanne might toss her off the dock again. Roxanne faces her square.

Still dripping, Lily stops a few feet short of Roxanne. Roxanne glances at Holden Caufield noting a cowed look, as if he had been the one thrown in the water. Roxanne speaks: "He said you two were split up."

"Idiot. He also said global warming was good for us." Lily grins. "And you must be the boyfriend. Feel a bit stupid, do you?" Her vengeful look dissolves when she sees no anger in Carlos. She faces Roxanne again. "Did you like sleeping with my famous husband? I hear he keeps it up longer with harlots. And I hope you enjoyed it because by the time I'm finished with you, you'll be the best-known tramp since Mary Magdalen. Young man, you have lousy taste in women." She walks away, dragging her husband by the hand like a little boy.

Tears of anger swell in Roxanne's eyes. "Bitch," she says quietly and looks at Carlos. "I'll understand if you just want to leave."

"Why would I want to leave?" Carlos asks, looking mystified. He has been practicing this look for months with his parents.

"I betrayed you. And I've lied to you." Roxanne's anger ratchets up a notch seeing the insincerity in his eyes.

"If this is the worst we encounter, I think we will be doing well. Our world is falling apart you know." He speaks the words with a practiced light tone. Carlos does not react to the sadness he sees. He believes it will make him weak.

Roxanne steps back from him. "How did you become covered in mud?"

"The mansion--it was almost washed away. They're all gone."

Her concern quells a moment.

--So that's it--

"Emile too?"

"Yes. Shall we eat lunch?" He takes her arm and leads Roxanne away from the dock; the crowd from the clubhouse has not dispersed and he wants some privacy. She follows reluctantly. The crowd means nothing to her. Carlos owns her attention.

"What about your parents?"

"They're the same. Let's walk."

He leads her along the destroyed sea wall. Stepping from rock to rock, Roxanne pauses on a flat piece of concrete, unable to contain her curiosity. "Don't even suppose you have me fooled," she says quietly.

"Jealousy and anger mean caring to you?" Carlos asks misunderstanding the statement.

She jabs his chest with her finger. "That's not what I mean and you know it. This is skin, not a cocoon," she replies sharply.

The comment stings; Carlos looks across the river. "That's a tough one. Skin is good, but a cocoon is safe." He looks at her. "What is the problem?"

"You are not in negotiations yet, Ambassador Jordan. You are a seventeen-year-old boy. Your friends at the Flowers mansion are gone. You have just been through a brutal storm that has killed God-knows-how-many people and you just found out the woman you have been trying to take to bed--who has told you she is a virgin--has been with another man, What should be the matter? Did your parents do something to you last night?" Tears fill his eyes and she fears she has gone too far.

"What about Holden Caulfield and you?" He asks quickly.

"There was nothing important going on there," Roxanne replies; she has gotten a real response from him.

"I see," Carlos says knowingly. Roxanne turns her back realizing his question about Holden was to deflect her questions from his parents. She walks away from him. From the corner of her eye she watches him discreetly brush the tears away. "You are right. It's pointless to get angry about what people might or might not have been doing. Look at the river."

She glances back at him incredulously. "The river?"

"The Hudson is comparatively calm today, but that only means it'll be raging again."

"Why does that mean and what are you talking about?" Roxanne's concern shifts to whether she should even be with this boy.

"Your friend Holden used to tell us these storms were part of a thousand-year cycle and they will go away. Does that mean the viewing public should shoot him because he was full of shit?"

This is the first time Roxanne has heard Carlos curse. "Shooting is too good for him."

"Don't you see it? Our damn grandparents knew burning hydrocarbons would increase global temperature. And they continued even though storms became worse and worse. They knew what was coming and they ignored it. They didn't stop driving their SUVs. They didn't try to fix anything. They didn't do anything--because of the economy. It's all the same now. Nobody gives a damn." Carlos leans over and picks up a small flat piece of plywood. "So should I be angry? I don't give a damn either. It's a tough life ahead of us. Of course every generation has trials."

"Carlos--" She cannot bear his pain as his analysis dams further tears.

"Bah. Anger is useless. My parents fight all the time." He slaps the plywood against his hand over and over. "I'll bet I have heard every ethnic slur and invective there is. What good does it do to fight stupidity?"

"You think I am stupid?" Roxanne asks.

"No, of course not. Should I be angry with them because they are insane? Why would you ask me if I think you are stupid?"

"Forget it. What do you mean insane?" Roxanne folds her hands behind her back now sure his parents did something to him. She wonders what she can do to help.

He continues. "You find a man attractive and sleep with him and you want to keep it private. So what? I respect privacy. Roxanne, we're all in deep do-do. I believe I can therefore choose not to be angry at a person who I care about and who likes to make love. There are worse things, much worse."

Roxanne gathers her hair in her hand and ties it behind her head not wanting to show the concern she feels.

"I am angry at you," Carlos says.

That was too much. She faces him. "What the hell is wrong with you?" She walks off the rocks and down the road.

"I just realized you want me to be mad so you'll know I care. And I do care. So I wanted you to think I was angry."

She stops on the road, but not before kicking a rock into the water.

"This is enough. One more shovel of bull manure at me and I'm leaving."

He approaches her. "I am no good at this."

Her gaze darts past him. A sight on the water stuns her. Roxanne pulls the field glasses from her bag. She fumbles with the glasses as she brings them to her eyes.

"What's wrong?"

"Oh, Christ, it's a demolitions barge. One of those they were using up at Storm King Mountain. It's loose." She lowers the glasses and looks at him. Roxanne hands him the field glasses.

This generation has learned to deal with death. It overshadows many parts of their lives. As a result they give the Devil its due.

Carlos peers at the water. "It is a barge riding awfully low. You think it's loaded with explosives?"

"I think we should run."

"And right now."

"What do you think--" Like the words are a detonator, the sky lights bright orange. Carlos throws Roxanne to the ground and covers her body with his own. A loud WHOMP hits them and immediately the air around the huddled pair is both wet and hot. Moments after, red metal falls. Despite the burning, Carlos will not move.

A few minutes later only the sounds of the flames that engulf the Tappan Zee Bridge can be heard. The center span points skyward. Neither speaks for a time as they watch the bridge burn. A fireboat arrives and begins to spray the flames. The center span collapses almost swamping the boat. Mesmerized by the incredible destruction, the two of them watch in fascination. A large twin-engine plane appears. It scoops water from the river and quickly douses the blaze.

Roxanne finally sees Carlos has been burned. Twenty black holes dot his back. The skin beneath the holes is already forming blisters. "We need to get you to a paramedic."

"No. I'm okay." Carlos replaces the field glasses in her bag.

"Come on, we need to get you some medical attention."

"Leave it alone, Roxanne." He stares at the smoldering structure. "It's all coming apart--right in front of us." Tears begin to fall from Carlos eyes. "Oh, no," he whimpers, and walks away.

She waits until he looks at her. She approaches him slowly then kisses his tears.

"Thank you." Carlos says.

"No, thank you."

Their caress will last a lifetime.

A few nights from now Carlos and Roxanne will make love for the first time. Alone in a large shelter belonging to a dead neighbor, they will ride out the new storm that batters the area. That storm will wash away the Flowers mansion and completely destroy River Road. Repair crews will not have time to replace the sea wall. Eight thousand people will die in New York. When the walls of their penthouse apartment collapse, Holden Caufield and his wife Lily will also die.

Carlos Jordan will never spend another night with his parents.

Chapter Three

Sitting in a crowded smelly bus, Roxanne churns thoughts. She knows her mother hopes this trip into New York City will clear her head. Roxanne plans are the same; however, Roxanne and her mother have different ideas of what a clear head looks like these days. Roxanne wants to find an answer to Carlos; her mother wants her to find Carlos' problem. Roxanne ruminates about last night when she talked about skipping school today and would Carlos like to join her on a trip into the city?

--He looked at me as if I might be from another planet and did he really think he could "help me see the truth?" The nerve of some men. Then when he asked me about college, my plans for the future--

"What future, tin man?" She responded and left him standing on the walk outside her home. Her mother's concern that weak men will try to control her still rings like an alarm bell. Along with the incessant warnings about Carlos' many problems, fear echoes into her head. Instead of enlightening her, the warnings feed rebellion. Even so, Roxanne understands his distance as a problem. Distance was dad's way of dealing with fear and her mother thinks Carlos' fear keeps him apart from Roxanne. Roxanne smiles; she fears Carlos doesn't even know what close means. Roxanne's other concern is the trips Carlos takes to the cemetery every week. Last week after he refused again to talk about what happened to that family, Roxanne refused to go to the grave site. He did not call for three days.

--Carlos makes such a big deal about stealing those flowers from his parents and the solemn five minutes of mourning for those three people; it is just morose. Why won't he tell me what happened to them during the storm? It must have been awful. Did he know the child? He must have, the way he stares at the child's grave. They were not relatives. I don't get it. Why does he think he needs to solve the problems of the world? I bet it has to do with his parents. Isn't it clear that the future holds little joy for us? He needs to grab joy, not stifle life so he can control his environment. A lack of love does not concern him. That bothers me most about Carlos. On the other hand, his sincerity and deep resolve to heal...perhaps that is the problem. I am impressed but not in love. So maybe we might be friends. He can do that--

Roxanne feels worse.

The bus bounces over a pothole. Her mind wanders to her resolution of not letting anyone interfere with the bits of joy left in this world. The decision of earlier years is in direct opposition to her desire to help those around her. She groans--that paradox becoming a major dilemma when dealing with Carlos Jordan. Along with the accolades from the audience--Roxanne has no problem with that, it makes him happy--service is all there is to life for Carlos. In that way he is typical of his age. Helping others for this generation is not simply volunteering to cook for the aged, work with unwed mothers, or put up recycling posters. For this generation community service is finding relatives for children made orphans, counseling shock victims who have lost everything, finding and burying family pets, or just listening to unending tales of grief and pain. This is a generation that clearly sees service as survival for the whole group.

Wisdom sometimes comes with an awful price.

She looks out at the lovely green pine trees swaying majestically, their wide branches dancing in warm winds. On the ground, the loggers remove the fallen trees. Beyond the cliffs, the Hudson flows calmly and the white sails from river traders proudly bow to the day. In the sky, fluffy white bits of dreams float like a child's toys in a blue bath. Smiling, Roxanne turns away and glances up. Three New U.N. soldiers stand within a few feet of her. Her grin fades.

The big red-bearded one with the round gut looks down at her and winks. He makes a comment to his thin olive-skinned friend in a foreign language. By the laughter she knows what has been said and wants to ask them why they speak in another language--other than the New U.N. mandated language of English. Jumping to the conclusion these New U.N.

soldiers are not evil, she decides not to tempt fate.

--They are just victims of the system--

This is one of the reasons Roxanne has no patience for school. For her, the school system is little more than a packing system for turning out good little workers and consumers who have the primary job of breeding more workers and consumers. The sugarcoated retelling of history, the sound-byte interaction with teachers, the dribble that pours forth to justify her society's myopic nature, it all frustrates her. Nothing in the education system, so far as she can tell, teaches awareness and action. Her fear of extinction breeds no patience for the tides of learning. This does not mean Roxanne is a bad student or a radical. Far from it, she simply wants nothing to do with a prepackaged life and pre-ordained slaughter. Determined to find her way in the world she sees as teetering on the edge of oblivion--she seeks to wrest from the world all she can before it tumbles into the abyss. Roxanne's innocence will last longer than most.

A man beside her wears a light blue bandage, his face a mass of bruises; he mumbles something as he stares out the window. The George Washington Bridge looms ahead. Listening closer to the wounded man's mumbling, Roxanne recognizes a series of invectives attacking the taxes that keep the bridge looking pristine. One of the few structures not visibly damaged by the storms, Roxanne finds the bridge enchanting--and a symbol of hope. Sadly, was this bridge to carry the twentieth century traffic volumes it used to bear, it would collapse. On the other hand, the hope it symbolizes carries millions through their day.

The man faces Roxanne. "Do you have the time?" In his unbandaged eye she sees a void.

"Almost ten."

"My house fell on me. Yours will too, young lady." Mumbling curses in a semi-self contained conversation, he looks away. "We loved what we owned too much. We loved our convenience. We really didn't care. A generation of swine, that son of a bitch was right. I'll make it all better. You'll see, Daughter." Like much of the older generation, he is overwhelmed with guilt and remorse. Too many have seen their children die.

Roxanne glances around the bus: From the number of people with red crosses on their seat backs, Roxanne figures this man is on his way to visit one of the Friday "free clinics" in New York City. Almost all the hospitals have a free day for outpatient care now. Another of the casualties of climate change is the importance of the profit motive. The systems for insurance payments have completely broken down. The battle for power, on the other hand, gathers force as if it were a tsunami. In a few years it will crash upon the shore of the society's consciousness swamping the remains of hope. Medical care will almost completely disappear as the well-healed demand more healing at the expense of care for all.

As if she can feel this coming, and to escape the pain around her, she closes her eyes and soon finds herself musing about life in turn of the century New York. Living on the East Side, attending dinner parties after work, taking trips to the country every weekend, her favorite fantasy is the excursion into Central Park after the theater. Around midnight, she and her friends enter the zoo to feed the animals. Roxanne would love to have seen the large animals, but zoos are extinct. Another fantasy is the early evening stroll with a lover along Fifth Avenue examining every useless luxurious item in the windows. In her fantasy she sees herself saying hello to neighbors as they pass. It is a city full of tall buildings and happy people. Thousands of taxis, noise filling every inch, commuters rushing down the streets, feet pounding on pavement pumping the city's blood. All is a mirror of the better life. A fantasy from her youngest days, one she will not shake for many years--it calms her in a perverse way; many, like the man beside her, never shake the fantasy.

She keeps her eyes closed to focus on this sunny bus ride into the city and her plans once she gets there. Roxanne believes being in Manhattan on the day the New U.N. tries to make taxis illegal should be quite an event. So far as she can tell no one has said no to the Greenies. Carlos' pain haunts her.

--If anyone is going to tell the Greenies to go to hell it will be the New York taxi drivers--

The thought thrills her. Oddly comforted, she settles into her seat.

The bus jerks to a stop. People call out angrily. Opening her eyes, she leans over the bandaged man. Looking both ways she sees abandoned cars along the highway's shoulder. They are in Fort Lee. This municipality has not banned overnight car parking. The result is a mud-covered caterpillar of abandoned vehicles stretching up and down the roadway. In the next two years other abuses of power will bring these cars back to Roxanne's consciousness. She will ask herself why powerful lobbies obliterate conscience. Roxanne will birth a paradox to deal with: She will want to both know the future and escape it.

The bus door opens with a whoosh. A tall man steps in the bus. He wears the same blue green uniform as the men standing in front of Roxanne, except his hat has blue and white checks around the cap. The man's angry deep-set eyes say trouble. "All right, everyone out. I want to see some E-passes." His voice is hoarse, as if he has been screaming all morning.

People begin to rise up. Roxanne stands slowly. She has no E-pass. It never occurred to her the New U.N. would be enforcing the rules about unnecessary travel so soon. She tells herself no one is going to bother a seventeen-year old girl who says she forgot her pass. It calms her as she follows the crowd passed the man. Roxanne flashes a smile; he smiles back. Feeling more confident, she steps out the bus door and soaks in the morning heat bouncing off the silver and black bus. The temperature this late May morning is ninety-nine degrees in the shade. The other passengers form a knot.

After inspecting each seat for people hiding from him, the police officer steps off the bus: "Everyone line up except you three men." He speaks to the three New U.N. soldiers who were on the bus. "Come here and lend a hand." The three men trudge over to the superior officer.

The crowd forms a line that stretches along the side of the bus. Roxanne makes sure she is toward the end of the line so she can get a better idea of what is going to happen to her. The four men talk among themselves. Roxanne looks behind her at the vehicles traveling along the roadway. The mix is what she would call typical: trucks, buses, a few government cars, and one or two private cars. Most speed, ignoring the New U.N. mandated limit of forty-five miles per hour. In one week private cars not sporting a large "P" on their bumpers will be heavily fined. She has no doubt all these private cars will have one. Anyone who can afford fifty dollars a gallon for gas and then waste it by speeding has the juice to get a "Privilege" Plate. In six months vehicles not having the "P" will be fired upon.

The four New U.N. soldiers start moving down the line towards her. They move much faster than she would have thought. Midway down they stop in front of a thin man with a tan cowboy hat and wide black sideburns. The man with the checked hat pulls him out of line merely by pointing with his finger. The man subserviently hurries by the soldier. Soon two other people join him. Two of the other soldiers stand guard over them.

The men continue down the line. Roxanne assumes she will be in that small group in just a few seconds.

"Madam, your pass please." The man stops in front of her and looks down. He no longer returns her smile.

"I, ah you see, forgot it," she says using her most flippant voice. "It's like, I didn't know I needed one. I like..."

"Step over there with the others," he says brusquely. He dismisses her easily, eyes focused on the next person in line.

"Captain, she is with me," says the big man with the gut. "This is my fault."

The soldier spins quickly as if he were the turret of a tank. His jaw tightens. "Explain, Corporal."

"She is local from New York. We ah, met. She and I spent a few days together. I was supposed to get her the pass, but you know how things are at Regional Processing. It's not her fault." He looks over to Roxanne with a display of affection that embarrasses her.

The inspector sighs. "Christ, how am I supposed to do my job with you soldiers boffing the locals?"

Roxanne bristles. Again someone has called her a tramp.

"I am sorry, Corporal, but you know the rules..."

"Be a mate. You already have three for the generators there, Captain. I know what your quota is..."

"That's enough, Corporal. All right. If this happens again with one of your tarts I won't be so lenient."

Her jaw clenches.

"Thanks, Brother." The big soldier winks and follows the other man.

Soon everyone, except for the three men pulled from the line, file in the bus. The man with the large gut escorts Roxanne inside the bus. He sets her down in the window seat previously occupied by the wounded man and leans over her. Roxanne stiffens. "Don't ever forget your pass again--or skip school--young lady. The generators those people will be sent to are quite harsh." He stands tipping his hat.

"Why did you do that?" Roxanne asks, concerned about her debt to this man; she will not tolerate anyone assuming she is for sale.

"You are young and beautiful. The world is yours. I am merely another servant--and a daddy. My girl was fourteen." He steps aside as the wounded man sits.

The wounded man leans close to her. "You know I didn't mean anything bad about the Greenies. I didn't know that guy was your...friend."

Roxanne flashes a sardonic smile. "Thank you so much. I'm sure he will take it into consideration."

The wounded man's eyes widen and he quickly looks away.

When the bus pulls into Columbia Hospital the three soldiers leave along with the bandaged riders. The man with the large gut slips on a Red Cross armband. He is an orderly. In a moment the bus is back on the street. His kind deed nestles itself in the young girl. Mostly because she is sure she will never see this man again. She is correct.

Twenty minutes later the bus pulls into an underground garage. "All out. This is the Port Authority of New York and New Jersey. Last stop." Roxanne looks around wondering why this smelly old parking garage is now the Port Authority building. Following the crowd out she asks the driver what happened. "The old Port Authority building collapsed a few weeks ago. Move along, miss." For Roxanne, temporary structures replacing storm-damaged structures underscore the pain of her life. She hurries through the crowded parking garage. Passed parked buses and makeshift stands selling newspapers, food, and trinkets she rushes out into the humid sticky heat.

The quiet strikes her. Roxanne glances up at blown out windows and pieces of curtain that wave like torn flags. Smoke rises from a number of windows. Slowly, she walks between the canyons of rubble that line the streets. The concrete and glass along the roadway rises almost twenty feet into the air. At the base, newspapers, cans, bottles, and plastic mound everywhere.

--The poor should not leave the glass and plastic there. They can recycle it--

Unknown to her, and most other people, the poor who pick up trash in the city are not paid in cash like the suburbs. Instead here they are given food vouchers for the city kitchens--institutions originally established to feed the poor and homeless with leftover food from the restaurants. The city kitchens, when open, now serve only a moldy gruel. It kills half of those who eat it.

"Miss, ya' got a buck?" A ragged panhandler dressed in a grease covered flowered jumper stands beside her. The woman's rutted face maps pain like a dark poem.

Roxanne pulls out a dollar and hands it to her. The severity of the storms again strikes home. Her mood sours.

"Bless you."

Roxanne hurries away knowing that in a few minutes other homeless people will try to find her. Roxanne never refuses to give them money but today she does not have much cash. Her mother said there was some problem with the trust account. Roxanne believes her family has more than she could ever spend.

She is wrong; the cost of energy has far outstripped script.

--The city has certainly taken a beating since I was here last month. So much for a day without a care in the world--

Passing a lot filled with thousands of old computers, she watches a huge crane grab PCs and drop them down a steel funnel on the front of the crane. The crunching and subsequent crushing of the equipment echoes all around her. Every minute, a two-foot cube pops out of the machine's metal anus onto the ground. A small robot conveyor system scoops the cube and deposits it in a waiting truck.

Huge garbage consolidation systems like the one eating and excreting computers replaces the next eight square blocks of buildings. Roxanne wonders what has happened here. She remembers Holden's comment that certain news events are no longer deemed "palatable for the population." A brief flash of Holden Caufield's caress passes through her like a cramp. "Excuse me," she says to a small woman in a yellow construction hat and torn green coveralls. "What happened?"

"A gas leak took it all out. Two thousand died. The rest happened in the riot afterwards." The woman never looks up from her pad.

"Thanks."

--Christ, what will happen at noon when the New U.N. edict of no more taxis in Manhattan is supposed to take effect, World War Three? I am glad Carlos decided not to come. He probably would have tried to straighten it all out--

Her nose wrinkles with an itch. A sweet sensation spreads. More welcome than a breeze the notion of Carlos Jordan nestles in like a fawn. She walks toward Broadway warmed by him and full of resolve to help him. Her watch: Eleven-fifty.

--If Carlos is not the man for me he is darn close. I wish it were all a bit easier--

A yellow and green taxi scrapes its fender on a trash heap in front of her. She stops walking. Fighting its way out of a parking spot between a crushed bus and the rubble, the taxi speeds off after clearing the obstruction. Horns blare as a taxi and a rickshaw aim for the same parking spot. Drivers inside the vehicles glare at each other--until the taxi driver pulls out a pistol. The rickshaw driver backs up. "Coward," screams the taxi driver. Palpable excitement crackles like static.

--This is going to be a war if the laws are really enforced. Manhattan will be a totally different place without the taxis. Surely the Greenies must know that if they gut the world of the icons no one will care what happens--

She turns the corner into Times Square. It is as if she has entered Oz. The pristine white-walled Valhalla that is Times Square glistens with fresh wash. Buildings surround the crossed roadways: live life-like lit Christmas trees. Offices on top of stores rise into the sky full of glass frames filled with people in suits. The smell of popcorn pervades the street.

Stopping and wondering how they do this: how they keep this area so clean, Roxanne takes it all in like fresh air. The lit billboards glow; the buildings everywhere churn. Music blares and motors hum. No exposed girders, nothing that would suggest anything other than glamour. Packed restaurants and theaters, the hotels and amusement parlors, police in traditional New York Police blue uniforms riding majestic horses--not a thing is out of place. She wonders how the city fathers make this happen and immediately she does not care.

--I must be a part of this play someday--

The clock on the large triangular white building says eleven fifty-eight. She stops so that she can see both down Forty-second Street and up Broadway at the same time. Others have stopped as well and mill about watching the seconds tick. Roxanne glances up at the ball that used to mark the coming of New Years. It remains permanently fixed to the front of the building like the last ball of a pawnbroker.

Twelve o'clock.

Horns begin to blare. The traffic slams to a stop. Every taxi driver exits his cab and walks away. So far as Roxanne can tell all the vehicles have their engines running.

Buses honk their horns. Rickshaw drivers stop, resting their loads and looking for a way through the stopped traffic. The taxi drivers form up into groups of three or four slapping each other on the back. Many laugh as they disappear into the subway.

"Let the damn Greenies deal with this mess," someone says. Roxanne stares about dumbfounded for a moment.

--So they did as they were told. But they left the vehicles in the middle of the street. So this is how you say no to the Greenies--

The crescendo of horns rises around her. A few people from the sidewalks jump into cabs and pull them out of the roadway--a cab driven by a bus driver rolls up onto the sidewalk.

A taxi sits in the middle of the intersection with its engine running. She bolts for it and jumps in the cab. This may be her only chance in life to drive a car. The man in the back of the cab leaves slamming the door behind him. Shifting the car into first, she notices people stream from the sidewalks to commandeer the remaining cabs. A fight breaks out between two burly men.

Rolling north slowly toward Forty-third Street, enjoying the feel of the automobile, for a moment she lives her greatest fantasy--until another taxi smashes into her vehicle. It backs up then crashes into another one. Stunned, she sees a madness spread. Vehicles ram into each other like bumper cars. Up ahead of her, across the street, a city bus plows its way south pushing aside more cars and honking its horn in triumph.

--There is no need for this --

A swarm of taxis like yellow jackets, rush at the bus attacking it from all sides. Smash, smash, over and over, the smaller vehicles run into the behemoth. Rickshaw drivers abandon their loads and run for safety. More taxis converge on the bus taking aim at the tires. Slowly they take their toll. Another bus appears. It approaches the fray knocking aside taxis like a mother dinosaur trying to protect its young. The buses link up, side by side and continue south. Pushing back taxis like soil from a plow, the buses toss rickshaws into stores and pedestrians. Roxanne jumps from her car just as the buses reach her. Her taxi flies back into a storefront. It explodes in flames. Looking up at the Bus driver, she sees a New U.N. soldier looking more like a man at work, than a madman bent on destruction. After he passes she looks in his wake. Broadway has two lanes clear for six blocks. She sees the method of those in power tonight when the bus drivers are labeled angry taxi drivers.

Sirens sound. The two buses continue down Broadway clearing a path. A black smoking cylinder lands near her feet. Twenty more projectiles land all around her: tear gas. Rushing into a small doorway beside a video game parlor, hustling up a flight of stairs, she opens a doorway and enters a tawdry tan lobby. Men and women in green coveralls stare out the window.

"It's the Greenies," someone says. "They're in helicopters dropping gas." The sound of thumping can be heard. "They're shooting." Other people hurry to the window.

Roxanne cannot move. "Get away from the windows," she says.

Like a herd in reverse, they back up--just as the glass shatters. The smell of gunpowder, onions, and chlorine rolls in the room. Two people bleed red pools on the floor. Roxanne turns and runs out rushing up the stairs. Kicking open one door, she slams the door behind her collapsing on the old tar roof. Her breath comes in short gasps.

Gunfire clatters below; screams echo around her. A trio of helicopters appears followed by three more gun ships. Like crop dusters they fly along the avenues spewing some kind of chemical and the occasional round of bullets. The smell of red peppers burns her nose. The brick edging seems to explode in red puffs as they fly by her. "What are you shooting at me for?" Roxanne hugs the floor as bullets whiz all around her; the helicopter gun ships pass. She crawls to the roof edge and looks down to the street. Chaos and flames dance like lovers.

-- Bodies. Those are dead bodies--

Flames spread from vehicle to vehicle. People rush from the buildings. Roxanne darts about the roof looking for escape. It seems only Forty-third Street has no explosions. She finds a fire escape and hurries down. The crowds rush away from Broadway. She follows them.

Every vehicle is abandoned including buses. When she reaches Sixth Avenue another scene of carnage and explosions await. More helicopters sweep the avenue with gas and gunfire. Roxanne weaves between burning vehicle formations, crossing the avenue.

Up ahead, one of the new subway stations catches her attention. Hurrying down the stairs she finds herself at the end of a long line. She calms despite the moaning and blood. At least safe, she leans over to help a young man bleeding through his white shirt. He pushes her hand away angrily.

"Leave me alone, bitch. I want to die."

Another young man screams at the crowd from a soapbox. "We are killing ourselves. Soon no place will be safe."

"So quit complaining. Live fast and die young." The reply comes from a pretty girl in the crowd. Roxanne does not know it is she who has spoken.

Chapter Four

A warm moist afternoon in early June: Carlos stops on a highway overpass and leans his bicycle against the guardrail. Clouds overhead, antique stereo headphones blaring music into his skull, Carlos taps his foot and stares at the empty freeway below him. He was back at the remains of the mansion yesterday. Battered by wind and storm, it looked like it had been a shambles for eons. No one has been there except to loot. The loss of friends heightens his concern about Roxanne. He cannot wait to see her. She has planned a trip see the new Energy Generation Camps.

He mentally kicks himself. The last time Roxanne and he were together--during a storm watch last week--he had said: "The Generator Guards rescue children from flood waters and they deliver food to storm victims. They try to help."

Roxanne had burst out of the bed; her face crimson. "Why would you ever believe something like that? You are sick."

Carlos had shrugged. Emile's comment a few months ago that the camps would be efficient generation facilities for rehabilitating criminals still sits silently locked inside him. Carlos tries to find some way to excuse himself for considering a job with the New U.N.. It is not that he wants to join them or their power. He wants to make a difference and he believes to make a difference he needs to be where the power lies.

"We are talking death camps here, Carlos, slavery. They make humans run in cages to generate energy. They eat, shit, and sleep in those cages. They run until they die." Her eyes glowed with anger from across the bunker in the light of candles; they mystified and called to Carlos' heart.

He stands in the bright June morning waiting for her after six days of being ignored. Last evening she stopped him in the mall and suggested they go on a date and see a camp. "Fine. Let's go find one of the camps." And in an attempt at humor he continued with: "But I think our dates are getting a bit morbid."

"You are the one who does the cemetery tours. This should be right up your grave site."

The rest of the night was ruined; his parents had asked when they might meet his "Storm-companion." After hours of their needling he made the mistake of telling them he may not be seeing her much and would they just leave him alone. The words lit dynamite. May's grin became hot poker against a rube and she asked Carlos what he had done to the "poor girl." His dad began a barrage of questions as to his virginity. Then mom wanted to know if "that girl Roxanne" had hurt him in some way. The barrage was going on at ten when he left the house to find a place to sleep.

Shell-shocked from his parents' abuse, Carlos suddenly worries Roxanne will refuse to be with him during the next storm alert. For the first time Carlos considers an anonymous bedmate to ride out the storms--many are alone. Fears that he may have to be with his parents during another storm dance in his skull. He gazes up at the cloudy sky hoping the storm season is over--too aware of his loss and no idea of what to do about it. Watching the long sloping hill, the twin black ribbons of empty highway, he spies a convoy cresting the hill in the distance. Carlos looks around seeing no one. He decides if she refuses to be with him during a storm alert he will ride it out either alone or wrapped in foreign arms. This decision will define most of his adulthood.

--Where is she? Ever since the New York Taxi Riots she has been very strange--

He is more frustrated with himself than her and believes he may have done something wrong. Carlos has no idea his self-imposed emotional confinement is both the match that lights the flame of Roxanne's ardor as well as the bucket that douses it. He also has no notion Roxanne may have other issues that keep them separate.

--If the world was not falling apart, we might have a chance. No, I need to tell her about the little girl drowning during that storm--

He senses Roxanne might think less of him once she knows what happened during the storm; nonetheless, he plans to tell her everything about the grave site he insists on visiting every week. To mitigate his feeling of betrayal he will do anything for her. Especially after the emotional beating he has taken the last few days from his parents.

He lingers under clouds looking for the afternoon sun--watching the New U.N. trucks crawling down the roadway toward him--waiting for Roxanne. The trucks creep closer. Carlos suddenly decides to work if Roxanne does not show up today. It is a response to pain.

The music stops and a bright voice barks over the airwaves: "The temperature remains above a hundred degrees throughout the New York metropolitan area and is anyone out there sweating? This is Uncle Ho with the two o'clock news. Last night in the final baseball game under lights the Yanks triumphed six to four over the Reds. Now for the boring stuff: The President calls for more flood relief along Lake Mississippi and film star Lee Oswald has agreed to play his famous relative in the newest remake of The Dallas Conspiracy. United Networks, having completed its takeover of the old United Nations, says the future is bright. The U-dot-N-dot, the conglomerate formed by United Networks, and the old UN, also says we've all been good little boys and girls and that energy usage is down fifteen per cent. Hoover Dam cracks a smile, and we'll be back after this New U.N. advisory. Put on your boots, kiddies."

An English accent crowns a deep melodious voice: "This is Arthur Conworth of the Global Revitalization Council reminding you that private automobiles are your responsibility to scrap. Cars left in roadways, driveways, garages, or anyplace after September first will be towed and the owners cited. We are on the right path now. Let us all work together for a better future. And remember, when going on vacation this summer make sure your yellow pass is valid--failure to do so might waste valuable energy."

Another voice, this one with a distinctly country and western flavor speaks: "This message has been brought to you by the Global Revitalization and Environmental Enforcement Agency. Stay cool partner. We're on the job."

A burp fills the airwaves. "This is Uncle Ho again. Hoover Dam has a splitting migraine and the WTO has demanded Congress pony up two billion to repair it. I say, why the hell not? It's funny money anyway. The death toll in Wednesday's Mexico City earthquake has risen to over one hundred thousand people. Scientists sight the event as conclusive proof there is no validity to the theory that tectonic change is accelerated by our warming environment. Why am I not surprised? Further details will be made available later this week."

Another burp.

"This final note: The cages of the Bronx Zoo will be auctioned off on Labor Day. The Greenies consider them a national treasure representing a valiant effort to save endangered species and fight global climate change. They want the bars preserved. They really want them preserved. Get it, kiddies? So, all you rich folk with a green conscience who want to kiss butt with the new Massas get on over and buy those bars. Happy summer you all, and Ho, Ho, Ho. I'll be back at five." Music begins again.

Overflowing with guards, dark green trucks belching exhaust pass slowly beneath Carlos. The noxious odor seems more caustic than he remembers it. Hand painted jagged yellow lightning bolts sit on the hoods of the vehicles. Looking at these men and women, they appear nothing like the handsome friendly guards on the public service ads. Many are passed out in drunken stupors; he sees no smiles. A couple of guards flip a middle finger at him as they pass. Feeling betrayed, Carlos counts trucks as if he were a member of The Resistance doing reconnaissance.

There have been a number of articles on The Resistance in the news. Mostly The Resistance is portrayed as bumbling fools. Carlos believes the media, except for Uncle Ho, is guilty of cowardice.

--Two-hundred-and-fourteen trucks in all. Well over four thousand guards. That's too many for just one reeducation facility. Roxanne may have been right about them building five more generators up north--

Leaning on his bicycle, he scans again for Roxanne. The trucks, even at their slow speed will be out of sight soon. There will be no way Roxanne and Carlos will be able to catch up on their bicycles.

The thought burrows in his head until a large green van lumbers up the roadway toward him. He guesses Roxanne will be inside. These last few weeks Carlos has heard a great deal about how the people in the Big Apple can do almost anything. When he sees the New York City license plates Carlos stands straighter. Sure enough the boxy van slows to a halt and the passenger door swings open.

"Put the bike in the back," says the driver, a slight woman in coveralls and a green bandanna. She sits next to Roxanne who wears a light blue sundress covered in pink crescent moons. Her hair is up and her eyes are dawn. Carlos melts.

Carlos picks his bike up and opens the side door of the van. "Hey, man, how goes it?" In the back of the van sit two skinny, scruffy-looking teens with scraggly beards wearing only shorts.

"Just great. Help me, okay?" Says Carlos. To Carlos they look like twigs ready to break. These two boys know hunger.

"Sure, man, beer?" The back is littered with cans.

"No, thanks." Carlos hands them the bike then slams the door shut. He climbs over beer cans and boxes to sit behind the front seat. Immediately the vehicle lurches forward as the electric motor and flywheel engage.

"Carlos, this is Lana. She works for the Greenies. I met her the other day in New York. I told her about our discussion. She offered to take us north to the Generation Camps. She has to drop off her younger brother and his friend at one of the camps later this week." Roxanne leans over and kisses him briefly. "Lana worries the camps might not be a nice place for her brother." Roxanne's darting eyes betray a span between she and Carlos he has never seen before.

The van enters the freeway and follows the trucks at a respectful distance. Silence fills the cab. Carlos wonders how much Roxanne has told this woman.

"Roxanne says you're going to one of those Ivy League schools down in Washington."

"Georgetown isn't exactly Ivy League, but it's good for me," Carlos glances at Roxanne. He could have gone to school closer to New York. They talked about it a few weeks ago. This time she does not react; it binds Carlos' heart even tighter than before. "How come we are not worried about being stopped?" He asks.

"I got myself a pass here." She pats her chest pocket. "No one messes with you once you have the right pass." Lana flashes a bright toothy mouth. "I hear you don't like the Greenies. Why would you work for them?"

"They're okay if you like guns," Carlos says with a grin. His gut churns. No part of him believes his companions acquired their pass legally.

"I like him. He has good sense--not like Beau, that stupid brother of mine." Lana rolls down her window and puts a hand into the breeze. "Too damn hot--you know what my dumb brother did?"

"No." Carlos watches Roxanne stare straight ahead. "So what did your brother do?" Carlos sits like a hunk of metal. To Carlos, this trip to the generators seems like the end of he and Roxanne.

She points back with a dirty thumb. "The jerk goes over to Greenie barracks in Staten Island and tries to steal some of those Privilege Plates. You know the kind they put on your bumper that says your waste of energy is okay. He figured he could make a tidy profit on the black market." She glances over to Roxanne. "Good money to be made there, aye, Roxie?"

Roxanne's eyes widen a moment. She does not like being called Roxie or having Carlos know she has contacts involved in the black market. "Look there they go. They are getting off."

"I got it." The van slows until all the trucks are out of sight. Following them, they enter a six-lane roadway full of shuttered strip malls, gas stations, and burned out fast food restaurants. Both Carlos and Roxanne gaze about the wasteland. No one even walks the street. The convoy remains two miles ahead of them until it slows to turn into a large fenced area.

"This is spooky," says Carlos. "They're using the big shopping mall as a prison."

"Look what they did to the mall." Roxanne says incredulously.

Lana negotiates the vehicle circling the empty parking lots; guard towers sit every few hundred yards. Between them rises a twenty-foot steel wire fence topped with concertina wire. The bright blue and silver vertical bands of the three-story mall glow in shafts of sunlight. Hanging from the roof is a white banner saying: "Building for the Future." The convoy stops and the guards begin to disembark.

Lana hauls the steering wheel over and pulls the van into an empty parking lot. They bounce over the concrete gutter and drive around back. "Easy Lana, take it easy," comes a voice from the back of the van. Stopping by the loading area of a large store, she shuts off the engine. From a shell shot wall a large dark hole stares at them like the ragged pupil of a battered eye.

"It's from an explosion. Looks like looters have been here before the Greenies had a chance to confiscate the inventory," Lana laughs. "Right on."

"Or the previous owners took it themselves," Carlos interjects. He keeps asking himself what he is doing here.

Roxanne shoots him with a glance. "The fence is shorter here. Look, there seems to be a hole under the fence for a storm drain. If Beau doesn't like it he can just leave," she says with a smile.

"Bah, this isn't the place. The fence is shorter because this is a construction fence. See? The poles are sitting in concrete blocks." Lana opens the small window behind her and speaks to the back of the van. "We're going in."

The two in the back of the truck tip their beer cans. "Have fun."

"Let's go," Lana says. Roxanne practically pushes Carlos out of the truck.

"What is the problem?" Carlos asks.

"We need to talk," Roxanne replies.

"What about?" Carlos asks.

"Not now."

Lana puts a small blue sheet of paper on the dashboard. "This signifies a repair crew. Beau won't get into any trouble while we're gone."

"Seems odd we should find ourselves at the perfect spot to enter. Look, they cannot see us from the towers." Carlos says staring at Roxanne. She appears to ignore him. A dark cloud settles over Carlos.

Reluctantly, Carlos follows as they cross the rubble in front of them.

They hurry over the edge of the concrete and down a short slope of rust colored weeds. Easily slipping under the construction fence, they follow the dry storm drain directly toward the bright blue and silver striped walls of the mall. They see no signs of the trucks or soldiers until they are fifty feet from one of the doors. A jeep with two guards appears on patrol. Rushing forward, Lana hauls them both down behind a light blue dumpster.

"They'll check on my truck when they complete their rounds. I'd say we have about ten minutes." When the jeep is out of sight they scurry toward the glass entrance. The doors open easily and the three of them sweep inside the mall.

--The timing was perfect. And the doors are open. How convenient--

The sound of construction fills the large space around them. Flashes of light from welders' sparks leap off bright metal railings. Heavy machines spew blue exhaust and voices of workers call to each other. Abandoned stores on either side of them lie safely behind metal roll cages. Roxanne, Carlos, and Lana, scoot past long dried-out plants in large terra-cotta planters. At the end of the corridor, they peek around a storefront filled with signs exclaiming the wonders of a sale.

A large cavernous hole runs down the center of the mall. Metal scaffolding cascades almost fifty feet down. The stores across the way are gutted and the mezzanine walkway is gone. Exposed steel girders crisscross the far wall. The girders form an odd looking ferris wheel. Workmen fill the pit and climb the girders.

"Whatever they are building, it must be big," Roxanne says.

"How nice we have such a perfect view," Carlos whispers.

"Look," says Roxanne, pointing at row after row of twelve-foot diameter cages that look like hamster runs.

"What are those for?" Asks Carlos.

"The prisoners call them home." Lana replies. "Look." She points to a brightly lit mock-up that hangs in mid air suspended by wire cables. Almost thirty feet in diameter and ten feet wide, it sways in the breeze like an executioner's noose. She hands him a set of opera glasses. Carlos counts two hundred cages geared into a large central wheel.

--Is the need for energy this acute? I thought there were alternative technologies; it cannot be this bad. What was Emile thinking? Surely they know we will not stand for this slavery--

"Life in those cages would be hell," he mumbles. Anger rises through his chest. To him it seems Emile was lying.

"Why is there another bank of them?" Roxanne asks.

"Double-decker, triple-decker, who knows?" Lana says, turning away, trying to catch her breath. She pulls out a note pad and begins sketching.

"They'll kill hundreds in this place every month."

"I can not believe it," Carlos says handing Roxanne the glasses.

"You better believe it, sonny," Lana says losing all her folksy charm in one breath.

Roxanne stares at Carlos--angry at what she sees as his need to remain blind. "See what is around you." She scans the construction mumbling invectives.

"Maybe we see things differently," Carlos suggests quietly.

"No doubt about it," replies Roxanne.

"And whatever you do," Lana says in an attempt to recover her folksy charm, "don't risk spending time on the bottom deck." Lana refers to life in the bottom tier of generator cages.

"Not him," Roxanne says.

Carlos clenches his jaw watching "You're angry at me for maybe working with them."

Roxanne makes no comment as Lana examines the supporting systems and the wiring around them. She makes notes alongside sketches. "From what I can tell the generators will be at least three decks high." Roxanne stares up and down the mall at the large stores at either end. "From the welding that's going on I'd say they appear to be closing the openings from the stores into the mall area. No air flow."

"I know this mall. There will be no place for a mess hall or sanitary facilities for this many people," Carlos says.

"They live in the cages," Lana says with a growl.

Carlos stares at the model.

"Time to go." Lana finishes her drawings and turns back toward the doors. Roxanne follows immediately. "Carlos."

Numb from all he has experienced today and angry from too much abuse, he can only calculate. Carlos backs up until he hears: "Don't move. Raise your hands." Carlos turns and sees two men holding automatic weapons standing by the glass doors.

Roxanne and Lana, their hands in the air, stand quite still. "Walk slowly toward us." The guard, a powerfully built man in his twenties, leans into his shoulder microphone to speak. "We've got three guests. No, they don't look like that resistance-scouting party. It's two kids and a woman. The woman is wearing Greens. They look like another set of tourists." He motions with his weapon for them to walk toward the doors. "No. I don't see a camera or weapons. Yeah, they're healthy. No, I said tourists--" The man clenches his jaw. "We don't need more people for this facility--Yes sir."

Carlos strides forward. "Do you realize you are building a death camp here? How can you--" The other guard jabs him in the stomach with the barrel of his gun. Gasping for air, Carlos collapses to the floor.

"Anyone else?" Growls the same guard.

The first guard looks at the boy on the ground then stares up at his comrade. "Are you crazy?"

"I certainly am," replies the other guard.

"Hey, Assholes."

The guards spin to see who is behind them. In mid-turn their feet fly out and their weapons clatter to the ground. The two men collapse. Lana's brother holds a weapon in each hand. Across his chest is a bandoleer of red-tipped bullets. "Lanie, the guns. I'll get the telecom."

As the others grab the weapons and telecommunications gear, Roxanne scoops up Carlos. "Let's get the hell out of here." Moments later they sprint through the deserted parking lot carrying Carlos and scoot under the fence.

"Whoa, were we good or what?" Comes the whoop from the front seat.

"How is he?" Lana asks. Roxanne has Carlos' head on her lap.

Carlos speaks: "My gut, thumps, but I am okay." In fact Carlos is blind with pain and anger. All he wants to do is hit back.

Roxanne speaks: "He will be all right. This was planned all along. Wasn't it?"

"Honey," says Lana, "You're either part of the solution or part of the problem. We're The Resistance. You've seen the sides of this now. Which side are you on?"

"You killed those guards," Roxanne says quietly, mopping Carlos' brow. "There was no need for that."

"Our job is to make the lives of the Greenies hell."

"Why didn't you tell me?" Roxanne asks.

"We had to see what one of those places looked like and you two were the perfect cover."

"So you endangered us?" Roxanne asks. "If you would have told me what you were planning I would have agreed. I don't like the Greenies either. Right now however, after killing them in cold blood, I do not see much difference between you and them."

"Get her? What a hoot," Lana says to her brother. "We're supposed to trust a couple of kids. Honey, we're all in danger from the Greenies. Are you with us or not?"

"She is not a killer. And who made you The Resistance?" Carlos asks, raising himself up from Roxanne's lap. He scans the van interior for escape and weapons. All he sees is empty beer cans, a passed out boy in the cargo area next to him, and Beau sporting a pink bowler in the front seat. In a few moments he will find an old Cub Scout knife in his pants.

"What's the pink bowler for, Sport?" Carlos tells himself he does not care how Beau reacts.

"I told you, we're in The Resistance. I think it maybe part of our uniform. Just a little bit of the old ultra-violence, aye mate. Others will join us," says Beau.

"Like him?" Carlos asks, pointing to the passed-out young man.

"Count us out," says Roxanne. "I am sorry, Carlos."

Carlos looks at Roxanne. She pulls back. It stuns him. He does not know the anger that surges from his eyes. Through the thin metal they hear Beau say: "We can't breach security by letting them go."

"I know," says Lana. "All right then, these two fail." She slams the window shut between the van and the cargo area.

"Hey, Lana," Roxanne calls. "Hey, what are you going to do?"

"Consider yourself martyrs."

Chapter Five

The tears remain like the leaks in an old concrete dam. The dam will not break--it will just leak. Through the tears, this July morning, Carlos whistles while he pedals his bicycle. The memories of the bloodshed, the screaming, the terror of the crash, everything but the look of horror in Roxanne's eyes has faded. Her blood spattered clothes in the flashing red lights of the ambulance and the way color seemed to drain from them everything--it was becoming a mist--except the tears.

--I had no choice. I can't think about this anymore--

Pumping the pedals harder he will focus on the clean air that fills a bright morning. Birds cheer. Flowers glow; warm winds caress the night's dew in a last bow. Sun glistens from the grass.

--Bicycle ridership and social interaction among community members grows with each day. In the three months since the Greenhouse Laws, crime, except for looting, has all but disappeared. Everywhere people wave to each other while riding bicycles; they speak in calm tones. I like that--

The local streets are empty of trucks--only the New U.N. trucks travel during the day. Buses are banned until noon and the four lanes of roadway feel rather luxuriant to Carlos. Autos must have special permission to be on the roads at any time. The other bicyclists, many more than last week, fill the thoroughfare. Listening to conversations, he feels lighter than he has felt in days; the pains cease for reasons unexamined.

--The tears are from the wind--

He tells himself as he hears new friends catching up on tales of change. The "Hydrogen Economy" is the topic of the day and observation moves from rider to rider like chat on the net: "The major impact of the Greenhouse Laws is economic not political." "That's right people must live close to their work." "I didn't think there would be jobs." "You call these jobs?"

"Perhaps, but the commute is heaven and what good is money if you are limited by the amount of energy you can use in a month?"

Carlos swerves back and forth on the wide roadway, enjoying the day. Before he knows it, other bicycles join in and a snake of travelers crosses the two lanes in a harmonious line. Sweeping back and forth like a Caribbean wave, the riders flow up the roadway in perfect synchronicity. Looking behind himself at the conga line of twenty or so bicyclists--Carlos almost crashes into a sleek red sports car that pulls out in front of him. A bright fluorescent "P" on the bumper flashes in blues and reds; the "P" signifies privilege, permission to drive on the roads. The driver honks, then roars up the street. Carlos and the other bicyclists wave good-bye.

A woman wearing a white shirt and jeans pedals alongside Carlos. "It feels like subservience to the auto. Foolish machines--oh, look how great." Up ahead a few of the more militant riders have blocked three of the four lanes. The car, honking its horn, passes in the last lane forcing an oncoming bicyclist to swerve and fall. The driver fists them for taking up too much space. In the car's wake, bicyclists ring bells and sound horns. Carlos looks over to the young woman who was beside him but she has disappeared; the conga line of bicyclists now follows her shapely form. In summer's praise, laughter and chatter flow freely the next few miles until he turns on a wide alder-lined drive that leads into a parking lot. Carlos waves back to those still on the roadway. Someone sounds a bell in response. Ahead of him squats a huge building--looking like a Christmas gift-wrapped in aluminum foil--even to the fake red ribbon and red steel bow on the top.

Erected on the site of an old distribution warehouse for automobile parts, George Washington Mall sells only New U.N. approved products. It opened soon after the Greenhouse Laws went to Congress for evaluation. Carlos notes the broad green ribbon of paint along the base of the building: "New U.N. Approved".

Passing a number of white buses waiting to begin their runs, Carlos scans the crowded bike racks. Even with all this parking he cannot find a space to leave his bicycle. He occasionally glances at the scores of empty bike racks set aside for the employees behind the line of white buses. His employee badge is in the saddlebag and he begins to circle on his bicycle and look for it--one hand groping the bag behind him. He cannot understand how he has become so absentminded this summer. All he need do is flash his pass at the sleepy guard and park his bicycle for a few minutes--Carlos is here to pick up a going away gift for Lars--not to work. Finding the badge he smiles at the guard and under a tree crowded with robins, finds a place to leave his bicycle. The white spots on the ground from nesting birds explain why the space is empty.

Hopping off the bicycle, Carlos attaches his bike to the twin locking pylons that clamp together around his wheels and frame. He takes out a small plastic tarp and drapes it over the seat. Passing the employee bike entrance, he waves to the portly guard who sits in a chair watching birds feathering their nest in the nearby trees. The man says: "You have the pass I know it kid--take advantage of it. I don't care. No one does."

"How do you know I work here?"

"My son goes to Vertwall. I know all about you." The man returns to watching the birds.

Carlos nods and continues down the pleasant pathway that leads to the building. Ever since the almost-riot on Earthday more people know him. The parents respect him for what he did that day and the children just wonder about him. The respect and notoriety ensnare him, more than Carlos will admit to himself. It makes Roxanne's distance a bit easier. As an adult, Carlos will often substitute notoriety for love.

On the ten-foot high green band it says: "U.N. Corporate Approved Building. Safe shopping Zone VII." Carlos descends the stairway into the mall. Most of the building is below ground, though you could not tell by the roof. It rises thirty feet from grade. Acting as a super insulation and power generation system, the mall uses convection currents to run massively parallel low output turbines for power. Weeks before the trip to the generator camp, Carlos and Roxanne went up into the roof to make love on every level. The tiny spinning tubes with colored wires snaking everywhere had made the task daunting--and fun. The memory bites Carlos. Since the trip to the generators Roxanne has treated him like a pariah. He tells himself he understands.

--She cannot possibly blame me for what happened there yet she does. Shouldn't she feel glad we are still alive? It was they or we. I saved us--

In disconnect, he looks out over the carpet of consumers on the mall floor wondering how many people are here. The law says any device that does not meet New U.N. energy consumption requirements must be turned off or the owner faces a heavy fine. And everyone has appliances or electronics that do not meet the New U.N. energy consumption standards. As a result the mall is always busy. The term "Captured Market," a term to describe consumers without choice, roosts in his brain. He saw the term for the first time while doing research for his senior project. Though it wasn't about appliances--it was about oil.

--It would be interesting to find out who controls these malls. After all that blather about a depression, what nonsense, it was all a ploy, some group's concern that a shift in power and wealth might hurt them. It certainly was not concern for the environment or concern for the common person. Why didn't they tell us this would result? It would have made it easier. New wind and waterpower industries spring up by the dozens every day; it has been a real boom to the local economy. Three months into the Greenhouse Laws, we have the Internet boom again. I bet the petroleum industry has a large hand in hiding it, somewhere--

Unlike the automobile industry or the tire industry, which spent record amounts of money on lobbying against the Greenhouse Laws, the petroleum industry, the industry that seemed to have the most to lose, remained largely silent about the Laws. The petroleum industry's lack of comment had confused Carlos for months. It led to a report on the petroleum industry as his senior project.

Midway through, it finally made sense to Carlos: the oil fields had become useless. The petroleum industry did not fight the Greenhouse Laws because they had run out of oil. That was the moment his senior project opened Carlos' eyes as to the timing of the Greenhouse Laws. He was sure had the oil run out sooner, the laws prohibiting petroleum usage would have been enacted years earlier. That small piece of the puzzle has led to a deep distrust of institutions for Carlos; of course at this point in his life he harbors a distrust of people as well. It will not get improve soon--but it will make him a better diplomat.

In college, he will conclude the scholarly approach to problems, the scientific method, is the only way to understand the meaning of life. Then he will recall the pageant of scholars seen on television screens over the last few years claiming that the impact of Global Warming was an economic impact, not a human one. "Only a few trillion dollars of cost--that's all." He will wonder why these scholars allowed themselves to be paraded like monkeys in a circus. Then, in his graduate work, he will uncover the ins and outs of the grant process and see how scholars are manipulated into protecting the economic interests of powerful lobbies. The "right" projects are funded; the wrong projects are not funded. He will conclude scholars are cowards and pawns.

Carlos will then seek to understand power. He will research why large organizations make trade-offs. He will examine the deals negotiated to soften the blow of the Greenhouse Laws, making them palatable to special interest groups--including the population at large. The result of all this knowledge, for Carlos, will be the insight that deals and compromises are important to maintain his society.

Carlos will also conclude unless you make the news, the news is useless, and finally enter the diplomatic service. He will return to this mall before his first assignment in Mexico, after learning this mall, and every one like it in the US, is owned by a consortium of industries who lost money as a result of the laws--the petroleum industry included. By that time it will all seem to make sense. He will conclude purity and ideals are merely delusions. Carlos will ignore love and warmth in favor of pragmatism, heroism and notoriety. The people who died in the van were the spark for that fire. While today, at the bottom of the mall stairs, at the age of seventeen, he can only continue guessing at how it all works and brush away tears--hoping no one will see.

--Van Waters had been right about one thing: It was all a fait accompli. So many changes were begun before the final approval by the people: this mall for example, the energy monitoring systems, the disposal and sale of automobiles, the layoffs at the auto plants with no apparent reason. What a lot of nonsense it is to fight inertia--

He shakes his head walking among the crowds concentrating on Lars' going-away present. He glances at the line of people waiting to get in the Cogeneration Shop: A store that specializes in microgeneration systems, it is always busy. Using wind power, methane conversion from kitchen waste, jogging and other exercising machines, this store sells ways for people to generate their power. No one thinks about spare parts yet.

In the store window, above the heads of consumers, he spies the cages where rats run on metal treadmills to generate electricity for the store. The cage keeps three-hundred rats busy and is a very popular item. The GeneRATors have even spawned another cottage industry, rat production, this despite the increase in the number of rats due to global climate change. The GeneRATors use rodents up at a furious pace and so a genetic strain that loves to run has been propagated. Harry and May, his parents, have already started a large rat farm where their flowers used to grow. Carlos stares at the treadmills. They are miniature versions of what he saw at the mall.

In the front display window: "200 WATTS! That's enough power for us. What about you?" Then in smaller type: "Once the rats die from exhaustion you recycle their bodies to make methane." This sign disturbs Carlos because he knows that same conversion will occur to prisoners in the Energy Generation Camps. Ever since the trip with Roxanne, the GeneRATors rile Carlos. He feels a crick in his neck. In his mind's eye, he sees people in those cages. Carlos moves on quickly passed the crowds of people waiting to enter the store.

Carlos stops into Happy Days, the electronics store where he works this summer. It specializes in low wattage electronic entertainment systems. A new sight and sound virtual reality system, small enough to be worn as a helmet is due in today. With a processor quick enough to allow completely smooth visual movement, as well as composition to augment canned programs, the system is eagerly awaited. The isolation from the world is complete with these systems--and therefore appealing to Carlos and many others of his time. Carlos wants one of these VR systems the way a male of a previous generation might have sought the escape of a Ferrari. He knows he will not be able to afford Head-Clamps--as they are called--in the foreseeable future. Even without his college bills the forty-five thousand dollar price tag is far beyond his reach. As a sales person he knows he will get to demonstrate it though. This is the main reason Carlos took the job here versus one of the other stores.

The idea of entering a new reality motivates many in this generation. The death and destruction around them, the decay of their lifestyle, it all beats on their psyches like a pile driver. Not unlike a wild party behind a steel curtain, the videos of the past showing an energy rich life and its wild ways mock this generation. Drugs had been popular, but they have almost disappeared; they take too much energy to make and transport--so the VR systems endeavor to take their place. VR will soon become a huge part of the entertainment business for this generation--everyone wants to escape.

Three weeks after taking the job Carlos has dismissed the business world as a career option. He tells himself he hates who he is for being a businessperson. His first day on the job, the owner, a tough looking bald man with a bright red nose and a large gut, said: "Successful sales people know an emotionally charged customer is a buyer." He instructed Carlos on how to get people excited about the products. Carlos found the man was right. People bought because of emotion, and no other reason. On the other hand, Carlos felt he violated people's privacy by touching their emotions; he has come to believe the stirring up of emotions to be detrimental to himself and others. He has taken to working long hours and seeing no one except for Lars. Carlos has not yet fully realized his friend will be gone in a week.

"Carlos, you working today?" The owner calls out across the store.

"I just came in to say hello, Pete."

"That and to see if the Aurora Head-Clamps have arrived yet." The man laughs at Carlos. Carlos colors. "I keep telling you they are not for those who lack." He laughs again. "They're not in yet."

"Ah, you got me again, Pete." Carlos dislikes this man for making fun of his desires. He says hello to a couple of co-workers who greet him with a cheery smile. They like Carlos' easy manners and quick humor. Carlos popularity has increased markedly since the Vertwall riots despite his isolation.

Carlos leaves the electronics shop and enters the Red Cross Store next to it. Here disaster victims make craft items. This store is usually empty because the crafts are so poorly made. Even so, he always checks in here when buying gifts. The ginger bread houses are still falling apart. The yo-yos do not work. The wooden toys made from two-by-fours splinter easily. The dolls made from rags smell of smoke. There is nothing new. In a month the Cogeneration Shop will take over this space.

Carlos hurries over to Good Times, the music store. Once inside, he quickly finds the music video Lars wanted and pays for it. On the way out he stops at the candy desk and picks out a hand-size red and blue hard candy heart for Roxanne.

He hopes Roxanne will add it to the collection of candy started by her grandfather. She has a huge collection of candy in her storm shelter. Many of the older examples are dark moldy-looking things; but others, thanks to her father's inventiveness, have been dipped in a liquid plastic that does not melt chocolate or wash out colors. Gumballs and sweets cover an entire wall of the family shelter. Various candy bars decorate the other three walls. Carlos thinks it the most interesting shelter he has ever seen and likes to contribute to it. He tells himself this gift will let Roxanne know he has no hard feelings toward her. Carlos wonders how well her family will do now. The plastic is petroleum-based. He pays for his gift and leaves the mall quickly. Once outside tears come in torrents and he is embarrassed.

Carlos steers his bicycle through the old front gate and follows the music and signs along the rutted roadway to "Lars' Blastoff!" The party is on the grounds of the old Lamont-Doherty Geological Observatory. Perched on the Palisades, the old college annex overlooks the Hudson River. A university once owned it. Sued into submission by a wealthy investor named Fisk whose son had died playing football, the university settled out of court giving the property as the settlement. A lawyer named Golding now rents the grounds out for Demolition Parties--another business thriving since the Greenhouse Laws.

Carlos finally stops at a twentieth century building that looks like a large gold match box with red striping along the top and bottom. Through every broken window, darting figures run about the building like demons. One large hole in the wall above the main doors reveals a bathroom where beer kegs have been set. Smoke from a couple of small fires burn on the roof, but they are still for food--not destruction.

Carlos dislikes Demolition Parties, but accepts their value. He knows a group of teenage partiers does remarkably efficient demolition, even while using no generated energy beyond that which is needed by a stereo system and a refrigerator. Fire or raw anger is usually used to trash the permitted buildings. The law allows no lawsuits and the partiers pay one of the local fire protection companies to keep a truck on site for the entire party. It is essentially a free-for-all. Sometimes it will take more than one party to destroy a building and the best Demolition Parties are obviously the first ones. It takes quite a bit of pull to get first crack at a building. This party is a second. The first group to use the building had been the PTA. As a result, all the walls and most of the windows are still in place along with some of the heavy furniture.

Once this former campus annex is completely razed, it will be turned into a members-only hunting preserve.

A large gray desk falls from the roof. Trailing smoke it just misses an oak tree landing in an explosion of sparks and flames. The bushes nearby light in a burst of flame; the crowds inside cheer. Three men sitting on the bright yellow pumper-truck shake their heads and begin to argue who will put out the burning desk. A fuzzyheaded firefighter with an orange mustache aims the turret of the fire truck toward the desk. A jet of water and chemicals spurts out, dousing the flames. The water and the turret slowly rotate toward Carlos as he parks his bicycle. Carlos darts to his left as the remains of gushing water splash his bicycle and others. The three men laugh uproariously.

Carlos hurries over to a red-painted pathway; it signifies a safe zone into the building where no desks or other lethal objects will fall. Scanning the building above him anyway, he quickly enters.

Just inside, Roxanne and Lars sit on an old green vinyl couch passing a bottle of Aquavit back and forth. The drinking age was reduced to sixteen with the introduction of the Greenhouse Laws. Theory goes: They will not be driving, so why not let sixteen and seventeen year olds drink? Roxanne jumps up and hugs Carlos. It is the warmest reception he has had from her since the trip to the generators. "You are stiff, Carlos. What is the matter?" She says. "Angry at someone?"

He takes the bottle submerged in questions. "Aquavit? Expensive stuff. I am impressed." He points outside with it. "I just dodged a blast of water directed at me by the three stooges. No. I am not angry." She sees a tear and he looks away.

Lars scowls. "Those guys piss me off."

It is macho to gulp Aquavit and he follows the custom, but Carlos does not enjoy it. Lars points to the bottle. Carlos hands it back and he takes a long pull. "I have a confession to make," Lars proclaims. He cannot bear what has happened to his friends but he will not talk about that.

Carlos sits on the arm of the green couch.

"Go ahead," Roxanne says, getting comfortable near Carlos' arm. Her snuggling feels like old times to him. He finds himself unable to trust the warmth and swims in confusion.

"I am filthy rich," Lars says quietly.

"No, I do not believe it. Tell us the gory details," Roxanne says quickly.

"My mother is the chairperson of Swedish Wheat."

Carlos and Roxanne look at each other quizzically. "So what is Swedish Wheat?" Carlos asks.

Lars looks at Carlos as if he has drooled on himself. He is insulted. "Swedish Wheat is the world's largest wheat production company. We have farms in fifty countries with more acres under the plow than anyone else. Who is Swedish Wheat? You Americans, I swear."

Carlos and Roxanne laugh; they have been teasing him. "Why did you tell us this and why should we care?" Carlos asks.

"Look around you," Lars says.

The room is a former reception area, the wallboard stripped away and the metal studs scorched. "Did Swedish Wheat do this?" Carlos asks dramatically. "I knew someone was at fault." He and Roxanne break into gales of laughter. In a sweet moment these teenagers forget the world.

"Go ahead Lars," Roxanne says when she sees Carlos stop laughing. His tears warm her. She has faced her pain and wishes he would face his soon.

"When I go back to Sweden, I go into corporate training. Do you both hate me?"

Roxanne cannot bear it anymore. She laughs so hard she tears. "Oh, Lars, you're drunk. We will still love you even if you are a corporate pig. Won't we, Carlos?"

"Sure," Carlos says, taking a swig from the bottle that has been in Lars' hand. "Where is your executive pony tail? Seen Pard recently?"

"No, I mean it. I'm a fake. I am going to the executive suite." He says the words like they are a death row sentence.

Roxanne and Carlos look at each other. In unison they face Lars. Roxanne speaks: "Whether you know it or not there is no way you will do that."

"You think so?" Lars asks, a ray of hope penetrating his funk.

"Remember those three guys that were waiting to beat up Carlos the day after the almost-Earthday-riot at Vertwall? A corporate guy would have bought them off--especially a corporate pig. You took them on. That's very un-corporate."

"What? Is that what happened? You said it was a climbing accident," says Carlos.

"Oops," says Roxanne. Carlos looks at her suspecting she did not let this slip because she is tipsy. In a moment of clarity he sees Roxanne wanting him to know he has friends who love him. Carlos cannot look at her.

"Forget it," says Lars with a sad look at Roxanne.

She purses her lips. "Don't worry. A hothead like you will never last in a corporation," says Roxanne.

"Count on it." Carlos smiles warmly at Roxanne.

"Well," Roxanne says standing. She hates it when Carlos flashes her one of those Ping Pong-smiles. "I have an announcement." She looks around cautiously, as if under surveillance, "I have a job in New York City." She grins wildly, then pushes her hands behind her back and begins rocking on her heels.

Lars cheers. "Oh yeah, way to go. The one with The Times Square Cooperative?"

"That very one," she replies.

"Huh?" Carlos knows nothing about this company.

Lars stands up and bows. "To the new Rockette."

Roxanne playfully slaps him. "I am not. I am Assistant Director of Displays and Light." She grabs the bottle. "And you know what is better? I'll get to go to California once a year."

Carlos, who has been clapping his hands, not missing a beat, kisses her on the cheek. Roxanne sighs at the hollow kiss. She tells herself it is all for the best. Turning to Lars: "Like I told you before, Lars, Carlos is just like my grandmother." She looks at Carlos. "Carlos, one must have fun. Period."

"You're going to hate the commute," Carlos says.

"Those buses stink," says Lars.

"I know. 'Ya' sure, Swedish buses are better," quips Roxanne. They all laugh. "Maybe I will find an apartment."

Carlos' eyes widen. "Really? I would love to be in New York more often. Now I have a reason."

Roxanne looks over to Lars; who is suddenly looking down the hallway. Then she looks at Carlos.

"Oh, I understand." He keeps his smile even and his eyes bright. His effort sears Roxanne.

A new song blares out from the rooftop speakers. "Come on, let's go Spindance," Lars says. Roxanne grabs both Lars and Carlos and they run down the hallway and rumble upstairs.

Teenagers bounce and twirl on the roof to a female voice and an electric be-bop violin. Waving trees swaying to the tune are topped by blue skies. Carlos, Roxanne, and Lars join in the Spindancing, a circular dance step done in tight circles. Whenever the whistle blows, a partner whirls off to dance with other partners like spinning solar systems joining new galaxies.

Carlos loves to Spindance and today it is an especially welcome step. He occasionally catches sight of Roxanne and notes that instead of her normally wild laughter, she maintains a shy smile and never looks at him. Passing from dance partner to dance partner Carlos quickly finds himself in the arms of a young woman with lovely pouting lips, dark hair and deep blue eyes. She will not release him. When the dance ends she stays in his arms.

"Dance with me," she says. A wild song; they jump and bounce around like jelly beans. It is a delight for him to dance with this beautiful young vixen. Neither speak and Carlos sees an advantage in lusty emotionless flirting. Her limpid eyes draw poetry from most boys. From Carlos they draw long goofy looks; she loves it.

When the dance is over Lars pushes passed Carlos pulled by a lithe young woman with short red hair. Surprisingly, in their wake, Roxanne threads her arm inside Carlos' arm and steers him to the stairs. Looking around for his dance partner he sees her watching him, a sly pouting smile on her face. Carlos winks. Roxanne heads him down the stairway.

The next floor down they follow the hallway. Someone in a fireproof jumpsuit waves at them. A moment later, that person breaks open a jar of flammable liquid and lights it. The room blazes. Instantly a blast of water from the hose outside douses the room, knocking the person onto the floor. "No inside fires are allowed until the roof is clear," someone yells. With the room drenched in water, a young woman pulls off the suit's hood. Debbie Gold begins to laugh hysterically. "How about you, Carlos?"

"I will be right back," Carlos says.

Roxanne drags him away. "I hear Pard dumped her. You are getting quite popular with the ladies," she says pulling him into an empty office. Pushing him down onto a gray office chair she closes the door behind her. The stamping of feet above thunders into her head as she faces him. "Carlos, even though I love you, we are done. Love me one last time." He cannot believe what he has heard.

"I am going to live with someone," she says as they lie in each other's arms on the large gray chair.

Carlos pushes through an unwanted surge of anger. "And I am supposed to say..."

"He is a man I met at Times Square Development."

"He would not happen to be the man you will be working for?" Carlos cannot handle it. "I am sorry. I know how mean that was." He stands up and begins to put on his pants.

The tart insinuation burns Roxanne. She sits, knees tight to her chest. Her arms encircle her knees. He is indeed the man for whom she will be working. Her eyebrows knit and eyes narrow. "That was not very nice. I expect better from you, Carlos."

"Can I go back to the dance?" He thrusts his arms inside his shirtsleeves.

"No."

"Sorry." He scans around looking for something--he does not know what he is looking for at this moment. The pounding above them and the sounds of breaking glass below come as mercy.

Roxanne picks up an old telephone database cube and tosses it through the window. It shatters on the ground below.

"What is it now?" He says. A tear stings him.

"Damn you." She stands and begins to dress.

"Still, I am glad you found a way to make it in the world--" He suddenly sits on the floor and leans against the wall. "Do we need to talk about what happened after the generators? I gather it doesn't hurt anymore." He glances at the top of her legs

"That's the past. Get over it. Can you understand that, Carlos?" She kicks an old garbage pail.

"Happiness is a luxury. You won't speak to me. You won't write me. I have to wait to hear what you are doing in a conversation with Lars. Are you afraid of me; is that it?"

"This has nothing to do with that. We will always be friends regardless of what has happened or what will happen to us."

"So it is about that." He looks away to hide a tear. "I was protecting us."

"Carlos, darling, it is not about that."

"Just level with me."

"I was protecting us also," she says, her arms out and her eyes moist. She looks around calming herself. "Carlos, in response to a hellish world and evil parents you have erected a wall to keep people out. I cannot--"

"I like my privacy. Roxanne, we humans belong in a cage."

"So you made one for yourself?"

Carlos' eyes blaze for just a moment. "That was a score. Good one, Roxanne. If I'm going to be any good as a diplomat, I'll need to be able to face comments like that without getting riled up. They were going to kill us."

"Carlos, you almost killed two people in a blind rage. You ripped open a boy's throat with your teeth."

"I was not going to let them hurt you."

"Listen to me. Damn it. Don't any of you men know how to listen? Shut up and listen." Roxanne stares at him. "Carlos, after what we saw that day I didn't care if they did kill me. Do you hear me? Do you know how bad things are going to get in the next few years? You were not protecting me. You were just so angry it took you over in a blind rage. None of it was about my safety."

"You think what you like, but it is up to us to make it better, not lie down…and die." He swipes his face to clear tears.

She can barely contain her anger. "Make it better? You were in a wild animal's rage. Or, you were trying to get yourself killed." She stands so close her body's heat touches him.

"Why didn't you call the police on me if you feel that way about it?"

"Why? Because, I love you. That's why. But you don't understand me. It is not about stretching out the time we live but making the time we live worthwhile." She kicks the garbage can again imbedding it between studs. "We are too different. But I want us always to be friends."

"Translation: I cannot love a man who did what you did." Carlos sheds more tears. "I saved your life. Doesn't that count for something?"

She cannot speak. She wonders if he will ever forgive her for what she had to do to save them.

He grabs a chair they made love on and throws it out the window. "You can leave now if you want. I have shown that nasty temper again just like my parents." He pauses. "That is it. You think I might do something to you, or someone else, or our child."

"No children for me thanks. Not with you. Not with anyone. But that is not it. You did save our lives. I know that. It was the action of a hero wrapped in the fury of an abused child. Carlos, I need joy, not remorse."

"Go away, Roxanne."

She wipes her eyes buttoning her shirt in silences. Turning to leave, she almost says something to Carlos about the girl he was dancing with-- then realizes he will probably spend the rest of his life in short meaningless relationships. Roxanne kisses him on the cheek. His tear tracks taste both salty and sweet. "This is not about you. It is about me." She leaves.

After she is gone from sight, Carlos pulls the hard candy heart from his backpack. Debbie-in-the-flame-proof-suit intercepts him. "Ready yet?"

"Not yet, but I will be back for you soon."

She stretches up like a cat. "Don't be too long."

"You will wait." He tosses her the hard candy heart. She catches it and purrs. Carlos wanders down the halls until he sees Lars leaving another wrecked office and yells to him. Lars waves.

Carlos speaks first: "Did Roxanne talk to you about what happened and that she is leaving me?"

"She told me what you did at the generator camp. But that isn't the reason she is leaving." He and Carlos walk slowly along the gutted hallway.

Carlos speaks: "I asked her again what a hero is supposed to look like."

"I know. She said you. She knows you were saving her life when you kicked those peoples' butts. If it helps I would have done the same thing. I don't think I would have left them alive." Lars shakes his head; he cannot bear what Roxanne did to save them. "You know what I love about Roxanne? Her ideals--she is the purist person I have ever met."

"Me too," Carlos says. "I just cannot have her think I am a beast like my parents."

"She doesn't. Come on," Lars says. "Let's go outside, take a few chairs and watch them burn this place to the ground."

They walk along the hallway listening to the music and screams. Dusk smiles and they park themselves under the large old oak tree near the remains of the burning desk. More and more of the building falls to the ground in front of them. "Carlos, did you really lose it?" Lars asks.

"Completely. They had us down by the old canning plant. They were hurting Roxanne."

Lars speaks: "All she was doing was diverting their attention, Carlos."

Carlos laughs ruefully. "I told the woman I was going to puke. I fell to the floor and asked for a handkerchief. I was blubbering so it was really convincing. Then I grabbed her and pulled on the steering wheel. After the crash, I went crazy. Next thing I knew Roxanne was hugging me. I was covered in blood. So was she. I kept asking her if she was okay."

"Anything happen? From the authorities, I mean."

"Not a blessed thing. I guess because they were terrorists the Greenies didn't care much about what happened to them. I saw an article the next day." He looks around with a grin. "You know the newspaper hinted the Greenies had killed them for killing those two guards." A burst of flames rose from the roof as if the devil had risen. The flames cast dancing shadows on his face. "I went nuts."

"And you two saved both of your lives," Lars says quietly. " I think you both did right."

"Well you are a hothead, Lars. For you battle is acceptable."

"Maybe so."

"So Roxanne and I really were a team that day. I will never let my emotions get the best of me again. I swear," Carlos watches students exit the building as the flames began to build. From the roof, royal red sparks mount the darkening sky while flames eat their way down into the heart of the building.

The Sixty-Fifth Anniversary of Earthday

Chapter Six

Outside the U.N. NorCal headquarters
(The former NASA Ames Research Center)
Mountain View, California

SETI had been a stopover, the only appointment in the San Francisco Bay Area after she received her doctorate in telecommunications, or Susan Willoughby would never would have taken the appointment. SETI--as far as she was concerned--was an absurdity. Who scrutinized the sky for aliens while people died? A vast waste of funding--but she took the appointment here because it answered her needs: Susan qualified for the Athens' Olympics--the last one for the foreseeable future and she needed a safe place to train. Being a backwater, SETI also allowed her the time to train.

Cycling along old Route 101, on her way to work, she noted the roads had been getting a bit dicey with the storms returning but she was handling that problem. The Bay Area's dry-cycle climate had been so beautiful; the long golden hills and flat stretches, perfect for distance bicycle training but now with the storms coming on for the wet period she was looking forward to a new government project for low wattage telephony opening in Virginia; old friends called her about it last week. Spring in Virginia was safe and many of the roads were still passable by bicycle. She had everything under control--she thought. A small dust devil ahead began to rise higher and higher into the blue sky. Susan took a hard left into the old SETI parking lot and headed for her office. Susan knew not to tempt fate.

In her tiny bunker of an office, Dr. Susan Willoughby looked at the report in front of her and wondered what to do. The coffee mug, the stacks of disks, the poster of Spock, her old green blanket on the floor, cracks in the cinder block walls, a moldy odor pervading the small office in the underfunded department and now this. Light limps through the bread box window overhead. The concrete office feels more claustrophobic than normal. She looks away from the documents on her desk and stares up at her window. Black garbage cans and brown grass mar her view of the sky. Cross from lack of sleep, she paces back and forth to her computers reexamining the numbers and occasionally making notes. Circling her desk, she picks up the wool blanket and tosses it on the chair-back. She returns to the printouts for the fifteenth time and studies them, somewhat amused but inexorably drawn to their content.

--Imagine Deus Ex Machina. What a hoot--

The plight of her generation owns Susan. She cannot fathom how previous generations could have been so selfish. And in that quandary there lies her Achilles heel: Susan's desire to return humanity to a prosperous past. Her passion to fix "The Problem," as many of her friends call it in polite company; it is all she thinks about. Considered a Quixotic notion by these close acquaintances, they nonetheless do everything they can to assist her. So how can she turn her back on what her computers tell her?

She wonders whom she might trust with this data--who might not laugh at her. She runs another system check. Her devotion to technology and computers has helped her make many of these friends. The theory is: By using bits and bytes for contact people will like her for herself and not her beauty or wealth. She is correct and as a result Susan has developed dear relationships despite her secret: She finds the computer more to her liking than most people--except when they come across as bits and bytes. The computer pays no attention to her features or wants. It processes and responds according to the best available data. The computer has no reason to "spin" information to please or entice her and it does not care about her looks. Susan's long blond hair and Javanese facial features give her an exotic beauty; she has had to fight off unwanted advances more than once. When her father's closest friend tried to assault her during prep school it led to recrimination and estrangement.

The resulting distance between her and her dad has never been breached. Beauty, she believes, is more of a nuisance than an advantage--a distraction from what is meaningful.

Poised at her desk, she outlines a set of questions then leans back against the cold cinder block walls. Glancing up at her trophy from the nationals, she ponders what to do now. A strong believer in focus she has plans to run the Department of Energy's office for telecommunications before she is thirty-five. An office that affects many defense issues, employment issues, financial issues, and security issues in a world where the population does not travel, data communication is king. Doing a remarkable job there, she believes, will make a difference and ensure her high visibility among Washington's elite. Susan also believes with visibility comes influence and with influence comes reconstruction.

But now, just hours after typing the first draft of her transfer, she gawks at the information on her desk, darting between it and her bank of three computers on the tables behind her desk. She has almost convinced herself that her team has not made a mistake. Her head begins to overflow with the possibilities of First Contact: help for humanity, a new start, life with hope, safety and prosperity for all. All this despite the feeling that the writing is still on the wall: Humanity's path leads nowhere.

--They better not be making a joke--

She gets up and leaves her room. Not letting the door close she sighs heavily

--Hope, real hope. Oh, what good does it do to pursue that anyway? So what if they're out there? We will likely be an extinct species before they could get to us. The gall of answering communication from a truly intelligent species after what we have done to ourselves is laughable. The numbers all look authentic, the numbers are right, but the odd communication, well that is just too peculiar. Why would anyone use that?

The door to her small concrete office opens and a dark handsome man in an old white lab coat enters. His gauntness is partially the result of severe hunger as a child. The rest is severe abuses of his body. Dr. Simon Weiss seeks to put an ugly past, an intolerable present, and a hopeless future behind him; he spends an inordinate amount of time dating and tasting the good life. He describes his activities as wallpapering the present. It is the prime reason he works for SETI. It leaves him with scads of time to enjoy the premium entertainment and activities in San Francisco, twenty miles north. Few cities in the world are as well tended as San Francisco and the U.N. bus that travels to San Francisco every four hours allows Simon access to every morsel offered by "Baghdad By The Bay."

The U.N. approved vacation spot stays pumped at high gear

twenty-four-seven; and that suits Simon fine. The merrier the night, the wilder the dance, the happier he feels. He travels up there four and five times a week sometimes alone, sometimes with a date. And with all the money spent on keeping San Francisco in repair and alluring, he can forget what he remembers, what he thinks he knows, and what he sees.

And although Simon might appear to be merely a bon vivant, certainly Susan, and everyone else he works with, does not consider him one. Susan knows the hardships and terror he encountered in his escape from southern Spain and the difficulties he had to endure getting his degree in the German sector of the European Union. Susan's view of his racing about savoring all life's flavors is one of sadness. She perceives it as a reaction to his early difficult life--unlike her early life of growing up with wealth and privilege. Susan calculates eventually he will tire of the trifling, once he rids himself of the ghosts from his youth. At that point she plans to give him a second look. Susan finds Simon a dear man. She studies his tired eyes and knows immediately Simon has again been out all night.

Before one foot passes the doorway, she begins: "In your opinion, this is factual? You are convinced this is not a joke, Doctor Weiss? Have you checked with CERN on these numbers?" Though innately shy, Susan is a stickler for the facts. When stressed she asks one question, then another, then another.

Susan Willoughby's quick tongue makes Simon fidget. A psychiatrist by training, he is not used to being so off-balance with anyone. It makes working with her difficult. And not just because of her intensity--her porcelain beauty and unsettling questions leave Simon hot and uneasy. He used to consider himself every-ladies' man--until he met her.

Simon clears his throat. "Dr. Willoughby, the answers to all questions are yes. I do believe it is real. I am convinced it is not a joke and I have checked with CERN. They confirm everything." His calm veneer shows no signs of his concern or present desires. It is an open face, angular and scared from his escapes. When under stress, his eyes sometimes betray the horrors of growing up in the Chaos of Southern Europe. For this generation Chaos is a place not a concept. Today his sparkling brown eyes and quick smile rest in a lined face. He closes the door behind him and sits.

"Doctor Weiss, there is a difference between unanswered questions and adolescent humor. I do not find this jape funny."

Simon finds Susan's abruptness curious. "Dr. Willoughby," he never uses her last name--except when she startles him. "This is no prank. It appears an alien culture is trying to contact us."

"Like this?" She shoves the papers off her desk. The action stuns Simon. He has never seen this side of her and wonders what is wrong. The pages flutter about the small concrete box of an office setting down on a gold Sarouk rug. "I suppose this is how they hail long distance." She shakes the printout. "Or perhaps they are just trying to get a good seat for the final act of the human comedy." She stares at him and he stares right back. Most dazzling human beings are in love with their looks.

Susan hardly cares. He finds himself pondering her unsteady gaze. This more than anything draws Simon to her. He quickly detects a slight grin that immediately draws into a tight glance directed at her desktop. He loves his boss' mischievous blue-green eyes. "Why bother with us?" She asks then looks up at him.

"It is possible they have a scientific interest. We would exemplify an interesting tragedy--a semi-intelligent species killing itself off. And we are no threat to them, given the state of our resources and technology." Simon finally notes the blanket on the chair back and figures she spent all night here. By her cross mood, he guesses she is thinking of staying at SETI. He has his answer. "You know they might assist us."

Her eyes flash. She inspects Simon and finds capacity. He nods yes, brown eyes darting about momentarily. Susan's preference for his eyes remains hidden; she has no time for individuals arrested in the tasting stage. Susan dates mature people who know their goals and can deal with her goals. "So I am supposed to march over to Quentin Conworth and declare we have contact, but we do not know why they communicate in this, shall we say odd design."

"Just say we have made contact and they might be trying to help us. No, Quentin would never buy that." He speaks with a puckered smile.

Susan circles the desk and plucks her blanket from the chair folding it neatly again. She does not intend to exhibit her smirk and arranges the blanket on top of her filing cabinet in the corner of the office. Simon waits, watching her replace the small red and gold biking trophy on top of the blanket. "Let's go see our people. I want to confer with them."

She strides down the dingy cinder block hallway weaving her way through the replacement fluorescent light fixtures that lean against the walls. Above, lighting the long hallway, the three incandescent bulbs sway in the aftershock of a quake. "What if they are trying to assist us?"

Simon follows her down the hallway wondering how long she will stay. Knowing her life goal, he speculates Susan has too much curiosity to miss this show. Simon allows himself to speculate on what she might be like during a walk in the jell caves on Mission Street. For Simon sex provides catharsis. Did her intensity level ever decline? He admits to himself he must find this out about her. He wonders if she knows his ardor is more than physical attraction--but only for a moment.

--Of course she knows--

Susan exits the shadows between bulbs, her eyes on the row of file cabinets to her right. They conceal a huge hole in the hallway that leads to an underground bunker. Once a munitions's storage area, it is now the final refuge in a large quake or windstorm. It has not been used in the year Susan has been here. The storms are less intense during the dry cycles. "We really need to install a door here now that the dry cycle is ending. Check on that will you? And see why these cabinets have not been relocated? Do you really think the aliens might help us?"

"I would say helping us or taking the planet from us are about fifty-fifty."

--No money, no resources, problems by the gross, there is no point in continuing here. Simon can handle all this. But what an enterprise, perhaps the last great adventure of humanity. And help, my God--

She leans on a prehistoric metal file cabinet just outside the twin glass doors of SETI communication control; elation courses through her. "A predicament?" Simon prompts, coming along side her.

"The illimitable possibilities." She shakes her head sadly. "Before this I acknowledged the facts. Humana Erratum--we are being expelled from the center line of this planet's gene pool. Now we have Deus Ex Machina. You appreciate; of course, a culture smart enough to contact us has likely untangled the obstacle we face. Otherwise they would not get to the point of technological development to dispatch us a message. This is real hope. I don't know if I want to cry or hasten away."

"Don't run away," Simon says. "Others will follow you."

Statements like those touch Susan. "Do you give that fluff to your patients?" She presses on the glass doors to enter the pitiful communications room.

--Why, yes, I do--

Her team huddles around the central readout system and does not even notice her entrance. Still arguing among themselves about what the printout means, they point at a large symbol and bark at each other.

"Good morning ladies and gentlemen," Susan declares, arms akimbo. The crowd of twelve researchers opens like a flower before her. On a blackboard in front of them dangles a large question mark formed by the characters from the telemetry data. It fills the three pages. This mysterious question mark design is what has prompted her to think it all a joke. Simon stands beside her.

"I will ask you all what I asked Simon--is this real?" She eyes her engineers suspiciously and points to the question mark.

They stare back, insulted that their operations director thinks they are making jokes. A broken dam of words gush forth: "Of course." "Hell yes, Susan." "I checked these Bozos out." "It's the fact, Jack." From their ragged hair, red eyes and disheveled clothes she can see they have been working all night to disprove it. Over the course of the last twelve months Susan has been impressed by their diligence--and their collective sense of honor.

She points to the question mark. "The pattern still iterates?"

"We continue to copying the telemetry, but it is not changing. That makes sixty hours and four thousand sheets of paper. Every fourth page repeats the same sentence over and over. Then there is the three page question mark," says a young woman named Dawn dressed in red jogging pants and a white tee shirt. Her bald head is tinted a light orange.

"And the sentence is?"

"'we are rostackmidarifians looking for this'," Dawn replies stumbling on the name.

"And when you tried to pinpoint the activator, you found you could not?" She pauses and they all nod yes. "The same message and question mark over all our primary channels?"

"With exactly the same sequence and only our primary channels," Dawn replies.

"Why can't you pinpoint the source?" Susan asks tilting her head to listen. Susan has a slight hearing impediment.

"We don't know," Dawn says hanging her head. "But we will."

"Then let me interpret what I think we have here. We are receiving a message. We believe aliens have sent the message. The message prints the design of a question mark and the design fits on three sheets of paper. A fourth page follows which says: 'we are rostackmidarifians looking for this' The message then repeats. And you all think this is a partial message."

Everyone nods. "So where is the rest?"

Susan continues: "This data means not only can they contact us, but they understand our language and they even know when to do a carriage return line feed so their message fits on our paper. How do they comprehend these things?"

"We don't know," Dawn says.

"Do you understand why I might think this is a joke?"

"Yes," Dawn says answering for the group. Too impressed with these peoples' thoroughness to contradict them, Simon, will say nothing about his opinion today. They all watch Susan in frozen anticipation.

"If I find out this is a joke," Susan says looking around the room, "I will have you all transferred to the equator." A ripple of nervous laughter rises from the dozen engineers and scientists. "I am serious." Susan takes a deep breath.

"We know," says Dawn.

"Nobody else knows besides yourselves and the team at CERN?"
They all nod.

"All right--if you get a different message, contact me immediately." She
takes a four-page run from one of the desks. "I will be at Quentin Conworth's
office. Simon, you convinced me to listen, perhaps you can help me convince
Quentin we aren't smoking our shoelaces in here." She looks back at her
team. "I'm proud of you all. This is a wondrous discovery. Or, you're fired."

Simon walks slowly beside her after they exit and continue down
the hallway to the stairs. All the polished metal fire doors glow brighter the
closer they get to the Director's office; she glances at her reflection, checks
her makeup and pats a stray lock of blond hair. Susan then smooths her
cream colored suit, Simon adjusts the collar of his white lab coat. Quentin
Conworth is a stickler about neatness. "Quentin is never going to believe us."
She opens the door to the stairs and pulls a flashlight from the rack on her
right. They scan the dark stairwell for new cracks. There is the latticework
of cracks that spread from the earthquake last week. "Once the rains soak
through, this basement will flood."

"We will have new offices by then," Simon says, scanning the cracks
again as they head up the stairs. "What do you think the question mark
means?"

"I don't know," Susan says. The echoes of their footsteps mingle with
their words. "I think they might want questions in response so they can help
us."

"A hopeful theory--that is good." Simon says.

"More fluff. We should see what my young geniuses come up with and
what Quentin allows. Besides, 'we are looking for this' does seem to be only
part of the message. Quentin may want to wait until we get something more
substantial before we respond. You saw his directive about never responding
to transmissions. I just hope our friends in the Deep Black do not ask any
direct questions. Quentin will never allow us to answer them. He hardly
answers questions from the U.N. Executive Council."

"That's because his dad is on it," Simon quips.

They enter another hallway of cracked cinder block and huge steel
reinforcing beams. This immaculate hallway is well lit but the bunker
mentality rules here. All the exterior windows are either taped or replaced
by a yellowing carbon fiber glaze. The patchwork of mortar on the cracks is
smooth and the walls are empty of pictures. In storms and quakes the cracks
return. Passed offices filled with people, they take the next flight of stairs to
the second floor of the building. She knocks on the nearest door.

"Come."

Susan takes a breath and enters the office with Simon following her. The door opens directly into Quentin's office. A lean man in an expensive dark blue suit sits at a tan metal desk. His broad chest is a bed for perfectly parted straight black hair falling in line to form a long executive ponytail. It hangs over his white shirt and ends in a gold clasp. Rising from his chair, he extends his hand. "Dr. Willoughby, Dr. Weiss, what can I do for you? It has been a while since I have heard anything from you SETI people." The Executive Director for U.N. NorCal motions for them to sit in paired gray chairs. As Susan sits, she glances at an elegant saddle mounted on a wooden stand in the corner of the office. The English saddle has intricate handwork and exquisitely complex stitching. She admires Quentin's handiwork and determination to create so beautiful an object. In stark contrast, above it, the ceiling is water-stained and sagging from yesterday's rain. Simon grins about that and quickly looks out over storm dikes to the salt marshes of San Francisco Bay.

Quentin sits. "So, made contact with any aliens recently?"

Susan narrows her gaze to Quentin's apparently open smile and bright gray eyes. Simon makes a mental note to call his date for tonight and tell her he will be late.

"We have made a contact," Susan says.

His calm eyes widen briefly to show surprise, but neither Simon nor Susan believes the show. Immediately stillness seems to descend over them. "That is wonderful, Susan."

She watches his every movement. He is a man with a course of action and clearly defined goals in life--in many ways the antithesis of Simon Weiss. "You knew," Susan says.

"Of course," Quentin says with a brief knot to his brow. "That is my job."

She breathes in a sigh now certain Quentin has all the offices under his command bugged; she assumes Quentin capable of anything and decides a closer alliance with Simon will be necessary. "It is such a strange communication. We should be cautious." She produces the printout and he examines the question mark on the page.

"This certainly looks like a joke," he says glancing over at Simon. The terse look from Simon has no effect. Quentin perceives Simon is a man capable of anything and Quentin does not like loose cannons. Quentin works to make sure Simon is tightly reined especially now that he might need him. "Is it possible someone is jamming your system with this message?"

"Our conclusion is we are being hailed with a partial message. The repeating pattern is there because they just want to make sure we do not miss it," Susan says.

"I know." Leaning back in his chair, he shakes his head. "Isn't this astonishing? We've been in react mode for so long something like this is likely to cause apoplexy. Imagine, an alien race knowing so much about us. Tomorrow when I tell the rest of the executive committee about this, the gasps will circle the planet in a heartbeat."

"You are planning to tell them about this so soon?" Susan asks utterly astounded. Quentin baffles her; regardless of his lack of scruples. She postulates, then concludes, that things must be very bad.

"I figured I should wait until you two came to me--then I would know it is real." He grins, pleased with himself, and picks up a copy of the printout. Susan and Simon exchange a quick bemused look. "We are looking for this. Well that is odd. What is this, Susan?"

"It could be anything. Perhaps they don't know what they are looking for. That would explain the question mark before the sentence. Or, as I believe, there is more to the message but they are waiting for a reply."

"So they want some kind of response before giving anything else away. That would make sense from a highly intelligent species."

"Or, they are asking us to ask them questions. We don't know," interjects Susan.

"No reason you should at so early a point." Quentin looks at his wristwatch. "I also think there is more to the message but we need to let them know we have received it. Do you think they know our situation?"

Susan answers: "The pages print perfectly. They have the language correct for the most part. I think they appreciate our situation."

"I want an update every day. Your team knows it will be sequestered?"

"They understand."

"Dr. Weiss, I want you to send me reports on my people's condition every four hours. Understand?" Quentin's voice takes on a lighter tone. "All that stress-thought training you had in Berlin will be needed. I am glad you are on the job."

Simon simply nods. He does not like Quentin--for many reasons.

"Seems odd we are contacted now. Why did they wait until humanity was in such trouble?"

"Perhaps it is the format," Simon replies. "A great deal of study has gone into getting this document correct."

"Mostly correct," Quentin says correcting Simon. "We need to understand why they made this mistake with the question mark."

"I do not think it is a mistake. I think it is a key of some sort into their culture."

"So Doctor, your initial analysis of our friends is that they are quite anal and somewhat moronic?" Quentin says.

Simon ignores the joke. "Our friends out there in the Deep Black did not contact us on a whim. I think they want to help us." Simon knows this possibility will seem unlikely to Quentin but he feels a need to keep the possibility as likely as any other possibility.

"Perhaps," Quentin says dismissing the idea. "But we are badly off and there is likely little we could do to stop an aggressor. I must assume they are a potential threat."

"Quentin," says Simon, "a threat to what, or whom? The last hurricane of the season was the size of the east coast. Washington, San Francisco, Denver and New York are the only real cities left in the U. S. The Chaos spreads in Europe and in China it rains twenty to thirty inches in twenty-four hours. Wind gusts typically reach two hundred miles an hour along the plains of Canada. The equatorial countries are uninhabitable. The population has halved in the last fifteen years. All the best estimates say the temperature rise is going to continue. The dry season is over and we are about to enter the 'Screamer' season. The infrastructure everywhere continues to decay--technology has already degraded to nineteenth century levels in some places. In fifty years we will to be little more than tribes--if there are any of us left. Quentin, we have nothing to lose by making contact." Simon catches his breath and looks into Quentin's alpha-dog stare. Simon knows he has gone too far.

Quentin nods shaking his head. "Perhaps, but because we have so few resources let us consider the need to be prudent. I do have a responsibility here." This is no ruse; Quentin Conworth takes his responsibilities quite seriously. He sees himself as a pragmatist with a mission. One way or the other he plans to keep order and reinvigorate humanity's climb to the top or make an elegant exit into extinction. "Let us assume they want questions from us as a way of saying we received their message. It would be the intelligent assumption since no one is going to broadcast anything significant to an unknown race."

"Just television," Simon mumbles.

"The question mark precedes their communication and it may be an insight into who they are...as Dr. Weiss was saying. The Spanish and Italians used to place upside down question marks before questions, I believe, so there may be something there. Have your team draw up sets of questions. I'll review them with you. If they're good, perhaps we can send a few out in the next week or so."

"Quentin, we are going to respond?" Susan says, shocked that Quentin has already gotten permission to reply; Quentin Conworth does nothing on a whim. "I thought I saw a memo from you that said standard operating procedure was to wait at least six months before responding?"

"We live in interesting times--humanity is on the Put side of life. Normally I would recommend a five-year wait before responding--but given humanity's current dilemma, I think we can send out a measured response. Besides, with some safe communication maybe we can get a little more funding so we can get you all out of the basement. Great work, both of you. When they placed SETI under me a few years ago, I thought it was a waste of energy and money. I was wrong. Good job." Quentin stands and makes a point of shaking both of their hands. Then he waits for them to leave; the meeting is over.

Susan walks out the door shocked that U.N. is allowing for outbound communication. She realizes the rumor about the failing infrastructure--the Chaos in Europe spreading to all continents--death, destruction, economic meltdown are riding headlong at humanity. The end of civilization; her surmise is the essence of a top-secret report to the U.N. Executive committee two months prior. All fifty copies have already been burned. Susan speaks in whispers. "Come on Simon; walk me across 101. I will buy you some tea."

"At that ugly place that looks like a nineteen-fifties A-bomb shelter?"

"Simon, every place looks like an A-bomb shelter now." She points around them. "Or looks like it has been hit by an A-bomb."

"Pretty loud music at Saint James Infirmary." They descend the stairs. "I did not know you frequented such places."

She looks around the staircase for bugs. "I know Quentin does not. But I will bet the next time we go there it will not be secure. How about we start an exercise routine of running? Say along the bay or up in the hills? We can vary it and I can use the extra workout."

"Sure." Simon understands and they walk out the door into the dry morning heat. He leans close. "But I doubt it will make any difference," he says with a note of humor in his voice. "Quentin will just bug all the trees or turn a satellite on us."

"If he has not done that already."

It is a beautiful spring evening with a light breeze; the dust devils are gone and temperatures in the mid seventies. Birds sing. In the bay, egrets and ducks thrash about in the mud flats. Horses graze in the corral by the parked bikes. In the sky there is only blue. Except for the snapped trees and scores of empty buildings around them, it could be paradise. Crossing the old parking lot filled with low drifts of dust and debris, they scan the ground for dustbowls; large pot holes formed from small mud-ponds in the rainy years that can be two or three feet deep. In dry years they form dust craters. Falling into one can easily break a leg. Mostly dying plants stick up from the craters.

Approaching the old overpass that runs over 101, the once concrete freeway below them looks like an impassable ice field; sheets of concrete thrust up every which way from the quakes. Even the repetitive roadways are not maintained anymore. Only a couple of North-South routes on the San Francisco Peninsula are open: Freeway 280 and the El Camino Real, but nothing else. Simon sees a family of three huddled under a concrete road looking up at him. They are dirt poor. They have no horses or sheep. "When my mom and I trekked out of the Chaos we came across many poor and hungry people. They would wander about looking for food and water, shelter and safety. Every time they built a small settlement and began to lay in provisions to make some kind of home, a warrior band would sweep in on their horses and take everything. Susan I will do anything to keep that from happening here." He looks at her. "Don't leave SETI. We need you to balance Quentin's paranoia."

"You have to give him credit though. He is a thorough man."

Simon shakes his head no. "I have known many individuals like him. He is a whore for power who sells himself for the illusion of control." Quentin Conworth reminds Simon of the warlords of Southern France.

They continue walking along the overpass in silence until they pass the stumps of old eucalyptus trees. Simon fears he has spoken out of turn until Susan speaks. "In the beginning there is the illusion of power for people like that. In time, and with good fortune, like... our... alien... contact," she says these words slowly so Simon will note them. "A person like Quentin can, in fact, acquire real power." Susan knows that if there is anyway to get something out of this contact Quentin can do it. "He is the person for the job because of his Machiavellian ways. Resources are worse than scarce and the battle for energy--especially for a monumental project like this one--will be fierce." Glancing about the torn buildings and shattered power lines of a former military housing development she speaks: "You don't like Quentin, but he can get us resources. Can you deal with that reality?"

"There is no problem here. The good of the many supersedes the needs of the few."

"I never should have brought in that poster of Spock," says Susan. "Come on, let's get some tea and plan our strategy for dealing with our boss' predilection for information gathering. Also I think we should work under the assumption the aliens will help us. That means we need to be as open as Quentin will allow."

--Hope. I did not know I believed in it--

Chapter Seven

Susan eyes four piles of papers that mark the bounds of her new office. The eight hundred and fifty questions sent out by the researchers over the past year meticulously fill the corners like medieval lookouts. Reaching almost to the top of the seven-foot ceiling, magnetic disks crown the knights. Between the pair of towers guarding the front door, Simon enters carrying changes to the budget. Mumbling to himself, leaning forward on the ox-leather couch in front of her, he appears bored in his budget numbers.

She glances away from him at the mica-veneer cabinet. Sitting under the wire reinforced window to the left of Simon, it holds her silver medal from the Athens Olympics. The fiasco and brutality of the last Olympics of modern times haunt her. The award's empty meaning, an anchor to her folly; the years wasted, a testament to her blindness. Susan displays the medal for all to see, and tells anyone who asks exactly what it was like in Athens: That twenty countries were represented at the Olympics, and in none of the twelve events had more than ten competitors woken up from the wild parties the night before. The long distance biking event had six riders--and fifteen armored personnel carriers. Two riders were wounded on the route, and had the rider from Norway not been hit by a stone--she would have gotten a bronze metal.

She would speak of the black uniformed soldiers and the high steel and barbed wire fence that had surrounded the venue. Carerra marble halls and the best food money could buy--while every night, over the parties' roar--the surrounding hillsides screamed in pain, often when lit by red tracer bullets. "They called like voices across the Styx." The curses of scared young men or the articulations of mothers testifying to their suffering children, came from makeshift loudspeaker: The hungry begged the Olympians for help. Those grainy utterances of the early morning with their calculations on the Olympics' waste of energy or the dusk of humanity--soliloquies by young girls weeping for their families still speak to Susan. One morning she had sat by a high window and watched those outside the gates. Dirty miserable humans wandered back and forth, the stench almost unbearable. Throughout that day and evening she had perched--until the "Dirties" as the Olympians called them--began broadcasting that day's dead over the loudspeakers. Then she found a partner in the lounge and made love all night in the deepest bowels of the stadium

"I don't understand budgets," Simon laments to break her funk. She continues to stare at the medal. He glances over to it. "Last night's news showed the opening ceremonies."

"A pre-staged vision of the Olympics--all scenes shot before the Olympians arrived. I saw it."

There were children playing on sunny fields or sitting in classrooms. The exterior shots showed fields under plow and a rudimentary transportation system. Cheering crowds and continued messages about how "Europe was Coming Back!!!"

She shakes her head. "My army friends called last night--the pavilion we turned over to the residents after the Olympics is now used by one of the local warlords as his palace. What good does a lie bring?"

Susan looks from her medal to Quentin's hand-written note on the front of the SETI yearly report. She reads the precise cursive letters Quentin used to assault the cover of her report: "They are laughing at us." Her eyes, wandering out the window to the huge sinkhole running down the center of the old NASA-Ames parking lot, watch mud on a smoldering wagon from last night's riot drip into the sinkhole. Above it, the curl of black smoke disappearing into the gusts, the vegetable wagon had been pushed over in the sink hole and burned; all because a U.N. NorCal executive ran over a boy in his car. Susan returns to work. She cannot think of anything else to do.

Simon, who has been watching her, speaks again: "The U.N. science directorate tells Quentin they think this signal we're receiving isn't really an attempt at communication--but instead some kind of jamming technique.

They want to cut funding to cryptography by sixty per cent. I hate budgeting."

Susan takes a small yellow pill and places it under her tongue. Simon worries more about Susan; her descriptions of the Olympics were horrific.

Susan looks up--blue eyes weary. "We haven't come up with a thing, Simon. Resources are getting scarce. They need to parcel out power carefully." Susan leans back on her desk and takes a deep breath. Unsure how Simon will take her latest input from Quentin, she decides the "Lesser of Two Evils" approach works best with him. "We need to give a little or they will eliminate all SETI funding."

The slight fraying of the material behind the heel of his pants catches Simon's eye for a moment. He unfolds one long leg and brushes lint off his blue linen pants. New wool pants are difficult to find--especially when project results are lacking. "If they are simply isolating us from the galactic output of EMR, why go to the bother of learning our language and formatting it? How many times do we have to go over this issue? It is just lies." Simon looks down at the paperwork trying to figure what to do next. It took him little time to realize Susan feels she has propagated a lie by her participation in the Olympics. Simon leans back frustrated with the madness of power and the need to put on a good show for the dying masses--instead of helping them. "We're in need of another jog."

For Susan, one of the bright spots of the past year has been working with Simon Weiss despite his occasional piques of frustration. Their runs out on the dikes of the bay every other day has done more than give them a secure place to talk. It has built a friendship. She occasionally finds concern in his not-to-well-hidden ardor but since he has never mentioned it, she has resolved to let it pass without comment. Susan, for all her intelligence, has no idea some ardor never quells but only simmers. "Quentin is under severe pressures. He has to agree they have effectively jammed our systems for locating them, Simon, and if they can understand our tongue and we cannot understand them, they are way ahead of us. Space command considers it all tactics." Susan rolls an empty pen under her fingertips. Ink should be arriving in a few days.

Simon watches her mouth noting she still wears the same sadness as when she returned from Athens. "On the other hand you could also say since they came to us they need something from us."

"All the more reason why the fear-mongers are getting a hearing."

He nods wondering how long it will take for her to bottom-out. "So what is next?"

"Simon, I think we are off-base on the messages we send." Susan sees something that tells her he is ready to hear what she has to say.

Sub textual cross talk is typical of their time. There is so much to deal with for this generation. She raises a finger off her dry pen figuring now is as good a time as any to give him the bad news: "We have struck a deal with the bean-counters. They will let us be in return for a watchdog. The new position is called Political Communications Consultant."

Simon shakes his head understanding the ramification immediately; he is no longer the number-two person on the team. "What is a Political Communications Consultant?"

"A commissar," Susan says after seeing the brief flash of anger in the form of his knitted brow.

"A jerk." Simon sighs. "I should have expected this from Quentin. So I'm being sacrificed because we are getting no response. We humans are amazing. Even with everything falling apart we still have time for petty politics."

Too many times Susan had told Simon to give Quentin the lip service he demands to repeat it as the real cause of what has happened. "Your duties will not change. And I know you don't like interference. But we are stuck with this decision."

Simon, seeing her rise from her funk, says: "Why are we getting a commissar?"

"Space Defense is concerned we might tell the aliens too much about our technology," Susan wears with a sarcastic smile.

Simon attributes Susan's cold grin to the time she spends with Quentin. The hair on the back of his neck stands. "Space Defense--three ICBMs modified to attack slow space vehicles. I could laugh if it all weren't so sad. Why would aliens want to contact us? We are just a group of morons who generate stupidity..." Simon lets the rest of the sentence drift away. He guesses correctly the choice for commissar has already been made and so he thinks he understands the return of her sullen mood. "I'm glad you are not happy with them putting someone in to replace me."

Susan passes on the attempted bridge because she feels duplicitous; Susan has held something back: Quentin is pushing for Simon's release. She needs to know he will stay even with that news. "So will you stay?"

"I never quit."

She looks out her window to the Santa Cruz Mountains for signs of the next storm. Susan wants to go riding this afternoon to clear her head and plan her strategy for keeping Simon around. The clouds are stacking and white capped mist streams between the peaks. So far it looks as if it could go either way: a big storm or a terrible one.

"Perhaps we can say the aliens worry that we will embarrass them at our first galactic dinner party and that's why they are being cautious in dealing with us. The powers that be would understand that," Simon says trying to lighten the mood in the room.

"More likely the aliens are concerned we will bring down the galactic property values as we continue to destroy our planet." Her smile is courtesy. Seeing light blue sky appear she immediately stands. Experience has taught her to take advantage of the calm whenever possible. She marches around her desk grabbing her gym bag and hoisting her training bicycle from behind the file cabinet. "I am going riding before the storm hits. My beeper will be on my personal code."

Simon follows her as she pushes her bicycle into the hallway. He has no idea she is calculating how best to bend he and Quentin to her will. When she stops at the door of the women's lockers, Simon speaks: "Susan, I have a theory on the signal. Can we talk?" His eyes dart around as he speaks. "Outside?"

They walk toward the dikes, the winds flapping their clothes. Passing the sinkhole with the smoldering wagon, she stops still holding her blue jogging clothes in her arm. "I am listening."

"I have been thinking about something and I just wanted your thoughts. And with this commissar arriving any day I felt I would do better to speak now."

She waits watching him fidget like a person about to propose marriage. "No fluff, please."

"Maybe they are looking for a question mark." He says the words quickly, then tilts his head with an embarrassed smile. A small earth tremor rolls through the ground in long shallow waves. "But then again, why would anyone be looking for a question mark?" He steps back from her.

"Looking for a question mark--and I thought I needed a rest. Go home Simon..." Then, only the wind speaks. She stands perfectly still for a moment, the wind fanning her golden hair. Staring into the dark muddy crevice, her head begins nodding over and over. Susan takes off her riding gloves. "They are alien, Simon--that's why they are looking for a question mark. Simon, would you take my stuff back? I am going down to the lab." She pushes the bike at him and drops her gym bag. She takes off in a run, her yellow dress flapping in the wind, hair flying like a comet's tail. She stops. "Leave the bicycle in my office. Then get down to the telecom lab."

Question marks cover the walls of the lab. Some of question marks are cut out from the computer paper, while other question marks are backgrounded in garish hues or paisley patterns. A question mark mobile spins in the center of the room and a basket of woven question marks holds plastic fruit. Simon particularly appreciates the two question marks intertwined over the main communications console with little hearts drawn around them.

The gaggle of researchers is draped over seats or sitting on the floor. A few sit on desks; one stands on his head. All look at Susan as she speaks to them in hushed tones. Seeing Simon enter she stops. "Good, let's let Dr. Weiss tell you his thoughts--Doctor?" He enters the center of the room brushing passed the mobile. Susan's bright cheer is sunlight. Clearing his throat: "Their message says 'we are looking for this'. There is no punctuation. However, there is the large question mark. The framework seems to indicate they are looking for questions. Or, it could be the point. Perhaps our friends out there are looking for a question mark."

Silence.

The eyes of the researchers dart like hummingbirds from question mark to question mark. "We are looking for this, meaning they are seeking a question mark," Dawn, a dark-eyed researcher, says. "That's bizarre."

"That's the definition of alien."

"A question mark. Why would anyone be looking for a question mark?"

Someone else laughs. "I like it. We can go into the question mark business. Earth, your source for question marks. After a few years we claim a shortage of question marks and become rich."

A researcher begins to applaud; the applause spreads. Embarrassed, Simon looks about the room. Susan puts her hands out to quiet them: "Dr. Weiss, your hypothesis may be incorrect. On the other hand, it may be accurate. In any case, we are applauding elegance."

"Your theory has resonance to it," Dawn says. Her skull has been painted dark gray for months.

Simon smiles, nodding his head. "I see."

"The question facing us--no pun intended--is how might we respond? Does anyone know how the question mark came into being?" Dawn asks.

"Funny you should ask," Simon says with a grin.

"Dr. Weiss, please, go ahead," Susan says.

"The Latin scholars used the word *questio* at the end of a sentence to indicate an interrogative. Questio was abbreviated to q. o.. Then people became confused that the two letters were part of the previous word. So, they put the q over the o. Over time, the o contracted to a dot and the loop in the q became open and the line lengthened. *Voi-la* one question mark."

"Thank you, Doctor Weiss. I had no idea you were a linguist," Susan says.

"Awe' give 'em a kiss," says a round fleshy boy with blond hair and a fez named Tommy; he winks at Simon. Tommy is brilliant at jury-rigging equipment, but he is only sixteen and he has no idea why Simon and Susan are both looking away from him.

Susan's embarrassed laugh is heard by all. "Okay, we send that data back to them. But I need to talk to Quentin before anything goes out." She glances at Tommy briefly. "Ladies and gentleman, tonight will be a busy one. I will see you all in a few hours, say for espresso around eleven? Simon, you'll stay as long as necessary."

"Of course. I'll need to call my neighbor. There's a storm coming in though I don't think it will be a problem until tomorrow--still I need her to close my windows."

Susan's eyebrows draw together briefly. Simon is notorious for underestimating the weather. "Just in case, have her close your storm shutters as well."

"She does not have net privileges and we have this system worked out on the phone..."

"I will authorize the wattage for a message out. Have someone at Datacom handle it for you and get back here. Simon, you are a hero." Susan hurries out the doors and down the hallway. Feeling dazed, Simon takes a deep breath and heads over to the data communications bunker to send his message. The researchers break up into small groups.

At eleven o'clock that night, everyone huddles around Susan. "I have gotten an okay to go forward with the description of the question mark. Also Quentin wants a question that will say: 'please ask us another question'. Quentin wants it all placed in a circle, and he wants us to leave out all punctuation."

"Why a circle?" Tommy

"Security," Susan says looking at Simon knowing he will guess the Political Communications Consultant is already making decisions that should have involved Simon.

He nods.

"I thought we agreed we could send them a few question marks," the same boy says.

"It's something they are interested in, so it's something we use cautiously. A question mark may be as valuable as a watt to these aliens. We need any currency we can get with our friends out in the Deep Black. Tommy, have you gotten everything set up for a response?" Susan worries about this boy, he seems unstable recently. Her gaze stops at Simon Weiss. Simon nods to let her know he is still working with Tommy.

Tommy speaks: "We are set. I can send within minutes, Susan."

"Send it." Susan tips her teacup.

Simon places his hand on the boy's shoulder. Tommy begins to tap out the message. Simon speaks to Susan in hushed tones: "Susan, we need to talk to Quentin regarding this erratic attitude about contact."

"Simon, consensus at U.N. NorCal is you're absolutely correct about the question mark. Save your chits and let this be." Susan knows that if this works Simon's job is secure--for a while. "For now, take your seat and watch other brilliant minds reach out with a billion dollars in technology."

"Surely it will take time for the signal to reach them," Simon says, deciding to let it go.

"Perhaps," Susan responds.

"We are ready," Tommy says.

"Go," Susan says quietly.

It takes only a few seconds to tap out Simon's message. Moments later there are just the sounds of the ink jet printer and the cooling fans. Simon watches everyone staring at the twin computer printers set up in the front of the room. At least one of them has been on, recording the same repeating message, for three-hundred, sixty days. The printer continues spraying letters on the paper with the same rhythm. No one speaks for ten minutes.

The printer's beat stops.

"Yeah, Baby--here we go," says Tommy. "Way to go, Doc."

"So much for the speed of light limiting communication," Dawn says. "I told you so."

"Quiet," Susan says.

Everyone stands quite still. Four pages prints and the printer quiets. "Damn," Simon says.

"No, the rhythm was different." A rush of feet moves toward the printer. Pushing passed the huddle of others, Dawn takes the pages and looks at them. After quickly reading, she takes a deep breath and closes her eyes to speak: "'you are a dying species send more about this'. The question mark repeats itself." Her eyes open with tears dropping down her cheeks.

The printer begins again. The same new message repeats.

Susan speaks. "All right. Let's get a response together to this little ditty. I want it in twenty-four hours."

"Susan," says Tommy, "we have something interesting here."

The crowd moves toward Tommy. He points to a screen that tracks the bands used by the aliens. As they watch, band after band ceases carrying the message. Within half a minute the number of bands carrying the message halves. The number continues halving every half-minute until it becomes a single tight band of data. Within five minutes of the second message, the location and distance of the source is verified. The source appears to be exactly sixty-five light-years away in the direction of Wolf 359. "I told you they want to help us," Tommy says, in apparent disregard for the message. Simon sighs quietly. The strain on Tommy grows with each day. He has seen too much death.

"Well team, they have decided to show us where they are and how far away they are. It is now up to us to bridge a measly sixty-five light years."

"Exactly sixty-five light years," says Dawn. "Yet it took ten minutes for the signal to get there and back. There must be a repeater within five light minutes. We will see if we can find it."

Susan nods. "Come on, Simon." Susan and Simon leave the communications room together. "So now the aliens have stopped jamming our detection systems and have shown us where they are," Susan says. "A good days work."

The doors behind them burst open. Dawn rushes down hallway. "Susan we have a problem. Tommy has sent a reply." She hands Susan a sheet of paper looking at Simon and trying to be calm. Susan reads it. She hands the paper to Simon. He reads it not really surprised that Tommy has done this but his gaze freezes at the words on the paper.

"Shabby management." Susan says loudly, "Get him away from the consoles. No more unauthorized outbound messages."

After seeing the message, Simon believes he understands her desire to tell Quentin via bug, rather than in person, what has happened. "Tell Tommy I want to see him when I get back," Simon says.

"Let me know when there is a response. We will be in Quentin Conworth's office." Susan and Simon leave the building. They walk out into a blustery night. The clouds obscure the moon but the storm promised since this afternoon has not yet arrived. They pick their way carefully around the mud bowls and the sinkhole. The wagons' ashes have blown away.

"Tommy will need more sessions with you," Susan says staring out over the tops of the swaying trees. "If Quentin does not have him hanged for planetary treason."

"Susan, I am glad Tommy sent a reply. His brother died in a twister and he needed to do something."

"Quentin will have a convulsion if he hears you say that, so don't mention it, okay?" She moves along clutching her cotton dress to her body for warmth. "You don't seem fazed by any of this."

Simon takes a breath, holds it, and then speaks. "We already knew we are a dying race. The fact that our friends in space know it may make our job easier. Tommy's response puts it all on the table. I think we have made some progress."

She lifts one perfectly sculpted blond eyebrow. He feels a distance between them, but has no idea it is her way of dealing with the notion he does not understand the dynamics around him and needs to be protected. Susan knows Quentin will blame Tommy's misstep on Simon. She steps up onto a new grass lawn to enter the just completed NorCal administrative building. After nodding to the guard on duty, they walk quickly upstairs and knock on Quentin's door.

"Come."

The door to his new office feels like the door on a vault. The inside is plush with a deep brown carpet and light wooden walls. Two couches of calf leather face each other and behind them sit his desk. The ceiling is steel. The saddle rests on a mahogany stand in the corner under the windows. Quentin stands off to the side, polishing his horn rimmed reading glasses. Susan has seen this look of gloss veneer before. She is certain Quentin has heard what she said in the hallway of the other building and he is trying to control his temper. "We have a response?"

Susan places the paper on Quentin's desk. "It is not pretty." She prepares herself.

Quentin looks at words. He looks up with a blank expression. "Why bother telling us this?"

"As in we already know?" Susan says quickly. Quentin nods.

Simon notes something passing between them that looks like intimacy. His gorge rises and he tells himself it cannot possibly be so.

Quentin speaks: "This is good. They still want something."

"That appears to be correct," replies Susan, quite sure Quentin knows exactly what she will say. She notes he appears in control of the situation. A brief glow from her eyes crosses the room toward Quentin Conworth. It is the first time Quentin has seen this type of warmth from Susan. He is drawn to it--just as she expected. "There is more."

Quentin circles his desk. He wears his white shirt open at the neck. His shoes are a deep blue, almost black. "Let's sit." After they all light on the remarkably comfortable couches, Quentin looks at Susan--his head slightly tilted to the left. "Yes?" Quentin tells himself he is immune to her beauty. He is, but he is not immune to her warmth.

"Against my orders, an immediate response was generated by one of my people." She watches Quentin hang his head then rub his graying eyebrows slowly. Simon wants to applaud the performance.

"What did it say?"

"please help us"

He sighs. "Did he use punctuation?"

"No," Susan pauses, "and there were no capital letters either."

"I suppose it could have been worse. Any response?"

"Nothing yet," says Simon.

"We are panicking." A knock on the door. "Come."

Dawn stands red-faced and out of breath. She walks over to Susan and hands her four pieces of paper as she looks around at the opulent office.

Susan nods. "How long did the response take?"

"Same--ten minutes--I'll let you know if there is anymore." Dawn leaves the office, but not before feeling the wood-grain of the walls. "Nice, very nice." The door closes.

Susan reads the message out loud:

"'because of your impending demise we will not help you ruin the ecology of other planets we still seek this'. There is the question mark covering the previous three pages, but this time the question mark is made of smaller question marks." She hands Quentin the papers. He examines them in silent anger; there appears to be no currency in the symbol. His dark eyes dart back and forth from Susan to Simon.

"So they do not really need question marks from us. What the heck is this all about?"

"It's a shame we cannot bug the offices of the aliens to find out what they are thinking," Simon says sharply. He tells himself he needs to get some sleep tonight. Susan would like to strangle him at that moment.

Quentin smiles. "Still they are not getting better at punctuation except for the question mark." Quentin says staring at the question mark design then spends a long moment looking into Susan's eyes. Quentin wants Simon to see Quentin can have her.

Simon instead sees nothing that looks like ardor in her eyes and finds himself dumbfounded at Susan's warm gaze. Simon has no idea this is all part of her strategy to keep him out of the shredder.

"Any profiles on our alien friends yet, Dr. Weiss?" Quentin says still caught up in Susan's warmth.

"Like what?"

"Are they coming for a visit?" Quentin asks, glancing at Simon for just a moment.

"Since they know so much about us, they are quite aware of our predilection for violence. Therefore, if they were coming for a visit they wouldn't announce themselves before hand."

"Why not?"

They would not want us to have time to prepare." Simon finds his palms sweaty. "Regarding the breach of security on Tommy's part, Quentin," he pauses to make sure Quentin is with him. "I think we need to take into account the issue of hope. As near as I can tell everyone involved in this project sees these communications as our only hope. These researchers are not your huddled masses. They know what the weather patterns mean and what the future looks like. I have even heard discussions of the message coming from God's angels. This second message that we are a dying species is quite painful. This third one, the response to Tommy's cry for help will be devastating."

"I am sure you are right," Quentin says looking back at Susan. Though he will not admit it to himself, Quentin seeks respite from the horrors just like everyone else. "How literal do you think we should take the message that we are a dying race, Susan?"

She shakes her head from side to side. "Hard to say, but I imagine fairly literally."

"Doctor Weiss?"

"Pretty damn literal--especially since it is a fact."

Quentin wears a poker face. He believes the demise of the species should be a burden drawn only by the leaders of the society. "Do you think everyone in your group has seen this message?"

"Of course. You know I couldn't hide anything like this from them. They're as close as family in there."

"Would they believe it?"

She shakes her head affirmatively. "I am sure."

Quentin writes a note. "How long did it take to get a response on the messages?"

"Ten minutes."

"So we have sphere of three-hundred seconds times the speed of light. Too large a space to search for their vehicle--but I want that search initiated anyway. Lets assume they took some time to come up with a reply. Search two-hundred seconds distant," Quentin says, a note of frustration in his voice. To Quentin's credit he usually carries knowledge about the future with little exterior hints. But it is not so easy a task tonight. His father has just told him all their wealth is useless. It is an unexpected horror this generation's ruling class must now face. Energy has become far more valuable than money and there is no recourse. "What do they want?" Chaos is inevitable.

"That is the question, is it not?" Simon says quickly. "Do you want me to try to get clarification from them?"

"No more messages." Quentin steeples his hands. "This new communication, while a problem because of a lack of discipline, nonetheless further demonstrates the need to get more information on these aliens in an appropriate fashion. Do they have faster than light travel?"

Simon glances at Susan. "We have pinpointed the source to be sixty-five light years away. It has also been speculated by Tommy, by the way, that they knew enough about us to know we do not have faster than light communication. Therefore any message that we respond to should take at least sixty-five years to get to them and sixty-five years to get back. That did not happen. Tommy speculated the only way to overcome our technological shortcoming for communication is park something nearby to propagate our message. As tonight proves, they have done this and so they therefore have faster than light travel. What is more important, they can transport mass across the light barrier."

"I see. So it is reasonable to assume they could transport human bodies?"

Quentin's words shatter Susan's calm. "Perhaps," Susan says. "But not many, I would think." She has heard mutterings of an escape into low Earth orbit for a privileged few. Now, escape or imprisonment on another planet is perhaps possible as well.

"I am taking my plane east. No more messages to anyone. Contact me immediately if there is more. Zurich is not going to like it that an unauthorized message went out tonight. Terminate the perpetrator by sending him to the Galapagos station.

"This boy Tommy keeps our systems up. He is brilliant," Simon says.

"That is why we are making him incommunicado immediately."

"I will handle it," Susan says hanging her head. "You can have my resignation also, if you like."

"None of that kind of talk. I need you." He looks into her eyes--and in response for a measured moment--Susan's eyes sparkle. Quentin looks away. Susan cannot believe the warmth has rattled Quentin. She will find out later today all her family's wealth has become useless and surmises Quentin's response to the stripping of wealth is her solice.

Simon asks himself if these two have something going on between them that he has missed. Susan tells herself she has made the first important step to keeping Simon around. Quentin tells himself there may be some refuge in this cold ugly world and grins at Simon thinking what splendid entertainment Doctor Weiss' ardor for Susan will provide to him. "Dr. Willoughby, join me for lunch after I get back from my meetings? I want to keep close...to what's going on." With an alpha-dog leer he turns to Simon. "We will note your attendance."

"I'll keep you informed," Susan replies. For now she has every confidence she will be able to keep things under control with Quentin. She does not recognize his cat-and-mouse grin. In a few months she will.

Simon stands, his hands behind his back--fists clenched--as if he were shackled. He and Susan leave the office and shuffle downstairs. They cross the empty parking lot in silence leaning into the lively winds. Susan speaks: "I'll take care of the mess. Go home, Simon. You earned your paycheck today. Did you get that message off to your neighbor?"

"No. She was not in and she does not have the energy allowance to keep a recording machine going. It will be all right. This does not look like a bad storm."

Susan cannot see the clouds but to her it feels like the storm may be a killer. They enter the building and Susan heads downstairs to talk to Dawn. "Be careful, Simon."

Simon gets his briefcase, then walks out to the empty parking lot just as a blue and green shuttle bus rolls to a stop. "A little messy tonight, Doc, but I think we can get you home in spite of the storm."

Simon steps in the small bus. "Forget home, Murphy. I'm going to the hottest, nastiest club in San Francisco. I'm going to drink until I can't stand then I'm going to drink more."

"You? You are getting drunk? What happened, Doc?" Replies the driver as he closes the door.

"Just a bad dance day, Murphy. I'm fine, thanks." Simon nods hello to the two individuals sitting behind the driver. From their green coveralls Simon guesses they are maintenance workers. He is correct. They plan to work all night on broken telecommunications links in one of the old BART tunnels under the bay. A third man sits behind them. The exhaustion in the man's face disappears the instant as he looks into Simon's eyes. A nod hello is followed by a piercing gaze. The gaunt face and cap of thick white hair parted in the middle allude to an easy grace. Simon does not believe the easy grace for a moment. He believes this person to be a soldier since he wears the lassitude of a soldier after battle. He does not know this individual dons his mask often now to confuse opponents and deflect interest.

"Hi," Simon says. The man turns toward the darkness. Simon takes the seat across the aisle from him. The bus rolls forward.

"Next stop, San Francisco, then the Half Moon Bay Terminus."

From experience Simon knows the trip north will take about fifty minutes; he settles back for a brief nap but his mind churns.

--A dying species, Quentin and Susan, it is all just going to crumble away--

At times like this, the past invades Simon's present. Memories of life's horrors steam into his brain like exhaust from an out of control engine. Anger rises. In his mind he sees his mother on the road selling herself for food. Blurred pain of grunts then a crisp memory follows; it is green eyes, a soldier's eyes. Simon sees himself as a child wondering if tired eyes will take his life. Simon glances at the man beside him and sees his memory like text over-striking itself. His thoughts retreat to nighttime fires and shadowy figures dancing like crazed druids. One bearded mountain of a man drinks blood-colored wine and boasts of killing more than any other warrior. A lullaby is overshadowed by the howl of someone in pain. He smells cooking flesh and hears his mother's death cough as they hide in a shattered gas station filled with drying human skins--and the soldier covered with blood.

As a younger man Simon had hoped learning psychiatry would quell the pain. It has helped but not eliminated it. A flash of lightning is the muzzle of a gun. The rumble of thunder is the hooves of horses; the man beside him is every soldier with a pistol. Simon knows the memories will never vanish but he remains stunned by their rapid slashes, like those of a sword, still cutting just as deep as they did years ago. For these, and other reasons, he is thankful that he can wend his way to San Francisco tonight. He knows otherwise he will lie awake in his bed, memories mixing with malevolent winds throwing up wintry images and repulsive sounds. Simon tries to forgive the stranger across the van for a crime he knows nothing of.

A blast of wind rocks the van. "Buckle up, all. I think we have a Screamer forming. All aboard for an E-ticket ride." Simon gawks out the window and notices the driver has turned on the flashing red beacon atop the van roof. The light is just in case they are swept off the road. Another light on the bottom of the van will activate if they overturn. The rooftop glow mingles with mangled deserted buildings snapped trees and ghosts of his past.

Darts of rain splatter on the windshield. Simon gets up and walks down the short aisle to the driver. "Hey, Murphy, can I use the phone? I forgot to close the storm blinds at my place."

"Sorry, Doc," says the driver. "Phones on the fritz and the radio is useless during a storm."

Simon watches the shadowy trees as they begin to rock back and forth. "Thanks anyway." He walks back to his seat.

"You can use my phone," says the man across from him. The man looks about Simon's age. His eyes are much older. The gaunt stranger beside him hands Simon a cell phone. Still thinking this individual is a soldier, Simon checks the mans wrist for cut marks. Many of the U.N. soldiers hate their jobs and scar themselves regularly. There are no scars on this man's skin. Simon takes the phone nodding his thanks. The phone looks new--unusual for a soldier. Simon watches him looking out the window giving Simon some privacy. Simon concludes he is wrong about this person being a soldier. Most of the soldiers he has known are cautious to the point of paranoia when they lend anyone anything. This man could not care less about the phone. Simon places the call. It rings once and a very loud matronly sounding female voice answers: "I know this is you, Simon. I already closed your blinds and storm shutters. I want you to know I am going to get an unlisted number. Is there anything else?"

"Thanks, Nancy," Simon says.

"Don't worry. Good night, Doc." The line goes quiet and Simon closes the phone. He hands it to the stranger.

"Feisty isn't she?" The stranger says, making light conversation to calm himself. He has had a fear of storms since he was a child. "I am sorry. I could not help hearing her."

"She is my cousin but she is a pistol. I'm Simon Weiss." He extends his hand.

The stranger extends his hand. "Carlos Jordan."

Chapter Eight

The gaunt face and deep-set eyes across the bus show no fear--and tickle a memory--the name Carlos Jordan is familiar to Simon Weiss but he cannot place the context. Ironically, Simon's training tells him this man Jordan is ice. "I don't think this storm will be too bad. Besides, Murphy is a good driver. He'll pull into a shelter long before we get into trouble." A gust rocks the vehicle and shots of rain strike the glass.

"I must say being snared in a Pacific Screamer is not my idea of amusement," Carlos says.

"This is a bit of a surprise, but we will be fine." Simon examines the man's face again. Other than the macho display, Jordan seems an honest sort but his obvious privileges make Simon careful of his assumptions. He remembers his first meeting with Quentin Conworth and how he was completely wrong about him. Simon scans his memory trying to remember where he has seen this face. "Will this be your first visit to San Francisco then?" Simon asks cordially.

"No." End of conversation.

--This guy Jordan is used to getting his way--

Simon notes openness is not one of this individual's attributes. For

Simon that confirms Carlos Jordan has full privileges. The bus swerves left then skids to a stop. The driver backs up, and then turns hard to the right rolling over the smaller limbs of trees blocking the roadway. After bouncing over the limbs, the bus takes off like a scared rabbit down the roadway. A rumble of thunder chases them.

Carlos watches the horizontal rain for a few minutes. Ever since his youth he has been afraid of storms that take their time appearing--like this one. He knew this storm was coming and chose the NorCal shuttle van because he did not want to be alone in his car during the storm. At thirty-three Carlos Jordan finally feels he has spent too many storms alone. When he told Roxanne this the other night she had whistled and cheered. It had been the first meeting between the two old friends in years. The last time had been in Hawaii when Roxanne ran into Carlos at the closing of Kauai. They spent the night together snuggled on a couch in the main lobby of an old hotel watching a fireplace. He had wanted more; Roxanne would have no part of it. Even so, their long friendship has, in many ways, sustained Carlos. He thinks about her comment from this afternoon regarding his now constant stone-like exterior. Carlos pushes his straight white hair back--and her from his mind--again.

The rapid blasts of lightening and the ever-increasing fusillade of thunder begins in earnest. Any moment the howling that characterizes the Pacific Screamers will begin. Only Simon will search the faces of the others for reaction. It is partly his profession and experience. Simon knows how important reliable comrades are in this situation. His gaze drifts over the two men in the back, they are chattering like chipmunks. He knows they are in trouble. He watches Murphy at the wheel. The driver works hard and he is competent. Simon looks at Carlos. The tightly knitted brow betrays fear but Simon sees no panic.

--He's seen it all. I wonder where--

The window frames Carlos in silhouette; outside the van, the high steel wall protecting the roadway from rifle shot reflects every lightning strike. Carlos holds his fear. Simon decides in a pinch Carlos Jordan can be trusted. Searchlights scan the roadway from the high steel wall. The riots have started--the rioters using the mayhem of the storm for cover. An armored vehicle full of soldiers passes by. Simon sees Murphy nod and fall in behind the carrier.

--This guy Jordan has serious juice--

They drive along in silence until Carlos sees a large minaret beside a Christmas-bow-topped building. "Excuse me, Mr. Weiss, what is that place, a shopping mall or a gold vault?"

"The Stanford Shopping Center--sometimes called the Bay Area Center--the walls and guards keep the unconnected out. Inside those walls you would think there was no such thing as global warming. It is a treasure throve of all those items you hardly see anymore. The wealthy tourists who come to San Francisco surreptitiously come down here to shop. It is a well-guarded secret."

"Only the privileged may attend...I have heard of the Bay Area Center." Carlos stares forward, as if his gaze might somehow have given respect to that mall. Carlos has seen too much suffering to excuse any vanity or excess; Simon notes this man quickly buries his contempt for the absurdities of wealth and says nothing further to Simon. Simon notes the dismissal and finds himself disliking this individual for being too abrupt.

Ahead there is an explosion. Murphy nods unconsciously at the incoming ordinance. He hauls the van to the left exiting the main roadway.

"Must be bad ahead," says Carlos, as the armored carrier in front of them speeds off down the main roadway leaving the van to negotiate the side roads alone. Flashes light up night from all around as the bus jerks back and forth in violent winds. The bus slows as the driver gives up any attempt at getting to San Francisco. A loud crack. "The trees are going down, folks. I'm sorry but the U.N. regulation says we need to find the nearest shelter." He peers through the boiling rain trying to thread his way among the flying debris and flooding street.

Simon looks around realizing he may have to walk back to SETI tomorrow morning. "Looks like you were right, Mr. Jordan," Simon says. "We have a Screamer."

"Call me, Carlos. I think we'll know each other quite well once this night is dawn."

The driver, wrestling with the bus to keep it on the roadway, says: "When we pull over, I want all of you to follow me to the shelter. Mr. Jordan, you are first. Doc, you bring up rear." The rain splatters hard against the side windows sounding like firecrackers.

"Are we safe out there?" Carlos asks, fearing the rain may shatter the windows.

Simon knows they are somewhere between Palo Alto and Menlo Park. Not a great neighborhood these days with all those angry children of bitter parents roaming the streets. "Well Mr. Jordan, eh Carlos, these neighborhoods were where the wealthy lived during the Silicon Valley heydays. Most parents worked sixty or seventy hours a week telling their children they were trying to make enough money to protect them from the angry planet. When the worth of money declined as energy became paramount many of these people came to feel they had been betrayed by the system. Their children certainly did; as a result, the decay and anger feed a survivalist mentality with no heart. I would say it is about average an the anger scale."

A pitchfork of lightning splits the sky then repeats in six or seven various patterns all around them. A bright flash strikes a building ahead of them. Simon watches a blaze of spark and flame rises in wildfire. The van scoots past the blaze while Simon scans the remains of other buildings looking for one that might provide shelter.

"Well this is some introduction to the west coast. This must be the reason the Bay Area is so often a vacation destination," Carlos says in an attempt a jocularity. Distant sparks fly in bright reds and oranges then immediately die in the torrent of rain.

The winds begin to howl a low evil sound, dark, full of pain and power. It moans, trees creek then the scream: A high-pitched note disgorged from the bowels of the planet through its winds. "Gaia wants us back," says one of the men in back of the van. Another barrage of lightning illuminates the driver's head. The winds pick up in pitch and the low moan turns to a guttural howl. Carlos stiffens in his seat and Simon wonders if Carlos' abrupt attitude change is born of fear for another.

"Let's go, Murphy," says one of the workers. "This Screamer ain't waitin' on us." They can all feel the small bus being buffeted back and forth in the winds. The radio crackles something neither Carlos nor the rest of them can hear. A high pitch warbling tone follows. Immediately the driver pulls the vehicle to a stop and opens the door to the lashing storm.

"Everyone out--get out into the field. We've got an earthquake for good measure. Stay low." Two passengers rush from the vehicle. For a moment Carlos waits for the driver to leave. "Just get the fuck out, will ya," says the driver. Carlos is out in a flash and running along the open area getting ten feet before the first jolt hits. The mud rushes up then drops away. He slides in the muck face first. The ground rolls and lightning strikes crash nearby. Sparks fly all around. A second red dart of light appears from the van then stops.

"The gas tank."

An explosion tosses Simon five feet through the air sending him face down into the mud. In the roar of oily flames Simon hears the driver scream. Looking up, Carlos sees Simon Weiss trying to get to his feet. The rolling quake pauses for a moment and both men stand. A wind's gust tosses them back in the slippery mud--this time within a few feet of each other. The ground rolls again in sickening waves. Filth splashes in Carlos mouth and he begins to choke. Simon crawls over to Carlos. "I guess we're allies tonight."

"The driver is still back by the van. I think he is hurt," replies Carlos spitting mud with his words.

"Stay here. I'm an MD. I will try to get to him." Simon begins to crawl toward Murphy. Carlos follows right behind him. Lightning lands like artillery fire around them. The rain is shrapnel in their hands and back. The wind screams in an opera of planetary pain and anger. Small pools form; an inch of rain has fallen in the last three minutes--five inches since they began their trek north. Carlos shields his eyes from the storm to stare at oily flames. The howling is unbearable; the rain splatters drops of flame in tiny exotic fountains. Then in a hellish downpour of water the fires are gone. The squall line passes and they hurry over to the driver. The wind decreases to sixty miles an hour. The low moan returns. Simon leans over feeling for wounds.

"He is not moving anymore," Carlos yells over the wind. A warm soupy mass of tissue and blood, then something hard, Simon's hands trace an angular rod protruding from the dead man--another squall line arrives. The screaming rages at them; furious winds pound both men. The sticky mess they cling to is a mix of blood and mud. Carlos tastes blood and tries to roll away jabbing Simon in the face with his waving hands. Trying to get to his feet, Carlos slips in the mix of blood and water and lands face first. Simon crawls across the mire putting his arm over Carlos. The wind's screams drown the human screams; then they are one. Astonished, Simon sees Carlos rising from the ground like a ghoul; Simon tries to hold on to him.

"You're okay; it is not your blood," Simon says.

"Let her in. She has a baby." Carlos begins to curse wildly, then: "They would have killed me." The winds abate for a moment and there is just the stinging rain. Simon scans for the other passengers however, cannot find them and stares at the wild-eyed man; there is no place to hide.

"Are you hurt--physically?" Simon asks.

"No." Carlos looks down at Simon. Like a computer resetting he calms, then sits in the mud. "The driver how is he?"

"The windshield wiper arm went through his abdomen when the van burned. He is dead." The wind and water calm. "It may be slowing. Did you see what happened to the other two?" Simon says. A loud wail calls from the winds. Another squall line is on its way in to the land.

"They made it to some kind of public shelter, I think. I saw a blue shelter-light back there, but I don't see it now." A distant flash of lightning; rain pours off Carlos' face mixing with his tears. In a second flash of lightning Simon places the face.

"You negotiated the Asian truce during the Monsoon Wars. Your picture was everywhere."

Carlos is pleased and he smiles faintly.

--What was he doing out there? How could he have done that? He's scared to death of these big storms--

"Come on; let's get to that shelter. The winds are getting worse again."

"Lead on," Carlos says appearing to have completely recovered.

Simon leads them to a concrete barrel vault bunker dug into the ground. The blue light is off. They slide down the stairway and pound on the door. "Hey, let us--hey." Simon yells. He kicks on the door screaming: "It's us from the bus." No one responds.

"It had to happen eventually," Carlos says feeling the joy of a person finally getting the retribution they feel they deserve. "They aren't full in there--of course--they are just saving themselves." The winds above them shriek again. "This storm is getting worse. Don't ever take up weather prediction, okay, Dr. Weiss?"

"They purposely turned the light off so it would not be seen. I have seen this happen before. People get into the bunkers and they go crazy. Bunker Syndrome is the official name for it. It can happen to anyone." Simon guesses Carlos has been involved in something like this before. "Stay here." Simon waits for the next set of lightning then hurries up the stairs. The winds have lulled for a moment. Carlos looks at the pool forming around his ankles. The drain system is plugged. When they open the door tomorrow those individuals will be greeted with a wall of water that will fill the bunker at least a foot deep with water. Carlos kneels down to pull debris from the grating so the drain works. A wild scream from the winds sends a chill throughout his body. He clears the drain waiting for Simon's return.

"This is downtown Menlo Park on the north end of town. There is an old theater across the roadway that was supposed to be a second shelter. It was torched six months ago but I think we are better off in there than out here. Of course we also might find some less than hospitable locals."

"That's probably why they turned the light off and locked the door against us. They are afraid of the locals," Carlos says, with a morose grin.

"Nice of you to be so understanding--and clean the drain system for them," Simon says of this apparently saintly activity. "I recommend we try for the theater." When Carlos nods yes, they crawl out and move again through the mud. An aftershock slows their progress as lightning illuminates the way. They pass the destroyed bus and stop at the roadway. The winds begin in earnest. The two men huddle in the lee of the bus. When the winds lower to a moan they head out in a run toward the street.

"It's flooded."

"Happens all the time. Can you swim?"

"Varsity letter holder," Carlos says, "But I think we should take the tree way." He points to a large oak across the roadway a hundred meters south. "If we ford there we will not have to deal with the current. The branches look as if they break up the flow also. But don't become caught in it." The winds ratchet down a notch.

They crawl to the sideways cypress tree. "We cross," Simon says. The two men haul themselves up onto the tree trunk using it as a bridge across the torrent rolling down the street. With all the handholds the crossing is relatively easy despite the increasing water. By the time they get to the other side the storm's winds are gusting to over a hundred and fifty miles an hour. A rattle of thunder rolls though the streets and into their bodies. Simon, now knowing who Carlos Jordan is, believes this individual must be protected from the storm--and the Pacific Screamers are like no storms on Earth. They scream just like people in pain. The effect is chilling. And for someone with a phobia about storms the effect is often madness. "It's going to start screaming again. Let's get inside. This way." Simon points to the doorway a hundred feet to their right.

They jump off the tree and rush toward the open doorway. A high pitched tone comes from everywhere and begins to modulate. The Screamer begins its peak phase. It is the sound of howling death. "God in heaven, that's the sound of a Pacific Screamer?" Carlos says. The wind lifts him off his feet. Simon, who was already holding onto an old parking meter, grabs hold of Carlos. Both men fall to the ground and Simon pulls Carlos close. The scream intensifies and Simon sees fear rise in Carlos. "The screams cannot hurt you." Simon urges him to crawl toward the doorway into the dark.

Tiny waterfalls from the roof look like silver bars in the lightning's glow. The howl now seems to speak the word "Who". Simon shoves Carlos toward the back of the building until they stumble into a comparatively dry corner between a trio of fifteen-inch I-beams. They form a pyramid for reinforcement of the walls and ceiling.

"This will definitely do," Simon says noting the sheets of plywood put in place by a previous occupant. The wind moan modulates. "Some say it sounds like a soprano being gored." Simon scans for others when the lightning flashes. He sees no one else.

Carlos has no voice, but he recognizes that this person is taking care of him. Carlos lies still trying not to be a problem. "Who," calls the winds. They drop an octave, and then increase their screaming like a tortured soul in hell. For every person the Screamers say something different: For Carlos they are the sounds of a mother calling for her child. Simon hears prisoners burning in a fire. It is far and away the worst part of the Screamers--people always seem to hear something different. The effect will overtime change the meaning of the word environment.

Rain pours through the leaks as gusts shake the entire structure. The winds' convulsion continues as Carlos works to control himself. He takes deeper breaths then tries a smile. "I am okay," Carlos says. Looking around, Carlos forces himself to speak again: "I always forget how bad it is for most people; and it just keeps getting worse."

"We are lucky. I think that sometimes it makes us blind," Simon replies.

"Where do you live?" Carlos asks with chattering teeth.

"Over the hill, near the ocean--that bus we took goes there four times a day because of the water processing plant in Half Moon Bay. I live nearby."

"Dangerous living near the ocean," Carlos says jerking his neck around to look at Simon. "I could never be that close to so much fury."

In a flash of bright white, Simon sees control in this man's eyes. "There is fury everywhere." He is amazed because, as he leans against Carlos, he feels the tremors of fear race though his body with each scream.

"Tell me someplace that is not dangerous and I will move there," Simon quips. "How come you tried to help those two individuals in the bunker?"

"I did not want them to get their feet wet," Carlos cowers at each blow screaming through the structure. The storm rocks the building. To Carlos the winds are now the voices of hell calling to him. "I should not have hesitated at the bus. The driver would have lived."

"You cannot control the whims of nature."

Silence.

"But you know that after the Monsoon Wars."

"I do not know what you are speaking of, Simon."

"You have nothing to be ashamed of Mr. Ambassador. You've saved too many lives in Asia and Southern Europe. I will not tell anyone about this."

Carlos does manage a smile this time. "So you finally placed me."

"In the rain you had the same expression on your face as the one from the cover of LIFE web page."

"The Sri Lankan storms," he says quietly. "Well now when you see that photo you will see fear as the truth in me and not the supposed determination. I always hated that picture." Wind tears the roof away and Carlos tenses into a hard mass of fear. Rain pours in around them as the girders offer protection.

"There is determination to face fear. The caption was right. Why don't you like it?"

"I do not like lies with longevity."

"Just the lies of the moment?" Simon asks.

"Like you do, Herr Doktor Freud."

"My boss calls them fluff instead of lies." The wind buffets the building and Simon thinks he can feel the girder they lean against move. He speaks again: "Are you from the East Coast?"

"Long ago," Carlos looks around the black, watching shapes appear in bright relief from the flashes. "I remember spending the storms with a friend.

She had a shelter that was decorated with candy. I'd sit in the shelter with her and her mother and stare at all the different candy bars and gum drops. Her mom would make popcorn on the stove and we would tell stories." Though Carlos stayed with Roxanne and her mom only once, he remembers the event fondly and has replaced many uglier memories with various versions that he has expanded that one time into many different storms.

"They were called Gum Drop Shelters, were they not?"

Carlos smiles into the dark. "That's right. Her father invented the formula for preserving the candy and the idea."

"Really? Now that person is a celebrity. Robert Gladstone right? The Gum Drop Shelters were very popular in Europe as well--until plastic became so dear." Simon tries to see Carlos' face or sense what he is feeling--other than fear--but he cannot. "I remember hearing his daughter tried to keep it running for a while. Too bad it all failed. She lives up in the mountains I have been told--oh, that's your friend--of course." Simon waits for some kind of confirmation but there is nothing. Simon wonders why Carlos Jordan spent the storms with Robert Gladstone's family instead of his own.

"And where are you from?" Carlos asks after a howl of wind.

"Spain."

Carlos turns suddenly and looks at him, surprising Simon. "So I guess each of us have interesting stories. When did you leave?" Carlos asks. "I'm sorry. I do not mean to pry. I have an assignment coming up that will take me to that part of the world."

"I left Madrid in twenty-nineteen. I got to Berlin in September of twenty-twenty-one."

"Bad time for travel." Carlos is impressed. Virtually everyone he has ever met who escaped the Chaos back then suffers post traumatic stress syndrome to the point few of them can hold a job. "And you work at U.N. NorCal?"

"That's correct."

Carlos nods as the winds abate. "You are a shrink aren't you?"

"A psychiatrist."

Carlos has begun to probe Dr. Simon Weiss. "Please don't write any articles about me being petrified all right? It would hinder my effectiveness in negotiation."

"Your secrets are safe with me, Carlos." The storm ratchets down a notch. They listen in silence for a moment.

"So what had you planned in San Francisco this evening?" Carlos asks looking at his watch. It is two AM. "Surely not a hotel room and a quiet tour of the sights tomorrow."

"No, I was actually going up to hear music and taste the flavors of the city. I am afraid I'm a bit of a child when it comes to pleasure. Today was a rough day at work."

"Unlike this evening," Carlos quips. "I think the storm has let up. You said something about the locals being a bit unfriendly?" Carlos looks for his cell phone but cannot find it. "I have lost my phone in the mud."

"It's probably being washed up in San Jose as we speak. You are right--we need to get going before the locals come out of their hiding places. There is a phone up by the Stanford Gate."

"They know me at the university. I've done some work with the people there." Carlos says.

"No, the university is a bit to the west. I'm talking about the shopping center we passed. Shall we get moving?" Simon says. "We have about an hour before the next storm band is due--or so the locals say."

"Thanks for the session, Doc." In the aftermath of panic Carlos stumbles out of the building onto the street. Carlos stands, finding the sky clearing and the moon coming out from behind the clouds. The wind has a bitter chill.

Through the wind Simon listens for the sounds of others. Despite the wind and dark, he is sure he hears no one. "We go this way." He points south but before they head out. Simon picks up a hefty branch and tests its strength by hitting the remains of an old light pole. The branch hits with a bang and does not break. It is not rotten. "You might want one of these," Simon says.

"A friend of mine died in a fist fight over the use of language. I made a pledge that if I could not get out of a situation without violence I would let it all go."

Simon immediately understands. "I have killed also. I have to say my view of death is different than yours. If I can't get out without violence I'm taking as many of them with me as I can." He looks at Carlos.

"Well you are obviously saner than me," Carlos says thinking about Lars. He picks up a stick; thinner than the one Simon carries, but sturdy enough to kill.

"Why would you do that?" Simon asks in a whisper. He thinks he has heard something in the distance and he needs to know his partner is reliable.

"I cannot bear the notion of you fighting to protect me while I jabber at a group of Klingons on how they should be respectful of our lives." For a moment the cold wind is gone. Simon finds he likes this individual who bares pain by complete disassociation from it.

They begin to walk, tripping on debris and slipping on sloping pieces of concrete sidewalk. "Shh." Simon puts his nose to the wind and sniffs intently. A moment later Carlos hears voices. Simon grabs Carlos and pushes him back into the shadows of a burned-out building. Neither man speaks or moves.

In the moonlight a group of men appear around the corner moving like a single multi-legged animal scanning the scene around them. One male speaks in a low snarl: "It was a water bus. I saw it--the Greenies' bus that goes up to San Francisco every day. "There, look--shit it burned." The men stand close enough that had Simon or Carlos swung their sticks they could have hit them. Simon prays the wet on their bodies keeps their scent down. "Look, two people there by the shelter. We got 'em." The men rush down the street whooping and screaming. Carlos and Simon jump from the shadows.

The mob fords the roadway oblivious to the current. "Come on," Simon says grabbing Carlos by the shirt.

"They will kill those men."

"They will surround the shelter. They cannot get to them. The Stanford Gate is half a mile away. We will tell the guards. The guards will rescue them. Come on." Simon pulls harder on Carlos' shirt. Carlos pauses a moment then the two of them rush off down the street.

Another quarter mile and they see the emergency lights of the Bay Area Center front gates and the outline of two large armored vehicles. "There are four machine gun emplacements you cannot see so be careful." Simon yells to the vehicles, "Hello the Center. We were caught in the storm." Quietly to Carlos he says: "Drop your stick. Keep your arms where they can see them and walk slowly." They approach the lit gate. The turrets on the armored carriers turn towards them and track their movements.

A guard in heavy blue body armor appears between the two vehicles. His face is hidden behind a light-enhancing visor. His weapon, hangs from his shoulder and points at the two individuals. "Stop and identify yourselves."

Carlos slowly reaches into his breast pocket to pull out his ID. When he opens it and the guard sees the light blue fluorescing hologram of lightning bolts he lowers his weapon immediately. "What can we do for you, sirs?"

"I am Ambassador Jordan, First League, North America. This is Doctor Simon Weiss. He works at NorCal in Mountain View." Simon displays his ID.

"We heard about you two being on the bus out of NorCal. Ambassador, there will be a car for you in a few minutes. If you just let me make a call--"

"There are two men in a shelter who were with us in the bus. They're about a half mile down the street. A crowd of men know they are in there."

"Sir, we have a job to do guarding this shopping center and you, if--"

"You see this ID, Corporal. It says First League. If you do not get your butt down there with a few of your men and rescue those two men now, I will have you guarding the shark stalls in LA--in your skivvies," Carlos speaks this in a voice that is just above a whisper.

The young corporal salutes. "Doe, take one of the APCs over to the Menlo public shelter. Bring the two individuals inside back. If any of the urchins gets in your way--remove them." Immediately one the armored cars lurches forward heading up the road. A bright red light on the top flashes and a siren's warble pierces the night.

"Sir," says the Corporal behind the black visor, "The roads north and south might still be a bit dicey when the storm returns but I think you'll be okay once we get you a car. Doctor Weiss, I'm sorry but you'll have to wait until the morning. There is heavy damage from this freak storm and all resources are on overload." He turns to speak into his shoulder radio.

"Why do they still call them freak storms?" Simon says as they walk toward the guard shack.

"I will give you a ride back to NorCal or to your house if you want." Carlos says.

"NorCal will be great." They enter the guards' concrete bunker and sit on a stool. The corporal in charge makes no movement to make them more comfortable. He remains outside at his post talking into his telecommunications unit.

"I'm going to the U.N. Language forum next month. You are speaking there right?" Simon says after a couple of minutes of silence. He has had an idea that he wants to fully explore. He needs to keep in contact with Carlos Jordan.

"I plan to be there. Here is my office number and my home number. Call me the week before. We'll arrange to have a nice dinner together--if I go."

Simon takes the card wondering how to get a guy like this assigned to SETI.

Chapter Nine

From the ancient upside down faucet, cold water arcs up into the scratched blue metal tray and bubbles within it. She adjusts the flow too much and dirty water runs down the sleeve to her elbow. Stepping away, Roxanne shakes her head then finishes tying back her straw-colored hair; only thereafter she pats dry the green canvas sleeve of her smock. The monstrous tide of events that has swamped her generation slides ever closer to possessing Roxanne. Looking down the line of cages with their square cutout near the wall for the trough, she inspects the three shepherd pups at play. Black and white fur mounds whine in protest, or bark, or just yelp--lost, hungry, and uncomfortable.

A memory of children on Manhattan streets floods into her brain. That brings forth the visions which thunder from her: hurricanes tearing the roof of her home, dead bodies and dying children, friends crushed by fallen buildings, stormy nights waiting for death's call.

Standing in the kennel area she grabs the rusting chain link fence. Then this morning's horror: the young girl with the empty eye-sockets crying. She remembers thinking to herself how odd someone can cry even without eyes. A moment later she feels nothing but a pool of purple-red haze.

Roxanne had stayed in New York for almost five years. She considered those years the best of times even though she watched the teetering city fight the madness and the storms--then slide into rubble and madness. She hears herself somewhere saying: "Those years were a moment in history--the last great hurrah of a great city." Then she is in a majestic party at Grand Central Station. The huge room festooned with balloons and flowers, black silk gowns and mourning coats of pinstripe gray. The last train was leaving Manhattan.

Her brain rewinds.

That day she had been filming children at play in subway stations recently converted into shelters. The city historian had asked for the shoot as part of a documentary portraying the city's rebirth. "This is more a headstone for the city," she said almost at the top of her lungs. "These absurd attempts at depicting revival with bad props and poorly done matte paintings sickens me." Nonetheless she sees herself at her tasks: all day long wandering among rubble, despair and pain painting it through the lens of the old Bolex camera to look like hope. Working as both camera person and editor she worked until the last possible hour arriving fashionably late for the party in a rather cross mood. But the party was a great bash--like the close of a long running play--and it wiped out every bad feeling in a way Roxanne had not experienced since she was a youth. The symphony played Handel, the catering came from restaurants all around the country. The Vice-President was there along with Arthur Conworth, Director for the New U.N. North America. The lights still bright in her eyes, the women and men beautiful, glitter owned every moment until dawn; a sinful night delicious in every way. She cheered the train as it left--like every good fool in the room.

Roxanne tastes the breakfast from that morning: warm honey buns. Her lover, a Belgium diplomat with one leg, pontificated on how there was no dignity in living every degrading step downward. "The planet is ridding herself of the human plague. However," he smiled with a leer that reminded her of a red-haired Mephistopheles: "Making believe it is not occurring has no shame." Roxanne laughed in their faces--then coped with the confused logic of her lover's cowardice for many years, until yesterday, when one woman's logic washed away the last of her youth.

The water from the trough begins to spill over onto the concrete; it will reach a prone Roxanne in a few seconds. Though at this moment, lying there, she feels she is bicycling from work; on the side of the road a tattered woman sits, a newborn cuddled in her arms. The woman screamed at her. "I figured since so many were going to die, the species needed as many of us as possible to fight the disasters. All anyone can do now is to have children. The next generation will save the future."

Roxanne saw herself walking alongside this woman. The squat matron rolling reason after reason upon her as to why humanity would be saved; everything from aliens to psychiatrists. Roxanne walked alongside, listening to her talk, cuddling her new son, horrified at the woman's need for creating baby after baby and handing them out like candy. "How can any mother serve her children up to die?"

"And what do you do? I have had twelve babies; eight are still alive. One is blind though." Roxanne had mumbled that she helped orphan blind children through Guide Dogs Inc.

It all dissolves into the eleven-year old that arrived this morning, starving and sick, claiming to have no family or friends. The soiled black silk bandages around her eyes and the beautiful long black hair. Roxanne suddenly feels the water; to her it seems like the truth. It soaks her entire side and she wakens to the yelping dog and the pain. Roxanne stands slowly thinking about the blind girl.

Taken in under the Orphanage Act, the girl now sleeps in a clean bed after a hot meal. Roxanne briefly wonders if she had really ever talked to that woman.

--Poor Molly will be a welfare case, but what a brave little girl. At least she'll be fed until she is fitted with a dog. Coping takes so many forms now. I wonder if the mother really did abandon her? Of course how could anyone bring a child into a dying world? A world where a child is more likely to starve, or be washed away, or killed in a food riot, than ride in a car? Death is all around now. No place is safe. There is just no way to judge the right or wrong of any logic that enhances survival. My God, I sound like Carlos--

Roxanne begins to cry on the cold wet concrete floor of the kennel.

Hours later Roxanne glances at the puppies' glowing eyes full of mischief. She envies the dogs. The puppies have no sense of the deserved punishment that sits fixed on every human, lashed to their souls. Death will come for the puppies like a sudden flash of lightning, without the horrors and fears lurking inside the people she knows. She sometimes convinces herself that she has joined the cognoscente of her generation in a toneless dance of stoicism, and the joy hardly matters. Then, after viewing the young blind girl's delight at petting a pup, the tears erupt again like hot lava and she knows her joy drowns under mounds of pain. This morning she feels like a bowl overflowing with misery.

Roxanne pets the puppy through the cage then rubs her hands on her pants hoping her love does not run out before she is wiped off the planet with the rest of humanity. A yelp of distress jars her back and she scans the tussle of adolescent dogs that scramble over each other. "You guys still do not have enough food do you? Well, I can fix that one. I will go talk to the nasty money-lovers again." The small Australian Shepherd with a white star on his head, nicknamed Bethlehem, yelps loudly.

--This dog is perfect for Molly, but the good dogs go to the rich children who have Head-Clamp Syndrome. I hate them. It isn't right; that girl has so much courage, not like the majority of my clients now, stroking themselves silly in absurd twentieth-century technological fantasies. Interactive nonsense with bubble-gum theories pasted on a fabled past--

Roxanne's wealthy clients disgust and sadden her with their cowardice. She detests the idea of rich children hiding in Head-Clamps, living their lives surrounded by synchronized sound and long-gone views projected inside their helmets to hide the horrors that surround them.

--They're using up all the good guide dogs while the really needy are left to wait--she scans the cages again. There are less and less dogs, too. Roxanne heads down the gray concrete walk between the cages to surgery examining each empty stall. Carlos' grim prophecy about the Earth's decision to cancel the next generation appears all too correct. They had talked last week after that storm caught him on the U.N. bus. When Carlos said another passenger had taken care of him Roxanne almost cried; no one, she thought, understood Carlos' fear of storms.

--God, Carlos, I hope you are always safe. If you had died in the damn bus during that stupid storm I think it would have been the end. It's sad I need hope now more than joy. What a melancholy creature I've become--

The wind-up clock at the end of the hallway says one thirty-five. Already five minutes late for the new client, she mumbles: "Well, let him wait." Roxanne stops at the large kennel holding the returned defective "merchandise" slated for destruction, the Goons, only the old collie remains. The dog lies propped against the cage, sleeping; her cast torn and covered with excrement. Roxanne bends down and puts a finger through the wire mesh stroking the top of the dog's skull. The guide dog broke her leg protecting its head-clamped young master from a mugger. Parents returned the canine three days later demanding a new dog. Their threat to sue, claiming the animal had not been fed well enough to keep its bones from getting brittle, put them in the front of the waiting line. They will probably get Bethlehem. The sad brown eyes of the collie opened. "Don't you worry girl. I'll get the orderly to clean you up too."

At the door, she stops once more and looks back down the long row of cages and listens to the yelping animals. "Sorry kids, they do not care about you. They don't even care about themselves," and opens the door.

In the vet's area, the orderly, his back to her, cleans a stainless steel operating table with a cloth. His shoulders move as a wave, his head and neck bop back and forth. The skull-shaped Head-Clamps are only partials. He can see, but he cannot hear anything.

--His last moment would be filled with music and detachment. Maybe it is better than a truth faced too late--

Roxanne sighs walking around in front of him waving her hand. He snaps his head back shutting off the music.

"Number three, with the broken leg--she has feces all over her."

The young, bearded intern stretches his arms over his head and looks at the ceiling a moment. The bloodstained cloth rests on the table.

"Will you clean her up, please? Also the puppies need more food."

"As soon as I clean the operating room, prep it for the next surgery and clean the last Goon out of the incinerator. That okay with you, Roxanne?" He makes no attempt to hide his dislike. Many in this younger generation mark time, waiting to die. They have seen all efforts of mitigation by Roxanne's generation fail miserably. "What's the big problem? That dog'll be dead as soon as we get a new shipment of Goons in anyway."

"Not if someone takes her."

"That's real bloody likely. Give it a rest will ya."

In one motion she picks up the rag and tosses it in his face. "Just do it."

A voice comes over the intercom: "Roxanne Gladstone, to the client area." She looks at the intern making sure he understands he will obey. He nods and she leaves.

Roxanne stops at the viewing window. Dr. Sullivan sits under the Guide Dogs Inc corporate logo, a German shepherd in silhouette, with the motto arching over its head: "Sight For The Sightless". She watches the fleshy, rotund figure of Dr. Sullivan as he speaks to a large man with his back toward the window. The individual wears an expensive white silk shirt and pants with bright blue serape over his shoulder. His black kinky hair is furrowed vertically and tightly knotted into a long pony tail.

--Wonderful another U.N. honcho of some sort--

Beside that man, a thin young man dressed in a blue kilt and green trimmed vest sits ignoring the world. A golden globe surrounds his sensory organs for smell, sight and hearing. The boy look likes a stereotypical man from Mars--except for the antennae.

Sullivan turns his brown-bearded face and bloodshot eyes to the one-way window as he speaks. His normally sour face shows even more anger today than usual. Roxanne figures the honcho has been giving him a bad time by the way his right eye twitches.

Roxanne enters the perfume-filled room and Dr. Sullivan shakes his head slowly, like an angry parent. She ignores him and faces the big man who has turned from her and now looks outside at the valley of redwood stumps. She wonders how he had rattled Sullivan so easily. Roxanne thinks Dr. Sullivan is a prick.

The customer turns and looks down from piercing dark eyes submerged in pillows of flesh. Eyes that remind her of a madrona stump. "Roxanne, this is Stanislaus Damube. He is with NorCal over in Mountain View," Sullivan says.

Roxanne shakes the muscular hand of the big man then turns quickly to the seated boy and holds out her hand: no reaction. He is typical; all externals are off to the planet. Roxanne watches the young man moving his head back and forth.

--He probably has no idea where he is, and given the stains on his teeth, he doesn't care--

She figures the boy has been wearing the Head-Clamps twenty-four hours a day, for at least a year or two. From his kilt style, he looks like an Easterner. She wonders what he is doing at a west coast guide dog facility with Mr. Damube.

Damube speaks: "My son here needs your help. Dr. Sullivan tells me you are the best trainer he has ever had."

Roxanne tries to muster a friendly smile but this guy seems like a vulture to her. "What is your son's name?"

"His name is Taylor." The man studies her from toe to brow. Instead of examining her as a piece of meat, as she had expected, he inspects her eyes trying to gauge her capability.

Uncomfortable, Roxanne taps the child on the shoulder. The child stops moving and waves hello. Immediately returning to moving with the sounds and sights of his clamps, he leaves the present again.

"Almost zero acknowledgment," Dr. Sullivan says, furry eyebrows raised in apparently deep concern. "Roxanne is our best trainer and I am sure she can help your son. She has the highest success rate matching owners and training guide dogs. None of her dogs have ever been returned." The bright, phony smile that lights Dr. Sullivan's round face disappears when Roxanne scowls at him for lying.

"How long has Taylor been clamped and cupped?" Roxanne bends down and stares at the gold on the child's helmet. It is not just paint.

"I do not know. I am not home that often. I travel a lot. My spouse says he has some older friends who involved him with isolation tanks a few months back. One thing led to another and here he is."

Roxanne examines the back of Taylor's neck. The small calluses at the base of the neck are well formed. "Bull."

Damube shoots her the predatory, practiced glance of a person used to shutting up subordinates. Roxanne does not have to check his rating. "Ms.

Gladstone," his voice is icy, "your job is to train my son and a guide dog so that he does not get hit by a bicycle or get molested--not to make insolent remarks."

Roxanne stands up, her voice even. "I am going to have to communicate with him and I need to know the last time he had the clamps off. You are not the only parent with this problem. Most kids know they have a better than eighty percent chance of being dead in ten years. They do this, poke their eyes out, kill themselves, and many other things to escape it. It's not the parents' fault. Understand? I need answers if we are going to help ease him out of the Head-Clamps. How long?"

The man's dark eyes narrow as he measures her. "It's been a year and a half."

"So ever since the information on the death rates came out over the nets?"

Sullivan interrupts quickly. "That was hard news on the kids."

"Cut the hype, Sullivan." He looks at Roxanne. "So you think he is running away from the future?" Damube stares down at the boy.

For a moment she glimpses both tenderness and stupidity.

--How do they get so powerful if they are so stupid--

"Has he signed all the forms?"

"All complete."

"Why don't I just walk Taylor to his cabin? You can call me in three or four weeks."

Roxanne taps Taylor's helmet with her knuckles three times. She places his hand on hers and points her index finger at him and then at herself. Then she retracts her index finger, and at the same time, sticks her thumb out as if she is hitch-hiking. Taylor stands. Almost six feet tall, he is a giant among his generation. He holds out his hand like a monarch waiting for supplicants. She shakes it up and down and walks straight to the door.

"Don't react when he hits the table," she says. Taylor takes two steps and bumps into a low table. He grabs his shin. A shrill tone sounds. Roxanne taps the helmet and curls her index finger twice. Then she grabs his shoulder and roughly pushes him out the door. "See you in a few weeks."

Stanislaus Damube, impressed by what he sees as competence, turns and leaves the office without saying good-bye to Dr. Sullivan. Sullivan, he ascertains, is nothing more than a leech.

Roxanne leads the adolescent down the hall, opens a side door and steps out to the garden. Then, as the boy leans forward in response to the music of his world, she slams the door on his helmet. He kicks the door wide open, slamming it against the building. That shrill sound comes again from his helmet. New green paint covering the scar on the inside of the wooden door adheres to the helmet. Roxanne leads him out along the grass path by the edge of the building. When he is around the corner in the dog run area, she sticks out her foot and sends Taylor sprawling in the grass and soft excrement. She deftly reaches behind the helmet in a quick motion and pulls the power jacks from the back of the helmet. The cooling system in the helmet stops.

"Hey, what the fuck is wrong with you." Taylor uses the same snarling tones as his father. She does not bother to answer and holds out the two torn wires for him to feel. "You blew my unit." When he tries to get up she trips him again. Then again. A third time--he reaches up and releases the pressure lock on the helmet.

A thin crack appears along the side by his ears and he lifts the helmet off his head. The barks of dogs mix with jazz bass and clarinet riffs coming from his ear speakers. Dog feces cover part of his neck. A ring of red calluses covers his cheeks. They run around to his neck where the seal and outside environment meet. A shiny metal band that loops over his head ties the black, foam-padded earmuffs of the ear clamps together. The eyecups, two pieces of white plastic half globes that look like golf balls, appear embedded in his face. Roxanne wonders if any human could look any stranger. She grabs the helmet out of his hands. His hands follow blindly, gripping after it.

"Shit," he says and sweeps the air again with both hands. Roxanne trips him again and pulls the exposed flat power pack from the back of his head. The music stops. The boy slowly reaches up and pulls the ear-cups from his head while releasing the air clamp holding it on at the base of his neck. Although there is much flaking skin, there is no fungus or skin rot. His skin is a deathly gray, but healthy, thanks to the well-made helmet. A small hiss sounds as he brings the pressure up on the eyecups. Roxanne examines the helmet.

The green Earth insignia of U.N. approval is embossed on the inside back edge under the cleaning and filtration system. The helmet is top of the line and she guesses it must have cost two hundred thousand dollars, minimum.

The half golf balls drop into Taylor's hands and two beautiful deep blue eyes look up at her, hate darting from them. "What the fuck is with you?" He begins to rub his eyes, as the unfiltered air makes them water.

"I'm Roxanne Gladstone. You do not like it out here, fine. You have gotten on the list and you have gotten the money to get a guide dog, fine. The sooner you learn to work with the dog, the sooner you can go back in there and hide. Fitting you to the dog will take about seven weeks--if you don't fight me. Longer if you do."

He keeps rubbing his eyes.

"Your ears will begin to burn soon also. It'll last for a few hours."

"I'm at a guide dog center?" He looks around and notices excrement covering him. "That's what I thought it was. Oh, you're a fucking trainer."

"I am your trainer--my name is Roxanne."

"Yippee." He looks down the rolling hillside to the Pacific Ocean. "Big waves out there. I can tell by your stink you're a Californian. You guys out here need to bathe more; you know that?" He looks at the steel buildings and barrel shaped cottages that make up the compound. "So, a California Guide Dog Center, what'd I do?"

"I do not know, but we are here to help," Roxanne says mimicking the commercials.

"Like this shit bath, but I guess your generation is used to handing that out to us."

"My pleasure. Do you like dogs?"

"Yeah, I guess so. The dogs are attack-trained, aren't they?" The boy is beautiful. Fifteen years ago she would have seduced him.

"Once you are hooked in with the animal, the dog will protect you, but it will not attack on command."

"That's too bad. I wouldn't mind seeing a video of you mauled."

In response, she pulls the filtration tubes from his helmet, making it useless and hands it back.

"Tough, huh? How old are you?"

"None of your business."

"Roxanne, you're some fox for an old bitch."

"Thanks."

"Sorry we started off bad," the boy says in a reasonable tone, "but let's get some things straight. You make it easy for me and I'll make it easy for you."

"Taylor, cut the crap."

"Then try this one on, Roxie. I'm sixteen and I'm gonna get screwed because of how all you older fuckers lived. So kiss my ass."

"Stop being a cry-baby. You're not dead yet."

"Sure, and you're Ralph Nader. Hey, who brought me here?"

"Your father."

"You are kidding? Daddy, huh? I haven't seen that Greenie fucker in years. What the hell is he doing dragging me across country?"

"Keeping you safe."

Taylor laughs. "You're tied into the Greenies in some way?"

Roxanne does not answer for a moment.

"I knew it."

"I am not tied into them."

Taylor laughs. "You're lying. The only thing my dad taught me to know was when a person was lying. And you definitely are." Roxanne leads him to a white barrel vault building half buried in the ground.

Taylor speaks. "Maybe we could make a deal?"

"No," Roxanne replies opening the door of the bunker. "This is where you will live. Take a shower; you stink."

"That makes me a Californian, doesn't it?"

"Bigoted little pain in the butt aren't you? Dinner is in three hours. In the meantime, look through the pamphlets and unpack. You will do all your own cleaning here."

He grunts and sticks his head inside the open doorway. "Are you kidding me? For what you guys get you don't clean the place? Oh that's right, you're the trainer, not the maid. You do anything else?" He puts his hand on his crotch and smirks at her.

"Oh, and, you will take care of your dog's pen. Ain't life a bitch?" She walks away leaving Taylor Damube standing at the open door. She hears it slam shut. A cold breeze blows in from the ocean and Roxanne looks to waving fields. A small figure walks among the brush. It is the girl from this morning Molly. Behind her clouds pile and darken. Roxanne starts down the hill to get her.

--Another storm. Give me strength to face it and the future where men like Damube and his son rule. There will be no past after that. No history to remember the brave children of this generation, or the cowards, or the cities, or the great men like Carlos. Has there ever really been a time of greatness or is it all ego--

Suddenly free of shackles, Roxanne smiles. Once Roxanne had planned for old age but now she will barely plan for next week. She wonders what Carlos will do if he can no longer sustain his isolation; she prays his disease of brain-first never happens to her and pities her dear friend. Being alone among all the destruction and pain is too overwhelming--for both of them. Roxanne calls out: "Molly, I think it is time to go in." She looks up at the clouds. "It's also time to introduce you to your guide dog."

The young thin girl in the white overalls and denim jacket stands, her face skyward. "I see. What's her name?"

"His name is Bethlehem. He's a bit young but I don't think anyone will mind you doing a longer training period than most." The young girl lets out a whoop of joy.

Chapter Ten

Standing in front of Simon and the researchers, thick arms crossed in front of his chest, Stanislaus Damube looks over the researchers in the room as if they were part of a private collection. Starched and creased with a seam in front, dressed in the same white shirt and pants as always--a style Simon had not seen for many years--the man pulls a small leather-bound note pad from his chest pocket. Thumbing through the pages, looking at this, noting that, Damube has the air of vassal as he points to Dawn. "I believe you have some paperwork for me?" She nods, handing him a small stack of papers. Across the table that separates Damube from the others, Simon settles in for another battle. These weekly meetings with the Political Communications Consultant have all the appeal of a dental appointment.

Damube scans the paperwork while the rest of the people in the small sunlit room anxiously wait. Simon folds his hands in front of him as Damube takes his time looking over each sheet of paper and placing it precisely on top of previously read pages.

Stanislaus Damube fills a room with his presence. After six months, every time Stanislaus enters it feels as if the air is being sucked from the room and the walls close in. His many nicknames are all derogatory. Simon does nothing to discourage this activity. He feels these people need an outlet for dealing with Damube's abrasive management style. Nor does it help that Stanislaus Damube has replaced Simon as Susan's number two.

A wall of steel, instead of a conduit, exists between the researchers and Susan Willoughby. As staff doctor, Simon only sees her once a week at Quentin's meetings--and that is only if Damube has not dreamed up another arcane task to keep him away. The long runs with Susan have become less and less while Simon's concern grows with each passing day. Communication with the aliens has been non-existent for seven months and Susan spends most of her time jetting back and forth with Quentin Conworth acquiring funding.

Simon has heard Quentin and Susan make an impressive team at presentations and dinners. They have earned the nick-name 'The Camelot Couple' because their pitch of hope of outside assistance is so compelling. The duo has upped SETI funding past the ten billion dollar mark. As of this December morning, Quentin Conworth and his queen firmly pilot the helm of hope. The search for the alien repeater station continues all over the world while rumors that the team here at NorCal are superfluous bounce about like Ping Pong balls.

Damube attributes the ceasing of communication to general incompetence. The researchers attribute it to Damube. Then there are these meetings--so orderly Simon wants to write a paper on them--which achieve nothing but to stoke the cauldron of anger. Simon's frustration boils with the lack of progress and he wonders where all that money sits. Certainly the facilities have gotten better--but not ten billion dollars worth. The transportation costs might eat up a bit of it--but most of that should be paid by the U.N. NorCal transportation budget. He has heard rumors of a new house for Quentin somewhere in Palo Alto, but that seems just too absurd--embezzlement of money for a new home. He wonders where the money is being spent. When he finds out later this morning the answer will make the notion of embezzlement seem almost saintly.

Dawn waits for some feedback on her work but there is none. Damube reads the last sheet of paper and lays it carefully on the table. He pulls a sheet of ochre paper from his notebook. As Damube places the ochre paper in front of him, Simon sees the latest communication the team plans to send to the aliens covered in red pencil marks. "Let's get down to it," Damube says, leaning forward. "Now, in the beginning, where we introduce me as the Ambassador, that is fine--but just my name and function should do. We do not want to detail my military rank. As far as these aliens are concerned I am just a diplomat. Also these sections on why we're trying to get together with them--you people provide too much data on our situation. They either know or they don't know so let's not belabor the negatives. Especially since our task is to get information, not give it."

Simon lowers his head and rubs his tired eyes with his thumb and forefinger. The political winds have turned against Damube, Simon believes--otherwise he might leave the room and march down the hallway screaming at the charade of Damube's leadership. Looking up at the researchers, he sees his sentiment shared by everyone. Damube catches his inattentiveness and shakes his head like some old school-marm. Simon bristles as Damube tries to embarrass him--again. He has no idea Damube is acting on orders from Quentin to make it as tough as possible on Simon. So far it has not achieved Simon's resignation but Stanislaus Damube is a patient human being. He believes he will eventually get under Simon's skin and Susan Willoughby will no longer be a factor in protecting him. Stanislaus has overestimated Quentin Conworth's steely exterior.

"Now, in section two, where we propose a meeting to discuss needs I think we should do it more forcefully. As I have said before, use more questions to get them to do as we wish while trying to capture their interest."

"I still think the messages are far too long," Dawn says in a weary tone of voice.

"So noted--"

"Captain Damube," Simon says, interrupting. "I think we are jumping the gun here. We need to go back to Tommy's line of thought which was asking for help--not trying chicanery."

"No."

"Since you got here," Dawn says looking crimson across the cheeks "We have gotten nowhere." Her skull colored a dull green to protest Damube's ways and eyes bloodshot from the stress of his constant badgering, Dawn burns. Her direct report to Stanislaus Damube grates upon her like sand rubbed in an open cut. "Why don't you lighten up and let those of us who know what we're doing do our job?" She stares at him defiantly.

"We must not appear weak." Damube stares back. "We need to be forceful. We need to understand what's so damn interesting to them about questions. We find that out and then we will know their needs. Information about your contacts is key. With information we will have the leverage we need to achieve our goals." He stops looking into her empty face. "Besides, what makes you think you are an expert? Just because you were here when they contacted us? That means nothing." Stanislaus Damube has concluded contact with the aliens was serendipity for this group because so far as he can tell no special talent resides here. He refers to his task here as baby-sitting when speaking to his superiors. He continues: "The rest of this discussion on climate and questions about their planet are out--for the time being. We also want you to add this note." He lays down a piece of paper.

Simon wonders how a person so incompetent can rise so high in an organization. He attributes it to a lack of talented people in a shrinking population. He has no idea that people like Stanislaus Damube have been rising through organizations as a result of embarrassing information for centuries. In Damube's case he possesses videotapes of a high official in Zurich during a six-month period of sexual indiscretion born of depression and hopelessness. Simon reads the note: "This message says we are in contact with another species who wishes to contact them on an important matter."

"This came from the top," Damube says, pandering to the disapproval on every face across the table.

"It's a lie," Simon replies.

"Lies are the essence of diplomacy," Damube says.

"I would like to put the message in different terminology, then pass it back to you for review," Simon says. "Is that okay?" All around him eyes widen in disbelief--unaware Simon has heard Damube is under pressure to get affairs progressing along. Simon feels anything he can do to slow things down works to the advantage of the team.

Damube nods his head slowly. "I want it back tomorrow." He has no anticipation whatsoever that he will allow any change to the message but Stanislaus knows his underlings must have a forum. "I'll expect to see your changes by noon tomorrow. We're through wasting time around here. It doesn't look good that we haven't made any progress since I arrived."

Seeing Damube's response as confirmation, Simon hides a smile and begins to wonder how to delay things even more.

"I have a question about funding," Dawn says leaning over to get a folder from her note pad.

"Doctor Weiss, please take over." Damube stands. "We can talk about it next week. I have another meeting so you will have to continue without me this morning." With no further comment, he leaves the room. Dawn stares mouth agape.

The moment he is out the door everyone speaks at once. It is a barrage. Simon waits until they quiet. "Dawn?"

"Simon, I hate that person."

He stares at her impassively.

"So I'll talk to you about the budget: remember that discussion about the ten billion dollars? I know where it's going." Simon sits back waiting for her speech. "They are building a ship in Huntsville," Dawn says. "The main effort has been shifted to locating the alien repeater station. That's why there's nothing happening here; he's just jerking us around. We are doing this as a diversion to keep the aliens busy. From what I'm told the ship will have weapons to force the aliens to help us. Of course don't ask me how they're going to get across sixty-five light years but that doesn't matter." She smirks. "This guy is no ambassador. He's a conquistador."

"And an idiot," someone mumbles.

"You have some proof--of the ship?"

"We need no proof about the other assertion," the same voice mumbles.

Simon thinks this the most far-fetched story he has heard yet. Even if they find the repeater, he wonders, what would they do; hold it for ransom? Simon's brow wrinkles.

"Will a photo of the ship do?" Dawn reaches into the folder and produces an analog snapshot of a bulbous steel framework; it houses retro-rockets and large engines. In the foreground, Stanislaus and Quentin stand by a large table reviewing plans. Overhead a banner says: "Huntsville leads the way." She points to a small pod hanging from a gantry crane. Cradled in chains is a large weapon with twin barrels.

Simon stares at the photo then recovers his composure. The answer to the funding question is clear. "This does not mean we are just a diversion-- probably it means we are just step one before they bring in--this thing." He looks at the photo dumbfounded by the audacity of humanity.

Just down the hall from Quentin's office is Susan's office--almost as large and filled with brand new furniture. Expensive tan rice paper covers the walls. A small Van Gogh hangs over a well-stuffed floral design couch. Across from it, behind the oak desk a large wire-filled window brings in sunlight. The sun's glow bounces off her pristine white blouse and her tightly bound hair. Flowers surround her as if she were in a funeral home.

"Simon, it has been too long. Come in." Susan stands up from behind her desk. The blue suit and stiff white shirt crinkle as she moves. Two black vases full of yellow mums flank her. Their smell fills the luxurious office. The glum pallor that had followed her like a train after the Olympics has disappeared but just what has replaced it still eludes Simon. It is not happiness and it is not love.

"Aren't these flowers beautiful?" Her secretary enters. Susan, despite her annoyance at the intrusion, gasps, and her face loses its tightness; she has not seen red and yellow roses in years. Light comes to her eyes. "They are from Mr. Conworth," her secretary says.

She glances around her office. "Well, I have finally run out of vases. Jane, do you have one?"

"I do, Doctor Willoughby." Jane places the flowers on the couch beside Simon. He sees the hint of remorse just before she leaves the room.

After glancing at Susan's glow, Simon wonders how so much beauty could be controlled by someone like Quentin.

As he glares at the flowers, Susan finds she pities Simon. She has no notion how heartless she appears at that moment and never will. Seeing more than she cares to, Susan has no time for looking back. The future rushes at her like a train, "I am so busy," she says awkwardly.

Seeing pity in her eyes, he concludes the devil has tied down her soul. Knowing nothing will be done in this office, Simon says casually: "It is time for our run."

"What? I cannot possibly do that. I have a new budget to review and there are some people coming from Alabama tomorrow. If you had told me that's what this was about..." Seeing his calm persistence to make contact with her, she sits and folds her hands. "Lets cut to it, shall we? I know Damube has tightened his grip on the project and we are getting caught up in his mania for security. Don't worry. Damube may have been given the title of First Assistant to Quentin Conworth, but he doesn't have the same power as me. I have him outflanked. It will just take me a little while to get the ducks in order so stay calm." She knows Quentin will hear this conversation. He listens to everything that goes on between Simon and her--even though he says he does not. It annoys her, but she has learned to bide her time rather than upset the apple cart. Quentin Conworth has taught her many lessons.

Hanging his head, Simon looks at the twin vases of lush flowers on her desk. "Quentin seems to care a great deal about you. I think you feel the same way about him. Am I right?"

"That is none of your business. Quentin knows what he is doing. You need to trust him more." Susan's hot anger at his intrusion calms. As a friend of course he would ask--considering how he feels about Quentin--and her. "I do feel quite warm toward Quentin and he feels the same toward me. Is this a problem for you? Is that what you want to talk about? I really do not have time for a run."

A cold nail rides Simon's spine. "Are you sure he does not have you outflanked?"

She relegates his comment to mere jealousy. "There is data you do not know. And you make it laborious for me to tell you."

"Well I guess it will just have to be that way. How about that run?" Simon says quickly.

She displays distance--Susan does not want to run with Simon. It will initiate an hour's discussion with Quentin over dinner. Simon ices over. His cold touches her when she sees the same look in his eyes for her that he reserves for Quentin. The expression stuns her because she knows it means disgust; Susan cannot bear that from Simon. She has met too many people she disrespects to have aversion from him. "You need to speak to me. A quick run--I will meet you in ten minutes."

"Right." Simon dons a counterfeit smile. Hearing her phone tone twice, he works to keep his jaw from clenching shut. Simon leaves the office. The two short tones mean it is an internal call.

On the walk downstairs to the lockers he passes a framed set of question marks outlined in gold. Simon asks himself again why Susan would allow Quentin so close to her. To him Quentin Conworth is evil. A memory from his childhood returns: A dark horse thunders through a pink stream. Two riders sit astride the mount; a man and a woman. Blood dots their arms and legs. Hanging from the saddle are loops of leather strung through bloody scalps. As Simon and his mother hide in the thicket the male voice calls out: "I am the future for you so you must love me." The woman sitting astride the horse weeps. Deep, spitish laughter succeeds the riders and Simon feels as if his gut were spinning inside his body.

A pathetic scene surrounds Simon as he waits for Susan--despite the warm sun and clear blue sky. It is as if the whole world has been axed. In the bay, the march of steel power lines sits broken in tinker-toy clumps. The Dumbarton Bridge is nothing but twin rows of concrete columns with spires of rusting steel. The far hillside is a saw tooth of shattered homes and the remains of destroyed shopping centers. Near Simon dismembered eucalyptus corpses stand like a petrified forest. No birds nest in the sloughs; no mammals move in the tall grass. The winds rush up and everything moves in a lifeless dance set to the quiet lapping of the bay waters. When Simon first came to SETI there was always the sound of some kind of equipment moving dirt, or hammers rebuilding a home. Voices would echo across the water of the bay. People jogged and others planted trees or bushes. Now there is nothing. Scanning the hillsides for the once weed-like plumes of smoke from fires he sees only a few dozen clusters scattered around the hills. He tells himself the fires are out because the weather is so warm today, then laughs at himself for a foolish lie. Surveying the storm dikes for other people running or biking, he sees only their ghosts. Moments later Susan appears, dressed in a bright yellow jogging suit.

"Sorry, I am late. Quentin and I had a conversation that took longer than I anticipated." She stretches looking out toward the bay. Her breath comes in short puffs as she tries to relax. Simon watches her to see the extent of the quarrel. Seeing him examine her, she shakes her head. "None of your business, Dr. Weiss."

They soon begin a leisurely pace north along the muddy dikes. Without a preamble she speaks: "The team is in trouble, Simon. Damube was talking to Quentin this morning and he was fit to be tied. I want you to help Damube while he is still here."

Simon notes the temporary state of Captain Damube's tenure and smiles. "That will be tough."

"I know. Can you get Dawn to back off? She has contacted U.N. North America and Zurich more than half-a-dozen times protesting the way the project is being run. She is making my job much tougher than it needs to be."

Simon shakes his head. "Those two have an ugly relationship. She dislikes Stanislaus the way a mouse hates a cat. Worse than that, he sees her as a mouse. Damube was doing security checks on everyone and found out Dawn spends her free time in Head-Clamps. I guess he has some issue with clamps and he dressed her down for it in the middle of a meeting last month. Since then it has been all out war."

"His son has some problems with the clamps. He has been in and out of a guide dog facility the whole time Damube's been out here. It has made it tough on Stan." Susan looks toward the hills for signs of a storm. "Simon, Dawn needs to fix her problem. You are the doctor; help her fix her problems," she says abruptly.

Simon runs in silence for a few hundred yards. "Damube is winning no popularity contests with his abrupt orders and Machiavellian ways-- regardless of personal problems."

Susan winces. "We are going to need Dawn running on all parts of her feet. I want you to help her." Their feet crunch on the gravel of the dike. "Tell her things will change and to lighten up. Many people are unhappy with the lack of results these last seven months. Very unhappy. Stanislaus will be gone soon and I need the new person to enter without negatives about her. Oh, I have gotten Quent to agree to bring Tommy back from the Galapagos."

"Tommy is dead. He killed himself two months ago--a drowning, I think."

Susan closes her eyes and sighs. "Oh damn. Quent never wanted to send Tommy away but he had to save face with U.N. Central. The First League is a rough group, Simon."

"I am surprised Quentin did not know about Tommy. My personnel report goes to him every month. I'm sure he read it--"

"Quit it, Simon," Susan says running with fists clenched. Neither of them speaks for the next mile. "Be happy we have someone like Quentin to run interference for us." The winds pick up a notch.

Simon finds himself looking askance at Susan as they run. "When is Damube going away? Is it for sure?"

"Yes. An edict from U.N. Central says meeting with the aliens is a number one priority. Stan had his time to make something happen. Now we go with someone else--then someone after that until we break through to them."

"So we make contact and we arrange a meeting. Is that the plan?"

"Exactly." The blue sky pours warmth.

"What happens at the meeting?" Simon asks, more cautious in his conversations with Susan than before. He feels dispirited about not being open with her.

"That is on a need-to-know basis. Quentin will not share that even with me. In fact I wonder if he even knows." Susan reads distance and finds her own elusiveness excusable.

"He knows," Simon says. "I am sorry that was unkind."

Susan ignores his words. "I think we are going to get better assistance this time."

"Where will Damube go?" Simon asks. He wonders how far to push the issue of the space ship being built in Huntsville.

Susan runs in silence skipping around mud puddles and avoiding collapsed parts of the dike. "Damube is going to take over the Armstrong construction project and start training for the flight. I assume you know what I am talking about here." Her tone betrays tacit agreement to the plan.

"The ship in Huntsville." Simon looks straight ahead and continues to jog even though he wants to scream about a heartlessness, he thinks, that has invaded her. "Damube is going to command that ship isn't he--regardless of who makes contact?" The stupidity of Damube in charge of a mission like that dumbfounds Simon. He marvels how idiocy seems to pile upon itself and we call that progress. "Why him?"

Susan cannot bring herself to look at Simon. "He has some powerful friends who have made the point he is the perfect person to be on the scene of a meeting--if diplomacy achieves nothing. Still that decision of command has not been made yet. But the flight--if it ever happens--will certainly be a military mission."

"Just like there was no decision on the political communications consultant when you told me about it. Did you know this in the beginning?" Simon asks. "When he was assigned to us, was the plan to send in the military to force our will?"

"Quentin informed me a couple of months ago." Her voice is soft and not very convincing.

He does not like Susan in this moment. Especially since her lack of openness and concern wears an elitist facade. Simon decides there will be no more runs along the dikes for them. He surprises himself in feeling no loss. "You have changed--become more savvy."

"I have and I know it." The colleagues look at each other and Susan finds herself hurt; the ardor that Simon once wore is now blown away like smoke from the hills. She runs beside him thinking of what she can possibly say to keep the friendship alive. "I once believed your trips to San Francisco were the wild play of a foolish child. Amazing how wrong one can be sometimes. There is no future for humanity. Yet you judge me as weak in feeling overwhelmed." Her harsh words come from even harsher eyes. She sees professional caring in Simon's face. Susan cannot bear it. "Do you know why they are throwing resources at us like mud against a wall?"

"The U.N. has no place else to spend it?" Simon jogs alongside her with that professional detachment spreading through his being like a virus.

"We have nothing else. All the calculations show we waited too long to address climate change. We missed saving our species by a decade at least. The carbon dioxide has a persistence in the atmosphere no one could have guessed. The deep ocean calculations on carbon uptake were all wrong. With the new numbers, every model shows continued heat retention in the atmosphere causing intensifying mega-storms for the next hundred years. Even with the drastic cuts in greenhouse emissions of the last seventeen years we have made almost no dent; the enormity of the system is going to kill us off. The models say we are riding an inertial tiger so big, if every creature on the planet ceased breathing and every gas-generating event culminated tomorrow, it would still be the end of life as we know it." Her eyes are the maw of tombs.

"The good news is the models are not worth a damn and never have been, Susan," Simon says trying to keep calm.

"Quentin believes them," Susan replies. "So do I. The negative delta of the population is increasing. Not enough people are producing food. Cities are being abandoned. Zurich and the rest of Europe will need to be deserted within five years. You cannot go some places in the US now without armed escort. Diseases decimate population centers like smart bombs. The technology is getting localized because of ambushes and our infrastructure is decaying. We will soon be at a point that we'll need to take on a triage mentality for basic services. Once that occurs we will be expending so much on keeping the chaos at bay we can do nothing proactive. From then on it is downward spirals until the chaos wins and those that are left crawl back into the caves."

Simon fears he does not have the strength of his youth to deal with the horror again. Terror looms before him then springs into his heart. He slows grabbing her arm. "So we need to do this right then Susan."

Susan stops. "Now you have it. You know what really makes me want to laugh? There are millions who still believe they will be able to ride it all out--as long as they do not give away too much. Let go of my arm." She runs her fingernails over her exposed arm leaving angry red tracks; he finally sees her pain and Susan steps back from him. "Don't try and help me. I need to do this my way." Transfixed, Simon watches her. A gust of winds slaps their jogging suits against their bodies. Clouds begin to pour through the lower ridges of the Santa Cruz Mountains.

She sees his tears. "I need him, Simon. I'm not a schoolgirl but if there is any happiness for me I want it now because soon happiness will be extinct. Do you understand?"

"I understand, but that's no excuse for giving up--"

"Like it or not, Quentin is a man for our time. I fought hard against the plans to militarize the mission," she screams. "I argued incessantly with Quentin about the expenditures claiming the money could better be spent on shelters for the general population so they can deal with the planet change. After agreeing with me, Quentin has done nothing nor will he. He believes in times of crisis only the strong should survive--since survival will only get more difficult." Susan wipes her tears. "I am strong enough to deal with what is coming at us. I am not a fool. Do not treat me like one. But there is a brutality needed for survival. And I do not want to be washed away."

He reaches up to touch her cheek.

She steps back. "And you should get off your high horse. Quentin is no saint but he does represent the future of humanity--if humanity is going to ride out the next hundred years. Without Deus ex Machina we are in trouble. So you better do what you can to make things work around here. I am doing everything I can--without complaint."

He looks up at the sky. "Pretty straight talk for you these days. I guess there are no satellites trained on us?"

"Far too few of them work for so foolish a task. That's what bothers Quentin about our runs. He can't keep current." Her rueful laugh brings forth more tears. "We cannot do this anymore." They head back toward the low buildings that make up U.N. NorCal.

Simon jogs alongside her knowing he has lost a dream today. He cannot bear the notion that Susan believes Quentin's kind is the only hope of humanity. He decides to pull out all the stops. "Whom do you think we can get to replace Damube?" Simon asks.

She smiles. "There is a short list. Your friend Jordan is on it, but so far there has been no decision."

"I like that guy," Simon says.

"He is not the kind of individual Quentin likes to work with; Quent considers him a loose cannon."

"The last time you told me we didn't have enough data on Jordan to make a good case for him. Well, I've kept in contact with Carlos these last few months and found out everything I can on him. Susan, if Jordan can't get the aliens to reply then I do not think anyone can. He's phenomenal."

"Is that so?" She asks impressed with Simon all over again.

"I am a doctor, psychiatrist, remember? I can get anyone's medical records under AMA Title 2. I just leveraged a little off that privilege. Want to hear what I found out about him? They--the Security Directorate--did not like Jordan from the start but he had a rabbi of some sort looking out for him. I could not find out who it was--but who ever it was they persuaded the diplomatic service to take him fresh out of school. They sent him out on the worst assignments. From the Colombian riots to the Monsoon Wars he goes in just before the U.N. military."

"I would not label them tough assignments by any means. Glamorous perhaps, but the information I have is he gets plum assignments. There has never been any need for military intervention in regions he worked."

"That's because he never fails. When the situation has been blown to smithereens by incompetent pedants they bring in the cavalry--Carlos Jordan. In fact the only reason there is military conflict in other areas is there just isn't enough of him to go around. He has saved millions of lives and billions of watts and he has won a grudging acceptance at the top but it is closely held."

"It is if I cannot find out about it."

"I tell you, Susan, eventually he is going to be the man here. The question is just how many failures do we have to go through before we get the best." Simon grabs Susan's arm again to stop her. He immediately releases it. She stops. "Look, I don't give a flying leap about Quentin Conworth's needs. I do care about the egoistic nonsense that is wiping us off this planet. First it was the scientists claiming there wasn't enough proof that the planet was really warming. Then there were the business people claiming the problem was an economic issue not a survival issue. Then there was the bickering about who should sacrifice what and how much. Then there were the incessant negotiations. Then the plagues of Southern Europe led to the Chaos and *voi la* we get the Greenhouse Laws: too much, too late. We fell behind the curve and stayed behind the curve because cowardice ruled us. And here we are, with no solutions because pure inertia is killing us off. So we have nothing except Deus ex Machina--the aliens. And our final question: Do we let the loonies kill us off? We need the best to break through to the aliens and get their help. Otherwise like every other damn thing in this climate change issue we are going to stay behind the curve of events and die off. If you need to give up fine--but don't stand in the way of those of us who have not given up."

Her eyes' blaze. "That was low."

"You have succumbed to the realities rather then curse them." He turns away for a moment. "Fuck Quentin Conworth and his truths," Simon says shocking both of them.

"I have been fucking him." She stares in cold silence for a moment. "How do you think I know so much? Why do you think I've become so hard? You think you see submission, don't you?" She asks. "Well let me tell you, Dr. Weiss. I'm not submitting to anything. I am working from inside the belly of the beast to beat this problem and I am not going down without cursing the realities. Period."

He faces her. "It's not worth it, Susan, to lose your soul."

"Keeping people like you on the project makes it worth it." Her breath comes in short bursts. "I was surer of myself before the Olympics. I thought I understood most of how it worked--in the largest sense anyway--and that I was equipped to deal with it. Then in Athens I saw madness on parade applauded by everyone. Simon, there are those who believe the planet is killing us yet they think that by digging deeper into the earth or snuggling up to the coral at the bottom of the ocean they will be able to ride it all out because of their wealth and power. I don't think you understand the fullness of that viewpoint. For them this horror is just another struggle for power with a different backdrop. Do you get it yet?" Her eyes blaze.

"They don't care," he says somewhat cowed.

"You're damn right they don't care. Everyone they know is someone they have had to beat to get to where they are now. Do you imagine a person like that can have any sympathy for those below them? I have seen their faces. There is no caring because they have no reason to care. I am like this because I can see how it all makes sense for them--not because of Quentin Conworth's ego. Quentin cares for me. He cares about saving us, but he has already taken on that triage mentality. So I walk a tightrope of influence. And I will do anything to keep fighting--even give up our runs." She kicks a stone. "Our fears have allowed the predators of our kind to control and so we pay with this horror. And we are left with only one decision: a choice to survive or not to survive."

"No--we are actually left with a question: Do we deserve to survive?"

"We are not beasts. They're not beasts. You don't understand. At the top it is easy to see others as either evil or weak. The good ones die off fighting a tide that washes them away. So the sane thing to do is fight on for yourself and your families not your ideals--they get people killed. And I'll tell you something else: The warlords aren't a throwback; they're just as current as computers. Our warloards are hidden behind desks. So you better do everything you can to keep them there."

"That's crazy."

"Every bit of it. We screwed up." She looks around; her eyes calm.

"Hell the system is set up on the premise that no one cares. Wealth trickles down and it is displayed as proof that we are civilized--thereby keeping the population from going rabid. We trade resources for stupidity and use the net effect as proof the system works. Crazy it may be, but it keeps the predators locked up in economic combat--not killing you or me."

Simon speaks softly. "Susan, there is more to life than becoming either a looter, a pawn, or a martyr."

"Well you almost said what you think--but at the last moment you tossed fluff. You think I'm weak." She clenches her fist so tight it hurts, but she does not stop.

"You secretly like my fluff," Simon says.

In the glint of his eyes she sees the artifact of ardor: humor. "Go to hell. Fluff in times like these is wasted. I will begin my own investigation about Carlos Jordan. If he is the man to help, I'll get him approved. I promise. Is there anything in his file that can be used against him?"

"Not that I saw. He apparently had a difficult childhood but his parents are dead. Other than that he's as pure as rainwater. Why?"

"There is a great deal of debate as to what might happen after we establish a dialogue. Zurich and Atlanta have to be convinced that should diplomacy fail the ambassador will do whatever is necessary--regardless of ethics or morality--to save our species."

"Don't worry about Carlos Jordan; he is like the rest of us super-achievers, Susan. Saving humanity is all he thinks about."

"We shall see." Susan looks away.

"I am sure he will do whatever is necessary." In that moment Simon's lips purse. He wonders if she believes his lie until she looks at him. Of course she does not believe him.

At that instant Susan sees the last of Simon's ardor die. "If there is a doubt about Jordan's ability to follow orders Damube will rise up in a howl of righteousness and smite the sinner," Susan says in deadly earnest. "He will be on Mr. Jordan like fire on a forest. Damube's job is backstop--like a guard dog--something he has done for Quentin over and over through the years."

"So Damube will be Quentin's eyes and ears out there."

"That--though I question the validity of Captain Damube's loyalty--and a videotape. Anything else I can do for you, Doctor Weiss?"

Simon would like to ask her to put a stake through Quentin's heart but he does not.

"Please, just for once Simon."

"I just don't understand," Simon says.

As he begins to speak, Susan interrupts. "No fluff, just say what I can do to help you."

He briefly reconsiders asking her the question but instead Simon says: "No, you are doing too much already."

"Some day you will be able to skip the fluff." The wind moans.

Chapter Eleven

With each seismic wave a metal pencil rolls back and forth on the Fairmont Hotel's red marble floor. Carlos Jordan bends over and replaces the pencil on the mahogany end table screwed into the floor. The brown leather couch jumps; colored snow seems to fall around him. Brushing back premature white hair, Carlos scans the high ceiling above. More cracking paint from between mahogany beams flutters to the carpet. A second large tremor sends a sickening wave through his gut. He grips the padded arm of the couch. The lobby of the Fairmont Hotel creaks and groans. A white cup shatters on the floor. Outside, limousines bounce from side to side. Behind the armored vehicles, the large Victorians of the Fairmont complex rock back and forth dropping windows and wood fenestration. Again the pencil drops, hitting Carlos on the foot. The missing toe which began to throb a moment before the quake calms as a picture window jumps from its frame and crashes on the marble floor spreading out a sea of crystals. Carlos hangs onto the couch breathing deeply, calming himself. Hundred-degree heat rushes into the large lobby. As the quake rolls on people cower in silence; among the privileged class, acknowledgement of the horrors is considered de' classe'. A half-inch crack appears in the floor and races toward Carlos. No one speaks, and then the motions cease. The crack stops at Carlos' feet, but not before swallowing the pencil.

Wordlessly, attendants dressed in red uniforms and brass buttons begin cleaning the glass from the floor. Shattered cups are swept away. Elevators ding as they restart. The long crack in the marble floor is inspected. The quartet on the low podium behind Carlos begins to play Vivaldi again. A second team of men and women appear from an elevator carrying a replacement window. Carlos notes the window says in white gothic letters: "American Hardware, since 1958"; supplies and repair items are getting scarce. White-shirted attendants scurry through the lobby carrying a covered stretcher. The person on the stretcher moans quietly as they disappear out the front door. The new pane is in place and the old frame removed before the start of Vivaldi's second movement. Seats are rearranged. Carlos leans over and touches the crack; waiters appear carrying tea--a Fairmont tradition after large quakes--and the conversations begin again. The tea announces the all clear in the best hotels now.

Other than the logistics of the physical repair, people will avoid mentioning the two earthquakes. The frequent violent tremblers are as commonplace as accidents used to be on California's freeways. Children are told polite company will not discuss this or other disasters. The damage, which has already utterly remodeled San Francisco, will continue on a stiff upper lip. A dismal future thunders forward--fed by old greed: its bastard child; inappropriate discourse rules the salon just as fear in the newsroom used to rule the media. In fact, the media still denies the link between global warming and earthquakes; outside the state, California remains "Paradise by the Pacific."

For some it still is paradise. Anyone with money enough to buy energy credits and still have adequate capital to spend on supplies can build a monolith of steel and concrete called an Eco-Home--a structure that defeats all but the worst natural occurrences. The luxuriant bunkers as large as fifteen thousand square feet are often supplied with every amenity. Use of the amenities is based on wattage; your League level defines the amount of wattage you can use. There are currently one-hundred Leagues in society with League ninety-one to one-hundred making up ninety per cent of the population. Privileges, or changes in League, are overseen by members of the U.N. Interior Authority who monitor "Population Wattage Expenditures." Access to excessive wattage is incorrectly called Privileges by the masses because a large "P" is fixed to every U.N. certified vehicle (League Five and below) that still cruise the streets. No one over the third league can afford the Fairmont or its complement of Victorian residences because venues like the

Fairmont charge a wattage fee as well as a room fee.

The vast majority of the population may not even vacation more than once in five years. On the fifth year the family--as a unit--may take an Earned Wattage Vacation based on watts saved over the course of the last five years. (The U.N. declared ten years ago the wattage to move humans around, feed them, and house them was far too dear for frivolous trips.) As a result when the unprivileged go on vacation--to places like the Bay Area--their money flows like water since money without energy privileges is useless. This pleases those who run the tourist industry. Their high league rating allows them all the energy they desire.

In the Bay Area, one of five U.N. approved tourist destinations in North America, wealth grows like moss. This boom in the tourist industry has added quite a few new souls to the wealthiest class on the planet. But the nouveau riche is seldom accepted by those with pre-greenhouse money. These new members of the aristocracy are considered "grief merchants"--but of course they do not care. They see their money as the path to paradise.

Unfortunately, the safety against the elements provided by wealth also prompts many to say things are not so bad ensuring that anyone who becomes too maudlin or boorish about the environment is ignored or silenced--in polite company. As a result, little information about the plight of the average person reaches those in power and so nothing need be done. This situation makes leaks about help from space even more unbelievable to the general population who cower in stopgap structures. Eating surplus food, or if they are lucky, local garden-grown food, the masses live a miserable life. Like ship-sinking victims clinging to makeshift rafts, most people merely hang on to life because they fear what is on the other side. Conserving energy so they can trade for essentials at the U.N. approved malls, most people exist on the brink--except for when they vacation. Then for two weeks, once every five years, it is as if the good times have returned. News is traded; regional goods are exchanged. People move about in crowds and the amenities are plentiful. New friends scheme on League climbing; rumors, like alien contact, are whispered over drinks--but only if it can buy someone a few extra watts.

An old man settles into a couch near Carlos. He speaks to a young woman just barely into her twenties who sits beside him scanning the ceiling and the cracks in the floor. She is new to luxury, this black haired beauty with the second skin of a black lame' dress. " Don't worry, Dolly, even though four hundred million people had died in the last year due to plagues and savage climactic events, only two thousand people worldwide died in auto accidents. This decline in roadway mortality is a reason why the aliens are a hoax--it is a sign. People are becoming more respectful of each other. We are turning a corner to new prosperity," he says. Carlos turns his head to laugh.

Carlos has come to love the absurd humor he constantly encounters as a diplomat. The blindness and lack of caring brought on by greed deliver choice lines through the teeth of the voracious. As if on cue the man continues expounding his world view: "It is an economic problem, first and foremost."

"Edward, people are dying." her voice is pleading for his silence but he will have none of it.

"Happiness belongs to those who own it. The climate models say everything will be fine."

"We humans are too crummy to be extinct."

"Now you understand dear. Go get us some drinks."

Carlos watches the lovely woman pass well-dressed young men bare in their styles and playing their roles. Unlike his childhood, he no longer idolizes these people. He has joined their ranks and found little he did not have before--except the senses of self-congratulation and competition that pervades all the parties. And even that has changed over the years: Unlike his youth, the members of this privileged generation mock concern to make up for, what they see, as their shortcomings in surmounting the challenge of global climate change. On seeing the pain around them, their feelings of inadequacy at being whipped about by the climate, in fact, form a common link across all the Leagues, but that is never acknowledged. Those who rule have ordained a cheery facade saying it promotes the common good. Translation: If the masses come face to face with truth it might upset the status quo and who wants to lose wealth and privilege in the hopeless cause of helping the unwashed crowd? Carlos watches the woman order three drinks. Before she turns to face her Sugar Daddy she downs a martini leaving two for consumption.

Dr. Susan Willoughby and Quentin Conworth appear, striding through the middle of the great room. She, like the girl next door who belonged to Mensa, he like Sir Galahad with a personality disorder. She with long, luxurious blond hair and haute couture light blue dress, he with a dark, chiseled jaw and razor front dark suit. Both of them cozy beside each other like prom-royalty; they move through the crowd smiling at polite waves. The "Camelot Couple" see Carlos and flash linen-white smiles.

As a sign of deference, he smoothes a wrinkle from his khaki pants and extends a hand: the sharp crease on his tan sleeve extends from a short-sleeved dark blue blazer. Dr. Willoughby shakes his hand first. Carlos notices a small pink broach on her lapel in the shape of a crescent moon. White gold stars surround the concave edge; diamonds on the convex edge glitter in furious colors. Carlos has a fondness for fine jewelry and smiles at Susan. "Doctor Willoughby, I have heard a great deal about you." Quentin thrusts his hand

forward as if to clench Simon's fingertips. Carlos finds these
alpha-dog types annoying. He backs his hand and grasps Quentin Conworth's
palm full on--no finger gripping for Carlos Jordan. "Mr. Conworth, how nice
to see you again."

Quentin smirks--a sign of respect: "Ambassador Jordan, I'm on my
way to another meeting with the contractors. I apologize for our tardiness,
but you know how busy we are now at SETI. I did want to make sure you and
Susan start off on the right foot, so perhaps we can go into one of the secure
rooms here at the hotel and chat?" He glances at Susan.

"All taken care of--this way." Susan leads Carlos and Quentin across
the cracked floor to a brightly lit hallway. Bellhops and couples rush about
as workers in white shirts continue covering cracks and applying quick
drying paint. Strolling along the hallway, they stop at a set of double wooden
doors. The coarse carving in the dark wood doors depicts a pine forest on a
hillside--cranes fly overhead. Quentin pauses briefly to admire the handiwork.
Susan also stops and begins to admire the door.

--He has her. She wants something, but not him. I wonder--

Carlos, aware of Quentin's scrutiny says: "There is no beauty which
humanity cannot improve upon." It has begun to worry Carlos recently that
this self-serving nonsense he spouts no longer bothers him. He thinks the
door is too busy and that the poor workmanship has butchered the natural
grain of the wood, but he has heard from Dr. Simon Weiss, and others, that
Quentin is not to be contradicted. And in a previous meeting he saw ample
evidence of this when a waiter disagreed that the vichyssoise was too cold.
After paying the check and leaving a large tip, Quentin had the waiter fired.
Carlos wonders how Dr. Willoughby can bear this individual's wounded
ego.

"They are beautiful," Quentin replies. He nods at Susan and she
opens the door. Carlos follows Quentin and Susan through and down a white
hallway past plain white doors. Each door bears a number beginning with
S-1, S-2, and so forth. At S-9 Susan produces a blue credit card. She runs it
through the door lock and it opens immediately.

Sparsely furnished in Danish pine, the small round room contains
four chairs surrounding a square table. From the ceiling a black coned shaped
light. Above it a vent. The bare walls are white.

"Well, let us begin," Quentin says, indicating the chairs. Carlos sits in
the nearest chair; Susan on his left and Quentin on his right.

Carlos thinks back to what his wise friend, Simon Weiss, had said
about her. "Susan Willoughby discovered the Rostackmidarifians' signal
because she was more dedicated to finding a solution than anyone else. She
shows a single-mindedness that only Quentin would dare try to control." He

reflects again on the implications of Simon's final comment: "Show Susan your commitment. Show Quentin Conworth nothing but admiration."

When Quentin interviewed Carlos for the position of Political Communications Consultant, Quentin appeared interested in Carlos and showed a light, almost wise viewpoint about the problem of the alien contact. To the uninitiated he would have seemed to have been completely above-board with Carlos about SETI--and its purposes. The job was to get the aliens to help--and not take "No" for an answer. Carlos understood immediately what it all meant and treated Quentin appropriately: like a dictator--showing the briefest hint of outrage when necessary and only stopping when he saw Quentin's smile of control. Carlos found the project fascinating nonetheless. Quentin called him on his fear of storms in a light, jovial way, chastising him for his glad-handing. Then he asked for more admiration, something Carlos has found typical of the type. In his life as a diplomat, Carlos habitually encountered warlords, dictators, and power junkies of every sort. The challenge of this type of person used to intrigue Carlos since discussions with people like Quentin were a deadly serious game--like Ping Pong with a hand grenade. The wrong move could easily lead to death. But now, after innumerable encounters with the powerful he found them merely impotent. After four meetings with Quentin, Carlos was offered the position pending Susan's approval today.

He watches Susan remove an eavesdropping detection system from her purse. She lays the small black box on the table and pushes a blue button. After blinking once, a red light dies then a green light flickers to life. Carlos notes the system also seems to make bugs inoperable. Carlos isn't worried about Susan's approval though he isn't really sure if he likes her. She will trade anything to win whatever she sees as important. That twentieth century attitude is, in Carlos' view, a major part of why the horror of climate change owns his generation. He wonders if she knows he is interviewing her.

"Well let's get this going so you two can solve the problems of the planet," Quentin says. "Let's get rid of that bug detector. We are safe here." His clear eyes sparkle over a boyish smile that appears like a red carpet of warmth. "As you know, Carlos, the Rostackmidarifians have stopped responding and we are running out of time. We need to break through to them. That's your task, Ambassador. There has also been a suggestion that Susan and I have talked about recently and I want your input on it. If we leaked information about the aliens to boost morale would it hinder your activities?"

Carlos, a practiced foreign services officer, comments: "There are already rumors, many of them, that SETI has made contact with a repeating signal. To have gotten any dialogue going at all will appear a major accomplishment. I can not see that as a problem." Carlos watches Quentin bask in his response--like a snake in the sun. Susan wears a brief grin.

Quentin glances at Susan Willoughby as if she has done it all. She nods her head in gracious acknowledgment. Carlos continues speaking: "I do not see any way general knowledge of contact will hinder me. In fact making it an open secret with media coverage might help us. I am assuming the aliens monitor our electromagnetic output."

"So you think broadcast dispersal is all right?" Quentin asks apparently keenly interested in Carlos' opinion. Carlos ignores it; he assumes the decision has already been made and this just another test of loyalty.

"You have steered a clear course. I think it is a grand idea," Carlos says sitting comfortably in his seat. This is not just a vignette for Quentin's ego. There has been no mention of alien contact in the media causing Carlos to wonder if the aliens have ceased responding. He will not say this to Quentin--that would be giving out too much information.

"Susan?" Quentin asks.

"I say we go with the release." She smiles sardonically and that surprises Carlos.

"Fine. I think we are finally going to get somewhere now that we have the first team in place." Quentin Conworth looks at his watch. "Your job, Ambassador Jordan, is to assist Susan in implementing face-to-face contact. Oh, and for the beginning stay out of the public eye. Is that a problem?"

--Here we go again. You are still worried I am a glory hound. Okay, so noted--

"I understand procedure. I prefer to stay out of the limelight anyway," he says, eyes sparkling with deceit. This performance is purely for Quentin's benefit. Carlos avoids the media spotlight but he wants Quentin to see media attention as something he craves. He figures it will keep Quentin off his back for a while as Quentin insulates Carlos from the media

"Good." Quentin mocks him with a wink. "I really must attend this other meeting. I also want to make sure there is nothing you need from me before I go?" Quentin stands up wearing a dry smile.

"Everything is in order," Susan says.

"Nice to have seen you again, Ambassador."

Carlos shakes Quentin's hand with a painful firmness.

Quentin leaves the room, closing the door behind him. Carlos sits back down and looks at Susan. She is an aristocrat and so he waits for her to speak.

"You can relax, Mr. Jordan. I have learned a lot about you in the last few months. You're unconventional, but may well be the best we have. Your last assignment avoiding the war between Eritrea and the Coast States was marvelously done. And you did stay away from the media." She wears a sly grin as she takes the bug detector out and turns it on.

Noting Susan has missed none of his performance, he only says: "Thank you." Carlos wonders if he should be concerned about her telling Quentin what goes on here. He reflects Susan treated him carefully so perhaps the detector being turned on again is not just a show.

Susan's blue eyes twinkle watching him weigh her response. "Our chief psychiatrist, Simon Weiss, has been saying good things about you all week. Tell me, did you bribe him?"

His weary eyes, deeply set under his brow and distant as the sun brightens as she curls the corner of her lip. "Not yet, but I have only known him for a year."

"Quentin is wary of you because of your friendship with Simon." Susan glances down at the bug detector on the tabletop. It still flashes green. "Your mastery of Quentin's ego has solved some of that problem."

Carlos is now less sure she will say nothing to Quentin. Her manor seems inconsistent with what Simon has said about her though he understands why Simon likes her. She is committed, but has enough perspective to laugh at it all. Simon is also a sucker for beautiful eyes belonging to beautiful women. Carlos has no such weakness--for him it is all a game. "Your words keep wild company."

"Perhaps." She recognizes the grace of a man used to charming women and teasing them with his distance. "When was the last time you saw Simon?" Susan asks.

An alarm bell goes off for Carlos. "At the English Language Conference in Atlanta."

"He was pushing that referendum to eliminate English as the official language of the planet again," Susan says. "You were involved in the early language negotiations were you not?"

"I am flattered you, or anyone else, would remember it," Carlos says tilting his thin face up inquisitively. He wonders if there is an unknown issue with Simon then decides this is just further testing.

Susan takes his measure again. He will be no pushover. "How did you become involved in the issue of territorial languages?"

He decides to bait her. "I worked with an exceptionally intelligent Swedish associate of mine who had a great deal to do with trying to change the U.N. mandate on English being the official language of the planet."

"Oh, who was that?"

"Lars Jensen." Carlos looks away, staring at the ceramic tile floor for a moment. He no longer tears; he just looks away.

"I met him once; just before he died. He was brilliant. His death was a tragedy. Did you know him well?" Carlos' association with Lars is well documented in his records.

--A complex test --

"I see you are not to be trusted yet." And he waits.

Susan's brow furls momentarily. Carlos knows she is interested in him now as a person. "You seem to be direct."

"Of course I'm not." He tilts his head. "Mr. Jensen hated the iniquity of the Greenhouse Laws. He fought for languages as a way to increase diversity of thought. He felt it might lead to new approaches for the greenhouse problem. Then one day he disappeared. I made inquiries, but nothing ever came of them. About a month later they pulled his body from the Arno River." Carlos decides to add to the mix; he wants to like Susan. "Did you have friends who eventually lost their humor?"

"And refused to compromise." She shakes her head yes. "I think everyone has had a friend like that. My friend did not understand that ideals made poor weapons and that they attracted enemies like arrows to a target. She was killed in a plane crash." Susan enjoys the repartee. "Your sense of humor appears in order. Or do you consider yourself more rigid than when you were younger?"

"I am an ambassador. My job is to find common ground; not be buried in it." Her intelligence is an advantage in Carlos' book; unfortunately for Carlos he never puts the book away.

Her expression changes abruptly. "Well, let's get down to operational issues. SETI is still a U.N. agency." She stops to allow Carlos to ask a question; when none comes she speaks: "You have read Captain Damube's reports and the reports of the team since initial contact two years ago. What do you think we should do that we have not done before? I ask you this because I am at a loss as to the next step." Susan worries about Carlos' reserved personality. Scholar, recluse, diplomat; in a difficult negotiation, he is supposedly like having a mind reader working for you. A man with an astounding ability to form bonds with strangers, and then pass on them like they were items on a hors d'oeuvre tray. Clearly, a man with a honed capability to keep everyone at a distance--she has concerns he may not have the imagination to engineer an initial break through. She thinks back on his dossier. His personal life is as unremarkable as a twig and she harbors a concern there may not be any life in this man--just a well-tuned ability to manipulate people.

He leans back steepling his hands trying to read between the lines of her questions. "I think you have all done a fine job--given the constraints of our time. Let me see...what might I change? Well our long-term goal is to get through to the aliens and initiate a meeting. At that meeting I am to get help. I believe I am to use any and every means at my disposal to achieve the goal of help for humanity. This assistance from the aliens is more important then me, or any other consideration. Therefore I conclude results count more than me. How long will we have to run every statement through the U.N. and Captain Damube?"

--That was good--

"You are the U.N. here, Mr. Jordan. It is your League rating if Zurich discovers we have said something we should not have said. I will not protect incompetence. You are the Political Communications Consultant--not Captain Damube. The decision on what is sent is yours."

He raises both eyebrows and takes in a deep breath. At that moment Susan believes he already has a plan. She is correct. "I do not know precisely what I am going to do but after reviewing the available data I will say the road less traveled appears most promising. All the reports indicate the question mark is of primary importance to them. So, we have been asking the aliens questions about themselves--I believe the notation in the report was that it was an attempt to appeal to their ego. Clearly that was wrong and so my first plan is to stop asking them questions and give more information about our plight and us. They seemed to respond to that--and I suspect there is concern in our plight."

Susan nods. "Are you worried about giving too much information?"

"Not in the least--we are far too deep in the soup to stop an aggressive force. If they have a repeater station out there they could just as easily have brought in a weapon. We have nothing to lose--in my opinion. And since I decide what is appropriate to send out I am planning on sending relevant data to solving our needs. Am I correct that this is still my decision?"

"Yes."

"Good, then my plan is to appeal to different emotions. They are often the key to entry."

Susan is unsure if they, or Carlos Jordan, even have emotions--but this method is opposite to Stanislaus' method so she will approve it. "As long as I can have a paper trail for protection you are free to do as you like."

Carlos speaks in calm tones as if trying to fathom this statement. "I understand the rules. I have no problem with them." His head tilts. "You do not strike me as a person concerned with covering your posterior."

Susan places one perfectly sculpted hand on the table and rubs it along the top. "You do not strike me as man who is afraid of people." She stares at him defiantly telling him he misspoke.

"I am afraid of people, but I see you are not concerned with your career." He appears to recalibrate and figure out his mistake. Eyes wide with surprise he says: "I admire your loyalty to Quentin. It will be a pleasure working with someone like you."

"Quentin believes you may cave in at the wrong moment. He thinks

Simon may lead you astray." Her eyes sparkle.

His mind clicks back to the memory of her participation in the Athens Olympics. The pictures he saw of her showed nothing but determination.

--Amazing the grace that event bestows on one--

"My friends are important to me. More important than any assignment." He has figured the point of the test. Carlos believes she wants to know if he is really Simon's friend.

"So if I told you Simon is a liability what would you do?"

Carlos is dying to get into the fray at SETI. Nonetheless, Carlos stands. "Thank you for this opportunity to meet. I believe I shall pass on working with SETI and wish you the best of luck." He extends his hand and keeps a cheerful demeanor.

She does not extend her hand. "Good. Simon matters to me as well. So then let's talk about Quentin," Susan says. "Please?" Her arm extends to the chair.

Carlos sits.

She glances at the bug detector again: still green. "You should not underestimate Quentin. He fights and he wins. He is making a difference--even though his tactics are unbounded. And we have to win."

Carlos nods impressed by Susan's candor. "You sound like Simon." He had expected far more distance after hearing Simon's description of her pain. He concludes that whatever has replaced Simon's former ardor it cannot bear her degrading relationship with Quentin. He is impressed again how she can bear it.

She brightens a moment. "We need Simon on the project. He has wisdom and an imaginative view. Did you know it was he who figured out they are interested in question marks?"

"I didn't see that in the official reports. I must have missed it."

"Quentin wants to get rid of him at the earliest possible moment. Your tasks will include keeping Quentin at a distance and Simon Weiss on the team."

"I understand." He examines her to determine if this is purely a professional decision. He decides there is more to it. Carlos will keep the information to himself since he believes there is nothing but pain for Simon with Susan: She has no time for him. He speaks: "We all have to give up so much."

There is no doubt in her mind that Jordan's words are meant to be sympathetic. "I will not allow humanity to be little more than a cruel joke told in an empty forest. Are you willing to risk your life to keep this endeavor from failing?" Force of will keeps her gaze clear and steady.

Seeing he has gone too far, Carlos says: "You will not allow me to do otherwise. We will not fail. We have displayed our limitations for the whole universe to see since our electromagnetic transmissions began to filter from our atmosphere into space. We have nothing left to hide. As a result, I believe they wish to help. I think it is we who are prohibiting help--not them."

As another mild shock rolls through California, the lights dim. The bug detector turns red. Carlos notes it, and then examines every facet of the featureless room. His eyes fix again on the pink broach; outside he hears the call of a crow. "I also think we will need to readjust our notions of causal thinking."

Watching his every move, her impression of him at that moment is of a hunting dog finding game. In the same moment she notes the red light remains on. There is an active bug in the room. His gaze settles briefly on the broach Quentin gave her last night. "Something wrong?"

--Well strange is certainly the word for this man. Carlos Jordan is a brilliant enigma. He will be invaluable if the Rostackmidarifians ever show themselves. He is so odd. No wonder they keep him under wraps. I'm surprised the media hasn't chewed him up like sausage--

"I have the notion that cause and effect is on a different plane with these creatures. The links are different."

"Why?"

He stares down at the red light on the surveillance detector. She taps her broach and he nods his awareness.

Carlo speaks: "I cannot reply to that. I do not have an answer. We will get it--despite my distractions." It is clear he will not say anything without complete security. "Sorry. The quakes in California take some time for me to get used to. I like my ground solid. On my first visit I was greeted by a Pacific Screamer."

"Simon told me about it. I must say that chance meeting has had a great deal to do with your being here today."

"I must thank him." Carlos continues to look about the room with darting eyes.

The lights in the room start flickering. They both glance down at the indication light on the bug detector and immediately the room lights all steady. Carlos says: "I think the correct approach with aliens is clarity; then we follow their lead--if I might be so bold. We are the junior partners needing assistance. They will show us the course. I am sorry to say I doubt we have any other direction." Carlos knows he is giving Quentin information. Carlos also believes Quentin's position to be weak.

"How do you feel about the military's involvement in this?" She asks purely to see how difficult he will be to protect. In months to come she will do everything she possibly can to avoid a collision between Damube and

Carlos. In the end she will fail. The red light of the detector ceases and the green light comes on.

Carlos looks at her right hand resting on her lap. She lifts it just enough to see she carries some device; it is this device that has apparently rendered Quentin's device inoperable. Carlos is sure Quentin's position is weak.

For a moment her beauty strikes him. "We thought policies tied to greed could control a planet. Now, absurdly, we think our policies might impact another world--after we have destroyed ours. Absurd, simply absurd--but you asked about the military: Weaponry to enforce policy is a last resort. It will always be a last resort but it must always be available to enforce policy. Sadly, our policy is survival. If we attack those that help us the assistance will be withdrawn. Nonetheless we must do whatever is necessary to secure aid for humanity. We are stuck in a fun house you and I." He lets in a breath and waits for her response.

Susan takes a moment to try to read him. "If you think I will put up with advertisements like that you are crazy. Want to try again?"

He will consider trusting her. "I believe you will do anything to make this work. I think you will protect the team and its efforts at any expense. You want to know what I think about the military? I have no opinion. You have been looking for my anchors. I have none. We are alike in that. I will get their help if it is possible to get." He pauses and looks deep into her. In that moment he understands what she wants from Quentin Conworth. "You would sell your soul or anything else to save as many people as possible. You are hiding that from Simon because you know there are some activities, and people, he finds reprehensible. You are concerned about selling yourself--or any potential relationship with him--because the means are atrocious from his standpoint. I believe you are right; he would not understand it. Your dedication is rare. So is mine. You can count on me to solve the problem--regardless of the cost." His steady eyes say he speaks the truth. Carlos also believes the only people he can really trust are those that love him.

Susan colors briefly--if only to hide her sense of transparency. "That was impressive. If you cannot handle any part of the assignment I want to know. I hope that is understood."

Carlos admires her in spite of himself. "There is nothing that can be taken from me. I am a gadget with a single task. I have nothing to forfeit. I understand the stakes and the potential issues. I love the game." In the ensuing calm it is the moment before a desert sirocco. Dead dry air fills the room.

An instant of despondency fills Susan's heart.

"What about your views on security for the meeting with

Rostackmidarifians? I might get impetuous in my task," Carlos says casually, with utter disassociation from the event.

"I am not worried about you being impetuous."

--This man has been emotionally eviscerated. His parents I suppose. Amazing he can function at all--

"I think I am flattered." Carlos admires her ability to show her ache at what she sees as her acceptance of his inability to bond.

Susan bears his smile with tight lips. To her, this person sums up loss without hope. A strong person capable of dealing with horrific humans, she finds she has no defense against his kind of agony. Everyone she has ever met fights the ache of desperation with every ounce of determination. He basks in it. Susan recognizes why his personal life is so vacuous. He has almost nothing to share beside torment and he keeps that decantered. She must change the subject. "Did you hear there might be a problem with your accommodations?"

"I heard a sinkhole swallowed the house I was supposed to rent."

"They are working on digging the house out as we speak. It should be ready in a week or so. What type of accommodations would you like in the mean time?"

"So you are approving me for the position?"

"Without reservation," she replies. Sorrow trails her words. Carlos hears the grief and pities her for feeling so poorly about the pain he believes he has long since accepted. It is a standoff between these two.

"Simon has offered to let me stay with him." Carlos has not decided if he will stay with Simon or Roxanne. "Once the house is out of the sinkhole, I will move into Mountain View."

"I will make sure the job is handled efficiently. We have no time for dawdling on any issue." Her deep eyes display a sincerity Carlos adores and he wonders about Simon's recent comment that she is sinking into the mire. Carlos concludes Simon must shed more ardor.

--Only then will he see Susan has no commitments beyond her task and no morality that supersedes her determination. It is a dangerous mixture for anyone who cares for her, or me--

Carlos will haul this perception into consciousness every time he feels himself warming to her. It will keep stillborn any feeling of closeness.

"Well I have to get back down to Mountain View." Susan says. She and Carlos soon exit the room and proceed into the lobby.

All hints of the recent quake are gone. Turning the corridor they pass the front desk and head toward the main entrance seeing only attendants and wait people. It is common after a large quake for guests to retire to their rooms where they try to calm. "May I drop you anywhere?" Susan asks. They exit the hotel passing a tall parking attendant dressed in a black mourning coat, starched white shirt and an English Bowler jauntily placed on his head. The heat assaults them as if it were tear gas yet this individual appears unfazed.

They scan the mansions of Nob Hill surrounding the hotel. Crews work from scaffolding to fix loose siding and repair windows. The clang clang of the streetcars echoes from somewhere on California Street. "Someday I'll ride one of those cars. Yes, I could use a lift to the airport." Carlos has decided to take Susan up on her offer since the cars will be crowded with tourists seeking out quake damage. It is an activity touted on the Net as a highlight of the San Francisco experience.

She looks around. "My car is not yet here. Shall we walk--do you want to see the cable cars?" Susan asks. "I will have them send the car over to the wall." A brightly colored wall eighteen feet high surrounds Nob Hill and the Fairmont compound. Strolling toward the large concrete partition covered with bougainvillea and wisteria they ascend a metal stairway. Decorated in the old time hacienda tradition of adobe, the wall's fragrant flowers cast a hot sweetness to the day. A glass enclosed walkway and its landing crowns the top of the wall. From this spot they see the crowds dressed in bright colors parading by. Carlos holds the door open as they enter the cooled glass promenade that circles the compound.

"They pump up cold air from the old BART tunnels. The hot air is sent down into the shelters to keep them dry and warm," someone says.

Carlos walks through the crowds looking for a bright red cable car on the street below. "It amazes me there are so many people in this city."

"San Francisco is very popular. I have heard it is the third most visited tourist attraction in the world. Did you know there is a building boom going on here? Not enough hotel space. You would never know the population had decreased but I guess that is the idea. I hate deceptions like that--but it is all for the best. Oh, the cable car is going away from us."

"Happens far too often," Carlos says.

Susan shakes her head as she pulls a small cellphone from her purse tapping in a code. An attendant who stands by a small glass booth near the base of Hyde Street hears a beep from his console. Entering the doorway he notes the League two request for a car at the Fairmont and takes the necessary action to send the cable car back up the hill.

"Is there no siesta in Northern California?" Carlos asks, looking back at the huge Victorian mansions inside the wall. His attention is off the car but he knows what has happened.

"In southern California there is siesta but not up here, yet. There might as well be. Very little is done--other than the tourists milling about. Those workers at the Victorians are only there because they are college students paying for room and board. The old time wood structures take a tremendous beating and require constant maintenance." Scores of workers race up and down the scaffolding doing repairs.

The bells clang again. She watches him look toward California Street. "So you have never been on the cable cars?"

"I was going to do that the first time I was here but I was waylaid by that storm. This time--well it will just have to wait. Is that your car?" He points to a sleek white limousine with bulletproof panels parked at the base of the wall.

"Yes. It looks like the cable car is coming back up the hill."

Her words elicit surprise from him in the form of a wide open-mouthed grin. "Thank you. I know you're busy and my bags should have arrived by now."

Susan finds disturbance in his pose. "I am sure Simon would be glad to show you the other sights. He knows the city intimately. Also we will make sure you have your car on site by next week. Did you know all Level Two SETI personnel would be equipped with cars now in addition to Level One personnel? Simon will be beside himself. He has this old time Italian sports car that he keeps saying he is going to take on a midnight ride. Of course I have heard rumors of that car though he never talks to me about it." Susan descends the stair towards the coming cable car. Her car appears at the bottom of the stairs. She speaks to the driver: "Stay close to us." Susan and Carlos climb on the running board of the ancient wooden trolley. They are immediately pushed and jostled further into the car. They sit on a long wooden bench inside the glass-enclosed center. The space in front of them fills with vacationers.

One of the great appeals of these trolleys is their egalitarian nature. Everyone gets treated the same. The brakeman nods to the man in front and the cable car lunges forward. The white car follows the cable car down the center of the hillside street passing pedestrians. Most adolescents gape at the car asking their parents if they can ride in one. Most of the younger children say to their parents, pointing at the car: "What is that?"

Carlos looks around wondering why the aristocratic woman beside him, now completely at home, insisted on this cable car ride--the question will bother him for a long time.

Chapter Twelve

Carlos speaks: "Susan is like Roxanne. She just has no time."

At the horizon, a large brown fog bank, dense as mud, shrouds a desalination plant. Neither Simon nor Carlos can see it--they sit in a protected cove's sandy, shallow chop behind the rebuilt rock jetty protecting Montara harbor. "Susan Willoughby has work time. That does not mean she is in the mire. She is in the midst of a journey that is an all out effort--like my trek through the chaos of Europe, Carlos."

Carlos keeps his eyes closed listening to Simon's wish-talk. Only the "real" need apply for Carlos. The ocean's water swells around the rock jetty and past the tide pools splashing him. Eyes open, Carlos sees the waves reflecting off the tan rock outcropping overhead. The merciless May sun pierces the stitching holes in their three-foot-wide sombreros speckling their lean bodies with a hundred dots. The seawater washes over ankles and calves. A moment later, their two plastic chairs tilt into the slowly rolling swell.

Where the seawall meets the land off to the right, families' barbecue foods in celebration of Memorial Day; young children sit along the water's edge building sand castles as their parents keep an eye on the sea. A wave rises over Simon's midsection. Then in front of him white-green water peaks the rock sea wall in fireworks of spray. "Surf's up, dude." Simon grabs snorkeling gear and begins to struggle into the ancient green fins that hang off the side of his chair.

"Looks like we finally have some waves from a quake coming in," Carlos says. "It is about time. I'm getting cooked out here."

Grabbing three small pieces of metal shaped like pitchforks, Simon leans over and pushes the metal through the white plastic base of the chairs into the metal bars sunk below the sand. He turns the rods ninety degrees to stabilize the chairs in place. Carlos follows suit then takes a white stuff bag full of snorkeling gear and ties it to his chair. Again, from the other side of the sea wall a curtain of spray raises twenty feet into the air. Horns sound and children scramble back from the water to the shore. The two men work purposefully and calmly as another slightly larger set of waves smash against the rock sea wall in front of them. A few moments later deep waves reach the chairs but by then both men have small breathing tanks affixed. With masks they sit belted into their chairs. An earlier generation would have thought this tempting of fate madness. For these men of this generation it is watt-free fun. Six more waves crash against the sea wall, the last one sending spray fifty feet into the air covering the sea wall in white wash and obliterating all the children's sand castles. Thundering off the rock cliffs that form a bowl, the water pours into the protected cove and douses the men again. From the shore, fifty meters behind them, young children yell "Ride it," as they encourage the men to stay affixed to their seats and ride out the waves. This is considered a form of modern day rodeo riding. "Cool." It is a culture intimate with death. It goes on for almost fifteen minutes as the men are buffeted about in the water.

Then, the water flows out. "That should be it for now, Simon says pulling off his mask.

Carlos moves the huge straw sombrero to allow the water to drain all at once. Simon ignores the water dripping from his sombrero; he appears mesmerized by a lithe jogger who seems to court death by running along the sea wall. He speaks reminded of Susan: "I am a bit judgmental about Susan. I might be able to deal with it if she didn't sleep with Quentin--that seems over the line--selling herself like a tart."

"That's a bit stiff," Carlos says replacing his sombrero. "What difference does sex make? You are jealous of Quentin, perhaps, Senor?"

"Disgusted. I find him offensive and the notion of intimacy with him pure degradation." His eyes remain fixed on the jogger wondering if she might just throw herself onto the rocks. It has happened here more than once.

"All the reason to applaud her journey," Carlos, says admiring the concern in Simon's eyes. "But why does sex make any difference?"

"You once asked me about my trek out of Chaos. I told you it was my mom and I--and that she died before we made it over the border into the remains of the European Union. My journey was paved by her love. She sold herself along the way for food, for our lives, for anything we needed. I can't bear seeing a person sell their body like that." The waves muddle over their legs.

"So you did or did not forgive your mom for what she did to save you?"

Looking in Carlos' eyes Simon sees no retort, just concern. "Been a therapist long?" Simon watches the jogger as she turns from the edge of the sea wall and runs back toward shore. Horns sound and the children return to the water's edge. "Better luck next time," he mumbles. Simon points his finger at Carlos. "How come we are talking about me again? This started as a discussion about your friend Roxanne and why she is just your friend. Suddenly the conversation has moved back to the story that was Simon and Susan...again. Just what do you want to know?"

Carlos pushes his sombrero off his head. Letting it rest on his shoulders he leans backwards over the chair. He watches the kites darting over wind generator blades on the cliff above. "We are talking about you because my life is so boring. I have no passions except winning. Roxanne cares for me but cannot love me because of my bottled pain. So what else is there to say about me?" His Adams apple points skyward.

"Or maybe we are talking about me because you are interested in Susan." Simon clears his throat.

Carlos' throat remains skyward. "It does not matter if I am interested in Susan. It will wither; she cares only for her tasks and I cannot care for anyone. Maybe after we solve global climate change I will take her out for a malted and a hot dog." He rubs his eyes. "Susan Willoughby is a national treasure. You really should give her a break."

"My computer analyzed your psychological fitness, Carlos. Seems you have a tendency to keep people away from you."

"Now there is a surprise, Simon. Golly, those tests you doctors do are marvelous. I am learning so much about myself. Did you know I had abusive parents also?" His head pops up and looks for the jogger Simon was watching. She is long gone. "If you psychiatrists were any good when you did those tests you would have written Damube and Quentin up and sent them out to some ranch in Montana where they couldn't do anyone any harm. That reminds me. I have just received the procedures to review for travel on the Armstrong. Is that guy Damube nuts or does he just like to display his shortcomings?"

"He is wacky as a dog in meat plant--if I may be so unprofessional as to say so." Simon sighs at the change in subject. "So why are you staying at my home instead of Roxanne's home?"

Carlos leans over and splashes water on himself. "I cannot bear to be so close and still be so far. It hurts too much."

Simon finds a cold shiver rising through his loins. In the two weeks of sharing his house with Carlos, Simon has been both amazed and saddened at this man's defense of distance as well as his lack of desire to change it. "If you share more of yourself, her emotions might relight."

"Even if I share more she is too smart to try and swim those waters. Roxanne cares about joy and therefore sees my depth of need as an anchor. It would take fifteen years of therapy to make my seas navigable. And I do not have the time to do that now." Two brawny women splash them rushing into the knee-deep water. The women begin to playfully wrestle in the waves off to the right.

Simon watches Carlos flirt with the women in the water by pointing at them and laughing at their antics. One of the brawny women winks at him. Carlos returns the gesture then looks back at Simon. The woman who winked swims away. Part of this friendship is the shared way of avoiding the impotence of their generation--countless trysts.

"Quentin--he is a man for our time: ruthless, voracious, and fully self-engrossed." Simon says. "You and Quentin are alike."

Carlos faces him with a look of mock consternation. "Thank you for that vote of confidence. I think I'll go slit my wrists."

"Neither of you can stand to be too close to people. And he, like you, has performed tasks that are...plainly monumental. So I would not push him too hard."

"Uh, huh--that was a leap." Carlos wonders if he has been discovered. "He does get things done. For example, when I need a spaceship to do my diplomacy thing, it will be ready; very impressive given the absurd notion of such an event--or the state of this sad world. So what is your point?"

Simon stands, scanning those around them. The two women have drifted off by the sea wall and the other adults on the shore show no sign of wanting to get into the water. Then he turns surveying the sea again. The fog has retreated, just beyond the desalination plant, it stands like a trylon and perisphere also soon to be useless. Far in the distance like a hoard of hungry ghosts the fog waits to devour the plant from sight. The bridges on the empty tankers, nesting alongside the water plant, tilt and roll. A bright yellow Coast Guard security dirigible circles the ships and the desalination facility. It will not be listening to those on the beach but concentrating on the sea around the water ships--two were hijacked last week. Simon sits sure he and Carlos have privacy.

"I doubt anyone in that plant will focus on two middle-aged men sitting in the water," Carlos says. "What are you angling toward in this conversation?"

"Here is my point. You need to give the devil his due. Quit pulling out the surveillance equipment everywhere you go."

"Really?" Busted. "This from the man who just scoped the area for surveillance. What is wrong with you people? Quentin has more bugs installed than a Moroccan meat loaf." Carlos shakes his head. "Why shouldn't I remove his reins of terror?"

"Nice pun. Carlos, if you keep shorting out his surveillance equipment you'll be off the project before your house is out of the mud. We need you."

Carlos tilts his head back again and looks toward a distant beach to the south and Simon's house. He notes the sea and sun will soon own that long, wood-faced waterside building. "So you are saying talk outside, like here, and otherwise consider myself a prisoner of Quentin's paranoia."

"Exactly. What are you looking for?"

"Roxanne. You are as nutty as Quentin is," Carlos says. He looks again at the house Simon loves. "That house could fall in on you in virtually any storm now. You'd be thrown about like a pebble. You shouldn't stay much longer. Yet you do. It is indicative of our time that we stay in places that are dangerous just because we are afraid of the consequences." His head snaps forward.

"Quit changing the subject."

"I am not ready to give him that victory yet. Besides, Quentin respects strength not submission.."

"That is completely wrong in our situation. He doesn't care a wit about your strength. Once you are on his team you are measured first and foremost on your ability to submit."

"His kingdom is on the line. He will put up with whatever I do until I either achieve something that makes me superfluous or he is sure I cannot help him. Besides he does not know yet who is disabling his bugs--and I like messing with him."

Simon folds his arms exasperated. He finds Carlos a most stubborn person some times. "Well then we are both fools. I am trying to hang onto a doomed house. You are trying to save a doomed species while keeping yourself miles away from anyone in that species. And to top it off you are jeopardizing your task by mooning a maniac. Quentin can get whatever is needed to make this work. The price for that capability is our being able to deal with his paranoia. Please, Carlos, just deal with it."

Carlos faces Simon and brings his sombrero over his head. "I was not expecting him to be so ever present." Carlos looks at the small waves around them. "How did you know it was me who was crippling the surveillance systems?"

"Dawn disables his bugs in a different way and no one else bothers. Susan told me you have a mania for security. The rest was easy. Quentin can't be far behind in his reasoning." Simon's catches a female figure on the shore watching them.

Carlos, like a boy caught peeking in his sister's drawers, immediately stares out at the desalination plant. "The gamble is too high you say. Okay, I will leave his bugs alone. I will not pull out, or soak down another bug, until I make some monumental advancement with the aliens. But then I am going to zap a group of them in celebration. Is that okay with you?"

"Still wrong. He is nuts. But that will do for now." Simon, who has seen Carlos' odd behavior, narrows his focus. "Someone is waving at us. I guess that is your friend, Roxanne." Simon sees Carlos turn anxiously flipping the hat from his head. The burst of excitement surprises him. Simon is dumbfounded when Carlos stands to wave and yell to the tall woman in the fluorescent pink bathing suit top. Simon has never seen this man so animate. Carlos, his face a Christmas morning, points to Simon beside them. The woman strolls out into the calm waters holding a straw bag in her right hand and removing a wrap of white cloth from around her hips to keep it dry.

Carlos' bright white teeth stun Simon; Simon has never seen this brightness either. "Don't look so surprised. As far as the other item--I mean what I say. I don't like dictators but I will do as you say," Carlos says, waving at Roxanne.

Simon watches this mystery woman approach and wants to ask Carlos if there can be such things as dictators of the heart. As a child of his time he does not fully recognize that problems of loving did not start with global climate change. But at this moment, Simon blames Carlos' distance from Roxanne, and his own failed romance with Susan Willoughby, on climate change. It has become common. "When appropriate I will help you zap our dictator's bugs."

"A partner in crime, at last." Carlos says, eyes again on Roxanne.

"Well you two look like the picture of leisure," Roxanne says, as she gets closer. After briefly seeing the light in Carlos' eyes she examines the man beside Carlos. "Hi," she extends her hand. "I am Roxanne Gladstone." Carlos had said nothing to her about another person being present for their picnic.

"One of my dearest friends--Roxanne. This is Dr. Simon Weiss, a very wise man."

Roxanne's eyes widen. "You neglected to tell me we would have your savior here, Carlos." She leans forward kissing Simon on the cheek, her right hand cupping the side of his face. "Thank you," she whispers. Without waiting for response she kisses Carlos hello on the cheek. Simon can still feel the touch of her lips. Noting Simon's disruption at her caress, Roxanne smiles as she places her bag on a chair. She looks down at Carlos' right foot. He has no socks on to cover his missing pinky toe--that means he likes this man, Simon. She adores the quizzical look that now owns Simon's face. "The kiss was for the bus ride in the storm. He hates storms."

Simon is astounded to see Carlos blush bright red. "I did not really save him. I actually arranged the whole thing so we could meet and I could persuade him to work with us. I am devious that way."

"I doubt it," she says watching the way his lips move and measuring the light in his eyes. His pain adds depth to the smile. She likes that in a man. It shows heart. The dark skin and thin physique appeal to her. She looks over to Carlos examining his cheeks and his eyes. He appears a bit angry, and she guesses it has something to do with the new assignment. He has called her twice this week to talk and insisted on this outing today--of course without full disclosure--but she is used to that from him. She looks down at his toe so Carlos notices. He smiles, proud of himself. She resolves to attend to the friendship of Doctor Simon Weiss. Roxanne has had a rough week and the notion of a new friend cheers her. She also decides this new assignment is a godsend for Carlos--despite those complaints about the dictator with the psychotic son she has been training.

Roxanne sits down in her chair pulling aside the straps of her bathing suit wondering if Simon is a pseudo-libertine like Carlos. Instead of continuing to go topless she waits seeing Simon react and decides to err on the side of conservatism. Fifteen years ago she would have wondered why his opinion of her might matter, but no more. She immediately feels this man owns a bow to her heartstrings.

"So have you boys been out in the water playing with quake-waves?" She puts sunscreen on her arms.

"Just chatting about work and the people we work with," Simon says. "Carlos has told me about you--I have been wanting to meet you for a year. My family and I had a Gum-Drop Shelter. They were very popular in Europe. I can't tell you the number of times I played with the plastic coated candy. It was a wonderful gift."

"My dad would be pleased to hear that--"

"I would love to swim out and catch some dinner," Carlos says interrupting them. He bolts out of his chair in a mad dash toward sea wall. Roxanne and Simon look at each other with mirth and confusion.

"He seems different around you," Simon says. His eyes slow the world for her.

"He keeps trying to convince me to love him. That was his attempt at showing that he is jealous."

"And he isn't?" Simon asks unsure of what he has seen. He thought he was seeing Carlos making room for him.

"Not in the least--when we were lovers he found out about another man and me. He did not quite catch us embracing but this man was holding me far to close as Carlos approached one day. Carlos made it quite clear to me he had no problems with sex. I made it quite clear that meant he did not care. Ever since then he has been practicing jealousy. What did you think of the performance?"

"He had me completely fooled. Are you sure about this?" Simon asks watching Carlos swim toward the sea wall.

"You thought he was giving us some space."

Simon worries this woman may be an entry into a vulnerable part of Carlos Jordan. She seems a bit too open about someone as important as Carlos. He does not know how bright and perceptive Roxanne is and how normally she would never be this open about Carlos. "He does not know you love him."

"He does. But he also knows we are not right for each other and he takes that issue up as a challenge--like a point in a negotiating session. His desire to resolve conflict is his greatest strength and his deepest weakness."

"But it isn't a conflict," Simon says puzzled by all this.

"It is all conflict, inside him. Shall we swim?"

Scrambling up the side of the jetty onto the sea wall, Carlos looks around behind him and watches the couple wade into the water.

--I have missed being with people these last few years--

Simon and Roxanne swim toward the sea wall. Simon's large white stuff bag containing his snorkel and mask trails behind. Carlos remains fixed on them, believing he feels an ache in his heart for the love he cannot have from Roxanne. After feeling as much as he can bear, he leans back looking at the sky. For the first time he sees more than just a lid to his world. He sees an escape.

Moments later, Simon and Roxanne climb the lee face of the rock wall. Simon looses his balance because he is carrying the stuff bag. Roxanne grabs him. In that moment, their hands link--so do their souls. Simon is taken completely off-guard. Embarrassed, he looks up furtively. Carlos has disappeared on the other side. Simon looks at her hand, then at her. "Why are you so open about Carlos? You might give an enemy an opening."

"Are you an enemy of his?" Roxanne finds herself flushed despite the cold water on her body. She brushes her hair back from her eyes. "How could

I not trust you?" She lets go of his hand. A moment later Carlos appears to take Roxanne's other hand and pulls her to the top of the sea wall. She sees a small rockfish. "Last one in cleans the fish." In trio they run wildly off the black steel structure that extends out the deep side of the sea wall and splash down into the grimy water. Underwater, Carlos swims away without looking back. When he rises to the surface a few seconds later he hears their laughter. Riding the large waves that bounce off the sea wall, Carlos spins quickly but cannot find Simon and Roxanne because they ride a different swell. Roxanne pops up from behind and splashes him. "That's for letting go of my hand." He swims trying to dunk her. "You can't get me Nine-Toes. I'm too quick." When just out of range she splashes him again. "And that's for not really getting jealous." Roxanne dives away under the water and Carlos follows her. They pop up and she splashes him again. "And that's for trying to sell me on your jealousy."

"Didn't buy it, huh? Simon bought it. I thought I was rather good."

Roxanne's tightly pursed lips open. "How come you didn't tell me you'd be here with Simon? You indicated you would be here alone."

"You can see why. I didn't tell you because I wanted to keep you two apart." A raucous play session follows with all three jumping, dunking, and splashing each other. Simon soon treads water watching them play tag in the waves. Roxanne is no match for Carlos' swimming, but she will not let him be; Simon sees love in her every move--the love of a sister. Carlos' wild play dumbfounds him.

"Cut it out, Roxanne." Carlos voice raises a notch as he is dunked repeatedly.

She looks deeply into his soul. "I am sorry, Nine-Toes. You have made me very happy today." Carlos quickly turns his head to find out how far away Simon is and did he hear that. "He heard," she says with a perfect smile.

"You are going to like him."

"I already do."

Carlos fruitlessly tries to dunk her and she evades him easily. Her face glistens with droplets of water. "So how is work?" He suddenly asks treading water just outside her reach.

Roxanne is used to this from Carlos and she lets it all pass. "Not great, that young girl, Molly, is gone and your boss' kid Taylor is coming back again."

"He might be my boss."

"Yes, Carlos--in any case it is a dreary story. Oh, Dr. Sullivan finally agreed to let me continue to teach rescue training. Guide Dogs Inc, is making money hand over fist because of it. My house needs a new roof and as soon as you get your car back, you are taking me for a long ride."

"You like the guide dog center?" Simon asks paddling over--glad the topic has moved on to something less personal.

"For most of the three years," Roxanne answers turning to face him. She sees Simon's worry and rolls over onto her back and floats. Carlos raises his right eyebrow. He wrinkles his brow at seeing the connection so quick to occur. "What about Damube? Know I cannot speak of him. I am a professional and the private life of our League One clients is of global importance." She bats her eyes.

"Is his son still there? Damube left two weeks ago," Simon says treading closer to her.

"He was returned again under order from the courts. He is a handful, that kid."

"So I have heard," Simon says.

"Our ever-lovable Stanislaus Damube?" Carlos asks. "Roxanne, Dambue is that looney-tune with the patent on anal retentiveness."

"See here. Again it isn't so good to be secretive with your friends." She smiles pleased with herself. "And you? What do you do at NorCal, Dr. Weiss?" She treads water now her hands moving just inches from Simon's body.

"I am a therapist," Simon says unsure of just what to do. He works hard not to look deeply at her but continually fails.

"I knew that," Roxanne looks over to Carlos with a question in her eyes. Carlos shakes his head no. He is still unwilling to share with Simon what he has told Roxanne. Her lips' purse; in truth Roxanne doesn't like it when Carlos is jealous.

Simon concludes she knows exactly what Carlos is doing and why he is doing it. The breach of security does not bother him. It just does not seem important at this moment. "You know what we are doing," Simon says without reproach.

Roxanne looks at Carlos as if to say: Trust us. "I suppose I do know what you are doing. But why does working with aliens require a psychiatrist?"

"I was hired as a second in command because of my background in communication theory. I became staff psychiatrist after Captain Damube came on board and I was demoted. And now, with Carlos here, I remain merely a lowly therapist."

"Too bad," Roxanne says, shaking her head. "On the other hand contact with aliens is something I would not talk about in polite company. They might put you all in the booby hatch."

Carlos then floats on his back with his toes under the water. He paddles with his arms to keep from being pulled toward the wall. "I keep telling you, Roxanne, they cannot put us in the booby-hatch because we is They." Carlos looks at Simon. "Roxanne does not really believe we are in contact with aliens. She thinks I am making it up to keep from telling her what we really do."

Roxanne smiles to herself. She decides to see how far it goes. "You have lied to me before about what you were doing...more than once."

"When?"

"When Lars died. You knew I wanted to look for him but you said you were too busy. Too busy looking for him."

"That was a dangerous time."

"Oh, and this is not?" She dunks her head under the water to cool off. When she pops up her eyes dart toward Simon. He does not look away this time. Only waves move.

"Well in a few weeks they will announce our discovery as a leak to boost morale, then you may apologize about all this," Carlos says mocking hurt.

"Do not apologize," Simon says to Roxanne. "Keep him guessing."

Roxanne suddenly thrashes about in the water like a butterfly shaking off a cocoon. "Carlos and I had a friend--this man Lars. For a while there we were the three musketeers. I long for those days. Will you be our friend?"

"My honor, madam." Glancing at each other, the eyes of these three people betray the light of coming home. It is clear to all of them they will know each other for a long time forward. Only Roxanne can guess at Carlos' detached analysis seeing her with Simon. Carlos tells himself Simon and Roxanne are similar: The joy of the moment owns their souls. Carlos cannot imagine the happiness that is filling their hearts and overcoming their fear of loss. He decides their caring for each other will keep them both near him. He decides that is important to him. In any case, he is sure Roxanne will ride it without remorse because nothing will hurt him. Neither Simon nor Roxanne have such knowledge and their emotions are in tumult.

"Lars would have liked you," Roxanne says.

Simon decides she is moving too quickly. "I am flattered," he says. He wonders for a moment if Lars and Roxanne slept together then chastises himself for being an ass. Carlos splashes Simon. In utter surprise Simon looks at Carlos. Roxanne jumps on top of both of them. For the next few minutes they splash about in a joy that reminds them of their youth. Soon they are diving under the water exploring the sea life and hunting abalone and shrimp for dinner. Pointing at this and that they glide under the waves like newborn creatures. Showing each other anemone and starfish, crabs and shrimp, the plentiful sea life is like a palette for their happiness and the sea floor a canvas.

Carlos rises to the surface and sees Simon and Roxanne alongside the metal ladder extending from the sea wall. He silently floats watching the glint in Roxanne's eyes as she speaks to Simon. Their song is as clear as the water around them. Carlos slips back under water unwilling to confront it. Within a few minutes he has hauled Simon's stuff bag filled with food to the surface. He sees his friends floating among the swells on their backs, talking. All hints of remorse, he decides, must appear purged from his being. In the distance he hears the sounds of motors and looks back at the desalination plant. The waterships remain tied in place but the dirigible seems to have changed its course from circular to linear and it appears to be heading north. Carlos peers into the yellowing fog but sees nothing. "I am getting jealous. How about some lunch?" Carlos says merrily to alert them.

"You two go ahead. I want to swim out to the raft and back. I'll meet you at the chairs." Without a word Simon is swimming at a furious pace toward the raft tied to an old buoy a hundred yards out in the sea.

Roxanne grabs the stuff bag from Carlos to head back to the sea wall. "We should wait," Carlos says glancing casually past her to the desalination plant. "You embarrassed him."

"Please, Carlos." She sees his shift in gaze and Roxanne places her arm on Carlos shoulder. "He likes me--a lot."

"I wish it were me," Carlos says, watching her dreamy look. "And you?"

Roxanne looks at him. "I would jump him tonight if I could," she says gleefully. "He seems blind to your indifference. He thinks you really do love me. Do you think he likes me?"

Carlos ignores the question looking for the dirigible but cannot see it. "Don't you have any concern for my feelings whatsoever?"

She places her arms around his neck and stares past him trying to figure out what he is looking for. "You and I were never meant to be. We both knew someday a man would enter our life. Is he a bad choice for me?" Her eyes scan the horizon.

"I wish you would not do that to me. It makes me feel like a kid again."

"You are welcome. There is someone for you, Carlos, but you'll never find her until you let go of me." He pulls back but it is not for her: His eyes narrow, focusing well passed her. Her gaze drops to the water. She lets her arms drop. "Carlos, I will tell you a secret I've kept from you for years. I am telling you because I see a chance with Simon I thought I would never have and I know if you say boo, he will head off in the opposite direction like a bullet. But first--what are you looking at?" His practiced casual gaze tells her he is weighing his options. "Carlos, dear, if I thought there was any chance whatsoever that you really could and would be my lover you could not pry me apart from you with a crowbar--" He stares at all her facades dropped. "--but it just isn't the case. I was your first love and I am your very best friend. Trust me--there is someone else for you." She sees concern and confusion. It is at times like this that Roxanne knows she is seeing the real Carlos Jordan.

The sadness in her eyes tells Carlos she believes everything that she says and this shocks him. It never occurs to him he might be the problem because he did not really love her. "I do not believe you," he says.

The warmth in her eyes flares. She has broken through Carlos' concerns into the moment of his heart. Her hand comes out of the water and her index finger points directly at his nose--not an inch away from him. "Don't even consider that negotiating crap with me again, Bucko. Cut it out." Her firm eyes stare straight into him. He blinks.

"Sorry," Carlos wears the goofy grin of a court jester. She knows this is the real him as well.

"I told you to stop that."

A dark emotion he will not talk about rides his face.

Roxanne worries about him now. He had that same sad look the day she went off to New York. She remembers him beside an old candy machine, leaning on it--hiding from her. One long arm at his side, the other arm across his chest clutching himself, he wore a plastic smile under tear-glazed eyes frozen in time and space. His bottom lip had been quivering. She had watched from inside the bus making sure he could not see her. Occasionally, a shudder had run through his body and then it would disappear like an object drawn into the core of his being never to be seen again. As the bus had pulled out she saw him cry.

Roxanne stares at him. "I have seen this look before and it means you are having trouble."

"I am not. You said I have already lost you and I am just blind to the cause."

"You never lost me. Carlos, I am just not the one for you. I am however the only one you let in," she says quietly.

"I know. I know, but," he treads water slowly moving his arms back in forth in a fluid motion. His eyes dart to the desalination plant after a puff of black smoke rises into the air. Carlos wonders why he does not hear engines anymore or see the dirigible. "Here we go again. Fire in the hole."

"You have developed a flair for the melodramatic," she says, concerned eyes glued to his distant gaze. Then she turns, sees the smoke and says: "I think this woman Susan has stirred something in you." Carlos admires her calm.

"Now who is negotiating? Susan and I have a commonality but it is not love." They both stare out to the plant as more puffs of smoke appear from it. His eyes display a mix of curiosity and resignation.

"Add maudlin romanticism to your resume, will you?" Roxanne keeps watching Simon wishing he would hurry up and get back here. Red flamed explosions and black smoke ascend from the tankers. Both see the dirigible appear from the sun. Bright red tracer bullets arc downward toward the sea swells. "Oh, damn." Simon, out of breath, appears beside them. "Let's go man," Roxanne says, pulling on Simon's arm. "There is a gun battle at the desalination plant." They all swim up to the sea wall. Roxanne first races up over the other side and scampers into the shallow water.

A moment later Simon and Carlos jump in the water. When they come up the sea is bathed in bright yellow light. Roxanne is transfixed staring behind the two friends. None of them can see anything over the rocks. "What is it?" Simon asks.

"The desalination plant--it just went boom." Trailing her words are the sounds of motors and distant machine gun fire. Roxanne watches a yellow glow fade as angry black clouds rise skyward. A bright yellow dirigible emerges overhead. "I cannot see what they are shooting at but they are coming this way--fast." She looks up from the sea wall and backs closer to the rock for cover. Moments later a small blue boat rounds the corner. Two individuals are on the boat--one driving and one shooting up at the dirigible. The boat crashes into Simon's chairs sending them flying. People on the beach scatter, as the dirigible peppers the boat with fire. The boat skis onto the beach area and two people jump from it heading straight into the crowd. Soldiers on the dirigible keep firing. Three vacationers fall to the ground. Those from the boat rush up the rocky hillside toward the wind generators. Fire control on the dirigible centers on escapees from the boat as it cuts one of them down before the top of the cliff. Reaching the tall white wind generator towers, the other terrorist dives under the sleek blades. Weapons fire immediately ceases. The terrorist scampers away through hundreds of towers and into an old abandoned housing development. A diver jumps from the dirigible into the water near shore.

"They will never get the other one," Roxanne says standing on a submerged rock between her two friends. "Why destroy a desalination plant?"

"It is destruction for the sake of destruction. I saw it in Spain. The population gets to the point where they don't buy it anymore and they just want to hurt those who have what they do not have. It's suicide--and unstoppable in a society once it starts."

"The hoarding of resources did this," Roxanne says. "Goddamn it all anyway." She looks at Carlos. "What the hell is wrong with you people? How much is enough?"

"What are you mad at him for?" Simon asks.

"You are 'They' remember? I am mad at you as well. You both have the inside track on this. You have comfort, and pretty much everything else you need because you just happen to be in the right place at the right time." The dirigible begins to circle above the generator blades keeping well clear of their wash. The diver emerges from the water. He ignores the bodies of the wounded civilians on the beach and hurries up to the dead terrorist.

"Hey, what about the living? That just isn't right." She yells looking at Simon. "That kid, Damube's kid, Taylor. You know why he is back here in California? He killed a blind girl three days ago."

"What? Why?" Simon asks.

"He wanted her dog." Roxanne begins to cry. Carlos watches the soldier check the dead body. Through her tears: "She had no family and he has connections so he is going to get off with an additional three months at the guide dog facility. If it had happened the other way the blind girl would be toast. It is not right."

"Was it an accident or maliciousness?" Carlos asks wanting to get more information on Damube.

"Oh, an accident--he was merely trying to break her leg at the time, but she fell forward hitting her head on a rock. Then the little shit threw her away into a garbage heap to hide his deed. I'm going home. You both sicken me."

Chapter Thirteen

The disagreement between environment and its petulant child, humanity, continues unabated.

A drought scorching the Iberian Peninsula spreads east during May turning many of the remaining French and Italian Riviera towns into ghost towns--except where Mediterranean storms have washed civilization away. The warlords, running from none but the planet's furies strike farther north for food and water. The U.N. forces hold the line for much of June until a Fujita Class Five windstorm flattens Paris, wiping out U.N. central military command for Western Europe. So badly has the area been hit; people are forcibly trucked into the countryside and given weapons to protect the city from the warlords. The city falls to a warlord from Kosavo on Bastille Day and preparations for moving U.N. command and control from Zurich to Reykjavik, Iceland commences in earnest.

In the Ukrainian desert, raiders scour the countryside for slaves to generate power. Like the Mongol hordes of centuries past claiming rights, raiders fight their way east to Viet Nam and west to Tehran. Bloody battles on horseback cover the Mideast and the Balkans. The remains of oil wells blasted apart form a common bond between invader and defender: Human sacrifice is common. Turkey ceases to exist as a state. Its citizens continue to succumb to the most virulent form of flesh eating bacteria. The plague forms a barrier, a wall, as the inevitable clash between the Ukrainians and the warlords of Southern Europe threaten to return Europe to pre-history.

Further east, in what was China, the now meager population clings to the coastal towns, backs to the water, their armies fighting raiding parties coming from the west, Korea and Southeast Asia. India's massive landforms still protects it. With population no longer a burden, India is quickly becoming a major power--despite its vulnerability to the massive cyclones and flooding. The Indian Air Force--a mercenary organization dropping bombs on enemies and picking up gold from clients--rules the skies over most of Asia. Absurdly, the funds go to pay off an old World Bank debt: the price the sub-continent pays to dominate the area.

Elsewhere on the planet, the intense storms brings death toll reports in six figures. Along the west coast of Africa, mining keeps the population steady as well-equipped forces guard the borders and food ships continue to supply food. Famine grows widespread in eastern Africa as the mighty corporate farms continue to fail one after the other. In South Africa, an iron willed dictator submits to the U.N. on only the occasional issue. Diamonds and raw materials keep flowing out of the country while Brazilians, in a reverse of the old slave traffic pattern are brought in to work. Rio is a slave port. The old dictator in South America, the jungle, breeds disease and anarchy. The Amazon is the true winner in climate change. In Australia, some parts of the continent have not been heard from in months. The pre-nineteenth century life-style feared by Carlos' generation is becoming a reality as the population dips just below two billion.

Virtual reality systems, Head-Clamps, and terrorism, grows throughout North America. Drug use, suicide, and civil disturbances are no longer reported by the news media. Riots break out on college campuses over a lack of educational materials and a new term enters the language: "Finalists." The word denotes the belief by most college students that they are to be the final generation of humanity. No one contradicts them. Escape rules the wealthy as they slowly come to see that their wealth is useless and recognition of their culpability rises with every dawn.

In the US Northwest, still essentially in tact, despite the horrific pounding of rain and snow, the flooding that began in April continues through June. Thankfully no one has built on the flood plains and the net result of the floods is good soil for planting. Efforts at replanting the forests continue with moderate success while migrants called "Walkers" wander the west coast in search of safe seasons and work. Most manufacturing in the US is done in the Northwest, due to the temperate climate and an abundance of waterpower. A ring of military bases surrounds the region.

Wheat and other grains pour out of Canada feeding North America and U.N. held Europe--thanks to the millions of tons of soil trucked in from the drying US Midwest. Unfortunately the market need--along with the population--decreases every day. In the East, the horrific windstorms that precede the hurricane season are again pounding what is left of the inland cities. In Texas, martial law has been declared and illegal aliens are shot on sight. Oblivion appears poised to overtake humanity.

California's snow pack from winter continues to decline. A good harvest is predicted for the San Joaquin Valley this summer--until a set of eight Pacific Screamers pounds the state over June destroying the water distribution system and devastating towns on the western slopes of the Sierra Nevada in tidal waves of mud. Showers again become a luxury and farming in the San Joaquin Valley ceases. The tourist industry booms as more and more people are drawn to San Francisco "The Earthquake Capitol of the World." In Mountain View, at SETI, due to ever increasing funding, people remain well off as privileges are extended and their knowledge of worldwide events is only available through hackers using the old ArpaNet--the precursor of the Internet. Those who fulfill administrative or engineering functions are given extra wattage and water allowances--lower level individuals get a pay raise. All SETI vehicles are bulletproofed--since travel on roadways always attracts gunfire. A U.N. catalogue mall is built near Huntsville. The SETI-Mountain View mall will open soon. Promises of regular shuttle service ferrying workers from SETI--and the local SETI contractors--to the mall thrill those who have never ridden in a vehicle. Many cannot wait to see examples of the newest industrial wonders: high tech protection devices, personnel hygiene devices, low wattage appliances, the newest pharmaceuticals, as well as other forms of the Head-Clamp--the ultimate entertainment systems. An eating area with ethnic cuisines and a small car dealership will also be part of the mall.

This extraordinary expense was pushed though after a report circulated at U.N. Central Command regarding the old time college-campus work environments of the Silicon Valley heydays. The report had displayed examples of employees biking, dining, playing volleyball--all discussing homelessness as if it were a scene from a TV show. The reports said a work-environment shielding employees from truth, making them feel elite--as well as disinterested in others' pain when they encounter it can also foster a total dissociation from the misery of their fellow humans.

A second report delineating how qualified technicians were increasingly scarce, and that problems with depression robbing key programs of workers followed soon afterward. The catalogue showrooms squeaked through--after Quentin finally agreed to allow information on the aliens to be shared with the public. Two more SETI technicians kill themselves despite the heralded coming of the catalogue mall.

Despite the best attempts of all, desperation grows this early summer. The Rostackmidarifians remain out of contact and articles begin to appear in the nets that people can expect more restrictions on their lives. Then in early July, news reports glut the airwaves that humanity has made contact with an alien race who has agreed to help solve global climate change. A number of reputable news people dare the General Assembly to deny the report. After two weeks of jousting, the Under-Secretary of Space announces that indeed there are repeating signals that might be from aliens but another year or two of research must be done before a meeting can be arranged with the unknown race. The mood in Huntsville and Mountain View changes immediately as SETI workers are treated like heroes by their neighbors--until someone in Huntsville lets known the dialogue has turned into a monologue. The environment's spanking of humanity seems to have no effect--the hoarding of energy and resources continues at a furious pace. Riots and wanton destruction can be seen from any window day or night. The environment of humanity's collective mind has finally surfaced.

Carlos walks back to his office, cursing the plague of stupidity that has descended this late July afternoon. It is one o'clock and already the technicians have had three major screw-ups with the antenna array. Another Pacific Screamer is due in tonight. The storm will be severe. People tell their managers they feel ill and leave--so almost no one is around this afternoon. It is a routine formed for dealing with storms. Carlos will be off line for the rest of the day.

He peers out his top floor window to the vacant grounds below; SETI looks as if it were populated by the dead. He tells himself it is understandable--almost no one has had time to complete repairs from the previous storm and everyone panicked with the news of another Pacific Screamer. Their ferocity kills by the thousands. Fear and mourning devastates any initiative and stalls thoughts of work--every threat takes all the workers' attention and mistakes proliferate. Carlos' eyes wander to the concrete bunker one-hundred yards distant; the disaster supply depot is jammed to capacity.

Plywood is plentiful. A peculiar event in Carlos' eyes. Plywood is usually in great demand--but not this summer. He has heard some no longer even try to effect repairs, as a result the once valuable resource abounds. People go out and buy food, or get drunk and wait to die--figuring if death does not meet them they can come to work the next day and deal with mistakes--if their boss is still alive. The chains of command crumple after every storm. Thinking about it, Carlos realizes signs of wind and storm damage still litter the SETI campus. Scarred buildings are being left to rot, trees remain on the roads; dead bodies can still be found in remote ditches. The decay of human society has changed from rust to fire and Carlos stands, sure, without the alien's assistance, humanity will end in a blaze of anger, self-involvement and denial.

Carlos looks away and logs into his computer running a diagnostic on the communication services--he has become an able technician in the last few months. The local communication lines show full usage, jammed with administrators and middle level managers up and down California making arrangements for dealing with the newest storm. There is nothing more to do today--but Carlos plans to stay at work. Of all the locations in the Bay Area he knows only SETI and the U.N. NorCal offices in San Francisco are truly safe. Besides, his house down the street has no meaning for him. If it is destroyed, it matters little--especially since he is not getting any response from the aliens. He had been hoping that the reports of alien contact he leaked out on the airwaves would help but so far every message might as well have been sent to a void.

To make matters worse, Carlos spends far too much time thinking about Roxanne. Somehow she has become his solace; her comments on the beach about being his first love, not his only love, still parade though his brain and the footsteps hurt. He tells himself again he can fix his feelings but his thoughts ring false. They have for weeks, and Carlos has taken to following Simon into San Francisco for wild times and trysts with strange women. Rather than healing his loneliness, the non-stop affairs with tourists and bureaucrats have made him even more lonely and depressed. Carlos doesn't care; he works harder.

Rocking back and forth in the squeaky green vinyl office chair and looking at his message files again, Carlos finds he cannot keep still; his pride haunts him like a hungry ghost while the announcement of contact with an alien culture mocks his efforts. "Three months wasted," he mutters. Carlos scans the list of messages sent by Damube looking for a pattern. The only pattern he can see is the incessant repeating of the question mark and the lack of punctuation. The constant interrogatory of all the statements initially seemed as though they might be a problem but Carlos changed that tone--still no progress. Looking at his notes and pondering what progress has been made on getting the search for the alien repeater station suspended, he checks for email messages from Susan; nothing is there. Simon had postulated that perhaps the search for the repeater station might be the issue since communication ceased soon after the search began for the alien's outpost. Susan seemed to pay attention but so far there has been no indication of her plan to deal with it. Carlos phones Quentin again; there is no answer still.

--Why did they stop? Did we send a message that said stop transmitting? Could they have possibly just decided to forget us? That would be too cruel of a joke and they would not do that, or would they? I do not understand--

Many believe the aliens are just ignoring humanity for some reason of their own. A few in Iceland have begun to say the alien contact was of no significance. All attempts at limiting funding however have failed thanks to Quentin's firm grip and increasing voice in the affairs of the planet. Carlos finds, despite his dislike of Quentin and his methods, that Simon was right. Quentin does a monumental job of keeping the program going in a difficult time. Carlos squints as sunlight bounces off the opening door handle; Simon enters the small bare office.

The neat spare office reflects its occupant. A parade of colored flowers: mums, fuscias, and pansies brightly line the shelves while mounds of paper and stock furniture add a tone of sadness to the room. The chair is simple with no back and the desk, clean and polished. Only a photo of some unknown tropical island hangs on the wall. Simon crosses the room and leans his arms against the windowpane. Looking out over the circus-top-building that will house the catalog mall, he says: "I heard on the radio the USGS predicted another half-degree increase in mean global temperature. And I said to myself, so what? There was a time that news would make me chew through a cinder-block wall."

It means a great deal to Carlos that Simon shares his pains. Simon knows this; he worries about Carlos' isolation. "Have you called Roxanne, yet?" Carlos asks.

"Nor shall I." A seige mentality has over taken Simon. Ever since that get-together with Roxanne, Simon has felt Carlos on the skids. Normally Simon would not worry about Carlos' pain--seeing it as a good step forward-- but depression is dangerous. Simon feels it is best to purposely stay away from Roxanne for the time being and keep close tabs on Carlos. Simon prays she will not call; his resolve weakens with every passing day.

"It will not hurt me, Simon."

"I know. This just isn't the right time." Simon turns from the windowpane, leans his back against the frame and speaks. "I was wondering if you want to come over and keep me company while I get my house ready for the storm?"

"Jest not, friend. I'll help you finish those storm doors and shutters but I will not spend another storm in the land of the thundering waves. Your home is my nightmare for a storm structure."

"I finished the storm doors last night."

"After you dropped me off at four in the morning?" Carlos asks, remembering the wild night they spent at the Top of the Mark. "Do you ever sleep?"

Simon wants to say he knows there will be plenty of time for sleep but he does not. Simon doesn't really share his pain with Carlos. "It only took an hour or two. So you'll spend a storm alone again? I thought you mentioned something about not wanting to do that anymore?" Then, seeing stubble on Carlos' face, Simon realizes Carlos didn't even enter his home when he dropped him off. "It looks like you did not sleep either."

Carlos rubs his chin. "I had some ideas I wanted to test out. And I'm nonplused the technicians have brought down the array again. We are not doing enough." Carlos continues after Simon nods: "I went through the messages one more time. I checked structure and subtext. I checked grammar and I checked patterns. I checked word usage and I checked the number and type of punctuation marks. The only thing I found was the same thing we already knew. Nothing. Oh, I tried to correlate time with responses this morning. I found nothing beyond our first take that we were being less than honest the whole time. And I still say lying can't be that big of an issue." Carlos squeaks back in his chair. "I have tried every emotional link I can think of: Sympathy, despair, concern, joy, love, pity--you name it I have tried it. Not a damn thing in response. It is possible they made some calculations. They realized we were going to be gone and decided not to bother with us." It is this scenario that haunts everyone at SETI: Suppose the aliens just decided to forget us?

"I still cannot subscribe to the notion that it was just a lark," Simon says. "I still think our search systems for the repeater interfere with communication."

"Technology as a limitation--The Galileo Syndrome. Have you talked to Susan again about suspending the search for the repeater?" Carlos asks.

"She is still working on it but so far there is no decision." Simon folds his arms. "Susan says she is having trouble with Quentin because there is no proof."

"Proof. I swear I am sick of proof. Just what does it take to realize our mania for certainty put us in this tragedy? We need to get Quentin to suspend the search for a week--or even a few days."

"If Susan really believes it is important she will get him to do it," Simon says distractedly. He has little desire to talk to Susan anymore. As Simon sees it, the infection in her heart has spread throughout her being. He does not yet know his ardor for Roxanne has spirited away his desire for Susan. "All right. I'll talk to her just before I leave."

"No, let me. You talk to Quentin. He has been acting odd towards me these last few days. He has some plan that I am sure I am not going to like."

Carlos frowns. "Or, we could try to meet with him for dinner. I can talk to Susan before that."

Simon marvels at Susan's magnetic personality. He believes Carlos is attracted to her--he is correct. "I am going back over the hill to board up my house soon. I cannot do dinner."

"What about that aunt of yours?"

"She moved after the last screamer--said those wind generator blades moaned like the dead," Simon answers. "I will talk to Quentin alone--especially if he is gunning for you."

"I will check with Susan as well," Carlos replies. "Maybe the aliens are just laughing at us for being so pompous and they cannot stop laughing."

"Have you heard the joke?" Simon asks placing his hand on the soft red petals of a silk fuscia.

"Which one?" Carlos asks.

"About the aliens? It's a light bulb joke. How many Rosts does it take to replace a light bulb? Answer: None. They don't care if it is burnt out. They are too busy laughing at it."

"Charming." Carlos hears the wind flutter his curtain. "I haven't tried humor with them yet. I'll try it."

"It cannot hurt," Simon says.

"So do you think I have missed something?" Carlos asks.

"You have not had enough time to mess it up." Simon says, looking at his watch. "Well if I am going to find Quentin I better get going. Try telling the Rostackmidarifians a joke. It cannot hurt."

"I will."

Simon waves his hand as he leaves. Carlos sits back in his chair and calls Susan.

The phone rings twice. "Willoughby."

"Susan, Carlos. Any word yet on ceasing the search operations for the alien repeater for a week or so?"

Susan looks up at Quentin switching on her speaker phone. He sits in her office sipping tea from a white porcelain cup. "Carlos, no decision has been made yet to cease the search for the repeater but it looks positive." She watches Quentin shake his head back and forth. "I will call you when I hear something." She places the phone back on the receiver terminating the call and picks up her teacup. The light breeze through the room calms her. "I think he may be right. He has tried everything else."

"It makes us look desperate," Quentin says admiring the way her bright blue dress waves in the wind from the window. "We cannot afford to look desperate. Central is still talking about cutting our funding."

"I'm laughing, Quent. We are desperate." She sips her tea. "Besides, you've a firm hand on the issue."

"The final message occurred before we began search operations. I need proof of a correlation." Quentin says, placing the teacup beside him on the end table and taking a small white napkin to wipe his mouth. He sees Susan purse her lips. "You know without proof to back up my actions I will be road-kill."

"Well then let's not do it." She leans forward and smiles. "But I did talk to Stan Damube and he said there was a maintenance cycle issue with the search arrays. Seems from his standpoint there will be no problem standing down for a few days for maintenance. I had the distinct impression he would see the break as a way to get peak performance from the system," Susan says--hoping Quentin does not find out one of her few remaining friends has been monkeying with the arrays.

"Let me see if I understand," Quentin says. "We should forget shutting down the array for Carlos because we think he is wrong. But, Stan wants the system brought down for maintenance so we should shut it down for a few days for him. Carlos is a wild hare and we are safe." He sips tea. "What did you do, sabotage the array?"

"Seven days is all I am suggesting."

"Three."

"Four."

"Okay," Quentin says with the glow of a proud father. "I have taught you too well."

Susan takes pleasure at beating him and brings the cup to her lips to hide her hatred. These last few months the strain of dealing with him has been mounting; Quentin's way of coping with disappointment is to control events and the people around him with the ruthlessness of a warlord. First he directed her every action, from meetings to dress, dinners to sex.

Only one suggestive command brings joy: that she build an Eco-Home nearby to show everyone that she and the SETI project are here for the long haul. Even though it consumes much energy and resources needed elsewhere the new home pleases her. Every day she can leave the vise of Quentin's fears and undertake an independent task. The house is half-done and within the next week she will decide the interior design arrangement. It is the light of her life these days, her sanctuary. She tells herself despite the selfishness of using so many resources, the house is a reward for a difficult job and she deserves it.

Sadly, Susan has just begun to see her easy morality as the cost of "handling" Quentin. The ensuing myopia of her hate so far, goes unnoticed by him except as resentment. The loss of Simon's attention is not even a memory. Susan has no idea she is less and less aware of anything but tasks. Her cache of friends has shrunk to a circle of implementers. Her awareness of suffering in others is now merely a distraction, a diversion from the important issue of solving problems so that she can vanquish humanity's pain. Even the dull ache in her soul has ceased. In short: she is becoming like Quentin.

Another change Susan is not aware of is her acceptance of a paradox: She tells herself Quentin's actions are more easily understood now and she calls her sympathy "a kind of growth." When she talked to her friends in Huntsville to realign the systems, so Carlos could have his shot at fixing the problem, that former friend, on hearing more about her and Quentin, responded with a comment on her growth: "But is your growth benign or malignant?"

Quentin stands. "You're distracted. Well you can let Carlos know you cajoled me into letting him have three days."

"You said four," Susan says quickly.

"He will ask for another day. Tell him he has three then give him the fourth." Quentin winks. "Oh, where do you want to spend the storm? My place?"

"You choose, Quent," Susan says certain he already has chosen.

"I will have some Chinese cooked by the staff and we can pick it up on our way out around three. Why don't we go to your place and eat supper then we can go to my place after to spend the storm? I am curious to see how things are going with your new home. I have a thought or two on decoration."

Susan spills her tea with her elbow. "Great."

Quentin leaves the office and ponders what he has seen until he spys Simon Weiss waiting outside his door. Smile frozen, Quentin waves hello. "Dr. Weiss. What can I do for you?"

"Can we talk in your office?" Simon asks.

"No, we are all on the same team here, Doctor. What is on your mind?" Quentin folds his arms across the front of his white shirt and adjusts his hair. The gold clasp at the bottom of his ponytail is a gold U.N. flag.

"Carlos needs the search system cut off for a while. He and I both think the search for the repeater has put the Rostackmidarifians in this mode of silence."

Quentin looks pensively at the floor. "How important is this really doctor--I mean in your professional opinion?" Quentin waits, eyes focused on Simon, apparently wrapped in anticipation of Simon's opinion--but in fact measuring his problem with Susan.

An alarm goes off for Simon. Quentin never asks his professional opinion anymore. "I think morale is poor and we cannot afford to lose more staff."

"Are you concerned about Carlos?" Quentin asks casually. "He does seem a bit...sad to me. Susan mentioned the same thing just now."

Simon lies: "No, it is not Carlos I am worried about here."

"But he is the one pushing for this. Is he not?" Quentin has little concern for Simon's lack of enthusiasm. He waits for Simon to slip.

Simon shakes his head. "Carlos is a professional. He has a suggestion that I think is prudent. No I'm much more concerned with the others on the project. We are getting nowhere and today this place is a ghost town--people are far more interested in the Screamer than the Rostackmidarifians. That is not good."

"But it is understandable. I'll tell you what, Doctor. I will go to bat on this if you will do me a favor?"

"Just ask," Simon says, hiding his glee that the decision has already been made. Simon is no one's fool.

"We had some equipment sabotaged a few months ago, just after Carlos Jordan joined us. It stopped but I am wondering if you would look into that?"

"Look into it how? And what happened?"

"Some surveillance systems were destroyed. Security contacted me on it. I told them to hold off because of how tough things are on everyone these days. But I want you to ask around and see if you can find out who was involved. Security thinks Ambassador Jordan is involved. I told them they were wrong but they maintain it was he. And you know me--I am careful about loose cannons. In your opinion, could he have done it?"

"I'll have him fired." Simon backs up to leave.

"Very funny--get back to me on that next week. And call on me for anything."

Simon spends the next fifteen minutes looking fruitlessly for Carlos then exits the building, crossing the new parking lot to his small sports car. Unplugging it from the charger he starts the engine. A low whine comes from under the hood as he backs out of his space. Simon passes the guard station as he leaves. Once outside the gate he curses loudly.

Crossing over the repaired entrance he makes a turn down a street filled with low, barrel-vault shaped homes. Similar to the old Quonset huts except that these are steel and concrete monoliths housing some of the more important SETI personnel, at the end of the line is Carlos' home. Just another muddy walkway with a concrete address molded into the structure. The same moonscape surroundings. The same tossed debris. Simon knocks on the front door. Simon tries the door and enters: "Carlos?" He scans the living room. There is still no furniture besides the large futon where Carlos sleeps and the bevy of fake flowers covering the rest of the floor like a mad carpet. Simon looks for paper to leave a message. Finding none, he walks outside again and looks for something to write upon. He spies two men dressed in bright orange coveralls pushing a large wheelbarrow. They are looking for objects that may become projectiles in a few hours. Simon asks them if they have seen Carlos. They say no. He takes a flat piece of wood from the wheelbarrow.

"Nice car," says the older of the two men. "An Alfa Romero, right?"

"Yes," Simon says noting their tight jaws and deep-set, angry eyes. They glance at each other then move on. Simon replaces the wood then reenters Carlos' house. He pulls a large paper petal from a daisy and writes a note. The note says: "You were right. Quentin is on the hunt for you. We have approval for the repeater to be brought down. Susan did it."

Closing the door, Simon scans for the men. After seeing them down the block talking to each other, he gets into his car and backs out of the drive. Simon motors past the men keeping an eye on them; he quickly leaves the neighborhood. Simon plans to call Carlos later today after preparing for the storm. He also plans never to see Roxanne again. Neither plan will occur.

Chapter Fourteen

Walking the patched wooden deck facing the ocean, Simon purses his lips at the malevolent sky and angry seas. The cold fog far beyond the sea wall, soon to envelop the house, blocks sunlight as if it were the roof of hell. Simon takes the large framing hammer and pounds down the head of a nail on the perimeter deck rail. The redwood, blasted clean of brown paint--has a slight silver shimmer this evening. Simon tells himself he will paint the house in a few weeks. Spray rises twenty feet in the air and a low shudder moves through the deck.

--It will not be too long for the storm surge to bring the waves against the foundation. This will be a bad one--

He figures in less than four hours he will know if he has to evacuate his home. Simon ponders his doom again as the gray proscenium sky begins to pitch from deep gray to purple in the coming winds. Death and Simon Weiss remain in the pitched battle that began when Simon was a child. Rolling back his shoulder blades he stands like a warrior daring his enemy to impale him. The sky rains wash from the deep green sea all around--as if to tell Simon "soon." He blinks, and then turns to reexamine the new iron shutters and doors he and Carlos had installed a few days ago. The metal's numerous flaws remind him of the class he took in blacksmithing. He loved the sparks flying.

--The skill levels in all the trades has declined precipitously, many have given up; an epidemic of my times, it can happen to anyone--

Crossing the long deck, he hauls the wicker table where he had eaten his supper through the sliding glass doors into the living room. A twenty by thirty foot room: The now-crowded space overflows with building materials for repair and outdoor furniture while his couch and tables sit stacked on wooden palettes, for the possible flooding, along the far wall. The debris hides white walls covered with prints by Goya and El Greco. The small dining area to the right has a stack of plates on the counter that separates the kitchen. Simon will not bother cleaning his dinner plates until after the storm. A green backpack full of clothing leans against the wall under the counter. Above, wallpaper depicting goofy farm animals reading newspapers peels in places near the ceiling. It bothers Simon that he can no longer find good glue. A drop leaf table in the center of the dining space holds a picture of his mother and father on their wedding day. His extensive collection of jazz CDs litters the tabletop. It is the only thing he will try to save in the event of evacuation.

Simon Weiss picks up his cell phone and immediately places it back in its charger. He can no longer get a dial tone. For two hours, he has been trying to call Carlos with no luck. He reached Security, Dawn, Susan, and a few others, but not Carlos. With the batteries dead Simon will need to use the land lines even though he expects them to be jammed with people making preparations for the storm. Crossing to the kitchen, he picks up the receiver of an ancient white wall telephone--and hears nothing; the land lines are down. "Oh, this is too much." He has run out of patience. Entering the bright yellow kitchen, he checks the oak cabinets making sure the plastic childproof locks are in place. After the last storm, plates and foodstuffs littered his kitchen from end to end. The cleanup was a nightmare of peanut butter and glass--dark red Madeira wine decorating the counter-top and strawberry jelly sticking to the floor. Light from the kitchen window, a dull white from the envelope of fog darkens as rain begins to beat against the house. "Well here we go." When he was afraid as a child, Simon developed the habit of talking to himself.

Simon walks out the front door of his home dressed in blue jeans and a sweatshirt. Looking up the cliff, he sees the telephone wire dangling from the telephone pole that leans downhill. In the sky above, the gray clouds that had marred the horizon stack overhead. Sand starts to sting him.

Two hours later, rain pours from the sky; it is whipped sideways by the wind slapping an oilskin poncho covering Simon Weiss. He walks the length of the deck--again. The wind flaps material against his legs while the hood over his head keeps cutting his vision. He pulls on each shutter, then checks the new metal covers that shield the sliding glass doors. Manically, he again tightens down the large thumbscrews making sure the rubber gaskets seal around the edge. Fierce winds scream at him and the house trembles with crashing waves. More than once, gusts pin him against his house. He tastes salty tears dripping from the poncho. He turns to see the white lick of the advancing ocean.

Mesmerized by the violence, Simon watches the winds rip white caps from angry waves stinging the shore. The thick fog now gone, he stares at narrow shafts of sunlight. Simon tells himself the storm looks rather tame so far. Smiling at his delusions, he circles around to the front of the house. The wind generators overhead spin furiously murmuring from the strain; they soon will feather--creating that terrible moaning blare that sounds to Simon like angry goats. Climbing the long stairway to the roadway he checks his car, opening the trunk to look for water and food. Satisfied the food will remain dry, he closes it and opens the driver's door. Leaning in, he sees the engine charge is full. The mounting winds feel like pins on the back of his legs. Simon sits in the car knowing he should leave. Looking around at the pounding rain and the spinning blades above him, his hand moves toward the starter.

--It doesn't make any difference--

Simon exits the car and slides down the hillside. Getting to his feet he enters the house, leaving his poncho on a hook he crosses to the kitchen. Pulling a plastic cup from the locked cabinet, Simon places a tea ball in it. Hot water from the thermos bottle steams, sipping tea he watches a small puddle of water grow on the kitchen windowsill. It appears to be from a drip--and not serious. He wipes it off and places a dirty cup from dinner to catch the rain then replaces the thermos bottle in the small towel like a swaddled child. Simon had turned off the hot water heater over an hour ago.

A crack. The side of the house shakes as two by fours break. He stares at the ceiling looking for drips. In the center it begins. "And, we're off..." Quickly opening the front door and stepping outside, he sees a tree limb impaling the roof of his house. "Now where did that come from? The damage is minor, little more than some scraped paint." He looks at the car and sees nothing amiss but climbs the stairs again for another examination--ignoring the need for his poncho. Satisfied the car is untouched by the incident, he reenters his house soaked to the skin.

Simon takes his tea crossing into the living room and sits in a rattan chair. The leak is incessant and getting worse. By rote, he glances to the sidewall where he has stacked a dozen pieces of plywood and various tools. The lights dim once then all is dark. Simon will not light a candle; they are too dangerous at times like these and he finds the black comforting. Sipping tea in the dark, his mind wanders to Spain. He thinks of the flowers in the mountains and starry nights: food around fireplaces and long swims in a deep pond--his mother's laughter and her strong arm close about him. A father who hugged him, an orchard ripe with oranges, the numbing winter evenings and he remembers how the cold almost took his life one night. He sighs sipping the last of his tea. For a few weeks Simon has been wondering why the human spirit fights to live even as the odds continue to stack against it. He muses how Susan has fought to protect herself and the cost to her. The leak has become a tiny waterfall. Simon finds he can think of no one who is not withering under the barrage of storms and pain.

--The battle appears pointless--

An earthquake rattles the area. The house cracks along the east wall. Simon does not get up to check for damage. "A tsunami might be nice." There are no figures on the number of people who have committed suicide in the past year. Some estimates say perhaps one third of the deaths in the last twelve months are attributable to people who just gave up; and like Simon, many of them had no idea they had lost the will to live. They just sat quietly watching the end come as if it were a scene on a DVD.

Spitting sand smacks the metal with low crackling sounds. Simon thinks of a dinner with the Mayor of Seville so many years ago. She had been a friend of his mother. He remembers a long wooden fifteenth century table with a hundred candles lit above it and piles of fruit and cakes. The Mayor sat at one end talking to Simon's mother telling her the trip across the Pyrenees was too dangerous to attempt. It was a long monologue full of hope for Spain and humanity. In the background a quartet played Gershwin; it mixed with his mother's laughter. He wonders if the Mayor of Seville, like so many others, has simply become lost in the wind. Just another grain of sand.

The madness of sound and movement surrounding Simon's small world--the wet, sandblasted chair he sits in--shrieks woe as the storm begins to moan. Waves batter the foundation as Simon repeatedly stands up patrolling the dark inside of his home, checking every window and door for water. But he is an actor playing a part; upon finding leak after leak, he just smiles and continues his patrol. Simon has not picked up a tool or wiped away a drip. He notes the new shutters and metal doors make him blind to the storm outside yet, Simon finds placing a name to the sounds of the objects thrown against his house a pleasing pastime. "That was a rock. That was wood, metal of some sort. Seaweed or kelp, more wood, oh, that was a mammal or fish. Where did that tree limb come from?" He turns on his portable radio and listens to the news.

"...And so we believe that the aliens have nothing sinister planned for us--but rather a desire to help us..."

"Bite me, Carlos." Simon retunes the station. "...The hurricane will most likely peak around nine o'clock this evening with sustained winds averaging a hundred and seventy miles per hour. All coastal residents are again urged to leave their homes. This Screamer is a beauty, folks. And tomorrow's another day--so hang in there. We're gonna' make it." Simon decides to wait until eight to make any decision to leave.

At eight-fifteen a piece of green steel slices through the metal covering the sliding glass door, shattering the tempered glass into a million rounded stones that rattle to the floor. The wind pours through the ceiling breach. Simon grabs a flashlight to examine the pierced shutter. He curses the poorly made metal as he picks out a four foot square piece from his repair pile, and his portable drill; he begins to drill holes in the shutter to screw the wood in place. While he does, the sand ricochets about and drops to the floor. The small piece of debris is part of a sign from the beach saying: "Danger."

"The hell with this." He tosses the signage over by his other materials. "I should go. This is suicide," he says turning. The surprisingly large pile of sand and glass on the floor stuns Simon. He grabs a broom and dustpan and begins to clean up the mess. Halfway though he finds he has no more room in his garbage bucket and sweeps the rest into a corner. Returning to the kitchen he looks for more hot water in the thermos but it is all gone. "Damn." Simon hears the shingles on the roof tear away and a large bang in the attic. Moments later water pours through the plasterboard ceiling in twenty places. More tearing in the roof; he looks up--the ceiling collapses knocking him to the floor.

Simon pushes the wet plasterboard off and sees the vicious dark sky above and the walls undulating back and forth around him as if he were staring at the inside of his pumping heart. Simon concludes the structural integrity of the house is irrevocably compromised and it is finally time to leave, but he has three-hundred pounds of plasterboard on him. He hears another crash and does not bother to look as he tries to extricate himself. Simon's groaning, shaking house will be dead soon. Buckets of water pour through the ceiling knocking old pictures off into the darkness. Simon feels himself lift into the air as if the carpet below him were from the Arabian Nights. Thrown against the oven by a wall of water, his grip is torn from the flashlight. Another wave strikes sending him up into the rafters. A backpack cushions his impact taking ten large nails that protrude through the wood.

The house turns on its side and collapses down. Salt water chokes him. Other parts of his house batter him: the chair, some tapes, a table and a cabinet--the glass from the picture cuts his hands. He turns over and over then finds himself slammed against something hard. The last thing he sees before going unconscious is a flash of lightning.

At two o'clock in the morning, rescue teams assemble at the jump-off locations. All along the state volunteers leave their families to examine power lines, water systems, telecommunications systems, and buildings. A seven-hundred-mile stretch of civilization along the Pacific Coast has been wiped away this evening. The wind has died down to gale force enabling assessments on infrastructure damage and loss of life.

These quick response disaster teams are small, usually no more than three people. They are equipped with radios, weapons, medical supplies, and a dog. One member of the team is a specialist cross-trained, as a paramedic while the second person is usually security. The third person is often a trainee. Life expectancy for these brave men and women is measured in months.

The job of these teams is to check infrastructure and find people who can be saved. They must ignore the severely wounded and spend time only on those who can be helped with the limited medical facilities available--unless the wounded have a high league rating. In those cases air ambulances are at the ready.

Roxanne and her dog Sid are part of Charley Team. Usually a three-person team checking on coastal power and sanitation, the third member of the team has not arrived at the assembly point. The individual missing from Charley team is a soldier who provides security. A utility technician, the other member of the team, cross-trained as an EMT, waits alongside the huge military truck replacing the batteries in his radio and checking his weapon. Ron Goldberg, the tech--who has taken to smoking cigarette after cigarette--appears to be smoldering. He recently lost his sister in a storm. Nonetheless, Roxanne cares about Ron and notes he appears to be fraying around the edges--like everyone else. In any case, she trusts Ron. He appears stoic and dedicated--traits that go a long way in times like these. The two of them listen to the other teams talking about the damage in their neighborhoods. Turning away from the details of storm damage, she walks toward a Red Cross worker with one arm. Roxanne takes a cup of black coffee. "This last Screamer is the worst one I have ever seen," says the worker who then inexplicably--for Roxanne--turns away as if she were not there.

Roxanne walks back to her teammate. All night long the reports of damage have been crackling over the radio. The death toll just on this bandwidth is well over a hundred. It is going to be a bad night. Like other members of her generation, she cannot believe that the storms could possibly get more malevolent--but they do every year.

The search team members climb into the trucks and move out from the hills towards the coast. Bodies sit jammed together with dogs quietly settled on the floor next to their dedicated handlers. No one mentions the search team members who have not appeared; they will see too much death and misery in the next few hours for that luxury.

The bumpy ride over downed trees and debris takes an hour and rattles every bone in their bodies. Finally Roxanne and Ron are alone on the cliffs of Montara. "We'll start at the lighthouse and check the pumps. Then we'll head north. Here are some bullets. Without security you may need them. And here's some food for your friend." Ron throws Sid, Roxanne's dog, a biscuit. Roxanne is aware Ron likes her but she has decided not to pursue him--mostly because of Simon Weiss.

"All right Sid, time for you to earn your dinner." This storm is only Roxanne's fifth search attempt, but she has learned many things so far--including trusting her dog's nose. If Sid begins to circle tightly in a search pattern, she will give him his head. The dog saved fourteen people in the last storm--more than any other dog--and it was his first time. The storm before she lost Sid's brother to the bullets of a looter.

The dog takes point and leads the pair along the cliffs. They pass wandering couples looking for shelters. Ron checks them over for wounds then directs them down the road to Moss Beach where an aid station has been set up. Pulverized homes from previous storms line the roadway. Snapped trees and rusting car wrecks from a bygone time lie rotting in ditches, an old gas station morphed to a church glows with candles from within. A few voices sing hymns in Spanish. Passing the remains of life and watching Sid sniff out wreckage, Roxanne begins to weep silently. Sid wanders about looking for signs of wounded humans and finds mostly empty hovels. Simon's home is still a mile north.

Roxanne turns to Ron as he emerges from another concrete power bunker wishing he would hurry up. She continually looks north as they inch their way along. So far she can see nothing of Simon's house. Roxanne had insisted on this search area when she graduated from the intensive four-week course because of, in her opinion, Simon's poor judgment in a dwelling. Only her skills with the dogs made the authorities finally agree to her demands.

"The damage isn't too bad here," Ron says approaching her and petting the dog that sits at her side. "Tell Base, power station Charley-Six-Twelve has only transformer damage and can be handled by a road crew." Roxanne calls the message in and they continue along the cliffs for another hour until they rest by the last standing structure. The beach in front of here looks clear--Roxanne cannot see Simon's house--after the last storm she could see it from this same spot with no problem. Her stomach knots; the sea wall is gone also. Ron, unaware of her pain looks inland and checks the wind generators by pulling a small scope from his backpack. He scans the generators looking for signs of broken blades. "Tell them a class three visual shows a complete loss of Charley-Six-One." He realizes he hears nothing from Roxanne. "Roxanne?" Her voice trembling, she calls in a preliminary report that none of the generators have survived. "All right let's run a thorough check on the generators."

"There used to be a house on Montara Beach by the sea wall," she says.

After glancing at the debris on the beach, Ron lights a cigarette in the lee of a low stonewall. He does not have to ask if the house contained someone she knows, or knew. The answer is obvious by her still eyes. "Let's go check it out."

What remains of the house glows in the ghostly moonlight like a lopsided pyramid; its roof leans against a back wall that slants inward. Even though the house is far from the rocky shore below, kelp and dead sea creatures rest everywhere in the ruins. A moment later the two-year old shepherd darts off. Sid barks once. Roxanne sighs. She hates this part of the task, even when she knows no one. One bark means a dead body. Roxanne follows the dog to the exposed side of the house. An old man and woman sit surrounded by beer bottles. A large home telescope sits on top of them crushed into their bodies by a steel beam that has fallen across chests. Dried blood from their figures cover the couch. Goldberg nails a red marker against the nearest beam. Roxanne radios in what they found.

"That them?" Goldberg asks, looking again at the generators stilled by the winds.

"Sid, are there anymore?" Roxanne asks her dog.

The dog just looks at her.

"You trainers all think your dogs are geniuses." Goldberg says. "Mercy, will you look at that Alfa? It's a beauty. I wonder what it's doing here?"

"It is from the house," she says.

"Oh, then they didn't get out," the thin bearded man says. "I am sorry."

They silently circle the debris of furniture and parts of the house plastered to the cliff wall. The rest of Simon's house appears spread out toward the ocean as if a large butter knife had pushed it out to sea. Waves lap against parts of the roof. "How does this happen?" She asks, trying to keep herself calm.

Goldberg points to the cliff. "The cliff and sea wall form a cup. The water came up, became caught by the cliff, came back around to the house, and just washed away what was not smashed against the cliff." A wooden kitchen cabinet lies jammed into the sand. Roxanne can barely speak.

"Sid, seek." Roxanne finally squeaks letting go of the leash. Moments later the dog begins barking by two pieces of concrete that form a corner. A metal door rests on top with its lower quarter buried in sand. The three elements form a tiny shelter. Seaweed and debris lie scattered everywhere. The dog starts digging in the sand, tearing through an old picture lodged between the door and the concrete. Turning on their flashlight, Roxanne and Ron begin digging as well. Something is alive in there.

"Hey, buddy, can you hear us?" Goldberg says, shining the light into the small triangular hole. Dirt and blood obscure the face Roxanne has seen only once but cannot forget. After a few more minutes of digging Goldberg takes hold of the wrist. "He has a pulse and it's regular. About eighty beats per minute, Whew, this is one lucky son of a bitch. By rights anything around here could have killed him." Goldberg scans for the tag everyone now wears for body identification; it is a tattoo on the shoulder. The next step is to determine league status of the occupant; it is a requirement.

Roxanne removes more sand until she can reach inside the small cubby. She begins to tap his face to waken him. "Simon. Simon."

Simon spits then suddenly begins screaming in Spanish.

"He's completely lost it," Goldberg says listening to the response on his radio. He purses his lips looking at Roxanne. He can finally speak after almost a minute. "Your friend is some big NorCal honcho. One of us is ordered to stay with him. Goddamn privileges--there sending in the Medicos."

Simon wails hysterically.

Roxanne speaks: "Easy Simon, you're okay. We're here. We'll get you out."

Simon hears her words but cannot understand them. His mind continues telling him he is tossed about and battered by his home. Drowning in sea and sand, he wishes only to die.

"What do we do?" Roxanne asks. "This poor man is going mad."

"Here, look out." Goldberg produces a syringe from his bright orange medical pack. He jabs it into Simon's hand.

"Isn't that dangerous without examining him?' Roxanne asks.

"Don't tell me my business. I won't tell you how to train dogs." Goldberg puts the empty syringe in his pack. "You need to stay here. I need to check the generators." Goldberg pulls out a strobe beacon. "If you do know him try talking to him about himself. That gash on his forehead looks bad."

He places the beacon on top of the concrete as if it were a light on an old police car. The red pulse cuts the night. "Someone will be here soon. There's a chopper on the way. Do privileges mean that much to you?" He doesn't wait for an answer. He just walks away. "I'll be right back."

Furious at his lack of caring, she hears Simon's cry dwindling into an unceasing mumble. Sid sits down beside Roxanne as she tries to make out the words, but all she can understand is the word: "madre."

Roxanne holds his hand, stroking it. Sid keeps watch.

"Simon, it's me, Roxanne. Tell me your name."

"Simon, Simon Weiss. Where am I?"

"Safe. Tell me something about yourself, Simon."

"Roxanne?" He says finally understanding she is talking to him and he is not dreaming this event. "What are you doing here?"

"I am with Disaster Relief. I am with a dog and we are part of a search team. You have been given a sedative and a rescue ambulance is on the way. You probably have a concussion but you will be fine. Can you feel your legs?" The next sound is Simon's hoarse laughing. She waits, surprised to hear humor rather than panic in the laughter. Finally she speaks: "What is so funny?"

"Damn, Carlos. He will do anything to get me to spend some time with you."

Roxanne sheds a tear. "You better stop. You need to conserve your strength. How do you feel? Can you feel your feet?"

Simon quiets. "I worked so hard to not see you again. You have no idea. Now I have two pieces of concrete on me to keep me from running away. Okay, I know when I'm licked."

"I like a person who can't run away from me. Can you feel your feet?"

"Yes. Everything hurts but, my spine is fine." Simon will never tell her it once didn't matter to him if he lived or died tonight.

Sid growls and stands. Roxanne looks over to see three people walking south down the beach. "Quiet Sid. Sleep." The dog stands still as death. She looks up at the beacon flashing above her. It is too late to remove it; they see it. She looks up but the night tells her nothing about the dirigible.

"What is it?" Simon asks.

"Quiet, Simon, some men are wandering down the beach. They look drunk." She feels around her waist and produces the pistol she carries. "Sid, rest." This is the command that tells the dog there may be a battle. The dog tenses with a low growl. The three men continue up the beach moving toward them. She hears glass break and she hunkers down close to the rocks loading her weapon. When she finishes, she looks back at Simon's hand then takes it with her free hand.

"So Roxanne, are you going to spend the night with me?"

"Sure," she whispers. "Of course I will spend the night. Now shut up."

The fingers on Simon's hand began to move in a rhythmic fashion to indicate he is thinking. His low voice fills with a gentle humor. He has no idea of the danger approaching them. "I have wanted to spend time with you since the first day we met."

Her attention leaves the danger and she gazes at his hand. "Shhh," she watches the men approach. "Be quiet." She takes her hand from his and grasps the leash. If the men approach, she plans to lead them away from Simon. Sid growls. "Sid, danger." It is the next level of agitation for the dog. The next command will cause him to strike. The dog quiets. Roxanne figures if a fight occurs Sid will be good for keeping at least one of them off balance maybe two. That means she will need to fire her weapon. She speaks quietly into her radio. "Ron, I have got three marauders about two hundred yards away heading straight towards me."

"I copy. You keep still and I'll get some support. Remember, fire your weapon only when you are sure of a kill."

Roxanne watches the men approach. Soon the men are no more than fifty yards away. Then they stop. The crashing waves seem to hold their attention as they stare out to sea. She wonders what interests them so much until a circle of light from above suddenly focuses on them. At that moment she can hear the sounds of helicopter blades. "This is the Global Revitalization and Environmental Enforcement Authority. Stand clear of our beacon or we will fire on you."

The men on the beach begin to walk away from the water--directly towards Roxanne. The dog tenses as they approach. The circle of light surrounding the men broadens and the sand around them puffs as the sound of machine gun fire fills the air. All three fall immediately. The machine gun chatter ceases. Roxanne bolts up and rushes to the closest man shot. Thin and covered with sores, the grisly-faced man smells of decay and disease--yet he smiles at her through rotted teeth. "Thank you, ma'am." And he dies.

"Roxanne?" Simon yells.

She walks back to him looking up at the car. She leans closer to Simon. "Well, I guess you are important--they sent a gun ship to protect us. And you are not running from me any more, Dr. Weiss." Now that she has found him, Roxanne resolves she will not let this man die before she does. Roxanne has just figured out he did not try to escape the storm. It is to become another link in their chain. "Why is your last name Weiss? It is German not Spanish."

"What? Why do you care about my last name?"

"Just curious." Roxanne cannot look at the dead bodies lit by the descending light of the ambulance.

"Dad was from Bavaria. It is where mom and I were heading. I have relatives there."

"Tell me about them," she says.

"Oh, I see. There's a bad cut on my head." The chopper lands nearby. Within a few minutes the concrete is moved and Simon is extricated. Two EMTs work swiftly examining Simon and loading him onto a stretcher. No one bothers to check on the other men. Just before they place Simon onto the gondola they call Roxanne over with a nod of their heads. Simon, who knows what has happened but has not seen the bodies, says: "Roxanne, contact Carlos."

"About what?"

"Quentin knows he destroyed some surveillance equipment. And with the lack of response from the aliens, he is the perfect scapegoat for our situation. I don't think he will run, but try to help him escape."

Hand drifting to her dog's coat, she strokes it slowly and asks: "It is really that bad?" Roxanne finally must know the answer. For years she has avoided asking anyone who might really know. "Do you think the game is over? Is humanity terminal?"

Simon closes his eyes. "You know I didn't run tonight."

"Is that why you fought the storm tonight--you foolish man?" Tears fill her eyes. "I'm crying. And I don't even like humanity."

"Go see him. Tell him someplace out in the open, away from SETI."

"Okay, you just rest and take it easy. I will handle it." She watches the medical technicians place Simon in the gondola and take off in a whirl of sand. She examines the bodies of the three marauders making sure they are dead then radios in the location. Watching the light disappear, she looks around at the remains of Simon's home and wonders where he will live now--but only for a moment. Later this morning when she finds she cannot reach Carlos, she will fear for Carlos' safety but Roxanne will not contact Simon. Roxanne does not equate love with dependence.

Chapter Fifteen

Above Palo Alto, California the sun shines yellowish-red from a clear blue sky. Crowds fill the street; another puff of wind moves the bright pink umbrella of the sidewalk café. It says "ZEKES" over the white fringe--and provides Carlos' shade. The cluster of tables sit, like circled wagons at a busy intersection of University Avenue. The chimes of the sidewalk restaurant mix with other chimes, from other restaurants. Carlos delights in the sounds of the outdoor eatery madrigal that bathes the quiet conversations, the good food, the Saturday crowd that flows around him like stream waters around a rock. Carlos reads a novel called "Living Twice" and drifts in between worlds. Susan had recommended the book last night telling him it spoke to her about purpose. A quiet shuffling disturbs him.

Looking up, he sees a dour waiter with a pock-marked face placing a dish of croissants on the small table; the waiter leaves without acknowledgment but smiling at his small victory over the relaxed aristocrat--as he saw it all. Laying the book down on the pure white tablecloth, Carlos takes in the aroma of the croissants and sips his iced tea. He replaces the tall glass in the saucer and adjusts the black linen napkin on his lap; he straightens it over freshly pressed khaki pants and a light blue cotton shirt, then tears a piece off the perfectly crisp delicacy. The croissant compresses with a light crunch and releases its flavor of buttered perfection. Above the umbrellas, a two-mile wave of fading blue tarps puff with each wind. The old steel framework from long-gone businesses supports ropes stretching over the roadway allowing a quiet snapping and rolling in the winds. The play seems to announce the pushcarts coming down the street--a weekly parade here. The brightly colored pushcarts: reds--from berries, dull green--from sea weed, yellow--from peaches, white--from chalk, purple--from heather. All arriving like small waves that wash around the restaurant in the center of the intersection. Two angled handles at the back of the carts soon rest on pairs of stilts to keep them steady. Large wooden boxes overflowing with produce burden the carts' center wheels. Spoked-wheels, which could have come from stagecoaches, soon hold metal hooks supporting dried wild flowers as the vendors prepare. The farmers erect American flags; the farmers market is open.

End-to-end pushcarts full of food seem like a dream to most. Their fruits' hues adding a rare flair to the day since bright colors are uncommon for most people now. Crowds swarm into the mountains of color drunk with prosperity.

For a while this year it looked as if there might not be a harvest. With each Screamer the local crops were battered but, though late, the storms have quieted and harvest is finally coming in earnest. Deep in his memory, Carlos remembers the brightly lit food markets with their unending shelves and gaudy neon. Most people of his age remember also--but they talk little of the memory. It seems cruel and shameful to recount.

Locals scurry about locating the choice fruits and freshest vegetables. Even though a sense of profusion fills the street, a feeling of competition pervades the air as men and women strive to take home the best offerings from the Santa Clara Valley. It is the curse of plenty--the desire to own the most excellent. It leads to absurd competitions since the notion of owning anything perfect is impertinent. Of course in other parts of the world any of these morsels is worth more than a human life so judgments about another's absurdity need be tempered by the savagery on which it rides.

Insulated from everyone, Carlos scans passed the people as if they were pictures from an exhibition. Looking down Ramona Street, he watches wooden bowls and ceramics swing in the breeze as less focused crowds meander among the goods. Rules are: Nothing other than produce can be displayed on University during the market days. So the side street carts display brightly colored cloth, dresses, or shirts. Untold racks of cookware hang from metal poles in the middle of the streets and brightly colored pinwheels spin on top. Firewood and plastics, sheet metal and salvaged bike parts flank the far ends of the streets in huge mounds. There are so many of these items, they are practically worthless. Beyond the mounds, large lots filled with consumers' bicycles glistening in the sunlight. Nowhere are bicycles kept as clean and shiny as this area of the country; it is tradition.

His revelry disturbed by the honk of a horn, Carlos turns to a clown and a mime arguing about a rubber chicken. The clown, dressed in a twentieth century dark blue suit, white shirt, red tie, and a white dunce cap, keeps honking a brass horn. He appears angry about a plastic chicken in the hand of the mime. The mime, dressed in a dark red leotard suit with a pancake makeup face, shakes his head and left hand like the pendulum of a clock--saying no. The clown grabs the chicken stretching it from neck to toe. Pulling the mime into the center of the crowd, the clown pulls out a toy gun and fires. The mime jumps but does not let go of the chicken; the comical confrontation between the street performers becomes a pageant of slapstick humor and physical comedy involving much punching and hitting.

Across the street, behind the mime's act, Carlos spots a dark-skinned woman in a white tank top and long blue skirt who had caught his attention earlier. She sits alone on a stone bench eating an ice cream cone and reading a book. Carlos watches her over the pages as she licks her ice cream. The woman's smooth skin glows from exotic oils, as does her black thick hair. A loose lace top of white silk blows in the breeze. Long fingers brush hair from her eyes as they rise from the pages and into his gaze. A pert smile of bright teeth framed by sensual lips ends with a wink. She kisses her vanilla ice cream cone and returns to her leather-bound book.

"And Simon was worried about you."

Roxanne suddenly stands on his right dressed in a blue and white striped sundress. A large German shepherd stands beside her, his eyes scanning the flow of the crowd around them. She steps under the pink umbrella and kisses Carlos on the cheek watching the woman's gaze. She returns again to the book--with no apparent interest in Carlos or Roxanne.

He does not believe it for a moment. Carlos is well studied in the interplay called courtship. Finding it similar to a contract negotiation, he has found it an easy game; at first he had thought it was his thin good looks, intelligent eyes, and quick humor that made it so easy. Then he realized his high League rating made it a bore. Carlos loves the solace of strangers' arms. So he plays only for amusement--and therefore always wins. "Nice timing, Roxanne."

"'Awe' come on; she is yours anytime you want her. Sid and I have been standing by the rope peddler watching you two for the last few minutes. It's lush at first sight."

"Oh, I didn't notice."

"She spikes the ice cream."

"Thanks." He motions for her to sit. "Is this Sid?" He examines the intelligent looking animal and decides it is safe.

Roxanne sits down and places her hand on the dog's head. "Sid, meet Carlos." The dog ignores him and settles in beside Roxanne.

"Not too convivial. How is Simon?"

"I just left the hospital. Simon says hello and the docs say he should be out in a few weeks. He has a broken femur and a broken tibia--a smashed rib and some lacerations." She leans in close. "Did you get his message about Quentin?"

"All the messages." Carlos looks down at the table and interlaces his fingers. "I'm sorry. I should have known he'd given up. "Carlos looks at Roxanne, remorse written across his face.

"I heard it the first ten times Nine-Toes." She looks back at the woman across the way; Roxanne takes Carlos' hand and bats her eyes. The woman immediately goes back to her book. Carlos hides his grin with a sip of tea. "So where were you yesterday, Carlos?" Roxanne asks.

He holds the glass of tea in front of him and stares though the green-brown liquid. "Would you like refreshment?" He lowers the the glass but receives no response--just a placid stare. He pushes the plate of croissants toward her. No response. "I was working."

Roxanne lifts an eyebrow and settles in her chair resigned to one of those teeth-pulling sessions with Carlos. She feels her frustration, then, for the first time in eons, realizes she may not have to spend the rest of her intimate life like this. She exhales deeply. The extraction of information suddenly takes on the tone of a game. Roxanne flags the waiter and orders an iced tea as well as a bowl of water for her dog. "He's not angry you didn't visit him this week."

Carlos appears to not quite grasp the meaning.

"Simon." She immediately senses she has been had; so she leans over to pet her dog.

Carlos is pleased to have another puzzle to solve involving Roxanne. She speaks: "We've already made some plans. I will be picking him up at the hospital in a week or so." Roxanne finds herself delirious with joy. The fog of clouds has replaced a weight of stone. "I am driving his car. He has no place to live. I think he will stay with me. "She lifts her eyebrows and sees him tear off a piece of croissant.

"You have it all planned--I see--but I would be wary." He wonders what has changed--beside Roxanne worrying about hurting him. "Simon has seven-league-boots when it comes to love."

"Exactly. He had nothing to live for. We're in love, Carlos." The words arrive with a combination of reverence and joy.

Carlos wonders why this takes pressure off her when trying to extract information from him. "That is great. I am so pleased. Do you have one of those emergency passes for the car?"

"The emergency driving pass is in my purse. They think I'm his sister." Roxanne plasters a smile on her face. Carlos sees Roxanne trying a new tack to get information from him. The dog pants under the table. "Where is that waiter?" She looks around. "Simon worries about you," she says staring at the wait station.

Carlos has noted she does not seem to be concerned--he concludes that means Simon will be all right. "Use caution with Simon, okay?" He feels a twinge of jealousy.

"Thanks, Dad. In fact, I've spent the whole morning fretting that some part of my checkered past will come and bite me. Do you think I need to worry?"

"Simon is a man of the world." Carlos glances at the woman across the way. She turns a page and peaks up at him. He winks. "Don't be silly."

"Silly, nothing--you are the only man I know who did not find something to disapprove of in me, or my past." The waiter places the large frosty glass on the table and then a small white bowl of water beside it. He has no plans of getting anywhere near the dog's mouth and waits a moment hoping to hear something of importance--until he sees Carlos watching him. The waiter nods and leaves. Carlos births another theory about Roxanne: He thinks perhaps she no longer fears she will be bound by his limitations. Roxanne continues: "Simon will find something to disapprove of I bet."

"Why?"

"He's a man. And that is the way most men are today--disapproval keeps their juices flowing."

He decides to test his newest theory about Roxanne as she lowers the ceramic bowl beside Sid. "I am not sure how much to tell him," Roxanne says, straightening up and wrapping her hands around the cold glass. Her eyes again peer at the woman. "I don't want to lose him to youthful foolishness."

Carlos looks down at the dog and smiles. "Tell him nothing you do not want him to resent or fear. Take your time. Explore each other slowly and make the discoveries fountains of joy, not sources of recrimination."

"That was poetic." Roxanne wonders what Carlos is up to now.

"Harry and May spewed recrimination constantly. My poetics may be a new line of work for me. What do you think?"

Roxanne curls a lip. "Carlos is tossing his bullcrap again, Sid. Can you smell it?" The dog remains unmoved by the words. "That's right he has not told me a darn thing. Well, beside all that talk-show-blah, Carlos, what do you think Simon might react badly to in my past?" She leans close over the white tablecloth--obviously wanting him to lower his voice--should he discuss specifics.

With Roxanne's parry and repost, Carlos believes he is correct: that Roxanne now feels less constrained by him. "I think you are referring to your days of wild songs."

"We are talking symphonies here not songs. The videos and that web page are the parts I am particularly worried about today." She sits back and tears a piece off an uneaten croissant.

"I would say leave it alone. Or was it so important to you?" Carlos asks, glancing at his watch then flagging the waiter for the check. When the waiter arrives, Carlos flashes his badge and the anxious waiter nods writing down his number. The account at SETI will be billed and an energy exchange ratio applied to the bill. The payment will be in the form of watts for the restaurant and a bit of cash for the waiter. The waiter nods thank you and leaves.

"It was nothing to me. Fun for the moment." She wonders why he has so abruptly decided to leave. This kind of rudeness is rare for Carlos. She knows it is not the woman--they are a dime a dozen for him; Roxanne wonders if perhaps he wants to tell her something in a more secluded spot. "I just do not want to mess things up with him," she says, glancing at the croissant and dismissing it as the source of his consternation. She cannot know he has a rendezvous in fifteen minutes.

"So forget it." He sits waiting for her to finish the tea and watching the blue tarps puff overhead. "Do you want to walk the booths?"

"I see. Disclosure time, eh Nine-Toes?" She asks, finishing the last of the delicious green tea.

"Yes." Carlos surprises himself. Originally he had no intention of talking about last night, but as the minutes tick by, he feels an overwhelming need to talk about it. The notion of intimacy has not entered his consciousness--only more time with a friend. Standing, Carlos picks up his book.

"What is that book?" Roxanne asks.

"Susan gave it me. It's environmental philosophy. She figures since no one has ever seen any aliens I might as well learn about them from a professional speculator."

"Too much censorship in those old books for me." They begin to work their way through the crowds. Roxanne notes Carlos seems to have a destination in mind.

"There are good works in every field." Carlos says, noting Sid walks close alongside Roxanne making sure his mistress is safe. It pleases Carlos that Roxanne has so dedicated a protector. "I never had a dog. I guess I haven't had the time."

"You should get one. They will guard what's left of your dreams."

"I don't dream anymore, Roxanne."

Without further comment they cross through the intersection and down Ramona Street peering into the different carts set up in front of destroyed stores. Only the mime still stalks the crowd--his rubber chicken in tow. Roxanne stops at a cart displaying objects d'art made from old computers. Not interested in memorabilia, she needs a moment to think, glances at the braids of electric cords woven into baskets, and picks up a rain stick. Made from old monitor glass and a hollow black plastic pipe, its rendition of rain is all wrong. She replaces it wondering what she can do for Carlos. Their pattern complete they will move toward the discussion now.

Carlos watches the crowds walking along the street. Sets of professional men and women, each with a child in their midst. They keep a wary eye out and lean on bicycles as if they were movable fortresses; healthy children are quite rare. Walking in groups, chatting in acronyms, many of these people work together at the university, or SETI, or the remaining high tech manufacturers whose buildings sit huddled in a walled compound a few miles away. The well-to-do attend to their peers--and kowtow to those with higher League rating. Carlos notes they examine each other for signs of success in the same way they examine produce for purchase. Only the best will do. When he sees a particularly pretty couple push past an old fat man with a dirty torn coat, Carlos turns away, saying: "Will your dog attack on command?"

Roxanne watches the couple move through the crowds like a pair of large buses ignoring anything smaller than them. "My dog is no fool, he ignores assholes." The pair continue their stroll until they begin circling the parking lot full of bicycles, Roxanne asks: "So...what did you want to tell me?"

He notes there is no anger or tightness in her voice the way there used to be when she was trying to extract information from him. Certain he is correct, that she rejoices in her new lover's lack of baggage, he says: "I went for a walk on the bay. Then I went to see Susan." It is Carlos' need for calm waters in their friendship that drives him to talk about last night. He needs to make sure Roxanne and he have a safe new harbor.

"Did you go see Susan for professional reasons?"

Carlos beams, glad the calmness remains in her voice. "Yes, but Susan had gone some place with the local dictator--"

Roxanne's attention fixes on Carlos. "Oh, hold it. Wait. Now *that* was jealousy. So it was not professional. Tell me more." Roxanne watches Carlos' lips tighten shut. These conversations used to drive her mad. This bright and sunny summer day, it is all a breeze.

Carlos folds his arms across his chest. He forms a featureless smile and shrugs his shoulders. Carlos is not trying to be difficult; he truly believes the events of his life are not worth the intercourse.

Roxanne reads the totally blank face and thinks he is trying to hide something from her and at the same time tell her something. She once believed this to be one of Carlos' most favored techniques for getting someone's undivided attention; over the years her empathy for his wounds became covered with frustration. Today, compassion resurfaces anew. She perceives she has been wrong. That he is not trying to get her attention--instead he is trying not to bore her with his pain. Touched by his throes, she cannot speak. Turning away, she stares at hundreds of bicycles, Roxanne tries to remember so many automobiles parked together; her mind sees only junk yards. "Come on. You need to tell me about her. Go ahead."

"No." He laughs. "I left SETI and I was alone until about seven. Then Susan showed up and we spent the night together."

Roxanne stumbles on a ledge of old sidewalk. She catches her balance and stands quite still looking at him. "Beg, pardon?"

"Susan showed up and we spent the night together."

"By plan? By the fireside? What?"

"Oh, there she is. Susan." Carlos calls. Roxanne practically wrenches her neck spinning around to see her. Over the bicycles, by a pushcart the tall blond woman with a black bandanna across her forehead and a white tennis outfit appears like an image from the past. All Roxanne can see is a woman with a mountain of trouble on her mind. Susan waves hello and waits. Rather than a smile, Roxanne wears the frozen face of confrontation. It does not help that Susan has history with Simon. Carlos guides Roxanne back around the bicycles toward Susan and the pushcart vendor.

--This is not about love. What is he doing messing with her? Perhaps it is the challenge of wrestling her from Quentin? That does sound like the kind of game he would play. Doesn't Carlos have the brains God gave a fence post? This one is not for warmth--

Examining Roxanne from head to toe Susan Willoughby registers disturbance--not unlike a small quake. Roxanne immediately beams back a warm smile. Truth be known, Roxanne is impressed this woman would register anything but resolve. Understanding there might be a link between Carlos and Susan, she worries a bit more. Determination can be a link between people but in a relationship, too much determination turns arguments into a vendetta.

They face each other across a cart painted in a dull red wash and filled with fresh herbs; a sign stretching across two poles at either end of the cart says: "Mills, the Herbalist," in black letters. The shop owner thinks they are customers and smiles hello. Only Sid, the dog, pays attention to the vendor--with a warning stare. No one else acknowledges him so the skinny man backs up to leave them alone.

Carlos speaks: "Susan, this is Roxanne. An old friend of mine." Susan shakes Roxanne's hand in a perfunctory way then recalls the cold stare she received from her at first glance. Roxanne bristles thinking the disquieted look she saw before was merely the disturbance of a collector who thinks they may have lost a trinket. Roxanne is wrong about Susan; but they are opposites. Susan lives for the future and is willing to sacrifice the present for it. Roxanne will not sacrifice the present for any reason.

"Carlos, I've a tennis date with Quentin. He is waiting in the car. I only told him I wanted some herbs for dinner. Can we talk--alone--for a minute?" She smiles at Roxanne.

"Don't worry about me," Roxanne says pleasantly. "I have to go buy a bone for my attack dog anyway." She takes Carlos' book as Susan takes Carlos' hand--leading him into the cluster of bicycles. Susan begins talking to Carlos watching Roxanne's face. Bits of emotion that look like pain flash from Susan. Carlos says something brushing his white hair aside; then a brief smile appears from the corners of his lips quickly disappearing beneath layers of protection. Susan's shoulders relax in humor. Roxanne notes Carlos has scored points--on Quentin--she assumes. She sees Susan then shrug her shoulder and shake her head no. Then her arms cross. Carlos leans closer and whispers something in her ear. A shudder of laughter breaks out and a moment later Susan leans her head forward on his shoulder. Roxanne is impressed by Carlos' technique--she has never seen him so good--and decides there is delight for this well-matched pair. Carlos touches her hand. Roxanne groans seeing Susan does not like the brotherly touch. Carlos steps back from her--a vision of innocence.

At that point Roxanne is convinced Carlos cares about Susan. She can tell by the amount of manipulation he appears to be going through to get her to like him. Susan steps forward to say something; and it's Carlos turn to laugh. They kiss; Roxanne is stunned. Susan lingers a moment longer then hurries to the cart by Roxanne to ostensibly get some herbs. They lock eyes.

"Try the, rue. It's good for the heart," Roxanne says.

Susan buys garlic as she flashes her badge to the herbalist and says to Roxanne: "You need not worry. I'll take care of him." Susan waves to Carlos casually and she is gone.

--Amazing. I guess this is why he was busting at the seams to talk to me. Well, okay. I can understand a little intrigue, but he plays it awfully near the edge these days. I think perhaps that Simon was not so far off in thinking Carlos is at risk. And Carlos is not that safe with her--

Carlos strolls toward Roxanne with a placid, joy-filled look on his face. Roxanne knows this is the look he wears after winning a Ping Pong game, but she does not scowl. She believes this time it may have meaning. Carlos takes her arm and leads her down one of the emptier side streets. They pass an old downtown residential area--now little more than a collection of rotting houses and burned out apartment buildings. Walking toward a tent city that replaces the lost residences, Roxanne remains quiet. After dark, these lanes between tents present little safety while ironically the rip-stop nylon and canvas walls of the tents could be made of steel. No one breaks into these tents. It is a crime immediately punishable by death. Skirting the tent city, smelling the fires and stews, Carlos now silent, Roxanne will not disturb the moment for him. She knows how important the feeling of triumph is for Carlos Jordan. Carlos speaks again: "Susan told me she is jealous of our friendship."

"And I'm Katherine Hepburn." They stop at an empty park. They are so far from any other people she fears for their safety until Sid brushes against her leg. She unconsciously pets his head.

"There is strong pressure from Iceland to cut funding. It looks as if the money can be spent in other places--preparing for the rest of the downward spiral. We have not been successful." He sees sad eyes confirming she already knows the prognosis. He does not know she is fuming because he has changed the subject.

"Simon told me the other day we have had it. You don't need to hide it from me." The strength in her eyes makes a part of Carlos glow with admiration--another part of him mourns a loss he still cannot fully understand.

Glancing around to make sure no one is in earshot Carlos continues: "She says Quentin is panicking because--"

She hands him his book slapping it down in his hands. "Who cares about Quentin? I certainly do not. I don't care about the warming. I don't care about storms. I don't even care about the end of humanity. I care about what is happening to you." Her eyes wide--she stares at him. Roxanne also strokes the dog's ears to make sure he knows she is having a fine time. Carlos tells himself he loves her at that moment.

If Carlos tells her what he feels, she will believe him for the first time ever. And with that admission their lives will attract even more turmoil. Instead Carlos says: "I have two more weeks to get in motion with the aliens. After that Quentin, hangs me out dry, ruins my reputation, and claims I am the reason the aliens are not responding--and generally places all the global warming tragedy on me. I am kicked out on my keester. We give up on the aliens and the rest is history. Or is that not history?"

Her eye's flash. Slowly she says: "You...and...her. If you don't tell me

I am going to have Sid rip you into shreds." She looks down at the dog. Sid looks back tongue wagging in the breeze, eyes bright with love. Moments later his eyes look away--to fix on a nearby cheese sandwich squashed on the pavement.

"If I was a cheese sandwich I would be scared." Carlos leans forward and pets the dog's head. "Susan says her tasks have always been more important than any person. She just told me I need to forget what happened in the shelter--"

"What happened in the shelter, Carlos? I know about the copulation."

"She also just said I am not that interesting--nor is my life."

"Carlos."

He looks around the barren park; then kicks the sandwich toward the dog. "Because of Susan, I have decided there must be a better way to die." His eyes search out hers. She holds her tears in check and places a hand on his shoulder. "When I got to SETI, I saw Susan's car in the parking lot. I thought about looking for her but I didn't--I went to my office."

"Why didn't you keep looking for her?"

"What for? Susan is not the kind of woman you look for in a storm or any other time. If she wants to be found she will be found. Anyway I went to my office to get some materials for work, and ointment for my wounds--"

"What kind of wounds?"

"There was an explosion and a window blew in on me. I have a cut on my back."

"Let me see. Lift up your shirt." He reluctantly turns and lifts the back of his shirt. A large gauze pad covers a wound that runs from his right shoulder blade to his ribs. A ribbon of dried blood runs the length. "Looks like a little more than a cut. Did Susan fix that up for you?"

"I headed down into the shelter and sat at one of the desks. I began to work. "

"What do you mean work?"

About an hour later Susan entered the shelter. She gasped so loudly I almost fell off my chair. I was bleeding on the floor and I didn't know it." Roxanne puts her hand over her mouth. This, and confirmation of humanity's demise, shakes her badly.

He sees this; and feeling guilty, tells himself he should not have talked about what happened. Nonetheless, he continues speaking hoping to find a way to cushion the pain he sees: "She tended my wounds and we began to talk. It seems she and Quentin had a fight about the decorations in her new house. Apparently an interior designer she hired was not up to Quentin's standards."

Still struggling with what she has seen and heard, Roxanne says: "She is building a custom house--and using an interior designer? Are you kidding me? I thought that mode of life was extinct. Has she had the Mercedes serviced yet? I am not sure I like her priorities, Carlos." She immediately regrets saying this.

"I knew this. You and her are not at all alike. Anyway, Susan and Quentin had a row about the design scheme. She desired plain walls and Quentin was predisposed to rice grass because it has the right ambiance for entertaining. Quentin detailed her shortcomings and then concluded she was being uncooperative. Susan withdrew--but not before placing egg foo yung into Quentin's lap." Carlos grins. "She started telling me this after she disabled the surveillance systems by tearing them off the walls of the shelter. My kind of gal." Seeing no response to his joke, he continues: "You have no idea how much she dislikes him."

"I had no idea she had so much fire. Carlos, you may be totally charming but that doesn't mean anything to a person like her. She is driven to perform success. Everything else is second--even her own love." Some women walk out from the tent city to investigate the strangers. Carlos and Roxanne begin to walk back to the street fair. Sid, the dog, walks carefully scanning everything with the eyes of a hunter. "Carlos, her commitments are to saving the planet and nothing else. If that cannot be done her world will collapse. I do not want it to collapse on you."

"So noted." He pauses watching the agitated dog looking around. Carlos sees no one.

"It is likely," Roxanne says trying to decide what is best for Carlos, "that she thinks helping you make contact with the aliens is worth any price." Roxanne is torn. As far as she is concerned, anyone who takes another's love for achieving a goal is dirt. Even if the victim is someone like Quentin. On the other hand, if a sham will keep Carlos alive, and interested in this woman, she wonders if perhaps she should support it and deal with the consequences later. "So you two just talked about her and Quentin...?"

"She was lonely, not manipulative. Believe me. I would know. We had dinner--some MREs--and talked until we got tired. Later I closed the door of the shelter and we cuddled up and slept in each other's arms." He quickly adds: "In the morning we had fifty-year-old coffee and she left. It was a great night. Funny how my best nights with women are..." Ironically, for Carlos, this discussion of what happened feels like an unabridged version of the Kama Sutra. He hates the feeling of exposing his sentiments. Carlos hides his eyes in embarrassment.

"So she left in the morning but you agreed to meet here this afternoon?"

"She said she wanted to talk to me."

"And when you saw her again she said?"

"She said there is nothing to talk about. We need to forget last night. I said no."

Roxanne pauses, then says: "You know by the time she left the two of you practically danced down the street."

"Susan said she made up with Quentin this morning. She knows we have to work together." He looks at the pavement. "She told me I was just a way to get back at him--"

"And I can still star in 'Woman of the Year'," Roxanne says.

Carlos brightens. "Really? You said she was using me."

Roxanne puts her arms around his shoulders. "Good for you, Carlos. She counts." Roxanne hugs him.

"After I get the aliens to solve global warming I will ask them to help me feel as well," Carlos looks down.

"Oh--" Surprise and hope stills her voice for a moment. "I think you also might want to consider what Quentin will do if he finds out about you two."

"I do not care."

"Of course," Roxanne wonders if this is truth or just another of Carlos' lies.

"I do not care because I have found someone else to care about besides you."

"You're different."

"And I am not all that sure worrying about the wrath of Quentin means much--given what may happen anyway."

Roxanne kisses him on the cheek. As she sees it, Carlos has finally taken the step Roxanne has been fearing and hoping for years. He is moving on from her and that means they are both finally free. "That is great. I hate her."

"Just in time for the end of the world," he says, face bright as the sun. They stroll along in silence until they enter the throngs marching up and down University Avenue.

Roxanne reminds herself that joy for a person, especially Carlos, is more important than any possible hurt. "And Carlos, I think you are right; the hell with Quentin Conworth. If you cannot get the aliens to respond his goose is cooked no matter what he hangs on you. And if you do get to the aliens he cannot touch you. You are free, Carlos. You truly care--and it is not the end of the world."

"It just feels like it."

"Finally. Carlos, do you remember that day in the van when those wanna-be terrorists took us to that mall the Greenies were converting into an energy generation plant and then decided we were expendable for the good of the cause?"

"Of course."

"There is something I have wanted to tell you for years. You did a wonderful job of protecting us. Thank you for keeping me alive. I thought it was a terrible mistake at the time."

Carlos puts his arm around her and the two friends walk along the crowded street. "Did you know anger is the core of all friendships now?" They cross through crowds heading to where Carlos had been sitting.

"I just thought it was love," she says sadly. "I knew it--she is still there."

Carlos watches the beautiful dark woman on the stone bench reading her book. She looks up and they make eye contact. "Come on. I will walk you to Simon's car."

Roxanne feels a deep ugly knot in the pit of her stomach. "What about her?" Roxanne asks.

"She works for Quentin."

Roxanne glances at the beautiful woman watching them. "How do you know?"

"She did not have enough League to pay for a chair at the restaurant but she was reading a leather-bound book." They walk arm and arm away from the woman, Sid close by. "Her purse was constantly facing me--even as we returned. And...I tapped into a security database the other day--don't tell Simon--I saw her picture as a contract operative hired for surveillance. Her code name is Gertrude."

"It seems to me you want her and she wants you."

"You are truly a sensualist." They laugh, wrapped in the comfort of an old friendship. Nonetheless, many who pass them think they are lovers. Including the woman with the book whom Quentin had assigned to trail Carlos this morning; she slams the book shut and gets up angrily. Tomorrow when her report contradicts another report--the one filed by the mime--that says Susan and Carlos are lovers Quentin will choose to believe Gertrude's observations. Even for Quentin Conworth, the dusk is becoming too lonely and cold.

Chapter Sixteen

Like a cuddling lover, calm waves bump the night shore. The smell of bay laurel ranges over hills mixing with smoky fires as families deeply wrapped, sleep in each other's arms. Crickets in weeds chirp under the blanket of night while dogs hug rustling leaves. A cool breeze rolls over the parking lots and through the alcoves between the SETI buildings while a lone figure maundering the compound looks up at the stars, finding a place to sit on the dew-soaked grass.

Carlos sighs, imagining Susan stepping around a building's edge and crossing the night to embrace him. The last two evenings, wandering the site, he had bumped into Susan well past midnight. The first night, he had cheered her up with a rendition of the ape-walk used in a schoolyard many years ago. They laughed about that before making love. On the second night, just before dawn, Susan cried when she said there was no future for them while their tasks remain unfulfilled. This afternoon, when Carlos thought he had finally broken through her wall of resolve; Susan left, with one hand by her side telling him not to follow.

Tonight, he plans to tell Susan life holds more than task. But so far tonight has been a bust. Carlos--no longer able to bury his feelings in some deep maw--gazes at the bay night bathed in moon-blue light. Wondering how his feeble heart can possibly bare the din he feels inside, Carlos rests his back against the new mowed lawn. He remembers as a child, the same wind and moon, the same night sky, the mowed-grass smell, the flowers' scent riding the breezes, the longing for a-Her to appear. Tonight, Carlos believes he knows her name and so waits--as best he can.

At four AM, Carlos passes the door to Susan's new office wondering if Susan is asleep with Quentin or has she thought of him at all tonight? He enters the hallway that leads to the control room stairs. Walking the hollow hallway looking at empty, spare offices, vision blurring from fatigue, he sees no colors just shadows. Moments later staring at one of the surveillance cameras wondering what it must be like to see people's lives from a distant control room--he tells himself it would all become boring, quickly. Yet, the omnipotence--the feeling has a lure he cannot yet understand. Crossing to the tan cinder block stairwell, going over the basics of his craft, wondering why none of his lover-levers work, he descends the brightly lit stairs. Carlos Jordan is an individual with too many questions, too little sleep, and an awakening heart.

Outside the control room, Carlos continues to jump from meeting to meeting, arguing with linguists, querying scientists, picking the brains of advertising people, as he relentlessly searches for a lever into Susan's heart and a conversation with the aliens. He cannot convince himself that there is not a tie--and that he finds maddening. What makes it worse is that two hours from now the search for the alien repeater station will recommence. The silence he requested and got from Quentin, is about to end. For Carlos, this signals the climax of humanity's chances for survival. He knows humanity waited too long to address the horrors of climate change and feels he as well has waited too long to claim Susan's heart. He senses Susan slipping away, takes out his cell phone, and again calls Quentin to ask for another day of a delay in recommencing the search for the alien repeater station. More static--Quentin's phone is off-line. A stab of rage wells up in Carlos; he does not know Quentin has been a ghost this last week, jetting back and forth to Iceland occasionally holing up in his office making contingency plans for Carlos' failure--seeing Susan only in meetings. Funding cuts killing the project are already underway; Quentin, Susan knows, may soon have little use for her. These two mine their path of intimacy waiting for battle. It is one reason Susan has been at home all night. She is trying to protect herself--and key personnel--from being furloughed and worse.

Carlos sits on a cold concrete stair and thinks back to a discussion about the space vehicle, Armstrong. Susan had appeared in Quentin's office like a goddess--dressed in a blue silk chemise and wearing a bright blue lilac on her neckline. Carrying a large bouquet of white roses in her hand, she made a point of circling the desk and whispering in Quentin's ear. She said he deserved flowers; that had elicited a wide grin from Quentin and headache for Carlos. Placing the flowers in a vase, she glanced at Carlos, and her eyes sang. They could have launched a thousand rockets. Her glow stayed with him as if it were a diamond appearing before a pair of coal miner's eyes. Carlos saw her later, her gaiety vanished: crying, having seen herself as a foolish shadow of the apocalypse.

Roxanne was partially right when she said Susan would do anything to stay on top of getting a response from the aliens. With Quentin, with Carlos, with the whole world, no cost was too dear for Susan. She was driven towards a single goal of salvation and in the process had attempted to thrust aside anything that got in the way of her goal. Finally, she felt this quixotic pursuit left her nothing more to shed--other than her self.

Susan had puttered about cleaning and writing notes for the artisans, telling them how well things were going on her house, and what needed to be done today. She had dreamed of the Athens' bicycle race paved with the bodies of dead women and children. That was at two o'clock. Now she sits up knowing where Carlos is and sought his touch, but her gratitude to Quentin for his work rebuffed every advance. After three nights she can no longer go back, finally recognizing that her fall may end hard and believing there is only a whimper left inside her. That like a rotting shell of a building, she feels she will soon collapse in on herself leaving only rubble. And in her collapse, she fears the obsidian heart she has groomed might crush Carlos; so she remains in her partially built home--nobility gone mad.

An hour later, Carlos stands at the glass wall, looking at the two rows of white consoles in the brightly lit control room wondering how Susan can be so distant from him. Dawn sits in the back row of terminals keeping track of nothing while technicians work on a glitch in the second row. Carlos gazes blankly past her as if she were one of the fixtures: banks of data screens on the wall, keyboards, chairs, the useless numbers everywhere.

--Perhaps there is no answer to this problem. Perhaps it is like our waiting too long, listening too much to the media pap: the oils' portrait of reality. This whole mess was caused by our insane need for certainty, and the questions that now laugh at our need to repeat, and be able to repeat, something, anything, over and over: The questions on the reliability of climate models during the turn of the century. The questions of certainty as to how much it would cost to deal with climate change. The questions of who would lose and who would win. The questionable nature of the wealthy and the questions about how much a human life is worth. The questions caused by misinformation and greed. The insanely ridiculous questions and answers about solving a global problem without causing any discomfort.

--Ironic, the planet was heaving and our ancestors were watching their stock portfolios. If they could have just seen how useless their money would become and how quickly it could vanish. It's all question, I hate the damn things. If we just knew why the Rostackmidarifians are so interested in question marks, we would have a chance. We could use the information. But they are too cagey for that. That's wrong. You do not question why someone needs something when you negotiate. You use the data. So the data is we have what they seek: question marks. Strange, silly, super intelligent creatures... Or maybe they aren't that intelligent. Maybe they are making a mistake, not us--

Carlos looks at the clock between the large data screen on the wall: a half hour before the repeaters come back on line. He stares at the hundreds of question marks around the room.

--So here we are my friend. What more could you want--

He stares at the door and walls. "No way." He hurries in passing the bank of printers. The door squeaks shut. Dawn spins in her chair. The five technicians on the other side of the console are too scared to care. They stayed all night hoping, guessing Carlos, someone, would try to make one last effort.

Dawn, who cannot do enough for Carlos, faces him. Wearing a ragged blue wool sweater and blue jeans his white hair strewn about his face Carlos looks like a man fresh from a mugging; his wild grin belongs to a groom at a bachelor party. She thinks it is the gait of Carlos' genius.

Carlos nods to Dawn and walks over to pour himself a cup of tea from the small table on the side of the room; then sits down at his console next to Dawn. Saying hello he notices the light gold of her scalp gleams like a halo. She wears this sunny paint for everyone this morning. He also notices her black and purple jump suit fits her like a designer dress. She speaks: "So, what's up?"

"We are going to try something a bit different since we have nothing to lose." As he types a new message, the five technicians glance at each other. Dawn taps sculpted fingers on the white Formica desk and watches Carlos push the enter key on his terminal. A bizarre attempt at communication reaches across the universe. If it fails, the review of practice will uncover it; and when the mud hits the fan Quentin will hang him with it. The others in the room note a message has been sent out without review. They look over to Dawn. She shrugs her shoulders. "Anyone care to complain?"

A second later a startled voice from one of the technicians yells: "Oh, my. We have a message. It is text." The technicians shake their fears and trip over each other to get to the stations in the front row. One of them punches a button that will alert all first line management as well as the rest of the technical staff. Within minutes the room will be swarming with people. "Confirmed. Text--and it's from our friends in space," says another voice. Carlos cannot move; he tells himself he is dreaming. The print head begins to sweep back and forth. Pushing her way passed all of them, Dawn reads the message out loud.

"Your humor, while far more advanced than anticipated, has a gruesome tone only tolerable."

"They didn't know we couldn't solve it." Carlos laughs loudly and taps out another message. He hits the send key.

"What the hell are you doing?" Dawn mumbles.

Immediately one old bulb in the corner of the room blows out. "Uh, oh." Carlos, stares at the bulb. "But they can solve it."

Dawn, glancing at the bulb and hoping his words are a joke, says: "What did you send?" She wonders if he only sees what he wishes to see. A malaise had taken over many at SETI these days.

Staring at the bulb, Carlos says: "I told them the question mark becomes extinct with the humans in my first message."

Dawn shakes her head "They think you told them a joke."

"I know that. So the second message was a joke...it was a light bulb joke Simon told me."

She looks up at the blown light bulb. "Uh, oh." Dawn speaks slowly: "Quentin will have us hung."

"Message coming in," yells a lanky boy named Kelly. "Text again--what the hell--where'd the message go?"

Carlos' screen begins to fill with question marks. "They've established a direct feed in the Ambassador's terminal," Dawn says.

"The hell they do--not without going through me," Kelly replies, vaulting over the consoles to begin pounding on the keys at the security station next to Dawn.

"Son of a bitch," says another older man with dark hair. "I can't trace it. Alerting Security that we have a hacker."

The question marks form a question mark design. "Hacker, my Aunt Manny's knees." Carlos watches the technicians try to figure out how he has gotten a direct feed. "Don't bother," Carlos says, "they are just establishing a negotiating position."

"What?" Dawn asks.

"Exactly," Carlos laughs, telling himself he is finally on the right path.

Even though he still does not have any good idea of what the "right" path is--other than that he needs to keep pushing an absurd threat, he types: "Your meager resources will fail. We know you need our resources. The question mark lives with us and dies with us. Prove you can barter." He sends the message. Another bulb blows.

"I guess," she says shaking her head, "the aliens have no idea we have so much control over all the question marks...in the universe." Carlos winks at her. She punches a key sending a recording of what has happened to a secure bunker a half-mile away. Carlos looks at the blown bulbs wondering how to take the next step in precipitating response.

Three more people enter the control room followed by two heavily armed guards. One of the guards says: "Ambassador Jordan, Dr. Willoughby is on her way in. She has contacted Mr. Conworth as well. His orders are to turn on the search system."

"No, keep it off," Carlos says forcefully. He immediately realizes Susan was not in Quentin's bed tonight. His smile broadens.

"But, Mr. Conworth said..."

"Off, and that is a direct order. Dawn, I want you to begin a draw down of question marks. I want them removed from all print media and sequestered in our most secure location. We have a point to prove." It takes some work for him to keep a straight face.

The guards stare at Carlos listening to the insane order. Dawn replies: "Right, Ambassador, I'll get right on removing all the question marks and immediately begin destroying them." She is not sure why she is playing along with this absurd charade other than she trusts Carlos--and two blown light bulbs. The guards lean over and speak quietly to each other, unsure of what to do here.

Carlos taps out another message: "Transport or else."

"Oh, lord." The technician at the security console interrupts: "Audio coming through at seven-hundred fifty meg, signal is frequency modulated. Source undetermined but it is not terrestrial." Carlos taps the recording button on his console and stares at the cone-shaped speaker that hangs between fluorescent light panels overhead. The lights begin to flicker but they do not go out. "Dawn, what are you waiting for now? I want those question marks sequestered and if anyone resists have the guards arrest them and then have them destroy their question marks as well. Oh, and make sure you tell security that I have confirmed our earlier concern that the control room may be under direct scrutiny by the aliens."

Everyone in the room, other than Carlos, loses all sense of amusement. The two guards understand the call for the electronic security teams to be woken up and delivered to this spot. One guard exits the room.

A dreamy voice speaks: *"Very funny Your reality verification system is charming Your gruesome humor is delightful I am pleased importance has so much meaning for you Killing so many is an odd way of showing respect though I do not judge But know that madness as the rule of law has no place Clarify your terms for propagation of that which we seek"*

Carlos brings forth a loud fake laugh and leans over to the microphone built into his terminal. The door bursts open and Susan enters. Carlos and she look at each other a moment. Her eyes fill with wonder, but little else; they cut Carlos like shards of glass. "Go ahead, Ambassador. This is your show. You are calling the shots. The rest of you get on helping Dawn remove all available question marks. This is priority one." Susan has been monitoring the control room from her limousine.

Carlos takes a breath and turns on the microphone. "There are no terms. The question marks die with us."

"You always speak with intentions of price"

"We seek community. Otherwise all the question marks will be consumed. We wish to discuss this but we will only do this in person. Since we do not have an effective system you are to show your good faith by providing us with a method of meeting." He watches the last few light bulbs. None blow out or even flicker.

Susan passes him a note: "Could this lead to war?" He immediately scratches out the question mark.

"This shall address this"

Five security guards enter the control room and begin to prepare for sophisticated electronics to arrive, which will supposedly locate surveillance equipment.

"Adorable humor"

Susan whisks the guards from the room with a flick of her wrist. She passes him another note. "Why do they think this is funny?"

Carlos looks up at Susan, "They screwed up."

"Dawn tap into my audio and get me out on a U.N. band." Susan speaks into her cell phone: "Tell the guards anyone who tries to hoard question marks is to be shot."

"More voice coming over," says Dawn. She is dumfounded by the madness that goes on around her. Carlos rides the tiger and does not have time to recognize the insane nature of the unfolding events.

"It is punctuation. Of course you are a dying world, you wish to stop a process your replicationists have created. This cannot be done safely. Even to provide a safe location, where some of you may ride out the disasters, the program they run under forbids this action. But the costs are so high. You may have the madness you seek."

Feeling comfortable at hearing what he thinks is the beginning of a negotiation, Carlos wonders if the stakes have risen or not. None the less he speaks: "We have great resources." Carlos shuts off his microphone even though he considers the action absurd. He is certain the aliens have heard everything that has gone on in this room for months. "Susan, do I have your commitment that all question marks--even the question marks owned by the U.N. can be taken under my control and that I have full right to negotiate their existence?"

"Absolutely," She replies without a pause. "All of you on U.N. Band One please note this commitment." It does not pass Susan's notice that Carlos will now control all discussion with the aliens.

He switches on the microphone: "First we will have a meeting. You will assist in arranging this meeting. There we will talk about our diminishing numbers as well as safe locations. In return we will not remove or sequester any question marks. We assume that is acceptable."

"No locale should be as fouled as your planet--regardless of its content or the resources of its inhabitants. We will keep any blight from spreading but one will not take on the infection. It is my task. I am Pilnouth and we will meet in compatible space-time. Period, end quotation, etcetera, etcetera."

"Audio is gone. Signal is gone."

Carlos leans back in his chair fingers interlaced across the back of his neck. "It's a home run."

"I'll make sure the repeater search is eliminated," Susan says.

Carlos looks up at her. "No more excuses." He grins like a satyr believing Susan will no longer have task as an excuse for distance from him.

Her eyes light and a short sigh comes from her breast. "We're a long way from success you and I."

"Perhaps," he says with the heart of a teenager in love. "In any case, I think we will have a meeting though I don't think it will be here. They are agreeing to save some of us in exchange for our commitment for their access to question marks. Oh, and I think it is important to stress with everyone that we are under surveillance. They hear and know too much."

"Whatever the hell that means," Dawn mumbles.

"Dr. Willoughby, Security is on the line." Dawn fears for Carlos as Susan leans over the console. She picks up the phone expecting Chief of Security to blast her about what has happened.

A moment later her eyes widen and her mouth drops open. Carlos worries about this atypical reaction to news. He fears he has overplayed his hand. "I will be right up." Voice trembling, she places the receiver down and stares at Carlos trying to calm herself. "Dawn, you monitor communication. All of you recognize security in here has been compromised. No discussion about anything that has gone on. Do your jobs and stick to the game plan. Ambassador, please come with me." She turns without waiting for a response and walks out of the glass doors at the back of the room.

Carlos stands up. "Do not fix those bulbs--and gather all the question marks you can find." He leaves the room as the technicians begin to gather the question marks that cover every wall.

By the time he is out the door, Susan is running up the stairs. Carlos breaks into a run, knowing he will never catch her; he just does not want to lose sight of her. "Susan, where are we going?"

Her voice echoes down the stair well: "Your delivery is approaching, Carlos." A door slams shut.

"Delivery?" Before he finishes his next breath he knows the answer. The sounds of his footsteps clatter throughout the stairwell until he bursts through the doorway into the day. Carlos sees Susan standing at the corner of the building staring out at the salt marshes. He rushes to her.

Then he sees it: A shimmering two-story white dome sitting on the edge of San Francisco bay less than a mile away. Over the far hills, rays of red sunlight paint pink bottoms on clouds. "Oh my God it has already landed," she says in a whisper. "How can that be?"

Carlos, struck dumb his mind running blind in every direction at once, knows this is just the beginning.

Sirens' sound and a large green truck full of troops speeds by them. Bright yellow dirigibles rise skyward and helicopter gunships take to the air. Incredibly a set of six jets armed with weapons roars overhead. Carlos cannot remember the last time he saw so many jets together. Pink contrails from other jets soon fill the skies.

Troopers pile out of trucks. Sirens wale. Helicopters with arms of white light radiating from their snouts surround the object on the edge of the salt marsh. Tanks head out to the marsh at full speed. People pour out from buildings, then stop, staring at the white dome on the marshland.

"They can do anything they want, anytime they want," Carlos says quietly.

Susan speaks over the roar: "Looks like they are seriously concerned about us taking question marks into the abyss." Carlos looks at her making sure she understands.

"Brilliant, Carlos. Absolutely brilliant."

"All pretense must be rational. Though I must say I'm not sure what rational is now. I am still not fully convinced they are concerned about embargo or if they just like the joke."

"From what I saw on my car's video feed the light bulbs seem to indicate a sense of humor."

"Whatever that means," Carlos says.

Susan would like to hug him at this moment, but she will not because Quentin's car pulls up behind them. Quentin exits the car and walks toward them wearing a communications Head-Clamp. A monocle over his right eye displays information. Carlos turns--and for a moment--thinks he sees an alien.

"Regardless of the effect on the media, by the time I am done with question marks, I will make the last oil embargo look like a kindergarten party." Quentin walks, speaking to every executive member of the U.N.. Detailing events as he understands them and initiating downloads of video clips from the control room to be sent around the planet, Quentin chatters as he stares. A squad of heavily armed officers piles out of a truck and takes up positions around Quentin. Then, like MacArthur retaking the Philippines, he surveys the scene barking orders to secure the area. Quentin removes the Head-Clamp and hands the headset to a General who places it on his head and begins speaking. Quentin stands silently alongside them staring at the white dome watching as more and more equipment surrounds it. A second squad of soldiers takes up positions around them. "Do you think this Pilnouth is in there?" He asks.

"I do not think so. They said we had fouled our environment to the point of blight. I doubt they would send anyone here. I think there are systems in there that will allow us to do a face to face. Are you in agreement on embargoing question marks?" Carlos asks.

Quentin looks at him with the seriousness of an executioner. "You have our full support." Quentin does not like the turn of events but tells himself he still controls the project. His only real concern is the apparent sophistication of the alien surveillance system. He will send an E-mail later today indicating the embargo of question marks must have the reverence of a national flag. The memo will say that violators will be dismissed from the program and immediately stripped of their League rating. Continued violation will be punishable by death. "What do you think they will want for their assistance in showing us a safe zone?" Quentin asks.

Knowing how Quentin thinks, Carlos decides to set the stage for his function as intermediary. "More than we want to give them. You can be sure of that."

Quentin nods knowingly. "Susan, good job. When did that vessel arrive?" The sky lightens a bit more.

"Security said the unit appeared in the troposphere without crossing the stratosphere. There was no plume. There was no warning. It just appeared on the screens, traversed the troposphere then lighted here. Total time of contact before landing was three point one four minutes."

" PI," Carlos muses.

"Why do you say that?" Quentin asks. He points to the General with the headset. The General repeats Carlos' observation to the world. Quentin hopes that by passing on premature conclusions by Carlos that he might undermine him. Both Carlos and Susan recognize Carlos' mistake and glance quickly at each other. Quentin appears to stare pensively at the vessel in the salt marsh.

"Using an irrational number for a time event, and a vehicle appearing when it should not have, can be seen as a form of power and intelligence gathering capabilities. I think they are chiding us about our primitive science." He actually thinks the irrational number is some sophisticated joke but decides to cover his situation with an unappealing option.

"So we have a threat situation?"

"That is as likely as anything else," Susan says.

Carlos has an effective cover for his admiration of her: fear. Carlos believes it is Quentin's mother's milk. "They've already proved their capabilities. Hard to tell what it means."

Quentin speaks: "I bet if we check the timing we can get a better fix on their repeater location."

The emotional minefield between Susan and Quentin ignites. "Damn it, Quentin. Wake up. Forget that mode of defense. We are junior partners here," Susan says in a huff. "There is no repeater. Keep the damn thing off and hope everyone forgets about it. It will save your career." She looks at Carlos. "Don't worry--I will handle this."

Quentin's eyes flash destruction. "What would I do without you looking after me and keeping me from making more mistakes? Thanks, Susan." He leans over and kisses her gently on the cheek. In a whisper he says: "Perhaps we do need to talk."

"No, Quent."

Quentin's chest burns in a white fire. "I am going back in to direct operations. You two go out there but be careful." He flags down a small truck. When it stops, he gives orders for the driver to take Susan and Carlos to the security perimeter. He also orders the squad of soldiers to provide security.

Susan enters the front of the truck. Carlos piles into the back. Carlos, because of who he is, cannot help noticing this event of severance took place at the exact moment he, not Quentin, became the key figure in saving the planet. It is a deadly arrow aimed at a heart he cannot trust; his own.

The small vehicle drives toward the white object. "How did you know?" She asks, leaning back. She remains glued to his eyes. "Carlos, you took an awful chance. What if they had gone to war over question marks?" She asks herself what kind of lunatic takes a chance like he has just taken.

Watching her eyes fill with calculation, Carlos prepares for the worst. "I just didn't care," Carlos says with a tired grin. The truck slows to a stop at a checkpoint manned by six soldiers.

Susan closes her eyes for a moment as she works to regain control. Task and purpose own Susan's heart again. Susan once told herself that on a brighter day she would seek out the attentions of Carlos Jordan--and not to help him save the planet. Today she tells herself the day is brighter but she must direct his actions to keep a wild hare on track.

The smell of exhaust fumes turns her stomach. "What about their surveillance--what gave you the clue?" These words are merely a ploy to get Carlos to look at her. Susan seeks to measure his state.

His gaze is empty. All Carlos' training forces him to wonder if Susan could really be so spare of heart. "I've had the notion distance was irrelevant since I joined the project. It was how I explained the instantaneous communication and the lack of success in finding the repeater to myself. I also think we have a vision of reality our friends out there think is hilarious. Which means their experience of existence may be well beyond our imagination. I am evolving the theory that our awareness of our own absurdity is the only link to our hyper-sophisticated friends."

"The question mark embargo is a joke between you and them?"

"We take little steps in diplomacy and hope something shifts." There is no chance Carlos will ever talk to anyone else without the appropriate reverence to the embargo. It is his training. Deep inside he harbors an old feeling of gray as the green truck comes to a halt. A team of soldiers assembles around them.

Susan speaks: "You have done an amazing thing here today. Some of us are going to make it." The bright glow in her eyes scares Carlos. He believes that he sees a lure.

"I don't want to be laughed at by you."

She misunderstands: "If what you say is correct I think they will be laughing at you anyway. And I do not know whether to laugh at you, give you a medal, or have you committed."

The white shimmering object starts to glow. The soldiers take their place as human shields in front of Susan and Carlos. As the object begins to pulse, the soldiers push Susan and Carlos behind a nearby tank. A second later the dome becomes transparent. Another moment later all trace of the ship is gone and only the two large gun-metal-gray-cylinders remain. Peeking over the tank skirt, Susan says: "The science directorate is not going to like this one little bit."

"If you are thinking about a padded room for me you all might as well take the one next door," Carlos says. He steps from behind the tank. "It will be interesting to see how their devices function." Carlos watches as two teams of investigators assemble a dozen meters away.

"I hope telemetry has recorded it. I do not want to be the one who tells them the game of reality has changed."

"And you know, that is exactly what has taken place this morning," Carlos says darkly. He reforms the notion that perhaps there is no one for him; it is the comfortable cloak of Susan's distance.

The radio in the tank nearby crackles: "This is Romeo One. We have two cylinders approximately three meters high and one and one half meters in diameter. The silver dome has disappeared from view. All telemetry shows a null set of readings. All telemetry showed a steady decrease in readings until null energy was measured. It just ceased to exist..."

"All you fans of thermodynamic law can go home now," Carlos says with a grin. Susan looks at him sure he feels at home with what is taking place. She wonders if this is the response of a man marveling at progress or a lunatic pleased to see the world bending to his warped ways. Susan decides Simon Weiss must be part of the Armstrong crew. She will never consider attending the meeting herself; Quentin needs watching. The prize of safety will be much too tempting a resource for him. She is certain he will try to control any safe location.

"This is Romeo One. Cameras were on and taping the event. NorCal we plan to approach per procedure. Do you copy?"

"This is NorCal. We have it, Romeo One. Proceed."

The men and women suit up then remove instruments from nearby vehicles; they quickly approach the cylinders. Within moments the teams are beginning their examination. "NorCal, we have two cylinders with smooth metallic surfaces. On one end we have what appears to be standard NASA telemetry fittings--"

"Romeo One, again. Please repeat again."

"I said we see standard NASA telemetry fittings on one end of each cylinder. Screw threads and couplings, terminated wires with solder, ribbon cable with data-connectors."

"All you fans of security can go home as well," Carlos says.

"We copy, Romeo One. What is the function of the cylinders? Can you determine if they are weapons?"

"Negative. We cannot determine this. On the sides of each cylinder are plaques. One says: 'Engines do not foul'. The other says: 'In friendship'. Based on preliminary field telemetry the metal is not an alloy or base metal we know of. Radiation is nominal. Biological activity is non-existent. Chemical analysis and biological examination are being transmitted now. NorCal we seem to be looking at a pair of engines but we cannot confirm that either."

"Proceed with containment."

"We copy that: Proceed with containment. Romeo One out."

Carlos asks for and gets a pair of field glasses. He examines the engines and their apparently extraordinary blandness. "Looks like steel--looks like it could have come out of our machine shop," Carlos says. "And two engines--one for each ship--that ought to clarify the uselessness of our security. Standard NASA fittings too, we should not tell anyone in the media about that. They will think it is a hoax." A pair of trucks, each with a crane on the back, motors on passed them.

"I am standing here, and I am not sure it is not a hoax," Susan says. "I am going to go examine the engines once containment is erected. I want you to get in touch with Simon and begin plans for a face to face. We know something is going to happen like that." Susan also wants to make sure Carlos is safe.

"We know nothing," Carlos says. "It is our saving grace."

Chapter Seventeen

For three months, SETI had been the center of the Earth. With scientists and government officials seeking influence into the plan for alien contact, business people and starlets looking for some way to become part of the safe site, visitors and terrorists, seekers and skeptics, descending on Mountain View like a landslide, the activity had been nothing short of madness. Quentin spending mega-watts sprucing up SETI with landscaping, a new reception hall, a huge new parking lot, and even new utensils for lavish dinners, every possible amenity in place: props for the visitors in Quentin's palace. The military was fierce guarding the base--everyone down to the lowest private knew he or she was humanity's only hope and assaults received crushing brutal responses.

But now, with the Armstrong launch only four weeks away the action has moved to Huntsville, Alabama. No more need for display, the landscaping is dead or drowned, the reception hall a barracks for troops--many of whom are loyal only to Quentin Conworth--the utensils stolen.

So begins the warmest winter ever recorded in Northern California, where odd weeds have taken hold of the new airfield-sized parking lot. Growing in pavement cracks, most of these weeds sport a dark green layer of dust that washes away during storms, revealing lighter red leaves. The green dust is chock full of carbonate--in a variance of photosynthesis--and some believe a significant potential carbon sink. However, the research shows the plant grows incredibly fast, but only in cracked blacktop; ironically, much of the planet's blacktop has been removed for trees. Examination of the plant has begun, but there is no energy budget left for anything besides the launch and the preparations for Chaos should contact fail. Another factor, the amount of CO2 in the atmosphere and its persistency making the effort more desperate every day.

Pulling his briefcase from the green limousine, Stanislaus Damube looks around the vast parking area; only ten other cars litter a lot that used to be the front lawn of SETI. He checks out the smaller, and more exclusive, executive parking structure in front of him. It girdles the first floor of the three-story white concrete building that is the new SETI mission headquarters--and Quentin's castle. Solid and noiseless the structure looks as if it might withstand an atomic explosion. White-painted government vehicles, with green bands along the bottom, sit neatly under a steel awning.

--When it comes to privileges, Conworth certainly knows how to work them. In the land of the blind, Quentin not only has sight, he has a tax on sound. But the gods tease Quentin, offering him ruler of the Earth at this time. However, his power wanes in four weeks. Another breach in Quentin's armor--

Damube knows people realize Quentin has an inside track on where salvation might lie. He also knows he will never run the big show, but he plans to make sure he has allied himself with the winning team. He admires Quentin's power; but the jury is still out on who will eventually own the critical information of where the safe location is located. Nonetheless, he has no plans to seek a new mentor, though he believes a few tests are in order.

A loud creak catches his attention and he looks to his right; a huge plastic greenhouse shudders in the winds. The greenhouse was a gift for the employees three months ago from the SETI contractors so they might grow their own vegetables. Convoys of fresh fruits and vegetables are regularly attacked by black-marketeers. Unfortunately, the first windstorm tore the recycled plastic siding off the greenhouse and mounds of dust blew in, drowning young seedlings. During the next storm, half the support poles gave way and the gift abandoned. He hears another sirocco whistle through broken building as "Do Not Trespass" signs slap hard against the snapped white poles.

--Like a shopping mall: A cheap gift for the ignorant--

Oddly, it is this building's structural weakness that has allowed Damube to keep his command of the project. The smart money says only a fool would trust a space vehicle built these days. He leans into the back door of the limousine speaking to his chauffeur: "I'll walk to the front entrance from here. Let them check over the car at security then park under the awning and wait." Damube watches the vehicle roll off towards a security station by the covered parking.

Walking sprightly to the front of the building, he avoids the dried puddles of fine dust that collects in the foot-deep holes of the cracked blacktop. He watches a sand devil appear then swirl across the parking area. Even for a large man like he, the winds can be dangerous if they suck him into one of the mini-twisters. Appearing like phantoms, they dance across a flat landscape eating anything in their way, then vanish leaving more debris. The tan sand devil swirling dust and sweepings moves towards him, then abruptly staggers off at ninety degrees toward the main gate. Five seconds later it disappears, again no more than a hot breeze.

Crossing onto the thin margin of grass, he steps on another new strain of plant. Its gray sick looking stalks and stumpy leaves are perforated by grit caught in the malevolent winds. It is called Endurium, because it uses the forty-mile-an-hour gusts off the oceans to pump water around punctured leaves. Five years ago these plants were everywhere around here but now the species thrives up by the Oregon border where it is a bit cooler.

--Even the plants know it's time to hide. Actually that's my jackpot, and that crackpot Jordan the problem. He refuses to push the issue of the safe zone. Though if he gets the information without anyone else being around, and that could very likely happen when he meets with the alien, Pilnouth, than we might have another game here. It would be interesting if the kook were wily as a fox. With the right information he could turn Quentin into dust. Men have been known to change like that when there is a woman involved. Damn her--

His formal white mesh shirt and white cotton pants flap in the hot breeze; Damube steps off the grass median onto the concrete leading to the covered parking area. He glances to the right; guards and their dogs swarm over his car looking for weapons and explosives. The Urchins--as Damube calls the populous--have been more aggressive with bombs of late so all autos are searched thoroughly. Crossing under the awning he notes the green and white cars have brown body rot in the corners of the wheel wells. Glancing into the passenger area he sees torn green upholstery and shot guns locked in their racks between the passenger and the driver seats. New U.N. regulations call for all drivers to carry these weapons. So what if the vehicles are dangerous; everything is dangerous.

At the heavy glass doors, he pulls his executive ponytail--which looks more like a dreadlock to his embarrassment--out of his collar. It ends just below his shoulders. A small gold clip in the shape of the Armstrong keeps the ends together. The doors swoosh open and he steps in the small heat lock.

The fans blow over him to remove the surface layer of dust. It is much cooler. Then, the second set of heavy glass doors open to a large reception area. Four shining steel sculptures hang on the twenty-foot high walls--decorated in brown rice paper. Looking like icebergs, the steel sculptures glisten from overhead spotlights. The upside down pyramids were Quentin's idea when this all broke. They are supposed to symbolize change.

Twin yellow steel doors lead into Quentin's kingdom. Damube walks up to the receptionist. She wears the same flower print green shift as she always wears. Only now it has brown patches on the shoulders. Damube is not proud to be part of an effort that has brought a little bit of prosperity to the poor of this area. He thinks this woman shabby.

Her bored glance brightens. "Captain Damube, welcome back. We haven't seen you in a while." Stanislaus decides to allow her to announce him. A show of respect for Quentin, it will also mean Quentin will either need to come get him or send an escort. Either way Damube will arrive with a flourish.

Damube surveys the breasts straining the material of her dress. Then he glances about the lobby. "Where is Wilson, the guard?"

"Ten years at the Richmond generators," she replies. "He took a U.N. vehicle and went off on a joy-ride along the ocean--after he heard he was laid off--dumb bunny."

"He got off lightly." Damube says.

Dana rolls her eyes. She does not like Captain Damube but she hopes another roll in the back of his limousine might make her permanent here at SETI. "By the way, you owe me a dinner. I told you Dr. Weiss would get on the mission."

"I stand corrected," Damube says bowing at the waist and still wondering what tidbit of information Susan Willoughby holds over Quentin's head to have accomplished that miracle.

"I wish my husband could take me for a ride along the ocean."

Damube frowns having no patience for her sob stories. "Tell Quentin Conworth I'm here." Looking at her pretty face he decides he will take her again if it is necessary for him to stay overnight.

She buzzes Quentin Conworth; Damube walks to the plexiglas-covered table that holds a mock-up of the Armstrong and her sister ship, the Constitution. The only difference between the two ships, unseen in the models, is a slight bulge on the underside of the Constitution. It is the reason Damube is at SETI today.

He stares at the silver colored ships and again congratulates himself on his command of the mission to the aliens--which he considers the greatest adventure in history: "A desperate voyage into the great unknown to find salvation for a dying humanity." He already hears history singing his praises as the individual who took whatever steps necessary for salvation, regardless of cost. He tells himself there is no price too dear to save his species and smirks that Quentin did not wish to command the mission. Stanislaus sees himself as an adventurer caught in a world of politicians and cowards who sneak up and attack each other with memos and innuendos. He finds politics disreputable, but a necessary evil of society and considers it a point of honor to subjugate himself to the needs of the political process. Though anyone who welcomes its intrusions Damube finds lacking. Stanislaus looks up from the models and winks at Dana. She smiles knowing she gets one more chance to keep her family safe.

A yellow steel door opens and Quentin enters wearing a custom tailored version of Damube's cotton pants and shirt. Broad-chested and tan, Quentin does not look like a man in his early fifties. His thick brown ponytail drapes over his right shoulder and rests on his broad swimmer's chest. Quentin has trimmed it so it hangs an inch or two above where his teat would be. His recent promotion to Director of Revitalization of North America allows him to wear it well past his waist. Quentin, in a show of bravado, is telling the world he defines his power and no one else.

"That new pool you put in at your house agrees with you. You look great, for an old man." Stanislaus walks toward him extending a bear-sized palm.

They shake hands. "Stanislaus, it has been too long. How are you?" Quentin hides his chagrin at this absurd show of camaraderie with sculpted teeth and a handsome open smile--like a carnivorous plant.

"How are things going?"

Quentin looks at the receptionist who occasionally shares Stanislaus' bed. Her sweet smile has no allure for him. He mourns the loss of his relationship with Susan--even though the parade of starlets that has passed through his office and bedroom these last few months has been a good ego massage. Quentin misses her wit and insight. "Let's go to my office."

"Anything you say, Quent."

Quentin decides there is a problem of some sort and that Damube wants to use it for leverage. It explains Damube's lack of decorum. The men walk through the door and up the stairs. "How were the meetings?" Quentin says. "You find everything straightened around to your satisfaction with our friends in Toronto?"

"We're all set except for a minor problem with the engine analysis. We have no data. All attempts at understanding the mechanisms have proven

 Daniel H. Gottlieb

useless. We are an armada of two," Damube says, as they walk along.

--So that's it. We can't reverse engineer the pod. Stan knows there will be no other ships and all our plans for a military solution will rest with him. That and my inability to produce the safe zone. Okay, I see--

The two individuals enter Quentin Conworth's new office. It smells from the tanned leather of a well-worn saddle. Damube sits on a green and white striped cloth sofa next to the door. Quentin props himself on the ledge between two corner windows. Between them rest a desk and chairs. Sunlight pours through the large windows and the winds are mute.

Damube points out the window. A blue pipe snaking along the tar roof leads to a pair of hourglass-shaped shrouds. "Do they work?"

"Taken some time, but I think we have it figured out. My office and a few others are now considered safe. It also looks like we will be able to piggyback off the alien's signal and bounce telemetry back here instantaneously once the Armstrong is in space. I will have the same data you do. I will even have pictures ready for the six o'clock news and the Secretary's speech--if I decide to let them out to the nets." Conworth checks Damube's response and sees an empty stare. Any plans of keeping secrets during the flight are now gone. On the other hand, Quentin's disclosure is another indication of Quentin's tenuous hold on the reins of power and both men know it. Quentin frowns and decides it is time to squash Damube's insolence. He reaches in his desk drawer and produces a picture that he hands to Damube. In the picture, two small movable disks about the size of pizza pans are visible like flat eyes. "As you can see the ion systems are in place but the shielding is being redone. I hear Huntsville does not agree with you and they think the defense systems need more shielding."

This bit of news immediately affects Damube. "I'm more concerned that the weapons have an effect on the Rostackmidarifians--if we need to use them. Shielding means little in the final analysis. We need to know how we can acquire leverage."

"Ambassador Jordan's visit will give us that data. We will need to make sure the shielding works this time. Will you handle the tests next week?" Quentin says placing some paper on the table in front of Damube.

Warily, Stanislaus gets up to look over the work orders. "Of course, but someone screwed up. This is the Constitution. I'll have the weapon's system moved to the Armstrong and be ready the week after next."

"Screwed up, how?" Quentin replies casually, feeling a bit better about his ability to control matters. He now knows that no one told Stanislaus about the change in plans while he was in Toronto. That means he has no important allies without Quentin's standard in hand.

Stanislaus blinks. "I thought you said if they got the ion systems finished in time they would place them on the Armstrong as well as the Constitution?"

Quentin sits in the chair and crosses his arms in front of him "I determined there is too much to lose by ineffectual shielding. And we need information--so I told them to go ahead and place them on the Constitution while you were busy in Toronto. I thought you were informed of this decision. I asked Susan to talk to you about it. She is so efficient--I never even checked to see if she had done it. Oh well, everyone messes up now and again. I promise you, if we need to use the Constitution--you will have command."

"If I get back alive," says Damube trying to hide his anger at being slapped down. "So I'm not an armada of two but an armada of one? And that one without a weapon system?"

"You know how important recon is, Stan," Quentin replies, looking straight at him. "We need to know what we are up against here. Do we not?" Quentin watches the veins pulse on the side of Damube's round head.

Damube stares out the window at the twin hourglass structures that shield Quentin's office. Later today he will uncover the bill of lading indicating their recent shipment from Huntsville and that these are not the systems ordered--they are the shields from the Armstrong. "Wise move to send a scouting party before sending an aggressor force." Stanislaus places the paper back down on the desk and sits back on the couch. He feels a pawn, something he hates. "I should have known."

"You certainly should have. By the way, how is your son doing?"

"Doing better now that he is back east with me." Stanislaus decides to return fire. "Did you know he was at the same Guide Dog facility as Weiss' new girl friend? In fact I met her once. She was Taylor's first trainer out here. Temperamental though, she refused to work with him after there was some problem with an Urchin trying to keep my boy from getting a certain dog. Strange coincidence they worked together, aye?"

"No coincidence. Small population of humans--lots of crossover." Quentin Conworth taps his fingers on the ledge of the desk. He didn't know about her. "Well I guess we should know more about her. How long have they been together?"

"I don't know. I just made the connection after talking to my son. He heard me on the phone with the doctors to see if there was some way to keep Weiss off the mission."

"He goes. But I want her checked out. What is her name?"

"Roxanne Gladstone." A quick smile emerges--then a plastered-on look of concern follows. "Quentin, are you all right?"

He sits frozen--a man so consumed by anger he cannot speak. Quentin believes he has been cuckolded. The report he chose to believe last summer about Carlos Jordan was incorrect. Susan and Carlos were lovers--and he believes the disintegration of his relationship was fostered by her misrepresentation. He stares blankly at the wall over Damube's head wondering how long Damube has known about Susan's betrayal. Quentin Conworth smirks: "I don't understand this thing that's going on with Weiss." He sighs looking at the smile on Damube's face. "Well who knows? Check her out and get back to me. So what happened in Toronto? Any more clues on where our friends, the Rosts, think we will be safe?"

Damube reaches in his briefcase and pulls out a disk knowing he scored well with that last one. He also knows Quentin did not know about Carlos and Susan and now considers it wise to broaden his allegiances. "This wasn't easy to get," he says getting up and putting the file on Quentin's desk. "Four days running I was up until three in the morning--poker with some bit-heads."

Still expecting little loyalty from Damube, Quentin is now certain the price of all loyalty is the safe zone location. This stance also conveniently explains Susan's preference for Carlos over Stanislaus as Ambassador. And though he does not recognize it, for Quentin, Damube's disclosure is a help: Before, Quentin found it difficult to cope with his sense of loss. Her departure being far more painful for him than he cared to admit. But this new information, while an insult to injury, has given him a focus for his anger--something Quentin can channel into satisfaction. "Did you review the climate data?"

Damube nods. "They started out talking about linear weather events but by the second night of drinking they opened the kimono and began explaining we had hit the knee of the curve sometime around two-thousand, fourteen and soon after that we phase shifted. The latest models show disaster after disaster and we can't predict them until they are forming."

"So we will have a few months notice still. Why aren't the models more complex?" Quentin already knows the answer, but he wants to see how far Damube's loyalty has degenerated.

"The stock answer is: we have a hundred individuals with PCs here, not a thousand PhDs running ten super computers and another thousand well-trained climatologists and mathematicians sucking up questions. Most of the people running the simulations don't even know how to do it right. By the time they finish a complex simulation it could be yesterday's news. The real answer is we believed our own notion that weather would act in a linear fashion."

"Meaning?"

"When we had all those resources we should have worked the problem." Stanislaus sees the stalwart stare that intimidates so many. He stares right back.

In those brown eyes Quentin sees how tenuous his hold on power has become. Stanislaus continues speaking: "They won't put a number on how many die. The only thing they're sure of is many more are going to die and infrastructure will continue to decay at an increasing pace. As to which locations look good, I've seen only pure guess on that as well. So far as consensus goes it could be Northern Canada. Of course there is still the concern about white earth--the next ice age."

Both men grin at the joke.

Once people were told the salinity of the ocean would decrease to the point that enough heat might not be transported by the oceans to the further reaches of the Northern and Southern hemisphere. The result would be a new ice age. History proved there was a slowing but no cessation and the heat increased from the elimination of Arctic ice in the summer and the decrease in polar albedo more than made up for the loss.

Quentin notes Damube has left Argentina and Greenland out of his report. "So we have nothing."

"Less than nothing--we have frightened politicians kowtowing to fear and their technical gurus scared that if they say the wrong thing they will be left in the dust."

A small beeper chirps. Quentin glances at the ID of the sender and smiles. "Susan wants to talk to me." He places the pager back on his desk. "Arrange a meeting that requires Susan's attendance. Make sure she has to fly. Make sure she flies alone. I'll take care of the rest."

Stanislaus Damube watches the leer of power. "So, its an American Pie for Susan. What about Jordan? Don't we want to get rid of him also?"

Quentin replies, "Jordan's doing a good job for us. You better than anybody knows how difficult that job is." Quentin grins. "So, how about a game of racquetball and some dinner?"

Susan Willoughby waits a few minutes for Quentin to respond then takes the short walk down the hall to Quentin's office. The alien's latest message telling them the venue for the meeting is not in space but on the Rostackmidarifians' home world worries her. In her opinion none of the spacecraft are even remotely safe and the stress of a planetary reentry in the shuttle Newton could be a death sentence for Carlos. Knocking on the door before entering, she finds an empty office and the latest pictures of the Constitution on Quentin's desk.

--That means Stan is here and they are chatting. But why wouldn't he respond? Perhaps another fit of pique. He resents being beaten at his own game--

Checking her watch, she seeks out Carlos. He has no intention of changing the meeting arrangements. Concerns about his bent toward self-destruction resurface for her. She returns to her office, sits back in her chair and closes her eyes.

--It was tough enough getting Simon on the flight; and even with Simon there for help, Carlos will be defenseless. Damube will jettison Carlos at the first possible opportunity. Now there is this threat to Carlos' life by forcing him to use another badly made craft for reentry--

Susan moans silently and wonders if she has made a mistake by not going on the mission. Her heart wants to go but her head tells her Quentin is not to be trusted. Opening her eyes she looks around disgusted with herself and everything she has seen the last few months. The shows by the frightened power elite, the fawning by young starlets trying to save their bacon, even her own remorseless focus for success--they all have just begun to seem like retribution to a stupid species. When do the problems end? She wonders. And why couldn't she have a life without doom or demons waiting around every corner?

Grabbing her computer and a large gray box, Susan closes the door behind her and tells her secretary Tom, he should contact her on the satellite phone if Quentin responds to her page. She lifts the gray box to make sure Tom understands this is serious since using this high priority system for communication is frowned upon. There are only a handful of transponder links that still work.

Exiting the new lobby into the late day, she scans the remains of Quentin's midway and shudders at memories of intimacy. Glancing at the dead landscaping, she knows his megalomania will have no bounds once he has the safe zone location.

--Rather than using the energy available to help others, Quentin commandeered every resource within a hundred miles to bolster his flagging status. Then he just lets his carnival of power die. The jerk. This is why I stayed here during the flight--

Walking under the awning to her white sedan, Susan opens the door of her car and notices the large chip in the back window. A rock was thrown at her last week. Another rock in the same place might shatter the window or worse cause her to lose control of the car on some roadway. The marauders on the roadways would swoop down on her like hungry crows. For a moment she considers the peace of death then tells herself she is not expendable.

--Or perhaps I am expendable--

She steps inside the car and flicks a switch that will disconnect the charger cable from the vehicle. The car's engine hums. Backing out, she passes the large green limousine belonging to Damube.

--Only he would have the ego to shuttle his private vehicle across the country--

She sees a small blue and red sticker that says: 'Support the Blind' on the back bumper. Not realizing she has seen the sticker once before, on Simon's car, she heads out of the parking lot.

Susan shifts into second gear, passing the guards and their dogs. After three more checkpoints--the last one a massive concrete wall with gun emplacements--she is out on what passes for roadway. The combination of blacktop and crushed debris from shattered buildings ticks and slaps the bottom of the vehicle with small stones. She directs the car by the scrub bushes lining the entrance to the single lane freeway heading north and tightens her grip on the steering wheel as she accelerates. The car's front wheels jiggle back and forth once she tops thirty miles an hour. Scanning the roadway for potholes, she drives in a pensive silence.

--I am doing nothing I want anymore. I should call Carlos and invite him for dinner. Or perhaps he might want to ask Simon and his girl over as well. We could have a dinner of casoulet and wine. I could bake bread. Maybe later we might go for a walk. Carlos and I could slowly become lost in the woods behind my house. We could wind up by that rock outcropping where the burned out mansion had been. Maybe I could have placed a bottle of wine nearby with glasses. He would know then. He probably knows now. No, he still thinks I am an ice-water vessel. He has not sat with me once, since we made contact with the Rosts. We could sip wine with the moon's rise and then make love on the rocks. We would spend the whole night out there and I could tell him how proud I am of him and how scared I am. He would love me. He loves me now. I will make it all up to him after this is done--

Like the tides of an ocean she reaches for the shore that is Carlos. But like the waves of those tides it is only an illusion of time that they are getting closer. Sadly, her caring is not an indicator of her locked heart's desires but an indicator of her alarm--something Carlos sees, fears, and therefore misconstrues as manipulation. Susan has no notion that her caring rises with the level of danger she faces then recedes in moments of safety. If she did she might change it, but she is too wrapped up in other problems to see her dilemma.

--I need to be more careful. I can't let Carlos know how I feel. It would be too dangerous for all of us if Quentin suspected treachery. He would kill Carlos and I. No, he would wait until after the mission to kill Carlos, or until he has control of the safe zone to act. I need to wait until after the mission to let Carlos know how I feel. Quentin is so dangerous. Anything could happen. Quentin would kill me over any betrayal. Even if he didn't I would lose access so I could not make a bit of difference. Quentin would wind up depending on Stanislaus and that would lead to God knows what--

The high security telephone rings. Susan slows the car and pulls over to the side of the road. Despite the danger of stopping on the roadway she gets out of her car and hoists the gray box onto the hood. Pulling the small antenna out of the box and fumbling with the emergency phone, she answers. "Susan."

"This is Stanislaus, Susan. You are booked on a flight to Huntsville at five tomorrow morning. Quentin wants you to examine the Newton. We're concerned of Carlos' safety.

She taps her fingers on the cracked gray plastic of the box. Glancing around her for marauders, seeing only the remains of small office buildings, she tells herself this is a stupid place to stop but not as stupid as taking a flight at five in the morning because Stanislaus and Quentin are concerned over Carlos' safety. "Will you be flying back with me, Stan?" She waits holding her breath.

"I can't."

Susan listens to the static on the satellite link.

--Oh Susan, you really burned the toast this time. Quentin knows about Carlos and I--

"This is important, Susan."

"I understand, Stan."

Chapter Eighteen

Simon clears his throat, a bored actor about to enter a stage. He pushes on the mission center glass doors and enters the control room. Seeing Carlos hunched over his desk, Simon notes the disheveled hair, blue shirt, and pants; Carlos looks in need of a pressing. Leaning lightly on a wooden cane, Simon smiles hello to Dawn and nods to the other technicians. The technicians get out their scripts, turn off their headsets and turn on all the recording devices. The U.N. Directorate now videotapes all control room transmissions. After three months of these scripted conversations, reciting Quentin's lines has taken on an air of the absurd. They refer to themselves as "The DaDa's dadaists."

Like a man in an emotional coma, Carlos speaks his line to no one: "What are you doing here, uh, Dr. Weiss?" He remains hunched over, still readying his next transmission for the Rostackmidarifians.

"Susan said we have a problem."

He looks up. "Your leg is bandaged again. What happened? Another house fall on you?" Carlos is letting him know something is wrong by leaving the script. His intercourse with the alien has not been duplicated by any one else and this has led to a kind of immunity for Carlos. He does as he pleases.

Simon wonders if he is the only person left alive who may.

"Roxanne brought home a dog yesterday. It knocked over a lamp that landed on my leg."

"Where the heck are you going to keep a second dog?" He mouths the word "Susan."

Simon wonders what the Directorate will think of that. He shakes his head no. Carlos frowns and Simon says: "Out by the barn with the other dog, Sid. This one is named Condominium. He was a return to Guide Dogs Inc; seems he tried to impregnate every dog in Hillsborough last week."

Carlos shakes his head back and forth and shrugs his shoulders to indicate he does not know where Susan is either. "Are you two going to stay in that place in the hills?"

"I think we might. It is close to SETI and close to the guide dog facility." Simon mouths the word "later." Simon wonders if she is worth his friend's frustration and worry--then reminds himself again how he danced to a similar tune.

Carlos begins to write a note explaining that a coded phone message last night from Susan said they were in danger from Above. "Above" always means Quentin. Carlos crumples the paper. He fears any extraneous text just before a communication might derail discourse with the alien. "It is dangerous these days." He returns to the script.

Simon looks up at the clock. "I see. Is that yesterday's message?" Carlos hands him a paper and Simon appears to scan it. In fact he saw the transmission last evening when he and Carlos met with Quentin and Stanislaus. He recalls wondering why Susan was not present. Simon reads aloud: "'Engines: Two inductive systems usable by replicationists. They will form a gap for traveling between gravity displacement zones. They will self-initiate function when your system reads an external gravity of point zero one four of your planetary standard. They will shut off when they arrive at our home. Use your reentry vehicle for our planet as they will not function on our planet.' Their planet? Since when are we meeting on their planet?"

Carlos sits back in his seat crossing his arms in front of his chest: "You are looking at the notification."

"Do we have a reentry vehicle besides the shuttle, Newton?"

"Nope," Carlos says. "Looks like I am going in by myself."

Dawn takes out a stick of gum and chews it. It means they should speed up the conversation. Transmission time with the aliens is always at three o'clock and it is past three now.

Simon speaks quickly. "A dangerous turn in the negotiations for you--one wrong move and the question marks die with you."

"And Captain Damube," Carlos drones out the words, "says there is no way to test the engines on the escape shuttle."

Dawn says her line: "I think we should forget this face to face. Let's try to get the data on the safe location via telecom." She leans back in her squeaky chair, knowing Damube sees glory. Quentin sees power. And Carlos sees adventure--maybe death. There is no possibility this mission will be scrubbed. She wonders what the alien, Pilnouth, sees.

Simon speaks: "We can try. Oh, this is bad news. Perhaps--"

"We need to talk to Susan. She has been out of touch since last night." Carlos says making it up as he goes along. "If something has happened to her there needs to be a full investigation." Carlos figures Quentin has done something to her, or plans to, and every member of the U.N. Directorate should know.

Simon, seeing Carlos' action as an attempt to protect Susan, says: "We don't know what will happen to any of us now. But we need to keep our priorities straight."

Carlos is suddenly mute.

"He doesn't care," Dawn says. "I think the question marks are better kept away from the aliens," filling in for Carlos.

Simon replies: "I've been studying the transcripts again. This Pilnouth character is like talking to a cloud of smoke." Silence. Simon sighs; he hates these performances. "Regardless we have work to do."

Seeing frustration from those in the control room, Carlos relents from his crusade--for the moment. "Sometimes I feel as if I am talking to an inmate in a lunatic asylum. One moment they seem to care. The next moment they just ignore us. I am getting the impression they misunderstand our powers."

"I'm worried--more than I can say," Simon says. He sits beside Carlos.

"You should be with leaden lines like that." Wondering what else he can do, Carlos pauses.

Dawn fills in again: "One thing is for sure. They are great engineers. Did you know we were able to install the engines with a single screwdriver and a wrench? All the couplings were perfect and the diagnostics showed the system ready to go--"

Carlos completes his line: "--In effect we have only to get the package outside the majority of Earth's gravity and then relax, until we hit the alien planet."

"Poor choice of words." Simon says.

Everyone waits. It has been postulated that the aliens will respond to certain commands without thought. Nothing happens. Simon shakes his head.

"The mission will certainly be dangerous: for us, and the question marks." Carlos rolls his eyes. "Transmission time." He leans forward in his chair and sends his message.

Then, after a brief silence in which Simon and Carlos stare in different directions...

"Incoming text--on the printer," says Dawn. Carlos raises the printer lid beside him and reads the message once, then again. The battle for the safe zone is about to go critical. He reaches over and types in a message declaring an emergency; this will require Susan to call in or appear in Quentin's office in the next five minutes. Failure to do so will evoke an investigation. Even if the message had not been this serious Carlos had already planned to provoke a crisis. Tearing out the message, he hands it to Dawn. She reads it silently then passes it to Simon. Who, after scanning it, wants only to scream.

The two individuals head out of the room knowing the team in the communications room will immediately begin a discussion of how they don't like the message and how this will cost a fortune in question marks. As they do they will pass a copy of the message back and forth knowing they may never speak of it.

At the top of the stairs, Quentin stands in front of his office door waiting. Simon hands him the message while entering the office. Tea and dim sum dressed in white porcelain sit on a low wooden table. Damube reclines on the couch behind the table. Nodding hello, Simon sits beside him. Carlos looks around anxiously--no Susan; Quentin notes his every move then reads the message after Carlos sits in a chair on the other side of the table. Tight-lipped, he hands the message to Damube and closes the door behind him. Damube hands Carlos back the message watching his every move. Carlos ignores him.

"They are devils," Damube says with the eyes of a warrior who believes the world is his stage. He begins to speak further but Quentin raises a hand to silence him. Quentin turns a small switch beside the door that looks like a light switch. A multi-phased interference pattern now percolates through the walls and floors of the office. The scientists at SETI believe this will isolate the room from alien inspection.

"Okay, we are clear." Quentin walks around his desk and sits. Hands intertwined on the desktop, he makes a point of smiling hello to Simon Weiss. Quentin clasps and unclasps his hands as he rubs the knuckles. Simon wonders if he might have arthritis. Quentin fears he does, but actually it is just a nervous habit he has developed these last few months. Quentin has no faith in the spacecraft.

Simon says: "There is too much here we do not understand. Why would they want more of us to die? Why would they place a price on helping us? Do they gain from our deaths?"

Quentin nods. "My guess is the Earth is about to become a conquered planet. I suspect that after this payment, or disaster--or whatever the hell happens there will indeed be fifty million of us safe--and then our friends the Rostackmidarifians are going to settle in and set up shop." Carlos sits mutely, waiting for five minutes to pass.

"The safe location could be targeted last," Simon says.

"Why bother? They want a local colonial government because we fouled up the environment--lucky for us. No, they want to see if we can do the job of running the planet for them. They need the question marks and they want to know if we are willing to give up a billion or so of our own kind to serve them. When we've said yes they will make a show of power and zap some of us off the planet to make sure we understand. Then, off we go as a satellite world of some hegemony. The rest is up to us," Quentin replies.

"So then we should not take the deal," Simon says. "Maybe it is a test of our morality." He is shocked to see everyone in the room hide a smile.

Quentin crosses his arms. "Think about it, Simon. If we just agree and they are testing, then we win because nothing happens. If they are being truthful then we better agree so at least we have a chance for survival. If we agree and they are wrong about the deaths of so many of our fellow humans, we have lost nothing. If we don't agree and they are right, then we are a dead planet. There is no choice here." Quentin's dark eyes narrow with thought. "Look team, my guess is after the event that requires this so called safe site they will clearly tell us what to do. We become their serfs--vassals if we're lucky--probably farming question marks or some other damn thing. I doubt there is much more to it all than that. Our only lever is they think question marks cost." A knock at the door. "Come."

Susan enters the office. Dressed in white cotton pants and a light blue jacket, her blond hair in a French braid; she looks like a person fresh from a vacation. Damube tries to smile but he is obviously bewildered. The temperature drops a hundred degrees as Quentin glares at him. His grasp on power is tenuous and it appears Susan has not only betrayed Quentin but outwitted him as well. Susan should be on a jet right now. One that crashed into the Atlantic one hour ago. Quentin speaks: "Ambassador, if you please--for Susan's benefit." His fingers tap on the underside wooden arm of his chair.

Wondering what was wrong, knowing things are okay--for now, Carlos reads the message aloud: *The need to find the location of a safe place is clear. Early discussion is not prudent. The location will only accommodate fifty million inhabitants. The use of the place further, will disrupt process. The net result: these are the only survivors of your kind.*

Carlos looks up at her; Quentin sees his relief and speaks in short breaths: "It looks like they are saying...the price for saving some people...is death for the rest of us."

Susan looks about forgetting her danger--as stunned as when she read the message that her plane crashed an hour ago. "The ante just keeps rising." Picking up a teacup, only will power keeps her hands from shaking. "Why do I feel that our friends out there in the Deep Black are connected to what happens here?" Susan sips green tea as she and Quentin shoot surreptitious glances at each other--like boxers before the bell.

Quentin taunts her gaze. "Fate does not favor those who lack. It seems we have been had." Deep inside he cannot help but marvel at Susan's manor.

Susan notes the admiration in his eyes. "They are connected, all right, but not in the way you think." Susan's eyes dart about the room; Quentin is surprised she seeks out Damube's eyes rather than Carlos. For a moment he wonders if somehow Damube kept her off the plane. He decides not, seeing Carlos sitting back to watch the proceedings with a practiced gaze. Carlos does not have the eyes of a conspirator; he has no idea what has happened. Then Quentin sees Susan's hand shaking. Wondering how much pressure Susan can really take--and will Carlos come to her rescue--he says: "Susan, do you think they caused the crash?" She spills tea.

"Of course not--perhaps they are trying to help us with a problem we do not yet understand." She cannot look at Carlos. She need not. She knows his practiced demeanor will show only interest in the words passing among them.

"Hard to say exactly what is going on," Damube says. He takes a teacake enjoying the show. Simon sits silently watching the discussion develop--feeling as if he is an audience in a devilish dream. He can clearly see the cat and mouse game between Quentin and Susan has turned into mortal combat.

"Or," Quentin says, "perhaps we are just being paranoid." He places his teacup on the desk seeing Susan's eyes as she looks at her empty teacup. "Something wrong with the tea?"

She decides a strong offense is needed now. "It's far more likely you caused the crash rather than the aliens." The tremors roll through her insides.

Quentin's eyes dart over to Carlos then return to Susan. Carlos guesses Quentin is hunting Susan. He fears her accusation is all too direct.

Damube crumples a napkin and speaks with a grin: "Well in any case it looks like we've screwed ourselves over, aye Susan? Carlos?"

"Sometimes we miss the obvious," Carlos says deflecting Damube's cobra-like stare from Susan to himself. "The strong feed on the weak."

Quentin stands up suddenly. "I do not think it matters. They have all the cards and we have hoops in our future." Quentin looks at Susan, but this time his gaze is as empty as a ruined building: "Well I am sorry to say I knew it all along." Quentin then looks at Carlos. "Tomorrow you tell them we accept the offer." His icy stare has no effect on Carlos. "Is there a problem, Ambassador?" Quentin works to pull Carlos into his game of cat and mouse.

Susan quickly speaks. "Why did we agree?"

Seeing her as trying to protect Carlos, Quentin's clenched fist balls even tighter. "Because a safe location for fifty million ensures that we continue as a species."

"What about those who will die?" Simon asks.

Quentin shakes his head. "Doctor, you are grasping at straws. We cannot even be sure the safe location will save anyone."

"The engines arrived immediately after their interest in the question marks was established," Simon shoots back. "I would say they have been rather direct."

"But our agreement will not be binding," Quentin says darkly. "Besides what difference does it make? We were playing a fool's game thinking we have leverage. All in all I'd say we are making progress in finally getting the big picture. Though I would say it will be tough to explain that to the people in Iceland. It would help if we had someone there to run interference with the Directorate."

Susan thinks of the dead pilot. "Are they giving you trouble?"

Anger seeps through Quentin's every pore and permeates the room; Damube credits her with bravery but thinks being openly hostile will lead to great to pain for her. Damube shakes his head. "You're getting to wound up about this, Quent. Susan. I think they are negotiating. There is nothing in the reports that show only fifty million people survive climate change."

"Exactly." Quentin spits words: "The worst case scenarios show a population decline then a passive population in a pre-industrial life-style: disease, poverty, starvation but a relatively steady population of three quarters of a billion as the net result. And that's without a true safe location to provide manufacturing, hospitals, a viable police force, and research facilities. Stan, you said the U.N. climate report shows no new climatic phase shifts on the horizon. Isn't that right?"

Damube nods, seeing this rush of words from Quentin as weakness. "Nothing in any of the models shows any single event that might offset our estimates. I am even guessing we'll be closer to one billion when the population stabilizes."

"See." Quentin says pointing a finger at the three of them like insolent children.

"Did the U.N. people check meteors, novas, and so forth, Stan?" Susan asks.

"Floods, locusts, pestilence, plague, you name it; they checked it all. Another few decades and we're over the hump--so far as a declining population is concerned."

"They are wrong," Quentin says leaning back on his desk. Stanislaus fails at hiding his surprise. Quentin congratulates himself on still being able to manipulate him. Again he finds himself admiring Susan's pluck. "They are wrong because they do not have this data. You said it yourself yesterday, Stan. Those scientists are hacks--amateurs with PCs that are better tuned for word processing than calculation." Quentin reaches to his right and picks up a small brass statue. It depicts a lanky cowboy in chaps. The statue's head bends forward, as if its neck is too tired to hold it; and the fatigued round shoulders are just barely able to support its arms. The right arm ends in a hand holding a battered saddle. The left hand rests on the butt of a holstered gun. "We need to know where the safe location is--from now on that's all we care about. If some die then we mourn. We must survive." Quentin points with the brass figure this time.

"What about the Rosts requesting this meeting on their planet? What happened to changing that? If the shuttle crashes, we are back at square one and I know how concerned you are about the Newton." Susan quickly glances at Carlos feeling she can now acknowledge him. "We don't even get the safe zone."

Quentin winks at Carlos, as if they might be old college buddies who share a secret. Carlos sees it as some kind of lunacy. Quentin speaks: "Stan will make sure that shuttle will not crash. Once we know the safe zone location we can take the gloves off and come out swinging. And that's when I am counting on the Constitution to provide me with a hell of a punch." Quentin runs his index finger over the small cowboy sculpture again. "Are you willing, Stan?"

"I will make a mess of their planet if they don't negotiate and I'll not return without a victory." Damube nods to Susan. Susan decides Damube is insane. If he is considering broadening his allegiances, she will try to enlist him--if she makes it through the day.

"That assumes our agreement or disagreement does not alter the mix," Carlos says. "I read the message to mean agreement to receive the data will effect the amount of deaths."

"As do I," says Simon.

"You mean the mere transmission of information might precipitate an event?" Quentin is surprised by this turn of discussion. "An interesting hypothesis. How do you think we might deal with their ability to use information to remold, Carlos?"

"I don't know what I think," Carlos says. "I am paid to tell you what the guys on the other side of the table are thinking and how best to get them to see the logic in our position. My senses tell me our agreement means nothing." His tense back and shoulders begin to hurt.

"But are you sure? We need a policy of safety here, not wild imaginings." Quentin appears pensive. "And our options are severely limited." Quentin looks at the brass sculpture in his hand. "Of course if they are somehow tied to the warming--which in truth I do not believe for a second--but let's for a moment suppose they are tied to it. We will still have no choice but to accept their terms."

"Why?" Simon asks, marveling at the way Quentin bends every piece of information to support his position.

"Doctor, you don't know this but when the reality of climate change could no longer be argued a fierce debate began. The window dressing that covered the debate was a mock discussion on how greenhouse gases might mean a major hit to the economy. This kept the tree-huggers and the yuppies off wrestling with each other and away from the real issue of population control. The dilemma went something like this: Addressing climate change meant the population would soon be too large for the planet to support it. It also meant too many people would then die because the system would be so bruised by dealing with the climate change that it could not help the needy. Later it was determined the total number of deaths was less by ignoring climate change--due to no increase in population."

"How does that apply to us?" Simon asks baffled by the madness of logic that kills people in exchange for economic certainty.

"Because the program said the weak are to be culled from this planet and since we are creatures of nature we should let nature take its course." Quentin continues: "Look, the numbers back then proved that a no regrets policy kept wealth from being diluted while other scenarios caused serious dilution and had little effect on the eventual death totals. So the decision was made not to bother with the already dead. Translation: In our case, today, the Directorate will opt for saving fifty million of their closest friends and sacrifice the masses. I am trying to tell you it is always a fait accompli on decisions like this. Human nature is to protect one's own and the hell with the others." He places the statue back on the desk and leans forward to pick up his cup of tea. "Those outside the circle of power are nothing more than data--sooner or later they go to the shredder." He tilts the cup toward Susan before sipping it.

Carlos watches Susan's face. In her anger at being toyed with he sees fear. "What do you think, Susan?" When she looks at him he wonders what could possibly have brought her back here--into the belly of the beast. He assumes from Quentin's blood lust she is now irrelevant.

Susan speaks: "Our goal is to save as many people as possible. I do not see how an agreement can possibly kill more. Unless the aliens somehow have a hand in climate change--but we have too much certainty that we have done it to ourselves to give that serious credence. Also, once the news gets out that only fifty million will live, we can assume civilized behavior is out the window as the rush for salvation enters a new phase. The crowds we saw here will return with a vengeance. I think therefore I would have to agree with Quentin that this is not a death sentence but some condition of species survival. We should not fight what is Above. And that is Above with a capital A."

Her words heighten Carlos' concern. Susan has just confirmed she is fighting Quentin. Simon is also stunned. Damube cannot wait to see the next act. So far as he is concerned these people are ripping each other apart. Quentin, wearing a demonic grin, says. "Carlos, you and Simon see if you can find any proof that agreement has repercussions here on Earth. If there is proof I will bring it up to the Directorate. But we do not have much time. Why don't you get on it?" They are being dismissed. Carlos stands already working on ways to provide escape for Susan. His first concern is Quentin's private army that surrounds SETI.

Quentin glows seeing himself again as master of his own fate; he sips his tea watching Simon follow Carlos out of the room, slamming the door behind him. To Susan. "You're right; this tea tastes like poison." He finds himself admiring her steady gaze and how well her eyes lie. A smile comes over him, as he ponders how she never retreats. Though different from Simon and Carlos in many ways, Quentin shares one trait: He adores brilliance and independence. Quentin lights at what he sees as her perverse desire to be close with an enemy.

Susan sees admiration. She tells herself she can take anything he has to offer. Susan refuses to live in fear. It is why she is here today. "But even if you are right, we cannot crawl to these aliens."

Quentin places his tea on the desk. "You will make a poor slave." There is an evil in his voice. In a need to recover he says: "We have been given our orders and the need for power always supersedes humanitarian interests. Why fight windmills? You know what the Directorate will say. Or do you have another answer, Supergirl?" This term of endearment, once uttered late night, is meant as a slash. It does not come across that way.

She wonders how Quentin could put-on that adoration so well--given his obviously agitated state. "Power is useless when all you rule is yourself, and a few friends."

"Touché" he says with a wink then waits, watching her.

An idea forms that seems so strange she almost dismisses it: "You have no desire to be a murderer like those in the generation before. Going back to your logic: Remember when government scientists calculated only a billion would die. They were off by four billion. Why risk it again?"

Quentin's adoration melts briefly. Then to her surprise he says: "Stanislaus, would you give us a few minutes?" He waits; Quentin works to appear friendly. The door closes.

"I thought we had an agreement about your silence regarding my father's calculations."

Susan had intentionally struck at his weak point knowing Quentin is sensitive to the pages of history when it concerns his father. She leans forward planning to charge the breach. "That was before the plane crash. Quent. I know how much your dad and his safety mean to you. I know you don't want him to be remembered as the greatest mass murderer in history. I am not trying to threaten you or him. I just want to make a point. The data is now ready to go--in the event of my demise." She is trying to shake him up.

He is calm--and somewhat amused. "Mistakes were made and too many died because of those mistakes. Let's not repeat them. And I'm sorry. If you are worried about Stanislaus and his plane crash..." He gets up walking back around his desk putting it between them--and sitting on the window ledge says: "It betrayed weakness. Though I must say I don't understand why you wanted Weiss on the mission. Unless it is to keep your boyfriend, Carlos, safe."

Susan remains on the couch, not a muscle moving; she quickly processes his words then says: "What boyfriend?"

"Jordan." Quentin pounces on his desk, and leaning forward on both hands says: "When we were no more last summer I have to admit it didn't make much difference to me. But knowing you were seeing Jordan on the sly cheapens you, and me. You could have at least had the sinew to tell me the truth. I have a responsibility here that cannot be fulfilled without respect." He walks back around the side of his desk and stops beside the statue. Schoolboy-eyes peek at her.

--There it is again--

"You are just angry your security people missed it." Realizing he might genuinely care; a plan solidifies. She ignores a wave of disgust and smiles warmly. "Quentin, I was not seeing Carlos."

He grabs the cowboy statue and slams an edge down scraping it across the desk top. "Now that I have your full attention, I have a security report from last summer. You met him in downtown Palo Alto--that day we went to play tennis in San Francisco. That was the night after you ran from the house before that Screamer--and stayed out all night." He tries to stare angrily but keeps blinking. His lips tighten and he looks away.

"We're all adults here." She loses control for a moment. "He's a very attractive man." The red boil that rises through Quentin pleases her. "Once. We were together. Once." She feels more in control of the situation than she has in months. "Quentin, I was mad at you. The next day before we went to play tennis I told him it was no good. We haven't been with each other since."

"What about those nights you spent walking around SETI with him?"

"Grow up, Quentin." She says watching his every movement. "You are jealous and afraid of him." She shakes her head in apparent amazement and humor. Her eyes twinkle. "And let's be truthful, Quentin. We both know fidelity is more like a good batting average than a promise. And if it helps: there has been no one else--beside you--and that one night with Carlos. It was once and that was it. Which is more than I can say about you and the Hollywood chorus-line that has paraded through here." She lifts an eyebrow. "Once people have been ruthless lovers, brutal clarity can be like the purr of a kitten." She laughs with little concern, praying there is no heaven or hell.

"Don't push it."

"I don't like that you kill. I don't like that you don't care about anything but power. You're a megalomaniac and a nihilist with a strap on soul." She stares straight on knowing her life depends on the next ten seconds. "And I don't like that sometimes you think I am just one of the gang. Did you really think I would get on that plane? Did you really think I would not kick you where it hurts?"

Quentin, his calculation flawed because his murderer's heart has begun to feed on itself stumbles. "You are not seeing him?"

"Never was. But I am glad it made you angry. Too bad you went overboard and killed others because you can't handle a little infighting. You're not handling your problems very well these days are you, Quent?" Susan watches as all pretense of conscience fall away behind his lonely eyes. Empty and dark, he nests in front of her like a bird of prey.

"You're no better than me. Your desires own you just as mine own me. Why don't you stop fighting me?"

"Never. We are doing the best we can with a hellish bequest." She pauses for just a moment seeing her path. Brushing her hair back with her hand, "I once wanted you to fight the horror. Now I see you are the horror. Too bad it doesn't disgust me." Her voice trails off as she sees the truth in her words. Susan lowers her head, resting it in her hands. For just a moment she remembers Simon running along the mud flats with her. Then a daydream of walking with Carlos bathes her heart's desires. It is only the sun-bleached cloth of Quentin's stare that wakes her. Nothing is left but the gray carpet at her feet and the battle for her life that seems to get harder with each day. "Neither of us are that easy to kill, Quentin."

Quentin turns to stare out the window. "Never before have I been able to fully see the absurdity of love. Imagine loving another for their ability to survive. Far stranger--imagine me loving you. We both see love as using the other. Did you know that?" She refuses to acknowledge him. "All right. We remain in neutral corners on that one. But if you and Jordan start seeing each other please have the backbone to tell me." His gaze remains fixed on the tar roof outside his window but he cannot see it. All he can think of is Susan lying on her back: candlelight on her face, her legs spread wide, on his bed.

Chapter Nineteen

The hovels raked by storms and quakes: shattered stores turned into housing, shopping malls filled with tribes, torn tents flapping in the wind, all give way to private homes that glow on the hillsides. The steel and concrete bunkers painted pastels of every color sparkle and shimmer row after row forming lines of blockhouses that look like rainbows on a bumpy sky. Up ahead, darts of red light sweep the heavens, even in this dusk slicing the evening like random swords.

The shining monument to technology, greed...and perseverance waits just over the next hilltop. Passing the Army Street exit, the black armored Hummer comes upon the domed trees of San Francisco alongside the roadway. These prismatic domes are San Francisco's latest attraction and a welcome sight after drab rusting factories, tents, wandering ragged crowds, and burning rubble.

"All the trees in the city will be like that soon," Simon says. Roxanne remains silent. They enter a short tunnel that quickly deposits the luxurious tracked Hummer near a group of triangular industrial buildings. Simon mourns the landmarks he once knew. At one time this was the SoHo, the literature and art district: full of wild nights, sweaty dance halls, and bizarre amusements. This rare urban bohemian district used to shimmer like molten steel but was condemned last year under the Greenhouse Laws' Restoration Provisions. "The domes instead of the SoHo District--well I guess beauty has worth whatever its task." The shimmering plastic skins torn from SoHo buildings now adorn the trees of San Francisco.

"There is little in most people's lives that they engage in merely for enjoyment. Tourists like it when the domes turn colors and they can breathe the purest air on the planet. I think the domes are beautiful." Like everything else in her life, the day overflows with fresh smells and a childlike rediscovery of wonders. Sitting beside Simon, she knows with him rests her second spring; even so, she cannot look at him. Launch time approaches and the media is full of spacecraft repair problems.

Simon, distracted by other events has finally noticed. He touches her shoulder with a light caress. "You haven't said much this morning. Carlos will be fine."

"You're not funny." She breathes deeply and tilts her head back to stare at the light blue sky through the vehicles bulletproof clear roof. "I spoke to Carlos yesterday. He said they let people play inside the domes during storms. He told me this just after he told me how much Susan Willoughby did not matter to him."

Simon looks at her. Her eyes remain fixed on the sky. Watching Roxanne's thick blond hair unfurling in the wind he says: "We could have never met."

"It's hard not to feel guilty." Roxanne takes his hand and holds it to her cheek. She wishes he understood what was bothering her.

Simon feels a tear. "We have this gift, Roxanne. It belongs to us and no one else. Not enjoying is the sin." For a mile, the only sound is wind.

"Perhaps." Roxanne closes her eyes. "Carlos was ready to deal with anything except Quentin and Susan together again." She stretches her arms above her head.

"Susan is not together with him," Simon says flatly.

"She is alive. She must be."

Simon closes his eyes frustrated by Roxanne's pigheadedness. "You don't like Susan and she is very able."

"Carlos will feel better once he is off in that space ship saving the planet. I just wish I could help him. He needs someone more than you do." Roxanne finally looks at him.

"Is that what you've been thinking about?"

"I wish he could love me, Simon. Then I could hate him and be all yours." She snuggles into his arm and he sighs watching a billboard pasted to the side of a tree proclaim: "Earthquakes are an Aphrodisiac!"

"Simon, is it true this hotel has rooms that can record the motion of quakes and replay them over and over or amplify of the magnitude up to a ten?"

Soon Simon and Carlos will be off in a marginally safe spaceship--and though she will not talk about it--she doubts she will ever see either of them again. Her hand caresses his; she believes in a few weeks the people she cares about most in this life may be dead and far away from her. With almost infinite strength she resolves to forget the future and instead make this weekend a joyful swing through hedonism and warmth.

"So I hear." Her funk seems to have faded and Simon wonders how he could have found someone so dear.

Up ahead, rainbow lights on gaily-painted arches appear at the next hillcrest: Gabled roofs, flying buttresses and small repair shops begin to line the roadway. The only city on the west coast that still receives disaster funds, San Francisco makes money for the U.N. every year. It is the number one tourist attraction in the western hemisphere. Everyone wants to taste its wicked pleasures before "The City by the Bay" finally succumbs to the environment. Oddly, it is its very decadence that means hope to people. The decadence seems to say: "Don't worry. Be happy. We've gotten it under control." Were these different times, this meaning of hope for humanity might elicit mounds of scholarly papers. But with people fighting just to survive decay--scholarship is without debate containing more rhetoric than contemplation. The most scholarly paper on the subject begins: "It serves no purpose to recognize the stones of history are well set..."

In the distance, over the prismatic playhouse buildings, Golden Gate Park rolls up Eighteenth Street west toward the sea and north over Pacific Heights into the old Marina district--now no more than a lagoon. Golden Gate Park had been Simon's favorite spot in the city during the day; he used to love wandering through the gardens and foliage, until the budget for repair was eliminated. Now the park is just another camping ground used by the poorest of tourists: dirty, abused, and denigrated.

Along the eastern crest of Pacific Heights, the red spring-shaped buildings of the USGS Earth Sciences Labs sit clustered together like old rouged tarts. To the west of them, the old military base, now a ragged set of uplifted cliffs, appears like a mesa. The uplifting of the Presidio provided a wealth of data on the ever-increasing tectonic plate pressure in the area and even funded the construction of these hyper-modern buildings. When no money could be made from the data and no energy shunts were buildable the USGS disappeared from budgets--its remaining people absorbed by other U.N. climate groups. The empty buildings squat boarded up and rusting.

The data collected sits unsifted--figures no longer relevant to this society.

"Did I tell you World Health tried to get the use of those USGS buildings, but the U.N. said no," Simon says, pointing to the line of buildings on the cliff. "Sorry. I am being a bore."

"Oh, let's take the freeway downtown," Roxanne says.

The vehicle turns onto the rebuilt section of Freeway 80 near downtown. Entering the three-mile run of restored freeway, Simon floors the accelerator until the Hummer reaches its top speed of forty miles an hour. Pitted concrete rolls beneath the tracks. Deep green signs with reflective letters calling out placebo exits pass in a flash. The four lanes are empty with waist high concrete bumpers along the center edges. High banked turns and painted lanes glow bright yellow; in one road-lane various twentieth century luxury cars sit gleaming in the sun. Nowhere else on the planet does a highway like this exist anymore.

They come upon a line of slow moving tourist buses. The people inside gawk and wave as Simon and Roxanne pass the parade of buses that stretch ahead as far as the eye can see. The buses are heading toward the orange bobbing bridge between downtown San Francisco and the floating jetport. There Roxanne can see a large bright yellow jet rising skyward. These tourists are going home. The buses slow to a stop in a simulated traffic jam for the bridge ramp.

To the right, the remainder of the original Bay Bridge, two vertical steel towers, blinks on and off with twin blue neon sky-slashes. Oakland lay dark on the other side of the bay. Not eligible for U.N. repair funds and lifeless except for occasional plumes of smoke, the city looks like a series of huge anthills, forgotten by the rest of the nation. "There are hardly any fires," Simon says. "I guess the Walkers have already started north this year." The people who live in Oakland now are called Walkers; a nomadic group of the west coast, they live with no running water, power, or sewer system. Others consider such people animals. Simon does not. He remembers how he had lived in southern France. To him civilization is more than gadgets and comfort. He sees it as cooperation, exploration--and hope--all items missing from present day society but abundant in Walker migrant society.

The road narrows. "Those nomads have the right idea," Roxanne says. "Get simple and learn to live that way. I could do that." Migrating north every year to work in what remains of Northwest forests, the Walkers are descendants of the twentieth century homeless. Considered unwanted migrants taking up space and continually harassed--Walkers learned long ago they were caught up in something they could not control. Luckily, they also wanted little to do with the 'civilized world' and left it behind. "We may have to follow their lead." Roxanne, and others, have come to see the Walkers as the future of humanity and millions of dollars are spent now trying to understand their ways. Simon thinks the Walkers should be a national treasure since the number of Walkers has remained constant for almost ten years--unheard of as the remains of the industrialized world withers away.

"It's my dream to live in nature--as long as you are there," Roxanne says.

"Not me. I've done the back to nature thing. You think I'm committed to saving the planet and humanity. Wrong. I'm committed to making sure I never have to use a leaf again on my posterior." She slaps him playfully on the shoulder.

The black Hummer rolls down the last exit onto the clickety-clack of the recycled trash that makes up the roadway. Driving by a ghostly bus graveyard full of rotting stripped buses: Manhattan Transit, MTI, SKAT, Florida Transit, the couple stares. "When did they start shipping buses here to shore up the San Francisco MUNI?" Roxanne asks.

"I don't know but it looks like soon there will be no more hulks to gut and the buses will stop." Simon quickly turns left onto a city street. They both know there is no point in discussing it further.

"It serves no purpose to recognize the stones of history are well set..."

They travel slowly until they come upon a low, square, sterile apartment building that goes on for more than a mile and surrounds the roadway on two sides. Flat and without fenestration like a bunker; it houses most of the city's middle class: the people that serve the city's attractions. This ugly dark building is reputed to be the safest residence in the country--despite the large cracks that have formed along the base from quakes. Inside, police roam the corridors and food is plentiful from hotel scrappings. As life goes these days--for the remaining members of the middle class--this dark fortress is quite pleasant. Translation: It is not dangerous.

At Mission Street the clickety-clack of the roadway ceases as the vehicle enters the South Hotel District. Crack free and pristine with raucous visitors, many cheer the couple in the Hummer. In San Francisco anger is breaking the law--especially anger directed towards the wealthy. Conviction of an offense against the wealthy leads to a lifelong ban from the funhouse-city.

Within a block, at Market Street, wide white sidewalks cannot contain the plethora of yellow and purple vacation-suited-visitors. The city provides the clothing as part of the vacation package. No one wants to vacation among raggedy-clothed crowds--or so the theory goes. The gaggle of colors overflow onto the city streets like peanut butter and jam; Simon makes his way slowly through the crowds carefully hiding pity and anger behind a plastic smile. Roxanne just enjoys the sight of so many people in one place and smiles at everyone.

Crossing Market Street they come upon an oriental circus group parading along the sidewalk swirling black plates on thin red sticks. In front of them, a genetically engineered dragon (it was once a bull) balances on a large blue ball leading the troupe, braying and snorting out smoke. A holographic lion runs above it in the air.

"It's incredible what they are doing with genetic engineering now," Roxanne says staring at the approaching parade.

"I hear they could replace whole organ systems if they just had the resources and the energy." Simon adds, stopping the vehicle to let the parade pass. "I think we try to control just a little too much."

Roxanne frowns at his morose humor.

Simon drives up Milk Street and passes the old Federal Building parking lot. Roxanne sees a woman in a red chiffon evening gown hand a metered piece of paper to a man in the green beret; then she hands him the keys. "She'll make sure not to lock the door as she gets out," Simon says, watching the increase in traffic. "These Green Berets, posted at ten-foot intervals around here, are charged with guarding cars in this lot. They take their jobs seriously. A person who locks his car might receive a scowl if well connected--otherwise the average visitors will likely return to find windows smashed and seats stinking of urine."

"She's safe. But that's a lot of power for a parking attendant."

"Those 'parking attendants' were the only way national entities could retain a military under national control; all other military resources were pledged as assets in the buy out of the old United Nations. The New United Networks Corporation, the New U.N., in putting together the crowning glory of corporate takeovers had strict requirements to bail out and take over the United Nations. One of the requirements was the elimination of all armies under national control. The rationale centered on the theory that the money put forth by the multinationals would mean nothing if a national state could just say no to United Networks by its military might. The first signatory, and strong proponent of the United Networks bailout of the United Nations, the United States, helped the takeover by pledging its air force first. The rest was easy."

"Always a trick." Passing the smiling hordes crowding the sidewalk, the Humvee glides by gayly colored buildings lining the street--almost all of them hotels--Roxanne hears the tinkle of bright green earrings. Worn by everyone, the earrings are given to each arriving tourist and encouraged at every turn. Locals wear them because it is the law; she notes the earrings make the city seem as if Santa's reindeer are just around the corner.

Nearing Van Ness, the best neighborhood in San Francisco, fewer tourists are on the street. Instead, skinny rag-covered Walkers move along the sidewalk shadows. Stealthy, like mice in a large animal's cave, they move head down, careful to avoid anyone's gaze. The Walkers still wear the dull green of recycled military uniforms and the mindless faces brought on by the illegal drugs always available to them. They also seem to wear a new sense of pride--even though the tourists take pictures of them as if they are just another attraction. Unknown to Roxanne, the Walkers around here are consultants to the U.N. on Walker culture and life-style. Projections show that in less than a generation the U.N.'s impact on world order will wither; to its credit the U.N. is doing whatever it can to strengthen the Walker society. It has already determined these peaceful migrants represent the form of society that will best support commerce. The myth of the market haunts this generation in many ways.

Roxanne sees the yellow-shirted city natives who, working in the tourist trade, openly sneer at the Walkers. Glancing at a newspaper headline that labels the antipathy between the San Franciscans and the Walkers as "Comatic Recessitude," she grins at the nonsensical term. It is typical of the news available to most now.

Passing a pair of armed guards, they come out onto the U.N. Zone of Van Ness Street. It is like entering another world. Mostly empty of tourists and filled with black and white limousines, the U.N. zone of San Francisco is only for the privileged. Even Simon hadn't enough league to be here before. And the tourists who inadvertently wander into the zone walk the tree-lined boulevard only briefly before turning and leaving. Green signs instruct the pedestrians not to wander out onto Van Ness--the U.N. limousines are not required to stop for any reason.

Roxanne points down the street to a golden sun burst flocked in brass. Above it arched pieces of chromed steel peak beyond a grouping of green plastic octagons stitched together by red steel wires. A second golden sunburst seems to sit above the spheres without support. Beneath it all is a large circular drive crowded with limousines. "Is that the hotel?" Roxanne asks, aghast by the opulence of the building. "This hotel is a bit gaudier than the Fairmont."

"I would say so," Simon says. "The Jack Tarr." He misses the tall hotel, the Fairmont, demolished this summer, but the continuous debris from the tremblers had become too dangerous. Translation: A man and his child with a high league rating were killed; the building was razed the next week.

"Why did Damube insist we stay there?"

"Security, same old thing."

They cross the street and park in the marble-walled parking circle. A pair of clean white sport vehicles pulls in beside them and disgorges two sets of families. The young children exit running about, oblivious to the world about them. A tall thin girl wearing a head-clamp exits the vehicle escorted by a guide dog. Roxanne looks away, to the sun's rays that beam down onto the marble floor. "This place is positively religious. Do we check in at a front desk or at a burning bush?"

"Good, I'm glad to see that twinkle again. I told you a little decadence would be good for your soul."

Looking around she follows with: "And I would say this fits the bill."

Simon shakes his head. "I am so far ahead of you on the decadence scale my memories positively creak. I'll show you decadence once we get into that room."

Roxanne grins mischievously. "What time is your meeting with Queeg?"

"Now. I'll check you in and be back." Simon congratulates himself on his poise. He believes Roxanne oblivious to his concerns about the meeting. Simon mistakes Roxanne's desire for joy with blindness--sometimes.

Simon crosses the plush deep red office and opens the door. "Captain Damube is ready, sir. Please step through that door." Damube's withered female secretary points to the walnut door that runs from floor to ceiling.

The wood paneled office is twice the size of Quentin's office and has a corner view of the old opera house through huge glass windows. Damube sits behind an antique oak desk in the middle of the room as if he had been erected there like a pyramid. Behind him, above the windows, is the deep blue rectangular logo of the United Networks Corporation, the U.N.. The logo--a spider web of linked computers surrounding the globe. Along the bottom is the word: "Success."

"Please sit, Dr. Weiss," Stanislaus says, pulling a thick blue folder from his top drawer.

Simon glances around this office's wooden walls. There is nothing on them beside a dozen coats of wax. "I did not realize you had an office at the Directorate--must be because you work so late."

"This is a guest office. I use it whenever I am out here since I prefer this area to the Spartan SETI surroundings." He opens the folder. "I placed you at the Jack Tarr, great hotel--one of my favorites. Are you all checked in? Is everything okay?"

"Yes, thank you."

Damube looks at him expectantly, but Simon will say no more. "I've just finished a security check on you and your friend Roxanne Gladstone and I wanted you to know that everything came out fine." Damube closes the folder and looks at him

Simon stares back. "And?"

"And what?"

"Why did you send me a summons to come to the Directorate?"

"Did I scare you? Actually I thought you might want an excuse to come by the Directorate." He wears the smile of a commissar. "Not buying it? How about I wanted to talk to you someplace where Quentin couldn't hear us?"

This throws Simon. He is unsure of what to say and tries to relax his face muscles telling himself he has gone through this type of meeting before--when he emigrated from Europe to America. He decides this is all a gambit, but unsure of the game, Simon tries not to display the fear of a child. He reminds himself this kind of meeting usually ends with some sort of payment. He wonders what cost he is about to incur. "You having problems with Quentin?"

Damube laughs. "Not me." He leans forward over his desk brushing away imaginary dust. "You are the chosen representative of the World Health Organization. I am here to tell you World Health is no longer part of the U.N. but part of the Asian Committee--due to some slick use of options. In any case, as of this moment, there will be no more reports to World Health without my okay. If you do, you're off the project and any provisions that were made for your survival with the Fifty will be terminated." The "Fifty" refers to the fifty million who are to be saved. It is fast becoming a very exclusive and dangerous club to be a member of--many have died.

"You cannot order me to disobey my orders."

"Doctor, I have been chosen to command the flight portion of the mission. I can point out those who I think will be a problem on the mission and remove them." He is, in his inept way, trying to show Simon how much power he has at the highest levels of the U.N..

"Nonsense." Simon stands in a show of bravado. "You do that and all hell will break loose. We both know Quentin will not accept any interference."

"Quentin is on the hot seat." Stanislaus' dark eyes narrow with thoughts of betrayal. His index finger points at Simon like the barrel of a gun. "Do you know how many see survival with percs as possible now? Hundreds of millions--yet they can't bet against Quentin--they have to support anyone with a chance. And that would be me."

"And that is you." Simon wonders who is listening in on this conversation then tells himself it doesn't matter. It might as well be Quentin.

"You don't like Quentin do you?" Damube stares watching Simon's every move. "Sit down, please."

"Quentin is in no danger. Quentin knows the information on the safe zone will make him monarch of the planet. He also knows not having the data yet makes things...difficult. I'm not interested in taking sides, Captain." Simon remains standing.

"Nobody's asking you to take sides. In fact that's the reason we're meeting. They're trying to break Quentin's lock on data."

"Means nothing to me."

"You need to understand the people whom you work for are no more altruistic than Quentin. Get it?"

"I do and I knew. There are no good guys at the top anymore. Just competing interests for safety. So I guess your question is why don't I play ball with you?"

"In spite of your lack of discipline, you are quite bright," Damube says. "We're giving you a choice."

"Who is giving me a choice and why give me a choice?"

Damube points his finger at Simon. "Jordan is unstable. He removed many surveillance devices and damaged others. He doesn't follow protocol. He oversteps his authority. He intrudes in areas he should not. Unfortunately he did make the contact and all attempts to use other negotiators have failed. We need him. He needs you. Now we know how much you want to help others but my friends will not accept any interference." Stanislaus Damube takes a deep breath. "If an accident befalls you Carlos will go on the flight--though he might mess up--he needs to live. He's in love. Don't you think they make a wonderful couple--assuming Quentin doesn't kill Susan?" Watching Simon's lip tighten Stanislaus continues: "So take your choice: Swing at windmills or win. Am I clear enough?" Damube is a stone behind the desk--unmoving and without emotion.

Simon glances up at the United Networks Corporate logo. It is no mistake Damube has chosen this place and this location. He wants to make sure Simon knows he is caught up in a power struggle between at least three warring camps--not good and evil.

Simon sits. Long ago Simon learned that a battleground is the wrong place to take a stand. A battleground is a place for survival--or a grave for dupes who fight for unknown reason. "And if I play ball, Roxanne and I are given spaces among the fifty million. If I don't, then I don't go on the mission, or Roxanne and I die in some accident. But then you worry it will make Carlos obstinate."

Damube nods his head in the affirmative. "It is nothing personal. You just need to understand the ever-evolving world in which we live--a world where deserving people take privileges and fools die. Those privileges however can be revoked at any time. So you need to decide if you wish to be washed away by ideals when no one gives a damn about ideals. We are down to the end game here Doctor: To survive is to win." Damube produces a cigarette and lights it.

"Funny how that high water mark keeps rising. I never would have guessed you to turn on Quentin."

"Quentin knows he has my loyalty as long as he has control. Right now, since Susan has let it be known he failed, trying to kill her, control is up in the air."

"So that's it. Susan is alive because Quentin is defending against the family of the dead pilot."

"He's lucky it wasn't a Seven-seven-seven. In any case, I'm merely broadening my alliances. As I suggest you do as well. It was always the battle of the fittest," he says with the grin. "Now it's blood-sport.

"Battle of the most ruthless, I would say. I can see why past generations did not stop this madness before it got here. Every time someone saw the danger they took the payoff--the smart move--knowing no one gave a damn about ideals. Except their children--too bad for us."

Damube's eyes light: "Too stupid, too comfortable, too easily corrupted."

"If I die in the deep black, will you make sure Roxanne is safe?"

"Of course," Damube says meaning it, and making his resolve clear. He has plans for Roxanne that are unspeakable.

Simon knows the unspeakable and he has no expectation he or Roxanne will get anywhere close to the safe location. He just wants to keep Roxanne safe until he returns. "You win." He lies.

"Good. Sign this non-disclosure agreement and we're set."

Simon notes the document has United Networks Corporation written all over it not just U.N.. "Are you kidding?"

"You betray me and everyone sees this."

Simon scans the document. Despite his stature in the organization this is the first document he has ever seen with the words United Networks Corporation spelled out. Everything else he has seen has said U.N. "Legal extortion."

"In essence."

"I plan to stay well clear of the blast zones as the battle of the warlords continues. You have my silence about what takes place but nothing else."

"Done."

Simon leans over and reads the brief paragraph that says all information he wishes to disseminate on the upcoming mission will require Damube's approval. After he signs, "Is this supposed to mean something to me?"

"The Directorate and I believe in the rule of law--regardless of how bastardized our society has become. It is the only barrier between the barbarian and us. At least with agreements and justice a person can be sure of what they own and do not own."

"Meaning I own nothing."

"You only own what you can defend. Unfortunately as a citizen who trusted the institutions he serves you can defend nothing." Taking the paper back, he smiles at Simon--a great hulking leer. "You're smart, Doctor. I can see how you made it out of the Chaos. As you know once the safe location is known it will be every man for himself and the gloves will really come off. Maybe if you fight hard enough this time you'll survive this as well." Lightening bolts rip the sky. "Looks like rain. Good evening, Doctor." Stanislaus Damube does not bother to stand as Simon exits the office.

Entering the teak-walled hotel interior drenched from rain, Simon finds himself too tired to walk the stairs so he sits on the nearest wicker chair. In the glow of this downpour the hotel appears to be located under the sea. Suspended soaring glass panels make up overlapping planes above the lobby. Swaying in every breeze the green lights criss-cross allowing air in but keeping water channeled outside. Glinting green flashes bathe the room during a two-minute fusillade of thunder as families and dignitaries wander the lobby. It is still bad form to show fear of the environment: Businessmen take cocktails at a white horseshoe bar listening to a quartet play Mozart. A short dark man wanders the expansive room watering ficus and ti plants. Two Hispanic women push a silver tea service about the lobby serving refreshments. Under the far glass wall, near a two-story waterfall, the men and women working the front desk chat among themselves. On the other side of the waterfall, a young family relaxes in a sunken pit, their children playing a board game.

Staring at the portrait of denial, Simon finds himself admiring Susan and her ability to swim with the sharks. He wonders if she knows her sacrifices make it impossible for him to run away.

--Of course she knows--

That old feeling of being used by her bubbles up then fades. He decides Susan's heroism deserves respect--no matter what her methods. Simon looks at the useless telephones on a far wall and thinks of Carlos. He knows Carlos comprehends Susan's depth of commitment. Simon is also sure Carlos does not understand why she has turned away from him.

Closing his eyes, Simon can only guess what horrors leap upon Susan at night as she deals with her decision to sacrifice love in an attempt to leash a maniac. He wonders if all dictators share the ability--and lack of conscience--to fork people between their priorities. In a moment of calm Simon thinks he may kill Quentin or Damube, if he has the chance. This moment scares him more than any other in his life as he sees death as a bit player in the saga of his species. Rising from the chair, Simon finds he embraces the person he has become.

Later tonight, as they lie in the dark, Simon will turn the bed motion amplifier to maximum and crank up the music. He will tell Roxanne what has occurred with Damube. Simon will say he cannot hide his hatred of "The Hungry Ghosts" anymore. She will further embrace this person as well.

The Seventieth Anniversary of Earth Day

Chapter Twenty

Continuing its tumbling descent, intruding into the alien atmosphere, Shuttle Newton tosses it lone occupant like roe in a can. Hellish noises rip through the hull. Heat has made a sidewall glow. A hissing sound somewhere behind Carlos sends a blue haze across the capsule. The vapor seems to coalesce into a figure that undulates in a dance. Another pop: A malfunction in the oxygen system allows carbon dioxide to remix with the nitrogen. A gas cocktail sends Carlos through consciousness and his mind drifts. He relives a difficult evening.

Before him, Susan again dances with Quentin at the officer's club. They sweep across the crowded floor as if they are king and queen. People applaud and her silver gown floats about on the wings of an angel. Then Carlos and Susan dance--cardboard movements, robot manikins in a tool shop website; Carlos, bowing in mock formality, sporting a bright sugar-glass smile, approaches a dripping canvas awning as hard rain pelts the sidewalk and lightning crackles overhead. He now stands outside the officers' club in Huntsville paying a check. Roxanne removes the picture from her tan coat pocket. Carlos feels the rigid paper in his hand. A tremor rolls through his body. "You need to try to understand her," Carlos takes the gift, turns, and immediately walks off into the rainy night. A dark green van waits. Opening the door Roxanne lies leg splayed, a bloody body on each side. *"None of them has to die. You don't have to kill it"*

His white titanium egg moans again rocking from side to side. Eyes wide, he stares at the photo taped to the metal bulkhead in front of him: Susan Willoughby dressed in white shorts and a blue jersey; she stands astride her red racing bicycle arms on her hips. A pert smile from her youth still haunts her curved lips. The sad blue eyes are from last month. It is a photo from Susan's office. Carlos believes he is hallucinating; the photo was not there before he blacked out.

Banks of LEDs blink on and off: first green then red then they go dark--again. Carlos feels heat on his side. The lights fail and the Newton heaves. In the dark capsule the picture glows.

--Of course Susan would think of that. How did she get it in here without me seeing it--

Spinning head over feet in the tight confines of the capsule Carlos keeps bumping his head on the lexan visor. He blacks out again. *"One of them must die."*

The physiometer directly in front of Carlos emits a low tone; he wakes. Inside his space suit, he smells sweat and feels himself sliding about as if someone had greased the interior of the suit. Blood trickles into his eyes. One alarm tone after the other begins to warble, but with the LEDs blinking madly, Carlos cannot tell which system is malfunctioning. Pure panic sets in and everything he learned about maintenance disappears in a scream. To him it seems every system in the ship is failing. The capsule lurches forward and spins one last time.

Calm black descends--except for humming fans and the clicking of the environmental sampling system. A heart-stopping thump: planet-fall--he believes. The quiet pattern of instrument sounds brings his own calming breath. Lights flicker on, then the LEDs. Gazing at the white painted ovum around him he tells himself the craft felt like it had been falling to pieces. Unknown to Carlos, he is correct. Without intervention the Newton would have burst apart due to mechanical and software flaws. This last time, the gyroscopic system had failed and the retro-rockets had misfired. He has no awareness of intervention.

Carlos looks for Susan's picture and punches the harness holding the suit in place. It releases with a hiss and the webbing falls aside. Immediately he removes his white and silver gloves. In one motion he stretches his hands and looks about for her picture. A moment later he cracks the seal on his helmet. He sniffs the air; the smell of burning wires and ozone fills the eight-foot cell. Carlos pulls the helmet off completely to search the capsule floor. Sitting straight, he decides indeed it was an illusion.

Extending his arm forward he taps on a set of keys above his head to evacuate the stale air into a tank. The smells subside. Reaching for the keyboard, he begins to test the ship's systems so he can contact the Armstrong. The red and green lights surrounding him continue to blink randomly--like a Christmas tree. Then, one after the other, red lights turn green and stay lit.

As Carlos waits for the CPU to uplink with the Armstrong, three hundred miles above him, he sheds his space suit and dons a dark blue jumpsuit. From the corner of his eye he still scans for a trace of her. A warning light off to the side of the main panel flashes bright red, another small leak in the auxiliary waste tank. He will ignore it until the primary goes down, per mission orders. Thankfully, he will never remember this moment nor recognize it as a moment of death.

A small screen between rows of LEDs in front of him lights with information; so far as he can tell everything works. Were he an experienced pilot he would wonder how all could still function after so many systems failed during reentry.

Like its parent ship, the Armstrong, the shuttle Newton had been built too quickly by nervous, frightened people. Both are basically unsafe, though through a pattern of denial familiar to Carlos and his peers he ignores what he knows as dysfunctional systems, considering it just a normal part of life in the dusk of humanity, and feels pleased at the absurd green lights telling him everything is okay.

Jumpsuit zipped up, he drops to one knee. The diplomat's sweaty hands search a side panel to find Susan's picture. Instead he releases the leather folder. It contains the contract to trade three-quarters of a billion lives for the safety of fifty million. Carlos might think the agreement depraved if it were not so bizarre. Sitting back down, he opens the folder and flips passed the death contract, checking the other documents. He stops at a young girl's letter to read it again.

Mattie Dent was a Topeka high school student who changed an entire race's chosen name from Rostackmidarifians to Genians, as part of a media-sponsored contest which had as its only requirement: that the name of the aliens be less than ten characters long. Her prize was a letter to the aliens. "Geek" was the name submitted most, but eliminated because the word is considered too "degrading."

To Carlos, the name change of an entire race so the media can pronounce it seems degrading enough to allow for virtually any name. He shakes his head knowing without this kind of absurdity, his career as a diplomat would have ended long ago. He glances again at the young girl's letter of peace. It contains no question marks after Quentin's editing. The touching text, full of heart and hope, rare jewels now, has become his favorite reading.

Carlos refolds the letter, making sure he separates it from the agreement on the Fifty. He closes the zipper of the folder then stuffs it into the leather briefcase. Accepting the picture of Susan as gone he says: "Okay, well we made it."

The communications link to Armstrong finally completes and a series of beeps sounds in the cabin as the computers identify themselves to each other. Simon Weiss is the first voice he will hear per security procedure.

"Newton, this is Armstrong, que tal?"

This is the signal for Carlos to establish visual communications and he taps a small black shelf with his fingertips to power the monitor and camera. Carlos' thin sweaty face appears on Simon's monitor. "A-OK Simon. Happy Earthday."

"You, too. You had us worried for a while there." Simon's dark, thin face and globe-eyes glow as he leans back in his chair. "Just a minute, Newton."

Damube's bulldog face fills the empty screen. Captain Stanislaus Damube, Queeg, as Simon now calls him, speaks. "Let's have the name of your dog."

Carlos scratches his ear in response to indicate he is okay. "Queeg." Then he blows the Captain a kiss. Damube's glare reminds Carlos of a monkey's posterior. He and Simon have discussed it often, but surreptitiously--using a new skill taught to them by Roxanne--sign language. It defeats the listening systems all over the Armstrong.

"Newton this is Armstrong--Damube here," the Captain's voice rumbles like a far storm. "Your dog's name?"

"Caesar."

"Jordan, we will begin hatch sequence in a few moments. Remember that under no circumstances are you to take any sort of lead in the proceedings. It's the Rostackmidarifian's show so you follow the leader. You do what they say. You're a platform for scanning, recording, and data gathering. After the first day, we'll instruct you on proceeding. Beginning hatch opening sequence. Good luck, Jordan."

Damube shuts down the band and grinds his teeth.

--Discipline, propriety, and vigilance are important here. Once we're sure of the safe location, then Bozos like Weiss and Jordan can joke all they want. I'll have what I need--

"You should have been down there, sir." It is his telecommunications officer, Carter Bruce. The thin college graduate has more degrees than a thermometer and more ways to suck up to superiors than a pump store. The readouts for Ambassador Jordan begin to fluctuate wildly. "Captain, we're getting some kind of interference. Damn, we're losing Mr. Jordan's link." Damube coolly walks across the small room to the junior officer. The bony fingers of the slight young man tap out a torrent of instructions to the CPU. "Link completely gone, sir, backups down." The skinny boy looks up at his Captain's broad face.

This officer is under-matched to his task due to a lack of experience in telecommunications so Damube merely shakes his head. "What happened, son?" Damube calls everyone in his command son.

"Right after we received confirmation of hatchway opening; the Ambassador's feeds began to degrade. Both primary and backups are down. His local recording systems are still functioning, I think, but we're no longer on-line with him."

"And the Newton, can we bring her back?" Captain Damube already knows all the answers. He and Quentin planned this failure of the telecommunications system.

"Yes sir, all nominal sir. Newton's data feeds say all normal with the Ambassador--except for his direct links. I think we will lose track of him once he steps out."

"Send a message to SETI with a report on the problem. Deep scramble it and mark it for Mr. Conworth." Damube looks at the flat line of the telemetry from the planet and scratches his chin. The young man notices the glint of the Captain's eyes and immediately understands what has happened. He smirks up at the Captain and conveys his understanding. That smirk will cost Carter Bruce his life when he later tries to secure the safe location by blackmailing Stanislaus Damube.

--Cutting off all telemetry and depending on those local recording devices of Jordan's will be a big gamble. Not that Quentin has much choice. Smart though, when the others figure out he sabotaged the remote telemetry they will see he still runs the show. Of course it puts Jordan in the driver's seat, if he figures out what has happened. Or until I get the safe zone out of him. Then we have a different game--

The big man's face seems to pull in on itself in a tight tiny smile. "Tell me the minute we re-establish contact." He turns, running right into Simon Weiss trailed by his armed escort. Damube snarls at the two guards. "What is he doing here?"

Simon looks back at his keepers. "I told them I need to see you. Did you want them to roll an oxygen tank over me to keep me in my room?"

"What is it, Weiss?" Damube examines the sephardic doctor's narrow face, thin curly hair, and aquiline nose.

"I have lost telemetry on Carlos."

"He is completely off-line. Having Jordan pucker up is your idea?"

"Just an extra security procedure. He's alone down there."

"He's fine." The Captain pushes past Simon. "And if you two let him out of medical again without my knowledge I'll bust you to alligator patrol in New Mexico."

Two thumps and a hiss sound through the small compartment. The octagonal hatchway of the shuttle begins to slide aside. Carlos lifts himself from the padded chair. Eager to get going, but with no bacterial or chemical filters to protect him, he hesitates. Damube had said it is safe, but Carlos knows that is like believing the taxman. Will he just fall over dead, frothing at the mouth? Carlos has already been told he will spend the majority of the voyage in the biological hazard's section, quarantined and that is good news from Carlos' standpoint. Otherwise he fears he may just kill Damube with his bare hands. The Captain has been living a megalomaniac's wet dream these last few weeks and Carlos is sick of it. The interior lights flash and Carlos checks the CPU screen.

--All your systems are nominal--

Carlos leans over and pulls the small keyboard from his forearm pocket. He taps a sequence of keys to test the two pen-sized cameras now resting behind his ears and the microphones in his suit. They test out perfectly. "Damube, I am on local recording. At this moment, the hatchway is almost open." The green light showing telecommunication glows red suddenly. "Okay, it seems my telecom with Armstrong is cut off. I guess that makes this a different ball game. I'll just have to wing it, but you can count on me to follow your orders to the letter, Captain." Carlos chuckles quietly to himself and bends his two-meter frame to peek around the open hatch.

--Just white mist--

He steps out into a cool mist that tastes like mint toothpaste.

"Mr. Jordan. I am Pilnouth. Please step through the hall. We apparently have a disjunction." Pilnouth's voice is like a distant bell, haunting, warm, mysterious--and utterly alien. Carlos straightens his frame and sees a large white room around him. In the center, directly in front of him, is a narrow black object. He steps closer, getting ready to speak the first direct words to an alien--until he realizes it is a sculpture of a black dog on a 'T' shaped perch. Oddly, while the body of the sculpture faces him, the head has been turned completely in the opposite direction. Carlos reaches out a hand and touches the sculpture. It is solid and the same temperature as his skin; it appears at first to be lifeless. But when Carlos turns his head to look around, the dog

sculpture moves its head in the same manner. Carlos keeps an eye on it as he slowly moves his head the other way. The dog head tracks along a parallel axis.

"Ambassador Pilnouth, I am Carlos Jordan." There is no response. Carlos feels stupid then turns his head fully to each side. In the periphery of his vision, he is startled to see two more sculptures in small alcoves; they are white birds, also on perches, flanking the short hall to the hatchway.

Turning, he examines the pair of white sculpted birds. Positioned to stare into the bare wall, their backs to Carlos, the sculptures remain an enigma. He wonders if the Rostackmidarifians Humane Society handled the interior design work. Carlos steps closer. The sculptures are exactly at head height and he is unable to get any view of the faces because they always look in the direction he is looking. Therefore all Carlos ever sees is the back of their heads. Turning back to the sculpture in the center of the room he watches the black dog track his head movements. Carlos crosses his arms half expecting the sculptures to cross their paws across each other. Nothing happens.

By turning first one direction, then the other, almost snapping his neck in the process, he is able to see that the left side of the dog's face is smaller than the right side. Believing that cannot be, he stands there a moment. Then, deciding this is a test, he walks across the room away from the hallway and alcoves. Figuring the dogs will be looking the same direction as he is; Carlos lifts a camera from behind his ear and points it at the three sculptures behind him. He feels like a child trying to see if the refrigerator light stays on when the door closes.

Carlos replaces the camera behind his ear and reaches out to touch the wall. A brief twang resounds, like a violin string breaking. The opaque wall becomes translucent. The "wall" breaks up like fog in a wind. Standing transfixed until the wall is transparent, he soon sees widely spaced trees in a pure white dirt meadow flowing downhill into a valley floor--where various sized thick red circles cover the field. Across the valley, the circles disappear; the forest is again dominant against a white canvas. The sky is pink.

He looks closer at the trees nearby. Apparently a single species of tree makes up the entire forest. They look like hemlock firs except for the top. From each tree a large green bell-shaped object hangs. He has no idea what the structure might do for the trees. At the base of the trees, a wind blows white swirling mists of powdery humus in knee-high dust storms. Carlos touches the clear wall. Still skin temperature, it is now solid and flexible, like the statues.

"*Please remove your receptor from the barrier and stay where you are, Mr. Jordan.*" The voice is melodious and precise, like a cello playing Bach. "*I am afraid we have had some miscommunication.*"

Carlos cannot determine if the voice is coming from outside his head or inside--he also notes another mistake on the part of the alien. "I don't see you in the room."

Unless you are one of these sculptures, he muses to himself. "Is there anything I can do for you?"

"How you are then. Well, it's something else to need to adjust. Ah pardon me, Ambassador, but questions are, ah...inherent to your species, but not to us. Try to keep the interrogative to a minimum even though they are the foci of our meeting. Foliage with less dispersion might help. We must arrange for it as soon as possible."

--They don't have questions. Simon was right. They are used to everything being self-evident. Yet they are looking for question marks. That's odd...and a lever--

"Ambassador look at the lightless dog." Carlos stares at the back of a black dog. It gazes away from him passively. *"Gaze at the full spectrum, not just visual."*

"Which one?"

"Dangerous and discouraging--interrogative with a response of either one. Yes, either one--triangulate from either dimension." Carlos looks at the sculptures thinking the alien has said the figures represent dimensions. He wonders if he is looking at length, breath, or height. All three guesses are wrong. *"Look up."* Carlos looks up to find himself staring at a pair of tan soles and a figure above them. *"Look straight down, now, please."* Below is a view of how he probably looks from above. He can see his small bald spot surrounded by neatly combed, white hair. He feels himself blush. Another set of dogs decorates the room below in exactly the same pattern. He moves his arm holding the briefcase. A second later the figure below does the same.

-- This is no reflection. A hypercube, perhaps--

"Non-directed. To impose this way, Mr. Jordan, because of the disjunction I cannot provide you with form and substance yet, as it would be too dangerous."

--I seem to be just fine--

A melody of laughter rolls through the room. *"Given your environment, this may seem so. This enclosure also presents challenges. But of course that's what you and I are here for."*

"Would you like me to tell you if I see anything more in the room?"

"Non-directed and terminal," returns the voice sounding tired. *"Mr. Jordan, step back into your ship. I will mitigate so we may continue."*

"Certainly." Carlos pulls the small keypad and enters the key sequence that opens the door. The airlock slides aside in less than a second. Once inside, he watches the door close with agonizing slowness behind him. The door locks with a thump and the communications link to Armstrong re-establishes itself.

"Ambassador Jordan?" a voice says.

"This is Jordan. Look I don't know how long the link will last, but the failure coincides with the hatchway opening. Telecom memo to Simon: Simon, the Rostackmidarifians maintain the same posture in conversation as text transmission. There is no indication of a question even when seeking information. They communicate only in declarative statements. Check my local recording system to see if the recording mode works. They also say questions are inherent to humans and they then said something about foliage--"

"Bruce, what the hell is wrong with you?"

"Captain?"

"Jordan." A pause that tells Carlos all he needs to know about his early malfunction in telecom. "Ah, this is Damube. I think I heard you say your exterior telecom link was down." The Captain curses his luck wondering how the systems he disabled could be functioning well enough to tell Jordan he was off-line. "Is this correct?"

"Confirmed." Carlos switches on the video. The bulky man with the pockmarked nose peers warily at him, like he has never seen Carlos before.

"Any news on the location?"

"No." Trusting soul, he thinks to himself.

"Perception has many flavors." It isn't Damube's voice, and by the lack of reaction, unheard by Damube.

"What is the last thing you heard from me, Captain?"

Damube tilts his head. His usual paranoia becomes a source of insight. "What did you hear?"

"I heard 'perception has many flavors.' It was uttered after I said no."

Damube puts his hand to his chin. "Any external links on?"

"Not a one."

"We will check your locals on this. You make sure they continue to function. Have you sent your locals up?" Damube turns to speak to someone else.

"It's in burst rate linkup on the backup channel right now."

"Good. You're my link and I'll do everything I can to keep you safe so don't worry." Carlos sees deceit and hits upon an idea. He leans over and touches a small toggle switch; it initiates the hatch open sequence and the link to Armstrong fails again. He is now certain the telecommunications failure is Quentin's doing to isolate the safe location information. The implication worries Carlos. It means the only one standing in Quentin's way is he. Carlos wonders if Damube's offer of protection contains the same betrayal as the meeting with Simon at the Directorate. He decides it is and again notes

Damube is planning an end-run around Quentin. Carlos, with no time for it, steps into the hatchway briefcase in hand.

"The slope between our words has disappeared. We are better at your repetitiveness--now that we have synchronized. Please join me." Carlos notices the audio counter does not increment.

--It isn't an audio link. Oh goody, aliens playing telephone in my head. That means the microphones are useless. So only the cameras work, perhaps. Interesting--

Carlos tells himself to guard his thoughts with these aliens.

"Genian is fine for addressing me." A response comes quicker to Carlos' mind than he can bring the questions to conscious thought. "Try not to fear this. It is my preferred way of communication at this moment; though it will disperse soon. I recognize your need to stay apart even though there is nothing in your being worth shame. And don't fear--it leads to useless questions."

--That's a hell of a way to greet an ambassador--

"Your modeled view of aggression can be shunted again when this dissipates. I will throw nothing at you. Please step closer. The gradient is wearing." Carlos realizes he is still immobile just inside the hatchway. He steps through the short hallway; the statues are gone.

"So, it is event over change that makes questions seem relevant to you." The voice--or whatever it is--sounds satisfied. "I am Pilnouth."

Carlos spins to face a figure in the left alcove where a white statue had recently been perched. The biped being is about Carlos' height. Striking widely spaced small white eyes peer at him under a corrugated membrane running above them. The eyes appear vacant and deeply set in smooth black skin. "Ambassador Jordan this moment has been a long time coming." The membrane moves in unison to the sounds Carlos perceives. The biped's skull is hairless; it also has small slits for a nose and a round toothless mouth that opens and closes like the blow-hole of a sea mammal. A simple flamingo-pink colored frock covers the body from neck to legs, which appear to be little more than round stumps.

"We can of course return the clear floor or wall. This darkness has allure." The wall mists and then it becomes slowly transparent. Carlos does not see the blow-hole lips move, though the corrugated membrane does every time the alien communicates.

The figure in front of him steps forward, halts, then extends a globe hand with four multi-jointed apparently fully opposable fingers. "Pilnouth." The blow-hole forms the words this time. Carlos grabs the hand and shakes it. The skin is much warmer than his own and soft like fur.

The floor melts. A large circular table and two chairs emerge from the molten pool that momentarily appears on the floor. "A place to sit."

Carlos follows Pilnouth over and sits down at the table. The chairs are the same pink color as the smock. Carlos sits and feels the chair's contour flow around his back and legs, apparently seeking his comfort. He places the briefcase on the floor beside him.

"I am limiting what you refer to as intrusion into your mind, but as a result I cannot see what is misty or dank, and respond. I must say however, this limiting is so delicious." Pilnouth's head moves forward a moment. "If? I see, how interesting. I shall rephrase for you. Is there... please tell me, I beg you, is this a question to be answered by you?" The alien's nose slits flutter. The black skin lightens a moment, and then returns to black.

"Yes, that is a question. Can you explain your need?" Damn, a question.

The alien lights from the chair with the grace of a dancer and walks around Carlos and the table inspecting him. "Perhaps you are not just for sensuality as I supposed. You are born to another task. The 'lies' are just blindness. How wasteful, but--I cannot say--you have my sympathy." The Rostackmidarifian stands behind the empty chair and moves its head rapidly back and forth. "I am just beginning to realize how noise-ridden your signals are."

Confused, Carlos leans back. He wonders what the alien means by "I". The chair immediately adjusts and he finds himself almost falling backwards out of the chair. He straightens up. Eyelids appear from the alien's corrugated membranes and move sideways in amusement; Carlos watches, fascinated by the movement of the heretofore-unseen structure.

"You are much more primitive than I imagined. To you I must be perfect." Pilnouth's white eyes close behind black vertical eyelids. "I wanted you to hear that."

"That is you, is it?" Carlos shifts in the seat. It adjusts, adding frustration to the conversation by its constant movement.

"Very impressive. My confusion is the result of previous conversations through your devices." Pilnouth points to Carlos' keyboard, cameras, and microphones. "My approximations are substandard as a result of linear repetitive structure... and I am limited for my kind. I now see just how much--the word retarded." The alien stills--it feels to Carlos like prairie-stillness before a storm. "Stupidly over-looking the notion that your signals are sources of pride for your species. I thought they were forms of humor. But of course I am so deficient." The alien ceases moving, appearing like a statue behind the chair.

Carlos holds out his hand to tap the table. "Deficient."

Pilnouth speaks: "In our world, we know other sentient creatures by their forced thoughts before sleep. With humans it is different because of your program, your ways, and your unique guards. It was my idea. Sadly I might bring your kind only life storms. My absurdity: your fallacy of wakening. But it all makes for an intriguing dance and undying loyalty between us. I wish to see your young person's greeting."

Carlos wants to ask a million questions but swallows them until he can think of a way to phrase the statements correctly. Carlos reaches in the leather case and hands the girl's letter to the Rostackmidarifian. It is only then the oddness of the alien's request takes hold. "You know a great deal more than I would have thought possible."

"Surprise is intense and intensity is a virtue. Even so, traditions persist." The alien takes the letter. "I am grateful. It is beauty." Pilnouth stares at the letter. "You also have a paper to formalize our agreement to guarantee the lives of fifty million of your kind. The document, the con-tract, contract exists to preserve the correctness of your many negligent leaders' decisions for future generations and to secure, insure the propagation. It is greed--not humor--how debilitating. Your tragedy again points out my deficient state. I am not grateful to see myself as such."

"Perhaps." He has never experienced discussions like these. As near as he can tell Pilnouth has been talking about a personal problem. After a moment of wondering why an entire race would send out a challenged individual as ambassador--he lights upon a notion. Does this individual represent an entire race or not? The perception triggers a conscious thought about an interest in question marks. A child's notion? Unable to accept the absurdity of the thought he concludes it is all tactic. He is partially right and partially wrong: Pilnouth's challenges are real but the alien does represent a race--just not in the way Carlos thinks.

"First your message to me from your government." Pilnouth's head tilts to the side. A light colored birch podium emerges from the floor. In front of the podium is a blank pink wall. Pink has never been Carlos' favorite color but glad to escape the ever-changing chair Carlos walks over to the podium carefully, and looks around. He taps the podium discreetly; it is wood. He had never appreciated the color of wood until all this pink.

"You're welcome." The alien's chair has spun and now faces the podium.

Carlos winces and places the briefcase on the floor.

Pilnouth's right eye begins to flutter; The central membrane also vibrates; a second later it stops. "That was the reason we must proceed so rapidly." The alien waits. "I see. I am a disabled Genian mostly immune to the damage your species might inadvertently inflict. My minimal capability, once a limitation, makes our meeting possible. Just like your limitations have facilitated your arrival here. I am, like yourself, pleased with this great honor. But I am cognizant I am here as much because of my limitations, as well as my abilities. Nonetheless, there is a race between my ability to adjust and your toxicity. That said, the fluttering you just saw would have killed any other Genian. It is a reason we meet through my disabilities. Not so negative, Mr. Jordan." Pilnouth motions to the podium. "When we finish with your world's commercial we can continue our intercourse."

Carlos nods uncomfortably. Opening the briefcase he sees Susan's picture; he forces himself not to stare.

"You were wise to bring the remainder of your divisive love. All need direction." Pilnouth's head ceases moving. It leans forward as if to speak, then stops. The alien's arms then rest by its sides. The figure becomes still. "I intrude. Pardon me. Please continue."

Carlos pulls out his speech. "You are a very different life form from us. We wish to know you better and we hope to become great friends with the Rosts-- ah, Genians."

"I am pleased you delight in the humor of lies as well." The alien's head moves back and forth like a metronome--the face a blank mask.

--And that is laughter from a disabled alien. This just cannot be--

Chapter Twenty-One

Alone on the podium he concludes a speech mixing desparate attempts at dignity with interstellar barbs meant to induce guilt in the Genians, who were: "apparently unconcerned by the plight of fellow intelligent beings. We seek commerce, camaraderie, and cooperation with the Rostackmidarifians. Thank you." Carlos, waits behind the podium looking through the clear walls to dark trees and a pink sky. He looks again at the alien, who, though sitting upright in the chair, appears comatose.

"You seek a response." The alien says after its eyelids sweep sideways across white eyeballs. "There is nothing to do--since curing your immediate problems will be worse than the current course of action. Insofar as the alternative, the survival of the few at the cost of many--there is agreement and commitment. Yet the short-sightedness of your leaders' surprises."

"Leaders often make mistakes." As Carlos has guessed, his comment has a startling effect on the alien; its skin ripples in light gray waves. Carlos returns to the table almost certain the demands of others can supercede the Genian's will. He wonders if it is part of the alien's infirmity and why this alien conducts these negotiations.

--Can humanity be that unimportant to the Rostackmidarifians? That must be it--

The alien's eyes follow Carlos to his seat. Carlos continues as he sits: "I am surprised those that care for you would allow so many of our kind to die." Carlos knows he needs to try to manipulate the alien and he hates himself for it.

"I, we, no I..." For the first time Carlos hears a slight stutter in the alien's speech. He awaits further clues. "...The decision to sacrifice so many for a selected fifty million equals crime. The simple numbers make it so. Regardless of desires to cease the cycle, competing with the art you know so well seems foolish."

"Meaning?" He says steepling his hands on the table in front of him.

"Your art of death."

"Death as art? Like it is a minor art-form?" An incongruous idea to Carlos, he is taken aback by the notion. Even so, Carlos catalogs the area of interest and influence as he has been trained. Carlos thinks for a moment, then: "We do not consider death, art."

The alien's head moves back and forth again like a metronome, while chirps of laughter come from the central membrane. "Perhaps that is worth another comment. Note my kind is without the events that force fifty million to claw for survival."

"The fifty million who will survive will be chosen for their probable ability to reestablish humanity on our planet," Carlos shoots back.

Pilnouth's head begins to rock from side to side, the chirping growing louder. "That is not your lie, but your delivery was extremely funny anyway. Pass our applause on to its originator."

Carlos nods his head to hide a mixture of confusion and amazement at the audacity of the alien. "You find lies humorous."

"Well put, Ambassador. Truth is self-evident. Truth is always there--a system, like oxygen is always there for you."

"A lack of oxygen would hurt us. Would a lack of truth hurt you?"

"Of course not. Attempts to change the truths are the quintessence of humor to, you call us, Genians. You see this as something impressive." Pilnouth picks up the contract from the tabletop. "You, alone among your species, carry this paper to us; even though the content appalls you. You guard this document and its absurdities with your life. When we finish you will take it back to your rulers so they can propagate. In the mean time those of you not ruthless enough to rule will be swept away. I think it odd your kind does not see the humor in this." The alien shakes the document. "On another level this agreement is a continuum of complicity not easily stemmed. Yet you seek to meander me into assistance even though you believe assistance will lead to a terrible set of events." The Genian's empty white eyes close sideways a moment. Then the digits on the opposite hand touch each other in a rapid rhythm. The document flaps back over the right hand like a wedding veil. "I will provide the safe haven on your planet. I will enter the information on this document then sign. The time of pause has passed us."

Carlos spends a moment trying to untangle the web of Genian logic then reaches behind his ear and turns off the cameras. Carlos knows as co-owner of the information on the safe location he is dead. As the only owner of the information he has leverage. He plans to tell Damube the recording system has malfunctioned though he need not have worried; the equipment has only recorded black dots and static. He has no idea what to do with the information that the apparent "savior of humanity" is deficient in the eyes of its peers.

Holding the pen between the second and third fingers, Pilnouth signs the document by pushing the paper up and down, keeping the pen still. The signature is a series of elongated loops barely legible. The alien then moves the paper about filling in the name of the safe location. Passing it back to Carlos, Carlos notes the location and sees why fifty million is a limit.

The Genian turns the pen over between digits. "It is odd that when you ask a null question you do not feel any sense of attack in the usage."

Carlos feels like a puppy on a leash, frustrated, and vaguely aware of limits. "We are different." He watches the Genian's eyes close, then open. A tiny band of blue appears around the once white eyeballs. Carlos wonders if the Genian's disability has something to do with it. He also cannot bear the madness of his situation: alone on an alien planet with a creature that claims to be able to save fifty million humans and also claims to be "challenged."

"Others' thoughts carry me away--that's my disability. My physical metamorphosis is the result of you and your species' focus on our activities. The Carlos effect--we may call it. An invasion of focus if you will. You shall see it in my slowly changing exterior. The effect is without bound. It is why I attend this meeting.

--Ah, that is it. The disability is a constraint in Genian life but between us it is flexibility. So then my presence changes the way the Genian looks and acts, or so the Genian says. Pilnouth may not really be challenged in my understanding of the word--

"We compliment each other. You are uncomfortable with intimacy. That shields me. This is why your resistance to connection has made this interaction possible without significant difficulty to me. Additionally, that which you call pain--your family experiences--are draining away into me; it is a kind of food to me since I have been sequestered so long for my own protection."

Carlos finds himself feeling defensive about losing pain from his youth. In the next moment, he cannot help smiling at the absurdity.

Laughter bursts forth from Pilnouth. "For you I am a shunt, a lower valley for the waters of mind to seek and then be drained away. For me you are the toehold I have never had. So I seek intercourse, and a loquaciousness you do not really mind. As I said, we complement each other."

Carlos looks less puzzled than he is: He understands that if he had been more connected to humanity, Pilnouth might be in severe pain--or even dead. He also understands that if Pilnouth had been more connected to Genian society the alien might also be dead. Their connections seem fruitful and, despite his trepidation, he sees a chance at influence--though he is not sure if he wants to engage it. He takes no notice of his own vulnerabilities.

"Ambassador Jordan, your isolation limits your options. My lack of isolation limits my connections, but without these attributes, our species could have never met. Your assumption I will be hurt is incorrect. Instead, had we not been compatible, your space ship would have destroyed itself. So you see our intercourse is a fait accompli."

Carlos tries to ignore an errant thought. "You kept me in one piece."

"Quite." The alien nods, then, shaking the treaty with one hand, speaks: "So you see we do not dislike your path. Therefore you may void shame if you desire--just as you void shame that your ship does battle reconnaissance as we speak."

Carlos had already decided to take the issue of reconnaissance head-on since he saw no way the aliens would not know the Armstrong is engaged in surveillance. "The reconnaissance was considered prudent."

"Your minds are lazy. Being from so fertile a planet, it is expected. The reports of war and death in your transmissions were alluring to me, as I have said, so I will permit it for a bit longer."

"Our art of death entices you."

"It is something I might be interested in seeing more of, but not participating in." The alien's mouth forms a silly lopsided smile.

Carlos grabs the document from the alien and places it on the table in front of him. "Perhaps we might be able to find a way to supply you with more information on our weapons of destruction." Carlos waits for Pilnouth's reaction. He sees a brightness from the alien's eyes and an increase in breath. "Or perhaps we might be able to limit your isolation by having more intercourse with humans."

Pilnouth slowly scans the empty pink room from right to left. The words then come slowly, "Even...if...I...were...greatly...tempted by your offer. There is little that can be changed in coming events. Be assured I appreciate your artistry in death and deceit." It is said with a throaty deep tone of excitement.

"I worry you might believe that in us evil is stronger than good." Carlos stares.

The alien fights to regain control, the blow-hole mouth lengthening and fluttering up and down in silent speech; the head moving back and forth. "This does seem the nature of things when viewed from your perspective. Evil supersedes good to exist for you, but that does not make it stronger. It is like your view that time is eternal, just as a second is not. There was great joy when I heard all these viewpoints. I particularly enjoy the chaos that resulted."

Carlos ignores the metaphysical insult and forms the words of his next query in his mind, making sure they will not come out as a question. "You never say we. You say I. I wish to know why."

"It is the state. Just as many of your kind die without reason or recourse."

Carlos is about to say: "From the human perspective, the Genians would always be seen as evil for killing so many."

Just as Carlos opens his mouth to speak, the Genian speaks instead: "Perhaps. I may be of use by removing the debris after the disaster."

--That was too easy--

Even so, Carlos seizes on the opportunity. "You have mentioned this before. It is interesting to imagine what you might do with the debris you collect. Perhaps your kind waits until materials are refined and the resultant pollution eliminated before you use materials--say after a terrible disaster befalls a planet."

The alien, for the first time looks angered. The gray waves of color lighten to a soft blue and the blow-hole mouth forms a tight flat frown. "Your planet as resource for me." The alien sighs. "Materials for material properties. Thank you for making me not feel less. As planets develop, dependency on the physical realm must lessen, or the species repeats the same sustainable development problem. Each time with less tools." The Genian moves, straightening up in the chair. Carlos is pleased to see some discomfort because he misinterprets it as leverage. The blue circle edging Pilnouth's white eyeballs deepens. The alien says brusquely: "In any case, I can eliminate the waste for you."

Carlos is not yet sure exactly where his score has landed and decides to push the Genian. "And it is because of a need for those physical goods you will not help us divert the disasters?"

More gray waves. "I have desires but not needs as you see them. While it is true that the aftermath could be displayed, touched, caressed, and even adored by members of my species, this is not central. Erotic events are always planned around artifacts."

"I suppose you, too, are tantalized." He expects to see denial but instead he senses envy.

"I cannot participate beyond our meetings. And while I, as much as any other Genian, am aroused by primitive pointless destruction, I am unable to attend to such matters." Physically, a slate blue iris forms around the outside edge of the Genian's white eyeballs.

"Perhaps we are not so far distant." It seems to Carlos the blue iris is possibly an indicator of Pilnouth's discomfort, or arousal, or more likely, a yardstick of Carlos' influence. He decides to try the 'side door'. "I'm puzzled still by your earlier comments about our guardians. You seemed to indicate they are dogs."

"You really do call them dogs--yet you pray to gods. And you do not find this at all funny. Dyslexia as a societal focus--how amusing." The alien pauses, seeing only a blank stare from Carlos. "You do not know without dogs those states you call sleep and its attendant events you call dreams would be far different. As would all the events of wakening."

"We did not know this."

"I believe your progeny will, as a result of our assistance. It is that continuum that restrains further action; I note the dramatic effects on your species may already be more than it will be able to bear. And, to assist further will reduce your progeny's ability to thrive."

"Sounds important."

"It is." The alien jumps to its feet as its chair melts into the floor.

To Carlos it looks as though the chair was not under Pilnouth's control. His mind rapidly considers the reasons and concludes Pilnouth really does have something that works in an aberrant fashion for Genians. Carlos speaks: "Tell me more of these consequences, please."

"When the path is fully formed I shall. Let us attend one of our city-museums. It will assist us." Pilnouth bows.

Carlos reaches behind his ear and removes the surveillance devices. "So then these consequences you allude to will change our lives. It has to do with the way our dreams are guarded...and the resulting waking time?"

"Please recognize we must attend to other activities before we can discuss such things further." The alien stands at parade rest.

"Let us continue." Carlos places the contract and the devices in his briefcase. When he stands up he has to work to hide his surprise: Pilnouth's face has changed again. A distinct narrow jaw meets in a cleft chin under an elongated toothless mouth. Above the mouth, a small bump is evident. The eyes also now elongate to the sides and the membrane between them, only a series of lines. The blue iris is deeper, but still without a pupil, just more white. Carlos wonders if the apparent scolding was tied to the rapidly accelerating change.

"You're looking more human every minute," Carlos says.

"I... I am learning it." There is a mix of sadness and pride in the alien's voice.

The sadness touches him; unknown to Carlos, he is also changing. Without surprise, he notices the Genian now stands in front of what appears to be a pink, ten-foot-tall English bowler.

Unconsciously, Carlos takes a step towards the alien. "I suspect the hat is a little large."

"This is our transport." Pilnouth points to the oversized hat. The rounded crown then flows back on itself. "Please step in--partner." Carrying the briefcase, Carlos walks onto the brim and over the hat-band base. A spongy, pink material on the floor heats the bottom of his feet. Two seats take up the small space; he cannot see any engines. "Either seat is fine." Carlos sits in the nearest seat, ready for it to adjust, while the alien enters the cockpit. Pilnouth sits down, and leaning over, pulls a white cowboy hat from under the chair and places it low over the eyes.

Carlos, in shock at what he sees, can say only: "Again, nice hat."

--This one has a childlike way--

The seat warms. Pilnouth tilts the hat from the brim. "Thank you. I just want you to know your previous attempt at humor did not go unnoticed and I conclude the cowboy-look best reflects our activities."

Carlos ignores the sentiment and concentrates on the white hat. It seems to be made of skinned beaver. He wonders about the significance of the hat and what it really means. It reminds him of a hat his father had once owned though for some reason he cannot remember his father ever wearing it.

"Sorry for the intrusion, but there is nothing of further importance about the design of the hat I wear. Oh, and if I appear to be parent-like, or obtuse, or pedantic, it is my own shortcoming, I apologize. I shall cease it as soon as possible."

Carlos breathes once very slowly. "About the hats, if I had known of the interest, I would have brought some as gifts." A thought begins to gather in Carlos' mind about maybe controlling Pilnouth more directly--however pirate-like--he buries it hoping the Genian will not find the thought.

"Your artistry in death again. Very odd." The Genian's hand, still holding the hat, sweeps the small cabin in an arc. There is a discernible hum. "This system is a pattern of simple machines combined to achieve a series of interrelated tasks. It is similar to your ship in that it complies with your God of repetitive activity--science." The instrumentation appears as a horizontal control panel of bright red lines, pulsing in the vertical direction. The remainder of the vehicle is simply pink transparent covering. Carlos' chair suddenly adjusts to cushion his thin frame and the low hum ceases. "Please relax," Pilnouth's lips seem almost human and the blow-hole mouth remains human in appearance--though without teeth. Pilnouth tips the hat and places it again, low over the eyes.

--That looks like a twinkle. Or perhaps the alien is not only deficient but somewhat mad--

The coverings flow back into place and the craft lifts off the ground. "This is an interesting method of transport," Carlos says.

"It is quite old. It was in storage when I found it. I thought it would be enjoyable." The gentleness of the alien's response, completely lacking the lecturing tone or madness that pervaded the earlier part of the meeting, reminds Carlos of friends from long ago: a distant, but careful caring. For a moment Carlos feels himself respond to it. Then, realizing it may be a tactic of negotiation; Carlos practices caution. A moment later, they silently dart about the green bell-shaped treetops.

"I wish to know the purpose of that bell-shaped structure on the top of the tree."

"That is the mechanism for expelling nutrients from the soil below. What the tree does not use it expels to the wind. Another plant, the red circular ones you saw earlier, uses the nutrients."

"I wonder if you have names for these plants." The forest breaks as they descend a steep hillside. The valley ahead is a series of red circles of various diameters. Below them is bare white soil.

"You may name the tree if you like, but the foliage in the valley is now called the Question Plant. It was named this after I examined your text."

"I need more information on the red foliage." Carlos holds his breath and concentrates on the word "flower", hoping to hear the alien say flower instead of plant.

"The Question Plant has been the signpost of civilization in many complex ways. We will go to them after we visit the ancient city-museum for inoculation. I am unwilling to have you inadvertently spread any infection of yours among the two remaining species from our home planet."

--Their home planet. Then this place is a colony--

Pilnouth's head tilts to the side and the ship follows the lower edge of the tree line in a wide circle around the valley floor.

"I would think the organisms in the waste you collect may also compete with your native plants," Carlos says, watching the red circles form a pink blur as the craft accelerates. Carlos repeats the word "flower" over and over in his head.

"I will neutralize them as I will be neutralizing the competitive organisms that still reside in your being. My kind are not novices to this type of event. This will be the fifth time we have transported materials from other planets, though none have attracted as much attention and enthusiasm. Also, you should be aware only a small proportion of earth material can be used here on this planet. This sun continues to cool so most of the nutrients, aside from the artifacts, will be used in preparations to settle the planet that orbits closer to the sun, thereby neutralizing heat loss. The atmosphere of that planet is under design right now."

--So, your kind will die if Earth escapes destruction--

"In another nineteen-thousand-years. Your disasters will occur in less than a thousandth of that time. So will many others. Yours is not the only planet I can use for adjustment."

"So you know when some great disaster will befall us. That information will help us." He can no longer look below him. The ground races by in a blur.

"I am considering providing that information."

"What is there to consider?"

"Many items--including the questions--as well as the awareness your artifacts contain significant, ah...spice and sensuality."

"You again describe our death-art in sexual terms."

"Yes, that's correct. I propose to you that sexuality--I use your word--is tied to each member of a species and therefore it is also tied to the species as a whole."

The concept of group sex takes on a new meaning. Carlos laughs briefly.

Pilnouth's, head moves side to side for a moment, then an odd, stunted laugh follows. "It is this ability of yours I admire. Sorry, I didn't mean to intrude."

Carlos is unruffled and tries to concentrate on the alien's words while formulating another attempt at getting some measure of control. He tries to form a picture of a rose in his mind to block the alien's intrusion then decides to table his attempts at getting a time fix on the disasters that will wipe out most of humanity. He needs time to think. "So, your civilization has been around long enough to put an artificial atmosphere around this second planet--with waste from a planet like ours--I suppose."

"The original planet was the seventh one in the system. It became uninhabitable after our industrial age. So, the atmosphere on the sixth planet was adjusted."

"But we are on the fifth planet of the solar system." The ship banks toward a body of water that appears on their right. The yellowish sand and a green river form a paisley pattern that empties into the sea. Pilnouth's head again tilts. The ship moves closer to the surface.

"I shall explain. We have been around long enough to spoil our home planet and to colonize another one. Then stupidly not learn from our cycle, also destroying that one. On this planet, we learned to stabilize the systems but as you see, the costs were enormous. All that remains are Genians, the single species of tree you see on the hillside, and the Question Flowers in the valleys."

--Bingo--

"And after many millenniums the sun's cooling has forced claim to a new world. You see, the problems your people face are not unknown."

"And you contacted us because you were unable to find other species from other planets to use."

Pilnouth looks at Carlos and sighs again. "Conquest is pointless when you can just wait for a problem to dissolve. I assure you your species is in the process of dissolving. When we began to lose species long ago, on the original planet, we tried other planetary species. They killed many of our remaining species of plants and animals. It is a horror of Genian history--born of the notion that full awareness breeds omnipotence."

Carlos sits back in his chair and looks from side to side at the unending water. When Armstrong had established orbit, no major bodies of water, other than a few small seas, had been detected. The ship steadies.

--This was a rather large ocean to overlook--

"The ocean covers one fourth of our planet. I thought it would serve as an object lesson on the limitations of your technology."

The ship skims above ice blue fifteen-foot waves then banks up to a cloudbank outside the sandy shoreline. "And the other species died off also, I guess."

"Guess. Quite a tantalizing word." Pilnouth's eyelids close briefly. "I am very careful now. It is why you have been in a controlled environment until I can use the membrane system of the city-museum to isolate you effectively. Of course, our partnership still continues. There is a hope that in another six hundred revolutions of the sun I will finish testing a promising mutation that is like your grasses."

"That's almost ten thousand years."

"I will keep you posted," Pilnouth quips. "Of course we could just take over another solar system."

--When their sun goes nova they will inhabit another solar system. They are warlike. We're finished, no--

The alien chortles. "You understand so little. No, Genians will not inhabit another solar system. The thirty different systems explored were abandoned after it was found out how many unknown species were exterminated. When this sun ends, it can be gone. I am told this. It is my blessing. So there is much work to be done. I sense no envy." Pilnouth's wide-eyed stare quickly ceases then the Genian looks away in apparent embarrassment. "In another hundred-thousand-years one will have to start seriously planning for a nova. The Genian race has never ended, so far as I know. To address the problem is one of the great joys of my time."

"For the Genian race to die seems a waste."

"I find this perspective of yours quite curious. It seems the unending cycles of your kind are what approaches pointlessness." Pilnouth hums and the ship begins to slow. "If it helps, adjusting this sun is an option..."

Carlos has a hard time believing the alien's words, but something in his gut says they are true. "You can keep your sun from going nova?" The ship rocks a moment and slips beneath the cloud cover. "I am sorry. I guess my question caused that."

"Yes."

"Pilnouth, I shall not worry about appearing too primitive to you. My friend, I am no longer worried about that because I accept that we are primitive, plain and simple. To pretend otherwise would be fool's play. You are challenged insofar as your species is concerned yet you speak like a god on vacation." Carlos is unsure if he is telling the truth or not.

"True or not, I suspect your confession will be frowned upon by your superiors." Pilnouth points to the recording cameras in Carlos' briefcase. "You are then pleased these systems are disabled."

"Let us just says the word disability has changed in context for me." Both creatures smile.

They pass over an effulgence of undulating colored light indicating the presence of a city that entirely covers an island in the vast sea. "You will probably be the only one of your kind to see this for many thousands of years," Pilnouth says.

Carlos stares. It is difficult to tell size, but half the buildings pierce through the clouds over the city. Some buildings look like huge arches. These arched buildings move slowly, like a luffed sail in a light breeze. All the buildings have a fluid, less than solid motion. He asks himself again if he believes how primitive humanity is compared to this culture. A spike of pain behind his right ear; it subsides a moment later. "Those buildings seem quite tall."

"Not very tall, a kilometer or two by your measurement."

"Oh, is that all?"

A chirping sound erupts from Pilnouth. "Humor in questions, I like that so very much." The ship wiggles a bit from side to side. The ship's motion stalls, then Pilnouth seems to be straining. After a moment, it comes under control.

The craft circles the irregularly shaped city. A light plays around the outskirts of the island, covering it like a dome. Amoeboid pods of land that hold structures snake out over the ocean surrounding the city, then retreat in a visual harmony with its shimmering distorted images. It seems to Carlos as though the land floats over, but does not really touch the sea. Carlos accepts the violations of Newtonian physics with a smile watching waves of color wash over each building in succession: reds and blues changing the earlier pinks and greens.

The same spot behind Carlos' ear begins to throb again. He presses his hand along the back of his neck and the pain diminishes just as they pass though a bubble surrounding the city. Images of his parents' flower shops appear in the puffy pink surrounding him, then sharply shifts into pictures of his childhood home by the Hudson River. A pulsing hum seems to expand and contract in between his ears. Carlos cannot speak or move.

Suddenly he is cowering under a table in the corner of the greenhouse. A small pool of his blood circles the leg of a table and he sees the bleeding stump of his toe. A voice booms: "Harry, you know the reason." Carlos feels a pain start at his toe and race up his leg into his spine and explode in his neck. He feels himself collapse onto a cold concrete floor. His mother then appears over him. Beside her is his father dressed in a black tee shirt. In his right hand he holds a beat-up white cowboy hat. Carlos lies in his own blood. "He's awake. It's just a toe, Carlos, see?" His mother leans over him; in her right hand she holds the severed digit between two brightly polished red fingernails. A sour taste fills his mouth as his stomach churns. Still displaying the toe, his mother's other hand caresses his head. "Carlitos, it means nothing." She tosses the toe behind her.

"Ambassador. I am sorry for the pain, but encapsulating certain psychological events is as necessary as physical containment. Infestation by emotional as well as physical events can cause great damage to unprotected species. You are fully encased and no longer a hazard to others. I suspect though you are a danger to yourself." The words and images cease like a bright light, echoes of the images fading in succession. The ship slows to a hover above the city.

Carlos barely hears the words; he feels as if someone has spray-painted the inside of his skull then wrapped the outside in a hot wet towel. He has trouble breathing.

"I am sorry to have not warned you. Without the encapsulation you would have been a deadly jolt to the Genian ecosystem, even though we noted you already seek to isolate yourself from us." The ship begins to move again.

In a daze Carlos watches the city: Translucent Genian figures float among the pathways between the shimmering buildings. Occasionally the figures simply step off the buildings, drop slowly, land on a walkway and continue along. Carlos can see no firm connection between the elevated walkways and the fluid buildings. The walkways appear to connect and disconnect to the buildings without reason. Nothing seems to repeat; that seeps into his being

Carlos' transport darts through the city and enters the city center. Genians crowd the walkways. At their feet, twin-spheroid black creatures roll among them. A thin translucent tube connects the two black spheres of the creature. Their shining surfaces reflect the light around them like polished pool-balls.

"Were those other inhabitants of the planet?" asks Carlos trying to regain his balance. Pain bursts into his being like flame. He fears for his life.

Pilnouth's eyes remain fixed on the scenery around them. These scenes are new to the alien as well. "This is an ancient time. These are only forms, but to answer your question, they were not inhabitants of this planet."

"These are only images, then." Carlos' seeks some defense or way out of the ship.

"If I flew into one of them, or a building, you would see they are quite solid. It is why I remain attendant to their time-space." A tear appears in the alien's blue eyes. "This city-museum is ancient, but comparatively speaking, closer to your age than to mine."

Carlos' ear throbs fiercely now. "I assume you visit this place often."

"This city-museum represents the time when we moved away from the replicationists--scientists--to a different set of priorities. A time just before I came to this planet. I do not come here often since it is so ancient, and my being would disrupt events. You counterbalance that. It is why I must provide that portion of it as a gift to your people."

"Thank you," Carlos says without recognizing the enormity of the offer.

"Later, others of your kind can explore and learn about us in a positive way. Of course, opening the container may be a bit of a task. I estimate it will take a few thousand years unless something interferes. When your progeny does figure it out, they will be pleased. It will be much more effective than spying on us and should allow access to most Genian knowledge, once you understand what that means."

Carlos is in too much pain to discuss Pilnouth's reference to the gift, or the container in which it will be presented. In that instant, the magnitude of Carlos' pain becomes apparent to Pilnouth who glances over at him. The odd alien eyes widen, showing horror. "Lonoc." The vehicle suddenly dives at a sixty-degree angle lengthening itself, forming a point in front.

Pilnouth's arm darts past Carlos' right ear. Carlos flinches in terror. Flailing his arms to protect himself he knocks aside Pilnouth's arm. A foot-long gash appears running from the alien's wrist to elbow. The vehicle enters a sharp right turn. For the first time Carlos feels acceleration. The craft dives straight down at a series of red circles on a pathway. Blood gushes into Carlos' mouth and he begins choking. As his vision explodes in popping orange spots on a black and green background he hears his mother's laughter: "Of course I threw the toe away. I hate him, stupid. Why did you think I did it, Harry? All right; we will tell him it was an accident. You understand Carlos, an accident?"

A howling impact with the ground, Carlos flies forward from his seat.

"Susan."

Chapter Twenty-Two

The ocean is close. Misty, it touches Carlos with cormorant tells. Expelled from the water, Carlos lands hard; a fish caught flopping on unyielding sand. Rolling over, he feels another wave wash him, tossing his body sideways into a boulder. Above it looms a ragged rock-faced cliff scarred with streaks of yellow stone and brown bands of sediment; a distant graphic of human pain. A rabble of waves rises and the cold drink covers him, filling his nose and throat with the taste of salt, briny and dark. In the sea wash he becomes a weightless bob of pain. Forcing him down, grinding him into the sand, the sea recedes again. Carlos coughs out tepid phlegm and rolls; his eyes open. The sensation of hot liquid sand torments him. Standing up, lost and blind, he blinks out the burning rasp, everything a painful blur. A thousand suns rise in an arc above him. For an eternity, he stares at them without pain, until a warm drizzle lands on his eyes. The rain speaks:

--I will play Ping Pong with him. I cannot lose him--

Carlos looses awareness.

Horrific torment rises, and then recedes like the tide--the cliffs around him collapse like a fallen soufflé. Waves of misery ram into him; Carlos, like a crag, endures the wash knowing echoes will never cease. As he straightens up, the smell of cut grass chokes his nostrils. The cloud in his skull parts slowly and the mansion by the Hudson begins to fill his view. On its porch, wait Ping Pong tables but nothing else. In the windows, a willowy figure in a long blue gown floating from room to room. "Susan?" Ocean waves wash over, throwing him face first onto the sand. "Damn it."

Crawling from the sea he pulls himself to his feet; Carlos looks again for the mansion. In its stead, a strange Victorian mansion stands. The building backs up against smooth bedrock shaped like a dam; it fades away into pink Genian mist. This queer building, ribbed in gray shingles and trimmed in maroon waits in silence then blushes rose like a bride in the dawn. Bright blue shutters reject the sunrise color and clank angrily in the salty winds. In harmony the zephyr begins to whistle through the porch front railing. The yellow railings run crisp across the front. And, repeated before the slate roof, other railings parade along the deep red scalloped edge of the building. In places, the railing bends with each gust of wind like glowing grass in a prairie storm. In other places it drunkenly marches off the roof then meanders back to its place behind a copper gutter. One piece of railing has fallen onto the second roof. It lies there impaled on a blood red lightning rod.

Two wooden and glass doors sit in the middle of the porch behind wide stone steps. On either side of the doors flowing glass windows parade across the house-front. Empty brass birdcages glitter inside the windows. The second and third floor windows, cut by red swagged curtains, are dark--except for the yellow silk fringes, glowing like the bird cages below, the yellow railing and maudlin gray sky above.

The front doors open in: a faceless being in a pink homburg and mackintosh emerges. A skin covers like a yellow corduroy. The being lights a pipe, without bringing it to its lips, then turns left and right as if looking for the kids to bring them in for supper. Then it steps back from the grand porch, closing the doors with impossibly long arms.

Carlos hears an engine; he turns to his right to see a black Cadillac hearse roll to a stop between him and the house. Inside the now silent hearse a legion of flowers, all gray, withering before his eyes. Carlos stares at the tableau until Pilnouth, dressed in surgical gown and mask, exits the far open door--the driver's door of the hearse--and crosses the lawn. Blood and yellowish body fluids cover the back of the gown. Carlos watches the hearse pull away disappearing around a rocky wall that now flows into a thick covering of moss; it gives way to the mists.

"Moss, it's always left behind. It is an honor." Pilnouth spins on the porch stairs: "A brutal interference. If not for one of my lesions, we would have been finished." The front of the gown is a paisley wash of flowers. Pilnouth pulls the mask down off its face. Its features are human from the thin nose to the deep-set eyes, from the small mouth to the short chin. "I could never have known your pain. It was not imaginable. Such brutality only in humans." The Genian bows formally at the waist. "I hope this emergency mode of transport is kinder to us both. Well, not to worry, come on up here." Pilnouth turns and opens the doors. After entering the doorway backwards, the alien closes the doors in its wake. "Look ma, no toes."

Carlos scans his feet. They are bare, badly cut and mud covered. "Nine toes." Then mute, Carlos crosses the gravel roadway and walks up the cracked concrete path, passing the just-mowed lawn. At the cracked stone steps leading onto the porch, he pauses. The double doors in front of him, scarred on the bottom wood as if a dog has scratched them, frame etched glass renderings of clipper ships in the upper halves; they open. The clippers, under full sail, appear to be heading toward each other.

--This is madness. In living color, and it belongs to me, or perhaps the madness of humanity's savior. We are doomed--

"Carlos, my old friend, how are you? You are free now to ask questions." It is Pilnouth again, now wearing khaki slacks and a red smoking jacket--above the tucked-in ascot, a full red beard and a mustache cover the lower part of the alien's face. "Well don't just stand there, you old fool; come on in. You do not want to bleed to death, or do you?" Pilnouth steps aside to usher Carlos through a second set of carved doors. The design in the white glass of each is long-stemmed roses. A diagonal crack splits the right rose and its stem down the center. When the door closes behind him, the two roses face each other forming a valentine heart.

Inside the colorless, bleached white hallway wait three passages. On his right is a wide doorway, with darkness inside. To his left, another doorway but this one glows pink. Ahead is a long dark hallway running along the underside of a staircase. "The stairs are backwards because of the event horizon. Here let me take your coat," Pilnouth says.

Carlos finds himself removing a bloodstained brown tweed jacket and tan muffler. Pilnouth hangs them on a set of four wooden pegs that protrude from the whiteout wall. "I had hesitated to use this more modern system. I wish I had not done so." Carlos stares at a second set of pegs, where a small toe hangs by a pink ribbon. Stunned, he cannot speak or even move. Then, like a puppet without strings he collapses to the floor bent forward over his crossed legs, his body wracked by sobs.

All at once the alien looks about, lost. "What is the matter, old man? Don't you like this place? I found it in the Marisol Courier after we crashed. Remember that, the Marisol Courier. I just had to show you." The alien stares at the shattered man. In this weeping heap Pilnouth finds the waters of its mind mingling and remaining--at long last. Then lost in the poor man's horrors, pulls a newspaper from the tan jacket Carlos had worn. The Genian leans forward a bit then whispers, "Can you see this is called the Marisol Courier." Pilnouth points with an index finger. It is a Genian finger. "The Marisol Courier. See."

Carlos looks up wiping tears from his eyes. "Pilnouth, have you decided to seek information by torture?" The ambassador straightens his body, but cannot yet stand.

"No. Otherwise my little doorway over there," Pilnouth points to the front door, "would be useless. Follow me so we may leave the horrors of your youth. I see this as my task." Pilnouth helps Carlos to his feet. The Genian leads Carlos through a featureless doorway into the pink mist. Suddenly frightened, Carlos glances back. An octagonal yellow sign hangs over the entryway saying: "You were there." An arrow points to a black hole in the pink.

They immediately enter a Victorian sitting room decorated with pastel blue wallpaper and woven pink roses set under a dark oak crown molding. The ceiling is black. Hanging from the ceiling is a U.N. banner of vertical green stripes. A green and red flowered couch sits beside a harpsichord. A heavy velour curtain with a moth-riddled swirling red design covers the windows--its color battling the couch.

"See, you need not worry," Pilnouth says. "It's approved." The alien now wears leather chaps and a dinner jacket over a pink and yellow flannel shirt. Carlos notes what appear to be breasts. Trying to smile but failing, the alien seeks to understand the new state of its body.

"Pilnouth, is this madness, part of the city-museum?" Carlos works to get control of himself. Otherwise he fears he may again dissolve into a blubbering screaming mass of pain.

A great waxed handlebar mustache blooms when the alien frowns. "You may call it a city-museum or a doll house."

"I wish to know where we are."

"Thank you. We are in recovery from the crash." The alien watches another tear form in the man's eye. When it drops from Carlos' cheek the alien catches it with astounding swiftness and places the tear on its cheek. "Sorry, I am challenged. This is the only way I would do this most important of tasks. Try not to fear."

"But--"

"We can speak of it later. I rented this house from Miss Biner. You must know her. No, I suppose not. Yet...you will though. Miss Biner--The Marisol Courier--her family has had this place for years." Pilnouth pulls a corncob pipe from somewhere and taps it on a boot heel.

"I am still on your planet, and it appears we are here in a dream."

"On the other hand you might be two places at the same apparent time," says the alien with a very human wink. The figure appears to have rounded itself into a female form with buxom hips and breasts. "I know. We will talk after we complete this surgery. You are to hear: "Moss, I will not make love while you watch.""

"I do not understand."

"That's because this is dream and it also a romance. Now listen, there is a pharmacy on State Street--in Marisol. You need to go there. It will complete the loop. Sorry for the slow linear information, but the search we are engaged in is over a two-squared distance." Pilnouth helps Carlos up and ushers him to the window. Sweeping the curtain aside, Pilnouth points to chairs hanging on the wall festooned by Christmas garlands. "Structure without function." When there is no response other than confusion, Pilnouth releases the drape and walks Carlos back to the couch. The Genian pushes Carlos into the comfortable couch. Dust sighs with his landing. The alien giggles like a small child. "At least that will work."

"And this is..." Carlos' words trail off; he sees plant trays--similar to those in his parents' florist shop--balanced on spindly sticks where the curtain used to be. The trays are full of scissors rising like silver junipers. "This healing system also does remediation," Carlos finds himself saying. He has no idea where the words have come from. It feels to Carlos as if someone else is using him like a puppet.

"A form of caring." Pilnouth suddenly falls back hitting its head on the hardwood floor then immediately sits back up with that odd lopsided grin. "Not yet--how frustrating you are. Matchmaking sounds like a scam to me." Pilnouth frowns at the words that have come from its mouth. "I am surprised. These are wondrous possibilities."

"You signed up with a matchmaker? Is that something you Genians do?" The tray of scissors crashes to the floor.

Pilnouth's head shakes back and forth. "Tsk tsk, we will have no more of that." The alien's eyebrows become bushy, like Damube's. "I have a date for you in mid-May. You will want to be in Marisol." Pilnouth, like a dog, jumps up from the floor and sits at the harpsichord. "I have a tune in mind."

"You mean I'm coming back to Genia?" The harpsichord collapses in scattered notes. Carlos feels like a stupid Alice in Wonderland.

Pilnouth claps hands like a child in an ice cream parlor. "Oh goodie. She is here." The alien bounds from the bench and saunters down the hallway, brushing off the chaps and mumbling Carlos' name. Hearing the front door open, Carlos jumps up and peeks around the doorway to the street.

The twin set of open doors wave back and forth like flags. A brown-haired woman walks up the path in front of the house. Her hair piled high on her head and a small black choker circling her neck holding a rare green and white cameo, she moves as if she were willow in a breeze. The upturned nose and blue-green eyes come into sharp focus above her flushed cheeks. Her button front skirt opens at the knee as she walks. Carlos' vision remains fixed on her legs as they flash from the tan skirt.

--A Genian female? She looks human, pretty also. I wonder what's going on? Or perhaps that is Pilnouth --

Carlos trots down the hallway. Pilnouth appears from the right side of the porch dressed in a top hat and tails. The alien grabs the woman's hand to escort her onto the porch. Carlos stops by the doors then steps back in their shadows as the alien and the woman approach.

--Odd, she seems confused. But she laughs at something said. These piecemeal events, they could be the intrusions of others--

He hears a rapid conversation of what sounds like French. Then it changes as the female responds to unheard questions.

"Of course I know who you are. Yes he is right."

"Of course I know who he is. Yes he is right."

"Yes, I am dying. It's the Dots. Oh, yes, of course I would--for both of them. But you are only part of a dream. Of course I will take the chance. Too bad you are only dreams. Good bye." Carlos cannot tell who was speaking Pilnouth or the woman. She strides down the stairs to the path and out of sight. A rush of sadness fills Carlos. He finds himself again thinking of Susan.

Pilnouth appears in the hallway. The alien now wears a pinstriped three-piece suit and pencil-thin mustache. Around the waist is a belt with twin holsters and two six-guns. A banner that says "Miss America" drapes across the alien's chest. "Miss Biner has told me Miss America has no choice but to betray you. Let's go into the garden. Another woman is waiting there."

Carlos approaches the alien. "This is difficult, Pilnouth."

"It is a beginning." Pilnouth leads him around a six-foot-wide mahogany stairway with a red Persian rug. Woven into the red runner is the word Rexall--in pink. Straight ahead is a glass solarium. Carlos finds the constantly changing interior pleasant. With a sense of anticipation he follows the alien inside; four wicker chairs sit around a large growing palm. The windows, whitewashed into glowing panels, seem to hum a low note. Wooden trays of blooming fuchsias are tiered upon each other; piles of scissors lay all over the slate floor. Through a distant glass door, an African woman appears. Dressed in a scooped-neck long white gown, it flows from her ample bosom to silver slippers.

"You are both quite nice." It is Susan's voice. "But neither of you knows how to ride in competition nor how to win. And, I seem to be the only one able to battle the night. That's too bad; you were both pretty." She stands quite still, arms along her side.

Pilnouth speaks: "She is lovely. Let us go upstairs now. I'm very excited to meet the other. She defines erotica for me and is the base of all I strive for." Like a twelve-year-old, Pilnouth races out and up the stairs. Carlos bends down and touches the scissors thinking he might use one as a weapon. Glass breaks and he looks up; the woman is gone. When he looks back down all the scissors have melted together like warmed white chocolate.

"Come on up."

Carlos walks to the staircase. Pilnouth waits at the top and peers down at him, arms akimbo. The Genian sports a child's white sailor's shirt and knee-high pink knickers. Next to him, a huge breast carved from top of the banister, drips milk. Carlos mounts the stairs tapping his fingers on the wood. He wonders what is next. The stair behind him collapses into the basement. Carlos barely takes notice as he continues his ascent.

At the top of the stairs, a painting of a luxuriant Genian landscape swings like a pendulum, or metronome. In the picture, waterfalls course into gorges of exposed smooth stone surrounded by riverbanks covered with masses of the red circles.

--These are the Genian question flowers--

"And so you can know now where laughter goes," whispers the alien pointing to the rocking portrait. Behind the flowers, trees arch, echoing the shape of the city buildings, except for the bell-shaped blossoms that wrap around each other in some kind of caress. The painting still rocks, back and forth.

Carlos cannot fathom the meaning but says: "The picture is laughing."

"Some of my essences are to be kept by my family. Come on," Pilnouth says insistently. Carlos sees the alien now covered in blue tree-printed wrapping paper. It is tight--revealing an exquisite female figure beneath. "In here." Pilnouth disappears behind a door intricately inlaid with light and dark wooden triangles. Carlos follows the Rostackmidarifian.

A woman lies asleep in a brass bed. It is Susan. Covered by a single thin white sheet, her strawberry-blond hair spreads like petals on a flower. The slightest hint of a smile escapes the corners of her pink lips. Beside her, on the bed, rests a huge dirty brown boar sleeping on its back. The room smells like a barnyard. Carlos can only stare.

"That was my first choice as well. Nonetheless, she will soon rest afar from you, returning like a willow does in the spring when appropriate," Pilnouth says. The alien wears the clothes of a bride with long brown hair hiding the face.

Carlos glances again at Susan; she stretches revealing a full breast and dark hard nipple. Pilnouth now in grooms-wear, top hat gone, approaches, leans over and kisses her on her cheek. Modestly, the alien covers her breast. "Thank you," says the alien to the sleeping body. "I can do no more than tell you that those you care for now know your sacrifice and yours is the worth of giants." Pilnouth then pulls the sheet up over her, as if she were a corpse.

Carlos, shocked, pulls the sheet away from her face and neck. She lies still without breath. "Pilnouth," he looks back at the Genian. The alien has assumed an Amazon's leather sash and loin protector. A brass sword hangs from a leather belt.

"Like a seductive glance across a cool lake during the hot summer night." The alien looks about confused for a moment, and then stares at Carlos. In those alien blue eyes comes the age of sighs. "I wish we could protect her from the course of her waters. Odd that in the courts of your time the heroine has nothing." Pilnouth looks at the floor, then clanks out of the room.

--Susan cannot be dead--

"Hey."

Carlos follows Pilnouth shuffling down the hall into another room; Carlos enters, then stops, startled. He knows the furnishings of the small blue room: the bed snuggled in the corner, the white wooden desk and small plastic dinosaur models on the desk top, the old stereo beside it, the huge drawing of the Presidential Range that covers the wall next to the bed. This room was his room in his parents' house. It is also his worst nightmare to return here. For Carlos it is not monsters, or falling, or horrible death that makes him wake in a sweat. It is the dream of finding himself in his old bedroom hearing the screaming and cursing of his mother and father. In the dream when he seeks them out they are not around--only their squawking voices; Carlos listens.

The rusty window above the bed creaks. Carlos braces himself against the doorframe. A light through the window flashes and a horn blares three times. Carlos crosses the room and puts a knee on the spongy bed. Against the calm ocean waits the black hearse. Its siren begins screaming. Beside the central silver horn, on the roof, twin gray coffins heave back and forth as if malevolent spirits seek egress from their tomb. In the vehicle below, two voiceless faces push tight against the hearse's glass; Carlos stares at the angry couple with cold calculation. The ongoing images and events drown him.

"We're certain she killed herself, Mr. Jordan. She left a note saying she pushed your father from the bridge then killed herself. In the end, the horror of her life took her." Carlos turns. A pair of police uniforms lay crumpled on the floor. Carlos launches himself from the bed at Pilnouth. The alien does not move or flinch. Carlos stops, milliseconds from striking a blow.

"Enough. The purpose. Why are you doing this?" screams Carlos.

"You've been hurt. Nothing else has happened--other than healing." Pilnouth turns and walks away. Carlos looks back in the room, then exits. He sees the alien down the stairs sitting on the banister. Transformed again, the alien is now clad in a red union suit with stocking cap and a brass candle holder in hand. The lit candle burns at the same forty-five degree angle as Pilnouth sits. The alien's blue eyes spill sadness and pain. "Carlos, we have been alone for so long."

In Carlos' eyes there is only the calculation of his youth. "Is this a test? Am I something to be studied?"

"No wonder you have been left to be alone. For me there was no fault--just the agg. " Pilnouth slides down the banister.

"Wait one damn minute." Carlos takes a step, then refuses to follow; he walks back into his room. It is empty except for the bed. He suddenly wants just to lie there and weep. Instead, breathing slowly and deliberately, he looks out the window. The street still holds the hearse and two coffins. The lids are open. Each contains half of a cow split down the middle. Yellow entrails float in a pool of blood inside the halved carcasses. Tacked to them, Valentine-shaped hearts beat.

Carlos screams in pain, then runs out the door and down the stairs jumping off the broken ledge. Landing with a thump at the downstairs entryway--now decorated with a thick mattress of rice grass carpets--he gets up staring at a skull and crossbones flag hanging from the ceiling. Pushing it aside, he sees no doors. Carlos smells ginger and steps back looking into the sitting room just off the hall. A table with a formal setting for twelve waits: Three wine glasses and three water goblets border each white porcelain setting. On the far wall, a chafing dish filled with mixed steaming vegetables sits on the sideboard. Beside it, a large fish sitting on a glossy red platter sings "Mammy;" tapping out the tune with its tail.

The same brown-haired woman who had appeared on the street, steps out from the red velour curtain wearing brown leather chaps and a white-lace body stocking. Her skin beneath is blue. Her hair, longer than before, drapes over the upper globes of her breasts. Carlos stares at the woman.

"Are you the Genian?"

The woman's face loses its luster. She fights it back to a smile. "It's the blue isn't it? Only Roo does not mind it. I thought it would be the Dots. So embarrassing not to die like this--for a man like you." Carlos watches her sit on the flowered couch near the ruined harpsichord; his ardor aroused.

A hand taps him on the shoulder. Carlos turns. Pilnouth resplendent in a long black jacket, a stovepipe hat and gray beard pulls a cigar from an inside pocket and breaks it in half. "We are all slaves. Oh good, your other guests have arrived." The alien removes the hat pointing back into the room.

John Wayne enters, then stands in the corner one arm crossed in front of the other--his boot heel against the wall. Marveling, Carlos watches J. Edgar Hoover walk over to John Wayne. They kiss. Across from them, a tiny Marilyn Monroe sits in the vegetable plate necking with Isaac Newton. The fish belts out another chorus of "Mammy." Then, three old women push past Carlos and sit at the table joined by Thomas Jefferson, Akira Kurosawa, Gammal Abdul Nasser, Golda Meir, Mahatma Gandhi, and Jeanne d'Orleans.

--My heroes. The woman is gone--

A large gurney rolls in on squeaky wheels. Stretched upon it, perfectly still and surrounded by a red Genian Question plant, lies Galileo Galilee flat on his stomach with a section of his exposed skull removed. The brain beneath it is sutured shut with a series of pink ribbons that form the symbols for Einstein's equation for mass-energy conversion.

"The myths of your heroes form the links of your chains," says Pilnouth, making a series of small jumps. The alien looks like a human female without facial features. "You know--we Genians live with a rather open-ended group of inputs and perceptions. Even I do, especially, when compared to all this. I still do not see why you create and ratify your reality by repetition though. Isn't life in this gravity-well boring enough?" Pilnouth does not wait for an answer and speaks again watching the three old women drink wine. "Correct me. If something is repeatable via your agreed-upon methodology, then it is real. And all must conform to that method."

"What? Yes, in some ways repetition is the basis of our science and reality, Pilnouth."

Pilnouth points to the figure on the gurney. "The Galileo Syndrome."

"Pilnouth, I don't want to discuss theories. Tell me about Susan. You said she was dead."

He is ignored. "Science as the gatekeeper of your reality--don't you see this is so because commerce is the core of your society, and it requires consistency? No surprises make for good commerce. Science cannot possibly reach the truths. Except for one: repetition makes certain events manageable by idiots." The alien purses its lips and a wash of sadness appears in the form of a furrow on the brow. "Doesn't the weight of that sameness feel like the slavery of your empty heart?" The alien pauses to shake its head in frustration. Carlos hears a rattling noise. The alien grins. "From a different approach: Your most ruthless seek to enforce the sanctity of science. It is similar to the churches in your, ah Dark Ages--how cute--locking up Galileo because he violated the agreed upon reality of God's will. Until his genius was recognized and its applications apparent: Think. But sadly one dogma follows another only because it was more efficient for commerce. With the rise of awareness the dogmas must become supplanted. The truths will not wait for your species. What do you think is removing your species through climate change? Sadly, you can only perceive your planet's ecosystem." Pilnouth stares at Carlos, then displays a kind, warm smile. "You are a planet of idiots. I am the reversed dog. I see I am home. The final home of one who lacks." The alien looks at its fingers by spreading the digits wide and staring at sculpted finger nails. "Well fine then. Let the market deal with the advances of course. Were we ever so primitive?"

"Pilnouth, I do not care to be enlightened at this point."

"You need not worry," says the alien with a sigh.

"Pedantic alien."

The cigar drops to the floor. "We were never this primitive." The creature grabs a handful of Galileo's brain and begins to place the matter on top of its head like a hat. Through the dripping bloody mass it says: "Of course I know this is difficult, but it's almost complete. It is my gift to you--no matter what the others have done."

"Go to hell."

One of the old women sneezes. Carlos turns. "Business as usual, aye Carlos?" she says, pulling her pearls off and tossing them into the air. The pearls land around Pilnouth's neck and somehow around every other guest as well--except Carlos. The old woman's clouded eyes, hidden under ancient folds of skin, look at Carlos. "Idiot. Because one is selfish it is no reason to build an entire society on the flaw. You will never know how to negotiate as one who lacks." She pulls an orange origami bird from between her breasts and hands it to him. Opening it, he sees the image of a computer chip. Confused, he looks back at the old woman.

"An analog." The old woman turns to Pilnouth. In that instant all in the room wear the same faceless face. "Ambassador Jordan is gentle and absurd--still, the corruption is distasteful. Isolation in their cycle is the sentence; there is no question. Pilnouth look for: The question mark becomes extinct with the humans. Find it."

"My only memory," Pilnouth says.

Galileo rises from the cart as he pulls brain matter from his skull. Throwing the gray matter to the floor, the scientist grabs a melon rind from the table and pushes it into the empty place. Kick-stepping out of the room Galileo belts out a song: "I get no kick from champagne..."

Pilnouth, still faceless and female speaks: "Weep for poor choice and accept it." The woman mauls Carlos with her eyes. "You are not evil in your blindness--just in the love of your pain."

"Well it was all I had. Too damn bad." Carlos exits the room. In front of him a new door opens. Inside, the brown-haired woman with the blue skin stands at the closed window. Carlos stares at the straps of tight chaps surrounding her thighs and the blue hue beneath white lace.

She turns moving slowly toward him. A small blue-hued hand touches his bare chest. "I have so little to lose--even if this is only a dream." Carlos is naked, his arousal apparent. One hand rubs his chest, the other drifts down along the outside of his thigh.

Her lace body stocking shreds as he pulls on it. When only bits of lace cling to her blue skin he bends over to lick a breast. The blue tastes like wine. Then they fall together into a thick warm wet and Carlos drifts between loving this woman and Susan.

He hears Susan speak, laughing hoarsely: "Only in the darkest night can I give myself to you, Quent. Only in the mud-covered hideaway of our fetid passion will I admit that only with you I feel whole. You are the evil I fight but without you I am nothing." Then, with a burst of lust she moans her love for Quentin; it spits Carlos away--as if he were the last bit of sticky wrapper on a candy heart.

In the remaining moments of consciousness, Carlos hears a baby cry: It is the echo of Pilnouth's sobs.

Chapter Twenty-Three

Carlos rubs his aching neck while the hum of the machines and the luminous readouts in front of him flash without meaning. Like the retold dreams of a maniac or the ludicrous distractions of a lunatic, the tightly packed interior of the Newton spits pure discord at him. Then, like the face of an enemy, everything seems to be in order. The diagnostic on the screen says: "Jordan." It remains a flat line. "I wonder if it is a bad chip?" Carlos peers around to the open hatchway of the Newton to make sure he is alive. On the floor outside the capsule lies Pilnouth, the alien looks fully human. A short brown mop of hair falls back from the face wearing a calm Buddha-like gaze. Deep-set eyes under light brown eyebrows, a small, feminine, turned up nose flares with each breath. Closed lips don a slight smile perching over a short chin. More the face of a wise youth than an adult, Pilnouth's narrow frame, outlined beneath the pink cloak, rises with each breath. Gazing at the thin slight features, Carlos believes he also has no idea as to the sex of his host.

Pilnouth begins to stir and the hatchway slides closed for a moment. When it opens again, the alien leans on one elbow. The human face forms an uneasy smile: small white teeth, petite features, deep blue eyes, all wearing sadness and joy at the same time. Carlos blinks. "It's all right. You're alive."

Pilnouth moves the slight jaw back and forth and clicks bright white teeth together. The alien looks around registering only short gasps of amusement. It becomes a stunted human laugh. "I am more human-like."

--And I suppose this means I have more influence over you--

"In many ways yes," Pilnouth says, standing; the alien takes an uneasy step towards the Newton. "But, the bastardization of contact seems pitiable." The alien pushes its two small hands together as if it were praying. "Thank goodness dreams provide no commerce, and therefore they have been made unreal to you. Your reality is e pluribus unum. May I enter?"

"Yes, if you promise to keep the lectures to a minimum."

A wink. Pilnouth leans over and enters. The alien examines the readout screens. "May I use your chains, er, communications system? I would like to hook into your computers."

"I'm sorry. I cannot let you do that. You asked me a question before."

"You mention that to deflect my request."

"You use contact with others as if it were a hatchet. I shall go." Turning away, the hatchway closes separating Carlos from the alien. The links reform for contact from the Armstrong. Carlos scans for his briefcase then finds it in the pocket beside his seat. Hurriedly he places the cameras behind his ears. As he does, he feels what seems to be a smirk from the alien deep inside him.

"Jordan. This is Armstrong. Are you all right?" The voice rides a mixture of relief and concern.

"I am fine, Mr. Bruce. I have a report."

"--Damube here, Ambassador. Be aware our computers and telecom are as open as a mall in December. We are fully compromised. Jordan, do you have the data?" Captain Damube's face looks drawn and sleepless; bright rivers of red streak his eyes

"I do."

"Send it up now."

Carlos places his empty recording disk in the telecommunications drive and hits Send. He hears. "Localized access by sense, with a profit made on every input. Delineation to the point of absurdity." Carlos watches the CPU processing load. It peaks at ninety-eight point six percent, hovers a moment, then fades.

"Pilnouth." The normal processing load of twenty-two percent returns.

Carter Bruce speaks: "Ambassador, be advised our firewall system now reports every file on psychiatry, religion, and metaphysics has just been downloaded."

"To where, son?" asks Damube from somewhere off screen.

"I don't know."

Carlos opens the hatch. The link breaks. "Well?"

Pilnouth who stands arms crossed and head bent low as if it were sleeping while standing stares up at him. "Those were the only ones that weren't completely self evident. I read them because I thought them an entertainment system." The alien steps forward into the capsule. Even with the hatch open the systems reboot. Pilnouth looks around the seat to stare into Damube's face. The Captain registers a mixture of horror and wonder.

"Jordan, what is going on there?"

"I have invited Ambassador Pilnouth in for a talk."

"The alien is inside your shuttle," Damube says with wide eyes and complete amazement at this breach of security. "Well, I guess that's unimportant, Ambassador--since your data files are blank." His eyes soften and smile comes to Damube's face. "Smart, Jordan. I want you to hold that information for me and only me."

"Yes sir."

--As soon as poverty is a virtue--

"And son, say nothing about Earth's space defenses, military activity, or anything that might compromise the planet's safety."

Carlos understands the implication of Damube's words. The crew of the Armstrong believes they have found an effective tool for battle. Carlos, again reminded of his reason for being here, responds according to procedure. "Captain, the Genian is deciding whether or not to keep a sun from going nova like it is rule change for a football game." Carlos has just said he thinks the alien invincible. "We sure wouldn't want them to know about our stones and knives." He has indicated he has only met one of them.

Pilnouth speaks. "Why are your people so afraid? Why do I look like an American settler in your American west?"

Carlos watches Damube's cunning leer. That will never do. "I'll get back to you when I'm alone. Jordan out." Carlos cuts the link and removes the cameras from behind his ears. Torn between duty and the Genian "healing" process Carlos wonders if he has made a terrible blunder by letting down his guard. Still he can barely fathom the situation of the disabled alien and he. On unsteady legs Carlos gets out of the seat and steps around Pilnouth. He reminds himself he has a duty to his species. Opening a small green cabinet on the side of the small cabin he exposes a set of white canisters and speaks. "The Native Americans, the Indians, were primitive agrarian people with little interest in conquest and riches. They were culturally superior though in many ways. The settlers conquered them with advanced techniques of colonization. We humans are concerned your kind may attempt the same type of aggression." He watches the alien nod, then: "Would you like some food?"

"Oh, I must not. I believe it would be harmful since while my form is human but my essences are still Genian--and for me the ingestion of other life forms would make me quite sick. Please do have some yourself, though."

Carlos lifts the container of warm thick nutrient juice and drinks. The liquid soothes a parched throat. Over the bottle he sees the Genian stir, eyes darting sideways, feet shuffling; he concludes the feeding arouses the alien. "So you do not eat?"

"I do not ingest other forms of life if that is what you mean." The alien constantly looks away as if Carlos had suddenly shed his clothes; in those shy glances Carlos finds himself a primitive entertaining a potentate.

"We must eat to survive."

"Only because you are ignorant," Pilnouth says with the blameless tone of a frustrated matron. "Your original sin was not the apple. It was eating the apple."

"For an intelligent species you seem unwilling to accept the needs of those less developed than you."

The voices of the lives being consumed call out to the alien. Pilnouth, heading toward the opening hatch says: "Only when those needs are self-congratulatory. After your food and report period, we will go to the truth. I think it will calm the fears of your superiors about a confrontation with me. Then, when the information you seek is complete, you must leave."

--Confrontation with me? Oh my--

Carlos screws the top back on the small jug. "Pilnouth, would your kind fight if our people came back to your planet without an invitation?"

The alien does not face him and does speak for a moment, standing quite still. "Destruction would not stem the tide of your destruction. And, you would lengthen the recovery period as well as multiply the horrors for your planet. Many of the fifty million would die. Still, I suppose you need to be aware the location of safety is almost useless without timing. And since the addition of chance to your leaders' demise will be unappetizing to them--your kind will not attack us."

--Then you are stupid--

The alien faces Carlos. A wash of pain seems to pump its heaving chest. Clearly this discourse is uncomfortable for the alien. "The random nature of the events, which will precipitate the massive death--you know nothing about. So I will not provide you with timing information until we are sure we will be safe." Pilnouth exits into a pink mist.

--Good--

After an hour's contemplation trying to untangle the mix of conflicts in his skull, Carlos concludes he has been given a part in, for some reason, an event that is paramount in human existence. It is a horrible, empty moment for Carlos Jordan because he feels this alien is nothing more than a fool. As such, he concludes all humanity's endeavors have achieved far less. Outside, the freedom Carlos might feel with this awareness is shunted away by the alien.

Ambassador Jordan opens the hatch and sees Pilnouth. Carlos is immediately suspicious of a wash of emotion usually reserved for Roxanne. He watches the Genian leaning on a translucent isosceles triangle while using another smaller one as a mirror. Above the straight, broad forehead, brown hair is now parted along the right side. The alien looks like the all American girl--except for the dark skin. "You look very human."

"Some of it worries me." The alien rubs its chin.

"The males have facial hair."

"I know. I'm a little too pliable. Do you like the direction of my bend?" The alien tilts its head in question.

"Very nice. Why the haircut?"

"I try to use one of my disabilities, my tendency to soak up traits from those around me, as positively as possible. When I was younger I would soak features up randomly. Sometimes the effect would be most distasteful. I must learn to remove this." Pilnouth points to its chin, then drops the mirror. It sinks into the floor. No wave is formed by the impact. "Would Susan Willoughby like to see facial hair?"

"Do you plan to meet her?"

"No." Pilnouth stares at Carlos. "You see yourself as a hero--also part of your being. I do not; I am merely one, now. Though I would be a prize for any Earth home." Pilnouth appears sad. Carlos is reminded this type of life is far from the Genian norm and he feels sorry for the alien.

--Damn it--

"A prize for any Genian home also I would think," Carlos says reminding himself to be careful.

"Crippled as I am? Never. I remain as you were, adrift. I'm sorry. I meant that as a parameter of aloneness or inability. No Genian mate could have touched me deeply because I am a repellent, let's see in your words: a pirate."

Carlos works to control his reaction.

--One pirate to another. Of course--

"Do you find the process of being with me repellent?" Carlos asks. An image of the sleeping stinking boar appears in his mind's eye. Carlos grins. "No, you need not answer further. I got it."

The alien seems to fade from view for a moment. "In our language I just said thank you. I had never become intimate in this--" the Genian sweeps an arc "--utilitarian space. It was always considered too dangerous for my kind. For me though, it is the only way. And so I said thank you for making it easier."

Uncomfortable with his remaining tasks of reconnaissance and finding a lever to bend the alien to his will, Carlos also experiences the alien's disgust as license. "And I have new freedom--and you are welcome." Carlos has no problem with the notion he is repellent to the alien; Pilnouth knows this.

"Our situation is not the same. I leak the waters of mind and therefore I am repellant to a Genian mate." Pilnouth pulls out a large black comb and runs it through over the thick brown hair. The left hand follows, patting the hair flat. "You are a product of your culture." Pilnouth's eyes search the floor apparently lost for words. "Did you like the gift, the 'dream'?"

"Pity doesn't suit you." Carlos is immediately angry with himself for the cheap shot--unsure of what to do next. "I have never been given anything like that before." He is having a hard time reestablishing his stance of negotiation and finds himself baffled about his tasks--all seems so pointless. "It was a wonderful gift. Now if I can just believe I have been healed."

Pilnouth looks quickly away. In that moment, the light-years are breached. "This is not one-sided. No Genian could have stayed with me in the 'dream' as long as you did. You merely saw my many adornments as façade or absurdity."

"The clothes were outside your control, and what else I wonder..." The woman's face from the dream flashes into his mind. "Pilnouth, I cannot help wondering what intimacy is like for your species."

"I do too. All the time." The alien walks to a clear wall and waits for Carlos. When Carlos steps alongside the alien, it points to its breast. "You see the beauty of our balance but it is an irritant to your kind's ecology. I suspect your training will seek to obviate the 'dream' in the name of investigation. Of course I am counting on that to solve the quandary of the Question plant."

"I do not understand. It feels like grace when perhaps you should be vigilant."

"Quite." Pilnouth touches the wall; it melts into the floor. Outside, a white path meanders into the thick monospecies forest and Pilnouth sets off on it. Carlos follows the alien--without a thought in his mind of the mission, the hatch on the Newton, or negotiation--a strange feeling has taken hold since the wall melted: Carlos seeks no end, merely camaraderie. As Carlos watches Pilnouth walk, the alien's hair grows longer--almost to its shoulders. Carlos finds Pilnouth more attractive with longer hair then again immediately feels manipulated. Carlos stops, and looking for a distraction, reaches down to touch the pebble path. It is made of closely placed white stones and sand filler. He is surprised to find, instead of grit, it is almost viscous in nature.

Between his fingers the sand feels more like tiny ball bearings, smooth and pleasing. He tries to push down with his palm, and resistance forms--like two magnets of the same poles being pushed together. Falling on this path would be like landing on a trampoline. He finds himself wondering about the mysteries of this place and what it might have been like for Pilnouth to be kept apart from it all. Carlos scratches his ear wondering about his concerns for the alien. In truth he cannot bear the notion of aggression against this being's species. "Droll isn't it? Connection with one outside your native species--let us walk."

The two ambassadors continue down the hillside. Around them, immense green trunks raise a hundred feet or more. Large green branches end in thin needles at the top is the bell-shaped structure. The ground around them lies carpeted, a shadowy field of needles and branches. "How thick is the layer of needles?"

"Hundreds of feet thick," Pilnouth says. "I have 'slept' on it many times. It is pleasing. Shall we walk to the valley so that your planet may see its might?"

Carlos says yes, a little too quickly, uncomfortable with the comment. He wonders if perhaps the Genians already know Damube has discovered a weakness. A sweet breeze fills Carlos' lungs with fresh air. The alien steps closer as they stroll along the path; Carlos can feel the Genian's cool breath. "I went into mourning when I received transmissions showing your aggression. Why is this ability to counter death so important to you?" The Genian looks at him as they walk.

"Mostly we fear it."

"But your fear is a coddled one. You nurture it and fertilize it with every action." Pilnouth's crossed arms and tilted head reminds Carlos of a young child for some reason.

"My species is complex," Carlos says.

--Score one for the humans--

"I see. You insist on approaching your most compelling of fears alone. Yet you refuse to acknowledge your guardians, your dogs, except as pets. You seem unable to make choices about what is correct and you seem to be unable to make choices about being with another." The alien looks at the sky. "Humans do disgust me sometimes."

"My friend Simon says I am loath to leave my parents' pains completely behind. Many humans are like that. Of course I find it abhorrent that your kind would leave you so alone."

"I understand that bond, as well as friendship. But the rest is a poor topic because it is too close to fresh wounds."

"I think I can take it," Carlos replies.

"My wounds." The alien continues down the path.

"Did I sustain wounds when we crashed?"

"They merely came to the surface and were eliminated." The path descends steeply and they follow it through the trees, now no taller than ten or twelve feet. The bed of needles remains thick even after the trees disappear. Carlos gazes at the valley that stretches for miles. Small red circles of flowers cover the valley except for a white canal-like band in the far distance. The plants increase in size as Carlos and Pilnouth enter the valley.

Pilnouth stops besides a striking plant specimen, close to two feet in diameter. The circular plant, anchored to the ground by thin stems, bears a narrow interlaced wreath of red petals that droops slightly around the outside edge. Carlos leans over to look at one-inch structures of perfectly shaped red question marks nestling between the ellipsoidal leaves.

--So that's it. I wonder why these were not displayed in the renderings I saw--

Beside the question marks, around the inside of the plant, tiny cilia sway rhythmically with every minor gust of wind. They look like a fine fur, their fluidity utterly enticing. Carlos can see nothing else special in the coincidental question mark structure, but he is careful to continue examining them. After a minute, he notes another ring of cilia bordering the leaves on the outside edge of the plant, but nothing else. He looks up.

Pilnouth stares with amused eyes. "This plant has been an enigma to my race since the beginning of time. It has been called many things over the eons." Pilnouth leans over a small hollow blossom about the size of a steering wheel and wrenches it from the ground. "Pulling and replacing the plants so they can fertilize has been one my major tasks. Many of these fields were my work--it was a great honor for me. But before I replace this one on the ground so it can fertilize..." The alien hands the plant to Carlos.

Carlos assumes Pilnouth's current tasks include dealing with humans. "So you are a gardener?" Carlos stares at the tiny question marks cluttered together and touches one. His finger feels like it is being tickled.

"A gardener, yes. In a manner of speaking. Do you have any plants like this on your world?" the Genian asks.

"We have none with this exact structure, but many that provide stimulation of nerve endings." The small structures he touches lose their red color and turn a bland gray. "I seem to have done damage by touching it." The area that Carlos has touched remains frozen for a moment--until cilia rise in the same spot and begin forming questions marks. Carlos is unimpressed.

Pilnouth lays the flower back down beside the path. "Watch."

A moment later the small cilium that covers the outside edge begins to vibrate. Deep red liquid, that looks disturbingly like blood, flows over the edges of the flower.

--So it's rooting itself--

The alien shoots a disgusted glimpse at Carlos. "Come let's walk a little farther. It will take too much time for this immature plant to fertilize and I seem to be boring you."

"Not at all."

But Pilnouth already walks farther down the path. As Carlos follows, not bothering to try and catch up, he gazes at the alien landscape and pink sky. A brittle quiet descends that both beings find disturbing. Carlos will wait to see what the alien does and so watches the small flowers bush larger and closer to each other as they approach the valley floor. Some of the plants up ahead appear to be almost ten feet across. The question mark pistils in the center of blossoms of the largest plants reach a foot in height. Surprisingly, some cilia remain tiny while others appear to have become the large pink branches that root into the ground. In the center of the larger plants, mounds appear and Carlos notices an occasional spouting of pink powder. Pollination, he speculates. Then he glances again at the pink sky remembering the color of the ocean. Unable to recall it, Carlos wonders if the source of the sky's color might be the Question plant.

"Correct. The mate grows below the surface and is stimulated by the cilia that flow into the ground." The alien's voice becomes quiet, almost a whisper. "A mate in hiding." A sweet, spicy scent, almost like a cross between cinnamon and saffron rides the breeze.

He has not missed the romanticism that seems to have taken a hold of the alien, and Carlos will hold it for leverage. "I assume the question mark is not used in your world's printed text." Carlos says, fishing for understanding of the awe and reverence Pilnouth appears to feel for the plant.

"Since for us the conception of a question and its answer are simultaneous events--in all but one case--there has been no need for such punctuation. You see we have no questions, except the plant, comma period, period." Pilnouth giggles foolishly. "Sorry. For a while, I am told, conversation like that was quite stylish." Pilnouth collapses backwards onto a plant.

Carlos rushes to help him, but stops. The question flower behind Pilnouth pops up and catches the alien's fall. It then slowly lowers itself stopping a foot or so off the ground. The smell is now delicate and fruity. Carlos, surprised by the response of the plant, still sees nothing that impresses him. In his mind, he likens the plant to a type of benign Venus Flytrap.

"Try it--just fall back," the alien says from a prone position. A vacant, almost empty calmness rests in Pilnouth's eyes. "Make sure it's a mature plant with a mound in the middle. They are better," the Genian says, eyes closing with delight.

Carlos hesitates a moment with visions of a man-eating plant swallowing him whole. He shrugs, chooses a large one and lets himself fall back. The plant comes up to meet him and the pleasure receptors in his body flash like a million exploding suns. A moan escapes his throat. Colors ride his vision and a glow of heaven lights his heart; it is much more like sex than death. When he becomes aware a few minutes later, he blushes and looks at his crotch.

"You need not worry. No fluid has escaped," Pilnouth says, still lying on the same plant as before.

Carlos sits up slowly.

--What do the trees do? Give you a blow job--

Pilnouth begins to rock with tiny twitters of laughter. After a few seconds the alien recovers its breath. "To fall on your planet is pain. To fall on my planet is joy. Watch when I get up." Pilnouth springs from the plant and steps back on the path. The plant sways with her energy; the fine pink powder on the plant's surface blows in the wind. "To initiate the change, the compounds in the plant attract and absorb different types of radiation. One of which comes from the waters of mind."

The plant undulates in red and pink waves of color. The pattern increases in intensity and vibrates until the roots break. Soon, only one stem remains connecting the plant to the ground. Then it too shatters and the plant ceases moving, but does not drop. Carlos sits, now impressed.

--It defies gravity, okay that's a good one--

Then the question flower disappears.

No sound of air rushing into the vacuum, no pops or whistles. Only a slight breeze from the valley floor touches his face. It is as if the plant were never there.

--A parlor trick--

Carlos stands up and faces the plant he had sat on just a moment ago. The same thing happens to his plant as well. He checks his scanning system for power trails. There are none.

--That cannot be. An interdimensional shift? Perhaps an incredible power source without residuals? But there is always a trace. No vacuum was formed. The plant just ceased--

"You see this plant as my ancestors saw it. Can you understand how this plant has defined my civilization? How the reality born of commerce never took hold here, like it did on your planet?"

"Easily. Every day you had proof of reality's scope."

"And your kind did not?" The alien tears. "Then one day we began to study our only enigma with rigor instead of joy; the plants began to die. We entered a difficult period. Our replicationists, scientists as you call them,

claimed the loss of the plants as the price of progress. A small group who saved
the plant secretively, then revealed its existence at an inopportune moment
for the replicationists reversing the misstep. It ended their tyranny."

"Where does the flower go? For that matter, how do you know it goes
anywhere?"

"Bingo, now you understand the enigma of the question flower.
Though technology had become sophisticated and measurements were
taken, the replicationists were never able to explain the occurrence. The plant
is an event outside the bounds of investigation from the replicationists, or
scientific method. I believe your kind called such things constants--or was
that a miracle." Pilnouth claps hands twice and smiles.

"Where does the plant go?" Carlos asks insistently, while thinking the
clapping of the hands has some religious significance. In fact it is applause
for Carlos.

"Almost a star's lifetime has been spent on that problem. It is the only
unanswered question left. An amount of energy enters some void, but where
is that void and how does it operate. There is no way to prove the existence of
the plant beyond base sensory input. Great sections of the Universe have been
explored looking for signs with no success. Can you imagine the reaction on
seeing the question marks in the text of your kind?"

"I do not really. It seems a coincidence." Carlos says with a grin. "I'm
joking."

Pilnouth places its arms around itself and shakes its head from side to
side while emitting a human giggle. The alien pauses. "Quite. Perhaps you
are a bit like me." The alien appears to ponder this notion, then says: "But
when you consider the usage in your text, well the excitement consumed
me beyond words. Always having an immediate answer can be tiresome, I
think, and occasionally dangerous. On the other hand, with your kind, if I
understand your ways, then I might understand where the Question plant
goes. Though I do not think it disappears as completely as affection does
with you."

"Meaning?"

"Nothing. Our Question plants go to you."

"Into our text?"

"And after--it is part of my task." Carlos recognizes that Pilnouth has
finally told him something that is a Genian goal. "And your kind believes our
notions and artifacts regarding death give clues as to how things happen to
your plant. You think our text is your Question plant's burial place and our
reading of it what?"

"Perhaps a stop-over. The flavors of death are something beyond erotic
my kind craves."

The hair on Carlos' back itches until he spies a smile. "Were you joking about that?"

Pilnouth's head rocks from side to side. "I have a fondness for lying, which I consider the best of humor, but I was speaking without it. Craving takes many forms--not all of them a form of gluttony." Pilnouth sighs. "That reminds me. It is time for you to see the strength humans possess over us. Soon you must go. We will be going there--" Pilnouth points to a white band that runs across the valley floor. "Let us go."

The discipline of training takes precedence over Carlos' curiosity. He will do his job of reconnaissance, even if in doing it he feels like the carnivore he feared the plant might be. The two proceed across the valley floor discussing the possibilities that might affect the Question plant. Both ambassadors find the discourse delightful.

Pilnouth stops twenty feet or so before the edge of the white wide space. It looks like a dry riverbed girdling the planet from east to west. "There is your answer. This is how your technology is for us: a proof, a replaceable circumstance, a reality."

Carlos can see signs of agitation in the Genian: a pulsing artery, sweat, and shortness of breath. Carlos hates his task of seeking a Genian weak spot for possible attack. In spite of it, he says: "What is this?"

"This area of devastation is the shadow, or perhaps reflection is a better word, of the highly organized mechanism, your space craft, in orbit around this planet. I suspect it never occurred to your kind that ecological balances are more than merely scientific events."

"Meaning?"

"You learned recently that waste from your form of power generation is killing your species. Is it then so surprising to learn a highly controlled--one might say over-controlled--system might do damage to other planets not trained in your ways?"

"Do all Genians give lectures instead of talk?"

"To grifters."

Carlos steps ahead of Pilnouth to measure the size of the dead white area. The answer appears on the fabric display: two-hundred, three meters wide. "It's the exact size of the Armstrong. The shadow, from where the ship is in orbit would disperse far beyond the width of the ship."

--Besides, they should be mapping the planet from a polar orbit. If Pilnouth were telling the truth, the entire planet would be laid bare. So I am a grifter, huh--

"Logical methods of verification are fine, but your kind has a mad fetish for certainty which can be taken advantage of with little effort." A hum seems to flutter from Pilnouth's top lip. "You refer to dispersion of electromagnetic radiation. Such phenomena have nothing to do with this effect. Yes we do lecture when we feel it is necessary for enlightenment."

"I never thought enlightenment could be boring..." Carlos says.

Pilnouth's jaw tightens. "One must sometimes be pedantic with the petulant. In any case, false readings to your data acquisition systems are common. Otherwise you are right, the entire planet would be laid bare and all, including the Question plant would be dead." The alien looks at Carlos. "If you walk out there you will be slightly ill, but the destructive power of your kind will be substantiated." The alien's hands close into tight fists, but they remain by the Genian's sides. "Science not only limits your kind, its methods destroy some advanced systems...and entities. In this case, science's child--technology--cannot coexist with what you label 'entropy' and overwhelms it. You cannot imagine the cost." Pilnouth's eyes appear to tear again. "If I did not interfere, the devastation you see would cover the whole planet. It is my only measure of control...and it is fading. That is the reason you must leave--otherwise this entire planet will cease."

It is time to press. "I wish to know if you can stop what will happen on Earth. This is also part of my task."

The Genian shrugs, the tears only tracks. "Blackmail. From each according to his needs, to each according to his greed. This is negotiation--or perhaps reality--for your kind. Your kind should be executed, not locked up. How can you stand to be so loathsome?" Pilnouth raises a hand, as if holding up the sky. "If your kind returns, we will cease." The alien's hand drops. "But there will be no alteration to events on your planet, other than making it worse for your kind if I interfere more than I have."

Carlos considers Quentin's theory about the Genians setting up the fifty million as a colonial administration for a conquered Earth and finds it absurd. Staring at the strip of devastation: "As I said before, we are primitive." Carlos takes a few steps. His stomach tightens and he stops. "Will I do damage to you or your planet by entering this area?"

"You have a comical sense of concerns." Pilnouth's eyes begin to twitch. "The damage is done. I urge you attend to this." Patience runs thin.

Carlos wonders at that moment just how deep the human changes in Pilnouth's appearance have embedded themselves in the alien. He looks at his friend and almost walks away from his task. Instead Carlos takes a step, then another. The tightening in his stomach increases and turns to nausea. Sweat pours down his face. Carlos notices the plants near his feet are wilted and gray. "How long did it take for the plants to die after we got here?" He asks Pilnouth, looking at the invisible wall.

"It is immediate. The sickness you feel is a wall, like a scar, or bandage. It is like a gateway into a dream, only this one guards from destruction. Move quickly across it."

Carlos puts his index finger across the space and pulls it back. He examines it. There seems to be no difference. "So do you have creatures, like our dogs, that guard your dreams?"

"Step across." Carlos steps across into the wasteland. A feeling of warmth and security washes over him. It is like lying in a warm bathtub. The air reminds him of the Southern California desert air, dry, empty and slightly acidic.

"I am okay, Pilnouth."

The alien seems to ignore Carlos. Carlos bends over to feel the white powder; the viscosity isn't there. Carlos takes a full scan: just lifeless chemicals and hard ground. He walks around the tedious space, which has all the interest of dusty rock. A violent wave of nausea assaults him at the border. He thinks for a moment about stepping back, but braces himself and continues on to Pilnouth. "It made me feel nauseous until I got inside."

"It is sad to see you were at one with the loneliness and devastation." They walk away until Pilnouth pushes Carlos back. He falls and is caught by a Question plant. His body stiffens. The nausea returns, but it is rapidly replaced by sadness. There is no sexual feeling whatsoever. Pilnouth steps forward and pulls Carlos up from the plant. "Look." The plant withers to a dead gray. Pilnouth whispers, "I have committed a sin just to add to your knowledge. I am too human now. It is time for us to part."

Carlos, suddenly short of breath, grabs onto Pilnouth, steadying himself on the Genian's shoulders: "With what I know now, our people will... All we have to do is arrive on your planet and use our technology. You must tell me how to change the coming events on Earth."

"I cannot. When you enter the atmosphere of Earth you shall know when the events of destruction will occur. And since you already know where the safe location is for fifty million I have done our best."

"They'll come back."

"Don't tell them about their might." Pilnouth takes Carlos' hands and covers them. "We will do our best."

"I am not strong enough to defeat their weapons of mind control."

"You can do that if I can do this." Pilnouth walks toward the shuttle Newton a hundred yards distant.

"The Newton should be a good kilometer from here. That can't be."

"Only to an idiot, Ambassador Jordan. Only to an idiot."

Chapter Twenty-Four

In a tiny white ward of the base hospital an overhead fan spins slowly. Dry dead light washes the room. The brown tile floor, void of wax, curls and rolls as if it were a dead ocean. Resting on the floor, four steel beds face each other like the points of a compass. A plump nurse stands in the middle of the room, scratching her back on the central post. She leans forward, clutching a clipboard in chubby hands. White as the wall, the nurse opens her eyes to stare at the only person in the ward. "You've been a good boy, Dr. Weiss. We'll be sorry to see you go."

Everyone who knows about the mysterious safe location has been working overtime figuring a way to get into the elite club of survivors. At first the nurse had been a saint; until she realized Simon was no longer in the inner circle of the fifty million. From that point on she became no better than she should be, taking her cue from the guards outside who treated Simon like a pariah. Kowtowing to Quentin and those he smiled on was rule number one. Rule number two: Undercut everyone else. Rule number three: There are only two choices left--either survive with the fifty million or die with rest.

As the nurse scans the papers flipping them over the back of the clipboard, Simon's eyes drift to a clock mounted on the post over her. He rises out of the bed. "Dr. Weiss, I said you'd be leaving early. I didn't say you'd be leaving now. You're a physician, you know the decontamination rules. You know how important procedures are."

"You said at nine o'clock. It is almost that now." Simon hates the dictatorial tone of the nurse's voice, but he settles back down thinking if he has to endure this--Carlos must be living in hell. He no longer wonders why he has heard nothing from Carlos. Roxanne had told him the other day the news nets reported Carlos ill, the result of some mysterious alien infection; of course neither of them believe that. Simon hopes Carlos is still being debriefed on the mission to Genia. Roxanne suspects he is being tortured. Both of them fear he may be dead

They have not talked about their fears because the last two weeks Roxanne and Simon have conversed across a glass wall using the old time handsets taken from a nearby prison. Quentin's single-minded efforts to extract the safe location--thinking that perhaps Carlos has told Simon the vital information--had prompted the phone installation at the hospital. At first, knowing Carlos, Simon had thought the notion absurd--but as the days wore on Simon has found the joke less and less funny.

In truth he feels as if he is losing his mind in this prison masquerading as a hospital ward. Susan met him the day he arrived and has not been heard from since. No one tells him anything except Roxanne and she has no conduit into the facts. Everyone he sees seems to hate him, and the sounds of gunfire are getting closer. Simon sits up in the bed; he has had enough. "Dr. Weiss, relax. The doctors say you are to remain quiet."

Simon gets out of bed and walks over to the wooden chair beneath the chest-high window. Picking up his blue pants, white shirt and lab coat he asks, "May I have some privacy?" The nurse exits the room between the far beds making sure she locks the ward door. As he dresses, he looks out to the empty parking lots and high concrete wall surrounding the compound. In the distance the sound of gunfire. The first night he arrived lights from guard towers had swept his window. He assumed it was Quentin's paranoia--then around midnight his worst fears were confirmed. A group of citizens attacked the compound; it was a massacre. The assaults occur every night with the same results. Mass suicide, Simon has concluded. Last night however the guard tower lights ceased after a huge explosion.

Since the return of the Armstrong limousines, trucks, and other vehicles are attacked with regularity night and day. Assassinations are a common event; food storage depots are raided by those with lower League ratings while people with no League rating remain at home or wander the countryside in large groups looking for sanctuary. Simon has seen it all before-in Spain as a young boy--even the jockeying for position by the once well connected. Roxanne has concluded the assassinations are as much to free up space in the fifty million as anger from the disenfranchised.

The door to the ward unlocks and in walks the nurse. "Time's up. Hurry now. We need this ward for sick people." Simon looks around then leaves an empty room.

Moments later Simon crosses the parking lot and approaches the employee entrance for SETI headquarters. He wonders if he will be allowed inside the wounded, pockmarked concrete building. Approaching it, he surveys the black-gashed exterior, the remains of gunfire and home made bombs. Cosmetic damage only, he hopes.

At the twin steel doors, the pair of U.N. soldiers pours loathing out from visored-eyes. "Badge." Overhead a narrow bronze plaque says: "Search for Extraterrestrial Intelligence--Employees Only." He flashes his badge and then pulls open the door. Another guard sits by a desk inside the small entryway. Beside him, a concrete staircase rises from a small hall; it appears like a page from a 1950's book of architecture--Quentin's newest favorite period of design. Simon flashes his badge again with no response. The flat chrome handrail bounces and jiggles as Simon springs up the aggregate concrete stairs supported by a single I-beam. An undernourished red-haired woman with drawn, gray skin stands at the top--waiting for him. "Oh, Dr. Weiss, Dr. Willoughby is looking for you. She wants to see you before the meeting."

"What meeting?" He stops.

"The one about Carlos Jordan and that Genian thing he brought back." She examines Simon from tiny brown eyes. "You did get the memos didn't you?"

"Every one," Simon says not bothering to hide his sarcasm. "Thank you. Carlos is still under guard?"

"I don't know. Dr. Willoughby wants to see you." Her downturn eyes and shaking hands display the fear that bubbles out from inside her. This meek individual fits the last category of the disenfranchised: those petrified who follow any group, hoping to die in a kinder, gentler way. She disgusts him and he strides down the gray-green hallway to a door at the end. Simon enters, knocking at the same time as he opens the door.

The director of Genian operations for SETI stands hunched over the back of a computer terminal; her tongue nestled in the corner of her mouth. Susan Willoughby looks up and smiles warmly. Her hair, now short and precisely cut, frames aristocratic cheekbones and weary eyes. The sadness that owns them seems unmistakable to Simon. He remembers seeing slaves with those same eyes when he was a child. He steps into the room slowly closing the door behind him. His anger drains away like water down a spillway. "Good Morning."

"Simon, you're out early. Welcome back to reality. Please sit down. Are you feeling okay? My damn computer thinks that occasionally isolating itself from the net is the height of humor." She sits down, but keeps one eye on the computer's screen in front of her. "We have armed the Constitution and she sits on the launch pad; they are waiting for information from Carlos to stall the launch."

"Nonsense."

"That doesn't help, Dr. Weiss."

"And Carlos is refusing to talk to them." He looks around the small room with the rice paper walls hoping Susan will not correct his assumption. There are no pictures, just her medal hanging on the far wall behind the desk. And other than a small mahogany table in front of the twin green chairs facing her desk, the room is barren. It reminds him of a desert.

"Quent is going to come by and talk to us about it." She points to a report on a small table. Simon's tension quells for the time being. Carlos is alive. "Those are the preliminary results of the truth-drug therapy program for Carlos Jordan. Look at it." Susan Willoughby watches Simon examine the document. "They've no plans for torture yet."

Her implication is that torture is next. "How long has the drug therapy been going on?" Simon gazes at her as if she were some disfigured masterpiece.

A deep breath expels words. "Last night was the fifth night. He has been held for two weeks." She wants kudos for holding the drug therapy back for over a week. She will get no kudos from Simon. She taps her fingers on the desk because Simon's now sanctimonious look annoys her. "So far he keeps talking about a Biner."

"What's that, a computer term?"

"None I've ever heard. I thought maybe you might know. All he says is 'see the Biner'. Any notion what it might mean?"

He notes her eyes blink constantly and she cannot look at him. He works to hide his disapproval, with a glance to the wire mesh window beside the desk. "Carlos told me none of what happened. I guess if he had I might be in drug therapy myself."

"Probably." She places her hands in front of her and interlaces them. He notes her fingernails are bitten to the bloodline. She places them on her lap.

Simon goes back to the report. "You've changed." He closes the folder disgusted with what he has seen today.

She grips her chair arms, angering at his luxury of piety. "The U.N.

committee is here today. I'm afraid they're going to pull out all the stops. Carlos should never have obliterated the safe location from the treaty. It opens the door for Quentin to get the information by any means."

Simon sighs. "I know. I told Carlos that when I examined him on the flight back." He wants more than anything to ask her about her. He will not; Simon knows what life under a dictator is all about.

Susan watches Simon stroke his chin. "He saved you from what he is going through, you know."

"I know. But heroes are like that."

"Thank you." She glances up at the clock over her door. "They'll kill you if you get in the way. Did you once have a beard?"

He looks down at his hand and smiles sadly at her feeble attempt at familiarity. "Yes, I did. A goatee, in fact. I had it in med-school. When I decided to become a psychiatrist I shaved it off for obvious reasons. We've talked about this." Simon cannot bear her cold calculated responses. "Maybe if I meet with him I can get him to see the logic of cooperation." He stands.

"That's exactly what we want you to do." Quentin Conworth walks in and closes the door behind him. "How do you feel, Simon?" His eyes drift to Susan. She stares at him--pure malevolence. Simon wonders if any of it is an act anymore and moves to shake hands with a person he considers a monster.

Quentin ignores the outstretched hand and motions for him to sit. Then he perches on Susan's desk; his back towards her. "We're launching Constitution--armed--and Simon, before you start your lecture, don't. If you have a gripe, take it up with the council. I'm informing you early as a courtesy so that you might better understand your assignment." He rests his hands on the side and crosses his legs with the casualness of a sultan. "Carlos isn't talking."

"I filled Simon in on our problem," Susan says, walking around the side of the desk and sitting in a chair beside Simon. A stranger in her own office.

"Good." Quentin doesn't bother to look at her.

"Who is in charge of the flight?" Simon says, through a clenched jaw, barely able to control his anger. He glances at Susan wondering why she does not stick a knife in Quentin's gut and cannot help but consider her a coward. Simon knows no one wins with a person like Quentin.

"There will be restricted data release later this afternoon, but Captain Damube is handling this mission also." Quentin rests his hands on the knee of his right leg. "Simon--we're going to lose millions of people soon. We have to try every avenue to get the information to save as many as possible. I will not stop until I get the data I need."

"What data?" Simon asks.

"One: The safe location. Two: Where and when the disastrous events will occur. Three: How do we get the Genians to help us. Four: Who can I save."

"What makes you believe Carlos knows these things?" Simon asks as casually as he can say it. He sees Quentin like any would-be emperor--an opportunist.

"We've gotten Carlos acting out Stage Five refusals, so let's cut to the meat. U.N. Security wants to know what he knows. So far we know the threats are real. Without timing and location, we're all dead. The location though is still paramount. We have nothing to lose now. If he continues to fight us…in the best of cases he'll be a vegetable." Quentin pauses; his tone dark. "Simon, Stanislaus thinks Carlos told you what went on down there."

"He didn't."

Quentin smiles at Susan then looks back at Simon. "That's what she said. You should thank her for protecting you and Carlos." He watches the lack of response from both of them and is satisfied Simon is unimportant. Now all he needs to do is deal with Carlos. "I need to know what happened down there."

"Sounds like you are well on the way to getting the information you need," Simon replies, understanding that Stage Five refusal means Carlos will soon lose all control over his body. At Stage Six he'll become a bubbling fountain discussing everything in his brain--and it will never stop--until he dies. "I recommended against drug therapy in my report. It may kill Carlos."

"Simon, Susan does the operational work. You do the shrink work. And I get to make all the crummy decisions. I need the information. I don't want to sacrifice anybody I don't have to, especially Carlos. Drug therapy will work with cooperation from you--we have this new Clipper therapy waiting in the wings."

"That's pure hell."

"I agree. If we get the data then we let him go and call it a night. Otherwise we go onto the extreme therapies and you already know the consequences of that: Carlos gives me the information and afterward we put him in a rocking chair, tubes stuck in every orifice, and we all wait for him to die."

"He's never going to talk even if I ask him to talk."

"I beg to differ." Quentin points to Susan. "My better half has convinced me you will do anything to protect Carlos." Quentin watches Simon's astonishment. The ensuing anger pleases him. "Therefore we are going to let you help us. She believes he trusts you more than anyone and will let down his guard with you. If she is wrong and she almost never is--my next step is to put his brain on a platter and dissect every goddamn neuron for the information." Quentin's voice lowers, almost to a whisper. "What do you know about that Genian contraption that was loaded in the Newton?"

"Nothing."

Susan speaks: "He said it was a machine, a museum of some sort we could examine and learn from--if we could open it."

"Some of our people think it may be a destructive device."

Simon glances at Susan Willoughby. "I guess it could be that." His eyes ask what has happened to her. She ignores the question.

"But it isn't. Carlos confirmed that last night; he believes it is called a city-museum. Help me and I'll make sure you and your lover are among the fifty million saved."

"Quentin, I'll see what I can do." Simon looks over to Susan who is watching them both. His brow furrows at what looks like the stare of a junkie. "Susan, you don't have to put up with this."

Quentin's casual smile cracks watching one of his marionettes fail to respond correctly. Susan sees Quentin's eyes flash. "Just do your job, Doctor I'm no concern of yours." Her lower lip trembles.

Quentin uncrosses his legs. "Dr. Weiss, the ship is sinking. We already know from Carlos that people are going to die unless the Constitution can get some leverage. We also need to know exactly when it will happen if we are to save fifty million of our fellow human beings. Carlos is our friend, but fifty million people are much more important. Get him to cough up the information or I will stop at nothing until our species is safe." Quentin walks out, closing the door behind him.

"How can you stand him?" Simon says.

"That man is a living paradox." Susan responds, well aware of the recording devices in the room. "All he wants to do is to save the world. I think he is just unwilling to sacrifice himself in the process. So let's put a cap on the holy routine and get back to work. We have people to save and you are the only way we can save Carlos' life. Or are you too holy to do your job?"

"You're being duty bound makes you blind."

"And your piety offends me." Susan believes he has lost sight of her ability to keep true to herself--even though life has become a beast. "Quentin's stuck in the middle. His life is a battle of leverage and trying to gain the upper hand. At the same time, he tries to do what's right," she adds quickly.

Simon gets out of the chair and turns his back seeing affection for Quentin. It is the biggest shock of his adult life. Steadying himself he faces her. He cannot understand how Susan could love that person. Worse than that he cannot bear the notion that she is on Quentin's side. "What's the

Constitution going to accomplish, besides getting the Genians torqued with us?"

"The Constitution would be a joke if it weren't so pitiful. Don't you see he knows we're outclassed by the competition and the coming disasters, so he's trying everything. The Constitution flying is a Hail-Mary." Susan picks up her mug and sips straight scotch.

"What about you and Carlos?" Simon asks.

"He isn't anymore." She stares him straight in the eye. "Tell me Doctor, why will Carlos not tell the safe location and the timing?"

"That's easy--his safety." Simon has now lied to Susan for the first time. He hates Quentin just a little bit more.

"Quentin would make him a deal."

"At the cost of his self-respect. No, Carlos has to fight until he can fight no more."

"We think he is protecting the Genians from us," Susan says watching a clinical mask descend over Simon's face. The calm emotionless gaze turns her stare to tears. "If Carlos tells Quentin exactly what happened, it might save some lives."

"He's a vengeful man--and any information is merely ammunition." Simon is daring her to defend him.

She will not because she considers his challenge an insult to her intelligence. "Quentin needs information and Quentin is the boss. You've seen the Chaos. Quentin is the last vestige of our civilization. We must support him. Simon, you know what it's going to be like better than anyone. Are you going to do your job or not?"

"You're right he is the last vestige of our civilization. I see little worth saving." Simon turns. "What has happened to you?"

"The end of the world. Too bad it takes a back seat to your self-image." Susan's eyes scan Simon crisply, like a general before battle. "You've become bitter. Can you do your job?"

"I can."

"If it helps I will try to save you and Roxanne." She returns a clinical stare to her cup. She finally acknowledges to herself that Simon thinks she has acquiesced to Quentin to keep herself alive.

"And who is going to save you?" He leaves without any further comment.

"You're a pompous ass, Simon," she mumbles into her cup--disgusted at the theatrics that own her life.

Carlos rolls over in bed; his eyes closed. The lingering drug cloud from last night floats him back to Orlando and Hong Kong: the rafts full of homeless people floating among swollen rivers. The ragged muddy humans caked with streaks of dried blood--feed for the flies. Crying children watching bodies floating in the dirty water, the bloated carcasses of animals, the rain and thunder overhead--the wail of holy men over a child's coffin. The five days of drug therapy have completely scrambled his memories. The face he sees on the inside of his eyelids belongs to his father. The reoccurring memory of a photo session with the President in Disney World is all wrong. He sees the children and the media, the popping of cannons. "You don't need to tell us, but you'll feel much better if you did..." These words were implanted in his memory by the drug therapy team. The President also continually asks Carlos to tell all he knows.

A bathroom light bounces off the highly polished blue and orange bathroom tiles; the shadow from the dresser casts itself on dark green curtains. The curtains, half open, hide a thick wire mesh covering the windows making the room look like it might be listed in the inexpensive category of a Greenie travel guide. A musty smell rides the stale air.

"No." His eyes snap open.

New words begin to grind on him today: "...Don't worry, it can only get worse. Help me..." They rise out of his unconsciousness like an overflowing cesspool. Soon Carlos will remember these words as screams from a young girl pounding on the door of his parent's bunker.

Like a drunk he looks around the room wondering where this is; the room changes every night while he sleeps. His gaze settles on the clock. It says four AM, but sunlight streams through the cage window. The reality of his situation does not register. Carlos has no idea where he is yet, and he doesn't care. Closing his eyes again, letting his arm drop beside the bed, he feels like a balled-up piece of paper. Carlos' hand lands on a scrap of paper; he picks it up and reads the fuzzy black letters.

"It can only get worse."

He drops the note to the floor and a triggered memory rushes at him like a train. "We want answers, Jordan. The Genians lied to you. They always lie. They've told us over and over they think lies are funny. Carlos, you'll feel much better without their lies in your head." It is Susan's voice with his mother's face painted on the inside of his eyelids.

Even with all this, Carlos tries to hold onto blurred anger at Quentin; but this morning it flip-flops into hatred of Genian lies. Voices bubble inside Carlos' head. "The Genians never had more than two plants." "Our scans show the soil is dead and empty." "The same is true of both of the other planets they were supposed to have inhabited." "That crap about losing plants to ecological disaster is nonsense." "They took control of our sensors. They took control of you." "Help humanity. It will feel better soon." Then

Simon's voice: "I'll see you today and we can talk about it."

Carlos hears himself speak: "Mr. President, there's nothing you can do. Our power doesn't amount to a hill of beans."

The drugs and his memory curdle in his skull. "...You'll feel better..." The words roll over him like crashing storms. "...It can only get worse..." "...Carlitos, it all makes no difference..."

Carlos begins crying. The gas jet overhead emits a sleep agent. He sinks back into sleep for a few moments. Then the jet emits a stimulant. When he wakes the taste of chemicals fills his mouth. Carlos realizes he has been tasting that for days. "Damn," he says, trying to gather himself. A phone beside the bed starts ringing; he ignores it. The clock now says eight thirty. Confusion and anger churn through his brain. His mind becomes his own again, and the room surrounding him, real. The jet shuts off. Carlos wonders if the drug team has made a mistake--or if perhaps he has told them what they wanted to know. In his head, Carlos keeps telling himself it can only get worse. His back begins to hurt.

"This bed is too soft," Carlos says loudly, opening his eyes again in panic. He finds himself staring at the glittery sparkles on the ceiling above him--and the brown water spot centered above the bed. It sags more than the last time he had seen it. The silver wallpaper below the sag wears mustached men, and bustled women holding lace parasols, sitting mutely on tandem bicycles. The fake silver clouds above them have been printed in such a way they always appear blurry. On the far wall, a dresser empty of drawers leans awkwardly to one side. He has a hard time remembering if the dresser was always that way.

An operator in the next room controls the pitch of the dresser trying to increase tension and a feeling of hopelessness. The operator has also been listing to Carlos intently and emails Quentin that Carlos is almost ready to meet with Simon Weiss. The outburst about the bed being too soft was a signal. The bed is as hard as a wooden board. A musty smell rides the stale air.

The phone rings again. A red light flashes from the little red dome beside a rotary dial. Carlos sits up, steadies himself, and stands. He wears no clothes; the lower half of his body smells of urine. Carlos walks into the bathroom to turn on the shower. Looking at himself in the cracked mirror he sees thick bags under his eyes and an unhealthy yellow pallor to his skin. The phone still rings. He spins the handles of the shower but nothing happens for a moment. Then a hot spray of water shoots out soaking the floor. "Damn it." He reduces the water flow then grabs a white towel and drops it on the floor to wipe the mess with his foot. Replacing the towel back on the metal towel rack, he steps in the shower.

Hot water runs off his body in small streams, steady and soothing. He begins to hack and cough. It feels as if hot sand is being pulled from his lungs. Carlos leans over to grab the low showerhead until the coughing subsides. Spitting phlegm Carlos looks in the swirling water for blood and thankfully sees none. Then, when the hacking eases, Carlos opens his mouth until water dribbles out and over his weak and shaking body. The warm water turns slowly colder. The phone bell changes to a buzzer emitting two short bursts, and then three short bursts. It starts cycling louder and louder. The room pitches from side to side. He tries to grab onto the tile walls but cannot. A moment later he slips to the floor and throws-up. Ice-cold water showers him for a moment; then it turns scalding hot. Carlos screams scrambling out of the shower onto the cold linoleum floor crying out like a sick, wounded animal. The misty bathroom fills with the smell of vomit.

As quickly as he can Carlos picks himself up from the floor and washes. He dries himself off then wipes the mist from the mirror. His now bloodshot eyes look sick and puffy. Leaning on the vanity, he stares at a small green toothbrush with a single row of bristles. It sits in a red plastic cup on the counter. The toothbrush head is again enclosed in a clear plastic wrapping bearing the legend: Sterilized.

--Me too probably--

The phone again. Carlos tosses the towel at it, missing it. "Shit." He pulls the rubber band off, ignoring the phone, and removes the plastic; he brushes his teeth and shaves. The telephone ring and the buzz of the electric shaver harmonize in his brain--just as they are supposed to. "It can only get worse," Carlos says out loud, finishing up and exiting over to the now buzzing phone. He picks up the receiver and drops it back in the cradle.

A white shirt and pants lie neatly folded on the bed. Carlos looks at the locked door. He picks up the clothes and the manila envelope under them. A matrix of rectangles full of crossed-out names covers the front of the envelope. The last name says Quentin Conworth.

Carlos unties the string. A note says: "Ten o'clock meeting today. Simon Weiss." There is also a flat data disk inside the envelope. It is one of his empty recording disks from Genia. Carlos turns the black disk over and over, then picks up the phone to call Susan again.

He is startled to hear a voice say, "Good morning Ambassador Jordan-- you have a meeting in five minutes." The voice speaks in perfectly enunciated English, like a butler.

"May I speak to Susan Willoughby, please?" Carlos does not believe Susan knows what is happening to him.

"Just a moment, sir. I'll ring her." The phone line goes dead briefly.

"Sir, Dr. Willoughby and Quentin Conworth are out together at a meeting. Would you like to leave her a message?"

"Tell her I'm being tortured and I'd like her to come by for dinner." He slams the phone down in the cradle. After dressing, he parts his white hair then finishes buttoning the clasps on the white linen shirt and pants. It has not occurred to him that he is dressing for this meeting with Simon as if Simon were some visiting dignitary.

A knock on the door. Carlos walks over and turns the knob. It opens.

A regulation size human: weight, manner, mid-fifties, well-healed, white male stands in front of him. He is dressed in an expensive blue polyester shirt and gray pants. A small green badge hangs around his neck on a chain. "Good morning Ambassador, I'm Pard. Michael Pard." The cookie-cutter human stands still blocking the door.

"You look familiar to me Mr. Pard."

The individual puts out his hand indicating Carlos should step back into the room. Carlos does this and watches the individual as he inspects the room briefly. "I just need to make sure Dr. Weiss will be safe with you. I'll be back with him in five minutes." The man backs out of the room and closes the door. Carlos stands alone for a few minutes. Five minutes later he sits on the bed. Two hours later he finds himself getting hungry. He picks up the phone. As he does so there is a knock at the door. When he opens the door, Pard stands there with a light green tray covered with a silver top. "Here is your breakfast." He hands Carlos the tray.

"Where is Dr. Weiss? Are you sure I don't know you?"

"It can only get worse. I told you, it can only get worse, Mr. Jordan." The guard closes the door and Carlos takes the food over to a small table and sits in the rickety chair to eat. Glancing at the clock, it indicates less than a minute has passed since Pard first arrived. Carlos opens the metal cover of the serving tray. He sees eggs, bacon and a large glass of orange juice. Carlos does not know what to make of it. Every other meal has been a dark gray gruel and cold, almost stale milk. He picks up the napkin believing he has told everything he was trying to hide. There is a knock at the door.

"Come in." Another more insistent knock. "Come in, damn it." More knocking. Carlos gets ups and walks to the door. When he opens the door there stands Simon Weiss. "Simon, I think I told them everything."

"You didn't, Carlos. That is why I am here." He enters.

Carlos looks down the hallway, thinking of escape, but instead he closes the door. He is too hungry for breakfast; until he turns to look at his meal. Instead of eggs and bacon toast there is a small bowl of gruel and a glass of milk. Carlos closes his eyes in frustration and walks over to the table to sit down and eat. "I hope you do not mind, if I have brunch as we talk," Carlos says ruefully. "Make yourself comfortable, Dr. Weiss."

"Are you okay? I'm going to examine you." Simon looks into Carlos' eyes and feels his neck. Like an old time physician he taps his hand on Carlos' back and listens to his lungs.

"My body's in fine shape. It is my brain that feels like crap. You know I thought this meal was eggs and bacon?" Carlos hits the bowl with the back of his hand sending it skidding across the table and into the wall.

When it dumps its contents all over the men and women plastered to the wall, Simon says "I saw them switch it when I walked in. There's a panel on the wall." He points to the wall next to the table. "Wait here." Simon pounds on the door. When it finally opens Simon goes out and immediately returns wheeling in a portable diagnostic center; he begins an examination. "It looks like anemia."

"I know. Too bad I didn't tell you anything. You too could share this luxury or have them scramble your brains. God, I really wanted those eggs. Simon, can you do anything for me?"

Simon pulls an apple out of his lab coat. "Eat this."

"I think they flog for this now," Carlos says, tearing into the apple. He is wrong, the apple came from Quentin.

"Carlos, I know you're not going to listen and I know your head says different but killing yourself isn't the answer to your dilemma."

Carlos sits still knowing Simon is trying to help him. He also knows it will only get worse. "How much information did the ship's sensors get on the surface conditions?" Carlos eats as Simon listens to his heart.

Simon pauses, while Carlos finishes the apple. "All they have is a strip of the planet. Analysis shows a lifeless silicon powder." Simon begins taking Carlos' blood pressure. A passive look crosses over Simon's face that would have made any poker player envious. "But is that your responsibility?"

"Ah, Doctor Weiss, there you are." Carlos responds. "Yes. Yes their annihilation is my responsibility. I do not intend to give crazies like Damube a weapon against the Genians. Simon, have you ever had your mind read and have your thoughts answered at the same time you recognized awareness of those thoughts?"

"I would think that kind of event for you would be rather disconcerting. Especially since it follows a certain pattern that we shrinks find symptomatic of mental and psychological stress," Simon replies.

"I don't mean its happening now--"

"It will--"

"Simon listen: For Genians, questions and answers are not separate. I am sure of it. And they like jokes because they are lies. We are insignificant and our future is fixed. I can't see taking another species with us."

"So how do we know when they are telling the truth?" Simon asks. He begins to draw blood knowing the apple will tilt the lab results. He hopes to use those skewed results to help Carlos. "Do you suspect the fifty million might not be safe?"

"I think they are," Carlos responds. "And actually I don't really think the Genians even care about that, but the plant, that's the key. With us gone, I think they believe they will not find the answer to the enigma of their Question plant. So they initiated contact. That's also why they will not kill us all. Did I tell you about dogs?"

"Yes about how others make contact through dreams. It will get better, Carlos." Simon can see Carlos' strength is failing. Another day, maybe two and he will lose touch with reality. "So why don't the Genians help us?"

"I think they tried, but this thing about dogs and the way we use them stopped them."

Simon places the vial of blood in the test-tube stand: "Be real, Carlos."

"Quit being a shrink, damnit." Carlos says angrily.

"Then quit acting like someone who is planning, and implementing, a suicide strategy. You know your mania for privacy has made you a perfect stooge for the Genians."

Carlos nods taking the comment in without examining it consciously. "Perhaps, but I need to figure this out." He looks around the room. "Do you really think I should tell Quentin what I know?"

This is the question Simon dreads. "The only issue here is how much pain you will endure and how much damage will you do to your body, mind, and reputation before you give in. Carlos, none of this is fair, or right, or even sane. It is however the fact of your life now and the way you deal with it will determine the rest of your life. Tell them what they need to know. The Genians can take care of themselves."

"You know, maybe you should be with Susan instead of Roxanne. It seems you two think alike now. Get out of my sight, Simon."

Simon nods knowing the anger of Carlos' words. "People love you, Carlos. We want you to live. The truth of your life is what you have tried to do. It is time to move on and let the Quentin Conworths of the world continue taking us into the mud." He pauses to consider for just a moment that his friend cannot see his sacrifice. "It has been happening for far longer than you or I."

Chapter Twenty-Five

After a bumpy hour on failing roadways, Simon steers his car into the driveway. Dry grass scrapes under the vehicle. Slowing the vehicle to a stop Simon opens the gate with a tap of the bumper. He stares at the fallen mailbox as the mechanical gate opens. Driving through and stopping, Simon gets out of the car to straighten the mailbox. There hasn't been mail delivery in months but he checks the box anyway. Opening the creaking door he examines the metal yawn. Just cobwebs. Closing the mailbox, Simon listens to a rocking beat echoing down the dirt road and around the stand of redwood. Raucous sounds bury the empty woods with a shrill pulsing flute. Wondering if Roxanne is having a party to welcome him home, he walks back to the car grabbing the gate and closing it behind him.

The drive sings home to the homeless.

Driving between the shadows he checks for bike tracks but sees none. Simon then looks for vehicles at the large rock-bordered turn around by an old oak. Only Roxanne's bicycle rests against the stooped malcontent; the tree stands alongside the sliding barn door permanently stuck in the half opened position. The red barn they painted, just before he left, still looks brand new but there are no signs of guests. He has begun to worry that something is wrong. The dogs are quiet; he had expected to see them bounding out of the house--but as he looks up to the stone house he sees only a closed screen door. Music pours out over the small porch and bright madras colored drapes flap out of the open casement windows. He honks the horn. Slapping open the blue screen door, Sid and Condo come pouring out of the house jumping from the top step of the porch down to the gravel drive trampling the remains of the flower beds and fearlessly assaulting the car.

Simon opens the car door and they back up greeting him at first with caution. Then, as their dog-brains remember his scent, they greet him with whimpers and circles of motion. Condo jumps on his chest and barks with joy. After petting him--Condo has adopted Simon--Simon pulls his bags from the back of the car expecting to see Roxanne when he faces the house; the porch is still empty. Over an old Jethro Tull tune he yells: "Hello?" and walks up the stairs to the house. He tells himself there is little chance of anything happening to her with these two well-trained dogs by her side--still he peers cautiously in the house.

In the middle of the living room an empty bottle of tequila leans against old books on the wicker table. The hanging couch rocks back and forth. The colored streamers above move in the breeze. Beside the couch, a tape player pounds out notes. On the wood floor beside the music box, a shattered glass litters a Guatemalan rug of reds and yellows. The glass' liquid pools on the rug. Simon enters the house glancing at the dining table in the far corner; it still has breakfast's remains: cereal and homemade bread--even though it is almost dusk. The dogs follow him inside. The stone fireplace looks cold. The banks of windows along the wall are all open splaying their bright curtains to the forest.

Simon crosses the living room dropping his bags on the wood floor and walking past the table into the kitchen. Empty, other than the dirty dishes on white counters, the small kitchen with its glass-front cabinets looks perfectly normal. He hurries up the two stairs at the back of the kitchen. They lead to the bedroom. The door is closed; Simon tries to open it. It's locked. "Roxanne, it's me--Simon."

"Sorry, no sessions today. Just take your stuff and leave."

The door swings open. Roxanne stands in front of him dressed in white pants and a blue tank top. Under disheveled blond hair, her red wet eyes glare at him. "What do you want?" Arms across her chest, she stands like a glacier.

He wants to kiss her. He can smell the alcohol on her breath. "What is it?" He steps forward to kiss her, but she recoils and he finds himself standing alone, arms outstretched in the doorway. "What happened?"

"Your buddy, Dr. Willoughby, sent a telegram. Seems your trip to visit

Carlos was successful. Carlos cracked--told them everything they wanted to know. She said to let you know your place among the fifty million is safe. Nice job, Doc, selling out your friend so you could save our miserable butts." Her eyes' flash. "How could you do that to Carlos?"

"I am his doctor." The doubts that have been playing in his head since his meeting with Susan are being replayed in living color. His arms spread; he begins pushing out on the panels of the doorframe until they creek. "You want me to tell you how awful I feel?" His voice becomes loud. "Or do you want me to beg forgiveness? Or no, I've got it; you want to tell me how what I did was right? That's it isn't it?" His voice lowers. "They were going to kill him to get the information. And one way or the other they were going to get the information. Oh, and so far as our miserable butts and the fifty million you can forget that. We aren't ruthless enough to make the cut."

"So you helped Quentin Conworth mentally eviscerate Carlos because...?"

"I had to."

"You had to stay out of it. It's none of your business. Do you have any idea what Carlos is going to be like now?"

"I know exactly what he will be like." He pushes past her into the room.

"Suicidal. Get it? You made no difference by helping them--except to destroy Carlos just before he dies. You think Quentin is going to let him go free with the information he has in his head?" She stumbles back and sits on the wicker chair in the corner of the room. She begins to cry again. "It's all he had, Simon. You took it from him. He's a dead man with no dignity and nothing to fight for."

"Well thank you, Doctor Gladstone." He picks up an empty glass and sniffs it: tequila. "I saved his life."

"Self serving stupidity. You took his pride." She leans back in the chair. "You took his self respect. You took the only thing his parents couldn't steal."

Simon groans. "So did you save me any of the tequila? I could use some solace." He looks at her well shamed but angrier than a hornet.

Roxanne clasps her arms about her-rocking back and forth. "I don't want to go through a Simon Weiss purification ceremony--especially about my reactions to your expediency. I have been here before with others." Her voice becomes cool. "Do you have any idea what Quentin has taken from you?"

He spins pointing his finger at her. "Do you have any idea how foolish you sound? He was going to kill him. Quentin was going to crack Carlos' skull open and dump his brains out. Then he was going to mind-fuck him until he told them everything they wanted to know. One way or the other Quentin gets the information and Carlos loses--"

"Get out."

"Whoa, Roxanne, wait a moment--"

"For what?"

"Roxanne, cut it out." Simon is yelling, drowning out the music.

"What do you want, Simon? There is no grace here," she says.

"I --"

"Oh...go find a shrink." She stands to leave the room. Instead the two dogs enter the room. One to each combatant nudging them with their heads.

"Roxanne. I did what I thought was correct. Tomorrow we'll go in and get him. Then, I don't know what. Maybe I can get them to erase the memory of the safe location. They have a system for that now." His eyes cast to the wood plank floor.

Turning, her eyes widen in astonishment, she says: "You know, you are awfully stupid when you want to be. I don't have any right to ask you to be contrite. I do want to know why you came back." Roxanne rubs the sides of her arms with her hands and then turns away again. Throwing her hands down as if she hopes they will tear from her arms, she says: "You want to know something?" She spins, tears pour from her eyes. She glares at him. "The hell with you." She pushes passed the dog and goes downstairs into the kitchen and out onto the porch. Simon immediately follows her outside.

She turns to see Simon inches from her. She steps back to the railing pushing into it. Fear rests between them as a long good-bye. Nonetheless, she says: "I'm not going to destroy my self-respect just so you can feel good. What you did was wrong." She crosses her arms in front of her chest.

"I made a decision to save his life. And no one's asking you to ruin your life. It was my decision--and that's why I didn't call you." A sad smile comes to his face. "Like I could have."

Roxanne explodes in a storm of tears and collapses on the deck, crying, a fragile baby with no mommy and daddy to help her. Simon reaches down to comfort her, but she throws his hand off her shoulder. "So is this all we have to look forward to now? Every day we are given some even more degrading event to deal with while bastards like Quentin pull the strings. Making us dance like his private toys as we grasp onto every hope sucking up to every morsel and selling ourselves to any bidder just so we get to breathe another breath? And all the time sick mother-fuckers like Quentin play chess with our lives--what the hell kind of life is that, Simon? Are we so afraid of death that we cling like little children to the apron of life and allow Quentin and his kind to strangle us? Carlos would have gladly died."

Simon cannot bear this truth. "Enough. I made my decision to save him. It may have been wrong but that was my decision. I will not discuss it anymore. Deal with it." He enters the kitchen and pulls down the last bottle of scotch. Today, this evening, he is acutely aware that this is probably the last bottle of scotch he will ever drink. From now on it will be that potato skin swill that masquerades as vodka, or the almost lethal apple-jack that people sell on the side of roads. He prays it kills him at this moment. "I am a doctor. I try to heal people." He unscrews the bottle top.

Roxanne enters the kitchen and sits across from him watching as he pours himself a small glass of scotch and downs it. Then she reaches behind herself and pulls a glass from the tan plastic dish rack. She fills the larger glass and stirs the brown liquid with the outstretched finger of her right hand. "I'd like ice someday. I'd really like to see some ice in a glass."

Simon sees madness. "Roxanne, there is nothing we can do but try and care for each other. Christ, if our grandparents had spent more time doing that and less time watching TV and sucking in products like trained leeches, people like Quentin Conworth would never have fed them the pap, everything that mattered was economic. I am very sorry if you think I have betrayed Carlos--but Carlos was betrayed long ago by every coward that walked the planet caring more for their own convenience than their children's future." Across the table they stare at each seeing only the maw of loneliness.

"So what happens next?" She looks down at her swirling finger circling the glass.

Seeing only concern for Carlos, Simon pours more scotch. "Tonight they will check on what he has told them after they put him to sleep. If everything checks, the drug therapy will be considered a success. Supposedly they will let him free tomorrow." The two dogs come in and sit on the floor. "Long around nine we'll go in and get him. I think it will be a long day."

"He might be dead by tomorrow." She cannot look at Simon.

"Susan will protect him. I wasn't sure she would before. But now, as a result of this, I am sure she will. I understand her a little bit better." He glances at Roxanne's reaction to the statement; there is none and that scares him. "We can go get him in the morning and it may take some time but we will all escape."

She only looks at his forearm. "Simon, I don't want a space with the fifty million. Things like that just cost too much." She continues to stir her scotch without drinking it. The music stops.

"Roxanne--"

"When I was a teenager, the one thing I wanted in all the world was to sail. We lived near the Hudson River, but my family didn't like the water. My mother used to get seasick all the time. To me though, a boat across the water was the most graceful object God ever created. I hated stink-boats but I adored sails. Unfortunately, at that time, the Greenhouse Laws were in the process of being approved and the price of sailboats was going through the roof. I had no hope of getting one myself--though I didn't know it at the time. I'd go down to the dock near my house and watch people sail their boats every weekend." She pets Sid briefly on the head. "There was a TV newsman." Roxanne laughs briefly. "From one of the local news shows in New York, he had a beautiful old Cal thirty-six. He was a master at handling that old boat. I swear he could make that boat dance. One day he asked me if I wanted to go sailing. He seemed like a creep when he spoke to me, but he had this beautiful boat and he was so skilled at sailing I figured he couldn't be a jerk--besides I was young and had decided I could handle anything." Roxanne pulls her fingers out of her glass and sucks the liquid off of them. "The Hudson was beautiful then. It still had mostly fresh water. The Atlantic hadn't intruded yet with brine and dead sea creatures. The mudslides along the shore were ugly but the water was a dream. I spent a year sailing with him. Actually I spent the year sailing and protesting the Greenhouse Laws. I got to be a pretty good sailor and a rotten protester. Carlos and I met towards the end of it. One Saturday, the newsman's wife showed up. She and I had a terrible fight. She called me a tramp. She was just sure we were fucking up a storm. Carlos was there--he smiled. You know how he is." Roxanne looks up at Simon so sad the walls could have shed a tear.

Simon nods, "You've told me all this."

She continues, ignoring him.

"The row was so loud I got a reputation for being a sailing hag." She looks at the ceiling, her head moving in an arc. Then she takes a deep breath. "I did sleep with him once or twice. As a result I could have sailed anytime I wanted from then on; you men, everything is a trade." She cannot bear to look at Simon, "But Carlos never asked for trade. There was never any charge for his affections." She brushes her thick hair aside. "We broke up when I realized he could not love. From that moment on I looked for someone I could love--someone who would love me like Carlos might have loved me were he able to love anyone. As I grew older I began to encounter more trades of love; I gave up on men in my early thirties and became a dog trainer.

"Then I was called into rescue a dumb beach dweller from that storm. That night I had been sitting at this very table considering what the rest of my life might be like--I was scared to death of being alone. Then I found you under a ton of sand. I decided to change my life. When it became perfect I told myself it would never last. God, Simon, I wanted it to last; but I need dignity. That is something Carlos taught me--dignity. That and forget trading your soul for comfort. He used to tell me: "It's the commerce of fools." She runs her hand through her hair pulling it back from her eyes. "We are humans--not ticks that suck out blood from anything we can attach to." She pushes the glass away without drinking it. "Well, so much for philosophy. To my way of thinking you owe Carlos for stealing his dignity. You say you had to do what you did because you thought it was right. I need you to understand that if Carlos gives up I want you out of here. For me life must not be so scary that I am willing to live in the shadow of fear. In a funny way Carlos taught me that as well. So if you are right, great; otherwise I cannot be with you because, Simon, I think you are willing to sell your guts to breathe. I hope like hell to tell you tomorrow how sorry I am for saying this to you." Roxanne stands up, leaving Simon at the table staring at the tabletop. "Oh, I'm glad you're safe."

He reminds himself he has her to thank for his life while wanting to strangle her and her sanctimony. He also remembers his discussion with Susan this morning and his own ponderous sanctity; he feels foolish.

Later that day, she sits on the couch rocking back and forth. His old Spanish blanket covering her shoulders. In her mind's course rolls questions of what she can possibly do for Carlos. She has already decided to tell Simon he must never confess to Carlos what he has done. Simon enters from outside. The tears locked in his eyes seem crystalline. "I need some time, Simon."

He again feels as he did this morning, a pariah. "I am going for a run."

"It is suicide to run that beach now, Simon. It will be dark in an hour or so. I just need a little time. Let's see what happens tomorrow before we do anything stupid."

"The lord protects fools and scoundrels. I seem to have a good measure of both." He crosses into the kitchen to leave.

Roxanne remains sitting alone on the couch looking at the black and tan German shepherd, Condo. The animal goes under the dining table and sits. Sid, her dog, remains at her feet.

"Condo, you protect him or do not come home." The animal cocks its head waiting for her next command. "Don't mess it up." Leaning her head over the back of the suspended couch, she stares at the wooden beam ceiling. Roxanne continues to hurt for Carlos wondering what he will do now that he has been mind-raped. As if her heart is in a tunnel, she can feel nothing else. The rocking of the couch makes her dizzy and she faces forward just as Simon walks back into the living room.

He stops in front of her. "I would like to kiss you hello." He leans over and kisses her on the cheek.

She pulls her arm from beneath the blanket and takes his hand to squeeze it. "Be careful." The other dog, Sid, barks.

"You, stay, Sid. Condo, come." Simon exits the front door and down the steps. Roxanne watches him then closes the door and walks into the kitchen. Taking that last bottle of scotch she dumps it out into the sink. She believes she has had enough wallowing for one day.

The dog is overjoyed as Simon puts him in the back of the car. The car turns left and heads down to the beach. The drive down is uneventful since most of the people who live in this area of the Santa Cruz mountains know Simon Weiss and Roxanne; they hold no grudge against the couple for having a car. All of these people have had the doctor into their homes for advice or to care for a loved one. Many consider his transportation a part of his life-saving duties and assume he has use of the car because he is a doctor. They are wrong. The people who live in this area, like most of the population, know nothing about the mechanisms that control their lives. Misinformation flows like pus from all the media outlets and most will never even hear about the fifty million who are to be chosen for life. So far as many of these people know, today is just another day--full of the usual disappointments and pains. All they have for information is the conduits fostered by the self-congratulatory policy that says the population cannot handle the facts. Ego still rules the media--even in the shadowy dusk. As a result the general population reads sketchy details of disasters, hears nonsense about the general well-being of the population slowly improving, and sees pictures of how the government is in control--in between reports of network soap operas, scandals, and sports gambling tips. Propaganda techniques perfected in the late twentieth century are about the only thing left that seems to be working--or so the leaders of this time suppose.

Simon Weiss opens the car door and steps out onto the beach. A grizzled security officer in green shorts and a white shirt ambles by and checks the license plate. Condo growls a warning from the back seat. The guard leans over ignoring the dog. The large green P attached to the bumper has fallen again. The man straightens the metal plate and smiles at the dog after comparing Simon to the image on his sleeve display; then he walks away. Had the image been different his new orders would have allowed him to shoot Simon and the dog on the spot. This means the patrol officer would then have the entire day to use the fuel in the car before returning it to the registered military base over in Mountain View. But, as it is, the individual walks away. He has heard about this Doctor Weiss helping the neighbors.

A cold Pacific breeze blows over Simon. It announces exactly where his pants do not reach his socks. All men's pants are one size now. Simon bends over and tucks his socks under the elastic of his green-fringed jogging pants, then straightens up, taking a breath of sea air. He rubs his hands together. The air tastes salty and fresh--so different from the recycled oxygen he had been breathing on the Armstrong. So different from the stink of the hospital room or the musty air of the tiny cell that had housed Carlos.

Condo barks again. Time to run. Simon looks at the animal thinking of what the Genians had said about dogs. He looks at his leash knowing a loose dog on the beach is almost never allowed anymore. Simon examines the guide dog dropout looking for signs of hidden intelligence; he sees none. All he sees is the dog's light brown eyes aglow and the rapid panting telling Simon to hurry it up. Then the dog rocks the convertible as he marches back and forth across the back seat. He pushed Roxanne from his mind. Simon is too embarrassed to contemplate it all anymore. It is why he runs.

"You are supposed to be more capable a creature than I had ever imagined." Simon finds himself unsure of how to talk to the animal. He thinks the authoritative tone taught to him by Roxanne now inappropriate to so noble a being. He places the leash in his pocket and pulls up on the silver latch to release the seat. Condo immediately pushes against the seat jamming it into Simon's face and pinning him to the dashboard. Simon grabs for Condo's choke collar as the dog leaps out wrenching Simon's right arm behind him. The force of the hundred-and-twenty pound dog might have spun Simon around, if his body had not been wedged in the tight space.

"Son of a bitch. Condo sit, you egocentric monster. Sit damnit. There's no bitch out there for you to screw. No wonder you failed doggie school." The dog pulls a moment more, then stops. He does not sit, but stares at Simon as Simon extricates himself from the car. Simon tries to ignore the pain in his arm. "You know, I don't care if you are some major metaphysical being jammed into the mind and body of an idiot. I'm your last refuge. Get it? After me, it's that great doggie kennel in the sky--dream guardian or not." Condo looks down the beach. "Fine." He attaches the leash to the dog then leans back into the car to reset the seat and close the door. Simon stretches his legs holding tightly onto the leash so Condo does not bolt off. After five minutes of stretching Simon pulls up twice on the dog's chain. "C'mon, heel." The dog follows alongside Simon as he moves down the small dirt path, surrounded by ice grass and weeds. Simon wonders again how the Genians could possibly be correct about dogs.

Gazing down the narrow beach, measuring the shadows--another forty minutes or so before dark--he watches the white-topped waves assaulting the beach like tiny storming troops. Turning his head to look down the high tide line, he sees the residents of Pescadero out walking the strand--the tsunamis and tidal surges from the deadly storms often leave items on the sand.

Among the debris, Simon sees two corpses on the beach; and while bodies are often washed ashore he notes these bodies are not bloated from the sea. Crossing the loose sand, cautiously Simon notices the others on the beach seem to ignore the dead. He guesses they are just too busy with their metal detectors looking for parts of the destroyed desalination plants, or jewelry from wrecked homes, or parts of old drilling platforms, to notice what is going on around them. The living wander about, like battery operated toys apparently unaware of the bodies they kick.

He steps over the bodies and sees dried blood on the sand. Turning over the corpse of a woman he can immediately tell her skull is smashed inward. The empty gaze of both the living and the dead strike a memory in his mind's eye: Simon sees people fighting for their lives in hand-to-hand combat. In a few years, Simon supposes, the ownership of the beach will change to the warlords--after they form war parties and begin organized raids.

To Simon anything is better than life in a world run by warlords yet he is willing to do just that so that he can feel right about himself. In a future moment he will conclude the decision belongs to Roxanne as well. It will be his true grace.

He decides to head north away from the bodies and away from the wandering survivors. Breaking into a slow jog, he approaches an area of old seaside structures: a few houses, a sea wall, some buried boats and the remains of an old oil tanker truck obscured to its wheels in the sand. The course of nature has taken hold, he believes, and it is merely a matter of time before the remnants of humanity that poke from the sand will be washed out to sea. He wishes he might see that time. Simon is one who perceives society's inequities and lives the consequences of conscience. His resulting anger has led him to see his civilization as a path toward chaos rather than bullwork against it.

As he leaves the shattered houses Simon crosses down to the white bubbly lines of the ocean foam and tries to clear his head by drinking in the misty smell of the salt and the ocean's march. He runs past brown bulbs of kelp abandoned on the shore and a spate of flies. It all reminds him again of how little there is to hold onto anymore and how much he needs to hold onto Roxanne. "I think I may have blown it, Condo."

The dog immediately becomes impatient and begins barking. Simon scans the beach to be sure there are no other dogs for Condo to fight with--or impregnate. He unleashes the dog. With the snap of the clasp, Condo darts at an incoming wave keeping his head low, just skimming the wet rocks. The dog breathes in the seashore's many smells, and lets the salty wave hit him just below his neck. He begins to romp and play tag with the waves.

Then, the distant sound of Simon's breath freezes the dog's play. Condo turns, ears erect, and sprints after Simon joyous at their game. First he runs parallel to the beach, still in the water. But when the dog realizes that Simon is getting away he darts to the hard beach and takes off after him. In five seconds he gallops past Simon, stopping fifty feet ahead to wait benevolently for his two-legged friend. Then together they run until a low moan fills the air. Simon turns and looks at a pair of passing ice tugs. The two belching machines pull a bright, criminally beautiful, blue iceberg that rolls and bounces on the waves.

The pristine water of the iceberg is well on its way to the dying sprawl of Southern California. In the land of movie-paste lies, muddy streets, and television tribes, water is life--and it will soon be devoured. This bit of ancient water is to be sacrificed in the world's most chaotic, and closed party. Ever since the return of the Armstrong, the center of Los Angles has been cordoned off for decoration. "The Party" will start when the Constitution launches. Called the most exclusive celebration of life in history, but broadcast on the Nets like a breaking news event, "The Party" calls anyone with a high League rating to attend the "Schmooz event of the century." The waiting list to get into the party is currently over a hundred thousand long and growing by thousands every day even though participants are to be charged hundreds of dollars and thousands of watts for each gallon of water.

Sanctioned by the upper leagues of the U.N., "The Party" will go on as long as there are celebrants alive who might be potential challengers for the fifty million spaces. It is the first in a series of events meant to cull competition for the sanctuary. So far, unknown to most, there have been three hundred deaths just during the preparation.

Simon turns, disgusted with his species and jogs back to the car watching the tugs drag the iceberg into the dirty, yellow mist shrouding the coast and swallowing the setting sun. He puts Condo in the back of the car. Then he leans on the hood to relieve his tightened muscles. Walking around to the driver's side he opens the door smelling wet sea dog. Simon reaches over, unclasps the roof, pulling it back. Condo looks at the red sky--all smiles--apparently sure Simon has opened the convertible top just for him. Simon takes the dog's leash and ties it to the metal runner that supports the passenger seat. Simon does not want Condo to jump from the car.

Simon drives toward the road. Route One; bicycle traffic is almost non-existent so late in the day, but he stops at the intersection anyway. There are, of course, no cars--just a single woman riding a bicycle with her child in an enclosed orange carriage behind her. The woman approaches, then stops, directly in the flood of headlights. Her eyes are pools of hatred.

"Must be nice to take your dog to the beach. I wish I could have had a car last week to take my son to a hospital when his appendix broke. I hope you and your dog had a nice time this evening." Perhaps soon my son will wind up in your dog's dinner some fine night." The woman peddles off and

Simon notes the toddler in the clear carriage. He is motionless, unbreathing, dead. Simon sits unable to move.

--Look what we have done to ourselves--

Chapter Twenty-Six

Carlos moans, lost somewhere on a California roadway. The irrigated orchard, a deep green shadow along the edge of the flat road, shields him from the rabid sun. He stops to stretch, cracking his back by leaning to his right. Dust clings to his lips in a thick crust. Below him sleeps a dead cat, desiccated, and untroubled, quiet on the dusty roadside. Carlos envies the animal's rest and looks again at the ancient, dented car in which he'd spent the night. He had never seen it, or the brown jeans and rag jacket he wears, until this morning. When he had woken in the car, his head still foggy, he thought this just another scene for pumping out his skull--until he remembered the laughter from Quentin Conworth and whoops of victory--was it yesterday? He lay in the car for hours staring through the torn roof at the passing clouds wishing for nothing, except an end to his shame. Only his body's need to relieve itself of urine had gotten him out of the car fifteen minutes ago. He had stood urinating in the dry winds, condemned and in shock--like any rape victim.

"An idiot trying to help other idiots. Or is it an idiot laughing at other idiots: God in heaven. It all means nothing." Every sound calls out his failures and every rustling branch seems to clatter like bones. "I failed. And it was all a fool's play--my whole life. I should have known." The winds holler his name; he tears at his sleeve with bare hands trying to rip away the material but it holds fast. Furious at his weakness, he pulls the jacket off and examines the label. "Brooms, San Francisco. Nobody around here can afford the most expensive clothing store in San Francisco. Well it's important to have nice throw-aways." In an odd way the clothes are both his badge of shame and a knight's armor. The dirty coat and manure-covered pants tell him his place is at the bottom of the world, in the dirt. He scans both sides of the two-lane roadway and sees nothing but orange trees, a straight roadway stretching like an unending scar, and blue sky. "Now all I need is a way inside the casket."

He wonders why Quentin has let him live then decides Quentin decided to torture him. The memories of the last week slap his brain as if the spokes of a bicycle were smacking a playing card. Images pour through his skull: rotating slides click from image to image to image the result of the fading drugs. The pain of his weakness rubbed raw, he pulls out a crumpled note from his baggy pants unaware of his programming.

"RUN", it says.

"The gray-brown paper could have come from SETI, but then again it could have come from anywhere. Maybe Simon has freed me. Be quiet, Carlos." He looks again at the note and laughs. "Christ, what a stupid note--run. I swear what am I supposed to do with this? Here? And why the hell should I care anyway? What the hell is the point?"

Carlos hangs his head and closes his eyes. "I betrayed everything I believe in to save myself. But there was nothing to believe in." He laughs till he cries. "Is this the way it will be from now on--all my thoughts pouring out of my big mouth? Shut up, Carlos. I think it and say it at the same time? Shut up, Carlos, your rusted failure." He screams a guttural blast of emotion to the blue sky scratching his throat raw with the outpouring. Standing alone on the empty roadway, a man at the bottom of his life: Carlos kicks the cat. It rips apart revealing white maggots on a feast. "What's the matter with you people?" he yells into the empty morning. "Isn't killing this planet good enough for you? Is it really necessary to try and kill another planet for the hell of it? You could have just had humans, birds, mammals and fish--but that wasn't enough. No let's take another species to the grave because we're so damn important."

Carlos' clenches his hands, fingers digging deeply into his palms. He looks straight ahead and walks. "Just how much pain can I bare?" When the cooling blood on his fingers startles him, he opens his eyes and gazes back at the blood trail that dots a sign in the dirt. No dust covers the words: Marisol sixty miles. "So that's it. Susan must have saved me. Who else would wipe the dust from a sign? Shut up, Carlos." He begins a feeling of caring from Susan

Willoughby. His romantic notion of what has occurred has only the slightest anchor in reality. Were he able to look into the sun, he would see a glider circling high above him, monitoring his every action.

"Where the hell am I?" Carlos yells, as he continues traveling down the roadway. "Okay, Marisol it is. First some transport. If she's there, well maybe... Imagine me, chasing after a woman. They chase me. I am Carlos Jordan. Why was I cursed with life?" He stops too aware of his inability to keep a thought private. "The drugs will wear off. Or I can just lie down and die. Walk Carlos, quietly."

Another dust-filled breeze rustles bare fruit trees. His mouth tastes foul. In the drainage ditch alongside the orchard a small drying puddle seems to shrink as he comes upon it. In the middle, a rotting orange is held fast as if the mud were trying to suck it beneath the surface before the winds dry it up and blows it away. "Those trees didn't produce you. So I'll talk too much for a while. I never did know when to keep my mouth shut. Looks like she is finally right about me." Touching the fruit with his shoe, he hears a noise in the distance.

Carlos glances up at what he thinks is an apparition: a red four-wheel-drive SUV encasing a sun-glassed family approaches him. "What the hell..." The couple sitting in front stare at him, happily disapproving of his muddy face and shaking their heads as they motor by him. Small blond children, their faces tight against the back window of the car, appear curious about Carlos; they figure him to be an indigent heading for the next field to pick fruit for the family's wholesome breakfast. The little girl waves--sad at his plight. The boy sticks out his tongue. Underneath their good-bye and beneath the back window a bumper sticker says: "Earthday, April 22--Please Care for your Mother."

"Hypocrites, fools, idiots." Unable to hear his words, the American-dream family fades away in the dusty morning shrinking into heat waves rising from the ground. The SUV slips behind a rise, near a squat building on the far side of the road. A freshly painted red sign hangs from a white metal pole impaled in the oak. It says: "Louise's Place."

His anger quells a bit; Carlos heads towards the building some half-mile distant. A crooked portico hangs along the building-front. Small back squares reveal themselves as windows. A wall of faded Coca Cola signs and red Coors signs come into view. Two dusty pickups sit beneath the signs in the parking lot. One truck is thirty years old, bright blue and buried to the wheel wells in sand--an old tire in back. The other truck, much older, is no more than a rusty shell with doors. A black dog rests on its tailgate. The dog appears married to the shade of a dying oak tree. As Carlos approaches, the dog moves to keep the sun from its body. To Carlos, the non-revenue generating oak appears ready to succumb to the winds that careen over the coastal range. Carlos jumps a small dry ditch that separates the road from the bar. "Okay with you, dog, if I lie down beside you and wait for the tree to fall?" The dog pants in response.

--We never had a chance--

Fiddler-twanged music now pours merrily out of the darkened front door. Carlos brushes the road off his brown pants and slaps the stained jacket against the wooden post. Beside the door, an eagle, with talons uncovered and wings spread, perches on top of a pole; Carlos salutes it, and then turns to salute the dog. He pushes his hand through the fist-sized hole in the green screen door, grabs the smooth bare wood brace, and pulls it open. The bar's cool interior smells of old beer and cigarettes.

On the right are four chrome-banded tables between five red vinyl booths, all-empty. On his left, blinks old pinball machines. The backlit paint on both machines say: "Rocket Man." The devices are mechanical, no computers or LEDs. "These machines must be close to a hundred years old." Even so they appear functional and their lights glow showing a fifties style rocket blasting off toward Saturn--as big breasted women shoot ray guns at bug-eyed-aliens.

Wondering where the power comes from, Carlos scans passed the machines and down a plywood bar running the length of the wall. The updated Tex Ritter tune ends with an echoing chord and a crack of pool balls in the dark. In the back, a pair of cowboys stand in front of a pool table. The walls, covered with fruit box labels and pictures, almost hide a fleshy woman who sits in a dark corner by the pool players.

The woman stands up and lumbers toward him. A Mickey Mouse face explodes on her shirt, drawn tight over a large gut. The shirt had been stuffed into tight blue jeans, but now ripples out along the sides adding more bulk to her basketball-like figure. In her left hand, she holds an old rag. Where her right hand should have been, chrome hooks balance a bar glass. Leather straps snake from her hook into a pin embedded into her skin just above her elbow. She stands in front of Carlos brushing her greasy brown hair aside with the rag. "What can I gitchya'?" she says, eyeing him.

"You should cover that arm. Where'd you get the power to run this place?" Carlos' eyes widen with embarrassment. "It's the drugs. Ah." He rolls his eyes. "Bad night," Carlos grabs a red leather barstool. "Any taxis in the area?"

She shakes her short, greasy hair. "Don't be a dope. Sit down, have a beer and relax. You ain't goin' nowhere." Carlos turns and looks out at the heated morning. The bright light hurts his eyes.

"What'll ya' have buddy?" she comes closer. A long scar runs down her right cheek. She waits while he stares. "Sorry I ain't looking for a boyfriend," and she scratches her petite, straight nose with the hook.

"Beer, anything draft." Pool balls crackle and he turns to stare at the cowboys' reflection in the mirror. They ignore him, concentrating on their game. Carlos then glances at his own face: muddy streaks running down. Happy with perceived anonymity, he tries to wipe the mud away and only manages to turn the hollow line into a smear under his bony cheek.

"Do you have a bathroom where I can wash up?"

Without turning, the bartender thrusts her head to the back of the room. "Just past the table at the end of the bar." She pivots quickly before he moves and puts a glass down on a red coaster. "That's a buck and a quarter. Our beer is cold."

"How can that be? Where'd you get the power?" He says wishing he could keep his mouth tethered.

"You want the beer or not?"

"I can't keep my mouth shut." He digs in his pocket and pulls out a crumpled ten. He tries not to look surprised at having found money in his pocket and picks up the drink. The cool drops on the slender glass soothe his hands as he sips. Moments later the glass is empty. Carlos puts it back on the bar top and walks to the rest room. "I just don't get it."

One of the cowboys, a blond bristly-faced young man, concentrates on a combination shot while Carlos looks over the table. Behind it are three doors. One door says: "Hombres." One says: "Mujares." The door in the middle says nothing. Two cowboy hats hang on steel pegs to the right of the doors. One hat is black, the other white. Carlos notices the cowboys are also. He wonders a moment which belongs to whom. He lingers, waiting for the shot. The white cowboy rushes it and misses cursing and stepping back so his friend can shoot.

Carlos walks around them and pulls on the white wooden door that says "Hombres." He notes a hasp over the front of the door and wonders why anyone would put a hasp on the outside of a bathroom. Carlos has no idea how scarce water can be in this part of the country. The door opens, responding with the moan of an old spring. The other cowboy grimaces as if the creak were a surprise and looks up from the table. He waits. Carlos, closing the door slowly, deliberately, plays the spring like a handicapped one note accordion. He reopens the door and looks out at the cowboys: "Please, beat me to death."

The men's room seems a bright blue plywood panel with a white urinal in a toilet stall. Grotesque pictures of men and women adorn the walls. Next to the urinal is a white sink with a brown teardrop stain from the leaky brass spout. Turning the single faucet a rush of water explodes from it, sending water over the basin and down the front of his pants. Carlos ignores it and pushes back his dirty white hair with one hand while vainly pumping the soap dispenser with the other hand and washing his face in the tepid water.

The unending towel dispenser above the sink fights him from the first pull, but finally complies when he beats on it with the side of his fist. He is surprised to see pressed and pristine whiteness appear after he gets the better of the eternal towel machine. "I guess these people have a way to hide, or hoard energy--and why do I care?" Unaware that he is chattering to himself, he dries his face and hands.

Outside, in the bar, the lanky black cowboy chalks up his cue, then spits his chaw on the floor--just as Carlos exits. "Wimp." Both cowboys watch Carlos' every move.

He sneers. "You guys are losers. Go back to your game." The cowboys make no moves as Carlos passes by them, angry that these two cowboys are about as dangerous as tumbleweed and walks back to his seat. "You're just normal."

His glass is full. Louise is nowhere to be seen, and another dollar and a quarter are gone also. Carlos sips his beer and studies the twenty black-framed pictures that lean against the wavy mirror above the empty bar shelf. One photo shows the ruined New York City skyline from the Jersey side. Many of the photos are of minor celebrities dressed in antique fashions laughing and mugging it up for the camera. A brown-haired ingénue and debonair looking older man are the focus of most pictures. Carlos leans forward and stares at the brown-haired woman. Could it be possible she is a younger, quite beautiful and less ravaged version of the bartender? "She even has two hands," he says out loud.

"Yeah, that's me. Funny what fame and fortune can do for ya.' I guess you never got any fortune from what you did. But you sure are famous. That's why the boys at the pool table didn't beat the shit outta' you." Carlos looks behind him. The bartender sits in the first booth with her feet up. An old laptop sits folded neatly on the table in front of her. A pair of wires runs from the back of the machine out behind the table.

"Been sending out email?"

"There's a news alert on you," she says with a smirk. "I gotta pay my dues you know."

"The hell with you. But maybe you've solved my problems. How about a free beer, Tubby?" Under normal circumstances Carlos seeks tranquility and is the soul of decorum; today he seeks anger.

She picks up the glass of clear liquid beside the computer and takes a sip. Then she wipes the water spot from her glass with a rag and stands up pushing the table tight against the facing seat. Louise leaves the laptop on the table and walks around by the flashing pinball machines to the alley separating the empty shelving from the plywood bar. She places the half empty glass in the sink.

"How come you got all this power to waste, Tubby?" Carlos asks taunting her.

"Local police." She comes back around the bar and glances outside. "They like their beer cold. Besides, there ain't no shortage of power. It's a shortage of people. Seems like it's easy to know everyone these days."

"Who do you think I am?"

She grabs her glass and fills it halfway with beer. Then she points with her glass to an ancient monitor sitting under it a sign that says: "NO CREDIT, ASSHOLE". "I git to watch a lot of TV and the Nets. My customers like it. In fact, two of my customers busted the joint up last month when you landed on that planet. One of my customers wanted to watch the news. The other wanted to watch a bullfight. The rest of us wanted to see the stuff on you and Genians so that's what we did. Mr. Jordan, I'd know your face anywhere." Her harsh face softens to a melodramatic pout. "Them Genian ghouls gonna' let us all die?"

"I think so. I really do." Carlos looks over the top of his glass, "You're a pretty cool cookie." Then he points to a picture showing a group of good-looking men and women sitting at a table toasting the camera. "Tell me about the pictures."

"You know who those people are?" she asks.

"No."

"They're judges who voted me Miss America. See the second guy from the end?"

The faded beauty queen seems interested in impressing Carlos. "I could use a friend about now." He balks. With his judgment useless from the drugs and brain as open as the sky, he tries to keep a rein on his tongue but says: "That guy looks like dirt."

She guffaws. "I can see why they hired you. We were married two years after this picture was taken. I useta' tease him that he voted for me just so I'd like him." She sets the picture down in front of him, carefully wiping the frame.

"He make a mess of you, Tubby?" Carlos picks up the last of the beer and sips it. "I don't care and I never have. Shut up, Carlos."

She holds the picture as if she were protecting a baby. "Beautiful, but dirt. And don't call me Tubby or else. What are you doing here and why do the bastards from the United Nations-Greenie-Gestapo-Dirt-Bags want you? You boff the Genian or something?"

Carlos cannot help but emit a short laugh. "Something like that." A blast-furnace wind slaps the screen-door open with a bang. Carlos stands up and closes it. "It is getting hellishly hot out there. "By the way Tubby, thats United Networks, not United Nations." He doesn't wait for a response. "Walking is out of the question."

"Goin someplace?" She watches him sit back down. "I don't know why I expect you to answer me straight. I shouldn't believe a thing you say anyway. You must be some sort of scumbag, ass-kissing liar to be selected to represent the human race."

"Amen." Carlos tilts his empty glass at her and checks out the cowboys. He decides they are just waiting for reinforcements--and that's just fine with Carlos. "So you busted someone up because they wanted to do something different than you. Yup, TV can sure teach you a lot." Carlos keeps talking, against his better judgment. "Buy this. Vote for that. Forget this, and do that."

She leans over the bar, her bulbous breasts jutting from each mouse ear. She laughs uncomfortably. "Man, you are one bullshitting son-of-a-gun. I once read this story where some aliens came to Earth and said they were our buddies. Then the humans found out that we were being bred for food. Think the Genians will do that?"

"The Genians don't like us much. I doubt they'll want us for dinner. On the other hand I know some humans that aren't far from breeding us for food. You going to help me?" he asks affecting her mode of speech.

She glances up suspiciously. "I don't like messing with the Greenies. They're tough bastards. I saw them close down a farm the other day because Liston Frew used an extra ten minutes a day of power. Don't make no sense. We got lotsa' power. Poor old Liston. I hear they got him in the squirrel cages out in Salinas. He won't last a month running in that heat." She glances out the screen door as a vehicle pulls into the parking lot tearing up the dust.

"Before we get into this tell me where you get your power from?" says Carlos. "There's no power to waste like this." His glass sweeps the room.

"What we got is no people." She watches Carlos look out the front door. "Or perhaps you think there's power only for your comfort?"

"Touché." He looks at her hook again. "How'd you lose the arm?"

She pats her hook with her left hand, then reaches underneath the bar and produces a pistol. She holds it casually in her good hand. "A couple of guys from Atlanta threw me out a window when I refused their kind offer. My ex-hubby was one of them."

The front door creaks open and an old man shaped like a question mark marches through the door. He is draped in a flapping green flannel shirt and red checked pants. His dyed black hair is tied back and braided, a mockery of an executive ponytail, and on his chest he wears a star.

"It's the Texaco man." Carlos laughs, tilting the glass at Louise in a small toast. "Golly, you're so cagey."

"Mr. Jordan, please step away from the bar." Carlos hears the police officer's humorless tone and sips his beer in defiance.

The law advances. "Lean forward on the bar and spread your legs."

"Just shoot me, buddy." Carlos says.

"Mr. Jordan. You're to be returned to your friends from Global Revitalization and Environmental Enforcement."

"What'd he do, Leslie?" Louise asks.

"I don't know. Louise, your email said he walked here?"

"Just came in the door bold as Dandy and twice as stupid. Said he was just wanderin.'"

"C'mon fella' let's get you someplace safe." The sheriff turns him around. Carlos kicks out at the man's knee. A crack ricochets through the room and the sheriff's face drains of color. The man's fractured kneecap gives way and he collapses grabbing at Carlos as he falls. Carlos wrestles the gun out of the holster and points it at the bartender but does not fire the weapon. She fires her pistol twice and misses him both times. Then her gun is empty. She looks at him and immediately lays the gun on the counter. Carlos sweeps the air looking for the cowboys. They're on the floor their hands over their heads.

"Oh, my." Carlos glances at the sheriff on the ground. "You two pick him up and get into the bathroom." He figures it will take the cowboys about five minutes to get out once he is gone and another ten minutes before the patrols find him. One quick gun battle and it will all be done. "Give me the lock to the bathroom." He circles around the side of the bar and watches her retrieve the lock. "You are one rotten shot, Louise. Let's go." With the two cowboys in front, the five of them walk towards the pool table. "Wait a minute." Carlos takes the handcuffs off the belt of the sheriff. "All three of you guys get in the bathroom." He snaps the lock in place over the hasp. "You really are one crappy shot." Carlos wipes some sweat off of his brow with his forearm. "You have a vehicle in back, Louise?"

She nods.

"I want the keys."

"I got 'em--just take it easy. They're in back, by my bed." She pulls on the center door and they enter an electric-green hallway with two more doors. One door on the right side is partially open. Inside, a huge wooden sleigh bed sitting kitty cornered takes up the entire room. Across the footboard hangs a brown-edged, once-white sash. In red, it says: "First Runner Up, Miss USA."

"Liar," Carlos says, pointing with the sheriff's gun.

"So what?" Louise leans over the bed and pulls a set of keys from under the pillow.

"Why'd they toss you out a window? Give me the keys."

"Seems I wouldn't agree to a set of public service commercials endorsing those hamster cages people run in to generate energy." She hands him the keys and they cross the short hallway to its terminus--a thick metal door. She pushes on the metal bar across it and they enter into the garage.

Posters from a hundred glittering cities cover old grimy walls. Carlos stares at the collection--and despite his pains and tears--cannot help but admire the posters depicting the glow from the buildings of New York, the blazing ribbons along the Eiffel Tower or the flash of headlights along the Autobon. "Your collection is worth millions."

"It's mine and nobody else's."

After a sigh, his eyes drift to a red and body-putty-colored wrecker from the late eighties. The truck sits nosed into the side bay in front of him. A wavy, hand-painted swatch of green paint runs between the wheel wells. It is supposed to signal U.N. approval. The sheet metal flaps in the hot breeze and a calico cat sleeps on the hood.

"That's Bert, my cat. Besides you, he's the only fat cat I know these days. Go ahead, get in." Carlos pulls on the door. It opens with the creak of metal against metal. The cab smells of cigarettes and chocolate. Bert the cat disappears into the day like an indignant bullet. The engine turns over but quickly dies. "You're out of luck."

"What's under the shroud?" Carlos asks pointing to the object next to the truck.

"A car, but it's not approved."

Carlos closes the truck door and walks around the wrecker keeping an eye on the bartender. He sweeps the cover off the car revealing an old white Chevy. "Yours, I guess. Does it run?"

"Nope."

Carlos opens the door and looks inside. A key is in the ignition. He walks around and opens the hood. Unsure of what he sees, he does recognize a battery--and a red coated lead floating just above a battery terminal. Replacing the terminal, he lets the hood drop and walks over to Louise. He takes her good hand and snaps the cuffs around her wrist. He takes the other end of the cuffs and attaches it to an old air hosepipe. Then he takes her hook and clamps it into a vise. He closes it down until it holds fast and wedges it with a small pipe and nails.

"There's no big P or green stripe, Ambassador. They'll get you in a few miles." She is lying; there have been no patrols in this area by the U.N. for months.

"Good point." He looks for and finds a can of green paint.

"No, not on my car," yells the bartender. She curses him as he hand-paints a green line between the wheel wells. Walking around to the driver's side he gets in and sits on the bright red vinyl seats. He turns the key and the engine immediately roars to life. He watches the gas gauge amazed to see it rise to over half full. He lowers the window.

"How far to Marisol?" He yells.

"About an hour. Get me outta' this. Ain't ya' got no respect for a cripple?"

"Good line, use it much?"

A fusillade of curses followed him into the dry day.

The old ninety-nine Chevy powers its way up the last turn of the switchback hillside. At the top, a forest-green sign says: "Welcome to Marisol." Next to it, off the road, a square brown twenty-wheel truck, bigger than most of the buildings he has seen today, leans to one side. Its two-note horn rips the morning forest. Ohhh-Ahhh, Ohhh-Ahhh, Ohhh-Ahhhh, over and over. Its large flashing "P", part of the chrome back fender, keeps time with the twin horns. Ohhh-Ahhh, Ohhh-Ahhhh. Carlos slows down. Ohhh-Ahhh, Ohhh--it stops. From the hood, a nest of wires is ejaculated. A moment later, a worker crawls out of the square hole above the front fender nearest the road. She lowers herself easily down the chrome spars welded into the side of the truck and lets out a loud whistle. She is the advance of a group of young marauders; her friends swarm over the vehicle to begin stripping it. Carlos accelerates down the hill wondering where the authorities are hiding. He hasn't seen a U.N. patrol or a police officer since he left the bar. He would be surprised to know how many police officers are just out of his sight.

At the bottom, the town of Marisol rests on a Route One intersection. Behind it the Pacific Ocean fades into the taupe fog. He slows again seeing no one following him and picks up the torn map from the seat next to him. For a second, he considers turning south on Route One. "Where are the police? Ah, what the hell? I might as well know the truth."

He folds the map back along the tears and crosses into the remains of town. An empty lumberyard and gas station mark the outskirts of Marisol. According to the map, State Street is supposed to be the name of the road that runs through the center of town. Carlos unconsciously nods at the sign like a man tasting fine tea. "So far that's right."

State Street is lined with a dozen small two-story brick buildings almost all of them battered in one way or another. He comes upon what was a fast-food restaurant with orange poles, and a rusting gas station. Ahead is a building that appears to be in use. He parks in front of a fresh scrubbed red brick building "Biner's Drugs".

"Biner. That was what the Genian had said in the dream. So that wasn't a lie." He has no idea he is speaking out loud.

Carlos finds himself tense with excitement as he watches an old Rexall sign swing back and forth. The stores surrounding it are wind-wounded and shut except for a combination hardware store and bar across the street. "Some setting for the fulfillment of my dreams. A dead town populated by struggling country folk and beachfront, rip-off artists taking down trucks. I suppose it's appropriate." He remains in the car, its engine off. "There's no telling if I'll ever see the light of day again, let alone Marisol-by-the-Sea and the girl of my intergalactic dreams, so what the hell? Love awaits me--"

Instead of getting out of the car, Carlos stares in the large, plate glass window. Behind it, the drug store is comical and quaint in its predictability. Empty aisles run back to a pharmacist's counter. An old soda fountain along the side is piled high with boxes. A young couple walk away from a lean white-haired man behind a raised counter. Someone else, a young boy is passing a carousel of paperback books and spinning it. Carlos feels as if this pharmacy were the inside of his mind, and he is shocked by how pedestrian it seems. The couple giggle as they walk out the door and down the street.

A skinny pharmacist, his white coat hanging loose around a thin frame, stares at Carlos as he enters. The young boy, now wearing Head-Clamps, rushes down the aisle, and bumps into Carlos. The boy pulls the VR system off immediately. "S'cuse me mister." The boy is redheaded and slightly built. His bright green eyes examine Carlos carefully as he bounces the helmet in his hands. Something is familiar about the boy.

"That's all right." Carlos steps around him and sees the light of amazement in boy's eyes. He has no doubt this boy knows whom he is speaking with. Even so the boy hurries out the store.

Anachronistic drugstore smells assault Carlos: perfumed soaps, liniments, and medicines. A moment later they coalesce into the single distinctive odor of every pharmacy he has ever entered.

"Can I help you?" says the pharmacist in a scratchy voice.

Carlos goes back to the counter. "Yes, are you the owner of this place?"

"No, I work for the owner. And you are not a salesman. We haven't seen one in a decade."

"I'd like to meet her, the owner." Carlos notices the medicine bottles under the counter are empty.

"Her, huh, why?" He leans over the counter looking to see what the rumpled indigent is peering at. Carlos looks up, smiling and friendly. The old man's stare could belong to a high school principal.

"Some pretty old bottles here. Your collection?"

The old man grins and puffs up like a rooster. "Yup. That's fifty years of medicine there. So what can I do for you?" His clouded eyes show the light of intelligence, and caution.

"I don't think you'd believe me if I told you I was a salesman."

The old man sports a wry, white-toothed smile. "Not in a month of Sundays I wouldn't." Carlos sighs and looks down at the empty bottles.

The pharmacy door squeaks and a female voice speaks: "Ralph, have you seen Roo?" The pharmacist looks up and his eyes widen.

Carlos wheels and stares down the aisle. Truth and dreams collide. She wears blue jeans and a blue flannel shirt, brown hair blown by the sea-wind and a shy petite face crowded with the same flinty blue eyes he'd seen millions of miles away, as well as on the boy's face. She brushes the wavy hair aside. Her small nose and odd turned out lips are slightly open in a question. Carlos gazes at her so hard he worries she might burn up from his stare. "So you are real."

Jenny Biner looks through Carlos as if he weren't there. Too many men have stared at her odd beauty for her to care anymore. She believes it will be gone soon anyway, like everything else, and she has little time left for self-indulgence or vanity. "Ralph what the heck is the matter with you? You been sippin' cures or something?" Her bottom lip covers the corner of her top lip and her high brow tightens.

"I think he's referring to me. I'm Carlos Jordan and I was asking to see you." Carlos turns to the old man standing over him. By his open-mouthed stare, the old man states he has just placed the name and face. Carlos turns back to the woman. "If I could talk to you a moment I'd like to ask you a question or two about a house. I think it is nearby." Her presence ratchets open his heart: "You are so beautiful."

Her mouth opens for a moment before the words come out. "You do look like him. What did you do, quit your job, and sleep in your car?"

He pats the front of his jacket. "As a matter of fact, yes." He brushes his hand over the top of his head, straightening his white hair. His missing toe throbs.

Amused he seems so frightened by her, she continues up the aisle wondering if this encounter is a fairy tale, or a joke. She stops behind a white metal spinner full of old paperback books. "What do you want, Mr. Jordan?"

--He is so bashful--

Carlos steps back from her and stumbles on the counter. "I am not bashful, what could I possibly want, besides you?" His face turns a bright red. "I'm sorry. No, I'm not. Is there an old Victorian house around with etched-glass entry doors--a picture of a clipper ship on them? And foyer doors with roses etched on them? I'm so lonely."

That surprises her. "No wonder they call you unconventional. There's a house like that around here--why?"

"Is unconventional bad?" Carlos looks down at the worn, planked-wood floor trying to gather the right words. "Did you have a dream about me? In that house perhaps? We made love." He looks in the same eyes he saw on Genia. "I don't see it, how can I possibly love after all this time. We're idiots, did you know that?"

"Anything's possible." Her face colors a moment.

"Jenny, step away from him," says an authoritative voice to Carlos' left.

Carlos faces a burly police officer defiantly--but Carlos is no longer ready to take a bullet in the gut. He has tasted wonder and beauty; he wants to feast on it forever. Then worrying a stray bullet might strike her he says: "Step back, Ms. Biner."

"Don't do anything stupid, Mr. Jordan. What'd he do, Sheriff?" Jenny Biner asks.

"He assaulted a police officer outside of Watsonville. Put your hands up, buddy."

The woman advances up the aisle to Carlos.

"Ms. Biner, please get back," Carlos says.

"Don't fight it, Mr. Jordan. I'll take you to that house when we get this straightened out." She stops a foot shy of him.

Putting out his hands to touch her, Carlos is cuffed to the counter behind him. He then notices, with jealousy, how the Sheriff affectionately puts his arm around Jenny to comfort her--until she removes his arm. A scowl rides her face. "Are you human? I'm sorry. I need your help. Would you please call SETI in Mountain View? A Susan Willoughby or a Doctor Simon Weiss, they're friends of mine. Tell them I'm here and that I came to see you. Tell them I need to talk to you."

"Shut up," says the Sheriff.

Jenny scowls at the Sheriff and wonders about this unlikely ambassador who, since his return from the Genian planet, has been called irresponsible and dangerous by the media. The part of her that knows her heart skips merrily above mountain tops cannot catch her breath. "I'll call them immediately."

Every cell in his body believes in her. Every sight that includes her is an answer to his life-prayer. Every sound she utters tunes his being to her orchestra. He ignores the angry hands of the Sheriff and the mundane surroundings of the pharmacy. The heat and the sun, the winds and the dust mean nothing; turning he sees her follow him to the street. "You and I belong together." The police officer shoves him into the patrol car. Only when she is out of sight does a teardrop emerge; it becomes a cascade of tears after dinner--the wash continues well into the next morning.

Chapter Twenty-Seven

--The alien was a moron--

Rhythmic breathing, the splash of his hands entering the water, the kicking feet: swimming is a visceral meditation for the planet's most powerful human. He thinks of nothing; he plans for nothing. All life is merely the water and his muscles, his strength and his breath. He pulls himself through the water breathing out bubbles and taking in air. The ride of the water over Quentin Conworth's body leaves glistening jewels reflecting the moonlight overhead. He notices changing water color as lights at both ends of the pool flash red.

--Damn. Someone is at the door--

He tucks in his legs to push off the concrete wall. The surge of his power through the water, like a missile, calms him. He has one more lap to complete in his two-mile swim. It will be done with the same control as the earlier laps, the water and his muscles, breathe, the water and his muscles.

--No one can know the alien was a moron--

Touching the tiled end of the pool, he pulls the swim goggles off his face and rubs his eyes. Pushing his long hair aside, feeling how thin it has become in the last few years, Quentin pastes it back from his face. As a youth, Quentin used to admire this tough guy look and since then has ended every swimming session this very same way. He considers this vanity his embarrassing secret.

Climbing the ladder, he feels his deltoid muscles and their vigor. The front bell chimes, and chimes again. Tingling from the night's breeze and cold water, Quentin glances up at clouds intruding on a bright moon. Machine gun fire tears the night. Laurel trees rustle, dropping dry leaves into the glow of a security light. Other leaves float on fading waves, then disappear into a corner of the pristine pool, sucked down by the filter.

Quentin nude, walking along the flagstone porch, checks his pulse. He is barely out of breath and his heart rate is just right--but the two miles have taken almost sixty minutes. That annoys him. The cape of aging weighs him down again. At the glass-top table impaled by the furled umbrella, he leans over to the telecom unit: "Yes?"

"Quent, it's me."

"Have you misplaced your key?" It is a joke. Quentin taps a sequence into the keyboard to unlock the front door.

--Now what is she doing here. I swear that sometimes it is like climbing a mountain of gelatin--

As he dries off his legs he recalls the first time Susan came over for a visit. She had sat out on the porch and watched him swim in the buff. As soon as he pulled off his goggles, she was in there right beside him. They made fantastic love that night--as he remembers it.

Looking at his black bathrobe deciding if he will cover his nakedness, he quickly grabs the thick terry robe and wraps it about his body. Quentin mourns a time when he would have never bothered to cover his nakedness--especially to greet a woman--but these days it seems his body hasn't the same allure it once had. In fact, it seems to him Susan finds him all too resistible. He ties the sash tightly around his waist. Philosophically, he tells himself these are difficult times and once he has secured the safe location he can spend more time on his health. He will pay no more attention to the notion the safe location might be the ramblings of an idiot.

Crossing the patio, to go inside his home, he opens the French doors with mahogany frames and multi-colored stained glass panes. Susan stands just inside the doors wearing white shorts and a bright blue leotard. Her hair is back in a tight braid. Upon her shoulders is a canvas rucksack. The white walls with their Monet paintings over black marble floors seem a perfect backdrop to this beautiful woman. He notes the two white straps from a rucksack tattoo on her shoulders and looks deeply into her eyes searching for traces of anger or trickery. Susan hates that action; as a result Quentin sees anger in her otherwise calm gaze. "You are brave to come into the belly of the beast."

"I was out running." Susan turns and lays the pack on the rattan couch that faces the pool. "Can your dinner wait a bit more?"

Quentin is surprised by the question "Why?"

Stripping off her clothes, she walks the cold marble to the flagstone and dives into the pool--a splash too soon for Quentin's stare. He follows her out wishing Susan would not use his pool as a bathtub. Nonetheless, he sits on the blue metal chairs watching her swim a lap. Seeing a grace he feels he does not posses, Quentin speculates she wants something for Carlos Jordan. Briefly the thought of entering the pool with her crosses his mind.

--There is too much work to do tonight to waste it away with sex, still with the absurdity of this life--

As if on cue, Susan exits the pool--the fading moonlight her servant. Quentin tosses her a fluffy white towel and asks: "So what's new?"

"This afternoon, dear Quentin, as you might remember, I spent the entire time keeping Simon and Roxanne from killing each other. She thinks we've killed Carlos and eaten him. Simon thinks we have him drugged for further study. When I assured them Carlos was okay, Roxanne looked at me as if I were a Nazi. When I told the pair I couldn't let them talk to him, Simon looked as though you put a spike through my soul. When can I let them know he is okay?" She stands nude for a moment then pulls a pair of sweat pants and a sweatshirt from her rucksack.

--So this was planned--

When they spoke this afternoon about Simon; Susan was fit to be tied. "First thing tomorrow morning you tell Simon we want him to go with you and retrieve Carlos. When he asks where, tell him. But wait until you are on the STOL. All right? I need that data on this Biner woman and that mansion thing." Quentin is playing with her. They both know it.

"So you think Carlos will get what he needs from this Biner woman by then? Is he out of jail?" She places the damp perfumed towel over her face for a moment.

Quentin takes in every curve of her body through the baggy white cloth. "I have given orders for him to spend the night in the jail. He will be let out around nine. See if you can arrange your arrival in Marisol around noon. Have Simon debrief him and we will listen. After that we can decide the next step."

She massages her head. "Talking about next steps: I went for a run inside the compound before I came over tonight. Are those goons with the body armor more recruits for your private army?"

"A man cannot control what he cannot defend. Speaking of that, guess what I now possess?" He looks up at the sky as the last moonlight drowns in dark clouds.

"What's left?" She says.

"An aircraft carrier." He follows her inside.

She begins to comb her hair. "Nuclear, I hope."

He grins like a little boy with a new toy. "I have renamed her the Susan Willoughby. Nuclear fuel included."

"Very funny."

"With jets and helicopters--all it took was a thousand reservations for the sanctuary. I have also given them an option for an additional five hundred places--if they come across with a few escort ships. Talk about the wealth of kings. My idea to just supply only reservations is going to make me billions. Do you realize with aircraft and my surveillance systems I will not only be able to keep an eye on the whole planet--once the disasters are done--I, and only I, will know when and where it is safe to rebuild. By the time I am done I'll own everyone and everything." Gunfire mixes with thunder.

"Then what?" She asks, grinning about his fetish for power. Another burst of gunfire follows an explosion lighting the night.

He shakes his head and faces her. "Can you believe it? I'll have won the game." Quentin deludes himself with a fantasy of final victory--even though the quest for power goes on day and night every day of the year. It is the central point in every meeting, every party, and every telephone conversation. Whether mentioned, implied, or just subtext, it pervades the life of people like Quentin. Every thought is in service; every lover is judged as a utensil for the meal of power. "What do you want?"

"The game is never over, Quent." Susan is amused, long passed fretting over Quentin's soul as he gloats over how he has won one "piece" or another. She is long passed fearing his influence is bad for the population. She is even long passed seeing the game as evil. She tells herself if Quentin isn't winning, it will be someone else and she much prefers Quentin to hold the reins of power.

Putting on her thick wool socks to keep her feet warm, Susan remembers a time when--as she views it--unfocused concerns with saving the people of the planet dominated her every waking hour. Viewing her former stances from the seat of power, she believes herself unsullied by the lure of controlling decisions. And though she does prefer power, to dealing with the weight of plans for knocking on the doors of the castle for the occasional favor, Susan is unaware of the snare she wears: Secretly Susan believes she can influence events for the common good better than any other individual. It is another commonality among those who seek the ring. To her credit, she still asks herself if the seat of power is worth the costs--while being thankful for the remains of humanity that still exist in Quentin's breast. Sadly, she tries not to judge others for their lack of understanding the way the world runs. Of late, she has been less and less successful. This afternoon for example, Simon's requests on Carlos' behalf seemed almost funny. And except that they seemed to placate his lover a bit--she could see no reason for the requests. There are questions to be answered--she believes--and Carlos is a clue. She often asks herself now what life would be on this Earth, if, like the Genians, all human questions wore their answers. She fantasizes that the power crazed would be rendered impotent. She looks up at Quentin. Her eyes blink and her pert lips part with distraction.

"Carlos safe." Her eyes peer at him. Quentin knows this look: it belongs to a woman when she feels the snake's tongue of power. He senses a burden over her recent change: from moralist on the issue of power to amused onlooker. He knows the next step is Player and he is unsure how he feels about that. In a battle, Susan might be real competition. "Did you finish all the reports on that woman, Ms. Biner?"

Surprised he has agreed she waits for the price.

-- He will approach it from a side door--

She speaks: "I have reviewed everything we could locate on her and I find it remarkably dull." Susan sits on the couch feeling the breeze from an overhead paddle fan. In the distance the sky lights. She cannot tell if it is lightning or an explosion.

"So this is quite a mystery: What do the Genians want from Carlos and this woman?" Quentin walks around Susan as the rumble of thunder rolls through the room. "Are you staying the night?"

"No." Susan knows her cues and waits for the real price. "It is tough keeping events at bay." Backing away from her, he picks up the pitcher of iced tea from a nearby table and fills two glasses. After he hands her one, he sips the cool tart liquid. "I'm starving, some dinner?" They cross the slippery floor to a long gray carpeted hallway. Various original oil paintings by Georgia O'Keefe dot the walls; this is Susan's favorite part of Quentin's home. Dark, yet beautiful, it is the place she thinks best reflects his life.

Entering the first door on the right they walk into his media room. Red cushions on the floor cover a thick maroon carpet. Behind them, three pairs of black leather couches sit on ascending risers with black cubes flanking them. The three aisles created are all lit by light strips. Quentin purchased these at an auction held in an old time movie theatre. Along the back wall hangs a black velour curtain running from floor to ceiling. It hadn't been part of the movie theatre sale but Quentin managed to acquire it nonetheless. Cowboy memorabilia decorates the dark red sidewalls: bull whips and six guns, straight razors and carbines. She notices new chrome spurs hanging from the wall in the far right corner over a small stainless steel cooler and oven.

The first time they had dinner it had been in the formal dining room. Since then they have eaten in this media room--Quentin's favorite spot in the small but luxurious house. From here he can see and hear almost anything of importance on the "civilized part of the planet," translation: the wired part of the planet. Quentin pushes a button by the side of the door and the black curtain slides aside revealing the sparkling blue pool and its diamonds of light. Massing clouds make the night moan. "Hear that? Should be quite a storm."

"Could be the powerful killing each other to ensure a spot among the Fifty." Susan stares at the high concrete wall behind the pool and sees no sentries. Unusual for Quentin to allow them shelter so early in a storm, especially since the SETI compound has been under nightly attacks. She watches huge bolts of lightning race across the sky. The evil spikes of light are called the Devil's Pitchforks. The media name comes from the fires caused by the intense lightning. This year has been particularly bad since no one will go out to fight the wildfires. "Where are the guards?"

"Training exercise, but I have the exterior walls manned. We'll be safe. This storm will keep the crazies inside tonight." He turns to face the front wall and a six-foot by six-foot central display surrounded by a set of sixteen monitors. Some monitors display data; some of them display the free networks pouring out incessant drivel. The main monitor shows a shadowy blue figure lying prone. Quentin walks up to the monitor and taps it with his finger. "I think this is the most amazing technology I have ever seen. Imagine being able to see through solid ceilings and walls." He cocks his head to one side and steps back staring at the image as if it were a fine painting. "There is no way anyone can hide from me. You know I spoke to the eggheads tonight and they said in a few years the pictures will be in color and the sound will have no background noise. Can you imagine it? I'll see and hear whatever I want. I'll be unstoppable."

Diverted from the storm, Susan says: "So you don't think the Genians are going to colonize us?"

He frowns at her. He does not like to be patronized by Susan. "Whether they are going to colonize--or not--any intelligence assets we control will help us. And seeing through solid walls and ceilings has to be a plus."

"Well that may be so but I'm not sure I would call that blur on the screen seeing through a ceiling. That image is little more than a bunch of blue dots. If someone came in and woke Carlos, moved him out of the jail cell, and laid down in his place, you would never know." The hailstones and wind begin to beat on the two inch thick glass. Susan is so tired of storms she refuses to even acknowledge them.

"Patience." He stands in front of the room as a college professor might, with hands folded behind his back addressing a lecture hall. "In a few years, say ten or twenty, these systems will have so much detail I can tell you whether or not the subject has any gray hairs or what kind of zipper they're wearing. I am even told these systems will be able to filter out all the garbage noise to three stories. Sadly we will not be able to get stereo. So odd, devices that can see through walls but the sound returns to monaural." He sighs, in love with his technology.

"So you are a total paranoid--what's next?" Susan is impatient with Quentin's fantasies, and spying a stack of plates, he keeps them out on the black-cube tables, she moves toward them.

Grinning at her, he says: "Am not."

"Look at how much money you spent for surveillance over the years. You've gotten SETI and most of civilized San Francisco wired up like your private stage. You've put bugs in every office that matters. You've spent billions on R&D and this new glider-borne peeping tom show could bankrupt a nation. You've purchased a navy for Pete's sake. And you dole out life to those who will not oppose you. Honey, if that's not paranoid I don't know what is." The honesty between these two is a scam.

"The future belongs to the vigilant. Think of it: We can be the king and queen of Earth. Quentin, the first, I like that." Even though his smile is there to say he sees the absurdity of his desires--his eyes glow with lust.

Susan laughs: "You are joking."

"In the back of it all yes. We have no future."

She sighs. He has told her future is nonexistent. Carrying a glass plate for him and a white porcelain plate for herself, she advances to the steel warmer beside the refrigerator on the far side of the room. Opening the warmer, she sees a white covered serving dish and a wilted salad. She laughs, inside herself, at the absurdity of her youthful notions: ideals of a leader having saintly qualities instead of the qualities that make for leaders now: amorality, a lust for power, pride, ruthlessness, a total disregard for any individual, and a love of weaponry. That any person could reach the pinnacle of power with caring properties strikes her as a miracle. And, so far as she can tell, the comparative abundance of caring Quentin seems to possess is positively phenomenal these days. Anyone else would have already had her shot.

She lifts the white serving dish from the warmer. When she turns to the blur of dots that is Carlos Jordan in his jail cell, she just stands there. Pitying Carlos for his lack of understanding, she watches the image intently misunderstanding the blurry back and forth movement of his body--assuming it is just the limits of the technology--rather than the truth: his body is wracked with sobs. "Might just be a great technology for watching people have a bad night's sleep," she quips to Quentin's back.

In many ways her conclusion about what she sees is the result of more than technology. One can only speculate on how she might be reacting at this moment were she able to perceive Carlos' movements for what they really are. But, as she is unable to see him clearly, his emotions remain without context or form, just a poor digital image. Susan walks down the set of risers carrying tarragon chicken. A monitor in the top left corner blips bright red. Quentin picks up a small keyboard sitting on a mahogany shelf. A face appears on the screen. It is an older fleshy man, a general that Susan has met at parties in Huntsville. He has a taste for orgies that usually end with some form of mayhem. The general stands in a glass booth. Behind him is mission control for the Constitution. His narrow eyes and angry gaze tell her something is not right; she is glad this man is a servant and not the other way around. From the posture of technicians in their seats monitoring the Constitution, it appears he bears grave news.

"Mr. Conworth, the Constitution is now officially on our threatened list. We initiated a series of pings and we have gotten nothing in return. All analog traffic remains off line since Captain Damube's report about establishing passive sensor contact with the Genian home world. All lines of data have also ceased." The sweat on the man's brow is ample evidence of his fears: So far Quentin has not bestowed sanctuary and the general appears worried he will be sentenced to purgatory for this mishap. Quentin turns toward Susan as she places the white serving dish down.

"Would you like me to serve the chicken?" Susan whispers, remaining out of sight watching the scene unfold. She turns for the two plates shocked that the Constitution has already launched.

Facing the screen again, Quentin asks: "So how are you going to solve this problem, General?"

"We've tried everything we can think of, Mr. Conworth--except for active calls that we all agree might alert the Genians to our presence. I'd like your permission to begin these more active procedures including remote actuation of sensors on the Constitution to determine the extent of difficulties."

"You have my permission, General. I will want hourly reports on your progress." Quentin taps out a sequence to disconnect the link. The monitor returns to one of the free nets. A commercial appears about the latest pepper spray available for self-protection. It's a booming cottage industry. Quentin rubs his eyes with the palm of his hands. "This is just what we feared. They told Carlos one thing and did something else. I'm going to order that Genian museum thing sent out into space. I think we have been co-opted to be the purveyor of our own destruction."

"Perhaps. But we are at least a month from getting a launch vehicle on the pad at Huntsville. And do you really want to risk a space launch? You wouldn't risk one of your super surveillance systems for a space launch. And wouldn't the Genians have detonated that city-museum by now--especially after discovering the Constitution was sent out to bend them to our will?"

He looks at her--an odd feeling of comradery for just a moment. "The risk of launch is marginal. I don't care if the damn thing is destroyed. Insofar as why they haven't detonated it; that's a moot point. They haven't and that is all we need to be concerned about. Perhaps the mysterious Question plant has constrained them?" he adds facetiously.

"Perhaps the Genians are constrained by some unknown forces that make them tied to a certain date." She spoons a small mound of salt on Quentin's plate.

"April twenty-second in three years? I doubt it."

She recovers the serving dish. "The cargo is in California--getting across the country will be tough. Everyone is watching that thing. Moving it could raise some fears. And if you do send it out into space for safety--I assume you are talking about a parking orbit?"

"Around the moon," he says standing by her. "We still have two old Apollo tapes."

"Then who is going to believe there really is a safe location?" Susan asks, handing him a glass plate with only slices of chicken and a small pile of salt in the corner. "The moment word gets out you are in doubt and your hold on the cards disappears. No one is going to trust the safe location. Next thing you know they'll find out the alien is an idiot." She watches him peer at the sliced white meat; unknown to her he wonders if she has poisoned his food. She has not.

"Who told you?" Quentin picks up a knife and fork.

"No one else knows but they will if I disappear."

"Do you think I'm being paranoid? Do you think the city-museum will be the cause of the disasters?"

"I think the device Carlos brought back may cause the event, yes," says Susan.

"We cannot take the chance it will not just wipe us all out. Or perhaps it isn't really a destructive device--or who knows? The point is we cannot take the chance. That object needs to be removed from Earth." He picks up a small slice of breast and dips it in the salt.

Susan believes she has bought herself some time. "The hull material that surrounds it will certainly stand up to space. We probed it every way we know, but we know nothing more than the day we started. It will be safe out there but this all begs the question: Why did they send two engines in the first place? Is one of them also a destructive device--is that why Constitution is off-line in the Deep Black?" She sits nearby watching him.

"I will send the spent engine from the Armstrong out as well." He stares at her plate piled high with meat and scowls in the way her cycling coach used to scowl at her.

"And, so why the second engine?" She ignores the look of disapproval.

"And we don't have all the data. Maybe they wanted to test us to see if we would send a warship. Then they'd know we weren't worth saving."

"Don't patronize me with my words. I think we need to know why they wanted us to send out a second ship. It could have been a test of our might?" She has again repeated his words back to him.

"Touché. I don't think we will ever know their plans for colonization--until it is too late."

"Do you want me to handle the shipment of the city-museum to Huntsville for launch?" She takes a bite of the aromatic chicken.

"I'm laughing. You are just barely holding onto breath."

"But that is everyone of us."

He smiles pointing his fork at her.

"Glad I can amuse you." She watches him carefully having learned his emotions are well hidden at times like this--but not completely unavailable. She sees a lifting of his top lip and a shake of his head. He is impressed with her, again.

"Well, it is not as if this were unexpected. I knew those Genians were cagier than they had let on to Jordan. They sure had him going about the moron thing didn't they? But it still doesn't explain this Biner woman and his dream."

Susan gears herself to reality, the price of her life has been agreed upon. "Well, we will get it figured out eventually."

"That woman Biner, are you sure we have everything on her? We are certain she has not been altered or abducted by aliens or something?"

"Apparently only in her dreams. We know everything else about her. Those medical records were checked over a dozen times and they are congruent with earlier records. And so far as we can tell she really is dying."

"I put my money on some alien inhabiting her body right after she dies."

"It is possible." She is grinning with that bright smile he has loved since he first saw it. She waits.

"You will see. A few months after she dies she will reappear. I will bet with ol' Pilnouth inside her body." He is joking. "She will probably try to take over the Earth." He works to appear as casual as he can. Susan sees Quentin really is worried about the alien's information. He does not like wild cards. "What do you think I should do with Carlos, Susan?"

She tilts her head ready for the joust. "You have your surveillance system to keep an eye on them. Mount one of your super-duper cameras wherever they land, wait and watch. If someone starts to twitch when we launch that city-museum into space--especially a resurrected Jenny Biner--you will know we have an issue.

"You are making fun of me," Quentin says, enjoying this place where he can make jokes about his fears. "But it is true. I worry about losing my hold on power from an unknown quarter."

"From Carlos?" Susan admires Quentin's perfect poker face of bemused attentiveness. "Look, let those people be. All Carlos wants is to be left alone--and no one wants your damn planet. Not even the moron."

Quentin stiffens with anger, then he immediately tacks in a different direction. "All Carlos wants is to die. Sorry, I just don't want him blabbing the safe location or anything else before he does himself in."

She halts unsure if this was a true statement. "You think that programming you did to change his memory of the safe location to South America will fail?"

"No. That's old technology. We can rely on it." He leans over and kisses her. She does not return the kiss.

"You really want me--knowing how I feel about you?"

"Defiling you is my pleasure and that is your choice Susan. It must be that puppy dog look in Carlos' eyes that angers me." She scowls at him. "I am afraid of losing you." He stands and walks up the aisle to a small cooler set by the warmer. Opening the refrigerator, he pulls out a glass dish with red jello. "Want some?"

She shakes her head no.

He sits close to her spooning into his gelatin. "I have no axe to grind."

Susan again realizes that asking Quentin Conworth to tell the truth about his fears is like asking a dog to pilot a jet. "You are still angry with Simon and Carlos because they fought you at every turn. Quentin, they lost. Send them on their way." She spoons mixed greens on her meat.

"You're tough to resist." He places a piece of gelatin in his mouth. "When you get together with Weiss and Jordan, please inform them they will get nothing from me and tell them to stay away from here. Tell them if I see them on the compound I will have them shot. All right?"

Susan understands this is his way of being magnanimous. Quentin owes no one and can do as he pleases at every turn. "So no quarter for Carlos."

Quentin wipes his hands. "Am I supposed to try to save them?" He asks. "I mean by allowing them a place among the fifty million? Tell me the truth."

She shakes her head. "That will be no place for them. They will certainly drown--or cause problems. No, for them the answer is a quiet life. They've done all they can. They're spent." She really does believe life among the fifty million will be a life of torment for them. Susan does not say she fears the same may be true for her. "Besides, with the vicious market for sanctuary these days a reservation can become a death warrant."

"Without armed guards--no doubt." He grins to let her know she now understands what their death will look like. Susan's heart sinks inside her chest as she listens to him speak: "It is getting nastier and nastier for a spot in the sanctuary. As the month's progress it will be more than just money, or wattage, or supplies, that will define the entrants--it will be brains and guts. A new phase of natural selection has begun; once again only the strong will survive. Mess with me and tomorrow's newspaper will extol the Ambassador and his accomplishments--soon after I will leak his place among the Fifty to some very anxious friends."

"And there is nothing I can do."

"Philistine is the new world culture. Like it?" He grins. "In some ways I wish I had some control over the secondary market but with the resources we have already collected, I suppose it doesn't matter. But if we could sell a spot after someone passes on it, it will multiply my resources by an order of magnitude."

Susan can again recognize her impact on events and finds her hands already covered in Carlos' blood. "Time for me to go."

"I'm putty in your hands," Quentin says, watching the monitor full of blue dots that represent Carlos Jordan on his bed. "I have not yet announced your place among the Fifty. I will do so if you interfere with my plans."

"And with that you have killed me." She stands to leave. "What will you live for?"

"Beatification." And he begins to laugh.

Chapter Twenty-Eight

Distant barking dogs rush towards Simon; he opens his eyes and immediately stares at the empty place beside him, "Ah Dios." He has slept alone. "Roxanne?"

He pulls himself from bed to see what bothers the dogs. Looking out the window he scans the back yard's carpet of wildflowers and fruit trees. The dew remains undisturbed. The garden gate is closed and the side door of the garage remains shut. The back porch is empty and the dogs still have not stopped barking. Roxanne, nowhere to be seen, ignores his call.

Putting on a bathrobe, he ties the cord around his waist and opens the bedroom door. Checking the kitchen, "Roxanne, why are the dogs in a snit? Roxanne?" He crosses through the kitchen then out into the living room. Rumpled bedclothes cover the couch. Roxanne, her back towards him, stands on the porch. He quickly traverses the living room walking out onto the porch--telling himself to be calm.

Beside his car, the two dogs bark at a long dark green object that looks like a log. "What the..." An alligator about four feet long stands hunched, engaged in a standoff with the two dogs. The dogs are circling feinting attacks as the alligator moves its head and tail in defense. "Why are you letting them do that?" Simon asks Roxanne.

She stands beside him mute--and apparently oblivious to the danger. Dressed in a white linen bathrobe, her arms crossed in front of her; she appears perhaps a bit amused. "It must have wandered up the hill from the swamp. It's the third time in as many months. If those dogs don't learn about these things they're going to be dinner one day. Sid, Condo. Come." The two dogs look up, then trot back besides her sitting one on each side. "I'm not sure if I will have the luxury of waiting to put up that fence. Too bad." With that she turns and walks into the house--leaving Simon and the two dogs looking at each other. The alligator makes a hasty retreat, off to the side of the driveway and down the hill.

--I cannot take another day like this--

"Roxanne?" He enters the house looking for her. Simon finds Roxanne outside the kitchen, lying on the chaise lounge, getting a body tan from the early morning sun. He studies, with distaste undiminished by familiarity, the small tattoo of a skull and crossbones on her right calf. After leaving SETI, she insisted on stopping in downtown Mountain View--at one of the tattoo parlors--believing Carlos to be dead. Tattoos are a common way of mourning now.

The dogs gallop passed them and down the back steps to the flowers below. Racing around the corner they appear to be heading out to smite the intruder again. "Dogs, rest." The two animals slow and stop. "I said rest. Leave the alligator alone." They begin sniffing the roses and snapping at bees. Simon sighs, already spent, watching the dogs and envying the simplicity of their life together.

Roxanne finally acknowledges him. "Sleep well? Susan called already this morning. She wants you to call her. No doubt to thank you for getting me out of her hair." Roxanne leans on her elbow, looking at him. A large white towel drapes across her body, stopping just above the tattoo.

The spring morning's charm has never bloomed for Simon. The battle that has been going on for forty-eight hours shows no sign of abating. He finds himself more angry with Susan than Roxanne wondering why she was so hardheaded yesterday about seeing Carlos. On the other hand he is vexed at Roxanne as well; her unfocused anger has him sentenced and condemned. Simon speaks: "She has probably gotten approval for us to see Carlos."

"Or take home the body." Roxanne picks up the bathrobe that lies crumpled on the small white table beside her. "Simon, why don't you call her?" The phone rings. Simon and Roxanne anticipate like gunfighters, waiting for signs of movement to draw their weapons. She backs away putting the robe around her shoulders.

Simon fumes. "You just want to fight."

Roxanne laughs. "I just want to brain you." She strides indoors and picks up the radiophone. "Hello? Yes, just a moment. Oh Judas, it's Pontius." She doesn't bother to cover the receiver.

"I give up." Simon takes the phone. "Susan, this is Simon."

"I see things have not improved. Simon, you need to be down here at SETI by eleven-thirty. We are booked on the STOL. We are going to get Carlos."

Simon looks up at Roxanne and repeats Susan's words. "Where is he?"

"I will brief you later. He's okay. I have also spoken with Quentin about you and Carlos. You are all safe, but without a place in the Fifty. I am sorry--on the other hand no one is hunting you."

"I will be there within the hour." There is silence on the phone except for the background hum of the scramblers. The phone disconnects and he shuts down the receiver. When Simon looks up, he sees Roxanne flipping through the pages of a thirty-year old gardening magazine. "Carlos is fine."

"I will believe it when I see it." She leaves him and walks into the living room. He enters and stands in front of Roxanne, watching her fold the bedclothes.

"Carlos' problems are not your fault."

Roxanne looks up at him over the frayed edges of a flowered sheet. "Thank you, Doctor Weiss, for that insightful analysis." She folds the sheet across her chest. "But we both know we could have done more. So please call the minute you see he is alive--or dead." Picking up her pillow, she leaves the room.

From behind the white door--decorated with small brown handprints--comes the rattle of pans followed by crashing dishes. Jenny Biner stares at her tofu-tuna sandwich. Sighing, she takes another sip of her tea, but Jenny does not enter the kitchen. Instead, she forces herself to swallow. Her weight has decreased almost three pounds since her last examination and the doctor has said unless she eats she will be dead before the end of the summer. Jenny is prepared for death, but death's creeping presence scares her. She wishes, most late nights as she lies in bed, for it all to just end. (Secretly, she thinks she and humanity have overspent their stay.) Even so, Jenny cannot picture her twelve-year-old son safe with someone else and leaving Roo alone seems a sin. She believes this a far colder, harder world than when she was a child. Roo's well-being prompts her to take another bite of the sandwich.

--Roo will be leaving for baseball camp in a few hours. Four days away from him will seem like an eternity. Still he has wanted this for so long--

Another cooking implement drops to the floor. A plate shatters followed by a yelp of pain. Her resolve to quietly sit by dissolves; Jenny races through the door into the kitchen. Roo lies on the tan linoleum floor, an over-turned chair on top of him. He kicks it off rubbing his elbow; the look of frightened child disappears from his green eyes as he focuses up at her. The slender boy stands and brushes off his blue canvas pants. "You said that you were going to wait outside."

"I though you might be hurt." Jenny surveys an array of kitchen tools on the scarred white counter top beside the refrigerator. On the floor next to Roo an overturned bowl spends drops of thick, yellow sauce. Above it, her mother's light blue bowl teeters half over the edge of the cabinet. Jenny rights it, but keeps herself from scooping up the banana halves from the floor or picking up the broken plate. "Were you trying to get something from the cabinet, Roo? Maybe I can reach it for you?"

He gazes a moment at the open cupboard above the refrigerator. "I was looking for brandy." Then, he wipes his hands on his blue pants and glances at his palms.

She quickly checks his scraped hands also--nothing serious. "Brandy? What for? To ease the pressure of cooking or just a mid-morning cocktail?"

"Wouldn't you be surprised if it was just a habit I have acquired?" He grins pleased with his retort. "I'm making Bananas Foster and I need the brandy to flame it. We have banana liqueur don't we?" He picks up pieces of broken plate and places them in the trashcan.

Jenny marvels at how Roo handles his world, and her imminent death--all with a combination of concern and humor--not an easy thing for a twelve-year-old-boy, or a forty-year-old-mother. "Bananas Foster? At ten AM?" Jenny rights the chair to pull down a small dusty bottle of banana liqueur. It had been her father's favorite. "Sorry, no brandy, how about cognac?"

"That'll do." He picks up the bananas, washes them in the clean bucket of water that sits in the sink, and puts them in the righted blue bowl. "Last night after you went upstairs I read a cook book. This Bananas Foster has lots of calories. I went out this morning and picked up the bananas from some Walkers after I did my chores. This is our last meal together, for a few days. I thought we'd live it up. Besides," the light in his eyes disappears for a moment, "you look too thin." He looks away to light the burner. Pulling a frying pan from under pine cabinets, he scoops some milky liquid into it then adds some butter and brown sugar. Her fading life sears his heart. As a young man Roo Biner will take the most extreme of measures to forget this pain.

Jenny walks over to him to put her arm across his shoulders. "Roo, I feel fine."

"I understand," he says quietly. They both know these lies do not help anymore. Jenny steps back to move the chair into the corner of the kitchen. She sits down and watches in awe as Roo begins to fry the three split bananas. He adds the banana liqueur to the bubbling liquid and asks her to flame it. As the flames fail, he sees mortality; Roo faces her. "The recipe doesn't use chocolate sauce, but I know how much you like it. Mind if I put it in a small bowl on the side?"

"Why not?" She is open-mouthed with admiration.

"We need to put the cognac on it. Would you light it in the dining room?" He empties the contents of the frying pan into his grandmother's old ceramic dish and tops it with the liquid. Jenny grabs the bottle and follows Roo out to the table. "Okay, light that baby up." Roo's eyes turn bright with more than just the reflections of the wide liqueur candle.

"It's beautiful, Roo." Roo looks just like her husband had when he was a boy. Long red hair, freckles and bright cheeks, her husband had never seen Roo. He died in a cyclone; the same night Jenny had given birth to Roo.

"The proof is in the eating, Mom." Jenny hears her words echoed back to her. Roo scoops out two large pieces of bananas with ice cream and sauce. "Chocolate?"

"Just a bit."

He ladles a rivulet of chocolate around the edge and hands it to her.

"Roo, you have talents I never imagined." Jenny cuts into the banana with her spoon and stares at the dessert. The doorbell chimes.

Roo darts from the table into the living room; spoon in hand. He peeks out the large picture window, then returns slowly to the kitchen. "Mom, you gotta' meet a better class a' guy. It's Deputy Dawg."

Jenny walks through the living room and opens the door. Matt Thompson, the Sheriff, tips his hat and cradles it in his arms; something is wrong. And Jenny is in no mood for another scene with her former lover, especially after Roo's last comment. She tries to smile. "Hi Matt." The words come out barbed on the edges.

"Now take it easy, Jenny. This is official business. I got a message from the Mayor, who got a message from the Senator, who got a radiophone call from God-knows-who. To make a long story short, that guy from the store wants to talk with you. I told you not to call those people for that guy Jordan." He speaks with that paternal voice she learned to hate over the last six months. "He wants to talk with you about the Genians."

"Carlos Jordan? So it really was him." Jenny leans on the doorframe blocking it. She wants to make sure Matt knows this is a business call. "What does he want to talk to me for?"

"He said to tell you it was about the dream."

Jenny flinches.

"If you're worried, I'll stay. We can pretend it was like it was."

Jenny did not want that at all. Having Matt here "pretending it was like it was," seems much more of a problem than Carlos Jordan.

"Carlos Jordan coming here? I knew it was him," Roo, who has appeared alongside her, whistles between his two front teeth. "Hypercool. Can I meet him?"

"Send him over...with a deputy waiting down the street." She steps back with a nod of good-bye. Matt replaces his hat on his head then waves awkwardly at Roo as she closes the door. Too late he has figured out her affections for him were merely tests for Roo's potential guardian.

"Mom, Matt is a nice man, but he is not right for us." Roo still holds the spoon in his hand. "If you married him and didn't get better I would be stuck with him, alone, for the rest of my life. Don't do that to me. He watches too much basketball."

"I know, Roo. A better class of person." They had both hoped at one time Matt would make a good parent. His drinking and sarcasm ended that notion for Jenny. His affection for what passes through the tripe of the free nets had ended his candidacy from Roo's standpoint.

Roo inhales the dessert as Jenny forces down a few pieces of banana. "I'm going to get fixed up. Want some help with the dishes?"

"Nah, I'll do them." He notes she has eaten less than half of her dessert. "I will save this."

After going upstairs to her bathroom, she gets undressed--and without bothering to heat the water, Jenny showers ignoring the lack of sensation from her skin. The blue powder that covers her torso from her knees to her elbows disappears down the drain in light blue swirls. She watches the last blue trace vanish then touches a few of the three dozen small black masses rising from her once flawless skin. To her they feel like scales.

--Damn--

She cleans herself then steps from the shower not bothering to apply the powder. The medicine is supposed to control the risk of further infection and help her live longer, but in her opinion, it is just another placebo--put out by a teetering pharmaceutical company trying to remain in business. Then, considering Roo, she reapplies the blue powder to cover her body and puts on a pair of blue jeans with a red flannel shirt.

--A blue skinned human in jeans. What a mess--

Putting on just a touch of rouge, Jenny hates looking sick, she stares in the mirror at small black dots visible by her hairline. Last week they were not there; she pulls the collar up on her shirt and dries her hair with the last clean towel. Jenny Biner reminds herself to do a wash tonight, but that will not happen.

Just as she gets downstairs the doorbell chimes again. "Shit, it's him." Roo blanches white. "Sorry, Mom, that must be the Ambassador." Roo is at the front door, banging it against the catcher's mask that he had placed there last night--so he would not forget it today.

A man stands at the door: Carlos Jordan, dressed in a brown corduroy jacket and light blue shirt and a pair of khaki pants, all pressed clean and neat. His brown shoes are polished. Carlos has no idea where it all came from; Susan had sent the outfit over last night. He is suddenly self--conscious of the set of clothes that fit and do not make him look like a derelict.

Roo sticks out his hand. "Hello." He notices the length of Carlos' hair and executive ponytail. The high league rating is a curiosity of just how much privilege this man has. For Roo's generation Privilege is a capital word--not to be messed with.

"How do you do?" Carlos extends his hand.

Jenny appears at the door and examines the man's face. The cold blue eyes would have normally looked a little too controlled for Jenny, except that he also stands, shoulders hunched and hands in his pockets, like a boy on his first date. A recollection of the dream in her father's mansion sends a shiver of delight though her loins.

Carlos looks at the young woman's almond-shaped eyes, even prettier than the dream. Her hair is thinner, but still deep red. He watches her rounded mouth form words and remembers her kiss. At her collar line he spies the blue-powdered skin; Carlos shuffles his feet again.

It surprises Jenny the first human representative to an alien culture could appear so awkward. "Hello, Mr. Jordan," She sticks out her hand. "This is my son, Roo. Please, come in." Jenny steps aside, her hand on Roo's chest, maneuvering him aside.

Letting a breath escape he did not know he had held, Carlos enters the house looking around. He smiles while examining her like an objet d'art. Then Carlos notices the watchful eyes of Roo, and the baseball equipment beside the front door. "Are you a baseball player...Roo?"

"Yup, I'm going to camp today. I could stay though--"

"Roo, get the album from the closet in the den. The old pink one. It's the one with grandpa's house in it." A wisp of hair falls by her eye and she brushes it aside.

Across the living room, inside the dining room, is the ship's clock from the dream. It sits on a sideboard under a mirror. In disbelief, he watches the hands move.

--What is with this guy? He appears friendly, but so detached. Those distracted stares give me the creeps--

Roo returns a moment later handing her the torn album, then looks over to Carlos. Carlos expects to see the pleading face of a twelve-year old. Instead he sees the appraising eyes of an older, wiser person. The boy is careful and Carlos likes that. "Mr. Jordan, why are you here?"

Carlos notices his mother does not correct him, or say anything at all. He likes that as well. "Roo, you know who Pilnouth is?"

"Yup, the Rostackmidarifian ambassador. It must have been fascinating."

He appraises the boy wondering what pains brought forth, in Carlos' lexicon, so much maturity. Carlos nods. "Pilnouth sent me here."

The boy's eyes widen and his jaw opens slightly. "Really?"

"May I look at the house pictures?" Pushing his white hair back, Carlos takes the album and slowly scans it. On the second page, a portly man and a young girl are sitting on wicker chairs staring out at the camera. Beside them are twin doors. The lower halves are wooden, the upper halves glass. Etched into the glass are clipper ships. The next page is a picture of the whole mansion. He closes the album. "Roo, the Genians communicate in many ways. They believe facility in communication, contemplation, and intimacies are a kind of intelligence. One of the ways they communicate intimacy is in dreams. I had a dream on their planet and the dream was about your mother and the house in this album. I came by to meet her and see the house."

"You must have been surprised to learn that communication and intimacy were important parts of intelligence," Jenny says somewhat dryly. She has no time for formalities anymore.

Carlos slowly turns his head from Roo wondering why she has said that. "The Genian view of my facilities," his eyes stare at her, "in that capacity is very similar to your assumptions--I suspect."

Jenny smiles; Roo snaps his fingers. "A-plus. Mr. Jordan, why did Pilnouth want you to meet my mother and see the house?"

"I don't know; that's why I am here."

"Will you clue me in on it later, Mr. Jordan? By email maybe?" Carlos' eyebrow lifts. The young boy's not-so-well-concealed smile disappears. "They are not so tough to write."

Carlos nods. "Okay. I will get the address from your mother. I'd like to go to the house now if we could?"

"Hypercool."

A bell tolls. Jenny walks to the window and sees the wagon for baseball camp and its large brass bell hanging from the side. "Roo, the wagon is here." The wagon's back section is piled high with baseball equipment and wrestling boys rocking the vehicle back and forth. A large woman with a straw hat and coveralls leans over to keep the clapper still and pet the two drayage horses. Behind the wagon sits an old military style jeep; she assumes it is Carlos' transportation. Her head tilts as she looks further down the street. "I didn't think we would be spied upon."

"I thought you requested a deputy?" Carlos looks out the picture window at the police car up the dirt road.

Jenny points to a rusty blue van down the road. "There's no Wilson Glass Company in Watsonville. And there are no trucks like that anymore--around here."

"Excuse me, Ms. Biner." Carlos walks quickly from the room and out the front door.

Roo tugs on Jenny's shirt and nods over to Carlos; then Roo sticks his thumb up in approval. "He'll do," he says. Jenny shakes her head slowly from side to side. She is put off by his oddness.

"Mom, I like this guy, and so do you," Roo says quickly.

"Mellow out, Roo. You'll bust a gut." Jenny places her hand on Roo's shoulder. "Go get your stuff." She walks outside and waves to the driver of the wagon. Jenny's attention is yanked away by the sound of Carlos banging on the side of the van, denting it. The back door opens. He reaches in and pulls a white-shirted, sun-glassed human.

Roo stands with his equipment in hand and his clothes in his backpack. "Mom, this guy Jordan is cool. Trust me." They both watch Carlos berate the man from the van. "On the other hand, he is one weird duck. But you like them like that."

Jenny flushes. Carlos pushes the man back inside and slams the door of the van. The vehicle drives off quickly since the driver knows the glider overhead will track Carlos Jordan. Carlos walks back into the house ignoring the people in the wagon and a few neighbors who stand outside their homes watching. Approaching Jenny he says: "Sorry."

"Is the Tarzan negotiation technique very useful?"

"Tarzan?" Carlos is taken aback by the comparison. "Ms. Biner, I use no force that is not necessary."

"I will bet you do."

Carlos stands at the door; his arms crossed. "I would like to visit that mansion of yours. Can you take me to the place of our liaison?" A moment of precisely measured innuendo trails in his voice.

"Before they declared you reckless and irresponsible--the tabloids said you were a lady-killer," Jenny replies instead of answering the question.

"I am, but if you do not mind, I am just here on business."

"I can see how it would be a business with you."

A grunt of approval comes from Roo. Amused, Carlos glances at him. "You deserved it...sir." He winks at his mother.

"And after we see the house, I'll not bother you further." Carlos is delighted she laughs--in doing so telling him he lies. "Are you a poker player, Ms. Biner?"

"My father once told me that if a man says he has seen you before, keep an eye on him. But if he looks like he has seen you before and does not talk about it, watch out."

No reaction comes from the precise, calm face of Carlos Jordan.

--This is going to be much more fun than I thought--

Roo speaks: "I've changed my mind. I don't want to go to baseball camp."

"As I remember my dream," Jenny says testing Carlos Jordan's armor again, "Pilnouth said we would travel together."

"Sounds like a note in a fortune cookie," Carlos says. "When did Pilnouth tell you that?"

"We spoke outside. He also told me we were to be lovers..."

"Perhaps, but you would not like the queue," Carlos retorts. "And I doubt the alien was male."

Jenny bristles. Roo, at first enthralled by his mother's reparte', reappraises the interactions worrying these two might not like each other; then when his mother looks down at him and winks his face brightens. She'll shake the surety and aloofness from her guest, by the neck if she has to. "Oh my gosh." Jenny looks out at the driver of the wagon--who wears a rather bemused smile. "Excuse me Mr. Jordan. I need to walk my son to the wagon. I will be right back."

Roo shakes Carlos' hand. "You two are going to have a dandy time. Do write to me, Mr. Jordan. I can't wait to hear your side of it. Gotta go now you two. Oh, by the way, let her drive your jeep. She will not ask and she's dying to drive again." He turns away--happier than he has been in months.

Carlos watches them hug each other good-bye.

A once paved, now pot-holed road, winds up a weed-dead hillside passing a fallen shopping center. The old mall, much busier than the town of Marisol, just down the hill, hums with the activity of nomads breaking camp. Many of the Walkers are packing for Oregon, or Washington, or other places less familiar. Jenny grew up with some of these people; they are former residents who only return part of the year. They claim to have said "the hell with it" and decided to become nomads. Others know the truth: they have to survive. Jenny drives slowly, but avoids looking at anyone too long. Carlos examines the black dots on her neck whenever she glimpses some long lost acquaintance.

A tall woman stares at Jenny while she watches a horse buck off its load. Tent parts ready to be packed on horses litter the area. When Jenny looks in the direction of the tall woman, she ignores her. Carlos guesses the woman knows Jenny, but is ashamed. In any case, he likes the nomads; mostly they seem to be thoughtful, decent people who rely on each other. "How ill are you, Ms. Biner?"

"I will be dead by next spring." Her face is a mask of resolve.

Carlos looks again at the black spots on her neck. He estimates she will be dead long before the end of next spring. "I have seen this disease before." Carlos says looking away, back at the Walker encampment. "And your son?"

"He seems to be immune."

"You're worried about him."

"Yes." She recognizes he has put his armor of reserve aside for the moment and sees pity. "Perhaps I will be dead sooner than the spring."

Carlos still stares at the Walker encampment with chagrin, noting to himself that love seems to always skirt his life. His gaze drops. "If I can, I will look after him. If not, I will make sure someone is looking after him."

"You are certainly an odd one. You've only just met Roo. Why would you offer to do that, pity?" She watches his every action hoping the relief she feels is more than just a temporary rein for her desperation.

"You worry about what will happen to him all the time."

"That's not an answer."

"I would rather not answer, if you don't mind. So do you want me to look after him or not?"

"Perhaps." In truth Jenny knows she will agree to the proposal--if given the chance. Jenny Biner slows the vehicle and turns off the main road, passing the remnants of a twentieth century suburban tract. Charred studs and brick chimneys are all that are left of suburbia--except for one white house where a large sinkhole has swallowed most of the pavement. At this single corner the mowed lawn smells like long ago. Above it, a line of drying laundry hangs on a rope stretched from an upstairs window to a half-sized telephone pole. The clothes flap and snap over the white-painted rail fence surrounding the property. In the driveway sits an old Porche convertible, marooned by the sinkhole and freshly polished, shining like the sun. Flowers bloom along the front of the house and inside the empty garage hang scores of garden tools. Jenny slows to a stop so Carlos might admire it.

Carlos gawks at the anachronistic scene, then faces Jenny. "I once thought that life would have lasted forever. The country had so much wealth."

"We were so stupid. " She wonders if he has conveyed any of this to the Genians. "Me too. I remember my Dad saying the businessmen of America would save the planet despite the ecologists."

"What did your Dad do?"

"He built sailboats for years. Then after getting into some legal problems with his partner, he bought the pharmacy. I wish he had been right."

"Everyone wishes that."

They drive around the sinkhole and start up the small winding road quickly cresting a grassy hill. The Victorian mansion of Jenny's father, and Carlos' dream, appears for a brief moment between some dying pines; Carlos stares until the house disappears behind a curve. The white capped Pacific Ocean, thundering into a hidden shore, appears in front of him. "Up there on the bluff he could have seen the ocean. Why did he build there in that hollow?" Carlos smells the ocean. "I suppose building here kept the house safe..."

"Dad hated painting houses. He used to say the sand was his enemy."

"Did he paint any less than his neighbors?"

"By thirty-eight percent--Dad was into statistics and money," she acknowledges. The vehicle descends into a shallow valley turns a corner and stops in front of the house. The car has taken the same route as the hearse in his dream. He sees the run-down house, again, knowing he will fall in love with it. He still isn't so sure about Jenny Biner.

--Why did the enigmatic Genians do this? Was Jenny a gift? Was Roo? What am I doing here? No questions, Carlos--

"I would like to go inside."

Stopping the jeep, Jenny steps out onto the broken concrete sidewalk. At the gate she turns, holding it open for Carlos who still sits in the vehicle. "Would you really take care of my son?"

"Probably in this house. I, ah need a place to live." Carlos gets out of the jeep testing the ground as if he might not find it solid.

--Roo would be safe with this man--

Other than a few paint chips and no birds in the windows, the house is exactly as in the dream. Even the grating on the roof is broken in all the same places. Carlos kicks branches off the pathway as they walk up to the rickety stairs and on to the porch. He looks along the covered porch at the rounded windows almost expecting to see Pilnouth in some outfit looking out; but nothing moves. After Jenny opens the door, he runs his hand along the clipper ship etchings and walks inside.

"Did you like the roses?" she asks.

"What roses?" Carlos knows perfectly well she is referring to the roses on the interior door. The doors he had seen in his dream. "Excuse me," he says looking at the heart-shaped etchings. "Yes, very much."

They stand in a dusty hallway.

In front of them, on the left, a wide wooden staircase climbs a water-stained wall. Carlos enters the sitting room across from it. The windows are blackened. It had been easier to blacken the windows in some rooms rather than not using electric lights--in the early days of the Greenhouse Laws. What looks as if it were a sideboard covered with a cloth reveals itself to be an old sleeping carton--after Jenny pulls the cloth off in a cloud of dust. Carlos runs his fingers over the words stenciled on the box "South Americares. Food for the North--with love."

"Would you consider selling this house?"

"Will Roo get the money?"

"Yes."

Jenny Biner nods her head slowly. "Yes."

Carlos wipes his hands looking around. "Good. Now we can both rest a little easier."

"Do you want to look upstairs?" She watches his eyes dart around the room. She could have stood there for hours staring at him--measuring him. When he finally looks at her, his caring completely naked, she grabs the wall behind her for support. "I believe I have just seen a miracle."

"What?"

"Your adoration. If I keep looking at you I'm going to fall."

He puts out his hand.

"Forget it." She exits the room for the staircase. Neither of them look into the drawing room off to their left. In the dream it is where they made love. Halfway up the stairs, she stops.

Worrying her disease causes her pain he asks: "Are you okay?"

She points to a red union suit hanging over the banister. "Your father's?" Carlos asks.

"I have never seen it before--except in that dream."

"I guess we have found something." Carlos stares at the union suit. It is similar to the one Pilnouth wore. "Might just be a coincidence."

"I had no idea you were stupid." He turns back to her; surprised. She ignores him. Her eyes wide, she stares passed him at the top of the stairs. Carlos turns back quickly. "And the union suit is gone." Jenny marvels at the great, stupid grin that covers his face. "And I thought you might be a boring date. So why are we together in this house looking at old underwear?" There is a bang from the kitchen. "It's the screen door--it always does that."

"Or perhaps it was your question." Carlos looks at her--then kisses her. When her thumping breast ceases, she rests a hand on his shoulder. Carlos walks up the stairs letting her hand fall away from his shoulder.

"Huh?" She looks up at the stairway; at the top it seems to fade to light pink.

Carlos stands straight and proud. "I am going upstairs--don't follow me."

"Right," she says, following him. "My, you are funny."

Carlos stops. "I beg your pardon."

"You couldn't keep me here with an anchor."

"You cannot go in--it'll be dangerous."

"Afraid I might get hurt and die? Did you mean what you said about looking after Roo?"

"I did." He stops three steps from the top of the stairs feeling a familiar queasiness in his stomach.

"Fine, you stay here. I'll go. I'll be dead in a few months anyway. You have a responsibility to my son." She advances up the stairs until she stands alongside him. The nausea reminds her of every morning now.

"There is no physical universe. So what is environment then?" he muses.

"Let's go." Jenny says. Carlos sees her resolve and lowers his head in thought for a moment. "I'm the Ambassador to the Genians. I have to go. You cannot go, Ms. Biner."

"This is not your decision, Bub," she says firmly. "This is my home and therefore my interdimensional doorway--or whatever the heck it is. I tell you what, you can come along." She buttons the top button of her shirt--as if it might be some kind of protection. "Carlos," Jenny continues, "You weren't getting anywhere without me. Now you've gotten a family, a lovely house--and a black hole, er pink hole. What else does a man need? Roo has a guardian so my work is done."

"That cannot be a Black Hole."

"Don't be difficult. Besides, the faceless goon told me in my dream we should go through together." She holds out her hand.

"You lie." Carlos tilts his head and looks behind them down the stairs.

"Hold my hand, please. If I am to die, I want to be holding someone's hand." She takes his hand.

"What about Roo?"

"I always thought it would be Roo's hand." Jenny drags Carlos. Their second step through the pink brings them to a metallic room with padded mats covering the walls and ceiling. The letter "C" is stenciled on everything; to Jenny it looks like the gymnastics room of some rich person who has monogrammed everything with an initial. To Carlos, the room looks like a storage locker room on the Constitution.

"What is this place?" she asks. A sharp pain digs into her neck. A moment later she collapses. Carlos knows the pain somehow--it is the same one he felt before the crash.

Chapter Twenty-Nine

Welcome back, Carlos.

This Extra-Vehicular Activity room looks exactly like the Armstrong's EVA except the gray pads wear "C's" instead of "A's." Carlos sits on the padded floor of the Constitution's EVA room and opens his eyes again; with each blink it feels like years have passed. Overhead, three of the four space suits still dangle on the chrome storage rails. Someone has removed a suit: Ms. Biner. A small red handle attached to a black pulley rocks back and forth. His eyes follow the rails across the ceiling. They converge above the huge gray changing chair. A rectangular communication console on the left side of the chair hangs by wires, ripped from the wall. Paired doors leading to the magazine and the stores' lockers flank the changing chair. Off to the right, a portal leads to a docking tube. Above the portal, a blinking yellow light flickers.

--The shuttle tube isn't locked. The floor heat isn't on but gravity is, so the ship is under Genian drive. Jenny Biner could have gone down the tube to a shuttle. But she shouldn't know the access codes for the corridor, let alone the ability, or motive, to tear the console from the wall--

Still dizzy, Carlos leans back against the foam mats, pulling himself to a sitting position. "Ms. Biner? Jenny?" He supports himself against the padded walls and takes a step. Down the tube, frozen floating pieces of white plastic ride the black night. The shuttle is gone. He looks back to the space suits.

--She doesn't know how to fly a shuttle. It couldn't have been her--

"Jenny." The magazine room lights as he enters. The shelves behind show no weapons; the Plexiglas doors are wide open along the far wall. "What the hell..."

The doors are not broken so Carlos believes whatever has taken place has not lead to a panic. Still, the communications console was ripped from the wall, the shuttle and a space suit are gone--plus the weapons are missing. To his left, the ten paired oxygen lockers are also almost empty of emergency air bottles; only three bottles remain. Surprisingly, most of the food supplies along the far wall are there--except for what appears to be a single busted bag of nutrients on the floor--and all the bottled water remains. "Jenny?"

Thinking he sees dried blood, Carlos crosses to the far corner deciding to examine the busted bag of nutrients. Carlos leans over the squashed mass that lies formlessly on the floor like an old parade float. "Oh, my lord." What was once human remains no more than a gelatinous liquid with leathery brown skin, spongy and dry to the touch. Carlos' legs began to buckle, but he keeps himself focused.

--Please, not her--

The only clue to the dead one is black hair that crowns a bump at one end. Carlos doesn't lift the head to examine the face; it is clear this is not Jenny Biner. He inspects the blood around the body. It is soupy and thick when it should have been dry. Carlos scans to the weapons' locker but finds nothing he can use for defense.

Crossing back into the suiting room, he attempts to use the intercom system but the torn console does not even have power. He opens the door to the main corridor. A male human form sits leaning against the far wall. The blue eyes are open and hanging grotesquely over sunken cheeks. The eyes, pulled up by thickening muscles focuses on Carlos.

--Oh, God, the eyes moved--

The spongy jaw moves to form words, then slackness...and the facial muscles relax; the eyeballs droop forward. A wheeze of air leaves the flattening chest and the body flops to the side. The body loses its shape as he watches it melt into a formless flesh bag. Carlos walks to the far side of the deflating body. A long black tube exits from the skull, just under the ear, and loops around to something spherical. Like a balloon, the skull begins to collapse. Carlos steadies himself on the bulkhead and kicks over the once-human mass to expose the rest of the black tube.

Resting on the floor behind the now flattened body, two black orbs are connected by the same type of black tube. The round orbs grow. The head section undulates, where the exterior tube ends. A slight squishing sound matches the small round dilation of material that travels the tube from the dead human head to the orb beside it.

--This is the same kind of creature I had seen in the Genian city. They're called Lonocs. Thanks for the gift, Pilnouth--

Carlos stumbles back to the magazine room and pulls one of the three remaining oxygen bottles from the wall. He runs back out and tosses it. The bottle hits the dead man's head and the tube coming from it. They both collapse like a rotten fruit. A flood of red and black liquid spills from the fissured skull, covering the black orbs; but otherwise the black creature appears unaffected and continues sucking its meal from the now lifeless body. Returning to the suiting room and closing the door, Carlos believes he needs some protection and enters his data into a small keyboard just beside the chair hoping his security codes are still in place. The system acknowledges him. Worrying about an attack, he glances nervously around the room for the twin orbs.

A small red light glows over the row of EVA suits. Carlos pulls off his shoes and steps into the gray changing chair built into the wall. He pulls a pair of boots from the racks on either side of him. Strapping himself into the boots, he hits Enter on the small keypad. He watches an orange suit conveyed over-head and placed into position. Already opened along the entire middle, the suit slides down along the chair back. His hands and arms slip easily into it. He grabs the blue handle in his left hand and releases the seat back. As it slides away the suit's twenty kilograms transfers its mass onto his back and shoulders pushing him deeper into the boots. He begins the process of tightening the legs and arms of the suit.

Thirty minutes later, Carlos seals the suit at the neck and turns on the cooling system. The self-contained power plant on his back runs with a soft hum. He places the helmet on his head and grabs a tote harness while retrieving a spare bottle of oxygen. After locking the helmet into the suit's systems, he leaves the room.

The black object, the Lonoc, is gone. Carlos examines the spot where the tube had been. A sticky gray clot covers the hole under the ear. He reaches for the area that should have been the collarbone. There is nothing there but the same spongy substance. Carlos stands up and makes sure his suit has a full charge of chlorine gas. It is the only defensive system built into the suit. He kicks the air bottle he had thrown at the Lonoc and sends it rolling down the hallway to the elevator doors leaving a dappled pattern of blood. He follows it, avoiding the gray liquid rivulet that streams across the hallway from vent to vent.

Down the hallway on the left is another communications console; this one is intact. He pushes the slide for motion detection imaging. The image of the Constitution's main communications room takes up the small screen. Lying on the floor crumpled over itself, as if a rag doll, is another crewmember. Next to it, another crew-person's clothes lie limply on the floor. A third person moves but he is in the same condition as the body in the hallway. Carlos manually scans the side corridors. "Where the hell is she?" No other people can be seen. He hits a paging sequence on the small keyboard built into the suit. "Hello? This is Ambassador Jordan. I'm by the EVA primary room. Ms. Biner, or anyone else, please respond." He waits knowing another suit is in use somewhere. "Jenny if you can hear me, just tap the bright red button on your left sleeve." Nothing happens. "Captain Damube?"

The elevator doors open; he spins: Two doll-like humans lie pleated in the lift. Carlos steps carefully towards them--neither are Jenny. Their arms are by their sides and the fingers are flattened by the liquid mass inside. Carlos considers cutting into them, but decides a cramped lift is the wrong place for that kind of exploration.

As agonizingly slowness moves the lift, Carlos' thought centers on Jenny Biner and what might have happened to her. The lift stops and the doors part. The hallway and glassed-in communications room are obscured by at least twenty identical black objects that appear to float effortlessly. Carlos is totally unprepared for what he sees next. The black sea separates: He stares at a body he had expected to see stilled in death. Jenny Biner appears to be waiting for him. She has no space suit, just the same pants and flannel shirt he had last seen her wearing in Marisol. At her feet crewmembers lie flattened on the floor with black objects lighting nearby, sucking life from their hosts.

Wondering if perhaps she cannot see them, Carlos turns on the external speaker of his suit. Taking a step forward, he says: "Jenny, there are floating black objects around the room. Can you see them?" He sees the figure flinch. The question bothered her. "Is that...oh, no. What have you done with her damn you?" He advances towards the control room again checking the charge on his defensive system. Carlos stops just this side of the glass wall staring at the person standing before him. She does not respond other than to gaze back at him. Not surprisingly, he sees both fear and concern filling her eyes.

The door to the room opens but neither party moves. Carlos points with his finger. "Pilnouth, where is Jenny Biner?" Jenny Biner appears stilted, almost mannequin-like as she reacts to the question and steps back from him. She spins quickly and stares at herself in the glass of a computer monitor. The concern immediately disappears.

Jenny glances over her shoulder at Carlos. Eyes full of defeat and sadness; tears well. She looks back at her reflection. "I am not dead. I don't see the alien. Where is she?" She turns back to him, the deadly gas obviously on his mind.

"I had thought you cared for me Pilnouth."

A tiny breathless scream comes from her.

"Finally the answer to our limits is brought forth but it wears no salvation--only recrimination." Carlos taps the charger priming system for the chlorine gas jets. In that instant, a mass of the black creatures begins leaking through the ceiling, surrounding the woman. A black wall forms between them.

She speaks: "Your soldiers had no pain, Tarzan. I took nothing. Now we have intimacy--you and I. Please do not try to stem the disasters that come toward your kind; you and I have not brought forth horror."

Carlos pushes through the wall of Lonocs batting them aside. He stands no more than a foot from Jenny Biner. "Pilnouth, return the woman. She is not yours to own like a coat. She is not something you can don like a new stole for a prom. She is a person--someone's mother. I want her back."

Jenny's eyes are red with tears and pain. "You see only fear, not me." She stares at him. He does not see the alien in those eyes. She looks at herself in the wall's reflection--then looks at Carlos; her eyes as soft as starlight.

Repelled by her he takes a step back.

Jenny looks around confused by Carlos' actions. "You want me to be the dead alien. Fine." The soft eyes cast down. "We need to be a team. There is work. The commander of this vessel at this very moment is moving about 'space' like a mad virus. We can work...together Carlos."

"That's Damube. How do you know this?" He says sarcastically.

She gazes at him. She sees none of the softness she saw earlier. "I forgot you were still bound by your disability." No tear is seen in the clear cold eyes. "The captain ran passed me just as I awoke. He took the shuttle." She looks around the room apparently in contact with the Lonocs. She nods. "Your Captain, in his ignorance, is a demon for our--I hate you Carlos Jordan--your progeny. The others fought so he might escape in a craft similar to the vessel you used on Genia. Now species madness flows out from him ripping the fabric into space and time. The tears he sows will be gathered up. They will haunt Earth's progeny--horror now awaits our children."

"Are you referring to Roo?"

"You are a denizen of the environment that surrounds humanity. Fault rests nowhere."

"You don't talk like Jenny." As Carlos peers at her, her gaze widens with amazement and a smile appears.

"You find me repellent." Jenny laughs ruefully. She tilts her head, again listening to some communication Carlos cannot hear. She sighs and looks at him full of sadness. "I assume it will be all right with you if we solve an immediate problem."

"Another of your kind's superior plans gone awry?"

"Follow me, Carlos--and try to keep your mouth shut. I don't like it when you appear a fool." Jenny leads Carlos through the communications room and down into the command center. The square room with the control panel covering every inch of wall space looks as if a tornado has hit it. Flat bodies litter the floor; burn marks from weapons scorch the walls and ceiling. Sets of panels are torn out of the far wall; they hang loosely from a bright blue--steel casing. Wires hang from the bottom and snake along the floor to the navigator's seat now crookedly placed in the center of the room. Another tangle of wires spills from a panel near the ship's engine controls and surrounds the chair on the floor. Carlos examines the board and the wiring system. He had not seen a blue colored box like this on the Armstrong. He keys an inquiry at the command keyboard beside it. The screen lights: Tenark Defense Systems.

"They fought you Genians in every way they knew how. I hope the damage to your kind was extensive," Carlos says, knowing the futility of anger but unable to control himself anymore.

Jenny looks at him. "Yes the damage is extensive--however to humanity--and it will get worse."

Carlos scans the dead bodies in the room for life. "Is this the damage that your kind has been predicting for humanity?"

She continues to glance at her reflection at every opportunity. When she sees him watching her she seems to color. "No. Where is the doll-house Pilnouth sent you in the pod?"

"Doll-house?" Carlos asks.

"Doll-house, city musuem, Pilnouth did not want to insult humanity."

"At our base. You refer to yourself in the third person."

"You must move the pod away from population. When the city-museum opens, the conductors will be dead and I will be there piloting it. Needless to say I'll be only minutely effective."

"Quite a task for someone used to running a pharmacy."

She scowls at him. "Quite a remark for an ambassador who belives life to be a Ping Pong game." Her eyes close squeezing away a tear. "The city-museum will expand violently. There will be immediate death to inhabitants who are above the ground when it opens." She recoils from his cold dead stare. "I know there is a problem. I am trying to help solve it. This doesn't mean

I'm some kind of alien monster. I am simply aware, Carlos. Nothing more."

"You're just little old Jenny," Carlos says calmly.

She narrows her eyes. "I never did like sarcastic men either. Those creatures, the Lonocs, killed many here. They have a symbiotic relationship with the Genian--protecting her in exchange for knowledge. Lonocs are in the city. They are why the city could not be opened before our world made more progress. Carlos, it will be a world wide slaughter."

"I am surprised you cannot stop the Lonocs from killing," Carlos says. "You seem to get along with them so well."

--These Lonocs might be a Genian defense system--

"Dominion is absurd--they have a right to exist. The universe isn't a jungle...Tarzan." She ignores the expression of disgust behind the visor.

"My kind died here for your amusement?" He purposely adds a lilt to his voice to turn it into a question.

"None of this amusing, Carlos. Your Greenie friends make war on the innocent instead of each other--in the name of profit to support their pleasures and fears. They teach this as progress: 'How nice that people die of hunger and neglect instead of bombs and bullets.' Now that is amusing. Damn you--I am not a sarcastic person. We must stop the Lonocs from cleaning the Agg as they have done here."

His thin face turns red with anger. "God in heaven what have you done here? I see. So I am to be co-opted again to save others and the hell with me." Carlos freezes, stunned by his words. A familiar calmness spreads over him. "You win I see. What must I do with the city-museum?"

She sighs too frustrated with him to care about his pains. "You must move the doll-house to an empty, dry location away from people."

"That's almost all Earth now, remember?"

"One of the deserts. It will slow the Lonocs from getting through the dome that protects it. Perhaps that time will be enough. But if the dome fails first..."

"I wonder how you could let creatures like that live."

She laughs. "They have a right to exist as much as you or I. Your opinions of each other are quite similar. They keep wanting to know why the Genians were concerned with so evil a species as humanity--"

"You are not human. We cannot communicate telepathically."

"Oh really? Well, knowledge cannot be pumped into a mental sieve and expected to stay."

"Cute. So the Lonocs are the horror that awaits us. Quentin deserves my apology."

"The Lonocs know the horror that awaits your progeny. They are trying to spare your kind from that horror."

"By killing us?" Carlos laughs. "You don't make a very convincing human."

"Neither do you." Jenny stares at him. "But at least I know who I am."

"I am not here to joust with you."

"The Lonocs cannot believe you would wish your kind to meet horrors rather than the simplicity of death. They do not understand we humans are so self-involved we think the program we call life is blessed and unique."

"On the other hand without this self-absorption how could we humans complete our tasks?"

"What tasks? Enlighten me," Jenny asks.

"That's apparently impossible."

She wonders how she can possibly deal with so much ignorance and looks to the floor trying to cope with the anger coursing through her body. The anger quickly subsides leaving her confused; it is as if a part of her has died and she cannot recall which part is now missing. She stares at him and her anger returns with a different pedigree. "You let them come to attack Genia without telling the Genians. If the Genians had known, it would have been different. Remember the dream?"

"Pilnouth, that whole dream thing was nothing more than a way for you to get out of the bonds that came with your birth." He swings wildly at her and she easily avoids the roundhouse punch. Creatures melt through the walls--their pulsing menacing bodies filling the room. "Damn you for stealing her from me. Damn you for killing all these people. Damn me for letting you trick me into thinking I could have love."

"You have not been tricked."

"She's dead."

"Idiot." Jenny Biner rolls her eyes. "Nobody tricks you--they provide you with a palatable truth."

"Beast," Carlos screams at her.

"Like Pilnouth you were also compelled to address the needs of those around you." She stands quite still.

"I was drugged and tortured. I did not willingly participate--"

"I was referring to the circumstances of your birth and its place in the environment."

"Why did you take her?" His hands clench at his sides.

"Me? This is all my fault?" She laughs.

He pushes off the wall rushing toward her, scaring her. This time the wall of Lonocs is unyielding.

She begins to cry. "You sanctimonious, self serving...savage. How dare you?" For just a moment her obvious pain touches him. In broken phrases she says: "The Genian...needed to solve the enigma of the Question Plant. It coincided with the acclimation of our art of death. That all this brings Pilnouth relief from the coil of life that owns her--well, so what is wrong with that? You found love. Or would you prefer some form of deceit." She looks at her hand back as if there might be something wrong. She looks up at him. "I think you love your pain too much."

Carlos counts silently to ten to calm himself. "You were the last of your kind, weren't you Pilnouth? You needed me because you were sick of living. You tricked me into bringing you this person who will function as some kind of conduit of death."

"You are right death is an imperative. Whom do you think is speaking to you, Carlos?"

He blinks staring at her. Carlos knows the right answer for this situation, even though it is not what he believes. Carlos remains first and foremost a player. In a soft voice he says: "Jenny."

"I am fine. How could you possibly not understand the final and lasting relief from the burdens of being."

"You killed Pilnouth so you could escape the pains of your limited existence?" He doesn't believe his own words.

Her eyes' flash rage and her forehead wrinkles with anger. "I do not see why you insist on crowning the glory of rebirth with anger." Her head shakes back and forth. "You are worst than a twelve-year-old. Oh my, God. I will see the man inside my child, Roo."

Carlos, too well trained to miss the meaning of the emotion he sees cannot speak.

From beneath her tears she says: "God, you are pig-headed."

Carlos tilts his head then looks around the room counting the floating Lonocs and the dead bodies. "I think you were tired of being a deficient Rostackmidarifian so you took her life. I further think you manipulated me. Lastly you killed my kind so that you might understand the quandary of death which you now face."

Jenny Biner's eyes widen with frustration then a glint crosses them. "You are happy. You misunderstand so you can swallow your favorite swill: pain. What gives you the right to kill and manipulate others?"

"I don't care if her death was a fait accompli." His rage momentarily sated; Carlos finds he has no control over his emotions and he grins also. "Who do you think you are?"

"You have a great deal of nerve asking that question. Your whole life was based on manipulating others and their circumstances so that no one would get close enough to you to see how much you hurt. Now I have pierced your keep. You are so scared of what your parents took from you so you cannot understand giving."

"What right does the Genian have to take life?"

She looks up at him. "None. Genians cannot take life. They are incapable of it. Otherwise, Pilnouth would never have been able to save you after the crash. Don't you get it, it was Pilnouth's inabilities that preserved you? That's why Pilnouth sees our facility with death as an art. The alien could not cause it or for that matter be one with it in any way--before all this." Her hand sweeps the ship. "You detest me. You do not trust me." A look of dismay crosses her face. "Do you really wish I were not here?"

"I do."

She grabs his hand and points to the gas release system. "Than kill me." Jenny Biner wears more tears.

"I will not kill you. I want you to live with your shame."

"Me? Shame? Shamed that I saved your love from extinction and brought you peace. You would be laughable if your blindness wasn't so self-serving."

"I would have gladly died to keep her from being murdered just to meet my needs of loneliness. She has a son, a small one who depends on her."

She looks around stunned at his statement. "I have a son. He is safe. Roo will be taken care of by me and my love." Tears cascade from her eyes.

"He will not be taken care of by you," Carlos says.

Her eyes flash; she advances toward him jamming his gloved hand into her chest. "You have no chance of keeping me from my son, buddy."

"Jenny?"

She steps back. "I am sorry. Carlos, I share some knowledge from the one you call Pilnouth so I know I am the object of your desires and the warmth of your cradle. Lord knows there's no other way of telling you can feel anything." Her lips purse. "It is odd to know I am both not myself and myself." She stops, eyes wide and mouth agape. As if lost in a forest, her eyes scan the room. "Do you have any idea what it is like to be so locked out of life?"

"I do." He grins. "Very cunning. So you know how it feels for me to learn once again I will not have love in my life."

"Imagine, the tin man rejecting me." She looks around.

He stands suddenly steely-eyed. "Maybe you did not know the whole plan. Maybe those who look after you arranged these events so that you might not feel so alone. Maybe you are innocent--"

"How gracious of you." She shakes her head. "I am alone. Or perhaps you are making a joke?"

"I think events occurred and your kind is trying to manipulate them."

"I am human," she screams.

"-- To your interests. Normally I wouldn't insult my hostess but I know you can read my thoughts."

Jenny Biner begins to weep. "I only see you loathe me. Fine." She wipes her eyes. "Now that we have that settled we have much to do. First of all--"

"That's it? End of discussion we have other topics? We were to be lovers. She had a son, and a life. You took it all. You're a cold-blooded creature."

"Just what do you want? First I am a monster then I am supposed to be sensitive to your needs. Get off it, Carlos. Grow up. But first change out of that technological diaper."

"What are you talking about?"

"Lose the space suit, Flash," Jenny says.

Carlos had forgotten he was talking to Jenny Biner from inside of a space suit. "Why should I?"

"You are going back. The suit has to stay here."

He considers the possibilities of it being a trap then begins to release the clasps. Carlos doesn't care if he is to die. He has had enough. As he yanks his helmet off he says: "If you had told me the whole truth about your defensive capabilities I might have been able to stop them. You deceived me."

"Odd that as artisans of death we would be so appalled at lies, but that is something which makes us kin to the Genians. Genians lie; we kill."

Carlos lets his suit drop to the floor. "I want to know how long before the portal explodes or whatever it will do."

"You want a Genian. You've got a Genian, Tarzan. The explosion will be imminent when the pink darts of light expand and turn blue. Be far from the pod when it opens, at least the length of this ship."

"So you know the explosive force. Odd the number of details you seem to know, then do not know."

"So I finally made you happy. Well, I am only human." She grins. "Sit in the seat."

He sits. "I want to take her body back for her son."

"It is in use. I will bring myself back with me."

"You cannot have the boy."

Jenny Biner cannot bear the rush of different emotions that course though her heart and mind. The conflict of caring and repulsion make her ill. "So thats it." She is speaking to herself.

Carlos bangs his hand onto the chair's arm. "I will take care of the boy."

When she smiles, Carlos finds himself lost. "We shall see, Mr. Jordan."

Her head tilts, as she appears to be listening to some far off communication. "But I think our time is finite here." She glares at him. "I am glad you are so concerned about Roo. It will be an interesting battle: for you--between your ignorance and enlightenment."

"You sound like an alien to me," Carlos says.

"Alien: As in a caring female? Think it over, Tarzan."

"Don't call me that."

She grins at him. "But it is so fitting." The room closes in upon him and he feels something like a blow in the spine bending him backwards. Unprepared, he feels his stomach empty itself.

California sunlight streams into the foyer of the Victorian as Carlos opens his eyes. He looks about for the woman. Instead he finds the broken glass from clipper ships littering the floor. Carlos pulls himself to his feet and pushes open the front doors to rush outside.

Matt Thompson, walking up the rickety staircase to check on Carlos and Jenny, reacts instinctively. As Carlos comes rushing out the door at him so his nightstick comes down hard on Carlos' skull making a distinctive pop. Carlos crashes through the rotting porch railing landing face first in the weedy garden.

Chapter Thirty

Holding onto the chrome rail with one hand and clutching her briefcase in the other hand, Susan ascends the metal stairs onto the jet. "...there is concern about his stability. Carlos may have just lost it. We fear he may have hurt her. Carlos claims the woman is missing and he doesn't know her location. We know that to be untrue."

Following her onboard the STOL, "What does that mean: We know it to be untrue?" Simon scans the jet's opulent cabin: a new color scheme. Mahogany walls, deep green carpet, four sets of tan high-backed leather chairs around tables, a stainless steel galley and a head. His two day stand off with Roxanne has left Simon surely and argumentative. "What is untrue?"

Susan does not say the data from the glider overhead had said two people entered the house, then after a brief overload of white noise, it was empty. She also does not say for twenty minutes there was no one inside the house until Carlos reappeared alone. Nor does Susan say that for the first time she finds herself impressed with Quentin's technology and its data gathering capabilities. Instead, Susan says brightly: "Quentin and his surveillance systems--you know." The thud of hollow familiarity embarrasses them both. Simon looks away and settles into the tan leather seat behind a green marble-topped table. Susan watches him knowing Simon will normally call her on evasiveness. He begins unfolding his small brown notebook.

It looks hopeless; so she begins paraphrasing her knowledge. "We had him in sight then we lost track of him. Before we could get a team in there this Sheriff Thompson arrives, clocks Carlos with his nightstick, and arrests him for the woman's murder." Susan wraps the seat belt across her blue pants suit. She clips it in place. "His hands were covered with blood. No one knows yet if it is her blood or not. Carlos said he cut them on the glass door. Problem was, after they searched the house, they couldn't find a trace of her. They're analyzing the blood now." Susan's fingernails rest on the table in front of her. "He also refuses to admit she was in there with him. He claims he went in there alone." She watches Simon adjust his seat belt. She wears a professional gaze.

Susan taps the wood paneled bulkhead behind her. The engines' exhaust create angry eddies of wind. The howl reaches inside the cabin. "In your opinion, Simon, could we have pushed him too far? Could he have killed her?"

The question galls Simon. "It is possible--but it is very unlikely 'We' pushed him too far. Everything about Carlos says he is wholly against violence. Furthermore I cannot imagine any motive that would lead him to hurt her. She was dying--"

That odd tipsy feeling of a vertical takeoff jet takes hold as they begin to ascend. Susan speaks quickly. "Ms. Biner may have rejected him. He may have had to see something he wasn't ready to come to terms with. Or perhaps it has something to do with the Genians. What do you think?"

"Truth Therapy is the only possibility." Forward motion begins and the queasy feeling fades. Immediately Simon gets up from the soft leather seat. "My throat is raspy. Is there bouillon? Want some?" Walking the narrow alley between the seats, Simon realizes he wants time to think before addressing Susan.

"No bouillon for me, Simon. Thank you."

He turns left into the small kitchen area unwraps a cup of water and places it in foot-square microwave. Simon stares at the controls--it has been a long time since he has used a microwave.

Susan pulls her laptop out and opens it. She is perturbed Simon is being evasive. "So then you agree the Genians are involved."

Simon looks around the corner. "Susan, at this point I might agree but I consider anything I tell you to be tantamount to telling Quentin--and not just because surveillance bugs fill this jet. Therefore I am sure you will accept my polite refusal to speculate on anything that might return Carlos to Quentin's care." He smiles and disappears behind the bulkhead. Lost in the roar, emptiness begins to gnaw on these two people.

The SETI STOL races south along the coast toward Marisol. Susan looks out the window at the clouds and shoreline below. The lines of huge cresting waves from a squall seem almost soft and musical from here. She had tried not to let Simon's comment about Quentin get to her but she is not doing so well. Susan shakes her head no. "Simon?"

He looks up from an old magazine. His eyes remain fixed and distant. "Nothing." Frustrated, she gazes at the multicolored waves of carpeting that decorate the wall between the main cabin and the kitchen. Quentin found the carpet at an airport six months ago and recently united the carpet with the small cabin wall because he finds it funny. She stares at the hideous waves of reds and oranges noting Quentin's new hobby seems cruel to her: He picks through the rubble of public buildings to find gauche examples of art.

"Quentin thinks the Genians are involved." Susan's voice has a tightness to it, raising the tone. Simon's gaze hides two days of recrimination from Roxanne. "We are to go out to the house after we pick up Carlos. If there is anything there, Quentin will have Carlos back in Truth Therapy the moment we get back to Mountain View. I would like to stop that from happening. I would like you to help me keep that from happening. Believe me--it is going to be a struggle. But that's life."

Simon looks at the blue cup bearing the acronym SETI in red. "It isn't a struggle for Quentin. It's a game. And dear, Dr. Willoughby, it has become a game for you as well. You have bought into one of the most foolish myths of our society." He picks up the cup and sips the chicken bouillon savoring its sweet taste. Simon loves chicken bouillon and Quentin's jets are the only place he can find it. He hates Quentin all the more for it. "You believe in your superiority. In your manifest destiny to control the lives of others--or worse than that--that you have the right to decide who lives and dies."

"Someone has to."

Simon stands before her: "Nonsense. In the Nineteen nineties we had six billion people. In the fifty years since then we have seen a decrease to less than one and one-half billion people. In three years there will probably be less than one-hundred million people. The death of those four and one-half billion wasn't a decision. Their death was merely a sidelight to the main events of fear and self-congratulation. Quentin's way of doing things is throwback. It had only seemed like it was rational decision making when there were ample resources, ample money, many people, and no serious problems." He sits. "Then along came climate change and everything fell apart. Stupidity, greed, and rule by egomania--it was all unmasked. Susan, you have seen the reports, if even twenty years before the Greenhouse Laws were enacted we took serious

Daniel H. Gottlieb

steps to reduce climate change there would be an additional one and one-half billion people alive today. That's double the current population. But people like Quentin kept those one and one-half billion from surviving because they were so afraid of what was happening. All they did was insulate themselves from events instead of taking on the responsibility of their positions. As a result, billions died so a few could be comfortable. Quentin's way does not work, Susan. It never has. He and the system he represents have a tragic flaw: they don't fight the evils of humanity--they kowtow to them in the name of progress. And so we are reaping the rewards of that system." He shakes his head. "Susan, Carlos has been through enough. Let him go."

Susan bristles at his sanctimony and works to control her temper. "I do not control Quentin--"

He looks away. "Too bad for you," Simon says sharply. He places the cup on the table having no trouble being so blunt with Susan. He tells himself it is nothing personal that her connection with Quentin makes her dangerous. He has trouble admitting his anger at what he sees as Susan's failures. The cabin becomes quiet except for the engines' whine. A calm emotionless exterior quickly masks his pride. "Sorry," he says for Carlos' sake.

Susan mourns for a moment. "You've become a pedantic shell of a man, Simon. You've been jealous of Quentin since the first day you met him." She leans over to the laptop computer. "That woman is someplace. I want to know where. She may save more of us."

"Well I guess we will just have to see what Carlos says." Simon again gazes out the window at the passing clusters of sunlight spotting the ruined kelp farms on the sea below. He looks back at Susan gazing into the screen of her laptop. Susan's finger lazily twirls her hair. The motion marks time like a medieval clock, winding and unwinding. Simon counts ten unwinds. He looks away reminding himself her beauty had hammered a wedge into his life from the first moment he met her.

The light for the intercom glows yellow and low tones sound. She turns and taps the button on the wall behind her. "Yes, Mitchell?"

"We'll be landing in a few minutes. We just received a report from U.N. NorCal. The blood sample was from Carlos Jordan. Mr. Conworth has asked that Carlos Jordan meet with Mr. Conworth upon his return. He suggested that if he is delayed perhaps Mr. Jordan might be checked over at the base hospital."

"Thanks." She turns front again to the angry glare of Simon Weiss. "What can I do for you?"

"You said if he cooperated that you would let him go. Quentin is going to put Carlos back in Truth Therapy."

Frustrated, her eyes dart around the small cabin. She leans forward so there is little space between them. "Stop being an ass." She leans back hopeful Quentin missed that. "There were unforeseen events. If the Genians have some kind of access then we need to know about it."

Simon pauses then speaks slowly. "When...I arrived here this morning I was willing to cut you some slack--"

"Is that right? You hid it pretty well."

Simon narrows his eyes. "So you are just going to turn him over to Quentin again?"

"I am." She stares right back at him.

"Must be nice to have a strap-on-soul."

"I am sure it would be for you with all that sanctimony. It must weigh a ton."

The STOL completes its final approach to the empty envelope of lights that is the county airfield just outside Marisol. Simon watches as the engines of the STOL rotate, slowing the jet. Turning his empty cup of bouillon round and round on the tabletop, his hands seek something constructive to do.

Carlos stares at the gray cracked concrete ceiling above him. The roar of a jet engine from the nearby airport is unmistakable. Carlos ponders who has come to retrieve him. Wondering if the jet is in answer to his arrest or the destruction of SETI and the surrounding community by the city-museum, he laughs at what he sees is the absurdity of existence; he taps the blood-stained wall beside him with his bandaged hands--even though his hands feel as if someone is sticking needles into them. The doctor had said he removed all the glass, but Carlos is sure shards remain. Loyalty to Jenny Biner, he supposes. Through the metal mesh door on the other side of the narrow hallway, clouds of dust swirl through the glassless window. Earlier thoughts of Jenny Biner's reincarnation returns to his consciousness as the engines' whine ceases. He asks himself over and over if it is possible that Jenny is reborn in a trade of death for the disabled Genian seeking relief from eons of life. Carlos, once comfortable at being alone, finds his head throbs again.

Carlos believes, were he to allow himself the hope of love, his being might blow away like paper in the wind. He fears this and so clutches despair ignoring his dread of another loss of love. Carlos tries to reconstruct his meeting with alien, Pilnouth. In his mind he stares at the piece of paper that bears the location and sees nothing but a blank page--along with Jenny Biner's face. He sighs in defeat.

--I need to know the safe location. They took it from me--

The deputy unlocks the cell door and opens it. The young blond boy with the thin pocked face curls his index finger. "Come on, buddy. The Sheriff wants to see you." Without bothering to reattach the foot manacles, the young man conducts Carlos down the dingy hallway into the brightly lit room that is the Marisol Sheriff's office. Three battered desks sit like islands in the center of the huge room. The room smells like a backed-up toilet in a cheap restaurant because it has been newly repainted. Paint is made now from human waste. Directly in front of him, Susan and Simon stand with their backs to him. They face the Sheriff who sees Carlos enter and ignores him. The Sheriff hands Susan the receiver from a battered brown radiotelephone that sits beside the desk.

Susan puts her ear to the phone but keeps away from the mouthpiece that smells like tobacco. "Yes that's right, Governor. No, it wasn't her blood. Yes, I know the Sheriff is concerned. We will do everything we can to help him find her. Good. Well yes and no. I have no say on the reservations. Yes. I know they are extremely difficult to get." She looks at the Sheriff who listens intently. "You will need to talk to Mr. Conworth about a reservation. Yes, I will let him know you were cooperative. Yes, thank you. " She nods, then pulls the phone from her ear and hands it back to the Sheriff.

The Sheriff takes the phone. His face sours immediately. "Yes, sir, I will." He lays the receiver among the clutter of his desk and looks up at Susan Willoughby. "Ms. Willoughby, Governor Enstein asked me to tell you he can arrange for more fuel for your jet--if you need it. What is this reservation thing you two were talking about just now?"

"I am sorry. I cannot discuss that, Sheriff." Her determined gaze brings the question to a close. "But we will help you find Ms. Biner."

"Bring the prisoner over, Deputy."

Rubbing his two bandaged arms against each other to quell the itch, Carlos walks up to them. "Sorry I can't hug you, Simon." Simon examines the dressings and notes the white gauze across the back of Carlos' head. Simon peeks under the gauze.

"A night stick and I collided this morning. Hello, Dr. Willoughby." He looks at his former lover. She sees this and grabs hold of the desk behind herself for support.

"Carlos, what happened?" She asks, having fully expected a chilly reception but not this.

"Can we talk about this someplace secure?" Carlos needs time to think of what he wants to disclose.

Simon carefully removes his hand from the gauze. "You will be all right. But be circumspect in what you say. Quentin wants you back in medical for an exam."

Susan's eyes widen with what she sees as a betrayal of confidence. "We can all talk in the STOL after we go out to the house." She faces the Deputy. "I understand you will be driving us out there?"

"Yes ma'am," says the thin man with blond hair. They exit the squat bunker-shaped building. Simon and Carlos both notice Susan does not bother to acknowledge the Sheriff as they leave. They mistake her hurt feelings for rudeness. At the two dented cars that make up the Sheriff's department transportation pool, Carlos finds himself light-headed and a bit confused at why they were going back to the mansion. To his surprise he finds it easy to embrace his confusion.

The twenty-minute drive is in complete silence. When they reach the house, the entire area is cordoned off by armed U.N. troops. Numerous individuals wearing stained lab coats move about the grounds taking notes-- some carrying samples of materials. When Susan gets out of the car, she meets with a short wiry man and they walk off along the rotted wood fence.

"You know any of these people?" Carlos asks.

"Not a one. What happened in there?" Simon asks.

Carlos leans close. "A quick trip to the Constitution. The woman is still there. Don't ask me how we got there. I don't know. We've got new problems. That city-museum has to be moved..."

Hoards of scientists stream from the doors of the building to congregate on the roadway. Susan has ordered everyone from the house while Carlos is here. Susan returns to the two men. Simon says quickly to Carlos, and loud enough for Susan to hear: "They will not believe you know nothing." Carlos wrinkles his brow then smiles at his friend's feeble attempt to help him.

Susan dismisses the men she was talking to then leads Simon and Carlos up the steps into the front entryway. Carlos looks around at short pieces of wire with small red and blue flags affixed to every nook and cranny. The glass still litters the floor and various instruments snake power cord tails out the doors. He grins thinking the technology will obliterate the functioning of any Genian systems.

They walk into the sitting room where five chairs surround a small table. Susan turns to Simon. "What in the name of Calvin Coolidge is wrong with you, Simon?" She slams her notebook on the table.

Simon darts across the room. First he tears a small camera from the wall disguised as a clock. Then he searches the lamp on the table and yanks out a microphone. "This--and this--and you. What do you mean what is wrong with me? What has happened to you? Nothing means anything to you anymore. Everything is all right as long as it meets your plans. People are tools and your facades govern you." Simon stands amazed at what he has said.

"You are the one who gave Carlos the key words and set up the last therapy pattern so he would tell us what we needed to know."

Simon's eyes widen, stunned by what he has heard and his own stupidity at trusting her. "You want him to stop trusting me, Susan. Is this really who you have become? Carlos, listen to me--" He stares into dull defeated blue eyes. Susan waits to see what will happen.

"You were trying to save my life." Carlos seems both shocked and relieved at the weakness of his friends. "And she's doing the best she knows how, Simon. Would one of you tell me where the safe location is? I can't seem to remember it and I have this gnawing pain in my head."

The absurd question elicits pitying stares. "You are better off not knowing. That knowledge could get you killed," Susan says.

"You stole it from him. Give it back," Simon says quietly.

"I made a decision--like you. I decided life was better than death--for him." She looks at Simon, whom she once adored as a friend; she can feel only contempt for his blindness.

Carlos, who feels as if he has been dragged through mud and laughed at, wanders out of the room; Susan trails him followed by Simon. They accompany Carlos around the lower portion of the house: through the sitting room and its fete of instrumentation and into the kitchen. They wander like tourists until Carlos returns to the bottom of the main staircase to stand on some power cables. Feeling whatever was here is now gone, Carlos tells himself perhaps it came from he and Jenny Biner. His downcast eyes remain dulled with pain. "We humans just keep tearing ourselves apart. It's the environment in here, stupid." He points to his head, then ascends the stairs trying to keep his gaze as neutral as possible. On the landing, he stops and looks down the long dry hallway. "Jenny's boy, Roo, where is he?" He looks back at Susan.

"Baseball camp--Quentin decided it was best to let him remain there. By the way, he confirmed to one of his counselors that you and Ms. Biner were coming out here. What happened here, Carlos?" There is no reaction from Carlos--or the house.

Carlos follows the pattern of feet along the dusty hallway. Suddenly a need to speak overwhelms him. He feels as if he were in Truth Therapy again. "We need to get the city-museum out of the Bay Area right away." Then an odd smile rides his lips.

"Why?" She appears at this moment, to Carlos, like a computer awaiting instruction.

With curiosity in his eyes instead of the pain of unwanted disclosure Carlos continues: "It's going to open with an explosion. The creatures that killed the crew on the Constitution are inside. When it opens they are going to spread all over the planet. It will be slaughter." He looks around marveling at the depth of his compulsion to tell her what he knows. "I guess there is wonder even now."

"You were on the Constitution?" Susan asks with astonishment. She looks around the building as if tracking Carlos' gaze might reveal some everlasting truth. Instead she sees he stares at a small black dot on the wall and knows Quentin has heard all of this quite clearly. There will be no protecting Carlos now. "You arrived there from here didn't you?"

"I think so. So did Ms. Biner." Carlos crosses the hallway to enter a small bedroom. He steps around rotted floorboards to look out the far window at the milling scientists. As he remembers it, the last time he was in this room it was an exact copy of his bedroom in his parents' old house. He feels none of the familiarity--just a need to keep talking. "She is still there. We don't have time to waste."

"Are they all dead on the Constitution?" Simon asks. He has been watching Carlos closely since they came upstairs. He can find no reason for this disclosure other than a fear of being drugged again--or madness. He does not yet understand the profound changes overtaking his friend.

"Creatures called Lonocs killed them. The Genian cannot do harm--but I suspect the Lonocs are very effective watchdogs." Carlos wipes his bandages along the dusty glass. He looks at the dust.

"So they were not so vulnerable after all?" Susan says looking at Simon. "Did you see the crew?"

Carlos looks up at Susan and again finds himself as unattached to her as a piece debris. "They are all dead except maybe for Damube since the shuttle was gone. Jenny Biner could not follow me back. She...died." Susan and Simon trade concerned looks.

"Is that what you meant by she is still there?" She watches Carlos respond with only a smile. "How sure are you the Genian arranged a Lonocian reception committee for the ship?" Susan asks.

"We did it. Not her, and according to...Pilnouth there are thousands of them waiting in the city-museum."

"Inside it?" Simon asks, inching toward Carlos by straddling two rotted floor members. Simon worries he may need to keep Carlos from jumping out the window.

"I doubt they are inside it. My guess is the city-museum is a portal of some sort." Carlos puts his head against the glass: He is a man in a dream.

Susan has a million questions but only cares about Carlos' fragile state. "Carlos, portals are usually two way." She hesitates to push too hard but she thinks the right data will set Carlos free from Quentin. "Once the portal opens, can the Genian or anything else come through this city-museum?"

"I suppose so," Carlos says gazing through the wavy glass of the window.

"Can the Genians help?" Simon asks.

"I don't think so. The Genian seems to have no control over these creatures."

"But they are pets, the Lonocs. What is the difference?" Susan asks.

"There is an ecological system out there that perhaps we do not understand. The Genian may not command the Lonocs, Susan." Simon is now within a foot of Carlos.

"Why the hell aren't we telling someone to get things moving?" Carlos gazes at Simon and notes the decrease in distance between them. "Do you think I am crazy?"

"Only because you have decided I am the enemy," Susan says seeing Simon inching closer to Carlos and understanding his concerns.

"Something has changed Susan." Carlos sees no hurt in her eyes. "You also do not know what the enemy looks like. Believe me Susan--I understand the need for making difficult decisions. I applaud that Quentin is able to make those decisions. Tell me the point of what he does?"

"Carlos, this is not the time--"

He points towards a small black microphone above the doorframe.

She moves towards the door apparently seeing the bug for the first time; she then shakes her head. "Quentin is keeping civilization alive."

Carlos remains beside his friend. "It's a perverse need to convince himself that he actually does have control over life. Look at us. Here we stand trying to figure how some woman and I could have left our 'here' and gone a thousand light years out 'there'. Not for knowledge or advancement--but for control. We are a society tied up in knots by our need to control the delusions we have created rather than accept our place. The Genian called it the Galileo Syndrome. And the proof: In three years virtually all of humanity will be wiped off the planet--just let it be."

"You know the real enemy now, don't you?" Susan says trying a different tack.

Simon watches his friend wipe the window again.

"Us." Carlos looks back at her. "Don't you get it? Don't you see it is our need for arranging our reality to fit our mass psychosis causes our problems? It isn't an attack on us--"

"I am not saying it is. But we do have a right to protect our fellow humans."

"You hypocrite. Explain the right to sell life to fifty million people? Explain to me our right to send a military force into space just so we might live. Explain how the need to save others repairs your conscience when the man you love is forced to endure torture. You don't have the right to love who you wish. You sold it for control." Carlos watches her face turn bright red.

"You..." For a moment she cannot speak. "Tribal recriminations are below you, Carlos."

"You were perfect for me," Carlos says. He takes a bandaged hand and rams it through the glass of the window. Simon yanks Carlos back holding him in his arms to keep him from moving. Carlos immediately stops struggling. He gently pushes Simon's arms away. "You know I think my days as an ambassador are over. I can't seem to excuse my actions, or the actions of others, as easily as I once could." He leaves the room saying: "You two were friends. Susan and I were lovers. We've lost all that and now we three are sinking deeper and deeper into Chaos. You and Roxanne as well, I bet. Too bad, really, we are lost." He walks out the door.

Simon speaks: I'll keep an eye on him."

Susan grabs Simon's shoulder, her rage finally bubbling forth. "Quentin was going to kill him. I saved his life."

Simon looks up at the water-stained ceiling and sighs. "Susan, you need to talk to Quentin and order the city-museum moved out to the desert and away from the city."

"You saw what Carlos is like. A judge would order a psychological evaluation before letting him go to the bathroom. We will need to verify that Carlos is telling the truth."

Simon speaks between clenched teeth. "For some of us truth is not so suspect as it has become for you. Have you gotten so wrapped up in the lives of the mad and powerful that you don't remember some people really do know, rather than merely pretending to sacrifice themselves while they feather their own nest."

"You have no idea what the word sacrifice means. If we display weakness now, there are others who would seek the controls. And believe me they are not as gentle as Quentin--" She stops, seeing Carlos re-enter the room.

"Screw the others," Carlos says, standing at door. "My days as an ambassador are definitely over." He rubs his head with a bandaged hand. "Have you really forgotten who I am? I am not some loony-tune. I am the person who got through to the Genians. I am the individual who talked to the Genians. I am the guy who held out against the Truth Therapy because I wanted to protect what was right. I am the man you once loved because of nobility. Do you really believe I don't know right from wrong? Do you really believe that I can't make my own judgments, that I am mad? Do you really think that Quentin gets to pump out my brain like an old septic tank so he can sift through the sludge of my skull to distill my convoluted, self serving, short sighted thoughts for the purpose of piecing facts together for the good of humanity? Are you insane?"

"I am not," she replies angrily. Susan has had enough of this abuse.

"You say get the city-museum out of the Bay Area. I need to get on the horn and get some approvals."

Simon speaks: "She is lying to distract you."

Susan shakes her head. "Again you do not understand. I am not saying we will not move it. It is just that any movement of the city-museum must be done quietly--"

"Good God, why?" Carlos asks.

"Any rush to remove the city-museum could lead to chaos. If the word gets out that we think there is a danger from the city-museum, Quentin believes the faith people have in the safe location might dissolve. The result will be panic and more death."

Carlos can only laugh. "So then you are willing to kill a few hundred thousand people just so Quentin can keep his hands around the throat of power."

Susan takes a breath and slowly exhales. "That's not right. We are trying to keep what remains of civilization in tact and orchestrate a healthy retreat."

"You don't really believe that crap." Carlos says. "Cut it out."

Without a word Susan walks pass them and out to the car. Carlos looks at Simon and shakes his head. "I shouldn't have been so hard on her." He immediately follows Susan to the car.

Carlos watches as she finishes dialing a number on her mobile telecommunications system. "Quentin, what do you think?" In the pause, her eyes search out Carlos; they fill with tears. "What Quentin? I don't think it's a hoax....Yes. Yes, I know. No. I think we have to act. Of course I can handle it. We already talked about security. The STOL will do perfectly. Carlos and Simon. I will handle it after we land. See, you doubted me. Right. Me too." She places the phone back in her briefcase and pulls out a form with Quentin Conworth's signature already on the bottom. She begins to fill it out approving the movement of the city-museum. Susan looks up as she caps her pen. Simon now stands beside Carlos. "You two self-righteous turnips love truth--well I hope you both choke on this one: My truth is I find that by helping all now, I can begin the wake for our dead friendship."

Simon blanches white; he is sure he knows her plan.

Chapter Thirty-One

During the flight from Marisol to Mountain View, Simon and Carlos speak in low whispers, mostly about Roxanne since the STOL is an ear for Quentin Conworth. Susan bounces between writing notes to herself and speaking to Quentin about moving the city-museum. She will not speak to Simon; with Carlos she asks questions that--for the most part Carlos is unable to answer. His thoughts center on Jenny Biner's boy, Roo: Carlos worries Quentin will want to interrogate the boy. He considers giving himself over to Quentin, but Carlos cannot believe that will forestall the event. Carlos seeks options.

As the jet descends through a sea squall storm, silence closes in as if it were the lid of a coffin. Suddenly, pelting rain slaps the windows and bounces off the white wings of the jet. The three comrades sit in the well-appointed cabin looking out at different directions until the jet banks for final approach; Conworth Field. Susan asks them to tighten their seat belts.

Troops line either side of the runway with no idea why they stand in the pouring rain to greet a U.N. jet. Ahead of the approaching aircraft is a pair of huge berms one hundred feet high flanking a rounded building. Buried by the berms twenty years ago for protection against the elements, the old dirigible hanger suddenly cracks open along the front sending a ghostly yellow light through the downpour. The building's vertical yawn looks like it could be a mouth of fire. The crack opens wider as the two enormous doors invite the jet to be digested by the anachronistically large, oval shaped building. When the plane disappears down a long ramp and the doors close behind the jet, the troops are dismissed; only officers remain on duty in the pouring rain. Laughing at the officers' plight, the enlisted men trundle off to the barracks. Those who remain silently grin as the storm thunders around them. The enlisted personnel have no idea those left on the flight line will attend and protect the safe zone.

Inside the building, light floods the STOL and wet mist thickens the air. The old dirigible hangar generates its own weather. Today it is foggy and cool inside the hangar. Yellow dirigibles the size of small clouds hang tethered halfway up the sidewalls. Rope ladders hang from their sides reaching all the way to the ground like flaccid bolts of lightning. Above the bags, waiting to be tethered, open-air aluminum gondolas hang like a dozen crescent moons suspended from steel cranes.

Although their duty was primarily as radar platforms for storm spotting, each gondola now sports a black, four-foot-long smart bomb nestled along the keel. The weapons were recently installed when the dirigibles gave most of their spy activities over to Quentin's new glider force--housed in an aircraft carrier anchored in San Francisco Bay. And although bombing missions had been rare, the increasing riots have caused more and more gondolas to rain down aging bombs on angry crowds.

Bumping over the gutters that funnel wastewater away for recycling, the jet rolls to a stop. Glancing around, Carlos sees various machines littering the blacktop but he can find no soldiers inside the hangar. All the external doors appear locked. Towards the front of the building a ten-foot-high security wall covered in white and green stripes and topped with looped concertina wire forms a security area. The heavy steel door in the center is open; Carlos stares at flashes of blue light coming from behind the wall as if someone were arc welding. "I see blue light sparking." The Genian city-museum pod waits.

Susan looks out the windows while Simon remains in his seat sipping what he believes is his last cup of bouillon. Susan glances at him then buzzes the pilot. "Mitchell, we will be here only about ten minutes. Would you please open the cargo bay then help Mr. Jordan and Dr. Weiss load our cargo?" Susan packs her laptop in its case and places it on the table top.

Simon leans back in his chair and speaks: "I thought Quentin might be around to greet us. But I guess not. What do you think Carlos, has our former boss headed for the hills?"

"I have a sense we are expendable." Carlos says. In his eyes cognition rises in the form of wide wonderment; he looks at Susan.

Simon immediately understands. "You too." He says to Susan.

"Your sanctimony slip is showing Doctor Fraud."

Carlos ignores the comment hoping Simon will do the same. "Are you sure the city-museum will fit in here?" Carlos asks diplomatically.

She forces her angry gaze from Simon to Carlos. "The pod is twelve feet long and eight feet wide. The cargo space is sixteen by nine." Her voice is all business. Susan watches the cabin door as it unfolds but when it does, she seems caught, unable to fathom what she sees. "Simon, I believe you have company." She points to a set of opening doors on the side of the building.

Simon rises from his seat and looks out the window. He shoots Susan a tight glare. "Nice guy, that Quentin." He bounces down the metal stairs before they lock into position and rushes toward Roxanne who has just entered the building. She crosses the red safety line on the hangar floor passing an empty forklift truck. On either side of her trot the two dogs. Simon and Roxanne hug as her chant of "I'm sorry," melts his rocky heart. The doors lock on their prison.

From inside the STOL, Carlos exits in front of Susan. He sees Roxanne and looks around for a guard, or Quentin. At first he cannot understand why Quentin would allow her in here by herself. When he looks at Susan all he sees is a clenched jaw and neck muscles tight as a steel bulkhead. Quentin banks on her determinations. She speaks: "Thank you." Carlos runs toward the open security gate pondering how both the women he loves could be here to die. He feels his heart sear; it reminds him of the dry white powder of the Genian planet.

Susan speaks quietly into her cell phone aware it will be a game of inches. She also ponders how she might gain time for Simon and Carlos to escape--without the airborne glider system detecting them. To that end she confirms with Quentin her flight plan will take the city-museum out to McClellan air base in central California. In reality she plans to take the city-museum to the southeastern part of the state near Edwards air base. The distance between the two sites means about two hours without detection--so Simon and Carlos can escape. She glances at Roxanne; her presence sentences her to death--or so Quentin might suppose.

Roxanne wears green jeans and a white dress to her knees. A pair of black, ankle high boots with thick green laces droop onto the cracked concrete. Susan finishes on the phone and exits, she approaches slowly. Simon and Roxanne cease talking to look at her. Susan gazes into the pale, distrustful eyes of Simon's lover. Roxanne shakes her hand. "Did Quentin arrange for you to join us?" Susan asks. Simon discounts her look of remorse and his eyes again contain no warmth.

"He sent a car--when I explained the dogs had to have a place to stay."

"Why would you do that?" Simon says picking up the thread.

"Quentin said we might be away for a few days--that I should tell the neighbors to watch the house and any pets. What's wrong here?" She steps back from Susan. "I should have known something was wrong when he jovially said Simon was a key member of the team again. What is going on, Susan?"

"Hey, Simon, how about a hand here?" Carlos yells from the security area. A spark of blue arcs toward the roof of the hangar and bangs against a gondola, just missing its black bomb. The gondola rocks back and forth as if it were the pendulum of a clock.

Susan watches the motion for just a moment then says to her: "Quentin knows that thing in there, the Genian city-museum may explode." Simon runs toward the open security gate.

"I am here to die?" Roxanne asks darkly. Roxanne, aware of the danger, is glad she is here; she does not want to live without love. And right now in this hangar are the two people she loves most in the world: Simon and Carlos. "Mr. Conworth seemed like such a pleasant person," she says facetiously.

"Not really," Susan says, turning away. "Get on-board as soon as possible. There isn't much time." She looks at the open gate. "Where is that damn thing? It should be waiting on a gurney." Heading back toward the jet she yells: "Mitchell, get it going will you."

At the STOL's stairs--the pilot--a tall handsome black man with graying hair approaches from the backside of the jet. "I had a message from the control tower that Fairfield control will be handling us once we leave here. I didn't say anything as you requested but there is no way the places we're going are the same places they think we're going."

She leads him by an idling engine and leans in to speak. "Do you have enough fuel to get us to Edwards?"

"They topped me off before we left Marisol. I thought we were going to McClellan?"

"It is better if you do not know why--but I need to know if you will follow my orders without reservation."

The pilot looks around the jet watching Carlos and Simon going back and forth appropriating tools and taking them to the security fence. "That signature on the order passed by me like a mosquito. Was it real?" He stretches his neck to relieve a cramp along the right side.

"Yes."

"Then obviously the orders you give me come directly from Mr.

Conworth. I'm required to follow all his orders." He tilts his head and removes his yellow-tinted sunglasses to see her eyes.

Susan says: "So now you can say I have told you we are acting under high security orders directly from Quentin Conworth. Any problem with the runway at Edwards?"

"After two years of dust I think it'll be interesting but I suspect it will be usable." He speaks with confidence. "Some of my buddies are still in the area. I was there during the Carson Prison shutdown. I'll radio ahead to get conditions if you want."

"No. If we're found out I can guarantee you strict security measures will be invoked."

"The kind where no one ever hears from you again. I get it." He grins. "You will need a truck to move that thing. I can make that happen."

"How can you get that to happen without alerting the tower?"

He taps the sunglasses on his palm. "You may not know this but sometimes we pilots move things from place to place. We do it by a bit of code when asking for weather information. I can handle it."

She squeezes his arm. "Thanks." She looks back and does not see the gurney with the city museum moving across the floor. "Help those two will you?"

"Ma'am." Susan watches the brave soldier remembering something her mother told her years ago. Sitting at tea one day she had said: "Make sure your friends love you. Then they will never let you down." Susan never forgot that--though today she believes her mother's advise was more of a curse than anything else. She longs for Carlos Jordan but is sure she has lost him. It is only this last problem that Susan Willoughby seeks a solution for in this life.

Behind the green and white striped wall, Simon continues trying to master the controls beside the gurney but nothing happens for him either. Mitchell appears and takes the controls. "You need to remove the interlock." He pulls out the small wire harness attaching the controls to the gurney. When the wires fall away Mitchell begins guiding the gurney with its cargo out of the holding pen. "A security measure." Simon and Carlos look at each then shrug their shoulders--until a spark of pink blinds them.

Small electric motors move the gurney across the floor until it stops beside the tail section of the STOL. Simon reads the plaque of a darker blue metal on the pod. It says: "In friendship." Around the sign, tiny bands of pink light leap out like the corona of a star. Mitchell lowers the gurney so that it can roll under the back end of the STOL. The pilot then centrally places the cylinder so that it can rise into place. "Need me?" Simon asks. Mitchell shakes his head no.

Simon begins to race around the building looking for an open door so that Roxanne might escape. Everything is locked and bared; he rushes back to try and convince her to stay behind but seeing her eyes he lets his shoulders drop. This generation knows the worth of dying well and respects it more than anything else.

The gurney rises up until six sets of arms from the STOL's belly slide under the bed and lift the city-museum atop the gurney into the STOL. A dart of blue light escapes the pod drilling into the ground leaving a bleached gray scar.

"We are running out of time." Following the pilot, Carlos hurries around the side of the jet. At the door, a small plastic bag flies out almost hitting him. "Hey." He steps back then sees a clock, two lamps, a wall sconce and a sprinkler head land on the cracked concrete. Someone is stripping the listening devices from the cabin walls. He assumes it is Simon, but once inside he spies Susan washing her hands and tending to a cut. She knew exactly where every device was located--and leaves just one in place. She immediately calls Quentin. "We've had a problem. Only one bug works. Do you want me to abort?"

"You lie. Get that thing out of there."

Simon nods in her direction and mouths the words: "Stay clear."

Carlos sits down as the pilot signals the tower; the front doors open. Moments later the jet rolls out into the storm. As casually as she can, Susan scans the individuals around the runway. Quentin is not here. She stares up at Quentin's office. His drapes are closed so he is not in there either. Susan's heart seizes like a worn out engine. She wonders just how far away from SETI he is at this moment; not because of her anger--but because she wishes she had another opinion on the possible size of the blast.

A few seconds later, the STOL is airborne, heading west. On the other side of the Santa Cruz Mountains it drops below radar detection and commences a long sweeping turn to the south and east. Susan launches another methodical sweep of the cabin to make sure she has every last surveillance device. The last one, a small red rose is crushed and tossed down the toilet.

Three minutes after the STOL disappears from radar, telecommunication with the cabin is terminated; two squads of U.N. interceptors leave Conworth Field heading west and east at full burn trying to locate the STOL--which they believe is now heading north and east. In fact it is crawling between the mountains heading towards the high desert. The occupants settle in for a game of cat and mouse with the interceptors. With satellites this kind of game would have been impossible; Susan however knows the last Keyhole Satellite burned itself in the atmosphere three years ago.

Bits of Simon and Roxanne's cozy conversation hang like a shroud on Susan Willoughby. She eventually gets up and walks toward the cockpit to speak with the pilot. The dogs lie quietly under a table. Carlos stands toward the back end of the STOL. Behind the bulkhead that separates the main cabin from the cargo area, the pod containing the city-museum is visible through a propped-open cargo door. Darts of pink and blue light spark the interior crackling off the metal bulkheads. The sparks leave whitish scars wherever they light.

--If the pod explodes while we're airborne in this rain that'll be it--

Carlos stares at the city-museum through a small round window, until he is distracted by short bursts of laughter from Roxanne. Turning, he catches Susan's eye as she approaches him; she wears the hollow stare of a bleached heart. A feeling of pity for her overwhelms him. Unable to hide it, he turns away.

"Carlos." She stands proud and defiant. "The STOL is cleared of bugs. I have arranged with the pilot for you three to be evacuated after the city-museum is loaded on a waiting truck. Mitchell has orders to take you wherever you want. I suggest you make it a low profile location." A spark of blue light startles her.

"It's making a mess in there. Any idea on how much more time we have?"

"Susan--this is a top security mission. Unfortunately today's notion of top security means dead participants. It isn't only him. It happens far more than you might imagine."

"Do not patronize me."

Simon speaks for the first time. "How could he believe you would kill us?" Carlos tries to wear that amused distant look he had practiced as a child. Everyone sees right though him. He frowns.

Her head nods back toward Roxanne. "My plan was supposed to give you two the time to escape--not add another notch to his gun."

Carlos taps his fingers on the metal door--frustrated his prized silence is no more. In that moment he cannot believe his focus. He turns and watches the pod eject a pair of blue sparks into the ceiling. Melting black plastic drips onto the floor. "He made sure Roxanne was here and had to be included in the security clean up--as icing on the cake. Quentin overestimates his influence sometimes. Carlos leans back against the bulkhead trying to remember how to be diplomatic. "We'll get out of this somehow."

"Not very likely." Her sad eyes seem to drift about the cabin. "You used to lie better."

"I know--damn Genian." He grins.

She wishes to touch him but she remains posed. "I'm sorry Carlos."

Carlos does not like the tenor of her words. "What are you planning?"

She points to the city-museum. "I am going to plant this puppy and drive that thing off to a blast area. Then I am going to wait for it to open and see what I never saw. You know I really did want to go to Genia."

"I know." For a heart as sequestered as his, her painful disclosure is only a cold breeze. He leans back on his hands. "Why didn't you go--really?"

"I think I was afraid. God, I wanted to go--but my duty to keep that lunatic in check kept me grounded. In more ways then one." Her sigh is practically a moan. "We're over--you and I. I am sad about that."

He crosses his arms in front of his chest. "It's the warm side of life that suffers around people like Quentin. That's their true crime."

"We've done well," she says--watching him breath slowly in and out trying to control his emotions. For just a moment she lets hope in but she abandons it immediately when he seems to gaze right through her.

He forces his gaze to return to her moist eyes. "Soon after the city-museum opens the Lonocs will break through the dome that surrounds it."

Susan shakes her head. "I am not so sure of the result of that. The Genian loves to lie."

"That is suicide."

"You made a career out of it. So why shouldn't I? The Genian was a female wasn't she?" A thud forces both of them to look into the cargo hold.

"That was the STOL engines rotating for the landing," says Simon, more for Roxanne's benefit than anything else. Carlos examines the outside to verify her words. In the still light from the sun low, he sees the engines moving. Below them, the neglected airfield is pitch black. When Carlos looks back to Susan, she is gone. The door to the cockpit closed.

The STOL descends in a maelstrom of dust onto an unused runway. Carlos sighs relief as the front wheel touches down, but gasps as warning lights flash and the cabin suddenly fills with smell of ozone. The STOL tips into a deep crater, hidden by the dust. The pod, still sparkling, wrenches forward through the cabin wall sending Carlos backwards. Sparks radiate out in a circle. Carlos gets up to try to steady the pod while the pilot applies more thrust to the engines. Simon rushes over, bracing it with his back while expecting the pod to break open like an egg. The engines howl as bright pink and blue sparks crackle through the cabin. No one seems to breathe. Sparks shatter three windows bringing forth the engines' roar and clouds of yellow dust.

A second later, the pilot, regains control of the STOL, settling it a few feet away. Carlos expels a lung full of air. With the STOL settled, Carlos punches the "Open Cargo Area" button. The cargo doors begin to arc out from the STOL. More hot, dry desert air pours into the cabin. Carlos stands waiting, sweat pouring from his body. Susan opens the cockpit door and enters the cabin. "Let's get going, team. Once it is out the pilot will take off. You have an hour of fuel."

The two dogs race out the cabin door and across the desert nipping at each other's necks. Reds and pinks bathe the tumbleweed and scrub. Simon and Carlos exit rushing around back to lower the gurney. The wheels do not roll. Simon takes the controls from his friend trying to employ the gurney's wheels. The wheels' engines finally engage, but the pod hits the metal skin of the jet twice. The sparking metal container cuts a deep wound in the STOL's skin. "The wheels don't roll right." Carlos runs back into the cabin to muscle the gurney; and on the third try, the gurney slowly rolls beneath the tail section. Simon looks at the gash wondering how serious it will be for flight. Then realizing he doesn't care scans the field around them.

In the glow of the front wheel light waits a dusty green panel truck. It is boxy, a corrugated metal cab that slopes up to the large corrugated cube that is the cargo area. The wind taps out a dead beat with the sheet metal. Under the glassless door of the cab are the stenciled words: "Rachel Carson Detention Center." Overhead, a tattered United Nations flag flies. Behind, the four wooden towers of the prison creak in the winds. Now, instead of energy violators, the towers stand guard over dried plants, rusting metal, bones, and scraps of wood.

The pilot appears around the front of the plane. Below his neatly trimmed mustache, gleam well-polished white teeth. He points to the small truck. "There are a couple of sleeping bags in the front seat and enough food and water for two days." He glances skyward every few seconds. He has not told them company is coming.

Susan speaks: "Mitchell, as soon as you're back at SETI, find Quentin. Tell him where we are." A blue spark rises skyward from the pod then explodes sending thousands of sparks crackling all around them. Susan leans over and puts her briefcase between her ankles and pulls out a manila envelope; she holds it out for him.

"Get them away once we have it loaded. I'll take the Genian pod to the solar well inside the old prison. Carlos says it needs to be in as warm a place as possible. Alert air traffic control to have the military approach carefully. We're pretty sure the pod is going to erupt with a good sized bang." She hands him the manila envelope. "You'll be fine."

"Aren't you going to just leave it?" Mitchell's eyes briefly scan the horizon.

"No, I need to get it inside something to absorb the shock--and keep it out of sight." A tone sounds from the plane. Susan's head jerks back and forth. "What was that?"

"I left the passive radar on; there's a patrol of jets vectored at us." Hot dry winds blow over them.

"Mitchell, can you get them away?" The pilot scans the clouds coming from the West. "In my sleep. But we have to get moving." He watches the gurney approach the truck for just a moment then reenters the jet to monitor the engines. The dust will ruin them unless he keeps modulating the speed.

Roxanne appears beside Susan watching Carlos cranking the back gate down to form a ramp. "He seems like a decent man, brave also," Roxanne says.

"I do not need your advice, Ms. Gladstone."

"I see. So you're not going to go live with fifty million egomaniacs and bask in the glow of their warmth." Roxanne tilts her head.

"Perhaps."

A moment later, the gurney rumbles up the ramp onto the truck. For a long minute the truck's front end lifts an inch or two from the ground as the gurney climbs the incline. The truck balances, and then resettles when the gurney enters the cargo area in back. The truck bed sets a foot closer to the dusty roadway. "Okay you two--thank you. We have no time for long good byes." A blue spark slices through the ceiling of the truck sending out a shower of red sparks.

Simon climbs into the front of the cab. "You're right. Let's get going." Roxanne calls the dogs and they scamper up the ramp and sit by canvas covered boxes smelling of rotten vegetables. Roxanne and Carlos climb in after them. "I snitched," Carlos says.

Susan stands still a moment then looks up at Mitchell telling him to take off. Carlos congratulates himself on still being able to read her. In the dust of the STOL's escape, Susan climbs in and taps on the glass window at the back of the cab. Simon winks and accelerates the truck down the dusty road.

Pulses of pink light bounce off the corrugated metal walls of the truck and ricochet around the ceiling of the cavernous cargo area. The dogs standing beside the pod appear completely unaware of the pink light show, even when a trio of three beams seem to bounce off a wall and through Condo.

"Where are we going?" Roxanne screams holding her streaming hair with one hand.

"I was going to an old solar complex," Susan screeches back. "The central building is a pumping and purification system for water. There's a nice deep basement lined with hot water from an underground fissure that appeared after a quake. It'll be hot, dry, and the perfect shock absorber for this thing."

"Can't. We need to contain the blast so those Lonocs won't get out," Carlos replies

"What's a Lonoc?" Roxanne screams to Carlos. She chokes on dust swirling through the cabin.

"Creatures that believe humanity seeks relief from its mortal coil--they ingest humans by removing their skeletal structure--" A blue flash lights the entire inside. With a bang, steel rivets pop; an entire metal panel on the side of the truck tears away. Simon slows and looks behind at them. Roxanne waves it is okay and the truck continues bouncing down the road. Carlos, now pelted by dirt and insects, moves closer to Roxanne. The dogs, wide mouthed and tongues flapping, switch to be nearer the wind. Susan hangs onto side handles in silence.

The truck approaches the four guard towers that stand stupidly at the corners of the collapsed prison walls. The walls, made of copper tubing for energy storage, had been ripped apart during riots. Carlos can see entire skeletons intertwined with copper pipe littering the sides of the roadway. The United Networks had regained control of the prison by killing everyone, including hostage guards.

They pass through the perimeter fence. On both sides of the road, the twisted thirty-foot diameter squirrel cages, the ones the prisoners had been forced to run inside to make power, peek up from huge rectangular holes in the ground. None of the cages are affixed to the inverted V-shaped steel girders that had once supported them. The girders remain paired over each hole, giving the impression of a graveyard containing sloppily exhumed graves that seem to go on as far as the eye can see. The human-powered generating systems, and their human recycling bins hidden beneath the cages, sit quietly in the eve. Ahead, the blast holes from the battle with the inmates of the prison and the Walkers, who had tried to free them, still scar the ground. Even after two years, the smell of death remains.

Carlos notices Simon slowing the truck. He looks around the torn away sheet metal to see what is on the road. Bones lie scattered all over the roadway and Simon is picking his way around them. "Go Simon. Go." He looks at Susan and shakes his head. She taps the window and points to her wristwatch. Simon floors the pedal and with a belch of exhaust the motor vehicle accelerates, crunching the bones of the dead.

They drive on toward the center of the prison where the farming area and solar well are located. Carlos remembers Susan in the mansion when he was on the Genian planet. The image of her death grows. He looks around.

Seeing nothing to explain it, Carlos puts his hand on the pod containing the city-museum. It vibrates, warm to the touch. For the first time he wonders about the being he met on the Constitution and her safety.

A small lump on the desert horizon rapidly becomes a cube shaped, green two-story building. In a frenzy they bounce down the roadway toward it. Narrow round lakes appear suddenly, but as they get closer, the illusion of water disappears and the lakes change into empty trenches with small white plastic pipes collapsed inside them. "What are those?" Roxanne asks. She does not want to think about the pink and blue flashes that now continually light the truck or the sound of dead souls' bones being crushed by the vehicle.

"They were the cause of the riots," Carlos screams, over the noise of the bouncing truck. "Those pipes carried electricity. Some of the guards figured a way to draw off energy for their own use. The prisoners figured it out and they rioted--nine-hundred people died. Soon afterwards most of these places were shut down. They said for humanitarian reasons. Truth is there was just no need for extra power after a while--not enough people to use it." He watches Susan for confirmation of his theory. She nods then looks away. They hit a bounce and become airborne a moment landing hard on one wheel. The truck careens to the side, but Simon gets it under control.

Another blue bolt blows a perfect one-meter hole through the remaining sidewall. Brakes squeal. Scraping to a stop they bump into the sand piled along the windward side of the building. Susan screams for Simon to back up through the barn-like doors. "There's a pit located in the center--hurry, Simon." Gusts of wind rattle the green building releasing metal moans as if the building were in pain. The truck pulls in reverse until the rear end faces a wide door. After backing in the building, flames of light from the pod immediately illuminate the once-black space. The engine idles as Carlos jumps from the truck and clobbers the back gate gears with a wrench. The gate arcs to the ground in a splash of dust.

A throbbing begins--then immediately modulates from a rumbling bass note to a middle C. Pink and blue flashes appear on every surface of the cylinder. Susan jumps from the front of the truck, grabs the gurney controls and starts the gurney to roll. Carlos climbs back in and pushes on it. The whine of the gurney's small engine mixes with the throbbing notes of the pod. Small sparks tap against the moaning building. To Carlos it sounds as if he were inside a maraca.

"As soon as it's off, Susan, you jump in the back. Simon, you take off." Carlos pushes with every muscle. The gurney continues down the extended ramp. First the front wheel hits the sandy floor, then the other. Susan sets it on forward so it will roll into the deep pit a few feet in front of it. Then she drops the controls and jumps onto the back of the truck. The pod disappears down the pit into the building. "Go, Simon." The truck begins a painfully slow acceleration away from pod, which now hums a steady C and blasts out eye-blinding bursts of crackling blue light.

"Simon, get going--" The building walls blow out and the ground begins to rumble in harmony with the spears of light leaping three hundred feet into the sky. The wheels of the truck bounce. Carlos lands on the dragging ramp jumping over the ground passing below. Susan quickly grabs the back of his pants, her other hand wrapping around the metal framing.

Another explosion and pieces of metal fly out across the landscape. One piece from the building tears into Susan's shoulder, sending blood in a pink spray. Roxanne dives across the cargo area and grabs her around the waist as Susan tries to keep a hold of Carlos. His body bounces with the ramp as it flops along the rocky roadway leaving a wash of dust. Only Susan's athletic muscles keep him on the truck. Around them bolts of electric pink and blue dance like crazed devils. First the left wheel, then the right wheel seesaws; slapped by giant waves of force.

Susan pulls Carlos into the truck ignoring her shoulder and severely gored arm. She will not let go to tend her wound knowing Carlos will fall from the speeding truck to be torn apart by the ragged rock roadway.

A third blast wave hits the truck sending it off the road heading straight towards a burning guard tower. Simon pulls the wheel violently to the right. The violence of his move sends the truck onto its side and tosses Carlos rolling toward a triangular metal fence post that juts from the ground like the teeth of some buried blade. Susan, with no time to think, jumps, wedging herself between Carlos and the fence, taking the full impact of Carlos against her front and the metal post from behind. Carlos feels the blade slice across her back. Her eyes lose focus and she falls away.

A tire pops. The rim hits the ground and bounces hard. The truck rolls and the earth turns. Roxanne slams against the ceiling and the dogs until the truck just slides sideways along the arid prairie. Screeching in protest heading directly toward a set of steel girders, the truck begins to disintegrate. Roxanne jumps into the dusty prairie screaming, "Sid, Condo, come." They all roll on the dirt.

Roxanne hears the truck impact against the girders and a sudden, short scream pierces the rumbling. The truck spins sideways, then drops into the huge rectangular hole, passing through the squirrel cage and into the human recycling area.

Carlos, stunned, stares at Susan's lifeless body, then slips down into a septic ditch. Roxanne clears the embankment. Frightened dogs roll behind her. A large rusted pipe fitting, three feet across, rushes up at her. At the last second, she pushes off with her feet, side-swiping it with outstretched arms;

breaking the bones. One of the dogs, Condo, crashes head first into the pipe. Its skull explodes. Blood and life drain from it. The other dog comes to rest a few inches from Roxanne.

Carlos, barely conscious, hardly knows where he is or what is happening--except that Susan and Roxanne have saved his life. He feels an intense cold. Then a bright pink flash blinds him; the air around Carlos begins to spark and pop. A weight descends pushing the air from his lungs; it feels like the gooey plastic. Every molecule of space seems filled with a plastic substance. The memory of Roxanne's storm shelter and its candy-covered walls comes to mind. His skin itchy, Carlos works to lift his head a few inches to breathe, but his face remains tight to the gravel. Choking, he struggles to slide down deeper into the air spaces of the trench. Small rocks scratch his face and lips as he strains to move his body lower. All fades into blackness.

Chapter Thirty-Two

Carlos can breathe again but the oppressive high desert heat seems to come from all around him--as if he were lying inside an oven. He rolls deeper into the trench. Platter-sized pieces of metal and various bones surround him. The small "stones" that had scraped his face earlier turn out to be human teeth. Carlos tries to stand. Blistering pain races across his lower back. In a moan he returns to the dirt and bones, struggling to remain conscious. The only sounds: the labored breathing of Roxanne, the panting of a dog, and the throbbing in his head.

"Simon, Roxanne?" The exertion makes him light-headed. "Susan?" No answer. A little more aware, he pulls himself up the wall of the trench and looks around. The tan ground appears as if a sizable grader has come through and scraped off the first two feet of desert. The truck, the towers, his friends, and the prison buildings are gone. Even the rusted I-beams are gone. The only visible landscaping: A thirty foot tall mound extending out in both directions blocking out the far peaks; Carlos twists his body to follow the berm. His head wrenches to his right, pulled by a glittering spark.

Oz stands less than two hundred yards away across an empty powdery field. Behind the blast-damaged outskirts and its plumes of brown smoke, a shimmering city glows and furls with typical Genian lightness. "Roxanne, Simon. Do you see the city?" No response. "Can you speak? If not hit something and make a sound of some sort." Nothing. Still too dizzy to stand, he surveys the rest of the city. Large bell-shaped treetops arise between the prismatic buildings, though no Question plants can be seen. The buildings, either cubed or in the strange horseshoe shapes he had seen before, appear edged in pink neon, extravagant in their undulating dance. Those structures partially destroyed or burning remain fixed, deathlike in their stillness. Carlos stares at frozen figures dressed in different colored smocks hanging from their shoulders to their knees. There is no style or differentiation to the apparently egalitarian costume. He wonders if these are style examples, or base clothing to be added onto like some child's dressing toy. "Hello," Carlos yells.

The Genian figures restart like images on a movie screen, but willowy and ghostlike. Their actions--walking, talking, entering buildings--betray no concern, or even awareness that the perimeter of the city burns and that rubble and smoke surrounds them. One Genian approaches the ragged edge of the city, then dissolves in a brief blue spark. As Carlos watches, other Genian figures turn and walk towards him. In silent puffs they all disappear.

--We destroy even their toys--

Close to where he sits, a repose of coal-black hunks make up the rubble. Their lack of fluidity seems stark in contrast to the serous dance from the rest of the city. An occasional fire-spout seems particularly ominous to Carlos. He identifies some remains of Genian figures lying among the fires--a leg here, a torso there, some burnt, some just decapitated. All of them with a fibrous exterior--like a coconut.

--They must be robots, or mannequins. Oh, oh. Lonocs, hundreds of them, maybe thousands of them coming from the buildings. They're floating around the city--

Looking for the dome Pilnouth had described, Carlos glances above the city. Until he scans the near horizon and recognizes the slight distortion telling him the dome is in place. The black-tubed objects begin their willowy rise.

At the end of the boulevard, the tallest building begins to blink brightly in greenish-blue. Thinking it is some kind of signal, Carlos watches the colors darken then decrease in fervor until the building becomes a deep cobalt blue. It begins to wave violently like a tree in a storm. Then the base on the left side bulges and the entire building begins to waver to the opposite side, as if it were in the process of falling. Carlos wonders incorrectly if the blast has weakened the structure.

A long flat vehicle appears then turns down the wide boulevard racing toward the building. A white ladder-like object covers the entire backbone of the hundred-foot pink vehicle. It pulls directly under the building and stops, as if it wanting to be crushed. Carlos, utterly fascinated, forgets his pains and hoists himself to a sitting position on the edge of the ditch. The ladder section begins to rise in a V from the center of the flat truck bed. He is unaware his pain begins to wane.

Carlos watches the building tilt to more than twenty degrees. Then, midway up, it begins to lean out even further; one leg of the V-shaped support penetrates the building's midsection. The vehicle, looking like a flat pink fire truck begins pumping a green fluid into the structure. Carlos finds the phenomenon an uncomfortable parallel to the tubes the Lonocs use. The outer edge of the building lengthens and accelerates its lean. The other leg of the V pierces the falling edge. Now, both sections begin pumping material into the building.

The building's edge and mid-section continue to lengthen, until it plants itself in the ground forming the horseshoe structure of so many of the other buildings. Material continues to be pumped in until the structure is settled and fully formed a few seconds later. The ladders rise away from the truck, remaining impaled on the now perfectly arched construction. A moment later, the characteristic flag-in-wind motion begins. The vehicle drives off leaving the supports stuck into the edifice. Genian figures appear from behind the remodeled assembly.

The supports fall to the ground as a series of frozen, glittering raindrops. The figures open their mouths to drink in the falling debris. Not even a single piece reaches the ground. A moment later the Genians walk away, some toward Carlos. As before, they disappear where the city's edge meets the desert. Unlike before, about half of the Genians avoid the burning edges of the city and continue their tasks. The Lonocs appear content in their floating dance skyward. His pain almost gone--he even lacks the memory of it.

Something touches his neck. He jumps. It is the dog, Sid, breathing on him. Carlos puts his hand to the dog's flank. "Hello." Carlos looks around for a stick to use as a cane. He spots a narrow board. "Dog, get the stick." Carlos points to an old two-by-four about twenty feet away. Sid looks at him. In that moment the pain returns to Carlos. Humanity has just washed another species from the planet.

"Carlos, say 'Sid, return', and point to what you want." It is Roxanne's voice.

"Roxanne. Are you okay?"

"I don't know." He can hear pain in her voice. "I'm in a ditch and my arms hurt like they're broken."

He points to the two-by-four: "Sid, return."

"Sid, follow," Roxanne calls. The dog walks toward the broken wood.

Carlos scans around wondering why neither of them were covered by the dirt as it was scraped away. He looks at other holes and ditches--none of these are covered either. This denial of Newtonian physics reinforces his notion that humanity has made some grave errors in its mad rush toward progress. Sid brings the stick to him and Carlos uses it to stand. "I can't see you yet."

"I'm down in some stinking pit."

Carlos hobbles over to the nearest chasm, keeping a lookout for Simon or Susan. He is pleased his wounds are not as serious as he once thought. The dog moans, but just briefly. The huge ditch, fifty or so feet across, looks as if it had held one of the generators. Twisted metal is sheared at ground level; the hole drops off steeply. Among metal lies a mangled body lying in a pool of blood. The bloody skull, ripped faceless, appears to have blond hair. Carlos stands still. "Susan," he whispers. "Susan is dead."

"Sid, come," Roxanne says.

Carlos follows the dog towards the berm away from the city. White canines suddenly bared, a fierce growl rumbles from Sid's throat. Carlos stops three feet from a ditch where he assumes Roxanne lies. Cold death flowing from the animal's eyes, the dog lowers its head and waits for attack. Carlos has no doubt the dog will attack if he gets any closer. "Sid--relax, buddy," Carlos says. It growls again in response, tensing for attack

"Sid, calm." The dog turns and trots back beside the ditch. "Sit." The last violation of Cause and Effect goes unnoticed by the two human participants. The dog lies on the dirt in apparent obedience to command--it is, in fact, the confused response of a noble animal to the death of its kind.

Carlos approaches the ditch and scans the debris. Roxanne lies propped against what looks like an old wooden barrel. Her limp body reminds him of the lifeless people he had found on the Constitution. Bloody arms hang along her sides. He looks at her quite unsure if she is alive.

"They're broken." She stares at him. "Carlos?" She watches his eyes ignoring the bloody scrapes on his face. And while she remains badly shaken by what has happened she recognizes little pain rides his being. But before she can speak...

"You're hurt." Like a location shift inside a dream, Carlos' world changes and he has no notion of a disturbance. The last remnants of reserve--and fear--are gone. He begins to work his way down the five-foot dirt wall leaving the two by four behind with his pains. "Have you seen Simon?"

"No," she feels his caring, quite confused at the event.

"Susan is dead."

Roxanne closes her eyes as Carlos slides down the last bit of embankment. She watches him take off his dirty corduroy jacket, making two slings to secure her arms; he ties the slings around her neck and waist. "The bones didn't come through the skin and the bleeding seems not too bad. Can you move?" He leans on her like a child needing a mother's touch. Momentarily full of relief that there is nothing more wrong with Roxanne, he tries to register stoic resignation.

"I feel like a piece of dough sent through a blender," she says looking around. "But I can walk. We need to find Simon." Roxanne watches Carlos stare at her arms.

His eyes fill with tears. "I don't know about Simon. Susan is dead. She gave her life for me." He begins to cry then quickly stiffens--immediately tears rush out again.

"I know." She tries to caress him as he sobs--and for the first time Roxanne understands her role of mother to Carlos Jordan. "Please get me out of here. It stinks like a toilet." Carlos, taken aback by her abrupt comment, helps her. After a few minutes of pulling she sits on the edge. "Oh my goodness. The Genian city?" She stares at the glowing buildings moving back and forth in symphonic harmony.

"Amazing isn't it?" He is overjoyed to see the light in her eyes--he hasn't seen it for fifteen years.

"Where is Condo? Condo." There is no response. Carlos helps her to her feet. Petting Sid's flank with her leg, she looks away from Carlos toward the berm. A gaggle of jets appears in the distance. Two break off and rush across the sky towards the city-museum. They bank sharply up from the city at the last moment, their afterburners lighting as they go ballistic. She cannot see them after they race into the reddish sun. "Sid--Simon. Where's Simon? Seek Simon," Roxanne calls.

The dog barks and begins running in ever widening circles; his snout to the ground. Directly in front of them on the third loop he breaks off in a run towards the berm. Then he stops by what looks like a pool of brown water. She waits to see if he sits. He remains active. "Thank God."

"Maybe the truck is in one of the generator ditches," Carlos says. They help each other to follow the dog.

A second pair of jets approaches the Genian city head-on. Carlos watches them through dome's transparent shimmer. One pilot begins a low-level reconnaissance approach: the jet disintegrates as if it has flown into a brick wall; blue sparks and yellow explosions ride the skin of the dome showing its immense size.

"Holy cow," Roxanne says. The other jet banks away in retreat. Carlos prods her to continue toward the dog and the deep crater behind it. He is first to look down the hole. Inside, a tipped concrete retaining wall appears pushed inward by the blast. Circling the pit they see it hangs ominously over the folded truck. The cab section, battered and sliced in half looks empty; the rear portion, buried beneath the front of the truck, has been doubled over flat. The truck rests on a shelf of wood and metal debris, hanging clustered together over a black abyss. "Sid? Rescue, Sid." The dog begins barking and scrambles down the dirt cliff until it meets the base of the tipped concrete wall. The dog walks back and forth seeking an avenue. Through a large hole in the base of the concrete abutment, Sid is gone.

"The truck is torn up pretty bad," Carlos says beginning to tear up again. Working to stop the emotional flood, he hides his face in embarrassment

"It's okay to cry, Carlos. You won't rust." She does not yet see how the recognition of her role has freed her. Instead she feels a bit betrayed by him. Roxanne stares down into the pit. The dog barks three times. "He has heard a noise. Simon."

"Roxanne, is that you--and the dog--of course."

"Yes, we'll get you out. Are you hurt? Sid, kiss."

"It's a little dark and I am hanging across a set of cables. Nothing feels broken. I cannot see anything around me. If it's daytime, I think I might be blind."

"Hang on. Can Sid get to you?" The dog begins crossing under some metal and wood until he sniffs passed the truck. He takes a few more steps then stops letting out three barks. "He sees you."

"I'll bet he can't get out on these wires. I cannot see him."

"Hold on, we're coming down. Sid, come here, boy." The dog darts out from under a shelf of wood and up the debris far to the right. In a moment the dog is beside her. "Carlos, put him on the leash in my pocket. He'll guide you." Carlos pulls a green webbed leash from her pocket and attaches Sid's red collar to it. He feels his leg and hopes it will hold out. He needn't worry; there is no damage not repaired by the Genian.

"You better not drag me anywhere, buddy. I've heard about you guys," Carlos jokes to calm himself while wiping the tears from his eyes. He slowly follows the dog down into the pit. "Simon, speak to me."

"I have been here before. I know what to do." Simon's voice is steady. "What'd you do, tie Roxanne to a post? How come you're coming down to get me?"

"Simon, her arms are broken." Carlos climbs under the wood and debris. "Can you see me yet?"

"I was so damn worried about my eyesight--"

"She's fine."

"That was some bang. Is everyone okay?"

"Fine." Carlos makes his way along the shattered wood and metal following the dog passed the crushed truck. This pit also smells like excrement. Sid immediately sits, waiting for him a few feet in front just on the edge of the chasm. Carlos lets his eyes adjust to the dim light then sees Simon lying face up across a set of old power lines. If they had been live, he would have been dead. He looks around. "Simon, do you see the catwalk that just passes over you? There is a pile of debris on top of the hand rails."

"I can't see anything," says Simon.

"Ask him if he has checked for broken bones." Roxanne calls.

"They're fine. How long have I been unconscious?"

"It looks like morning out there. We just awoke also." Carlos makes his way back to the truck then finds a passageway down to the catwalk. Small rocks and pieces of steel litter the metal stairs leading downwards. At the first landing he climbs on the catwalk. It wavers, then drops a foot sending dust and bits of rubble falling into the pit below him.

"Are you okay?" Simon asks, guarding his head to keep the falling debris off of him--frightened he cannot see.

"No problem, but that catwalk will only support one of us--or maybe one and a half." Carlos unleashes the dog. "Go to Simon." The dog remains sitting. Carlos grimaces. "Simon, just beside you is a torn girder." Simon gropes with his left hand until he feels the girder. The girder, twisted and rusty, feels clammy in his hands. Sid jumps up running until he is just above Simon's perch. Simon, scared by sounds of scampering feet, shields himself. "That's just the dog. Sit up slowly. That's good, now stick your hand out a bit further and say hello to Sid." The dog licks his hand. "There is a large flat metal grate there. That's the catwalk. Pull yourself up onto the catwalk. Simon, you can crawl onto the metal." Simon hoists himself, supporting some of his weight with his hands. "Crawl along but don't stand. The catwalk is covered with debris supported above by the handrails. It's a tunnel of sorts." The dog remains by Simon's side walking slowly, touching him with its flank.

"I still cannot see you," he says, wary of his blindness and frustrated by new limitations.

"I am not much to look at." Carlos sees him smile in the dim light then touches his friend's shoulder. The friends hug each other.

"Are you all right, Carlos?"

"I'm better now. There's a staircase and then a bunch of debris, and after that a hole in the concrete; put your hand through my arm and we can get out of here." He leads him along with the dog walking in front.

"What about the Lonocs--have they gotten out?" Simon asks.

"The dome held. I don't think any got out. The city-museum is about ten miles wide. Apparently transcendence of time and space aren't the only characteristics of Genian sentience. I guess the law of conservation of mass and energy is also a myth. Huge buildings appear out of nothingness wavering in the wind and glittering like a chest of jewels. We're surrounded by a self-supporting dome five or six hundred feet in height and a few miles across that scraped the top two feet off the entire desert area and it didn't fill in the ditches as it scraped along. And god knows what else."

"I wish I could see it."

"Maybe soon you'll see. Oh, the military is here also. A jet has already flown into the dome and disintegrated. We should have lots of company soon. Susan is dead."

"Oh, hell."

"She deserved better from me." Carlos stifles a moan of pain while rushing to get them both out of the pit. Once into the sunshine, Simon searches for Roxanne.

Carlos turns away from the couple as they seek each other's wounds. "Careful, my arms, Simon," Roxanne says. She steps back to look at the large gash that runs across the front of Simon's head. His eyeballs seem to have been bleeding. "Carlos." Carlos looks at her, then seeing she wants his help he gathers his wits. Tears again flow freely down his cheeks as he peeks at Roxanne. She winks.

A few moments later, following Roxanne's direction, he rips Simon's shirt and wraps it around the doctor's head. "Simon, you'll be blind for a time. I don't know how long," Roxanne says.

"I thought so. Roxanne, is the Genian city surrounding us?"

"Its just in front of us. There's a berm of dirt behind us." She leans her body against his, trying to keep control of herself.

"What does the city look like?"

"The sides of the buildings move like tapestries and they glitter in rainbow colors--although some are translucent. Some are arched over and some are squared. They appear alive. Most have a bright pink border. The building edges appear elastic--except where there is blast damage. At those places it's just a black hem."

"Are there round bubbles with wires or something in between them up there?"

Carlos glances at Roxanne. "Lonocs, Simon. You see them?"

"I think so."

Roxanne's face brightens. "Can you see anything else?"

"Roxanne, I have the notion I am not 'seeing' them at all."

"Maybe they will not be a threat," Roxanne says.

"Maybe." Carlos is not convinced.

A helicopter approaches from the distance but hovers well away from the mound. "I think we are being hailed," Carlos says. A large beacon in front blinks three times.

The trio approaches the mound, Carlos' heart aches with every movement. Sid guides the blind doctor. Roxanne follows, keeping an eye on all of them. The single helicopter is joined by a formation of four tan helicopter gun ships and twenty dark green transport helicopters. The transports land in a swirl of dust behind the mound while the gun ships hover. The red sun behind them clouds for a moment, then disappears in the prop wash. Climbing to the top of the mound in time to see soldiers piling out from the helicopters and fanning out in front, Carlos eyes them suspiciously. Mitchell, the pilot from the STOL appears with them; Carlos waves but the man lifts his arms to show he is in handcuffs. He and a squad of six soldiers approach. The rest take up positions behind them. More helicopters appear, some carrying armored vehicles slung beneath them. Carlos leans over, picks up a pinkish rock and tosses it at the shimmering barrier. The rock hits and falls to the ground without recoiling. The pilot says something to the officer beside him. The man says something in return; Carlos cannot understand the words. The men probe the dome wall with their gun barrels. No sounds. The pilot tries to yell to them again, then drops to one knee and scratches out the word 'Lonoc' in the dirt with a question mark beside it. For a moment Carlos cannot understand what the symbols are supposed to mean together.

"I think he is asking if there are Lonocs in here," Roxanne says.

Shaking his head to indicate the Lonocs are still inside, he fumbles trying to ask if the soldiers can--or cannot--see the creatures. Confusion reigns as a helicopter lands; Quentin Conworth hops out. All activity stops as he approaches. "Jesus, Quentin is here," Carlos says to Simon.

"Only in his mind, Senor," Simon responds.

Quentin speaks to the pilot, then pulls out a yellow sheet of paper and writes something. He holds up the paper. "Where are the Lonocs?" is written on the sheet.

Carlos shakes his head and points skyward.

"Any ideas on getting through?" Quentin writes.

Carlos shakes his head. Instead of sadness from Quentin he sees fury.

"Simon, sign something--there is a dog handler," Roxanne says watching the distrustful eyes of Quentin Conworth.

"I can't see."

"I will handle the reading," Roxanne says.

Simon, knowing Quentin cannot understand sign language, signs: "Quentin is an ass, isn't he?"

The dog handler's eyes widen. He turns and says something to Quentin who grins then says something to the soldier. The soldier begins to sign. "Thank you Doctor Weiss. Is Susan dead?"

"Simon sign 'yes'." Roxanne says. Simon signs the word, yes.

"We have a high power laser on its way over from SETI to cut through the wall--yes, you're right, he is," says the dog handler.

Roxanne translates then Carlos says: "Simon say 'wait'. Tell them 'the Lonocs are visible from our side and can they see them?' Sign 'perhaps the Lonocs will be invisible if you breach the dome and they get out'."

Quentin waits for the translation surveying the wounds of those on the other side of the dome. He then appears to glare at the pilot in unabashed suspicion. "How did you get in?" the dog handler asks translating Quentin's next query.

Roxanne shrugs her shoulders.

Quentin stares at her. "Think about it."

"Screw you," she says. Simon does not translate her words though her meaning is clear.

Quentin signals for the pilot to be brought over to him. Quentin places the pilot against the dome facing Roxanne. Quentin pulls out a pistol and places it to the back of Mitchell's head. The front of the pilot's face explodes as a bullet tears through it. Blood splatters on the dome and the pilot collapses. Suddenly, two black spheres bounce against the barrier, flatten against it and stick. Roxanne stares in shock at the cold-blooded act.

"What happened?" asks Simon.

"Quentin just killed the pilot." Carlos says keeping a fixed gaze on Quentin's eyes. "Simon, ask Quentin if he can see that?" Carlos points to the spot where the Lonoc has adhered itself. Simon conveys the query ending it with the word "murderer".

Quentin shakes his head and speaks; the handler replies: "All we see is the blood of a traitor." Roxanne repeats the comment in a quiet growl. She feels responsible for the man's death.

"Carlos, I see two black orbs and a now shimmering tube." Simon says. He points down at the ground.

Carlos glances down at the dog beside Simon. A black tube has entered the fur between the dog's shoulder blades. At the other end of the tube is Lonoc slung along the dog's side. Roxanne kicks out, still reeling from cold-blooded murder of the pilot. Her foot sends the creature sprawling to the dirt. It melts into the ground.

Quentin's interpreter signs: "What happened?" Roxanne repeats it.

Carlos shakes his head back and forth. "Tell them they cannot see the Lonocs. So opening the dome is too dangerous."

"Carlos, Lonocs, a lot of them, overhead," Simon says.

Carlos looks up at a dark cloud of floating creatures drifting to the edge of the dome; he scans the ground around them. "I don't see any shadows on the ground," Carlos says.

"We are coming in," Quentin says through his interpreter. Roxanne repeats it and Carlos shakes his head back and forth.

Quentin says something else to the man with the dog. Roxanne reads out loud: "Quentin says we're to stay here. And--you are going to love this-- it's an order."

Simon signs back with a raised middle finger. "Let's go." Carlos turns around, ignoring the flurry of hand movements. Sid leads them down the hill.

"He is going to open the dome for the Lonocs," Roxanne says. "He knows that can't be right."

"Suicide." Simon replies. "I think Quentin has finally reached that place we've all gotten to at one time or another. He must believe there is just no point to life any more."

"But that's the way it has always been: He who has the most toys wins. Oh, of course--don't you see it? That's what this is all about. It only makes sense: For someone like Quentin, suicide takes everyone else along."

"Climate change as suicide," Simon muses. "I wonder."

"How are we going stop him?" Roxanne asks.

"I think, I hope there is someone in the city who can help us," Carlos says.

"Who?" Simon asks.

"Pilnouth, or perhaps it is Jenny Biner. I don't really know." They walk down the dirt into the open fields towards the city. Crossing into the edge of the city; Lonocs are everywhere. Carlos has the distinct notion more keep appearing. "Susan conjectured this is a portal of some sort. I think she may be right because the number of Lonocs seem to be increasing."

"So we need to find the hole," Simon says. "On the other hand it seems there are already enough here to kill every human on the planet." In silence they walk toward the newly remodeled horseshoe-shaped building by following the boulevard of twin wide powder steps. Just passing the first set of burned buildings Roxanne gasps. Behind the rubble and previously hidden from view by the buildings blooms a field of bright red Question plants. Behind them, a tall building rises skyward. "Question plants," Simon says distractedly.

"What?" Carlos says.

"I see pink question marks. A plane of them--the rest was easy." He walks a little faster. "If I fall into one, will it disappear?" Simon asks.

"If it's real. You can check it out by touching it first."

Roxanne hurries in front of him and leans over to touch one with her limp hand. A shiver runs up her arm. "Yeow." She stumbles a moment and then leans on Simon. "They are real." Simon puts his hand on a plant, while Roxanne watches him in amazement. Simon's chest muscles tense and his face flushes.

"How did you do that?" Roxanne asks.

"Do what?"

"You knew exactly where to put your hand."

"I don't know. But now I guess I can see two things: Lonocs, and the proximity of Question plants." In shock at what has happened this morning he adds: "Imagine how we would have developed as a species if repetitive exceptions to science were obvious."

"They are, I bet," Roxanne says. "But devils like Quentin are indigenous to our species. I'm sure they would have found some way to nullify even this beauty." She kicks dirt.

"We just call them constants. Can you imagine what it would have been like for the blind on Earth to see objects the sighted could not see?" Simon says, knowing she blames herself for the death of the pilot and trying to engage her.

"The booby hatch?" Roxanne says. "Touch another plant, Simon." Simon turns away, walks directly to the next closest plant and touches it.

"Nice guess," Carlos says.

Roxanne falls back into a plant. She moans. Simon's head darts back and forth, but he does not speak. Carlos remembers that sound of hers also and smiles. "Carlos, did Roxanne just fall back into a Question plant?" Simon asks.

"Could you see it?" Roxanne asks hoping her experiment worked.

"No, but I know that moan." Roxanne sticks out her tongue. He sticks his out as well. "Just a guess. Was I right?" Simon asks. Roxanne smiles for the first time today. "The pain diminishes also."

Simon continues speaking: "No wonder they're an advanced race. With this kind of thing growing in the fields and available all the time I certainly would have pursued their study."

"When does it disappear?" Roxanne asks.

"You need to stand."

She pulls herself to her feet. The plant disappears. There is an amazed silence for more than a minute. "I saw it," Simon says. "I saw it turn red and blue--like the sparks of the pod. God, it passed right by me." Roxanne pushes Simon back into a plant. Simon's body stiffens and then relaxes. A deep sigh releases much of the tension and fear of the last day.

"I am still blind, whatever that means, what a gift." Simon straightens. He turns in the direction of the disappearing plant. "Well now, isn't that something," Simon says. "This time it folded in on itself, or perhaps me, instead of passing by me. You might be interested to know--the final image I saw was a question mark turning black then fading. No wonder our printed text held such fascination for them."

"Why does it change? Where does it go?" Roxanne asks.

"That was the Genian's whole point." Carlos scans around them, wanting to hurry his friends along, while wondering which direction to take.

"You are three for three on Genian life," Roxanne says turning away from Simon and facing the dog. "Sid--sit. Give Simon your paw." Simon brushes the dog's paw over the plant. Neither dog nor plant reacts. "That's funny. Did you see anything, Simon?"

"Not a thing."

Roxanne glances over to Carlos, who now stares beside a partially blasted building at three pink-frocked Genians. One of them has no facial features, like the figure in Carlos' dream. These are just like the other Genian figures Carlos has seen: Round blow-hole mouth, slits for a nose, deep set black eyes, no hair and multi-colored smocks. The Genians walk forward and stand before the humans. "Simon, look to your left about ninety degrees. See anything?"

"Just the plants."

"Then these figures are not alive," Carlos says. "I think you can only see live objects."

"He didn't see us or the others outside the wall," Roxanne says. "That can't be good."

"Makes me wonder which part of life we lack." Carlos reaches out and touches the figures. Their skin has a lifeless chalky texture, like powder.

"I am Carlos Jordan," Carlos says to them.

Two of the Genian figures begin to hum, pop, and trace wide sweeping circles with their arms. The third one, the faceless one, remains still. A moment later the glottal stops fade into a pleasant harmonic tone. Then they all turn and start walking away. Carlos takes a step, the tone becomes more pleasant. He stops, taking a step away and the tone becomes grating. "I guess we follow the dolls," Carlos says.

"Dolls?" asks Roxanne.

"City museum, I doubt it. This is a doll house." Bright flashes light the sky. Carlos and Roxanne look up at the dome's skin. It colors like a July fireworks' exhibition. Tanks and helicopter are firing various ordinance at the dome. "He is truly mad," Roxanne says; she explains what is happening to

Simon.

"We all are," Carlos says quietly.

"He is just running his program," Simon says. There is an unspoken consensus to ignore Quentin and his absurd weapons.

The aliens lead the battered company around the field of Question plants to an enormous blast hole in the side of the large building. Ragged edges glow pink near where the blast marks join the rest of the shimmering building. From the rubble around the building Carlos picks up a chunk of material the size of his hand. It is made of a flexible honeycombed substance. When he scrapes aside the charred exterior, the inside feels like the plastic goop that had oozed over him at the time of the explosion; the surface reveals a series of tiny intersecting arcs that mimic the building's structure. He breaks the piece again and again. The interior structure of the smallest piece mimics the largest structure. "A nonlinear fabric. It figures: chaos rather than science. Scalability rather than absolutes." The inside glows faintly green. "Can you see this?" he asks Simon. The doctor says no. Overhead ordinance glows like a prismatic lightning storm.

"Sid, get back here," Roxanne says. "Oh, now what?"

Carlos turns just in time to see Roxanne break into a run down a narrow tunnel formed by a series of horse shoe-shaped buildings. The Genians emit a cacophony of sound.

Carlos hobbles after her, leading Simon. The dark tunnel is about a hundred feet long. At the end, two structures form a small portico. "Roxanne?" Carlos exits the tunnel and stops. He stands staring, lost--as if he were suddenly alone in some strange place. Frightened, he turns fearing his friend is gone. The doctor stands beside him. "Simon, what does it feel like to you now?"

"A dream," Simon says. "Are those ocean waves I hear?"

"I can't hear them but the Victorian building and the cliffs are in front. I'm looking at sets from my dream--the repair after the crash." Even saying that he cannot comprehend how his dream locale could be standing before him, like a bubble of ancient gas inside a glacier. He looks up at the dome around him. "Simon, once we find Roxanne we are going for a visit inside one of my dreams."

"And aren't you glad you have your shrink with you?"

Roxanne's horrified scream pierces the air.

Chapter Thirty-Three

Running towards Roxanne's echo, Carlos descends six ramps to the bottom of the perfect square. In this courtyard, Question plants--like gaudy red steering wheels--hang vertically along the prismatic, terraced walls. Roxanne sits, hunched over, holding Sid by the collar and staring into a deep ditch. Behind Carlos, Simon gropes his way along the walls wanting to call out for help but stifling his fears; he touches the first plant. Feeling its thrill, he backs off with a loud yelp. Carlos looks up, and sees Simon by the plants. Knowing he is safe, Carlos hurries down the last incline. "Are you hurt?" Lying in a round hole between Question plants is the deflated body of the dog, Condo. "Oh, the dog."

"I, this isn't why I screamed." She takes in a deep breath. "Carlos, I saw you, and Lars, sitting on a couch--it was a dream. Do you remember the demolition party at Lamont?" Roxanne says quietly. Overhead an evil aura rides the dome's exterior from bombs and artillery shells casting an eerie light below.

"Where did you see this dream?" He looks around the courtyard at the plants and building walls around them. Carlos sees nothing out of place, except for a single Lonoc floating skyward.

"It was right where the dog is now. I followed Sid down here and came around the last terraced wall and there you both were--at the age of seventeen--sitting on a couch. You both turned black and began to shrink until you turned into a Lonoc feeding on the dog. I kicked it and there was nothing left just the corpse of the dog." Her words tumble upon each other like the leaves of a flooding creek. "I screamed. They are our dreams aren't they--the Lonocs."

"It wasn't a dream. It really happened."

"I dreamed that scene almost every night of my life Carlos. Simon, where is he?"

"Why? What? Simon, ah up at the top--I know it seems like an emotional warp drive here." Carlos lifts one eyebrow in an attempt to display his objectivity. "Try not to get carried away." He appears preposterous to Roxanne.

She looks back down at the dead animal. "I can't even hug him." Then she stares at Carlos. "I saw my dream turn into a Lonoc. And I know I will never have that dream again."

He nods thoughtfully. "Pilnouth said dogs guard our dreams and here we have a Lonoc feeding on a dog. Roxanne, do you think the Genian is evil?"

"Stop it, Carlos." She touches the dead dog with one of her bandaged arms. "Poor Condo. Where is Simon?"

"And your man is blind. He is on the first incline waiting. Simon?" At that moment, the sun seems to go behind a thick cloud and the glow from bombs and shells exploding against the dome take on a purplish hue. Looking up they see the patch of sky above nearly covered by the Lonocs.

"And now we have shadows. I suppose that means the Lonocs are making progress getting through the dome."

Simon speaks: "I'm here. I can hear you two but I can't find my way to you. The walls are covered with Question plants and by the time I reached you two I think my nerve endings might need a rehab clinic. Carlos--I'd be inclined to believe her notion of the Lonocs--no pun intended. Seems interrelationships in the real universe are nothing like we thought they were. And if these things are indicative of the rest of the universe--the term marketing will have all the negative connotations of a pitchfork."

Carlos cannot control himself anymore. He screams: "Intergalactic Pathogenesis? Life from dreams? First it was the Genian defenselessness. Then it was finding love--but Susan falls in love with Quentin, no she loves me--then Pilnouth kills Jenny Biner so she can bring death to Pilnouth, the one who lacks, and she tells me it never happened. Then this bull about dreams--there is something evil going on here. I am not buying any more

Genian lies. Pilnouth is a monster and she is using us."

"No one is using you, Carlos."

"You always did." He leaves striding up the incline. Roxanne stares at him wondering about this outburst. She stands wearily looking up at the cloud of Lonocs. Part of her understands, and wants, the Genian notion of the blessing of death. Retracing her steps up the terraced incline Roxanne finds Simon standing with his back to a corner hunched in fear. "It's me. Are you all right?" Sid leans against Simon's leg.

"I am all right. But Carlos went passed me like a rocket."

Roxanne brushes against him and he takes her shoulder; he has no trouble finding it. "I think Susan sacrificing herself for him was too much. If I had to guess I'd say the present holds too much hope while the past says hope is a joke--and it as all a cascade of stupidity--especially the future." Simon reaches around to find her face and kiss it.

He points up at the dome. "Let's go find Carlos. Dropping his chrysalis too quickly might be terminal."

His glib statement offends her: "Simon, it might just kill him."

"I know--but I think death is better than life inside a cocoon. Isn't that all we have seen today?"

She looks at Simon measuring his words. "We are manikins to fear." Her heart quakes with the emotional riot inside of her. "That's the house from his dream. It's so still. There he is." Carlos, running by a large boxy building heads across a field of Question plants approaching the Victorian home and cliff behind it. Simon and Roxanne hurry after him.

Carlos stands before them, in his hand he tosses a piece of shattered building up and down in some mad George Raft parody. "We have to find a way to do them in," Carlos says at their approach. "How, I don't know. I tried throwing this stuff at the Lonocs--it just bounces off them like the dome wall. On the other hand I'm really worried about Quentin and his laser-happy friends breaching the dome before we get some answers." He glances over to Roxanne. "There is my dream. It has not disappeared into a big Lonoc."

She has once heard madness before from Carlos and she closes her eyes briefly. "There is probably more than one Lonoc there, Carlos," Roxanne mutters opening her eyes. She wants to touch Carlos to calm him down but his agitation scares her. The last time she saw him like this he killed a boy.

"They might have a functioning laser already. We'll know when that cloud of Lonocs moves. I need to find Pilnouth," Carlos says. "I'm afraid we don't have enough time--We need to do something."

"I would say that visit to your dream locale is a good place to go," Simon says carefully listening to the tremors of confusion in Carlos' voice. Under the cloud of Lonocs they move out toward the house. "Is that dream tableau exact?" Simon asks. A low rumble moves through the ground and as they watch a turret section of the house crumble in a dusty silence.

"No more questions," Carlos says sarcastically. "They destroy the dreams. Which means they bring Lonocs." He grins pedantically at Roxanne. "Which means earthquakes are caused by the death of Lonocs." He cackles like a lunatic. "And you two believe that." Like a maniac he dances a waltz holding a phantom figure. "And I'm now dancing with the ghost of Susan who is keeping an eye on us all." He stops and stares at them. "Which begs the question: What have we gotten wrong about madness? You two are lucky. You have each other." He runs away like a wild teenager--across the city away from his dream. Exiting the district full of large buildings into what looks like a set of empty canals, he winds his way through the canals into a garden of Question plants to disappear behind some bell-shaped trees.

Roxanne stares after him. "We are all so mad. I'm sorry. This place is getting to me, also."

"Actually, I'm just scared silly."

"And I'm so angry I could kill." She looks around the city-museum. "We're not ready for this place."

"There's something about these surroundings that focuses us on ourselves. It's a peculiar taste from an advanced culture. Ah, shit. And Carlos feels it all full on." Simon sighs, again saddened by his loss of sight.

She looks at Simon's bloody bandages and the spectacular explosions on the dome's skin. "Self-involvement has been killing us for generations."

"Perhaps it's self-involvement only because of our primitive state," Simon says. "Let's go to the Victorian. He will be there soon enough." They cross through another garden of bell-shaped trees. "I would have never believed it. I see trees. In the tree tops are tiny pictures--they're too small to make out their content. They move like flags--tiny little flags. Funny, they remind me of grave markers."

Roxanne stares up at the treetops. "All I see are green bell-shaped objects."

"Stupid of me not to figure the trees had some mystical quality. They look like tiny TV sets. Or perhaps viewers into other cultures--or dreams," Simon postulates.

"There he is." The gardens give way to the rocky soil of the desert--then the rocks and grass of Carlos' dreams. In the center, a huge hole splits the roadway. "There must be something in the generator ditch. Sid will lead you over, Simon. I'm going to go talk to Carlos, alone." Letting his arm go she tells Sid to guide the blind doctor then runs across the desert--each step sending jolts of pain up into her shoulders. She comes upon Carlos spitting into the ditch. Tipped up on end is a black hearse. Open coffins hold mute bodies staring from a bed of purple silk tufts.

"Carlos, oh my God, are those your parents?" Roxanne asks, standing stunned beside him. The hearse falls over, tossing the coffins to the ground. The bodies of his parents roll together then shrink. As they watch the bodies form the twin orbs of a Lonoc. It floats skyward towards the dark cloud overhead.

Carlos stares. "So okay, Question plants become symbols in our text. Our dreams die and form Lonocs. The Genians keep the Lonocs as pets so they can have death. Dogs protect our dreams." He looks at her. "I am mad?"

Roxanne reaches out for him. "You are not alone, Carlos--"

He points his index finger at her. "Frankly, my dear, I am sick and tired of your mothering. I'm also sorry to say you may no longer make yourself feel better by measuring my pain against yours."

Roxanne's eyes widen with astonishment. "Carlos--let's try to remain calm. This place causes some kind of weird self-focus."

He barely acknowledges her comment. "Which all begs the question of why Lonocs would attack us--especially if our dreams birth them? What has changed about our dreams? What have we done?" Carlos rolls his eyes in confusion. "The dogs are dead."

"Don't be ridicules. I see Sid with Simon."

"Sure you do. I am going inside the building. My love, Jenny, waits inside." His acerbic words draw pitying looks. "And I'm going to get some answers." He strides away circling the pit walking to the gate.

"Besides, it's my dream. You two stay out."

"And so now we see the truth of this poor man," Roxanne says.

Carlos hurries up the path to the front door but stops to run his fingers over the etched glass heart; it bears no crack through the middle. "Bull." He opens the door and sees Jenny Biner and himself lying on the floor of the Constitution. Jenny looks up at him. She tries to scream but only soundless waves of terror overtake her body. He rushes in to help and immediately collapses as a wave of nausea overtakes him.

Roxanne sees him fall. "He's collapsed." They rush around the ditch and up the walkway to the open front doors. Neither of them notices the dog goes no further than the front gate.

Carlos lies on the floor of a hallway. Beside him is the unconscious form of Jenny Biner. Roxanne rushes over to Carlos to see if he is alive. When she concludes he has simply fainted she looks at the pulse of the woman. She also appears just unconscious. Simon checks them as well then walks down the narrow hallway to the wide staircase and peeks around the corner to see a glowing bipedal form.

"The touch of each species must be gentle because we exist in so many ways. Try to explain that to the others of your kind." "Roxanne, I need your eyes." She rushes into the room and sees Jenny Biner. She scans back to Carlos--he is alone.

Simon says: "Tell me what you see, please."

Working to control her fear she says: "Jenny Biner." A human-like figure with two legs, two arms, a torso, hips, and a blank face."

"I see exactly the same."

The Genian standing against the wall of the empty room reaches out to shake Simon's hand.

Carlos enters the room. "I am looking for Jenny." Silence. Carlos circles the room as if seeking an avenue for attack. "This thing and I met once briefly on Constitution. Carlos looks around the drawing room for familiar symbols. He scans for the body of Galileo but sees neither objects nor people from the dinner party in his dream. He takes it as just another indication of his own vacuity. "Pretty spare in here this time. So are you going to revive conversation in there?" She taps her knuckles on his skull.

She lowers her head sticking her hand out to shake hands with Simon. "Jenny Biner." She stares into his blindness.

Carlos speaks: "And I'm Mickey Mouse. Stow it, bub. We are here to keep the Lonocs from killing off our species. We want you to tell us how to save our kind." Carlos grins. "Or I could just ask a few more questions."

"That's enough, Carlos," Roxanne says. "Shut up and listen."

Jenny Biner tucks her plaid shirt into the blue jeans. The warmth that flows from her eyes melts Carlos' distrust for only a moment. The woman's wide open and friendly look then casts down to the floor. "I am not an enemy," she says looking at him.

"I don't recognize Pilnouth here. Are you Pilnouth?" Simon asks.

Jenny Biner appears to freeze lifelessly. She turns and exits the room heading for the front. They hear the front door close.

Carlos looks around: "No, not this damn time. I call." He rushes out of the room. Exiting the building, he finds Jenny Biner standing at the edge of the generator hole staring down at the empty coffins and the hearse. "Wait, please." Carlos' words end in the echo of cannons.

A shell explodes in the center of a distant arched building causing its instant collapse. Carlos turns to see helicopters swooping low over the city. "Simon, they have breached the dome." Small helicopters streak just above them firing rockets as they circle the city. Carlos looks for the cloud of Lonocs. They have dispersed from the roof of the dome and now float slowly toward the advancing helicopters. When he turns back to Jenny she is continuing to walk, circling the pit. Carlos runs to her and touches her shoulder.

She stops but does not look at him. "Is Roo all right?"

"Nice one." More explosions. "He is fine. Please look at me."

"The Lonocs will feed on this group first," Jenny says. "Then they will continue, just as they did on that space ship. Unless we do something, our kind will perish." The explosions from rockets and helicopters crashing startle him. Another shell explodes in a fireball. White-hot streaks of fire dart all around them. She faces him, tears boiling from her eyes.

"I just want to know who you are," Carlos says. "It looked to me like Jenny Biner had some kind of seizure back there on the Constitution when she saw me. I've seen enough death happen. It looked like Jenny died."

"You wouldn't recognize me if I were the Face on Mars." She turns away.

"Please--I cannot be lied to, or teased anymore, about this. I am going nuts. My life is empty. It's a sham of movement representing life. You cannot be so cruel as to tease me with your presence just for...for what?"

"I am no lie. You are," she says

"You are not Jenny Biner," Carlos says.

"You have no idea who Jenny Biner or, Ambassador Jordan is. And, I find it odd that it doesn't bother you soldiers are mounting an attack, firing weapons and destroying our dreams while you're trying to figure out how to prove I am evil. You're at home with cobwebs in your heart, but not me."

He reaches up and pulls her collar aside. "The cancer-black is gone. "Where has it gone...Jenny?"

"Carlos." Roxanne and Simon stand behind him. Simon stares in the direction of Jenny's voice. "Carlos, she does not glow." He smiles. "Her lack of a life-glow leads me to believe she is definitely human."

"Carlos the frigid, thinks I am a sham because the Genians cured my cancer," Jenny Biner says. She stares at him now wearing a pert smile. "There I knew a little pique would make you feel better. Was I right?" A nearby building explodes as more bombs rain down. Buildings begin to collapse. Fires break out all over the city. Genian figures are ground up by small arms fire even though they offer no resistance.

Roxanne watches Jenny's eyes continually move between the horror in front of them and the wild eyes of Carlos Jordan. Roxanne cannot tell which scene is more horrific for her. A formation of soundless black jets races overhead. Bombs begin to rain on the field all around them, though Roxanne and the others are not being targeted. A set of four helicopters appears through a wall of flame and approaches the area beside the Victorian house for a landing. Roxanne feels no concern and finds she enjoys this lack of fear toward death. "You cannot doubt the need to stop our kind."

An explosion erupts from the approaching formation of tanks. One helicopter falls to the ground in flames. Behind the burning helicopter, the vehicles rumbling along the surface begin to roll into each other; gunfire and screams grow louder and louder. Shells spit from cannon muzzles, beginning to explode randomly all around them. The remaining helicopters land as brave pilots losing consciousness guide their vehicles to the ground. A tank explodes from the inside. Its turret appears to lift from the base, then resettle crookedly, flames forking out in all directions. Another rocket explodes in front of the building, blasting part of the porch to burning splinters. Carlos and Roxanne duck, but Simon does not bother to react.

"You could help me die," Carlos says looking directly at Jenny.

Fear covers her face.

"So you are not Jenny Biner," Carlos says with a hint of self-satisfaction in his voice.

"What?" Her face contorts with anger.

"She does not care for me this much." He puts his thumb and forefinger within an inch of each other--then sports a smug smile. "Well we have that solved."

"Stop it, Carlos" Roxanne screams. "I can't stand this anymore. This house was kept here for you so you could climb out of your misery--something I suspect is no mean task but Christ on a crutch let it go."

"You are not usually a romantic, Roxanne." Carlos turns back to Jenny. "Is this the disaster you were predicting: was it the Lonocs killing us?" Another shell explodes into the roof blasting out the third story windows. Two Genians appear and stand underneath to catch the glass. It rains on them, ripping their bodies to pieces.

"I am beaten." Jenny says, looking over to Simon. "Any suggestions on dealing with this morose man?"

"More questions directed at him, I think," Roxanne says full of anger at Carlos.

"Pilnouth, the Lonocs--I want you to tell me if they are the disaster," Carlos says directly to Jenny Biner.

"I am Jenny Biner."

"You killed Jenny Biner," says Carlos, "in your mad rush to meet my needs."

"Carlos--" Simon says. "Enough. It doesn't matter who you think she is. We have a job to do." He wishes he could ascertain if his redirect worked.

"Let me alone, Simon, damn it." He points at Jenny. "So we must not be allowed to savage the ecology of other planets with our madness. Yet you kill without remorse. You lie because it is fun. You take bodies because it is convenient and your kind sentences billions of people to die then watches the game as a few million fight to keep themselves alive. You'll probably kill them all off anyway as your final sport."

"Carlos stop it." It is Simon's voice.

Jenny cannot bear the molestation and again begins to cry.

"I do not want to stop. She says she is here for me. Let her be here with me for my real pains."

"That's abuse Carlos," Simon says.

"Just another limitation on us poor humans." Carlos faces Jenny. "We want to stop the Lonocs from killing off our kind but we cannot stop that either. I want to know what it is we can do."

Knowing madness, she speaks. "There is nothing we can do for those that wish to destroy themselves." She looks to Roxanne.

Carlos hears the hint of an open door and seizes it. "But you would kill us all. We do not want death's blessing for our kind. We wish to exist--to continue to find our way. I know you can make this happen."

"There is no problem the Genians cannot solve," Simon says carefully. All around them tracked vehicles roll to a stop.

"Though I suspect in a generation or two there will be nothing but madness on this planet," Jenny Biner says, and then looks to Carlos.

"As I see it we are not so far from it," Simon says, looking blindly for Carlos. "Or perhaps it is fitting that the fifty million who will live on will do so in some purgatory where they must cope with the evil inside them."

"I like it," Carlos says. "I think it's just fine."

Roxanne stares at him. "You would have them condemn our kind to unspeakable horrors. I don't know--"

Carlos cuts her off. "I do. We've been grasping at straws for a generation because of our parents' selfishness. Now we have fifty million egomaniacs surviving while the rest of us are washed away in three years." He looks over to Jenny Biner then Roxanne. "We have no choice here, Roxanne. Don't you see, the Lonocs will not kill us? "

"What?" says Roxanne.

"Of course, our continuance has an unimaginable cost," says Simon. "Quentin and his kind are the future."

"We're the Neanderthals. We lose. They win. On the other hand, they deserve what they get," Carlos says, crossing his arms in front of his chest. The last flying helicopter dives into a Genian building. As the engines cease the screaming of dying soldiers continues unabated.

"Too bad your genes will die out also, Tarzan." Jenny Biner surveys the horrors around them. She stares shocked at what she sees and the indifference of the people she speaks with. "Carlos, you probably represent the optimal set of characteristics for the slave class in this new world order. Empty, longing, unable to love and willing to take any crap just to get a chance to display your worth--you're perfect." Jenny Biner finally sees a crack in the madness of Carlos Jordan. "Ah, a little cynicism also means home. So that's the path to your feeble heart. It figures." Jenny Biner sighs and looks skyward. "The Lonocs will leave now." The humans look around waiting for some momentous event, but nothing appears to happen. "The Lonocs have now ripped a hole in our future. To our senses, all will continue as before. Except for minor changes that only very few may notice--in the beginning. Know the many theories and rules you have erected will slowly dissolve. In time your kind will see itself: without the commercials, without the madness." A hollow, ugly laugh bellows through her body. "It is not your madness, Carlos. In too many ways you embody the madness of your kind."

Simon speaks. "So I see. It is true; there are no questions that do not contain answers, though sometimes the answers are quite distasteful. At least your joke of retribution will be worthwhile." Simon sees Jenny Biner for a brief moment as a slight glow: "Partial sentience in utter ignorance--our madness reflected back at us in a way it never has. I am glad I will not need to witness it." They look at the burning house. "It will be interesting to see, if I may quote Milton, how we will rule in hell."

Carlos stares at the burning building. "My dream burns, Roxanne. It didn't turn into Lonocs." Carlos points to Jenny with a smug smile. "In any case we are saved with less than a snap of the fingers. Just like the Phoenix here, Ms. Biner."

"Your ignorance embarrasses more than you. Jenny's eyes flash with the anger of exploding suns. Who I am doesn't really matter to you, Carlos. It is just knowing me that you detest." She looks over to Simon and Roxanne. "When we leave here please help me find my son."

"Not likely," Carlos says.

"Of course we will," Roxanne says.

"The curse is gone, Carlos. It is now owned by our progeny," Simon says feeling damned.

Carlos looks for any sign of the Lonocs. Except for the fires and the rapidly deteriorating buildings of the city-museum around them, they are alone. Vehicles appear in the distance reforming into columns. Six more helicopters approach through the smoke and begin to descend.

Carlos stares at Jenny, unsure if he should guard her or tell the advancing troops that he thinks her to be a Genian. He immediately realizes that if he tells Quentin what he thinks she will never get out of Quentin's clutches. Carlos cannot allow that--though he does not know why.

Wind-whipped dust blows up around them as a set of six helicopters encircle them and lands. Quentin Conworth, dressed in fatigues, jumps out surrounded by soldiers who immediately level their weapons at the party of people. In a moment, all the helicopters are empty and tens of soldiers advance toward Carlos' party. Anger owns the eyes of these men; in burning transports, behind them, lie the deflated bodies of comrades. Quentin walks rapidly, leading a pair of heavily armed men. The dog raises its top lip, exposing canines.

"Rest," says Roxanne.

Quentin stops a few feet away from them and surveys the wounded party. "Medic, take care of these people." He walks passed Carlos onto the steps of the burning Victorian mansion as if he owned the building. Flames, darting from the shattered windows of the first floor, thicken the air. "Looks just like the other building. Very impressive." Quentin turns, hands folded behind his back. "Looks like we won. I knew we didn't need to see them--putting a bullet or shrapnel into every square inch of space is just as good." He stares down at Carlos, who is watching a medical crew move Jenny Biner's slowly breathing form onto a stretcher. Quentin waits for Carlos to speak and studies the pyramidal piles of dust that once had been the Genian buildings. When Carlos faces Quentin, no words are forthcoming: "Mr. Jordan, report please."

Before Carlos can speak, he is quickly lowered onto a wheelchair by a medic. Quentin tells the medic to leave. Carlos speaks: "The Genians are gone. The city is gone. The Lonocs are gone. The 'Fifty' are safe. The Genians won't be back. You win. I quit."

Quentin steps off the porch, the heat from the fire much warmer than he had anticipated. "That's the thanks I get for saving your life." The guards that flank Quentin stare at him as if he is their god, their safety assured as long as Quentin lives.

"Of course saving his own arse had nothing to do with it." Simon says.

"What about her? We found no members of the Constitution's crew. Are there any others?" Quentin asks again approaching Carlos. The Victorian collapses in on itself, startling Quentin. He jumps briefly, then smiles. "There is nothing left for you to hide, Ambassador. We cannot get to the Genians anymore and we are in for a hell of a beating. I, and the rest of the people on the planet, need all the information you can supply." He turns Carlos' chair around and begins to push him toward a waiting helicopter. "If you have any doubts about how serious I am, I can tell you this--" He stops pushing the wheelchair and drops to one knee. "I am going to save as much of this planet and its inhabitants as I can. And if I do not get all the information I think you have, I will send you back into drug therapy and kill Ms. Biner and her son while you watch so I can be sure I break you down into sand. I hope I am being clear."

Carlos tries to stand but is immediately pushed back into his seat, by a guard. The movement sends a searing pain racing up his torn ligaments. "Quentin, as someone once said to me, 'it's a fait accompli'. I will be glad to tell you anything you want to know."

"Where did the woman go?"

Carlos pauses until he hears the last part of the Victorian collapse and burn. He watches to see if Lonocs form-but nothing happens. "The woman was hiding in the basement. She hid there because I scared her and she was worried about her son. You know how they are about people with privileges." Quentin points to one of the guards to push Carlos up a ramp into a waiting helicopter.

Quentin approaches Roxanne and Simon. "So do you two have problems responding to questions?"

Simon answers keeping his smile as neutral as possible. "All you need to do is ask me questions--for as long as you like. I have no problem with answers. I have no problem with death. I have no problem with you and your fifty million cohorts escaping. I just want to be done with you. If that includes death, then fine."

Roxanne stares at Quentin. "You really do serve a purpose, don't you?"

"And it's far more complex than you could ever imagine, Ms. Gladstone." Quentin ushers them to the ramp of a waiting medical helicopter. Under the slowly spinning blades he looks again at Roxanne. "Did Susan die well?"

"Like a hero, " Roxanne says.

"I knew she would do me proud," Quentin says, grinning at Roxanne's angry stare. "Take off, pilot."

Chapter Thirty-Four

Dressed in green fatigues, Quentin Conworth locks the door to his office for the last time. Slinging the saddle over his shoulder he walks down the hall keeping a straight back straight and shoulder's square--even though exhaustion owns every part of his body. His graying ponytail, which now reaches a still-trim waist, has two gold clips at the bottom made from Susan's Olympic medals. They click against saddle-leather like the tick of a clock.

The loss of her presence lessened as the plans for evacuation matured. This last year he found her memory a pleasant recollection of a simpler time. Stocking the island, arranging liaisons, fighting off the hopeless, saving humanity and solidifying his military control have all been wearing. Common knowledge says he is the only one alive with any real knowledge of the Genian disaster. Descending the metal stairs to the basement door, he sees his four faithful guards dressed in black jump suits with scarred body armor covering their chests. He looks to his keep for one last time. In fact there is no one, besides Quentin, who knows the real timing of the disasters; his guards have seen to that. For the rest of them, it is all just guessing when the disaster will strike this year. It makes them weak and him strong. Quentin laughs quietly to himself. His guards ignore this bit of madness.

--If they only knew about my television debut--

"Good morning, Sir."

He has already made sure he will be on the television the final day so that everyone remembers him when he comes back to reclaim and revitalize the planet--if there is anyone left.

The soldiers lead him into a darkened hallway, which will take them to the underground parking lot. The two individuals in the rear, who know they are the latest in a string of rear bodyguards, scan every corridor and listen to each sound as they walk. All four men know Quentin is their savior. He is their key to the safe zone. Ten have died.

Through the dusty hallway the entourage moves passed burned offices still thick with the smells of decaying bodies. Passing through the original control room where Susan Willoughby's team had made first contact with the aliens, Quentin glances around as if her ghost might be waiting. Only the black depths of an empty maw stare back. Mold and rat droppings fill the air. Sheets of computer paper bearing large faded question marks hang scorched and torn on the walls.

Out along a newer concrete lined-tunnel, they encounter a second set of guardians. These soldiers take up positions alongside the original guards. Two nights ago, during a rehearsal for this exodus, an ambush waited in this very tunnel; Quentin was forced to kill a young woman by bashing in her skull with chunk of concrete. He still feels lucky she was only armed with a crude spear. After checking the pistol strapped to his chest, he pops a small white pill in his mouth and chugs it back. Quentin then speaks quietly into a microphone resting on his shoulder opposite the saddle. "This is Knight--we are approaching the Snail. Two hours to rendezvous. Condition report?"

The captain of the aircraft carrier Lincoln responds: "All systems are nominal." Translation: The beach skirmishes and assaults on the fleet by rag-tag boats full of starving wannabe-emigrants continues without any noticeable effect.

"Make sure the hovercraft are on time. I'm looking forward to a nice sea voyage. Knight out." Quentin would rather have flown out, but he knows better than to fly these days. Three thousand spots have opened up in the safe zone in just the last six weeks from shoulder-launched missiles. In fact the missiles have destroyed most of what remains of the world's commercial and military planes--excluding the squadron of planes and helicopters Quentin has on his aircraft carrier. The carrier is his ace-in-the-hole at the safe zone. And while he knows of at least a dozen plots to unseat him once he gets there--they will be pointless because of the carrier's might.

Moored just beyond Land's End, the carrier Lincoln and its support vessels wait with enough aircraft, soldiers, missiles, munitions, and detection gear to deal with any Earthborne attack. Everyone that matters on the ships has been handpicked by Quentin. Like well-trained guard dogs, the ship's company anticipates their master's arrival. Another flotilla, this one of transports, awaits near the Hawaiian Islands. After linking up, the convoy of two hundred vessels will then transport the last of the Fifty and the majority of Quentin's munitions to safety. Using the carrier, and its convoy, Quentin plans to quickly eliminate rivals who have managed to gain a toehold in the safe zone--before he sets about building a better humanity.

--It will be the beginning of a new world once I am on the carrier. I will be back in full command and no longer exposed to every yahoo with a missile--

Fumes invade his nostrils--churning motors and diesel engines take over the sounds of breathing. The engine's of the convoy vehicles growl to life as if it were some wild beast straining at its chain. Quentin feels a rush of prideas he strides along the hallway. Smelling the thick smoke from the torches mixing with diesel exhaust, he believes the salvation of humanity is at hand. Up ahead, a large steel door opens and a guard rushes down the hallway. The guards all level their weapons--until the soldier quickly puts his hands up and identifies himself as a courier. "Let him by."

"Sir, all perimeter defenses have broken down." Sweat pours over the narrow face of the young man who wears the rank of captain. "We've let them inside then lit up the buildings as you commanded. We have also laid down suppression fire but they keep coming. The base choppers are in reserve."

"I see, Captain." While Quentin had expected the news about his convoy's purpose not to remain hidden, he has been surprised by the increasingly wild attacks against the base over the last week. He wonders if his decision to let Jordan and Weiss free last year was smart--believing perhaps they are behind the well-planned attacks these last few days--even though he knows neither Carlos nor Simon have any memory of precisely when the disaster predicted by the Genians is to occur, where the safe zone is located, or anything about base defenses. Had Susan not died Quentin would have kept closer tabs on them over the last year, but Quentin reminds himself the announcement of their place in the fifty million should have been enough to have Simon and Carlos killed. Quentin considers their lives are a memorial to Susan. A madness has taken hold of Quentin--it will never leave him.

He wonders one last time who replaced Carlos and Simon in the Fifty. "Captain, have the flame throwers and helicopters brought up to the north gate. I want a clear roadway north." The young man salutes then hurries away.

Exiting into the garage through the heavy steel door, Quentin can hear the increasing gunfire and explosions; he surveys the convoy looking for fear.

Eighteen battle-scarred tanks and twenty armored personnel carriers wait with engines running and headlights ablaze. Six two-ton trucks, sit among the shadows of the back wall. Men and women mill around the headlights huddled in tight circles. Quentin waves to troops and stops to talk with a group of soldiers.

"What about the passenger vehicles above ground? Will they get through?" Asks a female soldier with hollow angry eyes. "I've got relatives there."

Quentin reaches out and squeezes the soldier's shoulder. "I am committed to saving the citizens who won places in the nationwide lottery. They will make it. Do not worry, Soldier." The men and women stare at him unsure if they should laugh or jeer. He strides across the garage to his tank. He calls one of his guards over and tells him to kill the female soldier as soon as possible.

Looking around at the remains of his force he prays he has not miscalculated his influence and left himself with too few loyal troops here on the mainland. Quentin knows weakness invites more would-be monarchs. He waves to the troops as he climbs onto his tank and lowers the saddle carefully down in front of him through the turret into the crew compartment. He clenches his fists together over his head. "Let's go home."

The crowd cheers. He takes his seat in the center of the tank and waits for two guards to strap themselves in beside him. The tank is a monster of a thing run by a crew of four, not including Quentin and his guards. The engines' churning sends low vibrations throughout his body. "Send out the choppers."

The crew begins sealing the vehicle against chemical and biological weapons. Blowers begin recycling the oxygen. Bright green instrumentation comes to life and the various monitors around the tank's interior display information from various sources--including the squadron of helicopters now beginning an attack run on the forces overrunning his base. The nerve gas and the deadly accuracy of gattling guns are more than a match for the attacking forces in their steel-covered autos and trucks. As Quentin watches the tank's monitors, the vehicles and their occupants are shredded. Other attackers on foot fall to the ground writhing in pain. Over on the north wall, flamethrowers unleash fiery tongues at intruders sending them scurrying in every direction.

Quentin shakes his head at the carnage and looks around at the handpicked crew. The world has fallen apart and these individuals know it. The specially picked men, and their weapons' ability to deal death out faster than anything else, is all he can count on right now. Knowing this is his weakest moment, Quentin also realizes his real protection is the perception that he is in charge. He has no doubt the perception has saved his life many more times than he knows.

"Sir, the suppression fire has ceased."

"Get her going then," Quentin responds. The tank lunges forward, other vehicles form up around it. The convoy, like some nocturnal lizard, crawls out of the underground garage into the pre-dawn. Flames mark every direction of the compass. The smoke is so thick, Quentin orders a pair of small drones with infrared cameras to be launched. They show almost no movement around the convoy and he gives the order for the vehicles to begin their run toward the coast. Clearing the steel gates marking the perimeter of the field, the tank slowly begins picking up speed. A series of small explosions resounds through the armor. Quentin checks the camera drone that hovers silently above the rear of the convoy. As he had guessed, the guards left behind at the main gate have attacked the last five vehicles. The first vehicle of the five is destroyed and the remaining four, having stopped behind it, are quickly overrun by twenty-five heavily armed guards who slaughter the citizens. In a matter of moments, the carnage is complete. The fifteen families who had won spaces in the national lottery for the safe zone are left to die. Quentin watches the soldiers drag the limp bodies out and leave them beside the road. Then starting the vehicles again the pirates join up to the rear of the convoy.

"Initiate auto-destruct on vehicles forty-seven through fifty," Quentin commands emotionlessly. Immediately the four automobiles that had rejoined the convoy stall. The convoy proceeds an additional three hundred yards then the cars explode in fireballs. In a smoky dawn white phosphorous mayhem hides his old headquarters. In three hours it will also explode killing everyone within a two-mile radius of the SETI office. Quentin wants no one to remember SETI fondly.

The vehicles rumble along the freshly regrated dirt road heading north up the remains of Highway 101. Quentin continues checking the video input from four dirigibles that have been hovering over the rubble that once were part of the Silicon Valley industrial complex. From the rooftops small arms fire peppers the convoy. Occasionally the ping of low caliber bullets ricochet off the skin of his tank. "Ignore it." Tank commanders are under orders not to return fire unless commanded. Quentin has reduced the munitions in each tank to a minimum since he has no plans to allow a coup during this last phase of the trip. His tank is fully loaded. Peeping through the periscope, he sees people moving about in the early morning mist who couldn't care less about the convoy: Kids and older women preparing the for that day's cooking and cleaning disregard the weapons' fire as if it were the buzz of flies. "It is a great strength of these people to ignore so much vicissitude. I wish I could save them all." He pushes back from the viewer; his lips pursed and defiance in his eyes. Quentin wipes his brow. The soldiers in the tank ignore the parade of concern. All they care about is getting safely on the ships.

Approaching a perilous concrete bridge that leads to a narrow passage between old buildings, he slows the convoy and sends out scout vehicles to examine the bridge and the remains of an office complex. An ambush by anyone with a chance of hurting them will take place here. The rest of the trip is over wide unused roadways and the remains of an eight-lane freeway.

Watching the scout vehicles he notes the hollow between the buildings is still burning from yesterday's security check and fire-fight. Littered with bodies, most of them charred black, the battlefield also camouflages a few Sappers lying in wait. It takes only a minute for the machine guns to rake the bodies and the enemy to be cut into bloody hunks of meat. Suddenly, two modified trucks crash through fake walls from inside of each building. Each truck carries a swarm of armed citizens. Fearing they might have missiles, Quentin orders the lead tanks to engage them with their main guns. The two lead tanks advance quickly blowing the vehicles and the occupants apart.

"All clear."

Quentin hurries the convoy over the bridge and around the burning truck parts now littering the hollow. Through the periscope he notices a female lying on the side of the road; her eyes open. To Quentin she looks exactly like the woman he killed in the tunnel. "They all look alike now," he says, checking the chronometer on his wrist. He has more important things to think about than another dying anarchist; he directs the convoy west at an increased speed. Even as heavily armored as the convoy is, being caught on the embarkation beach might be dangerous.

An uneventful hour later the convoy rumbles to a halt along the great flat strand that borders the darkened remains of San Francisco. A few miles out, the blackness heaves and the huge flat hulk of the aircraft carrier lights up--like a jewel on the ocean. Quentin smiles at the carrier and its support ships. "Where are those damn LCACs? Anyone see the landing craft? Damnit, set a flare--contact the carrier." A moment later a set of three flares is airborne.

From the mist, five monstrous hovercrafts approach the beach. The distant engine roars the sound of music and the safety of home. The personnel carriers and tanks form a horseshoe around Quentin's tank. Soldiers begin joking and singing--as they pick off any curious denizens of the morning. Soon they are placing bets on where the bullets will land. Quentin, while he does not like these activities, knows the game will amuse the troops until the hovercraft arrive on shore and he has also learned not to interfere with the soldiers' fun after a difficult mission. Instead, Quentin turns his attention to coordinating traffic onto the approaching landing craft.

The loading of the tanks and other vehicles goes smoothly. Everyone involved in the effort works rapidly and efficiently. One hour after the convoy arrives at the beach only tank tracks and footprints remain in the sand. The last hovercraft spins and withdraws out to sea. Quentin, who is on the first hovercraft, waits a few hundred yards beyond the breakwater watching the final craft spin away from the shore; he considers it appropriate to be the last man on the carrier. Nonetheless, he will disembark under heavy guard.

Riding the waves to the ship he tells himself the trip to New Zealand will be slow because of the tankers and cargo ships. Other than a potential skirmish at sea by some competitor to owning the planet, he expects the trip to be uneventful to the point of boredom for the lucky passengers. Quentin plans to be busy every moment laying out the new world government and working with the three supercomputers he has had installed on the ships. The machines are currently busy going through every possible scenario in dealing with the Genians when they come to take over the planet--Quentin has convinced himself of the inevitability of this event. His fall back position--other than beating them in a battle which he doubts he has the slightest chance of winning--is to command Genian respect. The machines are also working to define that term.

It is a few hours later and a hundred miles down the coast; the cold ocean breeze blows in from a foggy sea. Carlos, dressed in white shorts and sneakers, hugs the tie-dyed canvas tunic closer to his body. Looking out to sea, he stares at the parade of large ships far in the distance. At his feet, the waves rolling up the sand hold still at their peak then recede in a gentle slide. Gulls call and the crash of breakers from nearby rocks sound flat and heartsore. Sure the exhibit of lights is Quentin's task force, he shivers feeling a cold he has not felt in over a year. "I'm sure Quentin believes us dead. He couldn't possibly conceive of us not showing up for roll call among the Fifty."

Beside him, digging into the sand, Jenny Biner pulls out a large manila clam with her spade and washes it off in the bucket. Then dropping it into a second bucket beside her left leg, she stands up brushing the sand from the front of her long woolen skirt. Rolling down the sleeves of her old blue sweater, patched with a rainbow of yarn she responds: "That's quite a set of boats out there. Your former host, Quentin I suppose."

"No one else would consider so gaudy a display," Carlos says, looking back at her for only a moment before he examines the bucket of clams.

"That's enough--I think," Jenny says.

He rubs the back of his neck. "I thought a lot about what this might be like when I was in that holding cell." He glances at Jenny watching her watch him with obvious surprise. This is the first time Carlos has spoken about the time he spent in Quentin's prison. "I kept drifting between my suspicions about you and my desire to be with you--so that we could talk. I think I never really expected to be released. It allowed me a fantasy of our life together: one I didn't have to be afraid of. Then I was released and found out everyone knew I had a place among the Fifty. I don't know how I stayed alive. Your brilliance saved me. I don't know why it has taken me so long to say anything. But I'd like to apologize."

She wraps her arms about her self to keep warm. "When Simon and Roxanne told me you were coming today I was surprised you wanted to be with us. I didn't think you would ever want to be near me."

"I am only here to keep Roo safe."

"I misunderstood you--thinking you were here only trying to protect him from me."

His puzzlement obvious, Carlos leans hard on his wood cane. "You misunderstand. I know you are just trying to help Roo. I want to thank you."

She pulls the bucket to the side and fills it with seawater. "I am glad you waited to apologize. I don't think I would have believed you--and I don't think I could have been very nice to you." She watches a harbor seal pop from the water to stare at them. The bobbing black mammal rides the swells effortlessly reminding her of life in a different time.

"I could tell," Carlos says, with a boyish grin.

"I think Roxanne telling me about her life in Hawaii was my clue the coast was safe. I was saddened about how she garnered a reputation as a party girl and that every man she met seemed to expect her to play that role--and how no matter what she did it was affixed to her like an albatross--"

"I did the same thing to you--regardless of who you were." He reaches out and touches her arm. "This is who you are now and what is more important we are here together, a family of six. The galactic significance means nothing."

Jenny freezes solid as a glacier. "I don't want your forgiveness, and I don't need your explanations." She stares in his distraught eyes. "You've gotten to the point of forgiving me for perhaps lying to you about who I am--"

"Wait. Wait. That's not what I meant," Carlos says with a bemused smile. "I said it didn't matter."

"Who am I, Carlos?" She waits arms akimbo--fire lighting her eyes.

"You are Jenny Biner," Carlos says trying to hide his suspicions under a cheerful grin. In truth Carlos has decided he will never know who she is so this war between them may stop--for Roo's sake. In truth, Carlos wants to be close to someone before he dies. He puts out his hand. "Please take my hand."

A straightjacket of emotions surrounds Jenny; her hands remain on her hips. "Not yet. Carlos, you're willing to bury your suspicions about me because you figure they just don't matter anymore, given the fate of the world. That's like love on a conveyor belt. It is not love for me. It is fear of our circumstance--and life's limited duration."

His arms interlace across his chest to keep warm. "All my life I've been alone--and when I was in that holding cell waiting for Quentin to make up his mind about killing me I was certain I had made a mistake. It freed me, Jenny. I realized that I was going to die all alone without love--even though love waited for me. The absurdity of it all shook something loose. I--like Quentin--was turning my life into an empty wasteland for some twisted notion of safety. I vowed that if I ever saw you again the first thing I would tell you is how sorry I am." He looks down at the bucket of clams. "It took me six months and probably a hundred trips here, watching you and those stinking buckets, to get up the nerve up to say I need to be close to someone--please don't stand in my way." In the distance the armada fades into the fog.

She takes his hand and squeezes it. Then she lets it go. Jenny leans over to take off her sandals and grab a second dirty bucket. She hauls it over to the water's edge leaving Carlos with the cleaned clams and a veil of hurt. She looks back over her shoulder wearing a smile. "Sorry Tarzan, the love scene has to wait a while longer. "Come on and give me a hand. I don't want to restoke the wood in that fish smoker anymore than I have to today." Moving carefully out a few feet Jenny hikes her skirt thigh high to keep it dry; bending over the cold water, she begins washing out the bucket in a small tide pool. Carlos watches the curve of her thighs into the frayed woolen skirt.

Jenny slips and her left leg slides off the rock into the cold water. Instantly, Carlos hurries out to help her, taking the bucket and pulling Jenny onto the rocks. The bucket goes into the tide pool and rather than loose it, she jumps to its rescue. Her skirt is immediately ten pounds more from the water's weight. Jenny grabs the bucket before it can float out to sea then scrambles to the side of the rocks.

She sees a look of triumph in his eyes. "You." Jenny cannot speak anymore she is so angry. She marches away from him to where her sandals await. Slipping them on, her back towards Carlos, she stills.

Approaching her holding the full bucket in one hand, he stands beside her. "Jenny--"

She leans over and takes the handle of the bucket. "Carlos, let's get this up to the house. I am finished talking to your suspicions… they bore me."

Walking along the strand, Jenny watches the grains stick to her clothes. Cleaning has become such a chore she hopes tonight's downpour will do the job of washing her skirt. Of all her tasks, cleaning of clothes has become

Jenny Biner's least favorite of chores.

Carlos thinks he is being purposely ignored: "I wasn't trying to trick you." She walks beside him silent for a moment.

Jenny stops and faces him. "Let go of the bucket. Go away."

"Not on your life. The moment I do, I'll be wearing it."

She looks to her feet, then at his feet in their sneakers. "Fine then I will." She lets go of the bucket and the bucket lands in the ice grass with a thud. By the time Carlos looks up, Jenny has started up the rock face towards the cliffs and house. "Jenny, stop this."

She halts and stares down at him. "Do you realize that in three months the world ends? Do you realize that the six of us are hanging on by our fingernails? Do you realize how hard you are working to make me shun you?" She turns and storms away up the cliff.

"How do you know it will end in three months? I see. Okay, I get it. No surety. But why not? Hey, I'm not carrying this by myself," Carlos yells pointing down at the bucket. "You know you drive me crazy."

"You just wait there. I will get Roo to help you--assuming I do not come back with that pistol and its single bullet and kill you." She disappears over the crest of the cliff leaving Carlos in the wake of her anger. He stares back out to sea.

"Carlos?" It is Roo heading down the embankment. The lanky boy wears a pair of cut blue jeans that end just above his knees and nothing else.

"Roo, go put on a shirt. It's cold out here."

"I know. I just got the same weather report from my mom." He bounces down the hillside and stops in front of Carlos. He leans over to help him with a bucket. The two men continue up the hill. "For a smart guy, dad, you sure can be an ass. Takes you six months to really talk to her and what do you do? You piss her off. Are you sure you're really Carlos Jordan: Ambassador to the stars? It's hard for me to believe he is such a boob."

Carlos adores Roo's straightforward ways and pinpoint humor. He finds them laudable. "Roo--I can't explain to you that I do not wish to be alone." Carlos blesses this young man who garners truth from him like water down a rain chute.

"The truth here is that you keep pushing my mom away because you care for her. Genian, Venutian, or Pond Lizard she is my mom. She is Jenny Biner. The rest of what's happened to her is never going to be shared with you as long as you continue treating her like a murder suspect. Forget what you think happened and stop trying to prove that you understand what's going on. 'Cause, Mr. Ambassador, the fact is you never will. I never will. It's too complex--dummy." This conversation is typical of an ease that Roo shares with most people. The universe has spared his mother--the rest just doesn't matter.

"But I cannot live with lies, Roo."

"Nonsense. You love only lies--you just have trouble adjusting to new lies--or truths--take your choice. I tell you I will not interfere with you two or take sides but I have to tell you Carlos, you are being an ass. Enjoy what we have and let the rest of it fade away. There just isn't that much left that we can afford to question whatever grace we are presented with."

"You sound like Simon," Carlos says.

"Actually those were mostly Roxanne's words."

Carlos stops even though they are only three quarters of the way up the hill and lowers the bucket. Roo follows suit wondering if perhaps Carlos has pulled a muscle. With his left hand Carlos reaches out and rubs Roo's head. "I wish I were more like you, son."

Chapter Thirty-Five

Standing on the cliff above the clam bed, overlooking a tan rock pointing to the ocean, a tall scraggly haired boy watches his mother and Carlos Jordan walking back from the rocks. Their canvas black clothes blowing in the sea breeze, their holy war continuing as they move unsteadily over the wet rocks, Jenny and Carlos avoid the moss trying to keep their balance. The couple seem attentive to each other, and Carlos' animate arms indicate he is beginning to tell another one of his fish stories. Through the crashing waves Roo hears his mother's laughter. Roo loves Carlos' fish stories because they are told only for humor. The last week or so, the lies have taken on brobdingnagian proportions keeping everyone in gales of laughter. The story of a ten-foot tuna that jumped into Carlos' arms when he was a child and kissed him is Roo's favorite yarn.

The boy notes his mother's crossed arms--as if she were afraid the other might freeze from the cold. Shaking his head at their stubbornness, the boy settles down behind the rock and stares skyward. The blue above and fluffy clouds signal another idyllic day on the strand. He believes the storms to be more benign even though Carlos constantly pontificates caution. Roo senses Carlos is trying to keep expectations in line; while his mother and Roxanne tend to accentuate the good days and play down the rough ones. To Roo, this is just another reason the two of them square off occasionally. And while Roo does not fully understand the reason for the their trench warfare, he believes, overall, a tumultuous relationship will develop--were there time.

Three weeks ago a herald appeared from Sacramento with a truckload of batteries and an announcement that Quentin Conworth was planning an important TV message. "...And all those with TVs are required to tune in..." Then soldiers began handing out the batteries saying they were to be used solely for "Prime Minister Conworth's message to the nation..." Knowing the implication, Carlos had hidden with Simon in the cliffs. The soldiers left totally unaware of anything but their errand to distribute batteries.

When questioned about it Carlos had donned the role of hero again. Jenny, and the other adults, had understood his duplicity and pity, but none dare deflate the sail of Carlos' altruism and love for the children. Everyone knows nothing matters for him, apart from making things comfortable and pleasant for them.

Quentin's message is to be broadcast in less then an hour. Carlos, knowing Quentin's plans for control of the planet, believes his world will end today. In a way, he is correct.

Roo, without this context, rises again from behind the rocks and watches his parents walk--noticing how Carlos keeps his shoulders tight and how he seems to get stiffer by the moment. Roo sighs, thinking to himself that this poor man has again succumbed to fear. Feeling that if anyone should know whether the woman on the beach were his mother it would be he. Roo, more than anything else wishes to cure Carlos of his pains. As a result, Roo and Roxanne have become very close; partly because of a shared world view and partly because they both seek to free Carlos of his chains. Roo has come to believe no one can put anything passed Roxanne--who continually reassures him that Carlos is just in too much pain to accept his mother's happiness. This has led to Roo frequently quizzing Simon about psychology and the workings of the mind. It occurs to Roo that Simon has all but ignored his lessons this morning. A troubling event, for Roo, because he has come to count on the doctor's punctuality and tenacity.

"Roo, they know you're spying on them."

The boy faces Simon and Roxanne who now walk towards him arm in arm. The boy points down the cliff. "I like watching the happy couple stroll along the rocks. They act so nice to each other sometimes I want to puke. They do it whenever they think I'm watching. But I'm not fooled. I'm pretty wily you know." For all his maturity Roo is still only on the cusp of manhood. "Or maybe you know something else is going on, Doc?"

Wearing a dark blue sweater and torn jeans, Simon leans over and pets Sid. "I guess they figured they didn't have all the time in the world." Simon refuses to lie and he also refuses to subject Roo to any more pain than necessary. Like most adults, he feels the youth of this time will have either a very short life or a very difficult one. "It'll work out soon enough."

Staring at the ugly scar that runs across his forehead and into his eye sockets, Roo has trouble with what he has just heard. The doctor's blindness tells him the world cannot be trusted. So far as Roo is concerned Simon Weiss is just too good a man to be blind. "You can say you know but you don't want to discuss it, Doc."

"I think he said that, Roo," says Roxanne. She wears a similar blue sweater and long brightly colored wool pants that Roo calls the barber poles because of the bright red and white stripes that run around the legs. She leans over to where he is sitting on the rock and hands him a fresh-baked cinnamon roll. The boy takes the sweet roll and bites into it feeling the pleasant brown sugar and cinnamon mix in a soft texture. He looks up at her short blond hair and bright friendly eyes. They are telling him this is not the time to push his questions. "Hope should be up from her nap soon and we are going to go for a short walk. Would you mind keeping an eye on her?"

He springs to his feet and heads off toward the house. Simon follows the footsteps with blind eyes then speaks quietly to Roxanne. "All the cinnamon is gone."

"You are the one who said Quentin's broadcast will be simultaneous with the ecological disaster or before it. We've still time before he comes on the TV--" She puts her warm hand in his and caresses his arm. He inhales her scent; it rides his consciousness like a rose. "Besides, a five minute walk before Armageddon should be all right. And frankly, I do not really need to see Quentin's show."

"I do. There might be some valuable information," Simon says bitterly. These last few days the pains of lovely people around him have become a burden. If he could, Simon would kill Quentin. In fact--if for some reason he survives and the rest of them do not--that is exactly what he plans to do.

Watching Carlos and Jenny begin the long trek up the rocks, Roxanne leans against her spouse. "They see us." She waves to the couple on the beach. Carlos points to his wrist asking if it is time. Roxanne shakes her head yes. "Do you think he'll ever let her in?"

"Not in this lifetime," Simon says. "But she loves him for the show he puts on for Roo--that's only when she doesn't want to kill him for being so angry." Simon is also frustrated by his friend's inability to let go of mistrust and fear. "I think he feels the closer we come to the end, the less he has to let her in--I thought he would do just the opposite. At this point I'm not expecting any miracles. But I want to keep him close to Roo. Without the boy, Carlos will implode."

"We all need someone to care for." Roxanne's attention turns back to Carlos and Jenny since she cannot continue watching Simon; she is too saddened by his circumstance. Last night he revealed his fear of living alone through another chaotic period like when he was young--but this time middle-aged and blind. Roxanne asks herself how the universe can be so cruel--while watching the woman who has taken an immense journey to be with Carlos only to have it mired in so much pain. She adores Jenny for her strength and kindness while at the same time considering her a bit of a fool to put up with Carlos. Had Roxanne not considered the same course of action--sacrificing herself for him--she might not be so judgmental. Then, no longer able to think about those around her, Roxanne stares blankly into the rolling ocean.

--It's hammer time--

Laughter startles her. Looking toward the Victorian house, she sees Roo with little Hope on his shoulders. He walks through the garden swaying back and forth dressed in an old clown costume they found last year. The pig-tailed child, dressed in a pink jumper, laughs at Roo's antics as he wanders about the yard like a drunk; she waves to her new mommy and daddy. Roxanne sees Roo pursue the show of all adults. "He is putting on a show for her. He knows something is up today."

"Of course, Love."

A little over a year ago, Sid discovered the little girl huddling in the corner of the shopping mall in Marisol one morning. About four years old, clutching her thin nightgown for warmth, her blond hair had been all but burned off in a fire. The frightened girl had explained to them she had lived in one of the houses nearby with her parents. The night before, marauders had set fire to it. "I escaped by crawling through the sewer ditch that ran from the house. My daddy and mommy died fighting the flames and the marauders. They should have run." Hope quickly astounded everyone with her ability to let go of her parents' memory. Simon has since found the phenomenon common among this generation, but it scares him a generation grows that cannot even mourn.

Hope removes her other hand from around Roo's neck to show-off. Roxanne smiles and claps.

"My, she is getting good at that," says Carlos, cresting the hill with Jenny alongside him. Roxanne marvels at his unending labor to keep emotional pain from the children's sight.

"Dad, do you know what Hope found?" Roo asks as he approaches the four adults who are whispering about the time.

Carlos shakes his head and looks away to hide a tear. He feels his life complete. "What did she find?" he responds.

The lanky boy casually swings Hope to the ground. "A frog, a big one, up by the pond. There's so much more life in the ponds these last couple of years--since the big storms have stopped."

"They haven't stopped. The greenhouse gases have an incredible persistence in the atmosphere. The storms will come back."

"Maybe," Jenny says.

Carlos nods. "We'll need to get back to the house, Roo. It's almost time for Quentin's broadcast." Staring at the Victorian, Carlos prays the home he found in his dream can provide some refuge for these children.

"Why so glum, Simon? You're the one who says frogs are the best indicator of ecological health."

"It could be an anomaly, Roo. Remember I told you about those," says Simon with tone of a serious uncle. He has taken to deflecting attention from Carlos when Carlos cannot maintain his facade. Roxanne cannot figure how he knows.

Roo tries to smile at Simon in a way that he can be seen. Believing every story Simon has told him about the visions he had witnessed in the Genian city-museum, the boy has no limits on possibilities. So far though, Roo notes, he has not mastered the techniques necessary for Simon to see his smile. It is another reason for his interest in the human condition. Roo glances at his mother and Roxanne. Their concerns are not hidden like Carlos' concerns. Jenny's bright eyes show no fear, but they are the same eyes he saw when she believed she was about to die. Roo thinks back to overhearing his mother and Roxanne discussing a secret supply of food just for the kids. He was, of course, meant to hear it. "Doc, what about spending some time teaching me doctor stuff?"

Simon shakes his head. "Let's let it go for today. I'm a bit tired."

In a flash Roo figures out what Carlos thinks he knows. Then, like Carlos, Roo modifies his facial expression immediately to hide any concern. He knows Carlos will hurt more otherwise. When Carlos looks away on feeling a stiff breeze, Roo looks at his mom then the man beside her. Their grim smiles tell him he is correct. "I see." Hope puts her arms out for him and Roo drops to one knee. The little girl's hug shields Carlos from the truth of Roo's awareness.

"What do you see, Roo?" asks the young girl.

Roo spins away from her and lifts Hope from the ground. Running along the hillside path on unsteady legs the boy tries to put crying distance between himself and Carlos. Draped over his shoulder, Hope cannot see the stream of tears that roll down his face. The young girl tries to straighten up but Roo, making a game of it, keeps her over his shoulder.

Carlos' eyes widen as he watches Roo avoiding Hope's gaze. "He knows," he says to Jenny. "I thought I saw him get it." Sitting on the rocks he hangs his head in his hands. The world has ended for Carlos. He believes he feels an insurmountable terror in the young man. "I failed him as well." Carlos jumps to his feet leaving the adults. "Roo, I want to talk with you."

Wiping his eyes, Roo puts the child down. "Hope, go over to your mom and I will be right with you."

"I want to stay with you," she says stamping her feet.

"Now," Carlos says. Hope trundles over to Roxanne.

"Walk?" Carlos asks. They look out from the cliff. Roo beside Carlos, his head up and a smile on his face--the boy takes his father's hand.

"What's up?"

"You tell me," Carlos says.

"We may have some troubles soon--as in the end of the world," Roo says. He feels so safe with Carlos. "The straight scoop, dad."

"That's twice you called me that."

"I can stop."

"Not funny." He watches the boy, his eyes filled with admiration. "Something bad may be coming--and soon I think. Quentin Conworth is the only one with any knowledge of when it is supposed to occur--"

"And he is coming on the tube soon--I got that. What will it be? Do you know?"

"Large scale devastation. The Genian predicted it. It's they who delineated the safe zone--and told us when it was going to happen. Are you afraid, son?" Carlos faces the boy and places his hands on Roo's shoulders. "I swear I will never leave your side."

Roo grins. "I know that. But I'm not afraid. I'm pissed. It's so difficult for you." The boy stops on the edge of the cliff watching the waves crash against the rocks. The rumble rises through the soles of his sandals. "Can you feel those waves?"

"Not through my sneakers."

"So take them off."

"Not right now," Carlos looks away. "What have you not gotten to do that you wish you could have done?"

Roo flinches. "I've always wanted to go for a ride in a really fast car." Roo hugs his father. Carlos, hugging the boy back can see Jenny on the porch of the Victorian now lying on a chaise. Simon and Roxanne sit beside her; Hope runs towards the house with Sid running out to meet her. Carlos looks back at Roo, then kisses him on the forehead. "She is Pilnouth--I know she cannot save us." Carlos lies. "You know it wasn't so different when I was young. I wanted a fast car too. When I finally did it I found out it wasn't so much fun with so many people suffering."

"It was different then. Now nothing matters."

Carlos tears. "I'm so sorry." He cannot stem the tears. "I keep asking myself how could we have been so stupid."

The boy steps back. He points at Carlos with his index finger. "Dad, you know when I first saw mom all healthy I was angry."

Carlos cannot control himself. "Me too," Carlos replies unsure of what he is saying.

"I don't mind dying dad--I just want my mom around--as well as my dad. She needs you, dad. If she could stop it she would have. Get it?"

Carlos put his arm around the boy. "Therapy does not work that way, son." And shaking his head, "Roo, this last year of my life has been infinitely better than the ones before. Even with the killings, and the lack of food this last winter, and all the rest. I don't want to die, and I certainly don't want the rest of you to die--but I've never been happier."

"You're not a God either, dad." Roo says, checking on little Hope as she trundles around the porch with the dog.

"I loved looking for ways to keep you happy and safe." Carlos' red eyes burn as he tries to wipe tears with his arm.

Roo feels he has never known a person so honorable. "Dad, I think you just don't want to live without mom. You're afraid you may be alone again."

"I am only sure I would not want to live without you."

The two hug in a cascade of tears.

Later, when Carlos can focus again he sees Roxanne point to her wrist. Carlos starts walking toward the house. "Have I told you about Susan Willoughby, the woman who saved my life?"

"Yes--many times." Roo almost said 'a million times,' but he keeps his face carefully composed--a technique he has learned from Carlos.

Carlos sees it. Pride wells up within him. He continues speaking. "Susan gave her life because she just couldn't live with people who had no soul--but she needed my caring and I couldn't give it to her."

"Again not your fault. She could have been with you but she decided to save the world instead. Sound familiar?"

"Clearly. Nonetheless, she could not live with certain people. And I do not want to live without certain people."

"Including mom?" the boy says insistently.

"Yes, including mom." They approach the back porch. "You see even though I'm all balled up about how I feel, and my pain gets in the way, I still care about her. I'm just...me."

"And that is?" Roo asks.

"I wish I knew. Please do not mention anything about our situation to Hope will you?"

"You mean about you and mom?" He grins. "Of course not--but I think she knows something is wrong." They walk in silence up the stairs. When Carlos steps on the porch Roxanne and Simon get to their feet. Roxanne looks directly at Roo. Jenny closes her eyes at the tear tracks.

"Come on Roo. Let's get some lunch and wait for the TV," says Simon, feeling the breath from Roo's heaving chest. "We will be there in just a moment." Roxanne motions for Hope and Roo to go inside. When Hope refuses, Roo grabs her hand and leads her away saying she may get to watch a TV show. As much as Roo wishes to drive fast, Hopes wishes to watch cartoons.

As the screen door closes behind them, Jenny opens her eyes and looks at Carlos. Carlos sighs and pulls a chair over by her. As he has done most mornings for the last weeks, he sits close beside her--without a comment. Discussions with Jenny have been few but these two sit together every day--for hours at a time. They both consider those periods the best of times. Carlos speaks before she can. "I want to thank you for letting me stay here with you. I want to thank you for many things."

She looks passed him through the screen door to Roo--who stands just inside the dark kitchen watching them. "Roo knows doesn't he?"

"He does."

"You need to be with him."

Carlos looks at the rock outcropping that separates the house from the view of the ocean. He shakes his head. Oddly, rather than leaving her, he sits quietly listing to the ocean and the sounds of Roxanne preparing a meal.

"The show is on." Roo calls.

Carlos looks at Jenny. After they stand, he reaches out for her hand. The action surprises her; she does not reach for his. "I have truth for you, Carlos."

Roo bursts through the screen-door. "New Zealand is gone. I was watching the show. It was broadcast live from the island--and the Prime Minister, your buddy Quentin, was saying something about how they were getting ready to bring another fifty million people to the island when the picture just blanked out. A second later the image cut back to the two planes that had been flying overhead showing how pretty New Zealand was--but the island was gone. All you could see was a bright pink mist. When it cleared a second later there was just ocean. One second there was an island, the next second it was gone. The whole island just went poof."

"The whole island went poof!" Hope says appearing beside him and repeating his words.

"Gee, what a surprise, that's too bad," Simon appears in the doorway. He begins to laugh.

Carlos totally baffled by Simon's reaction, stares at his friend. "And we are deliriously happy because the Genian lied about the safe zone--which means no humans will live through the disaster. This is funny because?"

Roxanne dances through the door looking brighter than sunshine. "We're safe, Carlos. How many Genians does it take to screw fifty million evil humans?"

"Perhaps only one lonely one," Roo says.

"The disease Pilnouth's kind could not cure," Roxanne says.

Carlos' jaw drops; it is a moment without end. He cannot speak.

"Those who were destroyed in New Zealand considered themselves powerful because they had the ability to take from others more degenerate then they--or so they believed. Of course the truth is: Only the most perverted of humanity would get to a safe zone in a time like ours. So the Rostackmidarifians created a belief that a disaster would happen. The human 'elite' huddles together inside a big net unable to conceive of power without depravity--and poof: scratch fifty million murderers." Simon reaches out for Roxanne to take her hand.

"You--they--lied about the planet being destroyed?" Carlos finally says. "It was a lie."

"And not a bad one either," Jenny says with a grin: "It seems the Rostackmidarifian followed through on the offer to remove the trash."

"But only the top layer." Roxanne grins.

"Mom, then we're safe?" Roo rushes into his mother's arms.

"For now." Jenny watches the mistrust in Carlos' eyes evaporate like fog on a sunny summer morning. She finds herself hating the curse of disease.

Carlos takes in a deep breath. He leans on a porch post. "It was all a set-up. I will be a son of a bitch. You weren't trying to lead us down the path of slavery. You--they were trying to help. You were really trying to help. Imagine that: Powerful beings who are not sick and twisted. I can hardly imagine it. Of course fifty million have died. And that's bad." His eyes begin to light with the glow of one who has heard a fine joke. "I should be sad." He looks at his smiling family. "Ah, screw it. They deserved it." He embraces the boy and his mother kissing Jenny hard on the lips.

"I wondered how the Rostackmidarifian could allow the destruction of the place where their Question plant nests," Simon says. "What's that sound? They are kissing."

"Quiet, dear," says Roxanne.

"We still have some challenges ahead." Jenny says between hugs and kisses from Carlos. She then just hugs him.

"You're quite a woman to figure those things out with so little training in the evils of society. I guess Pilnouth told you quite a bit before she died." Simon says.

Carlos holds her back so he can look into her eyes. "I am so sorry."

Jenny scans the quintet around her. "Are you? Well are you ready for another little surprise?" Hope snuggles against her mother.

Carlos grimaces. "Go ahead. I deserve it."

"In fact Pilnouth told me a very interesting story." The people on the porch watch Jenny seek out Carlos' down turned eyes. "Take off your sneakers, Tarzan."

"No, what for?"

"You have no reason to keep them on now. Take them off please." She steps back from him.

Carlos backs away from her. Stopping his protest, he sits. He slowly takes off his sneakers but then immediately tucks his feet under the chair in which he sits. Hope, with the candor of the young, bends at the waist and stares at his uncovered feet. "What's wrong with his feet?"

"How many toes does he have?" Jenny asks Hope.

Hope counts his toes. "Ten."

"No dear, count again," Carlos says.

"Ten," she says impatiently.

Carlos looks around at Simon and Roxanne then slowly brings his feet out from under the chair. He also counts ten toes.

Roxanne is mute.

"You once had nine toes, Carlos," Roo says. "Care to explain this slight of foot, Carlos?" He is teasing him for all the grief he has given Jenny. His key evidence in his articles of indictment against Jenny had been the evaporation of Jenny's cancer.

"That toe must be the leading edge of an invasion." Simon is deadpan.

"Oh my," is all Roxanne can say.

"This can't be." He looks down at his feet. "My mother and father cut off my toe. I remember it." He looks over to Jenny. "But I now have ten toes."

"I knew he wasn't really Carlos Jordan," Roo says teasing Carlos.

That pallor of mistrust that used to ride his spine like a tram collapses under the weight of Roo's barb. He stares sheepishly at Jenny.

She points to herself. "You are no more dead than I am, Carlos. You are no less human than anyone here. You are no more different now than you were before you were healed--"

"So does this mean I am another handicapped Genian like you?" Carlos asks. "One who has taken over my body as well as yours?"

"More than you will ever know--if you ask me," Roo quips. "Get a clue, dad. She made you whole."

"Kind of like putting a new face on the planet--only this time it worked." Jenny continues: "You are Carlos Jordan and I am Jenny Biner. We are here on the porch of our home with our son and our very close friends here in Marisol. I no longer have cancer and you have regained a toe. There is nothing more to it than that. And, we can be happy if we choose."

He looks down at his toe. "This cannot be." He reaches down realizing for for some time now he has put on socks and has seen ten toes without recognizing the change to his body. The paradox scares him. "But I don't feel any different. I feel like me. Why didn't Quentin's doctors know?"

Simon laughs. "Those clowns--are you kidding me? They'd have a hard time guessing your species." He grins. "Sorry. Besides, I destroyed your medical records during the truth therapy sessions. I didn't want them to have any links to you once you were released. I didn't know I was doing the work of angels. I thought I was just protecting you from further pain."

"I looked at my feet a dozen times. I don't remember anything different or abnormal. I don't know when it changed." He grabs his toe and moves it back and forth. "The Rostackmidarifian said things would change--"

"Nothing has changed, except you can be happy," Jenny says. She looks over to Roxanne. "Did you know? I was sure you knew but you never let on."

"I didn't know. I saw something changing for him and figured it was the force of your love on him." Roxanne smiles. "I never thought it was something as momentous as a toe."

The others laugh, but lost by all this Carlos looks around until his gaze stops to rest again at Jenny. "Where did I die? In the crash--just before the dream of this house? That must be it--" He takes in a deep breath then looks toward the sky. "That's not it." The others are laughing even harder. "This might be funny except the only real laughter is in a Genian's dreams." He stares wondering where these words came from inside him. "Nothing makes sense."

Roo puts his hand on his dad's shoulder. "Dad, it does not matter."

"You are human as we are, Carlos," Roxanne says. "But with a recycled toe--end of discussion."

"I do not deserve this," he says recognizing his grace at last.

"But you are the one that would be with Pilnouth when no other would," Roxanne says. Her caring floods into Carlos' consciousness. His vision fills with tears and he looks to Jenny--eyes locking in love.

"Amazing," Roo says. "He finally made it."

"We had all better go inside and let them be alone," Simon says. He and Roxanne turn to leave.

"No, wait," Carlos, voices. "Jenny, all I wanted was--anything."

Her eyes fill with tears. "And I have loved you in spite of it. Your love reaches across many lives to me. My door remains open to you. I love everything about you."

"But you do lie like a Genian," Carlos says, with a gentle smile.

"You too." Jenny takes his hand. "We are going for a walk. If you get a chance, Roxanne, stoke the fire. Carlos and I will return in a few hours--probably suffering hypothermia from waves crashing over us. And keep the spymaster with you if you please. We would like some privacy." She winks at her son as they walk off toward the ocean.

AFTERWORD

My hope is you have enjoyed "The Galileo Syndrome."

I first had the notion for a book about the colors of environment in the late 1970's. Then in the mid 1980's, global warming became a ripe topic for a novel: A vehicle full of speculation and precipices providing insight into the chaotic relationship between life's essences and the multiple dimensions served by time.

As weather events increased in severity far faster than the predictions, I began to see the book I'd written was far less esoteric than I had thought. It became clear, current science could not conclusively prove anthropogenic forcing of the climate. Modeling, and other forms of proof: examination of satellite data, trending, correlations between carbon dioxide and temperature, as well as other metrics, were employed in this search for truth. Sadly the limitation of prediction in a chaotic environment, the climate, showed itself to be more of a challenge to our current science and technology than we were prepared to work with. The conclusion: Proof of climate change by science became elusive and indefensible.

As a result of that doubt, the immediate imperatives of a sound economy supplanted the maybe's of future problems. Opening the door for groups that seek to nullify events which will negatively impact their balance sheet; proactive events became sequestered under the policy of "No Regrets". While perhaps considered a negative, under this policy, all parties are given and will continue to be given, a forum for their interests, not only myopic power bases.

Sound decision making is imperative to the continued functioning of governing a large population. Unfortunately, the climate, a system we currently do not fully understand or can predict, encompasses the thermodynamic balance of the planet. In my view it is turning negative to mankind's interests. We can mitigate the negative impact if we act. My proof?

Empiricism has little place in the process of proof because it has shown itself to miss complexities over and over again; this does not mean that empiricism is always wrong. For me, and maybe you as well, looking around and watching the interaction of humanity and climate yields awareness of change. Take your time. Just don't turn away from your environment; you are a part of it, not its master.

Too often events fostered by humans are seen as unnatural--crimes against the environment--needing to be modified for the good of the planet. Also as a result of reading this book you may acquire at least one other viewpoint; Events fostered by humans are integral to the environment--not sins against Gaia. There is a tendency on the part of environmentalists to affix blame on commercial interests for a lack of responsiveness to climate change. They neglect to take into account, among other things, that it would have been difficult, perhaps impossible, for our species to have advanced without inexpensive energy; Carbon dioxide is the natural by-product of cheap energy. Our use of inexpensive energy and acceptance of the commodity leads to wealth and power. That we have discovered tragedy in progress is not an indication of criminality or of malicious intent. It is an indication we have advanced in our awareness. But, on the other hand, if we seek to hide this awareness for the purpose of commerce, individual safety, or power, there is a crime: We lose that reason for place on this planet: our humanity.

Knowing that proof is elusive, I have attempted to stay away from the battle of prediction. There is no prophesy in this work. The science of climate change is only confusing if it is fostered by greed--making what is happening to our environment appear distant and confusing. I am not a crusader--I am an author--but the planet, and our children, demand our attention.

I cannot excuse inactivity on climate change when the chances are so high our progeny will suffer from a rabid environment. The trend, to me, seems clear: Larger, more active weather systems damaging more--killing at an increased tempo. As I said, I cannot prove this to you. However, as a result of reading this book you will, hopefully, feel the climate changing and our deep ties to that change.

And once you have seen the future, you might also speak for Carlos Jordan's generation and those that follow.

Daniel H. Gottlieb